CW00468075

THE NORDIC HEART SERIES

BOOKS 1-4

HELENA HALME

COPYRIGHT

The Nordic Heart Series Books 1-4 ©2018 Helena Halme
Published worldwide 2018
by Newhurst Press

All rights reserved in all media. No part of this book may be reproduced or transmitted in any form by any means, electronic or mechanical (including but not limited to: the Internet, photocopying, recording or by any information storage and retrieval system), without prior permission in writing from the author and/or publisher.
The moral right of Helena Halme as the author of the work has been asserted by her in accordance with the Copyright, Designs and Patents Act 1988.

e-ISBN: 978-1-9998929-8-2
ISBN: 978-0-9957495-0-4
Cover designs © Helena Frise

All characters and events featured in this book are entirely fictional and any resemblance to any person, organisation, place or thing living or dead, or event or place, is purely coincidental and completely unintentional.
Visit www.helenahalme.com for more books by the same author and for news and reviews of Helena's work.

THE ENGLISH HEART

BOOK 1

1

HELSINKI, 1980

K aisa's heart skipped a beat. She'd never been inside an embassy before nor attended a cocktail party. The invite, with its official English writing, seemed too glamorous to be real. She dug out the card and showed it to her friend, Tuuli. Kaisa glanced at her friend, wondering if she was as nervous about the evening as Kaisa was.

'Her Britannic Majesty's Ambassador and Mrs Farquhar request the pleasure of the company of Miss Niemi and guest for Buffet and Dancing on Thursday 2 October 1980 at 8.15 pm.'

'You look great,' Tuuli said.

'I keep thinking I should have worn a long dress,' Kaisa said in a low tone, so as not to be heard by the other guests gathering outside the impressive embassy building.

Kaisa's university friend looked down at her own turquoise satin blouse, which fitted tightly to her slim body. She'd tucked the shirt into her smart, navy trousers. On her feet, Tuuli wore a pair of light-brown pumps with low heels. Kaisa's courts for once made her the same height as Tuuli.

'What did the woman at the bank say, exactly, about the dress code?' Tuuli asked. Her blue eyes matched the hue of her blouse. Students and staff at Hanken, the Swedish language university Kaisa had gained entry to a year ago, thought the two blondes were sisters, but Kaisa didn't think she looked anything like Tuuli. As well as being much taller, her friend also had larger breasts, which made men turn and stare.

'Nothing really, but I assumed a cocktail dress would be fine.' She looked around her. 'But look at these women. They're all in fancy gowns.'

Tuuli glanced behind her at the small queue of people.

'Well, I don't wear dresses. Ever.'

Her friend had a way of stating her opinion so definitely that it excluded all future conversations on the matter.

'I didn't mean that. You look fantastic. It's just that she was so vague...' Kaisa continued to speak in an almost whisper, even though the chatter around them was mostly conducted in English.

She told her the conversation with her boss at the bank, where she worked as a summer intern.

'The woman who invited me is married to the Finnish naval officer. He organised for the British Royal Navy to visit Helsinki. She told me it's a very important occasion, as this is the first time the English fleet have been to Finland since the Second World War. Apparently the Russians are here all the time, so this occasion makes a nice change. It is 1980 after all, and a long time since the war. I guess they needed some Finnish girls at this cocktail party to keep the officers company. She knew I spoke English because I'd studied it since primary school.'

'Oh, I remember you telling me now,' said Tuuli. 'But she said nothing about the dress code?'

'No.' Kaisa sighed. 'I guess she thought I'd know what to wear.'

The British Embassy was a grand house on a tree-lined street in the old part of Helsinki. The chandeliers were shining, the parquet floors polished, the antique furniture gleaming. The ambassador and his wife, who wore a long velvet skirt and a frilly white blouse, stood in the doorway to the main reception room, officially greeting all guests. When it was Kaisa's turn she held out the invitation, with its ornate gold writing, but the woman didn't even glance at it. Instead she took Kaisa's hand and smiled briefly, before she did the same to Tuuli, and then to the next person in line. Kaisa tugged on the hem of her black-and-white crepe dress. When a waiter in a white waistcoat appeared out of nowhere and offered her a glass of sherry from a silver tray, Kaisa grabbed two. She and Tuuli settled into the corner of a brightly-lit room and sipped their sweet drinks.

A few people were scattered around the room, speaking English in small groups, but the space seemed too large for so few of them. One woman in a cream evening gown glanced at the Finnish girls and smiled, but most of the guests paid them no attention standing alone in a corner, staring at their shoes, in a vain attempt not to look out of place.

Kaisa touched the hem of her dress once more.

'Perhaps I should have borrowed a more formal frock?' she said almost to herself. The dress suited her well, but she still felt underdressed.

'Whatever, this will be fun,' Tuuli said determinedly and scanned the room. 'Relax!' She linked Kaisa's arm.

Kaisa looked around and tried to spot her boss from the bank, but she was nowhere to be seen. There were a few men whose Finnish naval uniforms she recognised. They stood by themselves, laughing and drinking beer.

'Couldn't we have beer instead of this?' Tuuli held up her sherry.

Kaisa glanced at the women in evening gowns. None of them were holding anything but sherry.

'Don't think it's very ladylike,' she said.

Tuuli sighed.

Watching her friend standing next to her with a straight back and relaxed shoulders, Kaisa wondered how Tuuli always managed to look more confident than she did. They'd both turned nineteen earlier that year, and had both started at the same university a month ago. During that short time their friendship had grown rapidly, and now they told each other everything.

Kaisa knew that Tuuli hadn't travelled much; she'd grown up in a small town just north of Helsinki. Kaisa had attended many different schools and even lived in another country: Sweden. Yet she was always more nervous than Tuuli about meeting new people or being in different situations.

An hour later, when no one had spoken to Kaisa or Tuuli, and after they'd had three glasses of the sickly-sweet sherry, they decided it was time to leave.

'We could go to the university disco?' Tuuli said turning towards Kaisa. She smiled wickedly. 'Tom and the rest of them might be there.'

'I don't think...' Kaisa began, but she was interrupted by a commotion.

A large group of men, all wearing dark Navy uniforms with flashes of gold braid, burst through the door, laughing and chatting. They went straight for the makeshift bar at the end of the large room. The quiet space filled with noise and Kaisa and Tuuli were pushed deeper into their corner.

A tall, slim man in a British Navy uniform walked over suddenly and stood in front of Kaisa. He had the darkest eyes she'd ever seen. He took her hand and shook it. 'How do you do?'

His touch gave her an electric shock.

'Ouch,' Kaisa said, pulling her hand back quickly. He smiled and his eyes sparkled.

'Sorry!' he said staring at Kaisa. She looked down at the floor then at Tuuli, who seemed unconcerned by this sudden invasion of foreign, uniformed men around them.

'What's your name?' the man asked.

She looked up at him. 'Kaisa Niemi.'

He cocked his ear. 'Sorry?' She repeated the name. It took the Englishman a while to pronounce Kaisa's Finnish name. She laughed at his failed attempts to make it sound at all authentic, but he didn't give up.

When happy with his pronunciation, he introduced himself to Kaisa and Tuuli. 'Peter Williams.'

He then tapped the shoulders of two of his shipmates. One was as tall as him but with fair hair, the other a much shorter, older man. They all shook hands awkwardly, while the dark-haired Englishman continued to stare at Kaisa. She didn't know what to say or where to look. She smoothed down her dress. Peter took a swig out of a large glass of beer, suddenly noticing Kaisa's empty hands.

'Can I get you a drink? What will you have?'

'Sherry,' Kaisa said.

She couldn't think of what else to ask for.

Peter watched Kaisa intensely.

'Stay here, promise? I'm going to put this old man in charge of not letting you get away.' The shorter guy gave an embarrassed laugh as Peter disappeared into the now-crowded room.

'So is it always this cold in Helsinki?' the short man asked after he'd introduced himself as Charles Collins. Kaisa explained that in the winter it was worse, there'd be snow soon, but that in summer it was really warm. He nodded, but didn't seem to be listening to her. They stood in silence, both glancing around the room. Kaisa tried to get her friend's attention but Tuuli was in the middle of a conversation with the blond British officer.

When the dark Englishman returned, Kaisa's breath caught in her throat at the sight of him. He was carrying a tray full of drinks, and very nearly spilled them all when someone knocked him from behind. Everyone laughed.

Peter's eyes met Kaisa's and he smiled.

'You're still here!' He handed her a drink.

He sounded surprised, like he'd expected her to leave. Disappointment flooded through her body. Didn't he want her to stay? Even if she'd decided to go, it would have been difficult to fight her way to the door.

The throng of people pushed Peter closer to Kaisa. The rough fabric of his uniform touched her bare arm. He gazed down at her.

'And what do you do?' He winced and added, 'Sorry, that sounds like such a cliché. But I really want to know.'

She laughed and told him about her studies at Hanken University. He said he was a sub-lieutenant on the British ship. She could tell he was proud of his rank and position.

Kaisa found it easy to talk to this foreign man. Even though her English faltered at times, they seemed to understand each other straightaway. They even laughed at the same jokes. Kaisa looked at Peter's lips when he spoke, and she suddenly found herself wondering what it would be like to kiss him. She shrugged the thought away.

'What?' Peter said softly, making those lips look even more inviting. His eyes twinkled with mischief.

Kaisa looked down at her hands feeling her cheeks redden, sure he'd read her mind.

'Nothing.'

They talked about books next, and Peter asked her if she'd read Thomas Hardy.

Kaisa shook her head.

'You must!' he said and, without his gaze leaving Kaisa's face, added, 'I believe character is fate.'

Is it fate that we met tonight? Kaisa wanted to ask but didn't dare. Instead she nodded, and decided to borrow a book by this Hardy person as soon as she could.

'You see, who you are determines what happens to you,' Peter continued. His tone was full of passion and he looked keenly at Kaisa.

She didn't know how to respond. She couldn't speak. Peter was so close to her now that she could see the stubble on his chin. He opened his mouth to say something else, but closed it again.

She lowered her head and bit her lower lip.

Peter surprised Kaisa by taking her hand and kissing the back of it.

'You're quite lovely, do you know that?'

She lifted her eyes up and for a moment they stood there, quite still, looking at each other. It was as if the whole room had emptied and the other guests had disappeared. To regain control, she pulled her hand from Peter's grip and turned back to the room. It surprised her to see that what had been a group was now just her and Peter, in one corner of the large space.

Feeling guilty, she remembered Tuuli.

'Do you know where my friend went?'

Peter took hold of her arm and pointed at a group of Finnish naval officers. 'Don't worry, I think she's OK.'

Tuuli was among them, drinking beer and laughing.

The music started and Peter asked Kaisa to dance. There were only two other couples on the small parquet floor. One was a government minister and his famous wife. Her long, black curls bounced gently against her tanned skin as she pushed her head back and laughed at something her husband said.

Peter held Kaisa's waist and she felt the heat of his touch through the thin fabric of her dress. She lifted her eyes to his, and for a moment they stood still in the middle of the dance floor. Slowly he started to move. Kaisa felt giddy with happiness. The room spun before her eyes in a delightful way and she relaxed in Peter's arms.

'You dance beautifully,' he said.

Kaisa smiled. 'So do you.'

He shifted his hands lower down Kaisa's back and squeezed her bottom.

'Naughty,' Kaisa said with a giggle. She removed them and whispered, 'That's the Foreign Minister and his famous wife. They'll see!'

'Sorry.' He looked sheepishly at the other couples on the dance floor.

After a few steps, his hands dropped to her backside for a second time. She tutted and moved them back up. His warm touch through her dress lingered, as if he'd branded her with his mark.

When the music stopped, Peter placed her hand in the crook of his arm and led her away from the dance floor. She noticed he had long fingers, and that his grip was strong. Surprised at her behaviour, Kaisa wished for this night to never end. She pushed back thoughts of the life waiting for her outside this party. Or, rather, *who* might be waiting for her back in her flat.

Peter found two plush chairs by a fireplace in a smaller room. It had windows overlooking a groomed, lit-up garden. As soon as they sat down a gong rang for food.

'You must be hungry,' Peter said and not waiting for a reply, got up.

'I'll get you a selection,' he added.

'OK,' Kaisa said.

'Promise not to move from this spot?'

Kaisa laughed and made a pledge not to move a muscle. She watched Peter disappear into the throng of people. As soon as he was gone she felt awkward sitting there, marking the time until Peter's return. She felt the eyes of the ladies she'd seen earlier in the evening upon her.

Kaisa fixed her dress again and looked at her watch: it was ten past eleven already. She saw Tuuli in the doorway to the larger room. She was holding hands with a Finnish naval officer, smiling up at him.

As if spotting her friend had awoken Kaisa to reality, she got up and walked towards them. 'Are you going? Wait, I'll come with you.'

Tuuli looked at the Finnish guy, then at Kaisa. 'Umm, I'll call you tomorrow?'

Kaisa flushed red. 'Ah, yes, of course.' She waved her friend goodbye and scanned the large room for Peter. It would be impolite to leave without saying goodbye.

Just then Peter reappeared, balancing two glasses of wine and two huge platefuls of food in his hands.

'I didn't know what you liked,' he said grinning.

Kaisa followed him back to the plush chairs. She watched him wolf down cocktail sausages, slices of ham and potato salad, as if he'd never been fed. He emptied his plate and said, 'Aren't you hungry?'

She shook her head. She wasn't sure if it was the formal surroundings or all the sherry she'd drunk, but she couldn't even think about food. All she could do was sip the wine. She leaned back in her chair. Peter sat forward in his. He placed his hand on her knee. His touch sent a current running through her body.

'You OK?'

Kaisa felt like she could sink into the dark pools of Peter's eyes. She shook her head, to shake off the spell this foreigner had cast over her.

'A bit drunk, I think.'

Peter laughed. He pushed the empty plate away and lit a cigarette. He studied her for a moment.

'I'm glad we met.'

'Me too,' Kaisa said, and felt herself blush. What was she doing? She should be telling Peter to go, not encouraging him.

But she couldn't tear herself away.

They sat and talked by the fireplace. The heat of the flames warmed the side of Kaisa's arm too much, but she didn't want to move an inch. While they talked, Peter gazed at her intently, as if trying to commit all of her to memory. She found this both flattering and frightening.

It was dangerous being here with Peter like this.

Once or twice during their chat, one of his shipmates came over and they exchanged a few words. There was a woman he seemed to know very well. She touched his arm and laughed at something he said. But when Peter turned back to Kaisa, the woman huffed and moved away.

Kaisa liked the feeling of owning Peter, of having all his attention on her. She found it easy to tell him her life story. He talked about his family in southwest England. He had a brother and a sister, both a lot older than him.

He smiled. 'My birth wasn't exactly planned.'

'Neither was mine! My parents made two mistakes: first my sister, then me,' Kaisa said and laughed.

Peter looked surprised, as if she'd told him something bad.

'It's OK,' she said.

He took her hands in his and asked, 'Can I see you again? After tonight, I mean?'

'I don't think that's a good idea.' She eased away from him.

An older officer, with fair, thinning hair, entered the room and Peter got rapidly to his feet.

'Good evening,' he said to the officer.

The man nodded to Kaisa and muttered something to Peter.

'Yes, sir,' Peter replied.

'Who was that?' Kaisa asked when the man walked away.

'Listen, something's happened. I have to go back to the ship.'

Kaisa looked at her watch; it was nearly midnight.

Peter held her hands.

'I must see you again.'

'It's not possible.'

She lowered her face to escape the intensity in his eyes.

'I'm only in Helsinki for another three days,' Peter insisted.

She didn't reply. Peter's hands around hers felt strong and she didn't want to pull away.

'Look, I have to go. Can I at least phone you?' Peter asked.

She hesitated. 'No.'

His eyes widened. 'Why not?'

'It's impossible.'

Kaisa didn't know what else to say.

Peter leaned closer to her. She felt his warm breath on her cheek when he whispered into her ear, 'Nothing is impossible.'

People were leaving. The older officer, Collins, came over to tell Peter he had to go.

Turning to Kaisa again Peter said, 'Please?'

Kaisa bit her lip, 'Do you have a pen?'

Peter tapped his pockets, before scanning the now-empty tables. He looked everywhere, even asked a waiter carrying a tray full of empty glasses, but no one had a pen. Kaisa dug in her handbag and found a pink lipstick.

'You can use this, I guess.'

Peter handed her a paper napkin from a table and she scrawled her number on it. Then, with the final bits of lipstick, he wrote his name and his address on HMS *Newcastle* on the back of Kaisa's invitation to the party.

Outside, on the steps of the embassy, all the officers from Peter's ship were gathered, waiting for something. The blond guy, who Peter had introduced to her and Tuuli earlier, touched his cap and smiled knowingly at them. She wondered if he thought she and Peter were now an item. Other officers also gave her sly glances. It was as if outside, on the steps of the embassy, she'd entered another world – the domain of their ship. As the only woman among the men, she felt shy and stood closer to Peter. Before she could stop him, he took off his cap and bent down to kiss her lips. He tasted of coconut and cigarettes. For a moment Kaisa kissed him back; she didn't want to pull away.

When Peter finally let go, everybody on the steps cheered. Kaisa was both embarrassed and breathless.

'You shouldn't have done that,' she whispered.

Peter smiled at her. 'Don't worry, they're just jealous.'

He led her through the throng of uniformed men and down the steps towards a waiting taxi.

'I'll call you tomorrow,' he whispered and opened the car door.

When the taxi moved away, Peter waved his cap at her. She told the driver her address and leaned back in the seat, touching her lips.

2

The dark Helsinki streets whizzed past the window. The city looked different at night; it had taken on a magical air. The taxi seemed to fly through the neighbourhoods. As they left the Esplanade Park behind them, the driver crossed the normally busy Mannerheim Street, now deserted, and, rattling over the tramlines, began the climb up the hill on Lönnrot Street. Kaisa loved the Jugendstil buildings in and around the centre of Helsinki. Their ornate facades and pale-coloured walls, built at the turn of the century, dominated the landscape. She wished all of Helsinki was built in the same style, instead of ugly, modern structures made of glass and steel. Turning into a small street the taxi slowed, and Kaisa wound down the window to get some air. On the top of the hill, even though she couldn't yet see the sea surrounding the city, she could smell it.

As the taxi crossed the bridge to Lauttasaari Island and made its way towards Kaisa's flat, she wondered how she was going to explain her actions to Matti. Even she didn't know what had happened during the magical evening she'd just spent with the British Officer.

Peter.

She looked out of the window, no longer seeing the passing scenery but his face and that smile. The white cap, which had accentuated his features, made him even more handsome. She grinned, remembering his hand on her backside when they'd danced to a slow piece. She wished now she'd let him keep his hand there for longer!

Kaisa shook her head. No, she mustn't think like that. She'd done a terrible thing and now she must pay for it.

She'd kissed another man, a foreign man. That was wrong, she knew that, but it was the feeling in her body from the tips of her toes to her fingertips that scared her. It made her feel like she was floating. Even though she'd betrayed her fiancé, it had felt so utterly right to respond to Peter's kiss when he'd grabbed her and lowered his lips to hers.

Whatever the reckoning with Matti, one thing she knew for certain: she had to see Peter again.

Kaisa unlocked the door to her flat and listened out for sounds. But she only heard the noise of the traffic outside. She blew a breath out that she hadn't realised she'd been holding. Her heart was still pounding by the time she got undressed and climbed into bed. The streetlight shone through the venetian blinds and formed a familiar zigzag pattern on the walls of her bedroom.

Remembering something, she jumped up and put the chain across the front door. Sometimes Matti came over without letting her know first, and tonight Kaisa didn't want see him. At the very least she wanted some warning of his arrival. She listened for the sound of steps outside in the hallway. When she heard nothing, she got back into bed and pulled the covers up to her chin.

What had she done? She'd given a man – a foreigner – her telephone number, and she'd let him kiss her. Feeling sober, Kaisa knew she couldn't see him again. Not only had she let him think she was free, but she'd also betrayed her fiancé. A cold shiver went through her when she imagined what Matti's mother would say if she found out.

Peter had hardly slept. The divers hadn't finished searching under the hull of the ship until the early hours of the morning. The excitement sobered him up pretty quickly after the party at the British Embassy. Perhaps the Duty Officer had been a little jumpy calling them back when it was probably only seagulls fighting over pieces of bread in the water. But, as the Captain had told them, any suspicious activity must be taken very seriously during this visit. By all accounts, the Russians had a more-or-less free hand in Helsinki, so who knew what they might try. Peter knew he shouldn't have had so much to drink on the first night ashore, but what could he do when he was required to attend three cocktail parties in one evening?

He stretched his legs over the narrow bunk and smiled. Someone had to do it. Who'd have thought the cuts in the Navy's budget would have such an effect on his personal life? The first visit to Finland by the Royal Navy since the Cold War started was supposed to include three ships, but in the end only Peter's had been sent to this small country bordering the Soviet Union. It was pathetic – and embarrassing.

I bet the Russians are laughing into their samovars this morning, Peter thought.

All the same, this was the closest Peter would ever get to visiting a country behind the Iron Curtain, so he planned to make the most of it. It wasn't that he hadn't heard the Captain's talk about honey traps, but Peter believed in the old proverb: you only live once. This was the most exciting trip of his naval career so far and he was sure he'd spot a KGB agent a mile off, however beautiful she was. And he could keep his mouth shut, he was sure of that too.

Peter's thoughts went to the girl last night. There was something irresistible about her. Those pale-blue eyes and the shiver of her body whenever he touched her. And she was intelligent. She'd kept Peter on his toes. Her ability to chat in a language not native to her was a huge turn on. He found himself wanting to impress Kaisa after only spending one evening with her.

Last night Peter almost wished the Russians had planted something – one of those minisubs they kept hearing about – under HMS *Newcastle*. He could see the newspaper headline *'Brave Royal Navy officer Peter Williams discovers Soviet minisub in the Baltic'* with a picture of him from his early Dartmouth days.

Of course, it would not have been him – as a sub-lieutenant, he was one of the lowest ranking officers on board. He'd only left Dartmouth a few weeks ago. And he wasn't even a diver. But the image of him as a hero was irresistible. Something like that would have impressed Kaisa.

He got up swiftly and found his mess undress jacket. The napkin was still there in the pocket, with the telephone number scrawled on it. Still legible – just. He took a long, deep drag on his cigarette and blew smoke to the side, away from his bunk.

Peter waited until noon to call Kaisa. He had nearly an hour until he was on duty again. He left his cabin and walked along the gangway to the wardroom.

'It's the lover boy!' A grinning Collins was sitting in the wardroom. He'd spoken to Kaisa for a while at the party, and witnessed much of their evening together. Collins was only jealous; he'd been married for years. But Peter liked the guy.

He smiled back at the lieutenant, and waited until the older officer had left before lifting the receiver. He felt a twinge in his groin when he heard the phone ringing at the other end. Kaisa had really been quite lovely and he could tell she'd been smitten by him too. The phone kept ringing at the other end.

'Your bit of foreign fluff not at home?' Collins said from the passageway.

Peter ignored him and dialled again, making sure he got each digit right. Pulling the long cord with him, he stepped into the mess and out of earshot of the older man. He tried the number four times, but there was no answer. He was standing in the gangway and was about to dial again when Collins passed him a second time and gave him a knowing look. He guessed everyone on board was talking about him and the pretty Finnish girl. There was nothing to be done now – he'd try ringing again after his four-hour watch on the quarterdeck.

As he spent the long hours of his shift thinking about Kaisa, Peter wondered if she'd already forgotten about him. A girl like that would have a queue of admirers. She was probably with another guy at this moment. *No,* Peter thought. She didn't seem that kind of girl. If anything, it was as if she'd never been kissed before when he'd taken her into his arms. She shivered but didn't pull back. Although, her reactions spoke of her having more experience, not less.

He hadn't planned on spending a long time at the British Embassy. Earlier in the evening, the Chinese had well and truly oiled them, probably hoping to gain vital information from a drunk officer. As if any of them would be that stupid!

But as soon as he'd seen the pretty, blonde girl standing in the corner, he knew he had to talk to her. And when they started talking, even with her accented English – which was so sexy – it was as if they'd met before. She was sweet, funny and clever. All he'd wanted to do was take her in his arms and kiss her. And perhaps, if he ever got hold of her before they sailed, he might take her to bed. Peter smiled and took a drag out of his cigarette, feeling confident that, somehow, he would meet Kaisa again.

'You must have it bad, old chap.' Collins slapped Peter on the shoulder as he passed. He'd lost count of how many times over the last two days he'd tried Kaisa's number. He'd called it all day yesterday and now, on a Saturday, it still kept ringing and ringing at the other end.

'Plenty more fish in the sea!' Collins shouted and, turning around, cupped his pretend breasts and pursed his lips in a mock kiss. There was dirty laughter all around him. Peter wanted to tell him to fuck off but he was senior to him, so he just laughed half-heartedly.

After about ten rings he replaced the receiver on the wall and slumped into an empty sofa in the officers' mess. Nick, the other sub-lieutenant onboard, sat in a chair opposite him, reading a magazine. A young steward was clearing away the dishes from a table, littered with half-filled cups of milky tea and cake crumbs.

Peter ran his fingers through his thick hair. He frowned at the paper napkin, trying to see if he'd missed something in the numbers.

'Still no answer?' said Nick.

He and Nick had graduated from Dartmouth at the same time, but it was really only during the last few weeks on the ship that they'd become firm friends. Peter waited until the steward, balancing a tray full of cups and saucers, left them.

'I don't get it – why would she give me a wrong number?'

'To shut you up?' Nick grinned at him.

Peter ignored his friend. With a sigh, he leaned back against the hard edge of the wardroom sofa, and flicked the now-tattered piece of napkin onto the table. He took a packet of cigarettes out of his breast pocket and lit one. Blowing the smoke upwards, he wondered why he was so keen to get in touch with this girl anyway. They were going to sail tomorrow, so there'd be no time to really get to know her, to have her. Still, there was something about her, something different.

The way she'd reacted when he'd touched her. The passion hidden beneath that cool exterior.

He wanted to know how she looked with the dress pulled down to her waist. She'd worn no bra and he'd clearly seen the outline of her breasts.

God, he mustn't think about it now.

'She was into me, wasn't she?' he asked Nick.

His friend nodded.

'She was more interested in you than her friend was in me, if I can put it that way. Her friend made a slip as soon as my back was turned.'

'You didn't mind, did you?' Peter said. He knew Nick had a serious girl-friend back at home.

Nick smiled. 'No, of course not. Still, it's nice to have a harmless flirt, but she didn't even want to do that!'

'Yeah.' Peter stumped out his cigarette.

'Here, let me have a look at that number.' Nick picked up the napkin and began studying it. He turned it this way and that. 'That last number – is it a seven?'

Peter nodded; he could recount the number by heart now, '2-4-5-5-2-7'.

'Have you tried it as a one? You know, Europeans put that little slash across a seven and this hasn't got one, so...'

3

Two days after the embassy party was a cold autumn day. The single tree outside Kaisa's block of flats had long since lost its leaves – it stood there, desolate, trying to survive the stormy winds from the Baltic that beat its tender trunk. She sighed as she watched its struggle from the narrow window of her kitchenette.

Living alone in a flat in Helsinki had seemed glamorous a year ago. Now the beige walls of the one-bedroomed place in Lauttasaari felt restricting. The flat, which belonged to her fiancé's family, wasn't even in Helsinki proper. There was a bus service but it took almost an hour to reach the city centre. While Tuuli could walk to Hanken from her place, Kaisa was forced to memorise bus schedules and carefully plan her trips into the city. She was always late for lectures.

When the phone rang suddenly, she jumped.

'Hello?'

'Hello Kaisa, how are you?'

The familiar voice left her feeling a mixture of emotions. She sat down on a chair next to the hall table, battling her guilt at what she had done, and the overwhelming sense of disappointment when she heard it was Matti.

Why had Peter not phoned as he promised?

'I'm not feeling any better,' she replied.

Matti had phoned twice the day before, and she'd put on a throaty voice to stop him from coming over. Kaisa couldn't see him, not yet. She'd never lied to Matti like this before. She stared at her reflection in the mirror above the table. The face of a cheat stared back at her.

She listened to her fiancé talk about the British ship he could see from his office window. Matti worked as a Customs officer at the South Harbour.

Her heart beat faster at the mention of it.

'You can see the English people coming and going?' she asked trying to sound nonchalant.

'Yes, their uniforms are very smart.'

Kaisa's mouth felt dry. She couldn't speak. The thought of Matti looking at the deck of the British ship and possibly seeing Peter walk along it made her feel dizzy.

'You still there?' Matti said. She could hear the irritation in his voice.

He'd been desperately jealous of her invite to the party and would have forbidden her to go, if he'd been able to. Oh, what a mess she'd got herself into. Perhaps Matti had been right: perhaps she should never have gone to the embassy party.

'I am feeling really poorly.'

She tried to make her voice sound croaky. She forced a cough and swallowed loudly.

'I'll come over. I'm sure I can make you feel better,' Matti said. Kaisa heard the smile in his voice and guessed the double entendre. She shivered. Feeling how she did, she couldn't be close to Matti now. She needed to buy more time.

'You don't want to catch whatever I have, do you?' she asked.

Matti hated being sick.

'No, and neither do I wish to pass it on to Mother,' Matti said, adding, 'I'll call you tomorrow.'

When she heard the line go dead, she replaced the receiver. Sitting there, Kaisa realised the embassy party had been the first time she'd been out without her fiancé since they got engaged. And that hadn't really been going out either – not according to her friend. When Kaisa first met Tuuli, on the first day of term in the autumn of last year, her friend had been surprised to see the ring on her finger.

'But you're the same age as me!' Tuuli had said. Of course, Kaisa was used to that kind of reaction – not many girls got engaged at the age of sixteen – so she just laughed.

Now sitting in the hall, next to the silent telephone, Kaisa looked at the invitation from the British Embassy. She traced the gold lettering with her fingertips and turned it over, gazing at the smudged lipstick on the back.

His name and address.

Like a fool Kaisa had sat in her flat for two days, waiting for Peter's phone call. During that time, she'd made only short calls to her friend and tried to get her fiancé off the line as quickly as possible. She was supposed to be studying, before her university lectures restarted next Monday, but all she could think about was Peter. Kaisa was furious with herself. At least Matti didn't know how dumb she'd been, so completely taken in by a foreign sailor. Thank goodness all he'd got out of her was a quick, stolen kiss.

She dialled Tuuli's number.

'No call?' her friend said with a sigh.

Was Tuuli getting bored with her talking about Peter?

'No,' she said.

'Forget about him. It was a bit of fun, that's all.'

Of course, Tuuli was right.

Kaisa changed the subject. 'Are you going to see your guy again?'

Her Finnish sailor had gone back to his barracks at Santahamina, a few miles down the coast of the Gulf of Bothnia.

'I don't know. He was a bit too – correct. You know what I mean?'

Kaisa said she did, but didn't really understand. Matti was very 'correct'. Peter wasn't at all like that, although he *was* serving in the armed forces, like Tuuli's sailor. He didn't seem to take anything seriously, he was always laughing. Perhaps that was why he hadn't called; perhaps Kaisa was a great big joke too? Or was it some kind of a game? Was he one of those boys who liked to conquer, and then chuck you as soon as they've won you over? But they hadn't done anything; all he'd got from her was a hasty kiss.

It didn't matter now, Kaisa told herself.

So why was she still waiting for a call from some foreign stranger when she was engaged to be married? It wasn't right. Sooner or later she'd have to come clean to Matti. But first, she needed to get over her own embarrassment. Matti's incessant questions about the party, the embassy, the foreign officers and the food and drink could wait.

Kaisa was putting on coffee and scanning her near-empty fridge for something to eat when her doorbell rang. She froze hoping, praying it wasn't Matti. But he was at work and only got half an hour for lunch. She glanced at her watch and saw it was a quarter past one. Perhaps he'd left work early?

The doorbell sounded again, this time more forcefully. Could she pretend she wasn't at home? No, that wouldn't work. She'd already told Matti she was ill and needed to rest.

Slowly, Kaisa made her way to the door and looked through the spy hole. She took a step back in surprise and opened the door.

'Dad!'

Her father smiled.

'Aren't you going to invite me in?'

Kaisa nodded and let him in to the flat. She hadn't seen him in over a month. They hadn't exactly been close since her parents' divorce, five years earlier. Unannounced home visits were a rarity.

He gave Kaisa one of his bear hugs, which always made Kaisa feel like a little girl. They reminded her of happier times when her dad used to call her his Best Girl, and joked and made up funny stories for her and her sister, Sirkka.

'This is nice,' her father said as he walked into Kaisa's living room. His large bulk seemed to dwarf the space. She nodded to the sofa, indicating he should sit down, and asked, 'Coffee?'

Her dad looked at her, as if he were surprised by the offer and went out to her small balcony instead.

'Sea view!' he said and smiled at Kaisa, standing in the doorway.

But it was still raining.

She nodded and stepped back inside, wondering how long it was going to take him to tell her what he wanted.

Her dad closed the balcony door behind him and said, 'I need new clothes.'

Kaisa sat down on the sofa. Since the divorce from her mother, Pirjo, her dad's appearance had slowly become more dishevelled. Kaisa remembered the old black-and-white pictures of a young handsome man, with wide shoulders and narrow hips, smiling widely below his light-brown hair. Nowadays he wore saggy pants with white shirts, which had long since turned a nasty shade of grey. He'd often sneer at the interest his daughters and wife showed in fashion; clothes were a waste of money in his opinion.

'And I want you to help me find a new outfit,' he added.

'But...'

'No buts. I'll buy you lunch afterwards.'

She was reluctant to leave her flat in case Peter called, but her dad looked so disappointed when she hesitated. It didn't help that she was slowly going mad waiting for a call that might never come, so she put on her coat and agreed to go shopping with him.

After her weird outing with her father, Kaisa decided to make bread rolls.

Turns out she'd really enjoyed the trip. Her dad had been his old self. He'd joked and teased her, and even flirted with one of the sales assistants. Looking at him in his new dark-blue cords and a Marimekko shirt she'd convinced him to buy at Stockmann's, she'd seen the return of that good-looking man from the old photos. The sales assistant clearly thought the same, judging by the smile she'd given him when he'd paid for his purchases. During lunch, her father had given her another surprise.

'I have a girlfriend. She's not much to look at, but she's nice. An artist.'

'That's good,' Kaisa had said, ignoring her father's unfavourable description of the poor woman.

She was glad that her dad was finally moving on. When the divorce became final, he'd vowed to, 'never let a woman run rings around me ever again.' Both Sirkka and Kaisa figured this statement included his two daughters and, true to his word, he'd hardly been in touch with either of them. Pirjo complained often about his lack of contributions towards the children's education and upkeep, but what Kaisa missed most was the simple presence of her father, the man he used to be before he started drinking and hitting their mother. He'd been the one person she could rely upon. Perhaps he'd stopped drinking? He'd even had low-alcohol beer during their lunch saying, 'Got to keep a clear head for later.'

When they'd parted, her dad had given Kaisa a bear hug and thanked her for the help with the shopping.

She looked out the window of her kitchenette. The temperatures had dropped and it was now snowing; the first fall of the year. Light flecks dropped slowly to the asphalt below and melted as they landed. She turned away from the cold scene and started mixing flour with water and yeast.

The loud, urgent ringing of the phone filled the flat.

Not Matti again, please, Kaisa prayed.

She picked up the receiver with her floured hands.

'Hello?'

'Kaisa, is it really you?' a familiar voice said. Her heart lifted and her legs felt as if they might give way.

'Peter,' Kaisa whispered.

'I told you I'd call.'

'You're late.'

'Sorry?' He sounded serious.

'Exactly two days late.'

Kaisa was surprised by the anger in her voice. She no longer felt breathless or weak.

'Let me explain...'

Peter talked fast and Kaisa listened. Even when he was being serious she could hear the smile in his voice. He'd rung the wrong number. The digit 'one' that she'd written in lipstick on his napkin looked like a seven, he said.

'Nick, you remember Nick, the tall, blond guy, don't you?' Peter asked.

'Yes.'

'Well, he told me that you Europeans write numbers differently.'

'I see.' She tried to hold on to her anger, but in truth she was melting.

'Please, please come and meet me!' Peter said.

Could Kaisa believe this foreign sailor's words? Everyone knew foreigners, and sailors in particular, had loose morals. She thought about her fiancé. How could she explain to Matti why she'd met up with the Englishman, twice? If they met up just as friends and didn't do anything, was it still wrong? Could she trust herself not to kiss him again? If Matti found out, he might leave her. Was she really prepared for that? She might lose the flat, owned by his aunt. Then there was Matti's mother. How could she face her?

'I would love to see you again,' Peter said, adding, 'We sail tomorrow.'

Kaisa heard the sincerity in his words. She closed her eyes and thought about the kiss.

'But it's impossible,' she whispered.

She sat down and held on tightly to the receiver, not caring about the dough sticking to the plastic handle.

There was another short pause. Kaisa held her breath. Was he giving up on her?

Peter said, 'If I phone again in half an hour, will you promise to think about it?'

4

_____

Peter arrived ten minutes late. Kaisa was early as usual; a Finn was always on time or early for a rendezvous. But as soon as she saw him walking towards her, wearing a dark navy mac, she forgave him for his lateness. He probably didn't know Helsinki that well. His hair was darker than she remembered, as were his eyes.

When he spotted her he opened his arms, scooped Kaisa up inside his coat and quickly released her. She looked around nervously; hugging wasn't something people in Finland did on the street, in public. What if some of her fiancé's family saw her? Kaisa dreaded to think what would happen if Matti's aunt spotted her with this dark-haired man. The old bat would know he was foreign straight away, with his features and the way he dressed – in a summer mac in October! Luckily it was a cold, windy evening and very few people had braved the outdoors.

'So,' Peter said, 'you're here.'

They were standing opposite each other. His dark eyes were, again, boring into Kaisa.

She looked down shyly at her boots and said, 'Yes.'

'Well, I'm glad.' He took her hand.

They walked long the deserted North Esplanade, their steps matching easily, as if they'd done this for years and years. Together, they sauntered along the streets of Helsinki, looking into the bright and inviting shop windows. But it was well past seven in the evening and everywhere was shut. Kaisa suddenly realised she hadn't given a thought to where they should go.

As if he'd read her mind, Peter said, 'Shall we go and have a drink?'

Kaisa looked up at him.

'A pub, perhaps?' he said.

She took him to the only place she knew none of her fiancé's family would go: Kaarle XII. 'Kalle', as the students called the place, was popular with young drinkers. There was a disco on Thursday nights that made it difficult to get in. Matti hated new music; he only liked the old-fashioned dances, such as tango, Finnish *humppa* or the waltz. Kaisa knew he'd never set foot in a bar like Kalle.

For a Saturday evening, the place wasn't too full. They found a table in the corner and Kaisa went to get two beers from the bar. When she handed the bottle and glass to Peter, he glanced behind him. A group of guys were whistling and pointing in their direction.

'Sailors from my ship,' Peter said and poured beer into his glass. He laughed as if it were a joke.

Peter put his hand on Kaisa's and smiled. She was bursting with happiness. Here she was, sitting opposite a man she'd met only once before. He was good-looking in an obvious way, which usually would make Kaisa mistrustful. Yet she didn't want to move even slightly in case he let go of her hand. She smiled at him, and he pulled her fingers to his lips and kissed them.

'I'm so happy you're here.'

The noise from the other patrons and the music grew louder, until they couldn't hear each other. One of the sailors came over to the table and, looking at Kaisa, said, 'Aren't you going to introduce me to the lovely lady, sir?'

Peter mumbled his reply, finished his beer quickly and said, 'Could we go somewhere else?'

Kaisa brought him to another place near the Helsinki train station, where they ordered some food. Peter ate a steak while she picked at a salad.

Over the meal he told her about his childhood, how he didn't do as well at school as he should have done.

'I was very lazy,' he said. 'My father wanted me to join the Navy, and I did it as soon as I could after school.' Peter smiled. 'And I love it.'

Kaisa told him about her childhood, about all the schools she'd been to, about how her family moved to Stockholm when she was eleven, after which she'd hardly spent more than a year in one school.

'How many languages do you speak?' said Peter.

'Just Swedish and English, and a little bit of French and German. And Finnish, obviously.'

'Wow.'

'But my English isn't so good.'

'You speak English wonderfully – I love your accent.'

Kaisa felt her face grow hot. She lowered her eyes.

Peter took hold of her hands and leaned closer to her.

'I love everything about you.'

'You mustn't say that.'

He rubbed the ring on her left hand.

'Why not?'

'I'm engaged to be married.'

He glanced down at her left finger, with the white and yellow gold band on it, and let go of her hands.

A silence followed. Kaisa held her breath. This would surely be the end. Next he'll say he has to get back to the ship.

Kaisa stared at a piece of lettuce on her plate. It had gone brown at the edges.

At last Peter said, 'But you're not *married*.'

She looked into his dark eyes, again feeling like she could sink into them.

'No.'

She knew she should be strong, leave Peter and return home, but something drew her to this foreign man. He'd be gone soon and she would never see him again. Still she didn't move, fiddling with her engagement band, rooted to her seat.

'So...you could come and see me in England?' Peter said.

'No, that's impossible,' Kaisa replied without thinking.

Peter took her hands in his again. His lips turned up at the corners into a bright smile.

'I told you – nothing is impossible!'

Kaisa smiled too. A waiter came over and, looking at her half-full plate of salad, asked if they'd finished.

'Yes,' she said.

The waiter pointed at Peter's empty glass of beer and asked in Finnish if he wanted another one. Kaisa exchanged glances with Peter. The waiter was being rude on purpose; surely he'd heard them speaking English.

'We're fine – just the bill please,' Kaisa snapped in Finnish.

After the meal, they did all the things would-be lovers with nowhere to go would do. They walked along the Esplanade under the steel-coloured sky, then flitted from one Helsinki bar to another. Kaisa was petrified that they'd meet someone she knew, especially as Peter insisted on holding her close to him. So she steered him to more places where her fiancé's posh family were unlikely to go. Of course, they bumped into his shipmates everywhere they went, inducing hilarity and cheering.

In Happy Days, a large bar that had opened only a few weeks earlier, Peter told Kaisa his commanding officer had warned him about her.

'What do you mean?'

'There are honey traps, you know.' When Kaisa frowned at him, he added, 'KGB agents posing as beautiful young women to trap young officers.'

Kaisa laughed. Her – a KGB agent? In Helsinki?

'But I'm not,' she said touching his arm.

'I know you're not. Very few of these honey traps wear an engagement ring, for one.'

He laughed and the sound made Kaisa smile.

'So you noticed the ring from the start?' she said.

He nodded.

Kaisa stared at him. 'But why call if you knew...'

Peter shrugged and took her hand between his.

'I couldn't help myself. You're very beautiful.'

She whispered, 'Thank you.'

'And we sail tomorrow.'

His eyes had grown even darker; Kaisa had to look away to stop from leaning over to kiss him.

With no more food or drink left, they braved the cold weather in Esplanade Park. At least it had stopped snowing. They sheltered from the chill wind by the statue of Eino Leino, the Finnish poet. Kaisa tried to remember some of his romantic works, but all she could recall was a verse from a poem about old age that she'd had to study at school, *'Haihtuvi nuoruus niinkuin vierivä virta'*. Kaisa translated for Peter: *'Youth disappears as fast as a river flows.'* She looked up at the imposing figure, with its heavy cape, and wondered if the great man was trying to tell her something. In the deserted park, they stood in the shadow of the statue. Happy no one could see them Kaisa relaxed a little.

'You're lovely,' Peter said, and hugged her.

She forgot all about the poem, or being cold, or her fiancé's family. She felt safe in Peter's arms. He took Kaisa's face between his hands and kissed her. She kissed him back. His lips moved to her neck and back to her lips again. His hands, now warm, roamed beneath Kaisa's jumper. She didn't tell him to stop. She couldn't resist him. His desire was hard against her thigh; she wanted him so much, her body ached.

'Can we go to your flat?' Peter asked breathlessly.

'My fiancé might be there.' Kaisa freed herself a little from his grip. 'He has a key.'

'This is our last chance to be together,' Peter said, his voice hoarse.

He kissed her again, this time more deeply and afterwards, looking into her eyes, he whispered, 'I know you want me too.'

She had no choice but to tell him her fiancé had a dangerous hobby.

'He has a favourite handgun, which he sometimes carries.'

Peter stared at her, and didn't ask about the flat again.

Kaisa's last bus was due to leave soon and Peter said he would walk her to the stop.

'I'll write, and you must promise to write back to me,' he said holding Kaisa's hand.

They walked slowly along the Boulevard, huddling for warmth. The hard wind swept along the tree-lined street, forcing them to hold each other even closer. When Kaisa saw her bus turn a corner from Mannerheim Street she felt tearful, but she swallowed her emotions and forced a smile.

Peter took hold of her chin and, looking into her eyes, said, 'We'll see each other again, I promise.'

He pulled something out of his coat pocket and gave it to her.

'It's a tape of a band I really like, the Pretenders. The best track is "Brass in Pocket". I want you to have this.'

Kaisa couldn't speak; she held the cassette tightly.

'Something to remember me by,' he said and kissed her again.

The bus stopped and Peter kept her hand in his. Kaisa tried to pull away but he wouldn't let go.

'One more kiss,' he said and they embraced again.

Over Peter's shoulder Kaisa saw the bus driver shrug, close the doors and pull away.

'That was the last one!' she said and they both laughed.

Past midnight, when Peter put her into a taxi and Kaisa was alone, she finally let herself cry. She knew she'd never see the Englishman again.

5

K aisa dreaded going back to her flat. She considered asking the taxi driver to take her to her friend's place in town instead. But it was nearly one o'clock in the morning; she couldn't wake up Tuuli now. But she wanted to remember Peter, to preserve the feel of his kisses and not lose the smell of him on her. Yet she knew she had to come clean to her fiancé at some point.

The taxi dropped her off at home. When Kaisa opened the front door and saw no lights on, she sighed with relief. She put the chain across the door and leaned against it. She had another free night to dream about Peter before having to talk to her fiancé.

Someone called her name, making Kaisa jump. She moved farther into the flat and saw Matti, sitting on her bed in the dark, wearing a pair of brown cords and an Icelandic sweater that Kaisa had knitted last Christmas. She hung back in the doorway to the bedroom, not knowing what to say or do.

Matti stood up and strode towards her. He grabbed her arm demanding, 'Where have you been?'

His brown hair was neatly combed to one side and his eyes looked darker than usual. He wasn't smiling.

When Kaisa told Matti about Peter he fell quiet. She talked more, trying to explain. 'I know he's a stranger, but it feels like I've known him all my life.'

Matti slumped onto the bed. He groaned, as if she'd stabbed him.

Kaisa sat beside him and carried on. 'I didn't go to the cocktail party in order to meet someone. It was just an accident.'

'Accident!' Matti's voice was sharp and loud.

Her fiancé, who'd been a calm and controlled man for the four years she'd known him, was suddenly shouting at her.

'You saw him again!' he bellowed. 'You're no better than those girls who hang around ports, prostituting themselves to sailors. How much did he pay you?'

'We didn't do anything!'

'Oh yeah? You expect me to believe you?'

Kaisa shrank back from his verbal attack. She'd never seen her fiancé like this. Despite his love of guns he was not a violent man. He was seven years older than Kaisa, and she guessed that had been part of her attraction to him. While the boys at school had drunk too much and hardly remembered what they'd done with a girl the night before, Matti would cook wonderful meals, or take Kaisa for long walks in the forest or read her poems. He'd never been in a hurry and he'd never done anything without considering the consequences. And he'd never said a cross word to her.

Until now.

'You know he has a girl like you in every port.'

Kaisa felt sick. She was so tired that tears ran down her face. It felt like ages that she and Matti had been sitting there on her bed.

'And what do you know about him – nothing!' Matti said. 'I bet you'll never set eyes on him again.'

Kaisa sobbed. She couldn't look at him.

'So what are you going to do?' Matti's tone was suddenly gentle.

Relieved, Kaisa looked into his brown eyes. It was as if the man she knew so well was back again.

'I don't know.'

They were both silent for a long time. Kaisa heard a solitary car somewhere in the distance. She wished she was in it. She wished she was anywhere else but here.

Matti put his arm around Kaisa's shoulders.

'Let's get into bed.'

His tone was demanding.

Kaisa nodded. It was late. She grabbed her nightdress and went into the bathroom, needing to be alone. Matti's fury had only validated her own worries. What did she know about the Englishman? Peter was young, the same age as her. She remembered him telling her at the embassy party that he didn't have a girlfriend, but was writing to someone at home. Someone he'd been to school with.

Kaisa hated the girl already.

Peter was tall, dark and handsome. He loved books and believed that character was fate. He'd told Kaisa to read Thomas Hardy. His lips were the softest and strongest she'd ever kissed. He laughed a lot, and when he did his eyes sparkled. He looked at Kaisa as if he wanted to wrap her up, protect her and devour her – all at once.

Kaisa realised she'd never felt love like this before, not even with Matti. This was the stuff she'd been reading about in books since she was a teenager; hoping for in the films she'd watched. This was how Ali MacGraw had felt about Ryan O'Neal in *Love Story*, and Barbra Streisand about Robert Redford in *The Way We Were*. Kaisa grinned. She'd wanted to pose the same question to Peter that Katie had to Hubbell, *'Do you smile ALL the time?'*

As she sat on the toilet seat, shivering in her thin nightwear, she couldn't get Peter out of her head. His smile, his dark eyes, his warm mouth. She sighed, flushed the empty toilet and ran the water in the sink for a second or two. She didn't want her fiancé to guess what she'd been doing in here – daydreaming about Peter.

Matti was already in bed. When Kaisa lay beside him, he turned so his face was close to hers. His breath was hot on her cheek and she knew what he wanted.

'I'm really tired,' she said as gently as she could, and turned her back to him.

Kaisa felt the tension in Matti's body. She curled herself into a ball and forced her eyes shut. He moved, pressed himself against her, but she remained still until his breathing steadied and she knew he was asleep.

In the morning, Kaisa woke early and went to make some coffee. She felt as if she hadn't slept a wink. The scene outside the little kitchen window was miserable; the first snow had melted and a hard drizzle was beating against the window pane. It was almost sleet. The street below was empty and only a few lights shone brightly from the block of flats opposite. It was too early on a Saturday morning for life.

She thought about Peter on board his ship. Had they sailed already? He'd said they'd be leaving early but not at what time.

For a mad second, Kaisa thought about getting dressed and going to the harbour to wave him goodbye. How wonderful it would be to see him once more – she imagined his surprise when he spotted her on the quayside. Then she remembered her fiancé, asleep in the next room. All her clothes were on the floor. If she woke Matti, he'd demand to know where she was off to.

Kaisa shivered when she remembered how he had woken up in the middle of the night, and seeing her awake had said, 'You know if I ever set my eyes on that sailor, I'll kill him.'

The coffee machine made gurgling noises. She turned, startled by Matti's large, looming figure in the open doorway to the kitchenette. Fully dressed, he walked over to her and slid his hands around Kaisa's waist.

'Coffee's nearly ready,' she said, turning away from him. His strong hand gripped her tighter and she felt sick. What was happening to her? It was as if she'd morphed into another person overnight; a stupid girl who believed a foreign man loved her.

Kaisa pushed his hands away gently.

'I'm going to get dressed.' She fled to the bedroom.

Returning to the lounge ten minutes later, she saw Matti standing with his arms crossed over his chest, facing the window.

'Breakfast?' she tried to sound normal, cheerful even.

He didn't reply. He didn't even move. Kaisa put out some ham and cheese and sliced the last piece of cucumber she had in the fridge. She'd bought some wheaten rolls from the small bakery opposite the bank a couple of days ago, and decided they were still soft enough to eat. She sat down and waited for Matti. He turned slowly and sat at the small table in one corner of the room, in his usual seat opposite Kaisa.

'So, are you still coming to the cottage with us?'

She looked at him holding half a roll in his hand, delicately balancing the cheese and two pieces of cucumber on top with his index finger. His face was serious, as if he was asking whether, with her new-found career as the local harlot, she'd given up all decent activities, such as taking his mother to the summer place. Every weekend between May and October – if the weather wasn't too bad – Matti would drive to Haapamäki, two hours north, where they'd spend the weekend in the cottage.

Kaisa frowned at her plate. She'd forgotten all about the trip.

When she didn't reply, Matti said, 'What shall I tell Mother?'

Kaisa shivered. 'OK. I'll go.'

All she wanted to do was stay at home and think about Peter, or go and see Tuuli and tell her all about the wonderful evening she'd spent with him. But she knew that if she didn't go to the cottage she'd never hear the end of it. She thought about asking him to say she was ill, but Matti never lied to his mother. (Although she truly didn't feel well.)

Kaisa shook the fantasy from her head. What did she think was going to happen with Peter anyway? He was in the British Royal Navy and she lived in Finland. He sailed all over the world, probably meeting many pretty girls. Kaisa needed to be realistic, to get back to normal. The cottage had to be made ready for the winter, when no one visited. She'd promised to help her fiancé rake up the leaves, and had told his mother she'd help pack away the fine china and glasses. Every spring his mother brought a box of 'her things' to the cabin, and every autumn she'd make Matti carry the same box back again.

This weekend was the last one they'd spend in the cottage. She had to keep her promise.

6

The three of them drove up north in almost total silence. As usual Kaisa was in the back seat, while Matti's mother sat in the front. Kaisa didn't know how to make conversation with her; all she wanted to do was stare out of the window at the greying landscape. The autumn colours were almost gone; on the road out of Helsinki, a few trees by the roadside had crops of yellow leaves still clutching to the branches. The sight of them added to Kaisa's sense of hopelessness.

For the first few minutes of the journey, Matti's mother had tried to make conversation. 'How are your studies going?'

'I'm not back at university yet.'

She knew this; why did she always ask questions she knows the answer to?

'That's a very long summer holiday!' Matti's mother tried to turn to face Kaisa, but could only bend her fair-haired head slightly towards the back seat.

Mother wasn't a well woman; she had rheumatism and made few trips without her son. She was also quite large, but had very thin ankles and wrists. Her hair was carefully coiffured but sparse; through the few strands of the up-do Kaisa saw the pink of her skull. Today she was wearing very little makeup: only dusty pink lipstick and black eyeliner that had been shakily applied. Kaisa often wondered if she should help Mother with her makeup, but was afraid to offer in case she got angry. She was a very proud woman with a quick temper.

She also held the purse strings tightly, something Matti was always privately complaining to Kaisa about.

'I'm an adult, for goodness sake. You'd think she'd let me have some kind of allowance.'

After their engagement, his mother had even insisted Kaisa call her 'Mother'. Matti had said it made his mother very happy to know she finally had the daughter she'd always longed for. To Kaisa it didn't seem right and she never called her that to her face.

At last the narrow country lane leading to the cottage appeared, and Matti drove onto the cleared bit of land in front of the one-storey building. It was a typical Finnish summer cottage construction: planks of timber cladding and each corner of the cabin perching on blocks of concrete. Kaisa hated the dark recesses below the house and was sure creepy crawlies, perhaps even snakes, lived in the damp soil. The cabin was painted pale yellow and had large windows looking out onto the lake.

The main room had doors for two small bedrooms on one side, and a small kitchen on the other. The front door led directly to the kitchen, so if anyone was cooking at the old electric stove and someone came in, they'd have to move to let them pass. Washing-up was equally problematic, but Matti's mother wouldn't hear of using disposable dinnerware. Kaisa had often stood at the sink after lunch, while the sun was beaming down outside, wishing she could sunbathe instead of taking dirty plates from Matti's mother. Mother's hands were swollen from rheumatism, but her long finger-nails were always perfectly manicured and painted with pink polish. Her arthritis made her clumsy, but she never let Kaisa do the washing-up on her own. During the whole, drawn-out procedure, Kaisa often worried there'd be a broken plate or glass to clear up from the floor.

But today, Kaisa didn't want to help prepare the food. Matti never had to do anything in the kitchen. She'd promised to help him rake the leaves; maybe she could use that as an excuse. Besides, they were here to clear up for winter, not to have a normal summer weekend.

She helped to unpack the car, noticing there was a cold lunch of mush-room pie and salad already prepared. Mother carried it inside and started to set the table, spreading out a white tablecloth. Not seeing how she could get out of it, Kaisa sighed and began to help her.

When the food was ready, Kaisa sat at the table. Matti's mother shouted out from the kitchen, 'Lunch is served!' But there was no sign of Matti.

'I'll go and see where he is,' Kaisa said standing up from her chair.

Mother gripped her bare arm; she was surprisingly strong.

Her nails dug into Kaisa's flesh.

'No, he should come when called!'

She couldn't see Matti from the windows. He must be at the back of the house raking leaves or clearing stuff from the space underneath the house, where the lilos and collapsible garden chairs were kept. Or perhaps he'd gone to the separate sauna cabin, where Kaisa usually slept.

'He might be getting the boat ready for winter,' Kaisa said in what she hoped was a soothing tone. She pulled her arm away, forcing Mother to let go of her, and walked out of the cottage.

She looked over to the sauna, but couldn't see her fiancé. By the cabin there was a long jetty to the lake and a rowing boat pulled up on the shore. Kaisa recalled how Matti used to take her to the opposite shore to pick blueberries in the late summer, and mushrooms in the autumn. After they'd filled the baskets, he would spread a blanket on a sunny cliff and make love to Kaisa. She shuddered when she thought about the times she'd been certain someone was watching from the other shore.

'All they need is a good pair of binoculars,' she'd tell Matti each time he started to undress her.

'Nah, there's no one here,' he'd reply and carry on.

'Where is that boy!' Mother shouted in a shrill voice behind her. Kaisa turned to see her at the kitchen door, her pupils dilated. With a large serving spoon in her hand, she shuffled past Kaisa and out into the garden, shouting her son's name at the deserted lake.

From the lounge window Kaisa saw a shape appear from behind the sauna. Matti slowly approached the house. For this trip, he'd chosen to wear the brown sweater she'd knitted him. As usual, he was unperturbed by his mother's outburst.

Every now and then during lunch, Matti's mother would mutter under her breath, 'I cook and clean but no one appreciates how much I do,' followed by, 'When I was a girl my mother never did anything – we had servants then, but oh no, not anymore. Not today.'

Kaisa was glad Mother was making a fuss; that way she wouldn't notice Kaisa wasn't eating anything. Her appetite had disappeared.

Matti muttered, 'We're not in tsarist Russia now.'

The fact that Matti's mother had never even been to Russia didn't matter. The tales her parents had told her of the place were enough for her to boast; the grand palaces, the acres of woodland the family had owned, the fine china and silver – 'All of it, left to the Bolsheviks.' But Matti's mother still appeared rich. She wore a mink coat in winter; she lived in a large house in Munkkiniemi, the good part of Helsinki, with a huge chandelier adorning the lounge. Kaisa never asked how her fiancé's maternal grandparents had come to Finland nor where the money had really come from. Matti had tried to tell her about it once, but she hadn't been interested.

As a Finn, Kaisa didn't want to think about the fact that Matti was half-Russian. She was just grateful that when her own father asked, she could say her fiancé's father had been Finnish.

When the light faded in the lounge, Matti took Kaisa's hand and said, 'I'll take you to the cabin.'

She looked into his eyes; they betrayed none of the anger he'd shown her earlier. This was their usual routine. He'd walk her the few hundred metres to the sauna and, unless Kaisa had her period, they'd make love. Sometimes he'd fall asleep next to her afterwards and not go back to his bedroom until four, or five, in the morning. On those mornings Kaisa would dread going into the house for breakfast. But Mother never mentioned her son's nocturnal escapades. It was as if sex didn't exist for her, or for her son.

'Goodnight, dear,' Matti's mother said and hugged her.

Matti led her outside.

'I'm really tired,' Kaisa said when he closed the kitchen door behind him.

He made no reply, and they walked in silence down the path towards the lake. The sauna was a much more recent addition to the summer place. Similar to the cottage it was also built on concrete stilts, and had steps leading up to a small veranda. It was a traditional log cabin, stained dark green.

Kaisa remembered watching Matti paint it on a late summer's day. She was sixteen and they'd been together for just over two months. It was only her second visit to the summer place. Matti told her later his mother had bought the cabin especially so that Kaisa would have somewhere to stay overnight. It never occurred to Mother that Kaisa would end up sharing her fiancé's bed in the main house and the cabin would go unused. At the time, this old-fashioned way to keep her and Matti separate had been endearing, even flattering. Now it seemed excessive to build a cottage, to stop your son and his girlfriend from sleeping together.

The cabin had a separate shower room next to it, and a dressing room with a single sofa bed. Apart from the sauna, there was no heating. The room chilled Kaisa when she opened the door. Quickly, she pulled out the trunk from underneath the sofa, where the sheets for her bed were kept. The duvet cover was also flower-patterned and pink, like the sheets.

'I'm really, really tired,' she said again, hoping he would take the hint. She turned around in the small space to see Matti was staring at the floor.

He lifted his eyes to hers. His face was so close to Kaisa that she could make out the slight wrinkles around his serious mouth. He breathed in deeply and his nostrils flared, as though he were angry.

Matti turned and left without saying a word. Kaisa locked the door. She lay awake that night, listening to the pine trees sway in the brisk autumn wind.

When they drove home on Monday back through the desolate landscape, Mother was quiet. Kaisa asked to be dropped off first. Matti stared at her through the rear-view mirror, as if to challenge her.

'We're both working early tomorrow,' Kaisa said, as nonchalantly as she could. She couldn't wait to be alone with her thoughts.

Matti turned his gaze back to the road and nodded.

Kaisa's stomach flipped. She'd lied to him again.

For the rest of the day Kaisa curled up on the sofa, listening to the Pretenders tape Peter had given her. She played it over and over, until she knew the lyrics by heart. Kaisa was sick of thinking about Matti, about the lies she'd told him, about his mother, about the future. She just wanted to relive the wonderful few hours she'd spent with Peter.

Kaisa longed for his touch, for his lips on hers. She wondered if he was thinking about her while he carried out whatever duties he had on that ship. She wished she'd gone to see him off now; instead she'd been forced to spend the Sunday at the stupid summer cottage with her stupid fiancé and his stupid mother.

7

When Kaisa entered through the glass doors of the Hanken building at the start of her second year at university, she felt almost as nervous as she had on her first day. The vast lecture theatre was barely full, with no familiar faces she could see. The high ceiling turned the hushed voices of the students into an echo. The first lecture was on employment law. The professor spoke too quietly and rushed through his notes at breakneck speed. Kaisa struggled to concentrate on the finer points of workers' rights and employers' duties. All she could think about was her handsome Englishman.

Kaisa had agreed to meet Tuuli in the Hanken canteen for coffee during the first break.

'Back here again,' Tuuli said, biting a large piece out of her doughnut.

They both loved the Berlin buns, freshly baked doughnuts filled with strawberry jam and covered with pink icing. The canteen only got a delivery once a week and they usually ran out by lunchtime.

Kaisa felt like an old timer, watching the first-year students queue up at the counter, umming and ahhing over whether to pick up a bun or not.

'They don't know how rare these are,' Kaisa said. Tuuli, with a mouthful of doughnut, nodded.

A group of boys walked into the canteen. Kaisa and Tuuli exchanged glances with them. She recognised two of the guys who had hit on them during their first week at Hanken, a year ago. The leader of the gang was a tall guy with long, light-brown hair. He and his friend had said they were in their final year, but Tuuli later found out that the pair had first started studying at Hanken in the early seventies, which meant they'd already been there for six years. All the boys in the group had rich parents. Maybe they didn't need to finish their studies and find work.

In their first week at Hanken, and knowing little of the whispers surrounding these boys, Tuuli and Kaisa had plucked up the courage to sit at a table in the Students' Union bar. Quickly they'd been joined by two of the four boys. Both girls had been surprised, and quite flattered, by the attention. The light-brown haired guy, who seemed the loudest in the group, had introduced himself as Tom and asked whether Kaisa ever went to the student disco.

'No, I don't,' Kaisa said and glanced over to her friend, who was accepting a cigarette from the blonde guy, Ricky, her head bent down to where his hand was cupped around a lit matchstick. Kaisa ignored the looks from people at other tables and from those standing about, smoking and chatting. Everyone at Hanken seemed to know one another, so when two first years had started talking to these two boys, it created a stir.

Kaisa and Tuuli chatted to Tom and Ricky for a while, smoking the cigarettes they offered. Kaisa avoided the hungry look in Tom's eyes that both scared and fascinated her. When she got up to leave, he gave her a wolfish look. Walking away, she felt his eyes on her backside.

Tuuli later found out that most of the boys in the group were rich and titled, and that they were often on the lookout for 'fresh meat'. Tuuli had been out with Ricky once and Kaisa had exchanged a few words with Tom earlier that summer when she'd bumped into him on holiday in the archipelago.

The rich boys now made their way noisily past Kaisa and Tuuli in the middle of the canteen, not even making eye contact. They spoke to everyone but them. Only when Ricky passed their table did he give the slightest of nods in Tuuli's direction, but when Tom passed by, he studiously ignored Kaisa. She widened her eyes at Tuuli when the group finally settled on a table on the other side of the room, but her friend's face was expressionless.

'So, have you heard from the Englishman?'

Kaisa had told her all about the wonderful evening she'd spent with Peter in Helsinki.

She shook her head. 'I don't think they're back in England yet.'

'What about your fiancé – you're still wearing the ring, I see?' Tuuli said with raised eyebrows.

The twisted gold band had been on Kaisa's finger for four years now.

Even though she'd thought about taking it off since meeting Peter and began having doubts about Matti, she hadn't.

'I don't know what to do,' she said.

'Are you still, you know, going to bed with him?' Tuuli asked quietly.

Kaisa lowered her eyes. She fiddled with a napkin.

'I don't want to hurt Matti.'

'Of course you don't.' Tuuli took Kaisa's hands in hers. 'You were too young when you started going out with him. And he knows that.'

Kaisa nodded. She knew her friend was right.

'If it's just sex you want,' Tuuli said nodding towards the rich boys, 'I'm sure someone else would oblige.'

The pair giggled.

Tuuli said, serious again, 'Honestly, you should have more fun – you can't go from being with one guy since you were sixteen straight into another serious relationship!'

On the following Friday, as usual, Matti used his key to enter Kaisa's apartment after his evening shift at the Customs office in the South Harbour. They hadn't spoken all week and she was surprised to see him. But he came in as if nothing had happened, took off his coat as usual and walked into the lounge. He was full of stories of the havoc the English destroyer had caused.

'I was there the morning they arrived. I saw the Finnish girls throw themselves at the foreign sailors. And they were well received, I can tell you!'

Kaisa said nothing. She knew what Matti was doing. Had Peter been tempted by those girls? Of course he had. When foreign ships arrived at the harbour women always went to the quayside, although Peter had never mentioned it.

Kaisa busied herself with spooning coffee into the percolator so that she didn't have to look at Matti. He sat down on the sofa Mother had given Kaisa when she'd moved into his auntie's flat. It was an old-fashioned rococo-style thing covered in green satin with carved wooden legs that perched on the floor, like some large bird's claws. When Kaisa had first seen the thing she'd recoiled. She preferred her mother's modern Asko furniture. Of course, Kaisa didn't say how she felt about the foul monstrosity; Matti's mother had been kind to give her the three-piece suite.

He stretched his arms across the complicated wooden carving on the back of the sofa and said, 'I bet your Englishman sailor took advantage of those girls too.'

Kaisa walked slowly out of the alcove kitchen, crossed the small living space and sat on one of the green satin-covered chairs opposite him.

They were both quiet. The only sound was the water dripping into the empty coffee jug in the percolator.

'I can't do this,' she said quietly, looking down at her lap.

'Do what?'

'I need to sort out what I want.'

She peeked up at him.

His face was paler than usual and his mouth was slightly open. For the first time, he looked untidy in the pale shirt and dark trousers of his Customs uniform. His tie was loose and the top button of his shirt was undone. He moved his hands to his lap and formed them into fists. A sudden fear flared up inside Kaisa and her throat went dry. Was he going to hit her?

She thought about her father.

'It's not fair on you, or on me, if I don't know what I want,' Kaisa said quickly.

'Don't do this, please.'

Matti's pleading surprised Kaisa. His brown eyes had filled with tears. She got up and sat next to him. She unfurled his hands and took them in hers.

'I'm really sorry, I didn't mean to hurt you.'

They hugged each other for a long time. Matti didn't cry, not really, but Kaisa did. Tears dripped down her face and onto his work shirt. She wondered briefly if she could live on her own without Matti. Would his aunt throw her out of the flat if she broke off the engagement? And would she have the nerve to break it off? If Kaisa didn't hear from Peter, could she love Matti in the same way she had before all this?

She held her breath. Was she really in love with Peter and not Matti? Is that how easily it happened? She'd only met Peter twice – how could Kaisa possibly know he was the man for her?

Matti had his head against Kaisa's chest. She stroked his hair, inhaling the familiar scent of his shampoo.

Now, here with her fiancé, she was certain of only one thing.

'I think you'd better go.'

He sat up and pressed his lips to hers.

'No,' she said and pulled away.

'Please, I love you.'

Matti kissed her neck. His body was so familiar to her. His hands roaming her body seemed natural. They made love, but after she asked him to leave.

'I'll see you soon,' he shouted from the hall.

When Kaisa heard the door slam shut she buried her face in her pillow and cried.

Peter sat in the wardroom with his pen poised over a blank piece of airmail paper. He was alone for now; a state of affairs that he knew would be temporary. He had to get on with it – and sharpish. Peter didn't want an audience for what he wanted to say. For this letter he'd chosen his fountain pen, which he'd bought for writing the official Navy correspondence. 'It was what was expected of an officer', one of his tutors at Dartmouth Naval College had told the whole class. Most guys had later sniggered at the comment, but Peter had taken it seriously.

He enjoyed the feel of the ink flowing from the tip of the fountain pen; it needed control to make the letters on the page legible. He liked to think it took some skill to write a beautiful letter. Now, however, he couldn't begin. As he sat there staring at the blank piece of paper, he wasn't even sure he should write it at all.

'A love letter, is it?' Lieutenant Collins said and plonked himself on the bunk opposite Peter.

Peter looked at the older officer's grinning face and forced a smile. 'No, I just thought I should write to my mother and father.'

He screwed the top back onto the pen and closed the writing pad. He needed to be alone to compose the words he wanted to say to Kaisa. The fact was, he did need to write to his parents, and more importantly reply to Jilly. It was over a week since he'd received her latest letter in which she'd asked when he was next going to be home in Wiltshire. Even though she hadn't expressly said it, she'd made it clear she was not seeing anyone else. She was saving herself for Peter.

Peter bit his lower lip as he watched Collins pick up an old Sunday Times off the table and begin to read it. The situation with Jilly was turning into a bloody disaster.

His mother had told him in her letter that, 'As a lovely surprise, Jilly popped over for coffee with me last week. She's such a nice girl.'

It'd been a mistake to ask Jilly to the Dartmouth Ball, Peter realised that now. But there'd been no one else to ask, and he had honestly thought she understood it was just a one off. He – in fact both of them – were far too young to tie themselves down. And surely she knew how he felt about the small town he'd spent all his life in? He'd told her over and over that the last thing he wanted to do was to settle down in Wiltshire.

Peter and Jilly had known each other since forever, but it had never been serious. Before he left to join the Navy, Jilly had cried so much that Peter promised to write. Now after the one evening (and a night, he had to concede), at Dartmouth, she was keener than ever.

Peter opened the pad of airmail paper again and began writing.

'Dear Jilly,

   It was very kind of you to accompany me to the Dartmouth Ball. I had a great time, but you know my life is devoted to the Navy now.

   Your friend,

   Peter.'

Reading back the words, Peter shook his head, tore the piece of paper off the pad, scrunched it up and put it into his pocket.

The first letter from Peter arrived ten days after Kaisa had said goodbye to him and twelve days after she'd met him at the embassy cocktail party. When she saw the blue air mail envelope on the doormat, she nearly screamed.

   She held the envelope in her hand for a moment before opening it. The paper was thick and silky, and she recognised the handwriting immediately. It was the same upright style as on the cassette Peter had left with her. She ripped the envelope open. The first paragraph took her breath away.

'It rained when we sailed from Helsinki and the weather seemed to echo my mood. I am sure I've never felt this way about anyone before. I miss you so much.'

Peter's words were like poetry. Kaisa read the pages over and over. Then, carefully, she folded the three full sheets of writing back into the envelope and pressed it to her chest. She thought about the grey weekend after that wonderful night with Peter in Helsinki. About the awful hours that followed which she'd spent awake lying next to her fiancé, listening to his steady breathing, too afraid to sleep. The days afterwards had been equally hard.

Kaisa read the letter over and over until the words became engraved on her mind. Peter wrote that he lived in a house in Portsmouth, which he shared with three friends, all from the Navy. He asked if he could phone Kaisa some evening.

She nearly danced to the bus stop and to her lectures in Hanken that day.

She and Tuuli were standing in the queue for the canteen. Tuuli frowned at the blackboard. Kaisa knew she was on a budget and had been contemplating whether to have the day's dish of fish soup (the cheapest option) or one of the more expensive rye bread sandwiches displayed in the glass cabinet. There were no Berlin buns today.

'Guess what arrived today?'

Kaisa showed Tuuli the blue envelope.

'Wow!'

Kaisa smiled and picked up a rye sandwich. Tuuli ordered the fish soup.

'So, what does it say?'

They carried their trays of food to the table.

Kaisa leaned over the table and whispered, 'He misses me and wants to phone me!'

Tuuli squeezed her arm. 'So have you replied to him yet?'

'Of course I did – I posted it on the way here. Imagine that he might call! What will I say to him?'

Her friend spooned some of the grey-looking soup into her mouth. 'You'll know what to say when he does.'

For the rest of the day, Kaisa couldn't concentrate on the lectures. Instead she took out Peter's letter and reread it. He used such beautiful words, but what she kept returning to over and over was the last sentence, '*Missing you. Yours, Peter*'. Kaisa had replied to him in such a rush that morning that she didn't check for spelling mistakes. She hoped he wouldn't mind.

When Kaisa finally put the letter down she noticed the other students around her were writing notes. This lecture was on international law, the part of her new course she'd been most looking forward to. Yet, Kaisa's mind wouldn't focus and she barely heard the professor. She was beginning to regret her choice of subject for second year. Business law was reputed to be one of the hardest courses in Hanken. A labyrinth of rules and regulations determined how society worked. Kaisa had wanted so bad to become an expert on something, and to be a lawyer in a top company had appealed to her. But the study material seemed frighteningly complicated to her now.

There were entire paragraphs on employment law alone that she didn't comprehend. On top of that, Kaisa found it hard to remember the names of legal cases – they sounded so similar.

It didn't help that she would listen to the Pretenders' tape while trying to study at home. And instead of memorising the legal cases, her mind would wander to the day in Esplanade Park and Peter's kisses. Like a woman obsessed, she couldn't stop listening to the songs, seeking meaning in the lyrics. Was there something Peter had wanted to convey to her? She knew the words to most of the tracks by heart and couldn't wait to discuss them with him. He was all she thought about, and the longing to see him again grew stronger with each passing day.

8

Weeks went by without another letter from Peter, but Kaisa dreamt about him nightly. The dreams were not all good. One night she woke with a start. As if it had been real, she'd seen Peter in the arms of another girl. He'd been laughing and looking into the dark-haired girl's eyes, telling her how lovely she was, just as he had said to Kaisa. She'd woken in a panic and screamed into the dark, empty bedroom.

Later that morning she woke up feeling groggy. It was a Saturday but she had a lot studying to do; she was falling badly behind in her studies. As she got up and dressed, she ignored the the Pretenders tape and got the books out. After a couple of hours' hard work, the doorbell rang.

Matti stood on the doorstep. She hadn't seen him since she'd told him to go. He'd phoned a couple of times and asked if he could come over, but Kaisa had told him she was busy studying.

Which was partly true.

'What are you doing here?' Kaisa asked.

The man she'd known for four years looked different to her. He was unshaven, and his dark leather coat was open, showing the brown jumper Kaisa had knitted for him.

'Can I come in?' he said in a low voice.

Kaisa felt sorry for him. She touched the ring on her left hand and opened the door to let Matti in. He stepped gingerly over the threshold and put his arms around her. At first she stiffened in his embrace, but then his familiar scent of pine cones and shampoo soothed her into submission. She relaxed and put her arms around Matti's neck. It was comforting to be held again, to feel safe. Then slowly, she moved away from him.

'You OK?' he said.

Kaisa smiled without answering. 'Would you like some coffee?'

Matti stayed the night. All through their lovemaking, Kaisa felt as if she wasn't there – as if all the things that Matti was doing, kissing her mouth, her ears, moving slowly but methodically down her body, were meant for someone else. Afterwards in the bathroom she looked at her flushed face in the mirror, trying to work out how she felt about it. Making love to Matti seemed right – they were still engaged – but she felt guilty about Peter, even though she hadn't promised him anything.

And that was ridiculous too; for all she knew he could be in bed right now with his old girlfriend – or a new one. The memory of Peter's face was fading by the day. Even with the letter contact, she started to doubt whether she'd ever see him again.

Matti's body was so familiar to her that their intimacy came easy. Yet, it was different from before. Kaisa didn't want to cuddle or kiss Matti afterwards; she no longer felt the closeness they once had. Studying her sad reflection, Kaisa made a decision. It wouldn't be fair on anyone if she carried on taking Matti into her bed.

The next morning, while she and Matti sat at the table having breakfast, he reached his hand out and said, 'I love you and forgive you.'

Kaisa looked at him, unable to tell him what he wanted to hear. Excusing herself, she fled to the kitchenette, where she gazed out of the narrow window at the bleak late autumn scene, wondering how her life had become so complicated. She needed to tell Matti that she couldn't go on as before.

When Kaisa returned to the table, Matti asked if he could stay another night.

'I don't think so,' Kaisa said with a shake of her head.

He got up and knelt in front of her. He placed his hands on her waist, but she removed them and said, 'Please don't. I can't do this anymore.'

Matti stayed on his knees, neither of them speaking.

When he got up, he said, 'You need time to think, I get that. But don't do anything rash.' He lifted Kaisa's chin with one finger. 'I am willing to carry on as if nothing had happened. I haven't told Mother – or my aunt – anything, so for your own sake, I'd think carefully about what you do next.'

. . .

Kaisa skipped Monday's lectures and stayed at home. Again, she avoided the Pretenders tape and managed to study. She hadn't heard anything from Peter for over three weeks after his first, wonderful letter. She decided he must have forgotten about her.

Kaisa touched the thick, gold band on her left finger. The weight felt so familiar, yet heavy and overbearing. She couldn't imagine life without Matti; at the same time she couldn't bear the thought of being married to him. She no longer wanted to be tied down by anybody. But how was she going to tell Matti? And what would his mother and aunt think?

It was notoriously difficult to find rental accommodation in Helsinki. The student flats went like hotcakes and were usually snapped up as soon as the universities announced their intakes. But her home, just like the ring on her finger, came with a price tag that was too high: Kaisa's freedom.

It was past one o'clock in the morning when the shrill ring of the telephone woke Kaisa up. As if in a trance she clambered out of bed and into the hall. It sounded ten times louder than it did during the day.

'Hullo?' she said, rubbing sleep out of her eyes.

'It's me, Peter.'

'Oh,' Kaisa said.

For a second she thought she was dreaming.

'Did I wake you?'

Peter's voice, low and manly, broke her out of her trance. He was real, and talking to her.

'Yes, but it's OK. What time is it there?' Kaisa asked.

'Just gone eleven. We're just back from the pub.'

'We?' The dream where Peter had a girl in his arms hit her.

'Me and my friends,' He paused. 'I miss you.'

Kaisa nearly fainted with happiness hearing Peter's last words. She pressed the receiver to her ear.

'I miss you too,' she whispered.

Until this moment and hearing his voice again, Kaisa hadn't realised how meeting Peter had thoroughly changed her.

Peter was quiet for a moment. Kaisa could hear his breathing, as if he were next to her in the cold, dark hall.

'I wish you were here right now. The things I'd do to you...' Peter's voice deepened more. And then he said, 'I think I'm falling in love with you.'

Kaisa tried to control her voice, to keep it from faltering.

'Me too,' she whispered.

What she really wanted to do was shout those words.

Peter ended the call with a promise to phone again soon. Kaisa replaced the receiver and climbed back into bed. The streetlight cast the familiar zigzag shadows into her bedroom. It took her a long time to get back to sleep. When she did, she dreamt of Peter.

On the following Saturday, just after six in the evening, Kaisa heard the front door open. She was in the kitchen making coffee when Matti called out to her. Kaisa met him in the hall and kissed him on the cheek. He smelt of the outside and his green jacket was damp with drizzle. Unlike other weekends they'd spent together, Kaisa hadn't bought any food. Since Peter's phone call she'd lost her appetite. Her clothes were hanging off her, including the black-and-white dress she'd worn when she'd met Peter. Kaisa now wore a pair of jeans that hadn't fitted her for years.

Matti took off his jacket and came close to Kaisa. She turned her face away when he tried to kiss her.

'What's the matter?' Matti said.

'Nothing, I'm just not in the mood tonight.'

'Have you eaten?' he asked and went to open the fridge door.

'I haven't had time to shop,' Kaisa lied.

'Let's go out, my treat,' Matti said.

Kaisa stared at her fiancé. It wasn't like him to spend money. Matti was saving money to buy a new car. He currently drove an old, green Opel Kadett belonging to his mother, even though she didn't have a driving licence. Between that and Kaisa's student loan that she lived on, the two of them rarely went out to eat.

They sat opposite each other at a local café, close to Kaisa's flat.'Why doesn't your mother just buy the car for you?' Kaisa asked him.

She pushed the food around on her plate. They'd both ordered minute steaks with French fries. Kaisa had eaten half of hers and was playing with the side salad. She knew Matti would be upset if she didn't finish the expensive dish.

'Because I want to buy this one myself,' Matti said. Seeing her half-eaten dish, he added, 'Are you going to eat that?' His voice was tight with anger.

Kaisa lifted her eyes to him and shook her head. 'Sorry.'

He exhaled heavily and asked for the bill, which he paid with a crisp one-hundred-Mark note. The waitress, wearing a pink apron, smiled seductively at Matti, wiggling her bum as she walked away from the table. But Matti didn't even notice.

Why can't he be interested in her? Kaisa wondered.

'Why did you come out and eat if you weren't hungry?' Matti said.

He was putting on his coat and standing up when the girl brought coffee, which was included in the meal.

'You've paid for it. It's part of the deal,' she said and flashed a hopeful smile at Matti. He sat back down. The place was almost empty; only one other table was taken, by a man nursing a large pint of beer.

Kaisa looked around. This was the same café Matti had taken her on their first date. It looked dreary now, but back then it had been a sunny, hot Midsummer's Eve and Kaisa had been so flattered by the attentions of this older boy – or man. She'd just turned fifteen that same April. He was twenty-two and doing his conscript service in the army. He'd behaved like a grown up opening car doors for her, and fixing her cardigan over her shoulders when it slipped down.

Kaisa looked at her fiancé now. His face looked strained, like he was tired from work.

She cast her mind back to when they'd first met. She'd been surprised – and flattered – to discover this older boy, a man, was interested in her. On Midsummer's Eve, while everyone else in the city was spending the holiday weekend by a lake somewhere in the country, Matti had turned up at the kiosk where Kaisa was working for the summer.

Everyone said that she was too young. Even Kaisa's mother had had her doubts, despite Matti coming from a good, wealthy family. One evening, after Kaisa had brought Matti home for coffee, her mother had expressed those concerns.

'He is very much older than you,' she'd said.

'I know, but he's very kind.'

Her mother had sighed and hugged Kaisa hard.

But six months later, when Matti had asked if he and Kaisa could get engaged after Kaisa turned sixteen, her mother had replied, 'Over my dead body.'

Matti had proposed anyway, ten months after their first midsummer's night together.

It had been a sunny and warm Sunday in late April. She remembered her mother being away at a conference, and Matti had taken Kaisa to Suomenlinna, an historic island off the coast of Helsinki.

On the ferry ride over, she wore a beige mac over the sky-blue dress Matti had bought for the occasion. It was only when they arrived on the former military island and Kaisa saw the old battlements with the guns pointing towards them, she sensed this was a momentous occasion. She knew she should be excited, but all she felt was a strange sense of numbness.

For a while they walked along a path that ran around the island. Matti said he wanted to find the ideal spot. Not too crowded by the groups of youngsters who, buoyed by the warm weather, had come out to drink their vodka in the open, yet beautiful enough for the pictures he wished to take. Matti said he wanted the images to look romantic.

'Our three children will want to see where their parents got engaged, don't you think?'

He took Kaisa's arm in his. For some reason Kaisa couldn't stop shivering.

'You're not cold, my little bird, are you?'

'Just a bit,' she said.

Matti settled on a place high up on a hill, from where they could see the outline of South Harbour. The riggings of the few sailing boats moored there after winter rocked back and forth, mirroring Kaisa's own shaking, which had got worse.

'You can't be cold – it's boiling here!' he said, looking annoyed.

She tried to stop.

'Take your mac off so that I can see the lovely dress,' he said.

'I'm cold.'

'You're imagining it. It's a beautiful day.' Matti frowned, as if annoyed. 'A coat will spoil the impression of a happy, sunny occasion.'

She breathed in and out slowly, and took off her mac.

'That's a good girl,' he said. 'Sit there on the stone wall and try to look pretty.'

To this day, Kaisa hated looking at the pictures Matti had taken. Her smile had been forced due to the goose pimples all along her bare arms. It also hadn't been boiling, as Matti had suggested.

Now, watching her fiancé slurp his coffee, Kaisa remembered her mother hitting the roof when she'd seen the ring on Kaisa's hand. She'd even thrown crockery and threatened to call Matti's mother.

'But it was she who insisted we get engaged,' Kaisa had said to her in tears.

Pirjo had stared at her daughter for a moment, ending the tense moment with a hug.

'As long as you're sure it's what you want,' she'd said.

Kaisa and Pirjo never spoke about the incident again, but to this day her mother and Matti still didn't get on. It was, of course, easier after her mother moved to Stockholm and Kaisa lived alone in the flat of Matti's aunt.

'Ready?' Matti now asked in that same manly tone that had impressed Kaisa when she was younger. He was staring at her plate, muttering something about wasted food under his breath.

Back in the flat, Matti tried to kiss Kaisa again. She moved away from his embrace, suddenly unable be close to him.

'What's up with you?' he asked walking into the living room.

Outside, the light had faded. Without turning on the light, Matti sat down on the sofa. He patted the space next to him.

'Come here.' In the dark living room his shadowy presence seemed haunting, threatening even.

'Look, I need to go to bed,' Kaisa said.

Matti got up quickly and said, 'That's a good idea.'

She shook her head. 'No...' He had to understand they couldn't keep pretending things were the same as before – that Kaisa couldn't just forget about Peter.

'Look, I need to sleep – alone. I'll call you tomorrow.'

Kaisa watched and waited in silence, rooted to the spot in the middle of the narrow hall as Matti slowly put his coat on, fastening each button of his Ulster carefully, as if he were a child learning how to get dressed. He picked up his leather gloves from inside the brown flat cap and held on to them. On the spur of the moment, Kaisa took her ring off and offered it to him.

At first Matti stared at her outstretched hand, not moving to take the ring pinched between her thumb and forefinger. Kaisa pushed it closer so it touched his coat.

'I'm sorry,' she breathed.

'So this is it, then?' Matti asked.

She lowered her head and tried to stop the tears, glad the hall was dark.

Matti snatched the ring from her, as if he'd never wanted her to have it in the first place.

'If you think anything will ever come out of you and that English sailor you must be dafter than I thought,' he said. His low voice had a bitter edge to it that Kaisa didn't like.

She lifted her head and said, 'It's not just that, you know it isn't. I was too young when we met.'

'Nonsense! Historically girls of fifteen –'

'Don't,' Kaisa interrupted him.

Why wouldn't he just go?

She suddenly thought of something.

'Can I have your key to this flat, please?'

Matti dug inside his pocket and began to unwind the silver key from a bunch of them. Fussing with it appeared to calm him down.

Finally, the thing came loose and he handed it to Kaisa. It felt hot in her hand.

'Thank you.'

'Well, goodnight then.' Matti kissed Kaisa stiffly on the cheek and left.

The next day, Kaisa called Matti and asked him to collect his things from the flat. There were a few of his LPs left, some shaving cream and deodorant she found in the bathroom, plus the brown jumper he liked to wear. Looking at the pile of things on the floor, she couldn't remember her feelings for Matti before meeting Peter. She couldn't understand how she'd been with another man so easily. Had she ever truly loved Matti?

Kaisa put on some coffee while waiting for him to arrive. The sound of the phone ringing interrupted her.

'Hello,' a grave female voice on the other line said.

Kaisa's blood turned to ice when she recognised the caller. When she didn't reply, Mother went on. 'Didn't think you'd hear from me, did you?'

Kaisa couldn't get any words out; her heart was racing too fast.

'So, what have you got to say for yourself?' Mother said.

'Excuse me?'

'You're a nasty young woman. First you seduce my son, then, when it suits, you cast him out like a used dishcloth. But I knew this from the beginning. Your mother's divorced, after all.'

Kaisa was speechless. She imagined the short, round woman, with piercing brown eyes and carefully coiffured hair sitting in her pink hall in the house in Munkkiniemi. The villa had high ceilings and the pink telephone was set on a dark, antique table with a pale-pink satin padded seat next to it. Pink was Matti's mother's favourite colour. She wore the shade nearly every day.

'Well?' Matti's mother demanded.

'I'm sorry, it's how I feel,' Kaisa said.

'Why? You don't think the sailor is ever going to marry you, do you?'

Kaisa opened her mouth to speak. What right had Matti's mother to interfere in her son's relationship?

'Well –'

Mother cut her off.

'You are a very silly girl. If you have any sense, you'll stick that expensive ring on your finger again and accept that life with my son is the best you can hope for. And as far as the apartment goes, let's just say my sister doesn't like whores living in her property.'

Kaisa's face grew hot.

Mother stopped talking. Kaisa heard her sniff down the line. How she'd pitied Matti's mother before now. Matti was all she had left after her husband died, many years before.

'I'm really sorry,' Kaisa said as calmly as she could. With shaking hands, she hung up.

A few moments later, the doorbell rang. Kaisa took the pile of Matti's things and handed them to him over the doorstep.

'Your mother called,' she said sharply.

'Oh,' Matti said and tried to step inside. She blocked him.

'I'm sorry, I didn't ask her to call,' he said.

Kaisa kissed Matti on the cheek. 'Goodbye.'

She closed the door and sighed with relief. It was as if a weight had been lifted from her chest. She was free! Free of Matti and his mother's oppressive judgement.

The coffee percolator made gurgling noises. From the kitchenette window, Kaisa watched her old life walk towards his moss-green Opel Kadett. He was holding the pile of things in front of him, like a robot. The sky looked dark, as though it were about to rain. Sure enough, the first drops fell as soon as his car disappeared from view.

9

HELSINKI, SPRING 1981

For five months Kaisa had been exchanging letters with the handsome Englishman, but there were times when she doubted his sincerity. Showing affection came easily to him. Yet they hardly knew each other.

The fights and recriminations with Matti and his mother had finally come to an end. Kaisa had returned the mink coat Matti's mother had gifted her the winter before. The engagement ring her son had given her was no longer on Kaisa's finger. At the end of every month, when the rental bill dropped through the letterbox, Kaisa feared it would include a notice to leave. But so far, she'd been allowed to stay in the flat. Kaisa knew they had no right to evict her just because she'd broken the engagement, but Matti's rich family might find a way.

During the lonely months following the break-up, Kaisa began to worry the affair with the English naval officer could also soon become a memory. Perhaps he'd just been a trigger, making her see the relationship with Matti for what it was. He, and the poet Eino Leino, whose statue she now made a point of visiting whenever she was in Helsinki centre, made Kaisa realise she was far too young to settle down. What she needed now was to concentrate on her studies at Hanken and forget about men for a while. On a crackly phone line from Stockholm, Kaisa's mother had reminded her she was still only twenty years old.

'You'll have many, many lovers yet,' she said. Not usual motherly advice, but Kaisa knew she was right.

In the middle of the stormy spring Peter called late, two o'clock in the morning in Helsinki.

'I've done it!' he said.

'Sorry?' Still drowsy with sleep Kaisa struggled to focus.

'I'm coming to Helsinki. I picked up the tickets from the travel agent today.'

'When?'

'Only twenty-one days from today!' Peter said triumphantly. 'And I'm staying for a week, if that's OK?' Doubt crept into his voice.

Kaisa gripped the receiver, fully awake now.

'Oh that's wonderful.'

In only three weeks' time Peter would be in Helsinki!

'I can't wait to take you to bed,' Peter said, his voice low and deep.

Kaisa caressed the phone as if she were holding Peter. She wanted to tell him she'd left Matti, but Peter had never asked about her fiancé. It was as if Matti didn't exist.

The second Kaisa put down the phone and caught her reflection in the mirror, she panicked. She plucked at her pyjama bottoms that cut into her skin. Kaisa must have put on at least three kilos since she'd broken off the engagement. And what would she wear for Peter's visit? A new wardrobe was out of the question; her funds were at an all-time low.

Kaisa looked around and her eyes settled on the bed. What if...they didn't get on? She'd only ever had one boyfriend. She couldn't bear the embarrassment. What would she do with Peter for a whole seven days and nights if it all turned sour?

At the Hanken canteen the next day, Tuuli was much more pragmatic and calmed her fears.

'Throw him out if you don't like him.' She smiled. 'But I know you will.'

On the day Peter was due to arrive, Kaisa agonised in her flat over what to wear to the airport to meet him. In his letters, Peter had told her he liked women who wore skirts and dresses. She lived in jeans and trousers. In her wardrobe she had one skirt and one dress – the summer one she'd worn to the embassy cocktail party. She'd made the skirt from a silky fabric, with a print of a mountain scene at the hem. In the end, she settled on the skirt with a pair of new high-heeled beige boots, and a cardigan with small pearly buttons that her mother had given her for Christmas. Standing in front of the mirror, Kaisa sighed with relief. She almost looked like a proper girly girl rather than the boyish, lanky thing who wore old jeans and an oversized jumper to lectures.

Sitting on the shiny air-conditioned Finnair bus to the Helsinki-Vantaa airport, Kaisa was full of nerves. The sky was grey and it was a cold and rainy April day. A few patches of dirty snow were still visible on the side of the road.

When the bus pulled up to the terminal, Kaisa rushed out the door. She couldn't wait to see Peter. Would she still recognise him after five months? And would she still like him – love him? What if he was disappointed when he saw her?

Her fears left her when she spotted Peter through the glass wall. The man of her dreams stood a few metres from her, impatiently changing position and staring at the empty baggage conveyor belt. She'd forgotten how handsome the naval officer was. It relieved her to learn she hadn't faked affection for this man so she could end her relationship with another. It pleased her that she hadn't fought with her ex-fiancé and his mother for nothing.

Peter had his back to her. She was grateful for a few moments to observe him without his intense gaze on her. At the same time, she was desperate to see that look of burning desire.

Peter's nerves were so unsteady on the flight he'd needed a gin and tonic to settle them. He could have done with another, but decided against it. He wanted to be sober to meet Kaisa. He could hardly believe he was doing this – going back to see a girl he'd met only twice. What if she'd changed her mind about him? Perhaps she wouldn't find him as fetching out of uniform as she did in it?

During the flight he'd listened to two middle-aged men behind him speak in Finnish – a language that was completely incomprehensible to him. The thought occurred to him that without Kaisa he'd be quite helpless on his own. New fears crept in. What had he done? If things didn't turn out well with Kaisa, how would he manage in this strange country? What if the warnings about KGB agents running riot in Helsinki were true and he was in real danger?

If this were the case, surely his Captain wouldn't have approved the trip?

Looking out the window as the plane approached Helsinki, he'd been shocked to see snow on the ground, and patches of grey landscape interspersed with tall, dark-green pine trees. Inhospitable was the word that came to mind as his panic rose. But when the tyres touched down and some passengers clapped, his stomach danced with similar excitement.

After his last visit to Finland, Peter had been teased mercilessly, but Lieutenant Collins had been a surprise ally to Peter.

'Give a chap a break,' he'd said to the others. 'You're only jealous because none of you scored like Peter did.'

During an onboard cocktail party, Collins had even asked him about Kaisa.

'I can't stop thinking about her,' Peter had admitted.

Collins put his hand on Peter's shoulder and smiled, creating lines in his high forehead. 'Well then, Williams, it's probably best you go see her. You're only young once.'

'I do have some leave coming up,' Peter said.

'What are you waiting for then? If I was you, I'd go straight to the travel agents tomorrow.'

And now he was here, waiting for his luggage in the near-deserted arrivals lounge. The stark difference to busy Heathrow, where people rushed along the long corridors, was palpable. As was the silence from his fellow passengers. Everyone looked sombre, gazing at the unmoving belt of the luggage carousel, as if trying to make it to move by sheer, collective willpower.

Peter didn't see Kaisa until he walked past Customs Control and through the automatic doors.

He swallowed. She was standing to one side of the arrivals lounge, wearing a Russian-looking fur hat. Her blonde hair was longer than he remembered, and the ends curled attractively on her shoulders. Then, her blue eyes met his and he knew he'd been right to come. Peter walked quickly towards her, dropped his luggage and kissed Kaisa.

She melted in his arms.

Kaisa brought Peter back to her flat where she had planned a celebratory dinner of prawn cocktail, followed by chicken fricassee. Peter ate heartily praising Kaisa's cooking, but she could hardly eat anything. Her appetite had again vanished. Peter's presence seemed to have that effect on her. When Kaisa served coffee with the small Pepe cakes she'd bought in the bakery that morning, Peter asked if they could move to the sofa.

Instead of coffee, they kissed and kissed.

'You haven't had any cake,' Kaisa said emerging for breath.

Peter gave her an intense look and asked, 'Can we go to bed?'

With a nod she took his hand, worried she wouldn't relax in the bed where she and Matti had made love so many times. But when Peter put his hand under her jumper and undid her bra, all thoughts went to his fingers running over her body. It was as if his touch was burning her, sparking a heat that lifted her desire in a way she'd never known before. First he caressed her back, then pulled her jumper over her head. He stood in front of her, watching while she lowered the straps of her bra and revealed her breasts.

'You're beautiful,' Peter said hoarsely and bent down to kiss her again, while gently cupping her breasts.

They undressed and Peter lowered her onto the bed.

For three days, they made love everywhere they could in the flat, often because they didn't make it to the bed in time. Kaisa had never felt such love before, the way she did for Peter. It was as if their hunger for each other could not be satiated. They even experimented, something she never did with Matti. Sex with Matti was good, but mechanical.

'I love you,' Peter said and kissed her eyelids.

They were panting and lying naked on the rug in the living room, where they'd ended up after realising the sofa, with its carved back, was too uncomfortable.

Kaisa giggled. What would Matti's mother say if she knew what they'd just done on her precious gift? She should be feeling guilty, but being with Peter felt so right, guilt didn't factor into it.

'Oh, you find that funny, do you?'

Peter lifted himself onto his elbow and traced the contours of her left breast with his fingers. Kaisa's nipples were still erect and sensitive to his touch.

'Never,' Kaisa said and looked into his dark eyes.

Desire rose in her again. Lust reached her inner core and she turned her body towards Peter.

Two days passed and Kaisa and Peter didn't leave the flat.

On the third morning of their seven days together, Kaisa said, 'We have to go for a walk.'

With Peter's arm around Kaisa, they walked along the shores of Laut-tasaari Island. The sea was stormy. Spring was late that year and the chilly wind blew against Kaisa's face. She didn't feel the cold in her winter coat, but Peter had not brought the right clothes for the Baltic spring storms.

They took the bus to the centre of Helsinki and Peter bought a waterproof coat from Stockmann's. On the way home, it started snowing and he pulled out his sunglasses. Everyone on the street stared. Kaisa laughed.

'What?'

'There's no sun,' she said.

'The snow flecks hurt my eyes.'

'Are all Englishmen sensitive like you?'

'They might be, but I hope you never find out.' He squeezed her closer to him.

Kaisa hadn't known happiness like this. They walked and talked. Peter told her about his childhood, about his parents in Wiltshire, about his love of music. She was hungry to know everything about him.

Peter had brought mixed tapes with him. Finnish radio played just domestic hits or a few foreign tracks by Elvis or Frank Sinatra. Kaisa had worn down the Pretenders tape Peter had given her on his first visit. His latest tapes included Billy Joel's "Just The Way You Are" and "She's Always A Woman" and The Isley Brothers' "Harvest For The World". They listened to the music and Peter sang along.

Kaisa told Peter about her love of opera.

'My mother took me and my older sister, Sirkka, to see *Tosca* in Stockholm when I was only eleven years old. And I loved it!'

On that night Kaisa had fallen in love with Italian opera. The tragic circumstances of Mimi in *La Bohème*, Violetta in *La Traviata*, or *Tosca* spoke to Kaisa in a way no modern film or TV series could. But the opera house in Helsinki was so tiny it was hard to get tickets. And she was always broke.

They lay in bed later, exhausted after a long and sublime lovemaking session. Peter stroked her face and kissed her lips gently.

'I've never seen an opera, but if you love it I'm sure I will too. You must take me next time.'

The words 'next time' rang in her ears. They hadn't discussed the future. Did his words mean he was planning another visit?

Kaisa burrowed deeper into Peter's arms and inhaled his manly scent. She loved the smell of the coconut shaving cream Peter used, often standing behind him in the bathroom and watching him run the razor over his square jaw.

They made love several times each day, and couldn't keep their hands off each other wherever they went. In Finland, public shows of emotion were rare, but Kaisa no longer cared if people on the bus or tram stared.

The day of Peter's departure loomed. While their time together seemed endless, it also felt too short. Kaisa tried not to think about being in the flat on her own again. With Peter leaving soon, her longing for him would be multiplied by a thousand percent. Could she manage it?

Peter watched Kaisa prepare food in the little kitchenette off from the lounge. They'd been to the centre of Helsinki that morning after sleepily making love. Peter had never known a girl like Kaisa before. Everything she did excited him. Just thinking about how she'd taken him in her mouth that morning made his groin ache with desire. Trying to control his thoughts, he turned back to the paper that he'd been reading. It was a two-day-old copy of *The Times*, which he'd found at a department store in town earlier.

He was also kicking himself because Kaisa had only just told her it was her twenty-first birthday today. He should have known – they'd talked about their age difference, eighteen days apart – but it had completely slipped his mind. Kaisa was so quiet, but he liked this about her. Now though, he wished she'd been more forthcoming. To make matters worse, Kaisa's mother would be making an appearance today. Peter had to be on his best behaviour.

Not that meeting Kaisa's mum worried him. His past girlfriends' mothers had always loved him. His naval career made him a good prospect, and he knew to be polite and respectful, like his own mother had taught him. But the language barrier worried him. Kaisa had told him that her mother didn't speak English. Still, she would no doubt ask what present he'd brought Kaisa. Would Kaisa complain to her that he'd forgotten?

Kaisa couldn't believe it when she got a surprise call from her mother to say she would be visiting from Stockholm. She'd only called the day before and although delighted, Kaisa was also nervous. Would Peter think she'd planned it? When Kaisa told him he seemed relaxed about it, but she worried it was too early to meet the parents. Pirjo was staying with friends in the centre of Helsinki as usual. She often popped over whenever she visited, but usually gave Kaisa a little more notice.

While they were waiting for her, Peter said, 'She's come to see if I'm good enough for her daughter.'

Kaisa looked at him and laughed. 'No, it's my birthday!'

Peter had apologised – again – for not getting her a present, but Kaisa didn't care. She didn't tell him, but having Peter in Helsinki was the only gift she wanted.

Pirjo brought a *Princess Tårta*, a layered Swedish sponge cake, and Kaisa's favourite. It had lots of cream in the middle and was topped with green icing and a pink marzipan rose.

Kaisa put out some bread, ham, cheese, slices of tomato and cucumber to have with coffee before the cake. She'd bought some white bread for Peter in town earlier. Kaisa didn't think he'd like the Finnish dark rye.

When they sat around the small table and Kaisa saw Pirjo assessing Peter, she wondered if he'd been right. Had her mother planned this visit?

There was an awkward silence.

'Please,' Kaisa said and nodded at Peter to start.

Both he and her mother took two slices of white bread, buttered them both and filled one side with ham and cucumber. But when Peter put the other slice on top, pressed it down and cut it in half diagonally, Kaisa giggled.

Peter looked up from his plate and smiled. 'What?'

'What's that?' Kaisa said pointing.

He grinned. 'It's a sandwich. It's what we do in England.'

'Oh.' Kaisa translated for her mother.

She showed Peter how they made sandwiches in Finland, filling just one side, and balancing the contents while she ate it. They all laughed, and the tense atmosphere lightened.

Kaisa relaxed in her chair.

When Peter sang 'Happy Birthday' to her, Kaisa squeezed his knee under the table. It made her happy to see that her mum liked Peter. When he excused himself and visited the bathroom, her mother whispered to her, 'He's so handsome!'

Kaisa nodded.

'When's he going back?' she said.

'Tomorrow.'

'So soon?'

Her mother knew her too well. The week coming to an end had been on Kaisa's mind since their first evening together. Like a ticking bomb, the last day loomed. How could she go back to living in the flat on her own? How would she sleep in the bed alone? The longing for him would kill her.

Tears filled Kaisa's eyes. Pirjo put her arm around her. When Kaisa heard the bathroom door open, she rushed to the kitchen to dry her eyes.

The day when Peter was due to leave came far too soon.

At the airport Kaisa felt a horrible dread. She'd been quiet on the airport bus while Peter held her hand.

'It'll be alright, you'll see. You'll come to England in August, promise?'

Peter's gaze was gentle and loving, his fingers tight around her hand.

August was four months away.

After Peter checked in his bag they had half an hour before the flight boarded. They stood looking up at the large display of flights. The white characters moved up the board, flicking old flights on and adding new ones. Only three destinations remained before London.

Peter said suddenly, 'Wait here, I'll be back.'

Kaisa stood and watched as Peter's flight moved forward once more. An awful emptiness filled her. Every molecule in her body felt Peter's absence. Why did he have to leave her now when they had spent so little time together?

Peter returned and handed Kaisa a red rose.

'This is for you.'

Kaisa inhaled the delicious scent of the deep-ruby coloured flower and started to cry.

Peter thumbed away her tears.

'I love you. Don't ever forget it.' He held her close and whispered, 'I have to go now.'

Kaisa nodded.

Peter kissed her one last time and was gone. She ran blindly down the stairs, clutching the rose, unable to watch him walk through to passport control.

The flat felt empty and was quiet – too quiet – when Kaisa returned from the airport. She put on the tapes Peter had left behind and loaded the coffee machine. She closed her eyes and listened to the music.

Kaisa could hear Peter's voice when Billy Joel sang "I love you just the way you are". How would she get through the night alone, in the bed they'd shared? Peter's scent was everywhere in the flat. In the bathroom, she found traces of his shaving foam on the basin. He'd told her he had the coconut-scented product shipped to him from America.

She scooped some up with her finger and inhaled. How was it possible to miss someone this much?

10

The flight to Heathrow was almost empty. There were two air hostesses and one steward, who all kept Kaisa topped up with orange juice and water. She was nervous. The steward appeared to pick up on it.

He smiled at her, flashing a row of white teeth.

'First time in London?' he asked.

Kaisa nodded. She was used to travelling on her own, but London was a big city, the largest she'd ever visited. As the plane swung over the Thames she saw Big Ben and the wide River Thames, snaking across the vast city littered with tall buildings.

A new worry took hold. What if Peter wasn't there to meet her?

They'd exchanged letters, several per week, during the four months that they hadn't seen each other. Peter had phoned Kaisa several times, confessing his love for her. He told her how much he loved her and was looking forward to seeing her again. Still, Kaisa worried. It had taken just one night for her to fall in love with someone else after a four-year relationship, something she still carried a huge amount of guilt over. Tuuli told her that Matti had taken advantage of her, that she had been too young when they'd met. But Kaisa had chosen to stay with him when she could have left any time. She now knew she hadn't loved Matti, hadn't known what real love was. But that was hardly his fault.

As the plane approached Heathrow, Kaisa looked out of the small window and saw rows and rows of houses below. There appeared to be no end to them. She closed her eyes and thought of Peter touching her skin. Soon, she would be able to press her body to his, look into those dark eyes and kiss his soft lips. And more...

It took forever to walk from the plane, queue up at passport control and get her luggage from the busy arrivals hall. A nervous Kaisa scanned the expectant faces on the other side of the double doors, beyond Customs Control.

At last she saw Peter. Tall and slim, and wearing a pair of jeans and a navy jumper, he stood on the other side of a steel barrier. She dodged reuniting families and passed an old couple walking too slow in front of her to reach him. He put his arms around Kaisa and gave her a long kiss. She inhaled his scent, feeling safe and happy for the first time in months.

As they turned to leave the airport, the steward from the plane walked past and waved to her. She waved back.

'Who was that?' asked Peter.

'Just the steward from the plane. He was nice.'

'I bet,' he said frowning.

It was the first time she'd seen Peter jealous and it felt good. Kaisa pushed closer to him as they walked out to the car park. The air beyond the airport terminal doors was warm and smelt of sour milk and traffic fumes. There were so many more people here than at Helsinki airport, all walking fast, all pushing past each other.

Peter opened the car door and handed Kaisa a Red Sox baseball cap. 'Here, put this on. It'll keep your hair in place.'

He'd told her in his letters that he owned an open-top Triumph Spitfire. *'The yellow colour isn't my favourite, but it does mean I won't be missed on the road!'*

The car looked tiny compared to the other vehicles in the dark, multi-storey building. The seats were black leather and very low down. She sank into the passenger seat. Peter slid into the driver's side and rolled the top down.

'The cap suits you.' He smiled and kissed her again. Then, he turned the engine over. 'It'll take us a couple of hours to get to Pompey.'

She smiled at the nickname Peter used for the coastal city he lived in – another detail she'd learnt from his letters. She'd never heard of the place before, but had looked it up on a map from the Hanken library afterwards. She'd memorised the entire map of England, including the place where his parents lived.

As Peter drove out of the car park and turned onto a motorway, the warm air brushed against her face. Rolling green hills, with the occasional cows grazing by the side of the road, followed the busy concrete spaghetti junctions. Kaisa felt so happy she could burst. With the Spitfire top down, they had to shout, but occasionally Peter would lean over, take Kaisa's hand and squeeze it. He'd smile and press it to his lips.

Suddenly, there was water on either side of the road.

'This is Southsea, the part of Portsmouth where I live,' Peter said and slowed down. He pointed out the Common, a large green space dotted with trees. At one end of the space was a large Ferris wheel. Then, the pale-blue sea opened up in front of them.

'Take in that sea air!' Peter said and inhaled loudly.

She smiled at him and turned her face to the water. A few sailing boats were moving fast across the glittering surface; a large passenger ferry was approaching in the distance. The sky was strewn with thin, fluffy clouds. Kaisa had always loved the sea, even the cold and inhospitable shoreline of the Lauttasaari Island in winter. She couldn't imagine the Pompey seafront ever being that uninviting.

There was a long promenade running alongside the sea. People in ones and twos, some with children or dogs, strolled along the pavement. The couples and families laughed and chatted to each other.

As Peter steered the car away from the water, Kaisa grew nervous again. They must be nearly at the house Peter shared with his Navy friends. What if they didn't like her? She'd chosen her outfit very carefully, but now she felt shabby and old-fashioned. What if his friends dressed smarter than her?

During the entire drive to Pompey, Peter kept glancing at Kaisa. He could hardly believe she was here. The two months they'd been apart had felt endless. He'd missed her far more than he'd expected. Every time he went out with his friends, he wished Kaisa were there by his side. In bed at night, the longing for her had been almost unbearable.

He looked at her again. The cap he'd given her really suited her. She was even more beautiful than he'd remembered. He touched her knee and smiled at her, and she beamed back at him.

He'd got to the airport ridiculously early, well ahead of the scheduled landing time, and had a long wait before she appeared through the automatic doors. His body had ached for her the whole time, and now, so close to home, he was nervous. Would the sex still be as passionate as it had been in Helsinki? What if she'd changed her mind about him when he saw where he lived?

His best friend Jeff's investment rental belonging to his parents was a small terraced house, which Peter shared with three other people. They wouldn't be able go to bed whenever they wanted, not the way they had in her Helsinki flat. Portsmouth wasn't exactly pretty or metropolitan, like London.

Peter had planned a busy schedule for Kaisa's stay. He wanted to show her how beautiful England was.

He turned to her and shouted over the wind whipping around their ears, 'Nearly there!'

Looking back at the road again, he knew his worries were unfounded. He was going to spend the next two weeks with the girl of his dreams. He could see in Kaisa's eyes that she, too, was on cloud nine.

From the seafront, Peter drove down one street and turned into another, then another. The streets all looked alike, with rows and rows of the same type of houses Kaisa had seen from the plane. The street names were displayed on white signs attached to low, brick walls. They passed by Canterbury Road, Devonshire Avenue, and Winter Road before Peter stopped on a tree-lined street and announced, 'We're here.'

The door to the house was ajar. Peter took Kaisa's hand and led her inside to the first room.

'Wait here,' he said.

Kaisa stood in a shabby-looking room with a worn-out sofa, a large TV and a stereo with speakers on either side. A stack of LPs were on the floor. A wooden staircase next to a narrow hall had a strip of carpet on it. Peter leapt up the stairs taking two or three steps at a time.

A guy with light-coloured hair in a faded T-shirt walked in from the dark, narrow hallway. He was barefoot.

'You must be the Finnish girlfriend.'

Kaisa shook his outstretched hand and smiled.

'Jeff,' he said and grinned at Kaisa. He was followed by a shorter man called Oliver, with tidy dark hair and well-pressed trousers, then a girl called Sandra. She had short, fair hair and dark eyes, and was Oliver's girl-friend. They both smiled and shook Kaisa's hand.

Peter pounded down the stairs.

'Here you all are.'

They stood in a circle, and for a while no one spoke.

'I'll show you my room,' Peter finally said.

The men sniggered until the English girl, Sandra, looked sternly at them. Embarrassed, Kaisa allowed Peter to lead her upstairs.

His bedroom was at the top of the stairs. It overlooked an overgrown garden with a patio area at its centre. Peter had a poster of a tennis player with half of her buttock showing, and a calendar with half-naked women above his bed.

Kaisa stared at the images. She'd seen similar – and worse – in the books Matti had at home, so she wasn't shocked. But she didn't want to be looking at them while she and Peter were in bed.

'Don't worry about those,' Peter said, coming up behind her.

As soon as he kissed her and began to unclasp her bra, Kaisa forgot about the posters. All she needed was Peter, to be close to him, to feel him inside of her.

11

The two weeks Kaisa spent in the UK, in the late summer of 1981, were the best. The sun never stopped shining and the music never stopped playing. Hearing Radio One for the first time, it sounded very American to her; all laughter and superficial chatter. But it played the hits that she never heard on the airways in Finland. The station was the only one Peter listened to, either in his car or in the house. He sang along to all the hits.

Every day while in Southsea, they would visit the beach and swim in the sea. Afterwards, Peter would drive them back to the house, which was empty during the day, and they would make love all afternoon in Peter's small, single bed. Every evening, they would meet various friends in the pub around the corner from the house, or in the centre of Pompey. Jeff's parents owned a pub in Old Portsmouth, where there'd often be a 'lock-in' and drinking until the small hours.

Halfway through the first week of Kaisa's stay, Peter drove her to the country to see his parents. She wore the Red Sox cap to keep her hair in place.

'How far is it?' Kaisa asked when they pulled into a large-looking town called Salisbury. She knew where it was on the map she'd studied, but not how long the drive from Portsmouth would take.

Peter must have noticed her nerves, because he squeezed her thigh and smiled. 'I'll let you know when we're ten minutes away.'

The image of Matti's mother flashed in her mind as they left the town behind and sped past green fields. She thought about what she had said to her during their awful last telephone conversation. Kaisa gazed sideways at Peter. He looked tanned and relaxed, holding the wheel with one hand, and his elbow resting on the open side of the car. She hoped a nice guy like him would have a nicer mother.

Instead of thinking about meeting the parents, she sat back and tried to enjoy the scenery. Peter drove past wooded hills and valleys, where tree branches hung over the road, nearly touching the tops of their heads. After Salisbury, there were small villages with pretty gingerbread houses. Kaisa felt like a character in a TV drama or an old English film. Her head filled with images from *Coronation Street* and *Mary Poppins*, both of which she'd seen in Finland. Kaisa almost expected a nanny with a large black umbrella to emerge at any moment from one of the chimneys, stacked on top of the red-brick houses.

When they arrived, Peter's mother was in the front garden of a pink house, attending to a flowerbed. She laughed lightly as she kissed her son and shook Kaisa's hand.

'Hello, I'm Evie. It's so nice to meet you at last.'

Evie had short, greying hair arranged in an old-fashioned hairdo, and large-framed glasses. She didn't look as scary as Matti's mother; but still Kaisa wanted to be careful. Not wanting to upset her from the start, she smiled and said as little as possible.

It was Wednesday lunchtime and Peter's father was at work. His mother cooked home-made chips and served them with thick slices of ham. Peter and Kaisa ate in a large kitchen overlooking a green lawn at the back of the house. Peter told his mother what they had been up to during Kaisa's two days in Portsmouth. She asked when Kaisa had arrived, when she was going home and where she lived in Helsinki. When Kaisa told her she lived alone in a flat, Evie raised an eyebrow. Kaisa wondered if Peter had mentioned that Kaisa's parents were divorced.

'I've put you in the blue room,' Evie said after lunch. She turned to her son. 'And you can sleep in the yellow one.'

Kaisa couldn't look at Peter. It was like a scene from a Jane Austen novel. She thought about the tennis girl's bare bottom, and the Pirelli calendar on his bedroom wall in Southsea. What would his mother say if she saw them?

Peter's father arrived home later. He was a charming man with a mop of white hair. His dark eyes fixed on Kaisa.

'Hello,' he said simply. He shook her hand.

The older man put on an LP of Sibelius in the long lounge, which had a green velour three-piece suite. He told Kaisa to sit down and told her how he admired the Finnish composer, as well as the soldiers in the Winter War.

'Brave men. You stood up to the Russians, eh?'

He smiled and nodded, as if to show her his approval.

That evening, Peter took Kaisa out to a pub in a pretty village called Lacock. The place was dark, with low rustic beams. They met Peter's school friends and chatted around a large, unlit fireplace. His friends gave Kaisa furtive glances, looking surprised that she could speak English.

Later in the evening, as they tiptoed inside the dark house, Peter kissed Kaisa softly and said, 'I'll come to your room in the morning, after my parents have gone to work.'

The next day, after they'd spent the morning in bed, Peter took Kaisa to Stourhead, a National Trust garden. He said it was prettier in May, when the rhododendrons were in bloom, but Kaisa couldn't see how the gardens, with deep ponds and sweeping lawns, could look any more beautiful. Another day's excursion was to an old English stately home called Longleat. They wandered hand in hand through the ancient Manor House. And they spent a full day in Bath. Kaisa fell in love with the Roman Baths, the Georgian architecture and the fancy shopping streets. She wondered cautiously if one day she might live there.

At the end of the visit, Kaisa thanked Peter's mother.

Evie said, 'It's my pleasure, dear. I try look after all the girlfriends my son brings home.'

Peter laughed nervously.

Kaisa pulled in a tight breath. It was something Mother might say. She searched Evie's face for signs of malice, but found only a kind, smiling woman. She hugged Kaisa warmly. As Peter drove away from the house, Kaisa turned back. Evie was standing by the door to the pink house, waving to them. She waved back.

On the drive back to Portsmouth, Kaisa looked at Peter's handsome profile as he negotiated a large roundabout. How many girlfriends have there been? she wondered. Was his mother trying to warn her? Was Kaisa taking this relationship too seriously – more seriously than Peter?

Perhaps the sightseeing, the introductions to various friends and the love letters were something he did for all his women. He certainly seemed practiced at making a girl feel special. The car sped up and the wind rushing past made it impossible to talk. Kaisa was grateful for the silence. She wiped the tears away gently, so they didn't smudge her makeup.

. . .

Peter concentrated on the driving, afraid to catch Kaisa's eye. Only after they'd been on the road for over half an hour, not speaking, did he dare to look over at her. Her head was high, but it worried him she hadn't said a word since they'd left his parent's house. Peter desperately wanted a cigarette, but it was impossible to smoke at this speed with the roof down. Outside Salisbury, the heavy traffic slowed the car to a stop. He peered over at Kaisa and touched her thigh.

'You OK?'

She turned briefly and nodded.

So, he'd been right, she was upset. Shit. What had his mum been thinking saying that? Perhaps she was trying to warn Kaisa that her son was fickle and not to be trusted? Or trying to tell him that he was too young to settle down? Of course the latter was true – but he had no intention of that, and neither had Kaisa.

As far as he knew.

When they cleared the town with its endless roundabouts and were once again speeding along the A31, Peter sighed with relief. As soon as they returned to Pompey, he would take her into his arms and remind her how much he loved her. He knew how to make her feel better. Just the thought of what he'd do to Kaisa later made his groin stir with longing.

They arrived back in Portsmouth to find the house was empty. It was midday on Monday and Peter and Kaisa had six more days together. As soon as they were inside, Peter pulled her close and kissed her mouth, moving to her neck and putting his had inside her jeans. She didn't resist, rather, she placed her fingers on his crotch, feeling his erection.

'Let's go upstairs,' Peter said hoarsely and Kaisa nodded.

Now and then during Kaisa's last week in the UK, the words of Peter's mother 'all of my son's girlfriends' replayed in her head. But as soon as Peter took her into his arms, or simply touched her, she convinced herself there was nothing to worry about.

She could talk. Kaisa had been engaged to be married when they'd met. Peter could have had serious girlfriends before her. Wasn't there a girl he'd been writing to? Maybe Peter's mum had wanted him to settle with her instead of a foreign girl.

But Peter's attentiveness during her two-week stay in England couldn't be misinterpreted. He had been eager to show his country off to her. For her last weekend, he took Kaisa to visit his older brother and his wife in Surrey, near London.

'I heard my mother put you in separate bedrooms in Wiltshire,' Simon said with a smile. Kaisa blushed. 'Don't worry, the same sleeping arrangements won't apply in this house.'

Simon, shorter in height than Peter, had the same dark features as his brother, but his hair had gone grey around the temples. Kaisa knew he was ten years older than Peter. His wife, Miriam, a wiry woman with cropped brown hair, kissed Kaisa warmly on both cheeks.

'You must be hungry,' she said and led Kaisa into the kitchen. Four plates, filled with ham and salad, were on the counter, ready to be served.

Kaisa smiled. 'Starving.'

They were lying in the guest bedroom later, decorated with Laura Ashley wallpaper and matching bedding. The bed squeaked too much, so their lovemaking had to be careful and slow. After, Peter surprised her with tickets for the English National Opera the following night. Kaisa was so touched tears welled up in her eyes.

'I remembered that you love Puccini,' he whispered.

Kaisa couldn't speak. The tickets were for *Tosca*, her absolute favourite.

The Opera House in London was larger than the one in Helsinki, but more modern, less classic. While drinking gin and tonics in the bar, Kaisa studied the programme.

'You must tell me what happens,' Peter said.

Kaisa recounted the sad story of Floria Tosca, the tempestuous singer, and her lover, Cavaradossi, who was imprisoned by the sadistic police chief, Scarpia.

'Scarpia is in love with Tosca, and she decides to use her power over him to save Cavaradossi. Of course, she fails and it all ends in tragedy.'

After taking their seats, the lights dimmed and the first notes of the opera were played. Kaisa squeezed Peter's hand. Bringing her to the opera made her fall in love with him again. He could not have given her a better gift than a live performance of *Tosca*. On cue, she cried during several of the arias, and let out a shriek when, in the final scene, Tosca jumps to her death from a castle wall.

On the way to the Tube station, Kaisa asked Peter what he thought of the opera.

'I loved it!' he said.

'Really?'

Peter stopped walking and turned towards her.

'Really. It was incredible. The music, the singing – everything.' He kissed Kaisa on the mouth. 'Thank you for introducing me to opera.'

Her heart filled with a happiness she had difficulty defining. Matti had never wanted to go and see an opera, however much Kaisa had asked him to. He'd always thought it was a waste of money.

While waiting for the train at Piccadilly Tube station, Peter said, 'You cried.'

Kaisa looked down. Her cheeks felt hot. 'Sorry, I couldn't help it. Every time I see *Tosca*, I hope that they've changed the ending. That they'll live happily ever after. It's silly, I know.'

Peter held Kaisa tightly and said, 'No it's sweet. You're sweet.' He looked deeply into her eyes. 'You've no idea how much I love you.'

He kissed Kaisa long and hard. Then whispered, 'I love everything about you.'

She melted into his arms and tried not to think about how they had less than forty-eight hours before they had to part again.

On Sunday, the day before her flight back to Helsinki, Peter planned a picnic in Hyde Park. It was a windy but sunny day. Before lunch, he drove Kaisa around the sights. The streets of London were quiet. From the passenger seat of the little yellow Spitfire, she took pictures of Big Ben, the Houses of Parliament and Buckingham Palace. It felt like a dream to see places and buildings Kaisa had only ever read about.

In Hyde Park, they spread a blanket under a large elm. A few boys were playing football in the distance. The vast lawns were incredibly green and even. Peter's ever-efficient sister-in-law had prepared a picnic of sandwiches, neatly cut into triangles and arranged in a Tupperware dish. There was a Thermos of tea and one of coffee. Peter ate heartily, but Kaisa just nibbled on one sandwich. Whenever she was close to Peter, Kaisa lost her appetite. Especially now, when their time together was ticking down so fast.

Lying on the blanket next to the man she loved Kaisa tried not to think about the future, although it was hard not to. This was their last day together and they hadn't made plans for their next meeting. Peter couldn't pin down his schedule in the Navy, Kaisa knew that much. But when he gave her a kiss and whispered hoarsely into her ear, 'I'm going to miss you so much', Kaisa couldn't delay the talk any longer.

She took a deep breath and said, 'So, what are we going to do? About the future, I mean.'

Peter released her and lay down on the blanket, breaking the spell between them. She wished suddenly that she hadn't said anything. It was as if she'd veered off the written libretto and brought the opera down to earth, down to reality, down to the present day. But Kaisa couldn't bear the uncertainty of not knowing.

She watched Peter put his sunglasses on and speak to the blue sky above him, 'I didn't tell you, but I'm joining a submarine up in Scotland next week.'

He turned to Kaisa; she couldn't read his expression behind the dark glasses.

'And you've got two more years at university?' he continued.

'Yes,' Kaisa muttered. She was beginning to feel sick.

Peter put his arms around her.

'If only Finland was in the EEC, then you wouldn't need a stupid work permit. You could just come and work here – in a pub or something. I'm sure someone would take you on.'

Kaisa moved away from him. She shivered.

'Are you cold?'

Peter removed his glasses. She saw concern in his eyes. He handed Kaisa his jumper. It smelled of his American coconut shaving foam and cigarettes. He retrieved a packet of Silk Cut cigarettes from the pocket of his jacket and lit one.

Kaisa was grateful for the interlude. Blood was rushing in her head and her heart was beating so hard, she could hardly breathe.

Peter blew smoke out the side of his mouth. Kaisa looked at his long legs. They were crossed at the ankles, and his white trainers looked shabbier than usual. She couldn't see his eyes.

'We'll just have to be friends,' he said.

'What do you mean?' she squeaked.

'When we're not together, we can be free to do whatever we want.'

Peter's tone was casual, as if he was talking about changing the make of cigarettes he smoked.

It was as if he'd hit Kaisa in the face.

'You mean we'll be free to see other people?'

Her words came out in a faint whisper, but she knew Peter had heard them.

There was a brief silence.

Peter took a long, final drag on his cigarette. He stumped it out on a small stone near the trunk of the tree and flicked the end away from them.

He faced Kaisa again and said, 'You know I love you.'

'So you say.'

Kaisa turned away. She started tidying the uneaten sandwiches back into the container. More anger rose inside of her. She'd been right all along: making a girl feel special came easily to Peter.

'Come here,' Peter pleaded.

'No,' Kaisa said.

She was no fool. She needed to keep her composure and keep away from Peter. Tears welled up behind her closed eyelids, but she could not – would not – let Peter see how upset she was. She opened her eyes and, from the corner of one, saw him sit up. She turned to face him properly. His long arms hugged his knees and he'd put his sunglasses back on. He spoke to her, while looking at his fingers.

'Look, this has happened to me before.'

Kaisa froze. So she was right! He did this sort of thing all the time. She'd been an idiot, a stupid girl thinking she was special to him.

Her heart was beating so hard against her ribcage that she thought she might faint. She slowed her breaths, tried to steady her heartbeat and went back to putting the sandwiches back into the plastic containers.

Peter continued, 'When I was on a commission in the Canadian Navy I met this girl. She...well, we fell in love. But it didn't last. She couldn't work in Britain and I couldn't afford to go to Canada all the time. So we slowly drifted apart. It was very hard.'

Kaisa felt dizzy. She dropped the Tupperware box onto the blanket and sat back down.

Peter took his sunglasses off again and put his arms around her. Kaisa didn't have the strength to resist.

In a low whisper he said, 'I just don't want that to happen to us.'

Kaisa looked into his dark eyes, at the straight line of his mouth. She couldn't be angry with Peter. If this was all she was going get, she'd have to be happy with that. She rested her head on his shoulder and twined her fingers with his strong, long ones. She wanted the world to stop here.

They sat like that while Kaisa waited for the tears to come, but there weren't any.

'You OK?' Peter said.

Kaisa looked up at him and heard herself say, 'Yes.'

12

HELSINKI, AUTUMN 1981

Kaisa had never felt as numb as she had waiting to board her flight at Heathrow after two wonderful weeks with Peter. There were just a handful of people sitting outside the gate for the Finnair flight to Helsinki. The labels on Kaisa's luggage read: Hel. It felt like hell was where she was going.

Peter and Kaisa hadn't discussed more of their future since the day in Hyde Park. Kaisa had accepted she was on the losing side, and that he meant more to her than she did to him.

It serves me right, she thought, as she watched a man in a pinstripe suit sitting opposite her read his *Financial Times*. Had Kaisa not done the same? Cast aside a man who was more devoted to her than she to him? Matti's heart must have hurt then as much as Kaisa's did now. What stung most was that Matti had been right all along. A foreign man, a sailor, usually had a girl in every port.

Peter didn't care for Kaisa – not in the way Matti did, or had done. Maybe she and Matti could try again? No, the thought of going back to her ex-fiancé made her shudder. She must learn to be on her own. How difficult could it be? Tuuli was alone and was fine. She'd never even had a serious boyfriend.

But sitting on the hard plastic seats of the airport terminal, Kaisa felt lonelier than she'd ever done in her life.

The man in the suit dropped his paper and gave Kaisa a quick smile. She nodded to him politely before looking at her watch. The flight was due to leave in five minutes. They should already be boarding, but there was no sign of an official by the gate. She felt shabby in her jeans and jumper. Maybe she should dress smarter and take an interest in financial matters, like the man opposite her. She was a student of economics, after all. Instead she sat there slouched over, like a lovesick puppy.

Kaisa straightened up and took out her book, Thomas Hardy's *Tess of the d'Urbervilles*, but she couldn't concentrate on the words. Peter had given her the paperback, saying it was one of his favourite books. Kaisa touched her lips, remembering the long kiss he'd given her by passport control only half an hour earlier. What was he doing now? Was he listening to Radio One, singing along to a tune as he drove back to Portsmouth in his yellow sports car? Was he thinking about Kaisa? On the way to the airport he'd told her it was the last night he'd spend with his friends in the terraced house in Portsmouth. He'd looked sad about it.

Kaisa had wanted to shout, 'What about me? This is the last time you're going to see me, ever.'

But she'd said nothing. Instead, she'd listened to him tell her about how the four friends were going out to the pub for a goodbye dinner.

Kaisa didn't even have a forwarding address for Peter. He'd told her only the name of the submarine he would be joining.

'I'll write to you as soon as I'm settled up there,' he'd said as they were saying goodbye at the airport.

Kaisa had nodded.

'I promise.' Peter then cupped Kaisa's face and kissed her. 'I love you, remember that.'

Kaisa hadn't replied. She'd given him a last quick kiss and turned towards the man in uniform waiting to check her ticket and passport. And she didn't look back.

Helsinki was cold and rainy. The leaves were already turning yellow and brown. Autumn was here. The airport bus dropped Kaisa off at Töölö Square. From there, she heaved her heavy suitcase down the hill to Mannerheim Street. She carried her luggage onto the tram and then onto a bus, which took her to the empty flat in Lauttasaari. Kaisa ignored the pile of post on the floor, mostly bills, which she'd received while away. Instead, she dug two LPs out of her bag that Peter had bought for her in Bath. She read *Tess of the d'Urbervilles* while listening to all the tracks on the Christopher Cross and Earth, Wind & Fire albums over and over.

Kaisa's lectures at Hanken restarted three weeks after she returned from her holiday in England. It was October and the afternoons were getting shorter in Helsinki.

On the first day of term she got up early, gathered all her bills, including the overdue rent for the flat, and headed into town. She needed to check the balance on her bank account. She hated being late with the rent, especially now she was no longer engaged to Matti. His aunt was certain to tell Mother if Kaisa ever fell behind with the payment. That would confirm all of Mother's suspicions about Kaisa's flaky personality. About how unreliable she was. About how she could not be depended upon. Just like her divorcee mother.

She arrived at the bank where she'd worked as a summer intern. Her former colleagues couldn't wait to hear all about Kaisa's holiday in England. When she eventually tore free from their chatter and asked for her bank book to be updated, she stared at the black printed figures on the small page.

'What's up?' the teller asked as she handed her back the book.

'Nothing.' Kaisa smiled and left.

At Hanken, she headed straight for the students' advisory office.

'My grant's not been paid into my bank,' Kaisa told the lady at the desk.

The woman remembered her from the first year, when Kaisa had filled in the forms. There weren't many students who were eligible for a student aid grant at the Helsinki Swedish School of Economics in 1981. Most students were from well-to-do families, not from a broken home like hers.

The woman with pale-blue eyes and messy blonde hair, with grey streaks, looked at Kaisa kindly.

'I'm afraid your grant was denied.'

Kaisa couldn't believe her ears. She asked her to check again.

The woman pulled out a sheet of paper and looked at it. She turned it over and pointed at a set of figures. Kaisa saw her name at the top of the print-out.

'You see, you only got fifteen credits last term. You need a minimum of twenty to receive the funding.'

'Oh,' Kaisa said and lifted her eyes slowly to the woman.

The woman opened her mouth, as if to say something. But she closed it again and looked down at her desk.

Kaisa ran out of the office, past the common room where other students were smoking and drinking coffee. Loud chatter and laughter filled the space. She dodged the people, keeping her eyes on the ground. As she reached the glass door exit, she saw a dark-haired guy lunge for the door and open it for her. Kaisa looked up and saw it was Tom, the boy who'd hit on her last year. For the first time in forever, he was looking straight at Kaisa.

'Thanks,' she said and quickly hurried out onto the cold street.

What was she going to do? Kaisa had just ninety-seven Marks in her bank account. That would last for a month, if she was very careful. But it didn't pay for the rent or the electricity bill. Both were a week overdue. Kaisa didn't have a job, and even if she got one now, she wouldn't get paid until the end of the month. Besides, good jobs were hard to come by, even for fully-fledged graduates. Kaisa had only passed her first year. How would she explain to an employer that in her second year she'd passed only three exams of the eight she'd taken?

On the Number 21 bus to Lauttasaari Kaisa's dread for her future grew. What would she tell her mother? She'd been so proud when Kaisa got accepted to Hanken, the Swedish School for Economics in Helsinki. As a bilingual country, Finland provided education in both Finnish and Swedish, and if you had the language, Hanken was much easier to get into than the Finnish-language equivalent. Kaisa had learnt Swedish when she lived in Stockholm for three years. She'd been eleven when the family moved there and fourteen when they returned to Finland. Kaisa even had a Stockholm accent, which made her stand out at Hanken. But she really struggled with Swedish academic text.

This is what she would tell her mother. As for her father, Kaisa decided not to contact him at all.

At home, Kaisa was greeted by another bill for the telephone. With dread she opened it: thirty-six Marks and seventy-nine pennies due. Underneath the white envelope was a blue one.

A letter from Peter.

Kaisa rubbed the silky texture between her fingers, trying to resist opening it straight away. Of course, Peter had been the reason she'd failed her classes. Instead of studying, she'd been re-reading his letters over and over again, lying awake at night waiting for his calls, daydreaming at lectures, or sometimes not even turning up after a sleepless, lovesick night. When Kaisa should have been studying employment law, she was instead planning a holiday to England. So many times she'd stared out of the large windows of the lecture hall, remembering the feel of Peter's kiss on her lips, when she should have been learning from a visiting professor in international law.

Unable to wait any longer, she tore the envelope open and read the letter.

· · ·

'When I arrived in Faslane it was snowing, can you believe that? It is so much colder up here in Scotland, just like Helsinki. And I got off at the wrong station and had to wait for another train for ages in the freezing cold. When I finally arrived at the naval base, I met an old mate who I didn't know was also joining a submarine. Of course, we had a few beers too many in the Back Bar and now I'm a bit worse for wear while writing to you, my love. I miss you so much. When I saw you walk through to the other side at Heathrow I thought my heart would break. The drive back to Pompey was horrible without you next to me wearing my Red Sox cap.'

Kaisa couldn't read on. She pressed the letter to her chest and closed her eyes.

Peter *did* love her. He missed her.

After a brief moment, she reread his words. Even though it was a short letter, just two sides on one sheet of paper, it was powerful. Peter ended by giving Kaisa a new address and telling her he didn't know when he would call, as he didn't know when or where they would sail.

'Even if I knew I don't think I could tell you, my darling.'

Kaisa put the letter down on the small dining table and went to the kitchenette to make coffee. She opened the tin and looked inside; there was just enough for one load in the percolator. Coffee was expensive, but she'd buy some for tomorrow morning.

I'd rather have coffee and starve, she thought ruefully.

And she'd rather see Peter than have coffee.

What a stupid, stupid girl she was.

13

STOCKHOLM, AUTUMN 1981

The smart, new ferry smelled of carpet freshener and paint. At the end of a long ramp a large-bellied man in uniform greeted Kaisa with a smile. Her arm ached from carrying the suitcase, and she barely managed a grimace in return. To her relief, the luggage store was close by. She placed the heavy bag on a shelf and checked she had all she needed for the overnight crossing: toiletries, a small towel and her purse. She placed the items into a small Marimekko holdall and went in search of a free bunk bed.

Fleeing Helsinki like this Kaisa felt like a refugee, but she didn't know how else to escape her unpaid rent bills and the wrath of her ex- fiancé's family. When Kaisa had spoken to her mother on the phone, Pirjo had said without hesitation, 'Darling, come to Stockholm.'

Kaisa had nothing to stay in Helsinki for. No money, no energy to study, no boyfriend.

After the initial elation following Peter's last letter wore off, Kaisa began to doubt his intentions again. She remembered his mother's words about 'all his girlfriends', and Peter's own wish to remain free to see other people. However much he said he missed Kaisa in his letter, she imagined him telling some other girl in the same breath how much he loved her. And he didn't seem worried he might lose Kaisa to another man.

During the long days planning her departure from Helsinki, Kaisa had decided not to write a reply to Peter. She hadn't known what to say. She really wanted to ask him if he'd changed his mind about them being friends, but was afraid of his reply. Besides, the wait for that letter would kill her.

Kaisa had already revealed too much of herself to Peter. She didn't want him to know how he had changed her life, or how much she'd believed they would have a future together. It was obvious now that Peter didn't think there was any hope for a long-term relationship. Hurting so much already, Kaisa didn't want to plunge deeper into misery.

But the night before she was due to leave the Lauttasaari flat forever, a phone call came.

'Hello, you,' Peter had said his tone soft.

Kaisa's heart had melted when she heard his voice, but she'd kept her reply simple.

'Oh, Peter, how nice to hear from you.'

'How's Helsinki?' Peter said sounding a little puzzled.

'Fine. It's late and I'm off to Stockholm tomorrow.'

'Wow, you off on holiday again?' Peter asked lightly.

'Actually, I'm moving there. To my sister's new flat.'

There was a silence.

'Really?' He sounded angry now. 'What if I hadn't called tonight? How would I have known where to contact you? I don't have your sister's address, or phone number!'

Kaisa said nothing. She wanted to sound like she didn't care, but his pain was hurting her too.

'I was going to write from Stockholm,' she lied and gave Peter the details of her new home.

Kaisa's mother embraced her at the ferry port in Stockholm. 'Your sister's at work; she'll see you tonight and we'll all have dinner together.'

Kaisa relaxed. For the first time in a long while she wasn't alone; her family would look after her.

Her sister worked at a large hotel in the middle of the city. One night, a few days after Kaisa had arrived, Sirkka suggested Kaisa meet her after a late shift.

'The staff usually go out together after we close; the bars and nightclubs are open till very late in Stockholm.'

Sirkka smiled at Kaisa over her mirror. She was putting on her makeup in the kitchen at a small table that folded out from the wall. The two sisters were sharing a studio flat. Sirkka had the bed in the alcove, and Kaisa slept on a corner sofa that their mother had bought when they'd all lived in

Stockholm. It was worn out but Kaisa didn't mind. Sharing with her sister was like being teenagers again.

Sirkka had fled Helsinki three years before Kaisa. Not because of money, work or studies, but to escape a jealous boyfriend. She was two years older than Kaisa and they'd always been close, spending their teenage years partying and going out together. Kaisa had missed her living in Helsinki.

'Just like old times,' Sirkka now said and put her hand through Kaisa's arm. She smelled of perfume and her hair was done up in large, bouncy, blonde curls.

Kaisa confessed she had no money for the evening but Sirkka said not to worry.

'Pay me back when you get a job,' she said with a laugh, shoving notes into her hand. Her job as *maître d'hotel* obviously paid well.

They arrived at the bar at half-past midnight. Kaisa couldn't believe how full it was. The music was playing loudly, and all the tables were taken. Her sister waved at a large group at the back of the room. Two empty chairs were found for them. Sirkka introduced Kaisa as Little Sister – her nickname from their childhood.

After the bar they all went to a disco, and for the first time since arriving in Stockholm Kaisa was having fun. She danced with several of her sister's friends, as well as unknown guys who came up and asked her onto the floor.

'It's about time you let your hair down,' Sirkka laughed later in her flat. It was well past 3am and she was making sandwiches.

They were listening to a new Rod Stewart LP, *Blondes Have More Fun*, when the loud ringing of the phone in the hall made them both jump.

Sirkka ran to answer it.

'It's Peter for you,' she called out, handing Kaisa the receiver when she stood in front of her sister. The phone was sitting on a small table. There was no chair so Kaisa sat on the floor, holding the receiver close to her ear.

'I've tried your number all evening,' said Peter.

'Sorry, I was out with my sister.'

'Right.'

Sirkka giggled and sang into the receiver. 'Do you think I'm sexy?'

Kaisa pulled it away and shook her head at Sirkka; her sister disappeared into the kitchen.

'What was that?' Peter sounded angry.

Kaisa shivered at his cold and distant tone. It killed her buzz and ruined what had been a good night. They ended the conversation shortly after without saying, 'I love you'.

. . .

Exactly three weeks after Kaisa had arrived in Stockholm, she was on her way back to Helsinki. She'd tried, and failed, to get a job in Stockholm. Her mother and sister had told her that the best option for the future would be to finish her studies at Hanken. But it was an encounter with a kind woman at a Swedish bank that had convinced Kaisa to return. The woman had said she'd employ Kaisa on the spot – her references from the bank in Helsinki were excellent – but she was doing her a favour by telling her to finish university instead.

'You'll earn twice as much and you'll have a brilliant career with us, plus a degree,' she'd said.

A good career was what Kaisa wanted.

She dragged her heavy suitcases onboard the ferry. It was a day sailing and a good book made the time fly by. As she watched the ferry dock at South Harbour jetty in Helsinki, she knew she'd made the right decision in returning.

That was until she saw her father, waiting for her just inside the ferry terminal. Had she made a mistake asking him to pick her up?

When Kaisa had phoned him from Stockholm her father had immediately promised her a temporary home in his house in Espoo, in the suburbs just outside Helsinki. Kaisa had hesitated at the idea of taking anything from him, but she felt better after her mother said, 'It's about time he took some responsibility for at least one of his daughters.'

Her grim looking father bear-hugged her, and grabbed the heavy suitcase.

'We'd better get you into the car then.' He grunted against the weight, and walked ahead of Kaisa into the already dark Helsinki afternoon.

My Best Girl: Her father's nickname for her growing up. But as an adult, his obvious favouritism of her over Sirkka had become a burden to her rather than a source of pride. When Kaisa's parents finally split up after years of fighting, the decision came as a relief to both her and Sirkka.

When Sirkka was fifteen and Kaisa thirteen, their parents had forced the girls to choose whom to live with. Kaisa's father hadn't taken her rejection well.

'You've made your bed, Kaisa. There'll be no more money from me.' That night he'd stormed out, and later he returned home, drunk again.

In spite of those early threats, her father had made an effort to connect over the last few years. On the rare occasions he invited his two daughters to lunch he always handed over a few one-hundred-Mark notes. When

Kaisa had told him she was going to study at Hanken, he'd even given her a small allowance.

After their shopping trip the previous autumn, when he'd been more like his old self before the divorce, Kaisa remained hopeful that her father might even be glad to have her live with him.

The next day at Hanken, Tuuli greeted Kaisa with a hug. 'Coming back to study is absolutely the best decision you could have made.'

The blonde-haired woman at the students' advisory office also agreed.

'Why don't you change your subject? Commercial law is a difficult one to specialise in, especially as Swedish is not your mother tongue.' Her kind eyes were on Kaisa. 'The next committee meeting is early December. If you get two exam passes by then, we can re-approve your grant.'

Following the student adviser's recommendation, Kaisa changed courses and became a student of political science. Her new department was small and homely. There, she studied the theories of Karl Marx, as well as those of Keynes, and her horizons were widened. While the other students at the university learnt how to make money, or account for it, Kaisa's new courses taught her the principles behind the desire for wealth and power. She found the subjects fascinating, which made studying for them easy.

At the house in Espoo, Kaisa rarely saw her father. He'd given up his bedroom for her, mostly staying over at his girlfriend's flat in Töölö. When he was at home and not drunk Kaisa cooked for him, and when he was in a good mood he made *gravad lax* for her.

Kaisa tried to move on from Peter, but his letters wouldn't allow it. He wrote at least once a week and called when he was on dry land. Most often he was away with the submarine, to unknown destinations for weeks on end. During those times, the letters would stop.

One night, the telephone woke her. She answered it to hear he had news for her.

'We've just sailed in, and I've been told I can take leave for Christmas. Can you come to England?'

Kaisa's grant would be paid in December. If she continued to live with her father she'd be able to afford the fare.

She told Peter she'd think about it, but Kaisa knew what her decision would be.

At Hanken the next day, Tuuli shook her head.

'Are you sure that's wise? You remember what happened last time you came home from England?'

They were standing in the semi-darkness of the Students' Union disco, in the centre of Helsinki. After her return from Stockholm, Kaisa and Tuuli had started going out, most often to 'Ladies' Nights' on Mondays. The disco was full of students from all the Helsinki universities, made up mostly of students from Hanken. The rich boys were always there, and that night they laughed and glanced over at her and Tuuli.

'Look who's here again,' Kaisa said, turning away sharply when Tom looked in her direction again. 'Do you think I should have gone out with him that first week?'

She often wondered what might have happened had she agreed to go out with Tom. Would he be with her now instead of the tall, red-haired girl next to him?

'No,' Tuuli said, 'he would have gone to bed with you and that's that. It's what the rich boys do: as many as possible in as little time as possible.'

Kaisa laughed, but she wondered was this what all men were like? Was Peter like that too? Was he only so loving and seemingly committed to her because he was lonely up in Faslane – or Faslavatory, as he called it? He said there were no pubs or clubs there. She read that to mean no places to meet girls in.

When Kaisa got home that night, she got another call from Peter.

This time he sounded impatient. 'Well, are we going to meet up at Christmas?'

'Of course we are,' Kaisa replied.

It might be a mistake to go back to the UK, but she couldn't resist Peter's invite.

He breathed in and out deeply and said, 'That means I'll see you in only two weeks' time!'

14

W hile in Stockholm Kaisa had discovered a company called Fritidsresor, which organised chartered trips from Sweden to London. If she travelled by ferry to Stockholm, flew to a small, new airport in London and spent a week in a cheap hotel there, it would cost half that of a Finnair airfare from Helsinki to Heathrow.

Peter said he'd never been to Stansted airport before. When Kaisa arrived, he was the only person meeting the plane full of Swedish tourists, apart from an efficient travel guide wearing a red-and-yellow shirt and holding a clipboard above her head.

Kaisa ran into Peter's arms. He smelt of the cold outside air. He gave her a long kiss.

'God, I've missed you,' he whispered and took her to the yellow Triumph Spitfire she loved. With the roof up the car was cosy and warm. He drove away from the airport and down a narrow road that met the perimeter fence for the runway.

'We're going to my parents for Christmas, and then Pompey for New Year. Is that OK?' Peter reached over and squeezed Kaisa's thigh. 'We'll be there in about three hours.'

Kaisa relaxed into the low seat and closed her eyes. She'd been even more nervous about coming to see Peter this time than last summer. But as soon as she saw him, and felt his lips on hers, all that he'd said at the end of the last visit seemed like a bad dream. She even doubted Peter's intention for them to see other people. His letters since, and his actions now, were even more passionate and loving than before. It was as if they were a real couple, not just two singles meeting up for occasional sex.

They pulled up to his parents' house and Kaisa sat in the car a moment, worried about meeting Evie again. But her fears melted away the second she embraced Kaisa warmly. Evie made a cup of sweet, milky tea and placed a slice of strongly spiced fruit cake in front of Kaisa. The kitchen smelt of her baking, which reminded Kaisa of her grandmother's house. Peter sat across the table from her, smiling while his mother fussed over Kaisa. She didn't dare say she didn't like tea, milk, or fruit cake, and tried to sip the hot, sickly drink.

Kaisa heard the front door open. Peter's sister walked into the kitchen. She hadn't met the woman before but had seen pictures of her in the house. Peter introduced Nancy. She kissed Kaisa lightly on both cheeks and sat down. She was dressed in a smart, navy-blue skirt and a white blouse. Nancy was seven years older than Peter and had the same dark features as him. Her eyebrows were plucked into a neat shape and her eyes made up with a discreet, pale-blue eye shadow.

Nancy smiled and looked from Kaisa to her brother

'I bet you two love birds are glad to see each other again.'

She sat down at the kitchen table.

Kaisa blushed and Peter shifted uncomfortably in his chair. It was as if Nancy had sensed their pent-up desire for each other.

Peter's mother got up and made more tea.

With immaculate timing, she said to Peter, 'I've put you in the blue room.'

Kaisa looked from Evie to Peter. That had been Kaisa's room the last time they'd stayed. Her face felt even hotter than before.

Peter got up abruptly

'Let's get your things from the car, Kaisa.' He led her out of the kitchen. Outside, he kissed her behind the car, shielded from eyes by the open boot.

'They've agreed to let us sleep in the same room,' he said his voice hoarse.

Kaisa relaxed her body against his. He held her and whispered into her ear, 'The things I'm going to do to you tonight...'

On Christmas Eve morning, Peter announced, 'I need to do some shopping.'

Kaisa was surprised. He hadn't bought all his presents yet? In Finland some shops didn't even open on Christmas Eve. Peter drove him and Kaisa into the nearest town, and bought some scented soap for his mother and a book for his father. Then he took her to a pub on the corner of the High Street. It turned out to be a bar in a hotel and full of people and noise.

In Finland, Christmas Eve was celebrated with a church service followed by a meal of special Christmas foods, which used to take Kaisa's mother weeks to prepare. When Kaisa and Sirkka were small they were allowed to watch a little television, but the highlight of the evening was the arrival of Father Christmas. It would either be their dad wearing a false beard and dressed in his sheepskin jacket, turned inside out, or one of the professional Father Christmases who roamed the streets on Christmas Eve, going from one household to the next. He usually brought a sack full of presents for Kaisa and Sirkka. The grown-ups would have a drink or two while the two girls played with their toys. But no one ever went out to a restaurant or a bar. Even visitors were discouraged until Boxing Day.

Kaisa couldn't believe how different the celebrations were in England.

'Everyone goes out on Christmas Eve,' Peter said, shouting above the noise of the revellers in the pub. He laughed. 'And then you end up with a hangover on Christmas morning,'

On Christmas morning, Peter and Kaisa exchanged presents in the privacy of the Blue Room. She'd bought Peter a leather wallet and he gave her a fountain pen. When she told Sirkka over the phone about their gifts for each other, Sirkka said, 'So sweet and so Freudian!'

Downstairs, the English house was busy with activity. The rooms were decorated with glittery paper streamers, balloons and tinsel. At around ten am, Nancy and her boyfriend arrived, followed by his brother, Simon, and sister-in-law, Miriam, who'd driven down from London that morning. His mother, wearing an old-fashioned pinny, rushed from one room to another, waving a tea towel and laughing. One by one the guests arrived for drinks, and soon the large sitting room was filled with cigarette smoke and noise.

Kaisa found the jolly people intimidating at first, but slowly relaxed when Peter introduced her to the various family friends. Then, as if by previous agreement, the guests left, wishing one another a 'Happy Christmas'.

Peter's mother rushed to get the food on the table. Kaisa had never seen so many kinds of vegetables – roasted, boiled and mashed. The gravy was dark and juicy, and the turkey slices large and white. She sat down feeling drunk, but Peter poured more wine into her glass.

'It's Christmas,' he said and kissed her cheek.

Everyone around the table smiled at Kaisa.

'How do you like Christmas in England?' Peter's father asked. He, too, was a little tipsy.

'I like it very much,' she said.

He patted Kaisa's hand and nodded to Peter. 'We like having you both here.'

Peter put his arm around Kaisa's shoulders and brought her closer. She smiled at the family gathered around the table, and felt as if her heart might burst.

15

W hen Kaisa arrived home from the UK on a cold Monday morning in January, her father was at work. She dropped her suitcase on the floor, exhausted from the travelling. First the late-night flight from London, then the overnight ferry from Stockholm. She'd hardly slept on the bunk bed, even though it had been a quiet enough crossing.

She checked the fridge to find no food in it. Maybe her father had forgotten she was coming back that day. Perhaps he hadn't been home since Christmas, spending it with his girlfriend, Marja, in Töölö. To refer to Marja as 'a girlfriend' felt strange. She was so much older than Kaisa, and still single.

Kaisa sat in the kitchen and looked out at the thick covering of snow outside. There was a sharp northerly wind and people passing by were huddled against it.

Tired and cold, she went to bed and put on the latest cassette Peter had given her. The words of *"Every Little Thing She Does Is Magic"* by The Police rang in her ears; Peter had sung that exact song to her on New Year's Eve. She could still smell the scent of his coconut shaving cream on her clothes. Kaisa curled up on her bed and slept.

She woke to the sound of the telephone ringing.

'Hello?' she croaked into the receiver.

'I'm coming home later. Is there any food?' Her father sounded irritable.

. . .

'Happy New Year, Dad,' Kaisa said sleepily. 'No, I haven't had time.'

'Yes, well, Happy New Year to you too. So, I guess I have to go to the shops?'

He hung up on her.

Too exhausted to care about her father's thinly veiled criticism, Kaisa put the receiver down and went back to sleep. He obviously thought she was a nuisance staying in his flat. After she finished her studies and got a well-paid job, she'd be gone. She couldn't wait for the day when she didn't have to be dependent on anyone, particularly on her cantankerous father.

Peter phoned the next day. Her father had been home, eaten some shop-bought raw herring and beetroot salad straight from the plastic container, and then left again.

Kaisa was glad to be alone once more.

'I love you so much. I can't bear to be without you,' Peter said.

She held the receiver close to her ear and listened to the sound of his breathing.

'Me too.'

'Listen, I haven't got much time to talk, but I've got news,' Peter said, speaking fast.

'Yes?'

'I've just bought a flight to Helsinki!'

Kaisa sat up straight and listened in stunned silence. She couldn't believe it. Peter was coming to see her in February. 'That means we'll see each other...'

He laughed. 'In just five weeks!'

Peter placed the telephone on its hook and walked back to the Back Bar. He ordered a pint and scanned the small room for anyone he knew, but the bar was quiet this Sunday lunchtime. Most of the other officers from his boat were down south visiting their families, or in their married quarters up here in Faslane. His old mate, Nick, had invited him out for lunch with his now wife, but Peter declined the offer. He was still on duty.

He thought about Kaisa and how wonderful it'd been to hear her voice. He just couldn't get her out of his mind. He knew he was foolish spending all his money on travel to see her when he should be saving to buy a house. He was on a good salary, more than any of his mates back in Wiltshire, but what was money for if he couldn't spend it when he was young? He sighed and finished his beer.

On his way back to the submarine, which was docked in refit, he thought about why he'd fallen for a foreign girl. And one from a country bordering Russia, no less. Was it the slight element of danger that made him more determined to not let Kaisa go?

He shook his head as he walked along the narrow gangway towards the control room to start his rounds. No, he simply loved her. He'd never felt like this about anyone else before. He just wanted to be with her, wake up next to her and spend his life with her. Just his luck that Finland wasn't in the EEC and Kaisa couldn't move to the UK and work without a permit. Which she'd told him was 'impossible' – there was that word she loved using again – to get.

Peter stopped suddenly. Why hadn't he thought of it before? There was an obvious solution to that issue.

He quickened his steps and nodded to the engineer peering at something on the control panel. He continued towards the forehead of the submarine. With a possible plan in place, he smiled. He was going to make it work.

Her father's face fell when Kaisa told him that evening about Peter's upcoming visit. They were sitting at the kitchen table. Kaisa had made meat balls with a creamy sauce, boiled potatoes and courgettes.

'What, he's coming here?'

'I suppose we could go and stay with mum in Stockholm,' she said, hoping he would make himself scarce in the house. She wrung her hands, but stopped and folded her arms instead.

'How did that woman manage to get a place big enough for you two to stay?' His pale-blue eyes were hard, full of contempt.

Kaisa sighed and ignored him. She wished she hadn't mentioned her mother.

Her father looked at the green vegetables and asked, 'What's this muck?'

'Courgette. It's good for you.'

He reached for the salt and sprinkled it liberally over the food.

'Just like your mother you can't season food properly.'

She looked down at her plate and bit her lip.

After a while he asked, 'When is he coming then?'

She told him, surprised when he agreed to stay at his girlfriend's place for the week Peter would be in Helsinki.

'But I do want to meet him,' he added.

Kaisa looked up at her father. His stare had softened, but was still serious. For a fleeting moment she saw her old dad, the one who called her 'My

Best Girl', and who took her to the park and let her sit on his knee, while she played with the soft flesh of his earlobe.

He got up from the table, leaving the uneaten courgette on his plate. He belched loudly.

Kaisa looked away.

'I'll teach him how to drink vodka,' he said and left the kitchen.

She heard him fall into a chair in the lounge and turn the TV on.

He shouted over the noise, 'You tell that Englishman there's no point in coming to Finland unless he's prepared to drink like a man.'

To Kaisa's relief, Peter didn't seem fazed by the idea of meeting her father.

'You've met all my family, it only seems right I do the same,' he said and put his arm around Kaisa. He'd just arrived from London, and they were walking up from Mannerheim Street tram stop to the bus station to catch the Number 105 to Espoo.

It was strange to meet up so quickly after only five weeks, rather than the many months they'd endured apart before. Kaisa relaxed against Peter's lean, taut body as they chatted about what she'd planned for the week. Again, she felt as if they were a real couple. Had she imagined his doubts in Hyde Park the previous summer?

At the bus stop, and in a bitterly cold afternoon in late February, he put his hands inside Kaisa's coat to warm them. When he kissed her, in full view of the other people in the queue, she couldn't imagine him being with anyone else. But Kaisa couldn't bring herself to ask him about it, or to discuss the future, afraid he'd repeat what he'd said to her before. If he did, Kaisa would surely die. She'd never want to see him again and that alone would kill her. Never mind Matti's reaction to it. He still phoned her on any pretext and asked, 'Are you carrying on with that foreign sailor?'

She took Peter back to her father's terraced house located in a shared development, then later to a cellar with a sauna and pool that he and residents from a couple of other houses could use. Kaisa had booked the space for that first evening.

Peter stood in his underpants in the middle of the small changing room, looking shy. 'I didn't bring my swimming trunks.'

After all they'd done in bed?

'Not a problem.' Kaisa pulled her top off and stripped down to nothing.

'Ah,' Peter said, dropping his pants and following her into the hot and dark sauna.

After a few moments, when she adjusted to the heat, Kaisa threw water on the coals. The hissing steam filled the space and the lovely prickly feeling of the heat touched her body. Peter swore and ducked, making her laugh.

'This is called a *löyly*.'

Like all Finns she loved the sauna. Her father had told her that when Kaisa was only three days old he'd taken her into the sauna in their summer cottage by the lake. Apparently Kaisa had enjoyed the heat so much her parents had called her 'sauna baby'.

She looked over at Peter, who was almost doubled over on the bench next to her.

'You OK?'

'Yeah, just a bit hot.'

'We'll go for a swim to cool down.'

Kaisa led a reluctant Peter into the pool, ignoring his protests about being naked.

'There's no one here!'

They swam in the cool water, then returned to the warm sauna. Peter seemed to relax with each round of *löyly* followed by another swim.

'I feel wonderful,' he said.

Kaisa smiled. She'd make a Finn out of this Englishman yet.

That evening, they met her father at a Russian restaurant called Saslik. Kaisa had never been there before. When her father had said '*she* likes it', Kaisa realised he was bringing his girlfriend.

The place was decorated with dark-red and blue colours; the table-cloths looked like satin, the wallpaper velvet. Lights hung low over the tables.

As they sat down her father nodded to an unseen waiter, who brought a round of vodka schnapps.

'To the Finnish ladies,' Kaisa's father said and lifted his glass.

His girlfriend, Marja, giggled. Kaisa took a sip, Marja managed half of hers and both Peter and her father emptied their glasses. Her father stared at Peter the whole time. The waiter, who was dressed in an old-fashioned Cossack's outfit, came around with the bottle a second time to refill the glasses. Kaisa's father nodded at him to leave the bottle of *Koskenkorva* on the table.

Kaisa glanced at Peter next to her, to warn him. Peter put his hand on her knee under the table and gave it a gentle squeeze.

'I'm fine,' he whispered in Kaisa's ear.

'So, you like Finnish vodka?' Kaisa's father said to Peter, and lifted his glass again.

'Yes, very much,' Peter replied and threw back his drink.

They hadn't even looked at the menus yet.

Everyone got very drunk very quickly, but no one fell under the table. No one said a cross word or had an argument. Kaisa's father didn't even mention Kaisa's mother. The food was excellent. Beetroot soup, rare spiced beef with dark sauce, garlicky potatoes, and a cabbage of some kind. They laughed a lot. Kaisa's father bought two long-stemmed red roses, one for Marja and one for Kaisa. He wanted them all to go dancing after. When Peter and Kaisa decided to leave instead, he looked sad and pulled them both into his bear hug.

Her father insisted on giving them money for a taxi and even got the Cossack to order it for them. It was as if the past ten years hadn't happened. It was as if Peter's presence had resurrected the version of Kaisa's father from her childhood. During the evening he'd even called Kaisa 'My Best Girl'.

'I think I passed.' Peter laughed when they stood outside the restaurant.

The taxi arrived and they climbed in the back. Kaisa curled up against Peter and fell asleep.

Peter's visit coincided with the annual Hanken Student Ball. The party was held in a smart, private club in the centre of Helsinki. Kaisa had never been inside before. Every room was decorated in a 1930's art deco style, with black marble and shining chrome.

Tuuli asked if Peter was going to wear his uniform, but Peter had already told Kaisa that this wasn't allowed. Kaisa had been a little disappointed, but thought it must have something to do with the Cold War, and Finland being so close to the Soviet Union.

In the end Kaisa didn't mind. Peter looked so handsome in his dinner jacket on the night, just as he had in his uniform at the British Embassy cocktail party, all those years ago. Kaisa wore a ball gown, made by an old school friend. It was a strapless, white silk dress, with a narrow black belt, tied with a small bow at the back of the waist. The long ends of the gown trailed behind her.

This was Kaisa's first university ball, but Peter told her he'd been to many black-tie events during his time at Dartmouth and after. Though he said none were quite like this one.

According to Hanken tradition, people at long tables were served rounds and rounds of schnapps, which were consumed to various drinking songs. There was a Drinks Master, who led the proceedings, and towards the end of the evening some of the people from the top table climbed onto the table to sing. One of them was the Finnish Foreign Minister. He'd come without his beautiful wife this time.

Peter took Kaisa to the dance floor where she glided around the space in his arms. She wanted everyone to see how in love they were.

Back at the table, Peter turned to Kaisa and said, 'You're beautiful, did you know that?'

She smiled. His warm hands covered hers and he looked at Kaisa intently. She basked under his hot gaze.

'Can I ask you something?' he said.

'Of course.'

He swallowed. 'Will you marry me?'

16

Just as Peter's words entered Kaisa's consciousness, she felt a tap on her shoulder It was Tuuli and she looked serious.

'Bathroom, now!'

Kaisa smiled at Peter. 'I'm really sorry. I'll be back as soon as I can.'

He lifted his eyebrows in surprise, but Kaisa didn't have time to explain. Tuuli was already dragging her away from the table. She pulled her through the throng of people on the dance floor and passed the bar, where Tom stood. He'd loosened his black bow tie and undone the top button of his shirt. He was leaning casually against the bar, with a drink in one hand and a cigarette in the other. Kaisa's eyes met his. He lifted his glass as if to toast her. Kaisa smiled confidently back at him.

Tuuli pulled Kaisa into the ladies' room.

'Guess what?' Kaisa said. 'Peter asked me to marry him!'

Tuuli dropped her hand.

'What?'

'Just now. Isn't it wonderful?'

'What about your studies?' Tuuli's expression was blank.

Kaisa gritted her teeth. It was as if her friend had splashed cold water over her face.

'Yes, I know. I'm not going to drop out, again, but isn't it –'

Tuuli cut her off. 'Have you ever read Doris Lessing's *A Proper Marriage*?'

'Well, no...'

'I'll lend you the book.'

Tuuli turned to face the large mirror. It was then Kaisa noticed the tears. She dabbed at them, smudging her makeup.

Kaisa touched Tuuli's arm, remembering she had dragged her to the ladies' room for a reason.

'What's the matter?' she asked.

'He's dancing with another girl!'

'Who?'

Her friend shot Kaisa an accusing look and said, 'The Incredible Hulk. I saw him kiss her. On the mouth!'

Tuuli's new boyfriend had a strong physique, and with his spiky dark hair he looked just like the cartoon character. The Hulk was her partner at the ball. Kaisa knew she was smitten with him, even though Tuuli had also said she no longer believed in love.

'The worst of it is, I know her,' Tuuli said between short sobs.

Kaisa was lost for words. She'd never seen her so upset about anything before. Especially not men.

Tuuli blew her nose. 'We went to school together, but she didn't get into Hanken. No brains.'

Kaisa hugged her friend. 'She's a bitch.'

Tuuli nodded and took a deep breath in. She returned to the mirror to fix her face.

'They can both go to hell. I was getting bored with the Hulk anyway.'

Kaisa loved how strong Tuuli was; Kaisa would never have coped with a betrayal like that.

'How did the bitch get in anyway?' she asked.

Tuuli looked away for a moment.

'I think she came as someone else's partner.'

She straightened her back and looked at Kaisa.

'But I don't want to talk about it anymore. Let's go back.'

They left the ladies' room. Outside, Tuuli turned suddenly to Kaisa and said, 'Promise me that you'll not marry Peter. You can't just become some-one's wife. You have to finish your studies.'

Kaisa looked at her wide-eyed friend. Tuuli was right. Kaisa had already been to England; she'd seen how difficult it was to get a job there. She didn't want to end up being a barmaid in a pub somewhere. Or worse, have no job at all and become a Navy wife, bringing up the kids singlehandedly while her husband was away at sea. She remembered the words of the wise woman in the bank in Stockholm.

'I promise,' she said and took hold of her friend's hands. They felt cold.
'Are you OK?' she asked.

Tuuli nodded and they returned to the large dining room.

Peter was sitting as Kaisa had left him, with one elbow on the table and holding a cigarette. He stubbed it out when he saw her and stood up. His politeness broke her heart. No Finnish boy would have known that's what you do when a lady comes back to the table.

'Everything alright?' he asked.

'It's a long story.'

Tuuli made her way to the other side of the long table. A mutual friend of theirs was waiting for her to return. Kaisa was glad to see she had someone to talk to. There was no sign of the Hulk.

Peter's gaze on Kaisa was steady. She knew he was waiting for an answer. He took Kaisa's hands into his. Feeling trapped all of a sudden, she wanted to pull away from his grasp. With control she lifted her eyes to him. His dark eyes were wide and expectant, his mouth set in a straight line.

'I still have a year and a half left at university,' she said quietly.

Peter let go of Kaisa's hands. He leaned back in the chair.

'I thought you might say that.'

To her surprise and relief, he was smiling. He gave her a light kiss on her cheek. The Drinks Master had climbed onto the table once more. It was time for another drinking song.

Kaisa was heartbroken when Peter left after his week-long visit, but she didn't cry. Clutching the red rose he'd bought her at the airport – a tradition now – Kaisa sat on the airline bus back to her father's place in Espoo, full of new determination to do well in her studies at Hanken. She was enjoying her new subject more and more. Learning about political systems, about the workings of the labour market and about the intricacies of parliamentary democracy, was a pleasure. And she felt more secure knowing that Peter was serious about their relationship.

Kaisa couldn't help thinking: the sooner I get my degree, the sooner we can be together. Though Peter hadn't said it, Kaisa knew she would have to move to England. Not a big deal. She'd moved countries before and didn't want to stay in Finland anyway. If she could get a good job in Sweden with her degree from Hanken, why wouldn't the same be true in the UK?

The house was cold and quiet when Kaisa got back. She found her father sitting in the living room with the lights off and a bottle of *Koskenkorva* vodka next to him.

'Gone then, has he?' he asked sarcastically.

Kaisa knew better than to answer. It was in these Jekyll and Hyde moments that she feared him most. She simply nodded and went to her room, locked the door and began reading Karl Marx's *Das Kapital* for an assignment due the following week. But she couldn't concentrate and put on the latest cassette Peter had brought with him instead.

17

As spring arrived and the snow slowly melted in the small patch of land outside the house, Kaisa's workload at Hanken grew. Tuuli was still upset about the Hulk and had immersed herself in her studies. She'd lent Kaisa all of her Doris Lessing books and Kaisa had fallen in love with Lessing's writing. She had never read a writer whose view of the world was so much like her own.

Peter wrote as often as he could, and phoned when he wasn't at sea. But it seemed like he was away most of the time now.

During that spring, Kaisa's third year at university, she spent a lot of time at the Hanken library, reading or borrowing books too expensive to buy. It was situated at the top of a modern office building, with one lift constantly ferrying students up and down. The stairwell doubled as the library smoking room. The library was affectionately known as the meat market; you could pick up both a book and a date for the evening. Needless to say, the rich boys spent most of their afternoons there.

Whenever Kaisa was there, so was Tom. If she passed his desk, where he had his legs sprawled out, he would pretend to examine the text in a book and would not look at her. But if she turned around abruptly she'd catch him looking at her backside. Kaisa found the game funny. She didn't care about him because Peter had proposed to her.

He'd written to say he was coming to visit again. She'd see him in April. This time they would meet in Stockholm, where Sirkka had promised the use of her flat for the week. Kaisa couldn't wait to show Peter her second hometown. Spring would be so much further along there; the city would be green and filled with Easter decorations and sunshine – the opposite of grey, cold, windy Helsinki.

On the 3rd of April at three in the morning, Kaisa got a phone call from Peter.

'We've declared war.'

He sounded grave.

'I know.' Kaisa had seen the news. How the mighty United Kingdom, a former colonial power, had been humiliated by a small South American dictatorship. Still, she'd been amazed that they'd declared war in the eighties.

'It happened on my birthday,' Peter said slurring his words slightly.

Was he drunk?

'And they've cancelled all leave, I mean ALL leave,' he added, this time sounding very clear.

Kaisa sat down on the floor next to the phone.

'Does that mean...?' she asked, unable to finish her sentence.

Peter's next words confirmed her worst nightmare.

'I can't come to Stockholm.'

He sounded so sad, so desperate, that Kaisa hid her own disappointment. How could the Falkland Islands, a group of outcrops no less and somewhere off the coast of Argentina, be spoiling her plans to see Peter? Kaisa had never even heard of the Falklands until they were mentioned on TV.

She asked, 'What about the cost of the flight?'

'Act of War is force majeure. I'll get all my money back.'

Act of War. That was all Kaisa heard.

'Are you...?' She hesitated.

There was a silence at the other end of the line.

'I mean, are they going to send you to – '

Peter interrupted her. 'Please don't ask. I can't say.'

He never did tell her if he went to war. During the Falklands conflict they spoke very rarely. Even his letters dried up.

No one in Finland understood what it meant to have Peter at sea, not knowing whether he was involved in the war or not. If a British submarine were lost to the Argentine Navy, would the Prime Minister, Thatcher, let the world know about it? Kaisa doubted it. If anything happened to Peter his parents would be told, but would they think to let Kaisa know? Perhaps they'd be too grief-stricken to remember.

Kaisa now wished she'd said 'yes' on that magical night at the ball. At least then as his fiancé, she'd have a right to know if Peter's submarine had been sunk.

Kaisa felt as if she were in limbo. Her isolation from the truth confused her and made her feel lonelier than ever.

She tried to concentrate on her studies, spending most of her time in the Hanken library. The main pick-up spot was busier than ever. She kept bumping into Tom in the lift or on the landing, where he'd lean against the steel banister, taking long drags on a cigarette. Once, when Kaisa and Tuuli were chatting in the stairwell, he came out alone from the library. His worn-out leather jacket was undone, and his dark-brown hair flopped over his eyes. He was so startled to see them that he stopped dead.

When Tom finally moved on from the door and pressed for the lift, the lonely devil in Kaisa said, 'Can I have a light?' She dangled a cigarette between her fingers. Tom stared at her for a moment, then lit a match and held it in his cupped hands. She noticed they were shaking.

Tuuli and Kaisa didn't look at each other until they heard the lift stop at the ground floor and the outside door open. They both burst out laughing.

'He's still got the hots for you, you know,' Tuuli said growing serious. 'Did you see how he was shaking? He was nervous being so close to you!'

On the bus home Kaisa thought about Tom. He was older than her; she and Tuuli worked out he must be at least twenty-six. Tom intrigued her. Perhaps we might have been together in another life, she mused. Her thoughts turned to Peter. It had been so long since they'd seen each other she was beginning to forget how his lips tasted when he kissed her. She longed for the day when she could feel his body next to her own. She tried not to think about the dangers Peter might be facing at sea, in what was a tin capsule, in constant danger of being sunk by an Argentine depth charge.

When she shared her worries with her father he was unsympathetic.

'You should find yourself a good Finnish man,' he said.

He seemed to have forgotten the good night at the Russian restaurant. But his change of heart didn't surprise Kaisa. He'd always been that way, saying one thing one day and the complete opposite the next. For the past few weeks he'd spent all his evenings and weekends at home, mostly in a bad mood. Kaisa wondered if he'd had a row with his girlfriend, but didn't dare ask.

The night the news reported the sinking of the *Belgrano* on TV, Kaisa's father had been drinking vodka all evening. The bottle of *Koskenkorva* stood on the floor next to his chair. The Finnish newscaster didn't say if there were any British casualties, but would they even know if British submarines had been involved? Kaisa had seen enough war movies to know subs hunted enemy ships in packs.

She sat on the plush sofa and watched the pictures, in silence. She put a hand to her mouth.

Her father narrowed his eyes at her.

'You know the Englishman is not there!'

Kaisa ran out of the living room. She sobbed quietly into her pillow. And then the phone rang. Kaisa heard her father answer.

He said, 'Just a moment,' in English.

Kaisa ran out into the hall and snatched the receiver from him.

'Hello?'

'It's me.'

Her heart burst with joy. Peter sounded as if he was far, far away, but Kaisa knew better than to ask where he was calling from. She sobbed into the telephone; she couldn't help herself.

'What's the matter?' Peter asked sounding concerned.

'I was just watching the news, and I didn't know...'

'I'm fine, except I'm missing you,'

Kaisa sighed with relief and sat on the floor in the hall. They spoke for over twenty minutes during which she cried, laughed and whispered into the receiver, not caring how much of it her father heard. When Peter said he had to go, Kaisa told him she loved him once more, put the receiver down and returned to her room.

That night, she fell asleep dreaming of her handsome Navy officer.

It wasn't until June that same year of the Falkland's War that Kaisa finally managed to see Peter. They'd been apart for four long months, during which she'd feared for her beloved submariner's life every waking hour. Peter telephoned her very rarely. When the news of the sinking of the HMS *Sheffield* came, she didn't sleep until she had a letter confirming Peter was OK.

How Kaisa wished she'd had someone she could call during those war months, someone who would understand what she was going through.

Instead, she distracted herself with her studies. By the end of the term she'd passed all her exams with good marks.

Watching now as Peter collected his bag through the glass wall of the arrivals hall at Helsinki airport, she thought about the two years she'd spent waiting for his letters and phone calls, counting the days until she could touch his body again. How her life had changed so dramatically, and quickly, after the British Embassy cocktail party, two years ago. Before she'd met Peter her path had been settled, planned even. She was going to complete her studies, marry Matti and move into a flat bought by his mother, in a leafy area of Helsinki. And, of course, Kaisa would have been expected to produce three grandchildren.

Instead, she stood in the deserted arrivals hall, nervously waiting for Peter to see her, with no idea what the next year would bring, let alone the next month, next week, or even day.

It was a hot and sunny afternoon, two days before midsummer. In Finland, the third Friday in June marked the start of the holidays. Everybody left Helsinki for the weekend to go somewhere by the sea, lake or forest. Most stayed away for two or three weeks, leaving the city empty and quiet. Having started another summer internship in the bank, Kaisa had booked a room for the weekend at a lakeside hotel an hour's train journey from town. Her parents had taken the family there when Kaisa was little. It was an all-inclusive package, which Kaisa's father, uncharacteristically, had paid for.

'Show the Englishman how beautiful Finland is,' he'd said.

His moods changed so fast they made her head spin.

On the airport bus home, the air conditioning was on full blast. Kaisa shivered in her thin, cotton dress. She'd just told Peter of their plans. He didn't seem impressed with them.

'We're going where?' he demanded.

Kaisa tried to explain better, but he sat in stony silence, holding her hand, his eyes facing the front. Kaisa looked at his profile, at the dark stubble on his chin.

'Don't you want to go?' she asked nervously.

Peter turned to Kaisa and kissed her lightly on the lips.

'Of course I do. No problem, let's do it.'

But he didn't sound at all certain.

The Aulanko hotel wasn't as Kaisa remembered it. The large, low-ceilinged lobby was shabby and there was a round stain on the carpet right by the reception desk. The small room they'd been allocated by a surly woman at reception had two single beds arranged head to toe.

When Peter saw the beds he laughed. Kaisa wanted to cry. She walked over to a large window and opened the curtains, seeing the view she remembered. Vanajavesi Lake was spread out in front of her. The afternoon sun, still high in the sky, blinded her.

Kaisa hugged Peter and tried to kiss him, but he turned away to put his bag down.

'Let's go, I'll show you around,' she said, grabbing Peter's hand.

She pulled him out of the room and downstairs.

Kaisa was eleven when her father had taken the family to have lunch at the then newly-built hotel. It had been an hour's drive away from Tampere, on the edge of the Häme National Park, and it was Mother's Day. She remembered the dining room had been a square space with large windows reaching from floor to high ceiling; the buffet had been laid out on a long table covered in a white linen tablecloth. As she led Peter through the hotel now, Kaisa wondered if the restaurant would look the same.

Peter said nothing. When they'd kissed at the airport, it had felt the same as before. When they'd made love last night, it had felt the same as before. But today he had hardly touched Kaisa.

The second they stepped outside, the sun disappeared. When Kaisa felt a few drops of rain on her bare arms, she began to regret the entire trip. They ran into an old, circular-shaped summer house, with chipped paintwork, and sat on a half-rotting bench to wait out the light shower. The warm summer rain fell softly on the old, pointed roof. Kaisa felt close to tears. Even the weather conspired to spoil Peter's week in Finland. Why hadn't she consulted him before booking this midsummer package?

Kaisa peeked at Peter. He was leaning against the railing, looking out to what Kaisa thought was the most beautiful view of the lake. But his tense back said he wasn't admiring it.

He turned around. His expression was serious. An awful thought entered Kaisa's mind. Perhaps he was not upset about the hotel at all. Perhaps it was her – them? Perhaps he'd come over to finish it and didn't want to do it in a hotel? That was probably why he hadn't wanted to make love to her on one of the ridiculous single beds just now.

Kaisa shivered.

Peter sat next to her and put his arm around her shoulders.

'What's the matter?'

His voice sounded soft. Confusing.

'Nothing,' Kaisa said.

Peter removed his arm. They sat in silence until the rain stopped. When Kaisa got up, he grabbed her waist and pulled her back down. 'C'mon, what's up?'

Kaisa looked out at the shifting clouds. The sun peeked over the tops of tall, dark pine trees on the other side of the lake.

'You know the sun won't even set tonight? It'll never get properly dark. It's supposed to be a magical night.'

Peter said nothing.

Kaisa continued. 'It's an enchanted, romantic night. Unmarried girls are supposed to put wildflowers under their pillows and dream about their future husbands.'

'Right.'

She glanced at Peter. He was looking at his feet, fiddling with a piece of bark he'd picked up. He didn't look like he'd heard a word she'd said.

'It's you!' she nearly shouted. 'Something's wrong with you, not me.'

Peter looked up, startled.

Now he'll have to say it, Kaisa thought. Now I've made him do it.

'It's this hotel...' he began, lowering his head again.

Kaisa waited for more.

'It's expensive, isn't it?'

She stared at him. 'Money? You're worried about money?'

Peter looked at his hands again and said, very quietly, 'Yes.'

Kaisa wanted to laugh.

'Oh, that,' she said lightly. 'I've already paid for it, or rather...'

'How, exactly...?'

'My father gave me the money.'

His jaw tensed and his eyes darkened more.

'Your father has paid for me to stay here?'

She didn't understand why he was annoyed.

'Yes.'

He got up and walked out of the little summer house. Kaisa followed him out. The sun was shining and it warmed Kaisa's bare arms. But it wasn't enough to counter the chill running through her entire body.

How could Peter – a warm, funny, passionate guy – have turned into this cold and angry person?

That midsummer's night was far from romantic. Peter told Kaisa he would pay her father back for the hotel, and then refused to discuss it further.

Kaisa wanted to him to understand that her father owed her big time for all the years Kaisa's mother had to scrimp and save for the school fees and food bills. That all he ever contributed was the occasional one hundred Marks for a birthday or Christmas present. And even those he often forgot. But Peter wouldn't listen to her. They left the hotel hardly speaking to each other. It was as if Peter had suddenly turned into someone she didn't recognise.

That night back in Helsinki, the old Peter returned in spirit – but his eyes still held resentment. He whispered lovely things into her ear like before, his touch was as wonderful as ever, his kisses as sweet as always.

On the Monday after midsummer Kaisa had to go back to work. Peter didn't seem to mind being left alone. In the evening, she cooked him steak and salad while he read his book. They visited the sauna and swam in the cool pool, then watched Finnish TV – which Peter thought was funny – and went to bed, where he was his old self.

One evening they were lying naked on her bed. It was a warm night and they'd just made love after visiting the sauna. Kaisa's head was resting on his chest. She felt closer to Peter now than she had during his visit.

She asked a question she'd been dying to know.

'Was your sub involved in the Falklands' War?'

She felt Peter's body tense.

'You know I can't tell you that.'

He got up and went into the bathroom.

Kaisa stared after him. Peter couldn't talk about the war, and she'd been foolish to ask. Still, the war had put a new barrier between them, created secrets. What else could Peter not tell her?

The night before Peter was due to fly home, he told Kaisa he was joining a new submarine at the Scottish base in Faslane.

'It's a nuclear sub,' he said.

Kaisa had been reading about the women at Greenham Common protesting against nuclear weapons. She was against them too. As a Finn she felt vulnerable, stuck between two superpowers – UK and Russia – wielding nuclear armaments. She shivered at the thought that Peter would be involved with the deadly weaponry.

'Don't you think the nuclear arms race should be stopped?' Kaisa said.

Peter looked up from his packing and regarded her for a moment.

'It's not for me to decide,' he said firmly and continued to put his things into the holdall.

When they parted at Helsinki airport, they didn't discuss the future. Peter bought Kaisa a red rose. She didn't cry when he waved her goodbye.

That same Sunday night, after Kaisa had said her tearless farewell to

Peter, she fell ill. Two days later, when she still couldn't keep a glass of water down, she phoned the student health service in the centre of Helsinki. They told her to come and see them straightaway.

The doctor who saw her wore a white coat. He wore round gold-rimmed glasses and had thinning, grey hair. Kaisa sat on the examination table while he took her temperature, tapped her knees, looked into her eyes and felt her glands and stomach. She hurt all over, but was so tired after two days and nights of diarrhoea and vomiting that she had no energy to utter a sound. He took two steps back and wrote something on his notes.

'I think you might have salmonella poisoning.'

Kaisa closed her eyes in relief. For a horrible moment while on her way to the surgery she thought she might be pregnant. All she wanted to do now was sleep.

The doctor regarded Kaisa for a moment.

'Did someone bring you here?'

'No.'

'Well, you look tired.'

Kaisa realised it was the bus journey from Espoo, a walk to the tram stop and another long walk to the health centre that had exhausted her.

'You need go to bed; take these and sip a mixture of this.'

He gave Kaisa a packet of tablets and a few sachets of some powder. 'If you don't improve within the next twenty-four hours, call an ambulance to take you to hospital. Can you phone someone to come and get you?' She noticed the doctor had kind eyes. He nodded at his desk phone. 'You can use that.'

Kaisa couldn't think of anyone to phone. Tuuli was travelling around Europe for the summer, and her mother and sister were in Stockholm. She hadn't seen her father since before midsummer, and didn't know if he was back at work. Kaisa dug in her handbag for her address book.

She dialled the only number she could.

'Yes?' her father said.

'It's me. I'm not feeling well. I'm in Töölö Health Centre. The doctor said I should have someone to pick me up.'

'What?'

'There's no one else I can call.'

'Can't you take a taxi?' Her father sounded irritable.

Kaisa was close to tears.

'I haven't got any money.'

'Of course you don't.' Her father sighed loudly. What's wrong with you anyway?'

When Kaisa told him, he agreed to meet her at home and pay for the taxi there.

'I don't really want to catch it, so I'll stay away until you're better,' he added.

Kaisa was ill for two weeks. She slept for most of it and had nightmares about sinking U-boats, nuclear mushroom clouds and men in uniform laughing at suffering women and children. She didn't go anywhere or see anybody. Her father phoned halfway through the second week. When he heard Kaisa was still not able to eat anything he said he'd stay away for another week, just to be safe.

'You do that.' She would never forgive him for abandoning her.

She hadn't told her mother how ill she was. It didn't matter. Both she and her sister were too far away to help anyway.

During her illness, Kaisa didn't hear from Peter. There was no letter or phone call. She didn't even know if he had reached the nuclear submarine in Scotland, was away at sea or on dry land at the base.

She also didn't know if they were still together, or if his disastrous week in Helsinki had been the end of the two-year romance. And she wasn't sure she cared anymore. She'd spent so much time thinking about him that not worrying about Peter – not longing for his touch or to hear his voice, or to read his letters – felt oddly liberating.

By the time Kaisa returned to her internship at the bank in mid-July, she'd lost five kilos in weight. She loved how her clothes fitted her better. At least something good had come out of the illness. The nice doctor at the health centre had signed her off the sickness register and given her a note to take to the bank manager.

'I was quite worried about you, young lady,' the doctor said and smiled.

All Kaisa could think was why couldn't her father, or Peter, be worried about her? Of course, Peter hadn't known she'd been poorly, but he should have phoned her at least once.

Finally, three weeks and three days after Peter had returned home, he called.

'You OK?' he asked after they'd said the usual hellos.

He hadn't said he missed her.

She told him about the salmonella poisoning and asked, 'You didn't get it too?'

'No.'

Hearing Peter's voice only reminded Kaisa of how angry she still was with him. Angry for spoiling their week together; angry for being an officer in the Royal Navy that was part of the nuclear arms race; angry for the secrets he had to keep from her; angry at not being there when she needed him; angry for not understanding how angry she felt.

But Kaisa said nothing.

'So...' Peter said after a few moments' silence.

'Yes?'

Her fury made it hard to speak.

'You OK now, right?' He tried again.

'Yes.'

'Right.'

Kaisa had enough. 'Look, I've made a decision.'

It was Peter's turn to be quiet. She heard noises in the background. Was he in a pub?

'Where are you phoning from?'

'The mess. I couldn't get away. We've been at sea all this time and I couldn't even get a letter to you.'

'Oh.'

'Hold on,' he said, and Kaisa heard him talk to someone. 'Five minutes,' he told them.

Of course there was a time limit. Foreign calls were expensive. He returned to the call.

Kaisa blurted out, 'Anyway, as I was saying, I've decided it's probably best if we stop this.'

'What?' Peter said softly. Then his tone sharpened. 'What did you say?'

Kaisa repeated for him, even though she struggled for breath and her chest felt heavy, as if a weight had been placed there.

'You can't say that,' Peter pleaded.

'I just have.'

There was another silence.

'Oh my God, Kaisa, are you saying it's over?'

Surely she was only saying what he thought, too? Or had she got it wrong...?

She felt dizzy.

But the facts didn't lie.

'We never see each other and I've got another year at Hanken. There's no guarantee I'll get a job in England when I'm finished. Or a work permit. And you're always away at sea. And...'

Kaisa sniffed. Tears ran down her face.

There were more voices in the background.

Peter said, 'Look, I have to go, but please don't cry. We have to talk about this, OK? Can I call you tomorrow night? Please.'

She whispered, 'Yes.'

She could never say no to Peter.

With shaking hands, she replaced the heavy receiver on the base and sat down on the floor. Her heart was racing inside her chest. It felt as if the weight was crushing her, as if her heart had no space to beat and no air could reach her lungs.

What had she done?

What if Peter didn't call back? What if, having thought about it, he agreed with her? The relationship would be doomed, their future together hopeless, impossible.

The last few weeks had shown their differences: they had a completely different attitude to money; Peter was still keeping secrets from her; Kaisa now had doubts about Peter's beloved career in the Navy. How could she be with someone who was part of the nuclear war machinery?

And how could they manage another year apart?

When she finished her studies and would be free to move to the UK, there was no guarantee she would get a job there – even if she got a work permit.

Peter had admitted he'd fallen in love before with a Canadian girl, and it hadn't worked out. He'd told her about his doubts in Hyde Park. And now it was happening to them.

Kaisa put her head in her hands and sobbed inside the empty house.

18

P eter didn't phone the following day, or the day after that.
A strong light filtered through the half-closed venetian blinds covering the bedroom window. It was as if the beautiful weather was mocking Kaisa. The summer in Finland was the hottest in a decade. It made everyone smile on the streets of Helsinki and in the bank, where Kaisa worked. But she had no desire to join them in their happiness. She just wanted to work, come home, watch TV and go to bed, where she'd lie awake trying not to think about Peter.

For the coming weekend, the temperatures were supposed to reach new heights. By the looks of it, the sun was already high up in the sky.

On the Saturday morning, three days after Kaisa had told Peter she wanted to finish it, a knock on her front door woke her.

Kaisa climbed out of bed and opened it to see her father there.

Even he looked happy.

'Marja and I are taking the boat out to the archipelago. Do you want to come?'

Kaisa considered it for a moment, then nodded and closed the door on him.

'Don't forget your swimming trunks, or whatever you women wear,' he shouted through the door.

Kaisa got ready, without thinking too much about what his good humour meant, or his strange desire to include her in the first outing on his latest purchase.

Soon, she was on board *Paula*, as her father had christened his new speedboat. Marja and Kaisa sat at the rear while her father, proudly wearing a blue seaman's cap, steered the thing at high speed under the bridges on the western shore of Helsinki. Marja shouted at him to slow down. That only made him go faster.

'He's your father. Make him listen.'

Marja spoke to her as if they'd known each other for years and were good friends. But they had nothing in common and had only met a handful of times. Kaisa didn't much like the way Marja spoke to her father. She often wore a disapproving sneer and made comments that constantly belittled him. Only that morning she'd made fun of her father's new boat, calling it 'A rich man's toy'. Kaisa also sensed that she was jealous of her relationship with her father.

She couldn't understand what her father saw in the woman.

But he was behaving like a child with a new toy, veering it this way and that making Marja and Kaisa scream as he accelerated hard and made the boat bounce.

Kaisa loosened her grip on the rail when, at last, he slowed for a small island and moored the boat under a steep cliff.

Marja had made a picnic.

'Did you have a good time in Aulanko? It's a posh hotel, isn't it?' she asked when they were all sitting around a checked tablecloth that she'd placed on the ground.

Not knowing what to say, Kaisa looked down at the food. There was a plateful of her father's *gravad lax*, a packet of thinly sliced smoked ham, a loaf of rye bread, butter and salted gherkins. Marja handed Kaisa a paper plate, while her father picked up slices of ham with his fingers and stuffed them into his mouth.

'Don't talk about that Englishman,' he mumbled to Marja.

She stared at him, the sea breeze blowing her hair messily over her dark-brown eyes.

'I just wondered, because it was so expensive...'

Kaisa couldn't believe her ears. Was Marja criticising her father for paying for the hotel? Or was she jealous that he'd given her the money?

'She doesn't want to talk about it – can't you see that?' her father barked.

Here we go, Kaisa thought, Mr Hyde is out. She lay back against the rock and shut her eyes, feeling tired from the tension. The surface felt warm against Kaisa's bare back. She hadn't slept through one full night since the phone call from Peter.

'Give her a *Lonkero*,' she heard her father say.

Marja handed Kaisa a cold bottle of the gin and bitter-lemon drink. She smiled her thanks at Marja, suddenly feeling sorry for her. She had no idea what she was taking on with Kaisa's father. Kaisa also felt a pang of guilt – should she warn her about his drinking and his moods? Should she tell her that he used to hit Kaisa's mother?

But Marja was old enough to figure that out for herself, and she seemed able to give as good as she got. As Kaisa lay in the warm sunshine, she wondered how, all through her life, she'd allowed men to completely control her. First her father, then Matti, and now Peter. Wasn't it high time she decided about her own life without considering a man?

They stayed on the small, rocky island for the rest of the day. The sun was burning their skin, so to cool down they each swam in the sea. Her father's mood improved and he talked of old times. He told Marja stories about when Kaisa was little. How he had to buy her a large box of chocolates to stop her crying when Sirkka started school and Kaisa was left to play alone at home; how he used to lie down and rock Kaisa on his belly when she was a baby; how wispy and thin Kaisa's hair had been when she was little. How Kaisa had been ill with diarrhoea and vomiting, and nearly died when she was only four. How useless Kaisa's mother had been, just crying, and how he'd been the one to take Kaisa to hospital.

Kaisa shaded the sun from her face to stare at him.

His large frame was splayed on the rock – the round, smooth shape of his belly mirroring that of the cliff. He finished his long narrative with pride.

Kaisa wondered if he remembered what had happened just a few weeks ago when she'd been sick with a similar virus, and the only concern he'd had was for his own welfare. But there was no sign that he'd made that connection. So she listened to her father talk now about someone in his office, smiling and laughing when expected. This brief interlude of good humour with her father rarely lasted. After the Jekyll would come his Hyde.

At the end of the day, when the sun moved towards the horizon, her father steered the boat into harbour. Even after her father's boastful tales, Kaisa was glad she'd spent a day with him – and Marja. She had become more tolerable, friendlier even, as the trip went on. After he moored the boat, he pressed a few hundred-Mark notes into Kaisa's palm and said, 'There's a bit of money for a *Lonkero* or two. Go and enjoy yourself!'

Then he told her he'd be staying with Marja for the rest of the weekend.

Her father was right for once: she should enjoy herself a bit more. With still no phone call from Peter, Kaisa assumed their relationship was over.

What else could she think? A lump formed in her throat at the thought; she tried to ignore it. She had no more room for self pity. It was time to move on.

It was only seven o'clock when she got home and still early. She admired her reflection in the mirror, noticing how the sun had bronzed her face and body. She wished Tuuli were in town to go out with. Checking her reflection once more, Kaisa decided to do something she'd never done before.

Wearing a bright-green miniskirt with a matching scoop-neck top, and black lace-up sandals, Kaisa walked into the university disco alone. It was half-full for a Saturday night. Most students were either Interrailing around Europe or at their parents' summer places. She went up to the bar and ordered a *Lonkero*. Turning around, she spotted him.

He was leaning against the railings of the bar upstairs on the mezzanine floor, looking down at the dance floor. Before Tom could spot Kaisa, she ducked out of sight. Her heart raced with the realisation she'd come out to see him. But now, she lost the courage to go and talk to him, or even invite him over with a covert glance or gesture. With a shaky hand Kaisa lit a cigarette, and tried to look cool. She gulped down her drink and ordered another. She needed to get drunk. Fast.

'What's the hurry?' the guy at the bar said when he handed Kaisa the second bottle.

She stubbed out the cigarette and said, 'No hurry, I'm just thirsty.'

The barman smiled, and from his lingering look Kaisa knew she looked good tonight. She smiled back.

Holding an unlit cigarette and the drink, she headed for the stairs to the mezzanine level.

Kaisa woke up with a dry mouth and a screaming hangover. Her limbs felt heavy and she realised she was pushed up against the wall in a narrow, single bed. The shape next to her moved. She rubbed her eyes and looked around the room.

There was a window covered with a see-through curtain, a sofa piled high with clothes and a table stacked with books. A studio flat, somewhere in Ullanlinna. Her memory of last night came back in pieces. She remembered him telling the taxi man to take them there.

She licked her lips for relief.

A hand slid around her waist, and she felt a bulge against her back. A hot mouth moved closer to her ear. She froze.

'Sorry, I feel a bit sick,' she said and closed her eyes briefly. The memories from last night flooded her brain. He'd been on top of her...

Oh, no. No!

The stranger removed his hand and got up.

'Fair enough.' He slapped Kaisa's bum. She watched his strong, hairy legs take him into the bathroom.

The sound of his peeing hitting the water in the pan reverberated in the bedroom. Then the noise stopped and started again. With a shudder, Kaisa stumbled out of bed and grabbed her clothes. She cursed her stupidity. Why had she agreed to go home with this guy? Because he was a tennis player, third in the Finnish rankings? Or because Tom hadn't even looked at her when she'd stood next to him in the bar upstairs?

She knew. It was because the tennis player was the only one showing any interest in her short skirt and sexy sandals.

Kaisa was sitting on the edge of the bed, fully clothed, when the guy came back into the room. He looked surprised to see her, as if he'd forgotten she was there.

'Can I?' Kaisa nodded towards the bathroom door.

'Sure.'

The toilet smelt bad. Kaisa held her breath and splashed cold water on her face, then wiped it dry with paper. She needed to leave. Now.

When she came out the tennis player was on the phone, wearing just his boxers. He was balancing the receiver between his neck and ear, while holding on to the base with his hand. Its long cord snaked over his clothes on the floor from last night. Looking out of the window, he laughed at something the other person said. Kaisa tiptoed towards the bed and found her handbag. She opened the front door.

'Bye then,' she muttered.

Startled, the tennis player turned around; a brief recognition passed over his face before he shrugged and nodded at her. Then he faced the window again.

She caught the bus home that she usually took into work and university. The same bus driver looked down at Kaisa's short skirt and sandals. It was obvious she was wearing last night's clothes. She hid behind her hair and slumped into a seat.

Is this what she'd wanted from last night – to feel cheap and used, not loved? Was this her life now? Skulking home the next morning after a cold, senseless one-night stand? Kaisa looked out the window at the people taking Sunday walks in the heat of the day – normal people with normal lives. She longed to be one of them.

When she arrived home, Kaisa realised the tennis player hadn't even asked for her phone number. Even though she wouldn't have given it to him, it would have been nice to be asked. He probably didn't even remember her name. Maybe she'd been disappointing. He was probably used to bedding women like the tennis girl in the poster in Peter's room. Slim things with tiny pert bottoms and long, lean legs.

Peter probably liked those women, too.

Kaisa was in the shower, washing away her shame, when the phone rang. She ran to catch the call.

'Hello?'

'I've been trying to ring you all night!' Peter sounded angry.

He had some nerve.

Her heart pounded with anger and guilt. 'I was out.'

'Must have been a late night?'

'I stayed over with a friend.'

'I see.'

Silence followed. Her heart ached over what she had done.

'So...how are you?' Peter asked. He sounded hesitant now.

'Fine.'

'Please don't be like this.'

'Like what?'

'Look, I've got more leave, and I've decided to come and see you. To talk. That is, if you want me to?'

Kaisa's heart beat harder.

'When?'

'Week after next. Is that OK?'

There had never been such a short amount of time between Kaisa and Peter seeing each other. Only four weeks!

But she'd have to tell him everything.

'OK,' she said.

Her father was grumpy when she told him the news of Peter's arrival, but agreed to 'stay out of the way'. Kaisa didn't care about her father's moods, not now. She had only ten days to prepare for Peter's visit.

She decided not to arrange anything special. Helsinki was still basking in glorious summer weather, so she decided to take him to Seurasaari, the open-air museum where those without summer cottages went for midsummer.

Or they could just walk in the Esplanade Park, as they had done on that first wintry evening, two years ago. They'd do as much or as little activities as Peter liked, but they would also talk. Kaisa would tell him how much she missed him and how lonely she'd been without him; how she worried about him being in the Navy operating nuclear weapons; how she feared she'd never get a job in England. And she would have to tell him about the tennis player.

Kaisa felt so guilty. But she had gone out thinking she and Peter were over and that she'd never hear from him again. He'd broken his promise to phone back the next day. What else was she supposed to have concluded from his radio silence?

But why had she been so stupid to jump into bed with the first guy who showed her any interest? What if Peter wouldn't forgive her?

What if he never wanted to see her again?

An hour after Peter had arrived at Helsinki airport Kaisa and Peter were sitting on her bed. At the airport Peter had hugged Kaisa tightly and kissed her for a long time. But now, before they'd even made love, he was looking down at his hands. He hadn't even taken his shoes off.

'What's the matter?' Kaisa asked.

Peter looked at her, then looked away.

'I've got to tell you something.' He paused. 'I've been so stupid.'

Kaisa waited. What was he talking about?

'I've slept with someone else,' he finally said.

She barely heard the words at first, then they pierced her heart, like daggers. This is what he had come all this way to tell her? She couldn't speak. Then, relief flooded through her body.

'Me too,' she said quickly.

'What?' Peter stared at her; his eyes were black.

Kaisa looked down at her hands, hoping he'd forget what she said. But Peter wouldn't let it go.

He grabbed Kaisa's shoulders and shook them.

'What did you say?'

His grip was strong and he was scaring her.

'You're hurting me.'

Tears ran down her face. She couldn't help it. She wiped her face with the back of her hand and stood up, moving away from him.

'This is it. We're both as bad as each other. What kind of a relationship is this? We never see each other. We don't even know if we can be together after I've finished at Hanken. As soon as we have a little argument, we both go off and have sex with someone else. We might as well stop here.'

She stormed out and into the dark kitchen.

A lone street lamp shone bright against the August twilight. Peter followed her. The refrigerator hummed, breaking the silence between them. Kaisa didn't know how long they stood there, either side of the kitchen table. It was as if time had stopped for her.

Peter had slept with another girl.

Images of him kissing someone else and stroking her hair kept playing in front of her eyes. Had she also told this other girl how lovely she was? A muffled cry escaped from deep within. Kaisa covered her mouth with her hand.

'Come here,' Peter said.

Kaisa looked up at Peter. He'd been crying too. She ran into his arms and started sobbing.

'Shh, it's OK,' Peter whispered. 'We'll be OK,'

He stroked her hair, then took her face between his hands and looked deeply into Kaisa's eyes.

'Let's go to bed. We'll talk after?'

After they made gentle love, Kaisa rested her head on Peter's shoulder. She told him, about the tennis player. She felt his body tense when she said she'd fled his apartment the next morning.

'You stayed the night?' he asked.

Kaisa nodded. Peter moved her off him and sat up, crossing his arms over his chest. Kaisa mirrored him and they both sat next to each other in the dark, not touching.

'I wish I hadn't done any of it. I felt so dirty, so awful after,' Kaisa said. Looking at Peter she added, 'And you?'

Peter faced her, his expression hard. Had he forgotten that he'd also slept with someone else?

He looked away 'It was a stupid accident,' he said, talking to the small desk set against the wall opposite her bed.

'Who was it?'

'No one,' Peter replied quickly.

Kaisa tried to look at him, to see his reaction, but he was still staring at the wall.

'Anyone I know?' she asked.

She tried to keep her voice level, but a terrible dread was spreading through her chest.

'No,' Peter said.

Kaisa gazed at Peter's profile. Why won't he tell me who it is?

'What's her name?'

Peter sighed and took Kaisa's face in his hands.

'She meant – means – nothing to me. I feel terrible about it. I was drunk, blind drunk. Jeff told me not to do it –'

'Jeff was there?' She pulled back. 'And he knows that you slept with someone else?'

He nodded. 'He won't tell anyone, I promise. I love you so much and... and he tried to stop me. But I was too drunk and you said you wanted to break it off, so, I don't know, I guess I was angry at you. That's why I didn't call you back.'

Kaisa widened her eyes. Peter added quickly, 'But I'm not angry now. I love you and want to be with you.'

He kissed her gently; she kissed him back.

Peter and Kaisa spent the week playing at being a happy couple. They stayed in every night, cooked together, and gazed into each other's eyes. In the mornings Kaisa went to work at the bank, and Peter went shopping for food. He told Kaisa how the women at the meat counter in the supermarket had laughed at him when he'd tried to use the Finnish phrases she'd written down for him.

Kaisa came home one evening and Peter poured them both a gin and tonic. They sat outside on the small patio at the back of Kaisa's father's house and enjoyed what Peter called 'sundowners'. Peter said that's what the officers called the first drink of the evening, while on a naval visit to a hot country. They'd sip their drinks while watching the sun set, before it disappeared into the sea.

'It goes, *psshht*.' He made the noise of a lit match dropping into water.

Kaisa watched the children from the surrounding houses play on the swings, in the middle of the communal gardens in front of them, beyond her father's small, neglected garden that was patchy and yellow from the scorching dry heat. The sun was still high. This far north it didn't set until much later in the evening. But sitting next to Peter, Kaisa could be in Gibraltar or the Caribbean, smoking a cigarette and drinking a fancy cocktail.

They didn't talk more about their infidelity, or about the future. At the end of the week, during their goodbyes at Helsinki airport, Kaisa nearly pulled Peter back, wishing she could start the week all over again.

Later in bed and alone, a chill spread through her as she wondered why Peter had been cagey about telling her who the girl was. She wrapped the thin summer duvet tighter around her body and tried not to think about who she might be. Despite her attempts to forget, Kaisa ransacked her brain for anyone – any girl who'd shown signs of being smitten with Peter. But she hadn't met many of his friends during her two visits to Britain.

Peter had blamed the drink. But how drunk did he have to be to accidentally sleep with someone? Kaisa had been drunk too; too drunk to realise that she shouldn't have had a one-night stand with a stranger, but she'd known what she was about to do, even if she regretted it in the morning. She'd even planned it, but her target had been a different man. Did that make her decision to cheat better or worse?

Similar to Kaisa, Peter had decided they were finished before his 'accident'. So, what had changed his mind after? Was it the girl? Why had he decided to come to Finland to kiss and make up?

The other thing that disturbed Kaisa was Peter had asked very few questions about the tennis player. It was as if he pretended it hadn't happened. But surely he must have been curious.

Jealous, even?

With him gone Kaisa couldn't ask him now. Perhaps she should write to him? No, the wait for a reply would be torture. Perhaps when Peter phoned next? Would she have the courage to spoil a rare telephone conversation with her doubts?

They had both been unfaithful. Why not forget about it and plan for the future?

At least they had agreed a time to meet again. In the New Year, Peter was going to be based in Rosyth, near Edinburgh. He said she should come over for a longer visit then.

The days and weeks after Peter left passed even more slowly than usual. His phone calls became more frequent, as did his letters, but they were poor substitutes for his presence.

In October, Kaisa continued her political science course at Hanken and negotiated a postponement of her December exams with her professor. He organised a pass to Edinburgh University library for her, and recommended books she should seek out while there.

Everything was finally falling into place.

19

SCOTLAND, NEW YEAR 1982

Peter drove Kaisa up to Scotland on Boxing Day, after a lovely, jolly Christmas with his parents in Wiltshire. The journey took a whole day. Peter had bought new tapes for the trip: ABC's *The Lexicon of Love*, *Night and Day* by Joe Jackson and *East Side Story* by Squeeze. As they sang along to the tracks, Kaisa tried not to think how apt the lyrics of "Tempted" were for them both.

They stopped for lunch – scampi in a basket – at a pub somewhere in the Lake District, in the shadow of an imposing mountain. The sun didn't make an appearance that day, and they arrived in Edinburgh under the dim light of a Scottish winter afternoon. It was raining, but the warm welcome given to Kaisa by Peter's friends made up for the bad weather outside.

Lucy, the wife of Peter's friend Nick, was the first naval wife Kaisa had ever met properly. She was heavily pregnant.

Her husband immediately went to 'mix the drinks'. Then he took their bags upstairs. Kaisa was embarrassed by the two heavy suitcases she'd brought. She wanted to explain that there were text books in the suitcase, but Nick just smiled and said, 'Don't worry your pretty little head about it.'

The next morning at breakfast, Lucy poured hot tea from a large teapot into two brown-glass mugs.

She patted her belly. 'I'm at the waddling stage.'

Kaisa smiled at her and looked down at the steaming milky stuff in front of her. She turned away from the smell. It was too late tell Lucy she didn't drink tea.

'The boys' as Lucy called Peter and Nick, had left early for work at the Rosyth base.

Nick had smiled. 'You girls can natter to your hearts' content.' Peter had winked at Kaisa and placed the white cap on his head.

She had not seen Peter in uniform since that first meeting, at the cocktail party in Helsinki. Peter looked even taller than usual in his black trousers and navy jumper with gold lapels. His eyes appeared darker, more seductive. When he kissed Kaisa goodbye, she caught a whiff of diesel from the scratchy wool.

Drinking her tea and trying not gag, Kaisa looked out at the communal garden set between the semi-detached houses that belonged to the naval quarters. The patch of grass was lush and green – different from the neglected space outside her father's house – but the grey concrete houses opposite, and the steely skies above, made the space feel oppressive.

She glanced at her watch. It was only nine in the morning, eight hours until she'd see Peter again.

'It's laundry day today,' Lucy said with a sigh, lifting herself up from the chair. 'I like to have a daily routine; makes the time pass quicker.'

Kaisa observed her. Lucy reminded her of the female character in Doris Lessing's books; she was just like Martha Quest, before she'd left her oppressive marriage. Just as Kaisa had imagined Martha to look, Lucy also had a pretty face, with large pale-blue eyes and a luminous complexion. Her long hair, which she kept in an old-fashioned loose bun, was very fair – almost grey. Her rounded tummy was out of proportion to her slender wrists and small ankles. Kaisa wanted to ask Lucy what her life had looked like before washing and ironing, dusting and tidying. Had she dreamt of a career of her own?

But Lucy liked to talk, not to answer questions. And it seemed as if she was trying to show Kaisa how to become an efficient naval wife.

Kaisa vowed to never, ever be like Lucy, and to never, ever have children.

Peter and Kaisa stayed two nights in Lucy and Nick's quarters. The day before New Year's Eve, a room became available in a flat in Edinburgh.

They drove in the dark to a part of Edinburgh called Leith.

'It's an old tenement building,' he said.

Kaisa shrugged; she didn't know what that meant.

'Where poor people used to live.' He smiled at Kaisa. 'But don't worry, it isn't like that anymore.'

Peter parked the car on a narrow street, shadowed by tall buildings on either side, and hauled the luggage out of the boot. All Kaisa cared about was that they'd have their own place for five weeks. It didn't matter what the place looked like. They could come and go as they pleased; they could stay in bed all weekend, if they wished.

The large hallway had a wide, stone staircase. Kaisa caught a strong smell of disinfectant. On the second-floor landing Peter stopped in front of a door, one of many similar looking doors, and rang the bell. A slim, dark-haired girl appeared, and immediately flung her arms around Peter. He kissed her cheek and, freeing himself from her embrace, pulled Kaisa to his side.

'This is my girlfriend, Kaisa. Kaisa, meet Frankie.'

'Hi,' the girl said and shook her hand. Her slim fingers felt bony and cold.

'Come in!' she added, moving aside to let them pass. She nodded to Kaisa and smiled at Peter.

The flat had high ceilings and smelled musty. It was as big as Kaisa's living room in Lauttasaari. It had a large bay window with a set of heavy brown curtains. Behind that was a set of yellowing net curtains, obscuring the view of the street. There was a single mattress on the floor, an electric heater in front of a small fireplace, a table with two chairs and a comfy chair covered in dark-green fabric.

Frankie left them to it.

'This is great,' Peter said.

'How do you know her?' Kaisa asked casually. The lyrics of *Tempted* by Squeeze again played in her head. Was this slim girl with cold fingers Peter's 'accident'? Would he really bring Kaisa to the same place as 'the girl'?

'Frankie? She's the sister of a friend.'

Before she could reply, Peter grabbed Kaisa and kissed her neck. She closed her eyes and decided not to think about anything else but the feel of Peter's body against her own.

Kaisa and Peter spent their first full day, New Year's Eve, in the flat in Edinburgh, kitting out the room with missing essentials. Their street was just off Leith Walk, where small shops sold everything from light bulbs to loaves of bread. On the corner was a place called Naz Superstore. In there, Peter and Kaisa bought a cheap reading lamp, a travel alarm clock and a small transistor radio. Kaisa felt like they were a young married couple buying the first supplies for their new home. An Asian man rang up the till. In a heavy Scottish accent he told Peter what they owed. They walked out of the shop hand in hand, carrying their purchases back to the flat.

It was cold and rainy outside but the second they stepped inside the tenement block, it felt even cooler. Frankie was standing in the hallway. She wore a short skirt, long leather boots and a black waxed jacket. Around her neck, she'd tied an expensive looking silk scarf. Kaisa felt shabby and inappropriately dressed in her new suede jacket, which wasn't standing up very well to the rain. Wet streaks had formed in the front and back, soaking through to the padded lining.

Frankie looked up and smiled. 'I'm off to a party tonight. You guys doing anything?'

'I'm on duty tomorrow morning,' Peter replied.

Frankie walked towards them, kissed him on the cheek and nodded to Kaisa. Disappearing out the door, she shouted, 'Too bad. See you in 1983!'

'How come she's got a big flat like this?' Kaisa said, scrutinising Peter's face. She still wasn't sure about the girl, though she couldn't believe Peter would be so stupid and unfeeling to bring her to the home of someone he'd been to bed with. However much of an 'accident' it had been.

Peter shrugged. 'I think it belonged to her aunt, or something.'

Peter had spotted a small pub opposite the tenement block earlier and thought it would be a good place to see in the New Year. But when they entered, he seemed to hesitate. The pub was full of middle-aged, chain-smoking men.

When Peter asked what Kaisa would like to drink, she said 'A pint of *80 shilling*.' In Finland, girls always drank what the guys did, and Peter always had a pint.

Peter turned away from the bar and said to her quietly, 'I'll get you a half.'

Kaisa looked around the brightly-lit pub, noticing she was the only woman there. Peter drank his pint quickly; the men, who'd stopped talking as soon as Peter and Kaisa had entered, didn't start again until he handed the empty glasses to the barman and headed for the door.

Outside Kaisa asked, 'What was that all about?'

Peter replied, 'They hate the English.'

She didn't understand.

It was bitterly cold and the air hung heavy with rain, or even snow.

'We can celebrate in our own way,' she said.

She took his arm and pulled him back to the flats. Kaisa and Peter opened a bottle of red wine they'd bought earlier and drank it in bed, clinging to each other for warmth as 1982 turned into 1983.

. . .

During their weeks in Leith, Kaisa and Peter fell into a routine of sorts. On the mornings Peter worked at the base in Rosyth he'd get up first and put on the electric heater, before Kaisa could even think of getting out from under the blanket. To keep warm in bed she wore Peter's thick, submarine socks and long, white uniform shirt. Kaisa would lie in, watching Peter get washed and dressed. Then she'd listen to him start his car each morning and, if it wasn't playing up, drive away. She was amazed how the noise, echoing between the tall tenement blocks, travelled up to the third floor.

She'd wait until the room got a little warmer, not getting out of bed until after ten. Then she'd either walk into town or take the bus to the university library. The flat was too cold for her to concentrate and she couldn't study like that. She also didn't feel brave enough to use the warmer communal lounge area in the block in case she'd bump into Frankie.

It rained every single day of the five weeks Kaisa and Peter spent in Edinburgh. Kaisa realised early on that she'd brought the wrong clothes. The suede coat, of which she'd been so proud, was now ruined, and the beige leather boots looked dirty. But Kaisa loved Edinburgh in spite of the cold and the rain. The city was dominated by the imposing castle, which at night was lit up and looked like a fairytale fortress. The sight bewitched her. The people she met in shops along Leith Walk or on Princes Street – the more affluent part of the city – or at the university, were friendly in a direct, almost Finnish, way. It didn't surprise her. This was Viking country after all.

Peter and Kaisa had so little money they had to count up coins for their drinks in the pub. They bought food every day, and always overspent. But being poor didn't matter. They laughed about it and promised each other they'd be rich one day. The most important thing for Kaisa was that they were together. And the longer she spent with Peter, the more in love with him she fell. Kaisa tried not to think about the future, or that time was ticking away; her return home got closer with every passing day.

Peter introduced Kaisa to gorgonzola in an Italian delicatessen on Leith Walk. They ate the blue cheese with water biscuits and a bottle of cheap, red wine on the cold floor of their flat, laughing and listening to Radio One on the transistor radio. In their tiny kitchen, Peter cooked new foods that Kaisa had never heard of: beef kebabs, shepherd's pie, chilli con carne.

Some nights they would meet up with Peter's many friends in the small, dimly-lit pubs scattered around the old part of the city. Its cobbled streets and low buildings were as charming and enchanting to Kaisa as the castle. She felt like she was living a dream.

The evening before Peter was due to drive Kaisa down to Newcastle to catch a ferry to Gothenburg, the first leg of her long journey back to Finland, she cried. The top of Peter's shirt was soaked with her tears.

'I know this is the end.' Kaisa sobbed. She had no idea when she'd see him again. Peter didn't know where he'd be based next, or even when.

'This is just the way the Navy is. You must trust me that I will tell you as soon as I know,' Peter said, taking Kaisa's face between his hands. 'You know I love you.'

Kaisa looked into his eyes. Before she knew what she was saying, the words came out of her mouth.

'But what if...what you meet someone else, another accident, like Frankie?'

Peter stared at Kaisa. He dropped his hands and walked over to the large bay window. They turned into fists and he looked down at the dark street below.

Kaisa held her breath. She wanted to take the words back, yet at the same time she wanted to hear what he had to say. She couldn't bear another long, sleepless journey across Europe, thinking about this girl he'd had sex with.

She had to know the truth. Who was she? What had she meant to him? Did Peter still want to be with Kaisa; did he still want to marry her? Or would Kaisa return to Finland having lost him? Or would they carry on as if they were together, but free to see other people. Kaisa had to know before she left.

'You know I love you,' Peter said, not turning around.

He folded his arms across his chest.

Kaisa got up and stood next to him. She put her head on his shoulder.

'And I love you.'

She burrowed between his chest and his hands. He laughed, briefly. It was a dry sound, almost a cough.

'I need to know,' Kaisa said quietly.

'It wasn't Frankie. How stupid do you think I am?'

He freed himself from Kaisa's embrace and walked to the other side of the room.

'Who was it then?'

'I told you, nobody.'

Kaisa said nothing for a moment.

'So what are we going to do?' she asked.

Peter returned to her and took Kaisa's hands in his.

'We'll find a way. I promise. You know I'm going to miss you so much. Being here on my own in this flat, in this room...'

'I know.'

His rounded eyes looked sad, his hands were trembling. She could tell he was speaking the truth.

'I'll never be a naval wife like Lucy, you know.' Kaisa looked into Peter's dark eyes. 'Never.'

He laughed sounding relieved.

'I know that. And I bloody well hoped you wouldn't.'

The drive from Edinburgh to Newcastle was much shorter than the journey had been five weeks earlier. Sitting next to Peter in his yellow Spitfire Kaisa wished time would stop and they could stay on the road south forever.

They arrived at the ferry. Peter accompanied Kaisa onboard the musty-smelling ship. Together, they stood in a four-berth cabin she'd booked for the crossing to Gothenburg.

'You must take one of these,' Peter said reaching into his pocket. He pulled out a packet of Stugeron.

Kaisa looked at the seasick pills. 'Why?'

'It's going to be a choppy sailing.' Peter put his arm around her. 'The North Sea in winter is unforgiving.'

It hadn't even occurred to Kaisa that she might be seasick. She'd never been sick on the ferry between Finland and Sweden.

When she tried to explain this to Peter he laughed and said, 'Just take them; believe me you don't want to take the chance. There's a saying in the Navy, "When you're seasick, first you fear you're going to die; then you wish you would."'

Kaisa put the packet into her handbag.

The Tannoy intercom announced that the ferry was leaving in fifteen minutes. She lifted her eyes to Peter's, trying not to cry.

Peter took her face between his hands.

'Your eyes are very blue today.' He looked at Kaisa for a long time and whispered, 'I love you.'

They kissed.

And then he was gone.

Kaisa slept through the ferry sailing for the most part. The short train journey up to Stockholm from Gothenburg passed quickly. At the central station, Kaisa's mother met her and greeted her warmly.

'I'm glad to see you back,' she said.

Kaisa spent the next two nights with her, thrilled to hear Sirkka was home from Lapland. The sisters slept on two thin mattresses on the floor of the living room. Kaisa told her sister everything about the trip to Edinburgh, and Sirkka told Kaisa about a man she'd met up in Rovaniemi.

'He's Swedish and the same age as father!' she whispered. Kaisa heard the faint sounds of her mother snoring in the next room. 'I've never felt like this about anyone.'

Kaisa hugged her. But a sudden thought alarmed her and she pulled back.

'He's not married, is he?'

To her relief, Sirkka shook her head. She told Kaisa the man had three grown-up children, but was divorced. He had his own restaurant on the Swedish side of the border and drove a huge Mercedes.

'But what will father say?' Kaisa asked.

Sirkka shrugged. 'Why should I care what he thinks?'

After two nights talking with her sister about everything, and planning their future weddings without speaking to the prospective grooms, Kaisa returned to Helsinki. Her father and his girlfriend met her at the ferry terminal. It was a Sunday morning and the sun was bright against the white snow at South Harbour.

'The wanderer returns!' Kaisa's father said. Next to him Marja giggled

He hugged her tightly; she felt as if he was truly glad to see her.

He said, 'I'm going to take you both out to lunch.'

Kaisa nodded and thanked him, though she wasn't at all hungry. In her ruined suede jacket Kaisa felt the cold too deeply, and shivered. They walked towards her father's dark-blue Saab.

'I see you decided to come back then,' Marja said, and added, 'Happy New Year!' She nudged Kaisa with her elbow. 'How did you celebrate?'

'We went to the pub.'

Marja launched into a long tale about a language course she'd attended years ago in Eastbourne. How she'd survived the month eating Mars bars, because English food was inedible. But she'd loved the pubs, the beer in particular.

Her stories bored Kaisa and she tried not to listen. This woman clearly knew nothing about England, not the real England anyway. There was no proper coffee, that was true, and the whole country smelt of milk that had gone bad. But there was some good food. Kaisa had never again tasted chips as good as the ones Peter's mother made, or the cabbage salad called coleslaw served with ham, in pubs. And the ham was thickly sliced and tasty, not like the thin over-salted stuff that Kaisa's father often bought from the local shop. And there was no cheddar cheese in Finland. Kaisa closed her eyes and thought about the gorgonzola she'd eaten with Peter, while sitting on the floor of their temporary home in Edinburgh.

The next day at Hanken, Tuuli was glad to see Kaisa. She hugged her.

'I thought you might not come back,' she said.

Kaisa looked at her. Her friend was being serious.

Is that what everyone thought, that she'd just stay, marry Peter and abandon her studies for good? Now that she thought about it, her mother, Sirkka, and his father and his girlfriend had all mentioned it in some way.

The possibility of staying in Scotland hadn't even occurred to her. Or to Peter.

Why hadn't it?

20

HELSINKI, SPRING 1983

In February, Kaisa got a part-time job at Stockmann's department store, selling fabrics on Friday evenings and Saturday mornings. She was short of money after her travelling the previous winter. All the money she'd earned from her summer internship at the bank had been spent.

In spite of her time away, her studies at Hanken were going well. She'd passed her remaining exams on her return from Edinburgh. Kaisa continued to get good marks for the coursework, even though she had less time to study because of the new job. Each week she and Tuuli went to the university disco. Once or twice she bumped into Tom there, but him ignoring her didn't bother Kaisa anymore. Once, she even saw the tennis player; he'd walked towards her and their eyes had met for a moment. A trembling Kaisa just nodded at him and turned away, fearing he'd come over and try to talk to her. Tuuli was preoccupied on the dance floor with a new guy. When he didn't, she breathed out a sigh of relief.

Kaisa missed Peter wherever she went.

He wrote nearly every week, his words full of longing and love for her. Occasionally there'd be a late-night phone call. Sometimes a fortnight would pass without any communication, and Kaisa could only assume he was away at sea, onboard his nuclear submarine. She replied to each letter, but often their messages to each other would cross in the post, and a question would take two or three letters to be answered. They never wrote about the future, or anything important, just what had happened during the week. Kaisa told Peter how Russian customers at Stockmann's would try to buy dress fabric with a bottle of vodka. She told him what marks she'd got in her exams. Peter told Kaisa about nights out with his mates, and about a trip down to Portsmouth, to see his old friends. He said very little about his work, merely referring to 'refits', 'work-ups', or 'programmes'. Kaisa didn't understand what the submarine did when it sailed, or what Peter's job was. She assumed she wasn't supposed to know or understand.

In April, Peter told Kaisa he'd visited his parents and they'd given him money towards the purchase of a new car for his birthday. He'd sold the yellow Spitfire and bought a more reliable car, a Ford Fiesta. Kaisa mourned the open-top sports car and couldn't imagine Peter at the wheel of anything else.

Kaisa spent her twenty-third birthday later the same month with her father and sister, the latter who'd travelled down from Lapland to see Kaisa.

The three of them were sitting in the Happy Days Café, where their father had taken them for a buffet lunch. For once, her father's girlfriend wasn't with him. The place reminded Kaisa of her first date with Peter. It seemed like an age ago now. She looked at the uneaten *gravad lax* and pickled herring on her plate and sipped the half litre glass of beer Sirkka had insisted she have.

'It's your birthday and he's paying, for goodness sake,' she whispered in Kaisa's ear when Kaisa had hesitated about what to order.

Their father got up suddenly and said, 'I'm off to get some more food.'

With him hovering over the buffet table and out of earshot, Kaisa asked Sirkka about the new boyfriend.

'Oh, it's over,' she said waving her hand, as if swatting a fly.

'Why?'

'Oh, I don't know, Little Sister, I don't think he's the one for me after all.'

'I'm sorry.' Kaisa squeezed her hand.

Kaisa looked her sister's appearance over. The blonde, with dark-green eyes, looked slim and athletic in her short, black skirt and stripy V-neck jumper. Living in Lapland obviously suited her. And she didn't seem to be too devastated about the end of her relationship.

'That's OK,' Sirkka said 'Hey, what about you and the Englishman? When are you moving over there?'

'Oh, I don't know. I won't be able to get a job in the UK without a work permit.'

'Get a work permit, then.'

She wished she could. 'You can't get one. There's huge unemployment in the UK, just like here, and no one outside the EEC can get one. Unless you're a brain surgeon or something. It's impossible. I'd have to marry him to live and work there.'

Sirkka smiled broadly. 'So, what's the problem? You love him, he loves you.'

'I know.'

'Besides, he's already asked you to marry him once, so just say yes!'

Sirkka lifted her glass and clinked it with Kaisa's.

Their father sat down heavily next to Kaisa in the leather booth. He'd brought a plateful of food from the buffet.

'Yes to what?' he said, looking suspiciously at Sirkka.

'I think Kaisa should marry and leave this godforsaken city and country forever.'

His nostrils flared as he took a deep breath in. Kaisa wanted to ask them not to fight on her birthday. But it was already too late.

'You'd think that, wouldn't you!' he said. 'You, who scampered over to Sweden to follow your bitch of a mother. Foreign men, that's what you're after, just because no Finnish man would have you. I bet you'll marry some soft, milk-drinking Swede.'

There was a silence. The little appetite Kaisa had had vanished. She didn't know what to say. Sirkka was looking down at her plate. She glanced at Kaisa. Her eyes were dark, angry and dangerous looking.

Their father was staring at Sirkka, holding his knife and fork upright. Like a man-eating giant about to pounce, waiting for the retaliation. But Sirkka stayed silent for once, not rising to the bait.

A waitress came to the table and broke the tension.

'Any schnapps here?'

Father's eyes lit up.

'Yes, we'll have a round of *Koskenkorva*.'

Kaisa glanced at her watch. It was barely 11.30am. The lunch went downhill from there.

'I don't care what he thinks,' Sirkka said later. They were walking along the Esplanade to a place where a friend of Sirkka's was working. In the restaurant business everyone seemed to know each other, even in different countries. It was a sunny, almost warm, day. Trees along the park were beginning to bud; spring was definitely on its way.

They'd left their father to drink himself stupid at Happy Days Café. Luckily his mood had improved after the first round of *Koskenkorva*. After they'd eaten, he'd told Sirkka and Kaisa to go out and have fun, pressing a few hundred Marks into each of their hands.

The same old routine.

'Might as well use the money as His Pisshead Lordship wishes.' Sirkka laughed and linked arms with Kaisa.

Peter phoned later that night to wish Kaisa a happy birthday. She very nearly told him what Sirkka had said about moving to England and marrying him, but at the last minute she hesitated. Even though he'd already proposed once, Kaisa still wanted Peter to ask a second time. She wanted to make sure he really wanted to marry her.

'I've only got three weeks of term left,' Kaisa said instead.

'Right, and then what?'

'I start at the bank on Monday 23rd May.'

'OK.'

The conversation was short and Kaisa couldn't get any more out of him. She tried not to worry that he may have stopped loving her, or that he'd slept with another girl – or even the same mystery girl.

In bed that night, she reread his last letter, in which he'd sworn undying love for her. No mention of his schedule. Perhaps he truly didn't know, or wasn't allowed to tell Kaisa what he was doing in the next few months, or even weeks. There was a Cold War on after all. Goodness knew who might be listening in on their telephone conversations. Whenever they spoke, it always sounded as if several lines were open during the overseas connection. Kaisa often heard a click or two, like someone was putting the phone down during their call. Peter's jokes about sleeping with a spy – or the 'honey traps', as he called them – that the ship's company had been warned about, still played on Kaisa's mind.

A month later, when Kaisa had already started her fourth summer internship at the bank, a letter from Peter arrived. That same day she'd discovered the British Council Library in a building next to the bank, and had borrowed Graham Greene's spy novel *The Human Factor*, in English. She was looking forward to curling up in bed and reading about England in English. But first, the letter. Kaisa ripped open the thin, blue envelope and read the contents.

. . .

'I have been so miserable here without you all this time. But now I finally know what my schedule is going to be for at least the next few months. As you know, our refit has been delayed so many times now, and as a consequence they've decided to send me on an OPS course in Portsmouth. I'll be on dry land and away from Scotland for six months! The course starts early June and will end at Christmas.'

Peter added that he would be living in his friend's house in Southsea again and he wanted Kaisa to come over *'for as long as you can, as soon as you can make it.'*

Kaisa sat down on her bed in the empty house. Her father was still at work. She hoped he wouldn't come home that evening; she needed time alone to think. She had no idea what an OPS course was, but it didn't matter. Her worry was asking for time off from the bank. She was only an intern. Would they understand she needed to go and see Peter? Kaisa had some money saved up from her part-time job at Stockmann's. At the end of the month she'd have her first pay cheque from the bank. Even though it was just for one week's work, it would cover the cost of the flight.

The next day Kaisa went to see the manager at the bank – the same one she'd had since her first summer internship. He'd graduated from the same university as Kaisa ten years earlier and kept calling her 'The Lady Economist'. When she told him about her request, he muttered and smiled. 'Young love. Take two weeks paid leave. I'm sure we'll manage without you.'

Kaisa couldn't believe it. It was unheard of for summer interns to get leave, paid or unpaid. They were supposed to cover the permanent staff's holidays. Kaisa shook his hand and thanked him. She danced out of his office.

That afternoon, walking back to the bus stop along Mannerheim Street, Kaisa hummed to herself. She'd just been to the Finnair travel agent on the corner of Aleksanterinkatu and reserved her flights to Heathrow. In only two weeks' time she'd be on the plane, on her way to London. In fourteen days Kaisa would be in Peter's arms.

21

Kaisa found Peter waiting for her in the airport, with a dark-red rose in his hand. He kissed her until she couldn't breathe. Kaisa had almost forgotten his familiar smell of cigarettes and coconut shaving cream, and how his mouth tasted minty. Her heart beat so hard she was sure everyone could hear it.

The new car was on the second level of a concrete parking lot. It was a grey-and-black Ford Fiesta and looked dull compared to Peter's old yellow Spitfire. But Peter was thrilled with it. He told her that the old sports car was always breaking down.

'I remember all those freezing cold mornings it wouldn't start in Edinburgh,' Kaisa said with a nod.

Peter squeezed her shoulder and smiled at her. It felt good to talk about an experience they had both shared.

The new Ford started like a dream. Peter kissed Kaisa on the mouth and drove the car out of the dank car park and into the bright sunshine. They headed down to Portsmouth. Along the way, Kaisa was struck by how bright-green the fields were that they passed. It was a hot June day and farmers were already cutting their crops of hay. In Finland they didn't start doing that until at least a month later. Summer is so much further ahead here, she thought. She wished she could stay in England forever.

'You didn't forget your dress, did you?' Peter said.

'Sorry?'

'For the Dolphin Summer Ball?'

'Yes, I remembered.'

'Great. It'll be fun!'

Peter had told Kaisa about the ball in his letter, which was held each summer at the submarine base in Portsmouth. She was nervous about meeting a new set of his friends. She'd brought the same dress (the only ball gown Kaisa owned) that she'd worn to the Hanken Ball in Helsinki, a year and a half ago. Kaisa was worried it would be far too ordinary looking. She was sure the other girls would be wearing designer gowns, not cheap material ones made by a friend.

Peter and Kaisa were the only ones out of the old group of Navy friends who stayed in the terraced house in Southsea that summer. Jeff, Peter's best mate, was now serving in Northern Ireland. The girl, Sandra, who had lived there two years previously when Kaisa had been to stay the first time, was working for NATO in Brussels. Her boyfriend, Oliver, was in Faslane, where Peter had been. It seemed strange for everyone to be scattered around Europe but, as Peter put it, 'That's the Navy for you.'

Again, Kaisa and Peter fell into a routine. Each morning during her two-week stay in the little house in Southsea, after Peter left for work looking handsome in his uniform, she walked down to the shops at the end of the street. She wanted to cook Peter Finnish dishes, and searched for the right ingredients at the small butcher's and greengrocer's.

Kaisa made Karelian stew out of diced beef, pork and lamb's kidney, pea soup from a hock of ham and dried peas, and fish chowder from cod and new potatoes. She struggled to work the gas oven and hob in the little kitchen at the back of the house, often burning her fingers on the lit matches. It seemed so old-fashioned and dangerous to cook with gas, but Peter said it was much better and cheaper than electric. Kaisa felt like a little wife in the kitchen, but strangely this didn't bother her anymore. What mattered to her was that she and Peter could spend every evening and night together, as well as the long weekends, while there was just the two of them and they could do as they please.

The long-awaited Dolphin Summer Ball took place two days before Kaisa was due to return to Helsinki. She'd been dreading it, and tried not to think about it. The invitation was written in the same gold lettering and on a similar card as the invitation to the cocktail party in Helsinki. Looking at it took Kaisa back to the days before she'd met Peter. This time, the invitation was issued in Peter's name. Underneath was space for an avec, where he'd written Kaisa's name.

Peter wore his summer dress jacket: white with gold lapels. Kaisa was still getting dressed by the time he was ready.

He kissed her on the cheek and said, 'No rush, darling. I'll go and fix you a gin and tonic.'

He sounded so domesticated, so husbandlike, as if he'd just stepped off the set of an English TV series like *The Good Life*, which Kaisa had watched in Finland with her mother.

She smiled to herself, took a deep breath and looked in the mirror at her pale reflection. She didn't want to wear too much makeup, so she just added more blusher to her cheeks. It was another hot summer's evening. It had rained only once during the two weeks Kaisa had spent in this house. But tonight she felt a chill run through her body. She couldn't explain why she was so nervous about this evening. Was it the fear of perhaps seeing the girl Peter slept with?

Neither she nor Peter had discussed the past, or the future. But she worried the girl was still a part of Peter's social circle. She had to be someone Kaisa had already met – otherwise why would he not tell her who it was?

The past two weeks had gone by in a blissful haze of domesticity. It was only now, when they were heading out together to meet other people, a thought occurred to Kaisa: she still didn't know if they were a proper couple. She'd not been brave enough to talk about anything important with Peter, and she certainly couldn't do it right now.

Peter drove the Fiesta to the jetty in HMS *Vernon*, where they boarded a pass-boat over to Gosport on the other side of the harbour. Peter went aboard first and offered Kaisa his hand to guide her onto the small vessel. When she sat down next to two other women in their evening gowns, made out of luxurious velvet and silk, and wearing long satin gloves, she felt as if she'd entered the last century. The ladies smiled at her. The men stood, holding on to the side of the boat. They took off their caps and nodded to Kaisa.

'Good evening,' one said.

'Good evening,' Kaisa replied. It was warm, but she was shivering.

Peter sat down next to her and put his arm around her. 'You OK?'

'Are Lucy and Nick going to be at the ball?'

Peter laughed. 'No, I don't think you'll know anyone.' As the loud engine started and the boat headed towards the other shore, he whispered in Kaisa's ear, 'But don't worry, I'll look after you.'

The Dolphin Submarine School knew how to organise a party. At the submarine base there were different areas for food, dancing, or just socialising. There was a disco, a Caribbean steel band, and a live group called The Smugglers, who played old-fashioned music from the sixties. It felt appropriate to be listening to the Beatles' songs in England, although the words of *Love Me Do* reminded Kaisa of her childhood summers spent in the wooden-clad cottage by a lake in Finland. One year, Sirkka and Kaisa played this same single their father had bought them in Stockholm over and over. Kaisa felt as if those summers in Finland had happened in another life.

Peter led Kaisa over to a huge balcony overlooking Old Portsmouth and Southsea. He handed her a drink and introduced her to a string of his friends and their wives or girlfriends. As soon as they told Kaisa their names she forgot them. She struggled to follow the conversation over the sound of the various music bands, which flowed from the different rooms. Everyone was happy; the men were making jokes and the women laughed out loud. Kaisa smiled too, pretending she understood the punch lines.

'You stay here, I'm going to check where we're sitting for supper,' Peter said and left.

A slightly older man, who appeared to be on his own, came over and stood next to Kaisa. He had watery eyes and thinning pale hair. His jacket had several gold rings on it. Kaisa guessed he must be more senior than Peter.

'He's not given you a set of Dolphins yet then?' the man said, bending to look down the top of Kaisa's low-cut dress.

She placed a hand over her cleavage, feeling exposed. She cursed her decision not to buy a proper ball gown. Hers was made of very thin fabric and had narrow straps, making it impossible to wear a bra with it. Kaisa had asked Peter if he thought it too revealing, but he'd just smiled and said she looked good.

'Sorry, I don't understand?' Kaisa said.

The man pointed at a small brooch-like pin on his uniform jacket.

Peter had told Kaisa about the emblem of the submarine service. Once you passed your exams and completed the required sea time in a boat, there was a ceremony onboard. You had to earn your Dolphins by knocking back a glass of rum with a pin in it and catching the pin between your teeth. She remembered how proud he'd been when he told her about it. But she thought the pins were for the officers only. Kaisa didn't know the wives and girlfriends could have them too.

'No, he hasn't,' she replied.

The man laughed at her confusion. 'I don't suppose he's told you he can't marry you, either?'

'What?'

Kaisa stared at the man's red face.

Just then Peter reappeared by her side. 'C'mon, darling, there's someone I want you to meet.'

'Excuse us, Sir,' Peter said.

Kaisa was still staring when Peter led her away.

Peter took her to the end of the long balcony. Her ears were ringing with the man's last words. She saw how the lights from the other side of the harbour reflected against the dark water. The floor beneath her felt uneven, as if she were still on the pass-boat. Or floating on water. Noises around her seemed muffled. Had she gone deaf?

Peter rested one hand on Kaisa's waist while drinking a pint of beer with the other. He was half-leaning over the low balcony wall, talking to three other officers, who'd appeared from nowhere. Kaisa couldn't remember if she'd met them before.

Their laughter sounded distant.

With a shake of her head her hearing returned slowly to her. Music was flowing out from the nearby rooms, and people were moving in and out of the long, wide outdoor space overlooking the harbour mouth. Lights from Old Portsmouth opposite flickered on the dark water. The men looked handsome in their pressed uniforms and polished boots, the women glamorous in their long, ball gowns.

She finished her drink in a few large gulps and asked Peter to get her another one.

Peter looked at her, puzzled. Kaisa knew, in England, ladies weren't supposed to ask for a drink, they were supposed to wait to be asked. But she didn't care.

'Alright darling, what would you like?' She nodded at the large beer glass in Peter's hand. 'A pint? Are you sure?'

She just looked at Peter.

'I'll get these, it's my round,' said one of the other guys Peter had been talking to, someone on the same OPS course as Peter and who had also been at Dartmouth Naval College. He walked inside the noisy mess.

'He's really, really rich,' Peter whispered in Kaisa's ear.

On another night she might have been impressed, but all Kaisa could think about was what the old man had said to her.

'Who was that man I was talking to before?' Kaisa said, trying to sound as if she were making polite conversation.

'He's Commander SM; he sort of runs this place. Why, what did he say?'

He looked away, as if he didn't want to know, and started surveying the crowd. Peter waved to someone. A pretty girl wearing a salmon-coloured silk satin gown, cinched in at her tiny waist, with a huge bow at the back, walked over. She was flanked by three men in uniform.

The buzzing sound returned to Kaisa's ears.

'Hello, handsome,' she said to Peter and kissed him on the cheek.

Peter introduced her. 'This is the lovely Tash. The girl we were all in love with at Dartmouth.'

Kaisa managed a smile, although the noise in her ears buzzed louder.

'Nonsense,' Tash said. She looked up at Peter through her lashes, feigning shyness.

The drinks arrived. When the man handed Kaisa the pint, there was silence. All eyes followed the glass of beer from the tray to her hand.

'Well, cheers,' Peter said.

'Cheers!' all said in unison.

'You know, I once knew an Australian girl who drank pints,' one of Tash's entourage said, nodding kindly at Kaisa.

'Yes, and I've heard all the girls down under do!' said the other.

'Do girls in Norway drink pints too?' asked the man who'd bought Kaisa the drink.

'I wouldn't know,' she said, 'I'm from Finland.'

Another silence followed.

Peter gripped Kaisa's waist and said, 'She can drink any of you under the table, though she hasn't grown a beard yet.'

Laughter followed.

Now I'm the butt of a joke, Kaisa thought. She drank her beer quickly. When asked, jokingly, if she wanted another one, Kaisa nodded.

By the time Kaisa sat down for the meal she was drunk, but all she wanted was to drink more. Occasionally, Peter took hold of her hand under the table and asked if she was alright, but for the most part he laughed and talked loudly with the other people at their table, one of whom was the famously lovely Tash, or Natasha, as Peter said her full name was. 'But everyone calls her Tash,' he'd added, as if it mattered.

Tash was sitting on the other side of the round table, with a handsome naval officer on either side of her. A dark-haired girl sat next to one of Tash's adoring male fans. Her plunging purple dress neckline showed off her plump breasts. Occasionally, Kaisa would catch one of the guys at the table staring at her assets, but for the most part he ignored her, leaning across her to catch what Tash was saying.

Kaisa felt sorry for her.

Whenever Peter got up to mingle, or she went to find the ladies' room, other uniformed men would approach Kaisa, as if she was fair game. Perhaps they'd somehow guessed she was foreign, so that made her inferior, even desperate, for attention. Just like the foreign nurses in English hospitals. Peter had said there was a joke among young naval officers: 'There are only two certainties in life: death and nurses.'

They didn't arrive back to the house in Southsea until two o'clock in the morning. Kaisa ran straight to the bathroom and threw up. Even after she'd brought up everything she'd eaten and drunk that night, she still couldn't sleep. She sat on the edge of the bed and felt like crying.

The alarm clock on the side table said: 5.30am. A sleepy Peter put his head on her lap, and said gently, 'You got room spin?'

Kaisa looked down at him. 'No.'

He shifted back to the pillow and closed his eyes. 'Come back to bed then.'

Kaisa knew she should have lain beside him and slept, waiting until later in the morning to talk. It was a Saturday and they'd have the whole day together, their last one before Kaisa headed home to Helsinki.

Still feeling lightheaded from all the alcohol, she couldn't help herself but ask, 'You're never going to marry me, are you?'

Hearing no response Kaisa turned around, angry that Peter had dared to go back to sleep.

But when she saw him lying on his back with his eyes open, staring up at the ceiling, Kaisa turned away.

Had he known what the people at the party would be like, looking down their noses at her – a foreign girl, daring to dream that an Englishman, a British naval officer, would ever marry her? He'd introduced Kaisa to Natasha, a girl who, she'd learnt later in the evening, was the daughter of an admiral. She would make the perfect wife for Peter. She'd know how to behave at cocktail parties and naval dances. She wouldn't wear a dress that was obviously cheap and too revealing, or drink pints.

'Well?' Kaisa said.

'Come here.'

Oh, how she wanted to lie next to him, to feel his strong arms around her, to put her head against his warm chest, to cry about everything. But she couldn't. She wasn't going to be charmed by his empty words, or by his warm kisses, or by sex. Kaisa had to be strong and not give in to seduction. She had to know if they had a future together.

'No.'

With her back to him she waited for him to say more.

She heard Peter sit up. He breathed in and out heavily, deliberately.

'You know how much I love you.'

Kaisa faced him. She was sick of hearing those words.

'You don't even mean that anymore!'

'But I do, darling. Please, I'm so tired...' Peter yawned loudly. 'You've been sick all night and...'

'What? I behaved in an uncivilised manner? Foreign girls are like that, you know. Especially us Finns, we're barely human, so we can't really be trusted to attend fancy balls. Unladylike freaks we are. We drink pints of beer like men, not tiny glasses of sherry, like the lovely Tashes of this world do.'

Peter got up and stood angrily before her. His arms were by his side, his fists tightly bunched.

'What's the matter with you?'

Tears ran down Kaisa's face. She wiped them away, swallowed hard and said, 'That man from last night, the Commander, he told me you knew you'd never be able to marry me.'

She sat on the bed. Peter sat next to her with a sigh. He put his arm around her shoulders but she shook it off. She didn't want his pity. She was shivering with hope that he'd tell her it wasn't true. That he loved her and would marry her as soon as she wanted, that he'd never been in love with that pretty Tash. That he would rather die than lose Kaisa forever.

'Look, I wasn't going to tell you...'

She couldn't believe this. It was all true...? Or was he talking about something else?

'Tell me what?'

Peter looked down at his hands, making it hard for Kaisa to see his face.

'I wrote to my Appointer and asked him if there was a problem with marrying someone from a near-Communist country.'

Not this again. She stood up and shouted, 'Finland is not a Communist country!'

'I know that, but as far as the Navy is concerned...'

Kaisa didn't know what else to say. She stared at Peter sitting with his head bowed. How long had he known about this? How long was he going to string her along, never telling her that she couldn't move to England and be with him?

Peter stood and took Kaisa into his arms. She remained stiff in his embrace. His voice rumbled in her ear. 'I was told by someone that it was a problem to marry a girl from, you know.' Peter took a deep breath and added, 'You've got to admit Finland is a bit different, and so close to the Soviet Union. Anyway, they told me marrying you might end my career in the Navy.'

Kaisa wriggled out of Peter's grip, but he grabbed her arm and held on to it. The buzzing noise started in her ears again. Peter's words sounded like he was speaking in a cave, or a deep tunnel.

'So I thought I'd ask directly, you know from the one person, my Appointer, who makes decisions on my career.'

Kaisa looked up at him. His lips were set in a narrow line, his eyes serious.

'So what did he tell you?' she prompted.

'I'm still waiting for his reply.'

22

HELSINKI, SUMMER 1983

I t was raining when the plane landed at Helsinki airport. The goodbye at Heathrow with Peter had been even more difficult than usual. Kaisa lost count of how many times they'd said, 'I love you.'

On their last day together, they didn't get out of bed until the afternoon. They talked about how they'd met. The two and a half years Kaisa and Peter had known each other seemed like an eternity now.

Kaisa had been sitting on the double bed, trying to pack. Sheets were strewn everywhere, her clothes mingled with Peter's. He'd come out of the shower wearing a towel around his angular hips. His hair was wet and he smelt of the special, coconut shaving cream that she loved. He sat next to Kaisa and took her hands in his.

'That evening we spent wandering in the cold park in Helsinki? I wanted you so much. But you kept saying, "It's impossible".'

Kaisa remembered the passionate kisses, the way Peter had looked deep into her eyes. And here they were, in love, longing for the day they could be together forever.

'Our relationship is still impossible,' Kaisa wanted to say, but she didn't. She didn't want to talk about the future when it was so uncertain.

'I thought I was going to die if I couldn't make love to you,' he said.

Peter held Kaisa's face and kissed her.

'I promise to phone as soon as I hear from the Appointer.' He added, 'I heard there is an engineer who married a Czech girl, but I think he's a skimmer.'

Kaisa looked at him. 'A skimmer?'

'A lieutenant on surface ships. They skim on top of the sea, not under it, like we do.'

'And why is that different?'

He kissed the top of Kaisa's head. 'It just is.'

Peter must have meant submariners had a higher security clearance than skimmers. But she could tell he didn't want to talk about it.

For their last few hours together they held each other. Kaisa listened as Peter said he couldn't imagine life without her. He kept kissing her, telling her she was beautiful. Did he do and say those things because he felt bad about putting his career before their future together? Or because he thought it might be the last time they saw each other?

Sitting now on the airport bus to home, she remembered him telling her early on that he loved the Navy above anything else.

'I hate being away from loved ones, but it's what I've always wanted to do,' he'd said to her.

Kaisa had seen in his eyes how much his job meant to him. It was what he lived for. The Royal Navy was his life.

What then, if the Navy said he couldn't marry her?

She couldn't move to England and not work; she wanted a career too. She and Peter were both ambitious – one of the many things they had in common.

The rain streaked down the windows of the Finnair bus. Outside, lighting flashed in the sky. How Kaisa wished to return to Sunny Southsea.

When Kaisa had told Peter she thought the name fit, Peter had laughed and said, 'It rains a lot here!'

'But you call it "Sunny"' she'd protested.

'It's called sarcasm. We Brits are full of it.' He'd pulled Kaisa close to him. 'You'll get the hang of it.'

Kaisa smiled at the memory, but it also made her sad. There was so much she didn't know about Peter's country, so much she needed to learn. And she didn't even drink tea.

The bus driver was listening to a sports programme on the radio. Barbra Streisand came on singing *Woman in Love*. The way the Finnish announcer pronounced both the artist and the song, in his heavily accented English, made Kaisa smile. She thought how it would make Peter laugh. She listened to the soppy song and dreamt of life in England, with Peter. How could she bear being without him?

Through the rain-streaked window, Kaisa looked out at the wet Helsinki streets. People were walking fast with their heads hidden underneath black, sombre looking umbrellas. No one was smiling, no one was holding someone else's hand, everyone was just miserable and alone. Kaisa couldn't believe she was back here again. The city, with its tall, utilitarian buildings and its unhappy people, made her feel oppressed. She was sure none of these people had known love like her.

A sports results announcement cut the Barbra Streisand song off half-way. Kaisa looked to the front of the bus. A luggage tag dangled from her suitcase in the rack. It read 'Hel', short for Helsinki.

She was back in hell all right.

The rest of the summer in Helsinki was glorious – the second warm summer in two years. But it didn't suit Kaisa's mood. If it hadn't been for Tuuli at Hanken she wouldn't have survived the latter part of that year.

By the end of July, Tuuli had finished her finals and submitted her thesis, which she'd written in record time. Now she was ready to party. And party they did. During the day Kaisa worked at the bank; at night the two friends went to the university disco, or the Helsinki Club, or a popular summer place called the Pikkuparlamentti. It was near the Finnish Parliament and only open from June to August. With some tables outside and sliding glass doors facing the park that sloped down to the sea, it was a perfect place to celebrate a graduation. There, and elsewhere, Tuuli and Kaisa bumped into the old gang of rich boys, including Tom, who sometimes exchanged a few words with them. Who spoke to whom didn't seem to matter to the boys anymore.

Unlike Tuuli, Kaisa would still see everybody at Hanken in the autumn. She had a few exams left, due to her loss of time when she'd changed subjects in her second year. But her future also depended on Peter.

The 'If we can marry, I can have a work permit and move to England, but if we can't, what then?' question was always on Kaisa's mind. But when Peter phoned, which he did at least twice a week, they skirted around the issue. At first, she asked him regularly if he'd heard from the Appointer, but after several short replies of 'No' she didn't mention it again. She knew Peter was in the middle of a tough course and he also had exams to study for. He'd told Kaisa it was very important for him to do well, so she let him be.

23

HELSINKI, WINTER 1983

As the nights grew dark and Helsinki descended into its depressing winter hibernation, Kaisa returned to lectures at Hanken that October. Her professor pressed her to make a decision on her thesis, but Kaisa kept putting off meetings with him. At twenty-three years of age, Kaisa had no idea what was going to happen to her life.

In his letters, Peter kept telling Kaisa how much he missed her and loved her. How much he longed for the day when she would move to England. Kaisa speculated whether she could get a work permit through the bank. They were opening a commercial branch in London, and in early September she'd got an interview with the man heading up the new venture. But when she'd attended the interview in plush offices just a few blocks from where she'd worked, it was clear she had no idea what the job entailed. When the man with dark hair, combed back and shiny, asked Kaisa what she knew about hedge funds and Eurodollars, She couldn't fake her lack of knowledge.

There was still no word from the Appointer and whether the Navy would allow a sailor to marry a girl from a country so near to the Eastern Bloc. Her life was resting on their decision. She couldn't even decide on a subject for her thesis. Kaisa had narrowed it down to three choices. The one she really wanted to do was on British party politics. But for this, she needed to be based in England. Handy if she was living there; impossible if it all fell through.

.   .   .

In the middle of November, Peter called. 'I have Christmas and New Year off! Can I come over to see you?'

Kaisa spoke to her father the next day.

'Christmas? Here?' he said incredulously.

'Yes, I thought we could get a ham and I'd cook the Karelian stew and the Swede bake, and you could make your *gravad lax...*'

Her father stated firmly, 'I'm not having any guests here. Christmas is a commercial invention anyway, for shops to sell more stuff.'

He'd been in an unusually bad mood for weeks. Kaisa guessed he'd had a fight with Marja, because he was spending all his evenings and nights at home, drinking *Koskenkorva* and monopolising the TV.

Kaisa stared at him. She wanted to say, 'What about me?' or 'Please can we have a family Christmas here, just like we did when I was little?' but she didn't.

What if he sneered at her or, worse, started to complain about her mother? Or tell Kaisa some story or other about how awful Christmas had been with his ex-wife? Kaisa wanted to hold on to her good childhood memories and not have them spoiled by her bitter father.

She spoke to her mother instead. Pirjo was delighted and said it would be a special Christmas with Peter in Stockholm.

There was no snow in Helsinki when Peter's plane landed on the Saturday before Christmas. The city looked grey with the lights over Aleksanterinkatu reflecting on the black pavements, instead of the sparkling, white snow. Kaisa took the bus to the airport and prayed the weather would turn colder. Everything looked so much prettier with freshly fallen snow.

Peter had two weeks off and flew first to Helsinki. Their plan was to travel together to Stockholm for the holidays, and then back to Helsinki to spend New Year with Kaisa's friends. When she saw him through the glass at the arrivals hall, waving at her and rushing towards her with a bag over his shoulder, Kaisa stopped thinking about the future. The next fourteen days were all that mattered.

When they arrived home, Kaisa's father was waiting in the kitchen. In front of him was a half-full bottle of *Koskenkorva* and an empty tumbler. He shook Peter's hand and took another two glasses out of the cupboard. He sat down at the table and nodded at the empty seats opposite him. He filled the two tumblers up to the brim and lifted one to his lips. Peter took his, glanced at Kaisa and emptied the glass. He made only the slightest of sounds as he swallowed the vodka. Kaisa sipped her drink.

Her father grabbed the bottle, and was about to pour more into Peter's glass when Kaisa took Peter's hand and lied, 'We're going out tonight.'

'Even more reason to start the evening off with style,' her father said and poured another round.

She glanced at the clock on the kitchen wall. It was just past four in the afternoon.

'It's OK,' Peter said.

He placed one hand on Kaisa's knee under the kitchen table. With his other he lifted the glass to his lips.

'C'mon we have to go,' she urged Peter after he'd gulped down his drink.

Her father looked at her. 'You don't have to leave. I'm off to Lapland today.'

'What?' Kaisa said. It was the first she'd heard of it.

Peter looked from Kaisa to her father as they switched to speaking Finnish. After three years, he still struggled to understand the most basic words in Kaisa's mother tongue. Although he'd tried – he'd even ordered a Lingua-phone course in Finnish through the Navy. But however much he listened to the dead-pan female's voice and repeated what she said, he just couldn't get to grips with the language. He could say, *Kiitos*, which meant 'thank you', and *Anteeksi* for 'sorry', and, of course, 'I love you', or *'Minä rakastan sinua'*. And as far as understanding active conversation, he was at a loss. It didn't help that when he'd tried to talk in Finnish here, most people imme-diately spoke English back to him.

Peter sighed. The vodka was having an effect on him. He watched Kaisa. Her features looked so delicate; those rosy little lips so beautiful, made even more attractive by her pale skin and blonde hair. He wanted to move his hand up her leg, but was afraid her father might see. If only he'd leave them alone, so he could take her to bed and make love to her. He'd been thinking about nothing else during the long journey from Scotland. The *Koskenkorva* didn't help matters; it turned him on even more. There was no way he could wait until the evening to be with her.

Peter was shaken out of his thoughts when Kaisa's father spoke in English.

'Since I won't see you until next year' – he took a wad of hundred-Mark notes out of his wallet – 'have a few drinks on me, or even a meal.'

He bear-hugged Kaisa and shook Peter's hand.

When her father left the apartment Kaisa rolled her eyes.

'Dad didn't tell me he was going away for Christmas. He and his girl-friend must have made up. He says they're going up to see her family in northern Finland.'

Peter didn't care. He pulled Kaisa close to him and kissed her. 'Can we go to bed now?'

They woke late the next morning, four days before Christmas.

'What do you want to do today?' Peter asked.

Kaisa had only one suggestion. 'Go into Helsinki for some Christmas shopping?'

It was drizzling out with a cold rain that was almost sleet. They spent an hour walking around Stockmann's department store, holding hands. Peter kept stopping to kiss Kaisa. He wore a padded jacket, jeans and a thick jumper. Even when he wasn't kissing her in public like a foreigner would, his dark hair gave him away. He attracted sideways glances from other shoppers but didn't seem bothered by the attention. He didn't say much, either.

When they queued up to pay for a box of Fazer chocolates for Sirkka, Peter suddenly said, 'So, your father. Am I going to see him again?'

Kaisa frowned. 'Again?'

Peter shifted on the spot. He didn't look at her.

'Yes, before I go back.'

A man ahead of them in the queue turned around. His gaze wandered from Peter's dark features to Kaisa's blonde head. Kaisa saw a strong disapproval there. She stared at him until he turned back to face the till.

Peter's eyes widened; he flicked his gaze to the man's back.

What's his problem, he mouthed to Kaisa silently.

She shrugged. Answering his original first question she said, 'No, I don't think so. My father's away for the whole of the holidays. Why?'

'Nothing.' Peter pulled Kaisa in for another kiss.

When they were walking out of the store, he said, 'Can we go for lunch somewhere?'

The sleet was still falling. It was only midday, and even with the bright Christmas lights the street looked dark. Kaisa spotted a sign for a new American hamburger bar opposite them, called Hesburger. She dragged Peter towards it.

'It's not McDonald's, but they do a great rye burger,' she said.

The place was full. When Peter and Kaisa entered people stared.

He looked around the small space. 'You sure this is OK?'

'We just want a quick bite, yeah? And it's raining.'

After translating some of the menu to him, they collected their bags of food.

'Let's sit by the window,' Kaisa said nodding to one of the red plastic tables and chairs.

They sat down, and Peter kept looking at Kaisa. She noticed he wasn't unwrapping his burger, and hadn't touched the chips. It was so unusual for him not to want food; he was always starving.

'Aren't you hungry?' she asked.

He reached across the shiny tabletop and took her hand. His fingers felt cold against her skin.

'You know I love you.'

Peter's mouth was a straight line. His eyes were wider than usual. He looked almost scared. Kaisa's heart sank. Had he heard from the Navy Appointer? Was this bad news?

'I know.'

Peter pulled something out of his pocket. It was a small black box.

'This isn't quite where I imagined I'd do this, but...'

He looked deep into her eyes and opened the box to show her the contents.

Kaisa saw gold and glittery stones. She dropped her burger and her heart started beating fast. She looked up at Peter.

'And I really wanted to ask your father first,' he added.

Kaisa's mouth went dry; she couldn't speak. She wanted to throw herself at Peter. Kiss him, hug him, feel him close to her. But with people around them, munching on their burgers, loudly sucking on the straws in their near-empty paper cups of Coca Cola, coupled with the smell of French fries everywhere, she thought better of it.

'So, what I'm asking is...'

Kaisa waited nervously while Peter struggled to say the words. She wanted to help him and say, 'Yes, yes, a hundred times yes,' and very nearly did, but then realised he hadn't actually asked her yet.

She looked down at the ring before her, then up at his tense mouth. How she wanted to kiss those narrow lips, taste the cigarettes and mint, take in the scent of coconut, feel the roughness of his stubble on her chin.

Finally Peter said, in almost a whisper, 'Would you please marry me?'

Kaisa grinned and said simply, 'Yes.'

24

Peter's last words 'Getting married in the summer,' rang in Kaisa's ears as she said goodbye to him at Helsinki airport, clutching the red rose he'd bought her.

'This will be the last time we have to do this,' he said, and stroked Kaisa's hair.

They were standing just outside the gates to the passport control. She tried not to cry. She felt closer to him than ever before.

'I feel bad about not asking your father for your hand,' Peter said.

Kaisa gazed at him. 'Don't worry, he wouldn't have expected it.'

He probably would have loved being asked, but to her it was such an old-fashioned idea. Romantic, yes, but against everything Kaisa believed in. She wasn't a "chattel" to be passed from father to husband. But she didn't want to spoil their last moments together by talking about her feminist views.

All too soon it was time for Peter to catch his flight. Kaisa held on to him for one final kiss. Knowing they'd be together soon didn't make the farewells any easier. She rubbed the ring on her finger and prayed her last few months in Helsinki would pass quickly.

As she watched him disappear from view down the gangway, it suddenly occurred to her that she might have to organise the wedding in the UK. She ran out of the airport terminal and into the waiting bus. There was so much to do!

At home, she put the red rose into a vase next to her bed and went into the kitchen to get dinner ready.

Kaisa's father was due back from his travels that evening. She'd planned to cook his favourite meal: meatballs in a creamy sauce with boiled potatoes. She made a salad too, but knew he wouldn't want any of the 'rabbit food'.

He turned up an hour later, and they sat opposite each other for dinner at the small, kitchen table.

'Did you have a nice Christmas?' she asked.

She wondered if he'd spotted the ring on her finger yet. She'd placed her left hand in full view on the top of the table.

Her father lifted his head and looked at her from under his unruly eyebrows. 'In Oulu?'

'Yes.'

He put down his knife and fork and said, 'In Lapland they don't even know how to bake a ham properly. They're not really Finns; they're too close to the North Pole.'

She noticed he looked tired. He paused a moment, then a smile flitted across his lips.

'But the Christmas tree didn't cost anything. We felled it from one of the forests her family owns. They're big landowners up there.'

'That's nice,' Kaisa said resting her chin on her left hand, showing off the ring. When her father went back to eating, ladling the food into his mouth as if he'd never been fed, she sighed.

'I got this,' she said impatiently, stretching her arm across the table, shoving the hand with the sparkling diamond ring under his nose.

He stared at the band, as if it were on fire. Or infectious. His eyes moved slowly from her hand to her face. She smiled at him. He returned to his food and ate in silence.

Kaisa waited for his to reply, unable to eat.

'You're getting married and moving to England then?' he said finally.

'Yes.'

'Getting married in England?'

'I...I don't know. We haven't decided yet. It all depends –'

He interrupted her. 'I'll pay for it all if you get married in Finland.'

'Oh.'

Her father's rough gaze was on Kaisa. He coughed as if nervous, and said, 'Anyway...are you happy?'

The question surprised her. He'd never asked her such a thing before.

She didn't think 'being happy' even entered his consciousness. He was moody most of the time and thought happy people were weird.

'Yes, very.'

'And I assume your mother has met the young man, and approves?'

Kaisa realised her mouth had gone slack. She closed it and tried to remember the last time her father had called her mother anything other than 'that woman', or worse, 'that bitch'. Had he undergone a personality change?

'Yes.'

'Good, good,' he said, nodding vigorously.

A long silence followed. Kaisa looked out of the window. It had started snowing at last. Large flakes hung in the air, slowly falling onto the ground. The orange glow of the single lamppost brightened the small patch of dead grass outside the house.

'I think this calls for a celebration!'

Her father got up and took a bottle of *Koskenkorva* out of the fridge. He filled two tumblers and lifted his glass.

'*Kippis!*'

Kaisa nodded and lifted her own glass. They sat in silence drinking the neat vodka. It burnt Kaisa's throat, as it always did. She took small sips and tried not to grimace.

'There's a lovely church in Espoo, you know,' her father said.

Kaisa didn't know how to answer; the conversation was getting more and more surreal.

'Yes?'

'Have a look and tell me how much it's all going to cost. I've got the funds, so don't worry about that.'

He downed the rest of his drink and walked into the living room. She heard him put on the TV, sit down in one of the chairs and fart loudly.

The old church in Espoo stood at the end of a country lane, set away from a newly-built shopping centre. It was flanked by high-rise blocks on one side and a wide motorway on the other. Kaisa and her father went to see it for the first time one Saturday in late January. It seemed odd to plan a wedding in a church she'd never been to, but her father said it was the prettiest in the parish. Kaisa wondered how he knew this. Over the past few weeks, he'd been full of surprises.

The stone-clad church was empty when they both wandered down the narrow aisle. Kaisa shivered in the space that felt colder inside than outside.

It was strange to think she'd stand here in a few months' time, arm in arm with Peter. There was so much to do before she could get away and finally be with him. Kaisa looked from the simple altar, with its two silver candlesticks, to her father. He was standing perfectly still, with his hands in the pockets of his light-grey overcoat. His shoes were unpolished. Instead of his smarter work clothes, he wore the same shabby jogging pants and cardigan that he did when lazing in front of the TV.

His eyes met Kaisa's. 'What?'

'Nothing,' she said and looked away.

Her father had been in a funny mood all morning. In the car he kept asking Kaisa how long the visits to the church and the venue would take, as if he had a more important appointment to go to. Had he changed his mind about paying for the wedding? Kaisa wasn't sure he had any idea how much it would all cost. But neither did she.

She walked to the exit, afraid a pastor or a warden might appear and start asking questions. She wasn't ready for that; she didn't even know the date of the wedding yet.

'We have to be in Bastvik in fifteen minutes,' she called to her father over her shoulder.

The Bastvik Manor House faced a central courtyard, with a converted barn on either side. The woman showing them around the rooms smiled at her. There were bedrooms in each of the outbuildings for the use of overnight guests. The ceilings were low and the furniture antique. It all looked perfect, even if there was only one bathroom in each corridor for the guests to share. Surely Peter's family wouldn't mind? Back at the Manor House the woman checked a large book, and confirmed there were still dates available for a function in the summer.

'How many wedding guests are there going to be?' she asked Kaisa's father.

'Not too many, I hope,' he sneered.

The woman's smile froze into place.

Embarrassed, Kaisa looked down at her own hands.

'How many can you accommodate?' She looked at the woman again.

'The maximum number is seventy-five.'

'That many!' her father shouted.

'That should be more than enough,' Kaisa quickly added.

'Good, good,' the woman said. She attempted another smile, but ended up giving them a lopsided grin.

On the way home in the car, Kaisa didn't speak to her father. When they got closer to the house, her anger had peaked. After being so keen on the wedding, he'd just embarrassed her in front of the woman in the Bastvik Manor House. What must she think of them? How would Kaisa arrange the wedding with her now?

She looked at the leaflet the woman had given her. The rates seemed reasonable. After Kaisa's father's snippy comment about the number of guests, the woman had suggested a domestic sparkling wine for the toasts and a cheaper meal option. No fish course and chicken as a main, instead of veal.

Kaisa sighed. She didn't really care about the food or drink. But she also wanted Peter's family and friends to be impressed with the wedding in her home country.

Later that day Peter called. Kaisa's excitement about the wedding returned when he told her his news.

'I've got the whole of my programme set out for next the twelve months. First, at the NATO base in Naples until the last week of May then two weeks off, and the rest of the year I'll be based in Pompey. So, our date could be Saturday the 2nd of June.'

'The 2nd of June.'

Kaisa could almost taste the date on her lips. Could this be true? Was this going to happen?

'My father wants to pay for the wedding here,' she said.

'That's wonderful!' He sounded thrilled. 'I'd better tell my parents, Jeff and the others.'

They spoke briefly about the arrangements and Peter promised to let Kaisa know how many would be coming from the UK.

'So when can you finally come over to England for good?' he asked.

Kaisa's heart flipped. This was for real. Soon, she would be living in the UK with Peter as his wife. They'd agreed that she'd travel over as soon as possible, and then return to Finland for the wedding.

'My Professor says I can take the final exams at the Finnish Embassy in London, so I can come as soon as I have arranged everything here. I think perhaps the middle of February.'

'Great! I'm going to Italy in March, but you can stay in the house in Southsea. I'll be home at least every other weekend.'

For the rest of the evening the words 'I'll be home' repeated in Kaisa's head. How would it feel in England to wait for Peter to come home after being away? Would Kaisa be as lonely there as she was in her father's house in Espoo? More often than not, though, Kaisa was glad her father hadn't been around much, especially after his behaviour today.

At least it will be warmer in Southsea, Kaisa thought. And she'd be working just like Peter's sister-in-law and sister, taking the bus or the train to an office where she'd do important work. She still had no idea what that job would be. First she needed to marry the man.

Kaisa pulled out the *Yellow Pages*. She ran her finger down the names of printers. Now she knew the date she could have the invitations made. And she needed to let everyone know.

She lifted the receiver and dialled her mother's number in Stockholm.

The date for her move to England was set for the 25th of February.

She'd take the train through Europe, and cross the English Channel over to Harwich. That way she could send all her worldly possessions separately to her new home country, rather than be limited by the number of suitcases she could take on a flight. Personal luggage sent in this way cost nothing; sending it by international mail would have cost Kaisa money she didn't have. However, she expected that while in England she would have to live off Peter's salary – something she tried not to think about.

The next day, Kaisa went to pick up the wedding invitations. She and Peter had spent a long time on the telephone drawing up a list of guests. He'd come up with only ten names, including his parents, godmother, sister and brother with their spouses, and Jeff, Oliver and Sandra. He said the flights were so expensive that many of his friends couldn't afford the trip to Helsinki. The same conversation Kaisa had with father was equally as fruitless.

'You must decide,' he said. 'How am I supposed to know who wants to come to your wedding?'

After sitting in front of the TV for half an hour, he shouted, 'Invite my mother and my step-sisters. I guess they'll want to come now my old bastard of a step-father is dead.'

Kaisa sighed. He always had to put someone down.

The conversation about the wedding guests was more enjoyable with her mother. Over the phone they made a list of over thirty people, including grandparents, aunts, uncles, cousins and Kaisa's friends from school and university. Whenever she spoke on the phone with Pirjo she'd make sure her father was out first. Kaisa couldn't bear the thought of him saying nasty things about her afterwards when he heard who she'd been talking to.

They had a long chat about the wording of the invitations. Peter had given Kaisa the text traditionally used in the UK, but she wasn't sure if the Finnish translation should reflect the official tone of 'Mr-and-Mrs-so-and-so have the pleasure of inviting you to the wedding of their daughter and Sub-

Lieutenant Peter Williams, RN.' There was nothing similar in Finnish that didn't risk sounding pompous and old-fashioned. Eventually they settled on a simple wording, in slightly more formal Finnish.

The printers were in Lauttasaari, in a small industrial park at the far end of the island. As she passed the street where her old block of flats stood, Kaisa felt a little nostalgic. Life with Matti had been dull, but it was safe. When she saw a light on in her old window and a new set of dark curtains, Kaisa couldn't but wonder if she was making a grave mistake moving to England. What if it turned out to be a difficult country to live in? What if people were unfriendly – even prejudiced – against foreigners like her?

The prejudice she'd endured at the Dolphin Summer Ball could happen everywhere she went. On the bus, at work, in the pub. What if she didn't get a job and ended up being a Navy housewife, like Lucy in Scotland? What if Peter, once married, turned out to be as possessive and jealous as Matti had been? What if Kaisa found married life to be as unbearable as Martha Quest had in Doris Lessing's books?

When Kaisa's father got in from work that evening, she showed him the invitations that didn't exceed fifty in total. It was at least twenty-five fewer than the maximum he was expecting.

He sat down heavily in one of the chairs and perched his reading glasses on the end of his nose to read one.

'What's this?' he said looking at Kaisa over his glasses.

She'd been hovering nearby, but sat down when her heart started to beat a little faster.

'The wedding invitations.'

He looked down at the card Kaisa had handed him, saying nothing.

'It's in English as well as in Finnish, because...' she started to say.

Perhaps he's offended by the bilingual text, Kaisa thought.

'No, what's this?' He pointed at one sentence and read, 'Mr and Mrs Niemi have the pleasure of inviting...'

'It's the English text. I thought, since less than half don't understand Finnish...it would be better to have both languages.'

Kaisa was stammering now, her heart beating so fast she could hardly get the words out. Her father looked livid.

'Not that!' he said loudly. 'It's me who's inviting these people, not your mother.'

Kaisa frowned. 'Yes, I know that...' What did he mean by 'not your mother'?

'It's me who's paying for it.'

His pale-blue eyes, over the wonky glasses, focused on Kaisa. His lips turned downwards. His hand, holding the card was trembling.

'I don't understand.'

A chill ran down Kaisa's spine. Even before he said it she knew what he was going to say.

'I don't want that bitch on the invitation. And I don't want her anywhere near the wedding.'

He threw the card at her and tucked his reading glasses into the top pocket of his shirt. He reached for the remote and turned on the TV.

Kaisa picked up the invitation. She felt sick and faint.

In the long silence that followed, she struggled to find the right words.

'You mean my own mother can't come to my wedding?'

She willed her voice to sound normal or firm, but she heard the tremble in it.

Her father stayed silent, his expression grave. Turning to Kaisa he said drily, 'I'm paying for everything. Not your mother. Me. And I don't want to see that bitch there. That's my final word on the matter.'

He returned his gaze to the TV and increased the volume, probably to drown out any protests Kaisa might have.

He needn't have bothered.

Kaisa ran to her bedroom clutching the plastic bag of invitations. The hate she felt for her father in that moment was greater than the love she felt for Peter.

25

Kaisa lay face down on her bed. Her head was spinning and she was trying to make sense of what had just happened, when she heard the front door slam shut. She waited for a few minutes.

She crept out of her room and walked into the darkened kitchen. The house was quiet. She looked outside. The parking space where her father's Saab was usually parked was empty.

Kaisa took a deep breath and wiped her face with the threadbare tissue she had in her hand. She walked to the telephone in the hall and lifted the heavy receiver.

'Mum?' she croaked.

'What's the matter?'

Hearing her mother's concerned voice made tears prick the backs of her eyes. Kaisa dabbed them with her tissue to stop the flow. 'Dad, he...' Trying not to cry took such an effort; she couldn't finish the sentence.

Her mother sighed heavily. 'What's he done now?'

Kaisa hesitated. How much of what her father had said could she really tell her mother? She didn't want to upset her, but she needed to speak to someone.

'He said you wouldn't be allowed to come...' The tears fell. She sobbed down the line. 'He said because he's paying for the wedding you are not welcome. He said I'm not to invite you.'

'What?!'

Kaisa imagined her mother getting up from the chair in the hallway of her flat and straightening her back, ready for a fight. When it came to her daughters, her mum was like a lioness. Kaisa felt a little better – and a little safer.

'Oh Mum! What do I do?'

Kaisa was full-on crying now. Should she get married in England? She couldn't see how she and Peter could afford to pay for the wedding. And she wouldn't ask Peter's parents for the money.

Without her father's contribution, there was no way she'd be able to marry Peter.

Kaisa heard her mother's quick intake of breath. 'I cannot believe he'd do that.'

It was a relief to hear her mother take her side, even without hearing the awful things her father had said. It assured Kaisa that she hadn't been over-reacting.

Her mother said firmly, 'Don't worry, I'll pay for your wedding.'

'But you don't have the money!' Kaisa felt guilty. 'That's not why I called –' she began.

Her mother interrupted her.

'I do have the funds. It's not a problem.'

A weary Kaisa leaned against the wall and slid down to the floor.

Her mother continued, 'I knew he was going to be trouble. Always the same, he just doesn't change.'

They ended the call and Kaisa felt better about everything. Her father had not yet returned. She enjoyed the time alone to process everything.

Half an hour later Sirkka called.

'Bastard!' she said. 'But don't worry, mum and I have discussed every-thing. We'll organise the wedding in Tampere; it's where you were born after all. And it's only a couple of hour's train journey from Helsinki. You can stay at grandmother's place and the English guests can stay in a hotel. I'm thinking of the cathedral for the wedding. I can't imagine the June date will be a problem, we have nearly six months to organise things. I also think that we should have the reception at Rosendahl Hotel by Lake Pyhäjärvi. It's a perfect location for the foreign guests.'

Sirkka shared her ideas about the menu – even the wines and cham-pagne they were going to serve. The more she talked the more Kaisa relaxed. She'd forgotten that as a qualified *maître d'*, Sirkka was the perfect person to organise the wedding. Why hadn't she thought to ask her before?

'All you have to do is turn up for the wedding. I'll take care of every-thing.' Sirkka said.

Kaisa's thoughts turned to the gown. She was going to ask Heli, a school friend and a dressmaker, who'd made her evening gown for the Hanken Ball. Kaisa couldn't wait to chat to her about designs. Ever since Peter's proposal in December, Kaisa had saved several pictures from magazines. In the fabric department at Stockmann's, where she worked weekends, they sold dress patterns. A Vogue design of a simple, silk tulle dress was her favourite, but she had no idea if her friend could make it, or where she might find the correct fabric. There was nothing even close to it at the store. There must be places in London where they sell soft, feathery tulle fabric, Kaisa thought.

'You still there?' Sirkka sounded concerned.

Kaisa tuned into the conversation again. 'Sorry, I'm just tired.'

'That's OK. I'll call you tomorrow with more details.' Sirkka hung up.

Kaisa phoned Heli next to tell her the news. She congratulated her and immediately agreed to make the dress. Exhausted, Kaisa fell into bed and slept soundly.

The next day there was still no sign of her father. Having to be at Heli's place on Lauttasaari Island at nine, Kaisa hurried out of the house. She hoped her father would stay at his girlfriend's for as long as possible, where she presumed he was hiding. She didn't think she could endure one more evening like their last with him. She couldn't wait to leave his house, and Finland, for good.

There was little snow left on the ground, just a few dirty patches on the side of the road. But a harsh northerly wind bit her skin as she walked along the streets of Lauttasaari. For the second time that week Kaisa was back on the island and wandering past her old flat. Why was she torturing herself like this? Was it because she was beginning to doubt she and Peter would ever make it down the aisle together? So many obstacles had been put in their way. Kaisa shrugged off such fatalistic thoughts, and marched past her old place without looking up at it.

Kaisa spent her last few days in Helsinki arranging the practical details of a move to another country.

On the Thursday she had an oral examination in methodology with her professor at Hanken. Kaisa was ill-prepared for the exam in his office on the fourth floor, but she somehow managed to pass.

Leaving his office and closing the door behind her, Kaisa stood for a moment in the wide, empty hall. This could be the last time she'd stand here. The space flooded suddenly with a bright sunlight, filtered through the large windows on one side of the sixties-style building. When she'd first stepped inside this building, four years ago, she'd been proud to get a place here but scared that she wouldn't be accepted by the other students. Kaisa had known little about the Swedish-speaking community in Finland. It never occurred to her that this place would turn her life upside down, or that it would mark the start of the end of her life in Finland. She felt older and wiser now.

Yet as Kaisa stood there in the empty hall, listening to the familiar echoing sounds of students' footsteps in the stairwell, she was less sure of her future than she'd ever been in her life.

She glanced at her watch and cursed. Kaisa was due to be at Tuuli's place in five minutes' time. She and Tuuli were going to the university disco that evening for old times' sake, even though they rarely went these days. Tuuli had already finished her degree, and was now working in a bank in the centre of Helsinki. Her flat in Töölö was a couple of tram stops away from Hanken. When Tuuli suggested that Kaisa stay the night she agreed. Kaisa didn't want to spend any more nights in her father's house than she had to.

She ran down the stairs, taking two at a time, and exited through the glazed, double doors of the main Hanken building. The tram approached the stop on the other side of the street. She just made it before the doors closed.

When she arrived at Tuuli's place, Kaisa was touched to find her friend had made an early supper. They shared a bottle of wine while reminiscing about their years at Hanken.

'I'll miss you,' Tuuli said, touching Kaisa's arm across the table.

Tears welled in Tuuli's eyes and her own. She was suddenly aware of the life-changing decision she had made. In December, accepting Peter's offer of marriage had seemed natural, even a relief, after so many years of uncertainty about their future together. She hadn't even considered how hard it would be to leave her best friend behind.

'This is not goodbye. I'll see you in June, before the wedding,' Kaisa replied. She tried to swallow down the lump forming in her throat.

Kaisa reminded Tuuli she'd be back for at least two weeks for the fitting of the wedding gown, and a hen party, which Heli and her other school friends had already started planning.

'Of course,' Tuuli replied. 'But you promise to write, yes?'

Kaisa stood up and gave her friend a long hug.

'I promise.'

·   ·   ·

Friday afternoon was Kaisa's last shift at Stockmann's. When she saw her colleagues, she realised she would miss them too. But their endless questions, about what she would to do in England, when she was going to get married and where she would to live, exhausted her. The doubts in her mind about her decision to move weren't helping. She wished for the shift to end.

Half an hour before closing time the floor manager gave Kaisa a card and a present: a pinnie made out of blue-and-white checked fabric – the colours of the Finnish flag. Kaisa hugged each of them in turn before returning her name badge, uniform and discount card to the personnel department on the top floor.

When she returned home later that evening, her legs ached so bad all she wanted to do was sit. The house was dark and quiet; still no sign of her father.

Kaisa had just settled down in front of the TV and put her feet up when the phone rang.

It was Peter.

'Oh, hi,' Kaisa said flatly.

'What's up?'

They'd been talking forever about the day she'd finally move to England. But now that day was almost here, she couldn't put into words how sad she felt about leaving. Instead of explaining she talked about the wedding, about how them finally being together forever was what kept Kaisa going. She talked about the arrangements for the big day, and that Sirkka was telephoning her daily with updates and questions about guest lists and table placements at the Rosendahl Hotel.

'Oh,' Peter said sounding distracted. 'Where did you say this hotel was again?'

Kaisa fell silent. She'd told him on several occasions about the changed venue, why it had happened and how upset she was with her father.

'You still there?' he asked.

'Yes. Look, I'll call you from Stockholm on Sunday, OK?' Kaisa snapped and put the receiver down.

She felt stupid for getting upset over such a small thing. What was the matter with her?

That night in bed, Kaisa heard the front door open and her father's familiar sounds. He kicked off his boots, rattled the clothes hangers in the hall and, after a while, flushed the loo. Then all fell quiet. Kaisa checked the time: it was well past midnight. She wondered if he was drunk. But his movements had sounded controlled enough.

For the next few hours she tossed and turned in her bed, sick at the thought of seeing her father. She'd managed to avoid him since their row. The previous Monday, rather than ask for help and risk seeing him, she'd ordered a taxi to take her and the two cardboard boxes containing her belongings to the railway station. They would take a month or so to arrive in Portsmouth. The taxi journey to Helsinki station had cost more than the transport to England, but it had been worth it.

But here he was back at home. And tomorrow, Saturday, he would be off work. How could Kaisa avoid saying goodbye to him in this small house?

Then there were the books she'd stolen from him. He owned two expensive volumes of Finnish/English dictionaries. In her fury following his outburst, Kaisa had packed both volumes in one of the cardboard boxes. They were currently in a container ship somewhere in the middle of the Baltic. She hoped he didn't notice the large gap in his bookshelf before she left.

26

A t around three in the morning, Kaisa finally fell asleep. She dreamt she'd hit her father with an ice-hockey stick and drawn blood; he'd been trying to lead a scared Kaisa into a darkened room. She woke with a start and heard movement in the kitchen. Her alarm clock showed it was five to seven in the morning. There was a strip of light under the door of her bedroom.

Kaisa got up to go to the bathroom. She looked from the open doorway to the kitchen to see her father. He was sitting at the table staring out of the window. Kaisa sighed.

She'd be out of here soon. She was due to take the train to the ferry port in Turku later, then the ferry to Stockholm and onwards through Europe to Harwich, leaving her country of birth for good.

Kaisa approached the kitchen, seeing that her father was still in his nightwear: a pair of long johns and an undershirt. He had a cup of coffee with no saucer in front of him. It was still dark outside and she wondered what he was looking at. But then he spotted Kaisa's reflection in the window and gave her a sheepish smile; she didn't return it. She didn't care if he was back to being nice, Dr Jekyll again. She looked forward to never having to deal with his dual personality again.

'Coffee?' he asked.

In spite of her anger Kaisa sat down. She wanted to take his cup and pour the hot coffee over his head. That he tried to appease her with that boyish smirk of his – as if all he needed for Kaisa to forgive him was to be nice to her again. She briefly wondered if there was vodka in his coffee, but when he poured her a cup and passed it to her she didn't get any hint of alcohol from his breath. He sat down heavily in the wooden chair, its faint creak the only sound in the kitchen. Her father's gaze was still on her, but he no longer smiled.

She looked elsewhere.

'So you're off today, then?' he asked.

Kaisa nodded.

'I'll drive you.'

She opened her mouth to say there was no need, but hesitated. His eyes were bloodshot and had dark circles under them. He was unshaven, and his hands shook when he fiddled with the ear of the coffee cup. Kaisa looked down at her own hands, seeing she'd inherited his bone structure. He was her dear father.

She chased the nostalgic thought away.

She wasn't going to fall into the trap of thinking he was the man she'd grown up with. This time Kaisa couldn't forgive him for the hurtful things he'd said about her mother, or for backing out of organising the wedding. Sirkka said he'd only done it to get out of paying for it, and Kaisa was beginning to suspect this was true.

'No, I'll take a taxi,' Kaisa said.

'Nonsense, you need to save your money. I'm taking you. No discussion.'

He looked serious.

Kaisa shook her head at him. Not knowing what else to say, she got up and left the kitchen. She trembled as she sat on her bed. What game was her father playing?

'What time is your train?' he called out.

'Three o'clock,' she shouted back, realising too late that she'd just accepted his offer of the lift. She put her head in her hands and groaned. Kaisa checked the time: twenty-five minutes past seven. In eight hours she'd be on the train to Turku and in twenty-four hours she'd be with her mother and sister in Stockholm.

She got dressed quickly and got on with her last-minute chores. She needed to go to the shopping centre in Tapiola, where she planned to withdraw all her money from her bank account. That would take an hour; the rest would be spent packing up her room.

. . .

Kaisa returned later to find the house was empty. Relieved, she dialled her mother's number and told her about her father's offer of a lift.

'Calm down,' Pirjo said. 'If he wants to take you to the station let him.'

Her mother sounded so strong, and Kaisa wished she were already with her in Stockholm. Her relationship with her father was so draining. Wasn't this supposed to be a happy time? She was about to marry the man of her dreams, the love of her life. Why was her father trying to make it so hellish for her?

She finished the conversation up with her mother and went to the bathroom. There, she washed her face, in an attempt to pull herself together.

With half an hour before Kaisa had to leave, her father returned. She'd been about to call a taxi when she heard the front door open. Kaisa had no idea where he'd been but was glad he'd stayed away while she packed. She was sitting in the kitchen eating a rye sandwich and drinking a cup of coffee when he walked in. Her stomach churned with nerves when she saw him, and it killed her appetite. But just like Matti her father hated wasted food, so she forced down the last piece of bread and cheese.

'All ready?' he said from the doorway. He nodded at Kaisa's suitcase in the hall.

'Yes.'

'We'd better be off then.'

He picked up the case and grunted. Kaisa let out a short laugh that came out more like a snort.

She knew her luggage was heavy. She'd bought a set of wheels that fitted the base of the suitcase, to make it easier to transport. Without them, she wouldn't manage the long walk between the railway station at Turku Harbour and the ferry terminal. Maybe it was good her father would be driving her. He could help to lift the case onto the train at Helsinki – something a taxi driver would not do. Or at least that's what Kaisa hoped he would do.

But in the car, she soon regretted taking a lift from him.

He was crossing the long bridge by Lauttasaari Island. Under the dim light of the car interior her father said, 'So what's happening with the wedding?'

She couldn't believe her ears. How could he ask her about the ceremony after what he'd done to her? He'd nearly made it impossible for Kaisa to marry at all, and now he was curious about the details?

'We're getting married at Tampere cathedral. Mother's paying for the wedding. So you needn't worry.'

Kaisa hoped he detected the sarcasm in her voice.

'She can afford it, can she?' he sneered.

She looked at him. His eyes were on the road and his lips were set in a straight line. He looked a little tidier than he had that morning: clean-shaven and wearing his striped Marimekko shirt with the dark-blue cords. This was the outfit she'd chosen for him that day when they'd gone shopping. It had been a strange day; she'd been torn between choosing Matti and Peter. Her father had been nice, behaving like a normal, loving, funny man who was simply taking his daughter out shopping, and then to an expensive restaurant for lunch. Kaisa wondered again how he could change from one extreme to another so quickly.

As if he'd read her thoughts, he said, 'It all went wrong with us when you moved in, you know.'

Kaisa's anger rose again. 'Really!'

'Yes. And I bet it was your mother's idea.'

'What?'

'It's all her nasty plan to get me out of the way, I'm sure. You and I have always got along, unlike your sister...' When he mentioned Sirkka he had the good sense to stop. But he continued with his incredible theory about her mum's motives.

'Your mother knew our living together would cause a rift between us and that's exactly what she was after.'

Kaisa fell silent. The car idled at the traffic lights at Hietaniemi. She looked at the red lights and counted to ten. But ten wasn't a high enough number to calm her rage.

'So it's nothing to do with the fact that you're a selfish, nasty bastard who doesn't love anybody and will never be happy? You're mean and don't want anyone else to be happy, either. You don't think of anyone else but yourself. You never have. You and I have never "got on", as you put it. Have you forgotten how you tried to hit me? You weren't satisfied with hitting mother black and blue in Stockholm, you had to strike your sixteen-year-old daughter too. I guess I was just a little annoying, wasn't I?'

Kaisa's father looked from the road to her. 'But I never hit you!'

He looked back at the road.

'No,' she said quietly. 'But you came very close, raising your hand. That's enough.'

His breathing grew heavy. They passed Arkadiankatu and the university disco.

Kaisa spoke again.

'And another thing: last year when I was really ill and phoned you from hospital, you didn't want to help me. You stayed away just so you wouldn't catch the stomach bug. During the two weeks when I was so poorly, who were you thinking about then? I had salmonella poisoning and, frankly, needed to be looked after. Where were you? Hiding at your girlfriend's place, that's where!'

He said nothing. Kaisa, too, was now quiet. Her little speech had exhausted her. Her father drove in silence down Annankatu, past the bus station, across Mannerheim Street and parked outside the railway station. When she got out of the car her father was already by the boot, lifting her luggage out. Kaisa hurried out and lunged for the handle of the suitcase, not looking at him. But her father nudged Kaisa's hand away with his elbow, locked the car and, struggling with the heavy bag, dragged it towards the station building. Kaisa couldn't move. She'd rather carry the case herself than speak to her father again. Why wouldn't he just leave her be? She'd told him what she thought of him now. She didn't regret one word, but she had nothing more to say.

She picked up her Marimekko shoulder bag and the wheels for the suitcase, and followed her father into the station.

Her father stood next to his daughter on the platform, his shoulders hunched, looking lost. He was breathing heavy from carrying the case but Kaisa felt no pity for him. A bitterly cold wind blew through the station matching the chilly mood between them.

He had asked her what carriage her pre-booked seat was in. Kaisa told him, but those were the only words to pass between them since their fight in the car.

The train pulled up.

'Go on,' he said nodding at the door of the train carriage.

Beads of sweat marked his forehead, but Kaisa didn't care. She couldn't wait to tell her mother what she'd said to him, how, after all these years of biting her tongue, she'd stood up to him and told her father exactly what she thought of him.

Kaisa found her seat on the train. Her father tried to lift the heavy bag onto the parcel shelf.

'No,' she said and motioned to a space between the seats.

'Right.' He slid the bag in and looked at his daughter.

She returned his gaze, feeling strong. She was in the right. He was a mean bastard, just like Sirkka had always said.

Her father surprised her by moving closer. He gave her a bear hug.

She froze.

Holding her tightly he said, 'I'm sorry.'

He let go of Kaisa and hurried off the train.

27

T he last leg of Kaisa's train journey across Europe, from Harwich to London's Liverpool Street Station, seemed to take forever. She was dead tired from three days of travelling, and had not slept a wink during the Channel crossing. By the time she got to the train at Harwich it was full, with the only free seat left in the smoking compartment.

When the train at last pulled into Liverpool Street Station Kaisa waited until most people were out of the carriage. Once she'd fixed the wheels onto the suitcase Kaisa quickly wheeled it down the long platform, towards a busy station concourse. She looked around for Peter. He was tall so should be easy to spot. But she couldn't see him. Kaisa waited for five minutes before she began to worry. Businessmen dressed in pinstripe suits and dark overcoats frowned at her. Their glances made her feel self conscious. She looked shabby next to them in her dark-blue jeans and tennis shoes.

She spotted several phone booths in the middle of the station. After another ten minutes had passed with no sign of Peter, Kaisa considered joining the queue. But who would she phone? She didn't want to talk to Peter's mother in Wiltshire. Evie probably wouldn't know where Peter was anyway. And Kaisa didn't know if anyone was at home in the house in Southsea. Had she even written down the telephone number of the house? She'd never used a phone booth in England. She worried she wouldn't be able to use it. Everything – trains, the Tube, buses, banks and shops –

worked differently to back home. They even drove on the wrong side of the road.

Both of the booths in the middle of the station concourse were occupied, with one person waiting outside. Kaisa decided against using one. She didn't want to risk people getting annoyed at her while she tried to work out the telephone system.

She would stay put and wait. The large clock at the end of the station concourse told her the train had arrived on time. Perhaps Peter had got the wrong day? Kaisa was sure she'd told him the correct date and time when he'd phoned her in Stockholm. She'd smiled when Peter had told her how much he was looking forward to staying in the house together, even if it was just for a couple of weeks. He would be leaving for his NATO job in Naples in only ten days' time.

Perhaps something had happened and he had to go early? No. He would have arranged for word to be sent to her, or for someone else to come and meet her instead.

As more time passed, Kaisa began to feel angry. Why was he late, this time of all times? She imagined how delighted her father would be to see his stroppy daughter now.

'I told you, foreigners can't be trusted,' he'd say.

Standing in the middle of the station concourse, feeling shabby and foreign, getting in the way of the people hurrying past her, Kaisa pictured a satisfied look on Matti's face.

'See, he's left you in the lurch, just as I told you he would.'

Kaisa took a deep breath and shook the negative thoughts from her mind.

She spotted a row of plastic seats by the side of the stairs and walked over to them. She sat down opposite the station clock. She dug the carton of tax-free Silk Cut out of her bag that she'd bought on the ferry for Peter. She got out a cigarette and lit one. She didn't usually smoke unless she had a drink, but she needed something to calm her nerves. She checked the time and decided to wait until two o'clock. That was over an hour from now. If Peter hadn't turned up by then she'd take a taxi to the nearest hotel and book a room for the night. Kaisa had just about enough money for that. She hoped it wouldn't come to that. Any minute now Peter would appear in the station concourse and look around, spot Kaisa, run to her and fling his arms around her, apologising profusely.

But Peter was nowhere to be seen.

. . .

Kaisa waited on the orange plastic seat at Liverpool Street Station for over three hours. It was a chilly February day and as the light began to fade in the late afternoon, she finally saw a tall man running through the throng of people, dodging an old woman pulling a large suitcase and several men in smart suits carrying small, black briefcases.

'God, I'm so sorry!'

Peter was panting. He took Kaisa into his arms.

'I was afraid you'd gone.'

'I have nowhere to go,' she replied quietly. The annoyance she'd felt earlier had turned into relief as soon as she set eyes on Peter.

Tears she'd been holding back for several lonely hours rolled down her face. Kaisa wiped them away carefully, trying not to smudge her mascara.

'You poor darling,' Peter said and cupped her face.

He kissed her and hugged her. She drew in his familiar scent of coconut shaving cream and tobacco.

'You're safe now,' he said.

Kaisa relaxed in his arms.

Peter explained how he'd been waiting at Waterloo. After an hour he had enquired about the trains from Harwich. To his horror, he realised Kaisa's train was arriving at Liverpool Street instead.

'The traffic was awful and I couldn't find a parking space anywhere,' he said, as he lugged her heavy suitcase down the stairs to the busy street outside. It was already dark and there were lines of traffic. Kaisa realised it must be rush hour.

'It's a bit of a hike to the car,' Peter said taking Kaisa's arm in his.

They walked along one narrow street after another.

'Are you OK?' he asked. He looked so miserable, so apologetic.

She lost her anger when she saw Peter. The warmth of his fingers against her cold hand felt so good, she didn't care that he'd left her in the station.

Kaisa smiled. 'I'm fine.'

28

They spent the ten days together alone in the little house in Southsea. Peter's friend, Jeff, whose parents owned the place, was still in Ireland, and a new tenant wasn't due to arrive until later that summer.

They lay in bed on their last Sunday morning together. Peter was returning to Naples early the next day. Kaisa tried not to think about having to say goodbye to him again so soon.

'I hope you'll be OK all alone here,' Peter said.

She'd practically lived on her own for the past four years – even while staying with her father – through the tumultuous affair with Peter and her difficult separation from her fiancé.

Kaisa laughed and threw a pillow at him. 'Of course I will be.'

After she waved Peter off at the train station the next morning, Kaisa took the bus home. Alone, the walls of the little terraced house closed in on her. The hallway was cold and dark. For the first time she noticed how shabby the house in Southsea was.

Perched on the edge of the lumpy, three-piece suite Jeff had inherited from his parents, she looked around the bare room. There was a TV on a cardboard box in the corner and a record player with two large speakers on either side. Perhaps she should get a coffee table, or a throw and a few cushions, to brighten the place up a little.

Kaisa went upstairs, and began arranging her books in one of the small bedrooms that Peter had set up as her office. They'd found an old trestle table in the conservatory at the back of the house, which Kaisa had wiped clean and set the old typewriter on that she'd lugged all the way from Finland. She had a thesis to research and write, as well as several deferred exams to pass.

As she opened one of the large volumes on Futurism, in the end she was glad for the peace and quiet to study. She was a Finn, and being alone came naturally to her.

Kaisa spent most of the first two months in England studying for the final exams she would take at the Finnish Embassy in Chelsea. Sitting at the rickety table in her office, Kaisa would find herself gazing across at the neighbour's garden that backed onto theirs. The identical looking house was occupied by a young family. The mother was always at home. Kaisa usually saw her washing dishes at the kitchen sink, or pegging washing onto a line in the back garden. She usually wore a skirt and a blouse or jumper, never looking up. Kaisa guessed she was too busy to care about her neighbours.

Kaisa wondered if her life would be like that a few years after she got married. Sometimes she even daydreamed about having Peter's children, something she swore she would never have. Horrified at the thought, she would turn back to her exam revision.

She had even started drinking tea. Even though the smell of the milky drink made her gag, she was determined to make it her new, very British, habit. She wanted to surprise Peter when he returned home.

That evening, as she lay in bed listening to the now-familiar distant noises of the city, Kaisa thought about how far she and Peter had come. From meeting at the British Embassy four years before, to walking down the aisle together in less than three months' time. She reminisced about all the happy and tearful phone calls they'd had; the heart-breaking goodbyes and the blissful reunions; the many misunderstandings and the realisation they couldn't live without one another. Kaisa's stomach tightened with joy when she thought about the wedding. She could hardly believe it was going to happen.

The invitations had been sent. The ten English guests had all replied. They had even bought tickets for their flight over. Sirkka had booked the hotel in Tampere. It was all arranged. Kaisa would fly to Finland two weeks before the wedding. Peter would fly with the guests a few days before the ceremony.

The only thing left for him to get was something called a Certificate of Non-Impediment, so that he could marry in Finland. Kaisa still had to find a suitable silk tulle fabric for her dress and send it to Heli. She had planned to look after her first exam in London. She knew exactly what she wanted and had the addresses of three shops that sold fabrics near Oxford Street.

Before he left, Peter had given Kaisa a map of London and told her how to take the Tube from Waterloo Station to Sloane Square. Being alone in London was scary but exhilarating. Kaisa followed Peter's directions and found the right line and the right stop on the Tube.

Emerging from the dark tunnels and dressed in a sombre black suit, Kaisa carried her black-leather briefcase containing her study books. Not wanting to appear like a tourist she avoided looking at the map, and walked out of the station in what she hoped was the direction of Chesham Place. It was around noon on a Tuesday in mid-March. She matched the rushed steps of the people around her, pretending that she belonged in this part of the city.

The Finnish Embassy was just beyond a large green park, fenced off with a set of freshly painted wrought-iron railings. A sign on the gate read 'Private'. Kaisa assumed the park belonged to the owners of the white stucco-fronted houses surrounding it. With fewer people about, she slowed her pace and dared to look at her map. She was very close. Turning a new corner she saw the Finnish flag.

Over March and April Kaisa travelled to the embassy five times. She got to know the staff well during the three-hour exams. The same Finnish lady, with brown hair and dark-rimmed glasses, would stand by Kaisa each time she pulled out the exam papers from the sealed, brown envelope. Her makeup was always heavy, but carefully, applied. Even when the weather got warmer in April, the invigilator still wore the same tweed skirt and white blouse, often with a blue-and-white silk scarf tied loosely around her neck. Each time the woman closed the door and left Kaisa alone, she'd say, 'Good luck, see you later.'

After Kaisa finished her last exam, in late April 1984, the invigilator said, 'It's our staff sauna night, perhaps you'd like to stay?'

She told Kaisa how one of the previous ambassadors had built a Finnish sauna in the basement, and that evening was the scheduled bathing night for the female employees. If the Ambassador wasn't entertaining, they'd have a sauna session once or twice a month. Kaisa told her she hadn't brought a towel or a change of clothing, but the woman said she could borrow some items kept aside for guests.

Kaisa spent an hour alone in the wood-cladded sauna in the dimly-lit basement. The sauna smelt of pine and soap, and the bite of heat on her skin, as the *löyly* water hit the hot stones, made her suddenly feel homesick. After, the invigilator hugged Kaisa and made her promise to say hello to her when she came next, to apply for a new passport.

Kaisa usually left the Finnish Embassy feeling tired and glad that another exam was over. She was always in a hurry to get away, whether it was to go shopping on King's Road or take the train back to Southsea. But that evening, after her last paper, feeling fresh and relaxed from the sauna, she didn't want to leave. It felt too much like she was severing another tie to her mother country. Even though the embassy would always be there for her, it wouldn't be the same to return as an ordinary citizen to renew a passport. She'd never again be offered a sauna, or be allowed to sit in that little room – officially a part of Finland – feverishly writing, straining to remember anything she'd learnt at her desk in Southsea.

The following day, Kaisa had a meeting with the naval padre. Peter had organised the appointment before he left for Naples. According to him, the padre would issue a Certificate of Non-Impediment for Peter, the final piece of red tape before the wedding could go ahead.

The padre, a tall man who towered over Kaisa, wore a black priest's outfit. As they shook hands at the front door of the Southsea house, the padre smiled.

She asked him in and made him a cup of tea. They sat on the sofa in the front room facing each other.

'And how may I help you, dear?' he asked.

'I am from Finland. My English fiancé, a lieutenant in the Royal Navy, and I are getting married there next month. He said you can issue him with a Certificate of Non-Impediment.'

'Ah,' the padre said, and drained his cup. He looked around for somewhere to place his empty cup and saucer, before carefully putting it down on the floor. He placed one hand on the other and said, 'There may be a little problem with that.'

'A problem?' Kaisa's heart sank. Peter had told her this was a mere formality.

'Well...what is the date of the happy occasion?'

Kaisa told him they'd be married the first Saturday in June, in just under five weeks' time.

'Hmm, well... Oh dear. You see, I don't issue these certificates. What happens in England – and this may well be the same in Norway –'

'Finland,' Kaisa interrupted him.

She got a sick feeling in the pit of her stomach.

He gave Kaisa a sheepish look and smiled. 'Of course, yes, Finland.'

The expression in his eyes did not change when he spoke. He reached his hand across and patted Kaisa's knee.

'For your fiancé to get a Certificate of Non-Impediment he needs to have the banns read in his home parish. Has he had his banns read?'

She hadn't heard of them before.

'No, I don't think so.'

'Well then he needs to do that first. But it takes six weeks.'

Kaisa drew in a breath. The padre patted her knee again.

She pulled her leg away and stared at the padre.

He placed his hands on his lap. 'Can you, perhaps, change the date of the wedding?'

It was impossible. Kaisa thought about how much organisation Sirkka had done for the day. How all the English guests had bought their expensive flight tickets. How Peter's mother and godmother had already bought their outfits and matching hats. How the cathedral in Tampere had been booked, how the hotel for the reception had been reserved, how the menu had been decided...

'No,' she stated.

'I understand, dear.' The meek expression on the padre's face barely changed.

Kaisa knew she needed to find a way around this, but her mind was blank. Did this mean they couldn't get married? The pastor in Tampere had said that without this certificate he couldn't marry them.

The padre explained. 'The purpose of the banns being read in the groom's home parish is to establish that he's not been married before...' He hesitated when he saw Kaisa's shocked face. 'Which I'm sure he hasn't been, of course, but when a young man marries abroad the foreign, or in this case the Fi...Fin...'

'Finnish.'

'Ah, yes, the Finnish church has to be certain that he is not committing a crime.'

'But...' Kaisa stared at the padre. What the hell was he telling her? 'We don't have six weeks.'

'Well, no,' he said and went for Kaisa's knee again.

Kaisa moved her leg away before he could touch it.

The padre coughed. 'What you could do is have a civil ceremony here in England, at a registry office.' – he said the last two words slowly as if Kaisa was half-witted – 'and then have a blessing in the church abroad. The wording of the ceremony is almost the same, and in the eyes of God you'll still be married in the church in...hmm...your country.'

The padre smiled weakly.

'I have the telephone number.'

He rummaged in his worn-looking leather satchel, fished out a number and gave it to her.

After the padre had left, Kaisa went straight to the telephone under the stairs and dialled the number for Portsmouth Registry Office.

The friendly man who answered the phone listened to Kaisa's rambling explanation of the situation. How her fiancé was in the Navy and stationed abroad, how moments ago she'd only just found out that the wedding they'd planned for months may not happen, and how the only solution the naval padre had suggested was to have a civil ceremony in England and a blessing in the church in Finland.

Occasionally he said, 'Oh dear,' or 'I understand,' or 'Yes, yes.'

When Kaisa finished, he said, 'So would you like me to have a look in the diary to see what dates we have before the 2nd of June?'

'Yes please!'

She exhaled slowly and waited for the man to come back to the phone.

'Well, I do have a date this coming Friday, but then the next weekend date I have is the 9th of June.'

The first date was four days away and the June date was seven days after their wedding in Finland, which was too late. As they discussed the dates, she realised that day was Walburgh Night, the student festival back home, and felt suddenly homesick. All her friends in Helsinki would be going out to celebrate, wearing their student caps and drinking too much. Meanwhile, Kaisa was stuck trying to organise something that felt very much like a shotgun wedding.

Then it dawned on her: she could be married in four days time, not in five weeks time!

'Which date would you like me to book?' the man asked.

Kaisa considered the question for a fraction of a second.

'Friday 4th May, please.'

He went through the cost over the phone and asked if Kaisa could post a cheque as soon as possible. She promised she would and hung up.

Next, Kaisa called the number Peter had given her for Italy. Peter sounded surprised when he heard Kaisa's voice. They never telephoned each other during the day.

'Are you OK?'

Kaisa hadn't realised how furious she was with him until she heard his voice. During almost every phone call from Finland, she'd nagged Peter about the certificate, and again when she arrived in England. He'd arranged the meeting with the naval padre just before he left for Naples and assured Kaisa it was a mere formality.

'No, I'm not,' Kaisa said.

'Really?' Peter sounded worried.

'The padre told me this morning that he can't issue the certificate. You know, the Certificate of Non-Impediment you need in order to marry me?'

Keeping her explanation short and trying to keep calm, Kaisa told Peter the whole sorry tale. Including the change of date.

'We're going to get married this Friday?' Peter asked.

He sounded calm, considering the circumstances.

'Yes,' she replied simply.

Neither of them spoke for a moment.

Finally losing her patience Kaisa barked at him, 'This was the ONLY thing you had to do, and you couldn't even be bothered with that!'

She held back tears. She wanted to scream at him. She wanted to tell him that if he didn't want to marry her, he should say so. Kaisa listened to the sound of Peter breathing down the line, feeling numb. When she had arrived in England Peter had been late meeting her at the train station. Then he had delayed the meeting with the padre. Was he trying to stop the wedding from going ahead?

'I'm really sorry,' Peter said whispering. 'Look, I'll call you back in an hour. I need to arrange a pass to come home. But I'm going to do it. Don't worry, everything will be alright.'

'It will?'

'Yes. And Kaisa?'

Peter spoke in a whisper. Kaisa knew he was trying to say something without being overheard, 'I love you, don't ever forget it. And I can't wait to be married to you. The sooner the better.'

29

T wo days after the padre's visit, exactly one month before they were due to marry in Finland, Peter returned from Naples. As the evening sun was setting at the end of the tree-lined street in Portsmouth, he stepped out of the taxi. Looking tanned and so handsome in his official Navy jumper and trousers, Kaisa had to catch her breath. Peter kissed her on the doorstep. They walked arm in arm into the house, with Peter carrying his Navy issue 'Pusser's Grip' over his shoulder. He took her upstairs, and before they had a chance to talk about the wedding they made love. His body looked leaner and his tanned skin made his eyes look darker.

Peter and Kaisa lay in bed after and she rested her head on his chest. She breathed in his scent that included something new, and they talked about the wedding.

'So this time on Friday you'll be my wife,' Peter said and kissed Kaisa again.

He jumped out of bed, opened a new carton of Silk Cut and lit a cigarette.

'Sorry, I've been smoking a lot more in Italy. Everyone on the base smokes.'

Kaisa smiled. Italy suited him; his body was bronzed and muscular; the black hairs that covered his legs had turned slightly lighter. The sight of him mesmerised her.

Peter got back in bed and started telling Kaisa about his journey from Naples to Rome, from where he'd caught a plane to Heathrow.

'The driver they gave me was Italian. He drove like a maniac along mountain roads that had sheer drops down to the sea and dark tunnels that seemed to go on forever. He scared the living daylights out of me. He drove through every red light. He said you didn't have to follow traffic signals in Italy, that they were just advisory. My God, I thought I'd never make it back to you alive!'

Kaisa stared at first, and then laughed. But the thought that she could have lost him in a stupid car accident hit her. She would rather have her Englishman hopelessly disorganised than not have him at all.

'What did the others say when they found out about the certificate?'

Peter gave Kaisa a sheepish look. 'The Italians just shrugged their shoulders and the English said what a prat I was.'

She play-punched his side. 'They were right.'

Peter took Kaisa into his arms and kissed her.

'But I'm happy because it means I can marry you sooner,' he said.

Peter got up and put on his boxer shorts and a worn-out T-shirt that he dug out of the wardrobe. Kaisa had tried to arrange their clothes as best she could, though there was very little room for their things in the tiny space. Once they were married, Peter had told her, they'd get a large three-bedroom married quarter right in the centre of Southsea, though he didn't know exactly where. Kaisa couldn't wait to move into their own place.

'Thank goodness we're alone in the house,' Peter said walking out.

She heard him take the stairs down. He shouted up to Kaisa.

'I'll phone around to let people know about the wedding. Then we'll go to the pub, shall we?'

She answered yes, then stretched out on the bed and listened to his footsteps through the open door. She heard him dial a number and talk to someone. 'Yeah, this Friday, can you make it?'

Back at home Peter was all action. His second call was to Jeff, who was also his best man. He returned to the bedroom and filled her in on their conversation.

'He's going to try to get weekend leave from his posting in Northern Ireland.'

Next he got in touch with Jeff's parents, who owned the Southsea house and also ran a pub and B&B in Old Portsmouth. Hearing Peter's news, they offered to give Kaisa and Peter a small reception after the registry office wedding, in the breakfast room upstairs.

Peter laughed when he told Kaisa how the conversation with his friend had gone.

'Me: Listen, I'm getting married. Him: Yes I know, I'm your best man. Me: No, I'm getting married this Friday. Him: WHAT?'

After a few more phone calls, Peter managed to gather about twenty people for the short-notice wedding. Kaisa was amazed by his capacity to get things done.

She dressed in a pair of jeans and one of Peter's old submarine jumpers. Sitting on the bottom of the stairs, she watched in awe as he made his phone calls, laughing with people, joking with them about his inability to organise the certificate, and about how angry Kaisa had been.

'But I'm not mad at you anymore,' she said to him after one such jokey call.

'I know, darling,' he said. He looked her over. 'My clothes suit you.' He gave her another quick kiss.

Leafing through his black notebook again, he dialled another number. The truth was, Kaisa was blissfully happy; happy to watch him arrange everything; happy just to hold him; happy to be married to him sooner than planned.

A thought occurred to her. What would her mother and sister say when they found out she would already be married when she walked down the aisle in Tampere cathedral?

The day of the registry office wedding was gloriously sunny. During the two days of frantic organising, Peter had enrolled the help of their neighbours in Southsea, a couple who lived opposite them and who Kaisa hardly knew. The husband had deep sideburns and grey hair. All she remembered about him was he'd got very drunk at the parties she'd been to in their house. In his inebriated state, he'd get his guitar out and sing. His wife was a short, jolly woman called Sally. She was in her forties and had jet-black hair, with white roots at the parting. Sally had always been incredibly kind to Kaisa. When she found out about the wedding, she called over immediately and demanded to know if Kaisa needed her help.

'You must have something old, something blue and something borrowed,' Sally said, ushering Peter out of the way.

The next day, she took Kaisa shopping on Palmerston Road, a small high street in Southsea. She promised she'd be over the night before the wedding to make sure Kaisa had company. Peter was planning to go out with his friends, 'to commiserate his last night of freedom.' He was going to stay the night in the bed and breakfast Jeff's parents ran above their pub.

Peter squeezed Kaisa's shoulders. 'You going to be alright on your own?'

She nodded. She'd lived alone in the house in Southsea for weeks. Why would this one night be any different?

But on the night before the wedding Kaisa was glad of company. She and Sally sat on the velour sofa in the front room of the terraced house and emptied half a bottle of Smirnoff that Sally had brought with her.

'I remembered you said Finns drink vodka.'

Kaisa told her about her ex-fiancé, Matti, about the night at the British Embassy when she first met Peter, about his 'accident', about the tennis player, about her father, and about her mother and sister. Sally held Kaisa's hand and listened. Kaisa had never told anyone so many secrets before.

On the day of the wedding, Kaisa sat in the back of her neighbours' car, clutching the posy of white-and-pink roses Sally had ordered for her. Sally sat with her while her husband drove. Kaisa took her hand and thanked her. Her body shook and Sally put her arm around her shoulders. The black curls of her new friend's hair touched her cheek. She smelt the strong musk perfume she wore.

'You'll be fine, girl. You know you love him and he loves you, so there's nothing to worry about,' Sally said and smiled.

Her husband nodded vigorously from the front seat, as if agreeing with her.

Kaisa smiled. She knew they were both right. But last night alone in the large bed, listening to the empty house creak all around her, she'd panicked. She would be marrying Peter and there wouldn't be a single person there who knew her – except for Sally who she'd only known a matter of weeks. Kaisa was abroad and utterly alone. She didn't have the heart to tell her sister or mother about the civil ceremony. She didn't want to spoil the real wedding in Finland for them. But while Kaisa had lain there, wide awake and still drunk on vodka, she realised this was it. In a few hours, she and Peter would be joined together in law.

Forever.

'You look lovely,' Sally said. The car stopped and she helped Kaisa out of the car gently.

Kaisa was wearing a new white hat, that she'd bought while shopping with Sally, and a white skirt and top her friend Heli had made, before she'd left for England. The only blue in Kaisa's outfit was a lacy garter she'd bought at the same time as the hat. Her white shoes were the something old;

they were the same shoes she'd worn to the cocktail party the night she'd met Peter. Finally, Sally had lent her a gold bracelet, which was the only item of jewellery she wore, apart from a set of pearl earrings and her diamond engagement ring.

Outside the registry office were a few smiling faces. The second Kaisa walked towards them, they hurried up the steps to the registry office and disappeared inside.

Kaisa's nerves would not let her be as Sally accompanied her inside. Ahead was a mahogany staircase leading up to the registry office. When she saw Peter standing next to Jeff at the top of the stairs and smiling down at her, her legs almost gave way. Peter came down and met her halfway.

He kissed Kaisa lightly on the lips and said, 'You ready?'

She looked into his eyes and nodded. He placed Kaisa's hand in the crook of his arm and nodded to Jeff, who disappeared behind a set of double doors.

'We'll wait here just for a second, and then we'll go in,' he whispered in her ear.

30

K aisa and Peter fell sound asleep at about five in the afternoon in the huge bed at The Portsmouth Hilton Hotel. They were both exhausted after the ceremony at the registry office where – with her trembling voice and in his confident, sure words – they'd promised to love and honour each other for as long as they lived. At the end of the ceremony when Kaisa had been told to sit down at a desk and sign a large book, she was glad to rest her trembling limbs. Peter gripped her shoulders and, bending over her, also signed his name. There were pictures; everyone wanted to take one.

At the lunch reception, they'd stood to receive the congratulations, had lifted their glasses of champagne hundreds of times, and had cut the cake with a naval sword acquired by Jeff. Kaisa's jaw ached from all the happy smiling.

Most of all, she was relieved she'd made it through the afternoon without bursting into tears or collapsing in a heap. She'd worried she would somehow forget to breathe, that she wouldn't be able to say anything during the ceremony, or afterwards at the reception. Kaisa was afraid she would say the wrong thing when she spoke to all the kind and happy people, who'd gone to such trouble to make the day special for her – a foreign girl no one really knew – and Peter.

Everything had been a new experience for Kaisa; she'd never been to an English wedding before. Apparently, the sword was how a naval officer traditionally cut his wedding cake. The cake itself was different too: a dark and fruity tea cake rather than a sponge, which was more typical in Finland. The vows were similar; although as soon as she'd said the words she forgot them. The small paper flowers that were thrown over them, 'confetti', Peter had called it, was also different. In Finland they threw rice at the newly-weds.

Then there was the strange tradition of spoiling the bed at the hotel. Jeff had somehow got into their room and put sand between the sheets.

'It's what you do.' Peter laughed as they stripped the bed and shook the sand off.

Lying on the duvet cover, unable to even drink the champagne the hotel had left for the newly-weds, they both fell asleep.

When Kaisa awoke early the next morning, the first thought that entered her head was that in only a few hours' time she'd have to say goodbye to her new husband. It was pitch-black in the room, and for a moment she had to remind herself where she was. A thin strip of light bled through a set of dark, heavy curtains.

'What time is it?' Peter murmured next to her.

She heard him tumble out of bed. 'Bloody hell!'

Kaisa giggled. He cursed again and after a few minutes of crawling, he finally managed to switch on a light. When he pulled open the curtains, only then could Kaisa fully appreciate the huge size of the bridal suite that occupied one corner of the top floor, with large floor-to-ceiling windows on two sides. The exterior of the hotel was ugly; a seventies high-rise situated on the outskirts of Portsmouth, but it was the best one in the city. It had been a complete surprise to Kaisa when, at the end of the lunch reception, Jeff had put Peter and Kaisa into a taxi. A small holdall had even been packed for her.

Peter said, 'I'm taking you for the shortest honeymoon in the history of naval weddings. It will only last twenty-four hours but I promise it'll be memorable.'

With the honeymoon nearly over, Kaisa stood next to Peter as he gazed out of the window towards the harbour. The sun was about to rise up from the sea, separating the sky into steel-grey clouds at the top and a bright-white light below. Peter put his arm around Kaisa. She pressed against his body.

'What time do you have to go?'

'The flight leaves at five thirty pm.' Peter turned to her. He looked into her eyes. 'But I'll be back before you know it.'

. . .

Soon after the registry office wedding Kaisa became somebody in England. She had a banker's card and a cheque book, which her new husband had organised for her all the way from Italy. Kaisa also had a title: Mrs Peter Williams. It immediately brought respect, whether she was paying with her brand-new cheque book in the local butcher's or arranging driving lessons over the telephone.

Over the next two weeks in the house in Southsea, Kaisa forged a new life and a new set of rules to live by. Gone was her solitary life in her father's house, her nights out with Tuuli and the long hours spent in the Hanken library, cramming for her exams. Instead, Kaisa spent the mornings writing her thesis on her old typewriter on the rickety table. At around noon she'd walk down to the end of the road to buy food for the day and post that day's letter to her husband. In the evenings she'd either watch TV or pop over to Sally's house, where they'd sit at her kitchen table and chat. Kaisa would tell her the latest news on getting a married quarter. Peter was waiting to hear when they could move in and, more importantly, where. Even with her elevated position as a naval wife, Kaisa couldn't find out from the Navy's housing officer what kind of place they'd been allocated. She wanted to know where their new life as a married couple would begin so she could picture their home life together. Living in the terraced house in Southsea felt too much like being in limbo.

Three days after Peter had returned to his posting in Naples, the phone rang. It was Sirkka.

'Have you thought about who's going to give you away?' her sister said.

She sounded out of breath, as if she'd been running.

'No,' Kaisa said. It surprised her that she hadn't thought about her father much, or that his absence from the wedding meant there'd be no one to hand her over to Peter. It was such an antiquated tradition anyway. After the ceremony in the registry office, Kaisa hadn't given much thought to the wedding in Finland. It didn't seem that important anymore, but she couldn't tell Sirkka this. No one in Finland knew she was already married to Peter.

Talking to her sister now, Kaisa regretted not being brave enough to tell Sirkka or her mother about it. But revealing the truth now would only spoil the day for both of them and make all their hard work seem unimportant.

'Well, you said you didn't want to invite him...' Sirkka said.

'I don't.' Was she warming to the bastard?

'Yes, well, in that case mum was wondering if she should ask our uncle?'

Kaisa agreed. It was the safer option.

Sirkka then launched into a long conversation about the hotel in Helsinki that she'd booked for the English visitors. She also thought it would be nice if everyone got together for a meal on the day Peter's family and friends arrived in Finland.

'It would be a good way for everyone to get to know each other,' she said.

Neither Sirkka nor her mother had met Peter's family yet.

Her sister had decided on Sahlik, a Russian restaurant where Kaisa's father had taken her and Peter, all those years ago. It was a good choice: the food was different and they could accommodate a large group. Kaisa had not been back since that same evening. She wondered if returning was a good idea, if it would bring back bad memories. But Sirkka didn't care about woolly emotions, so Kaisa agreed.

One late afternoon, a few days before Kaisa was due to return to Finland to prepare for the church wedding, she got a phone call from a girl called Samantha. She'd been one of the guests at the registry office, a large-bosomed girl with streaky blonde hair. She'd hugged Kaisa warmly that day, even though they were strangers.

'I'll call you and take you out sometime when he's away,' Samantha had said and winked at Peter.

Kaisa had agreed to go out with her that evening. Just after seven o'clock, Samantha rang the door bell. Kaisa answered and Samantha stepped inside confidently before she had had a chance to ask her in. She kissed Kaisa on both cheeks, rising on tiptoes as she did so. Samantha was shorter than Kaisa remembered.

She must have read Kaisa's mind because she laughed and pointed at her shoes. 'Oh God, don't look at my flats. I just wear these to drive in; my proper ones are in the car!'

Kaisa glanced at them and just said, 'Oh.'

'So you ready?' Samantha asked, her heavily made-up eyes wide and expectant.

She had bright red lipstick on. Kaisa felt underdressed in black cropped trousers and a simple top she'd made herself from a piece of faux-suede fabric. Compared to Samantha's flowing, deep-cut dress, Kaisa looked like a boy.

Samantha chose the naval base where, on Wednesday nights, there was a bar and a disco. Kaisa had been there once before, with Peter. He'd told her it was an after-hours place for young naval officers to go and find a date, and that it was full of nurses looking for officers. Kaisa remembered the saying about nurses being easy, but she didn't tell Samantha this.

It felt strange for Kaisa to go to a place like this without Peter. As they sat at the bar and some of the young officers gave the pair hungry looks, Kaisa's discomfort grew. When a blond guy asked if she wanted a drink, even though Kaisa already had a full glass of wine in front of her, Samantha lifted her brows.

'No thank you,' Kaisa said, holding up her hand and flashing her rings. Next to the diamond was a simple gold band. The combination still felt heavy on Kaisa's finger.

'Ah, sorry,' he mumbled and moved away.

A lot of the men were already drunk by the time Kaisa and Samantha had arrived. After only two drinks Samantha decided she wanted to go, and asked if Kaisa needed a lift home.

Kaisa couldn't wait to leave.

Sitting next to her in the car on the way back from the base, watching the already familiar streets whiz past, Kaisa felt relief that the evening had gone well. It had been the first time she'd been out in England without Peter. Kaisa looked warmly at Samantha and asked if she wanted to come inside for a coffee before driving home.

Samantha looked surprised. 'Yeah, sure.'

Kaisa entered the kitchen and asked Samantha to wait in the front room. She made instant coffee with milk for Samantha and black for herself. As Kaisa handed her the mug Samantha said, 'It's jolly decent of you to be friends with me.'

Kaisa frowned at the girl in the now-wrinkled cotton dress. It was an odd thing to say. 'Why?'

'Well, you know...' She gave Kaisa a sheepish look and lowered her eyes.

'I don't know – What?' Kaisa pushed.

Samantha stirred her milky coffee, shifting her position on the sofa a little. With Sam's gaze elsewhere, it suddenly clicked. Images of Peter – Kaisa's new husband – and this voluptuous girl with the perfect English upperclass accent flashed in Kaisa's mind. This was *the* girl; the 'accident' Peter had wanted to hide from her. Her face grew hot and Kaisa hoped her blush wasn't showing through her makeup.

'Look,' Samantha said, 'it really didn't mean anything, honestly.'

Kaisa was speechless. Her throat was dry. She doubted she could speak, even if she knew the right words to utter.

Samantha's eyes met Kaisa's. 'You did know, right?'

At last Kaisa found her voice.

'Yeah, of course. Don't worry.'

Her heart was beating so hard she wondered if the girl, the 'accident' sitting with her legs crossed, wearing her 'driving shoes' at the end of her little plump legs, might hear it. She concentrated on breathing normally and added, 'He told me right away.'

Surprise flashed in Samantha's eyes. She straightened her back and lifted up her bosom.

'It was a total accident. We were both so bloody plastered; I mean it could've been anybody.'

Kaisa forced a smile. Samantha had used *that* word – the same word Peter had used. Had they agreed what to tell Kaisa afterwards?

'We've known each other for donkeys, and of course we were friends, because you know, I went out with one of his Dartmouth pals,' Samantha babbled on.

'And don't take this the wrong way, but the last thing I want to do is to marry a naval officer.'

Kaisa was barely listening. She wanted tell Samantha to shut up and get out of the house. Instead, she sat at there with a fake smile on her face until Samantha finished her coffee and left.

For the next two days, Kaisa couldn't concentrate on her thesis. She tried to write to Peter but as soon as she started a letter, she tore it into bits. The house felt more empty than usual. The only person she could talk to was her neighbour.

Sally patted Kaisa's hand kindly and said, 'But it happened once, and that's it. I know Peter; he's a good man. He won't make the same mistake twice.'

Kaisa knew her feelings were unjustified. When it happened they'd been far apart and had just had a fight. Even she'd presumed they'd broken up at the time. And Kaisa had been with somebody too. But it wasn't the act that made her feel so bad; it was that 'the accident' was here, close to Kaisa. Close to Peter.

She'd come to the wedding and had even tried to be friends with Kaisa. By keeping her identity a secret, Peter had put her in an awkward position. What fool did he take Kaisa for? Did he really think she wouldn't find out who the person was? And why had he invited Samantha to the wedding?

All this Kaisa wanted to ask him, but she couldn't find the right words to put into a letter without sounding madly jealous, or hypocritical. But more than those things, she was afraid for the future. What if Peter couldn't be faithful? What if that was the reason for his previous doubts, and why he'd said what he had on that sunny day in Hyde Park?

And if so, what had changed his mind and made him want to marry Kaisa, after all?

31

FINLAND, SUMMER 1984

The temperature in Finland soared suddenly the day before the English party arrived in Helsinki.

At the airport, Peter's mother carried her trench coat on her arm and asked, 'Is it always this warm here in Finland?'

Kaisa smiled and said the summer weather was very much the same as in England – it could be cold and rainy, or hot and sunny.

When her gaze met Peter's at the airport, Kaisa tried to brush away thoughts of Samantha. She walked into his arms and returned Peter's kiss.

'I love you more than ever,' He whispered in her ear.

Kaisa directed the English group onto the Finnair bus and when the last of the luggage was in, including the two hatboxes Peter's mother and auntie had carried as hand luggage, she sat with Peter at the back of the bus. With him here and so attentive, Kaisa wondered if she should mention Samantha.

She looked into Peter's eyes.

He smiled at her. 'God, I've missed you.'

'Me too.'

Later in his hotel room, where Peter had brought her saying he wanted to escape the wedding party, he took Kaisa into his arms. But she pulled away too soon and looked down at her hands.

'What?' He bent his neck to look into her eyes.

'I went out with Samantha a few weeks ago,' she said.

Peter slumped onto the bed. He ran his fingers through his thick black hair and sighed. It was dark in the room and she couldn't see his reaction properly; brown curtains had been pulled across a wide window.

'Come here,' he said and patted the silky bedspread.

Kaisa crossed her arms. How easy it would be to just give in to him. To sit next to him and to be loved. But she had to know what had really gone on between him and that girl.

'No,' she said and stood by the window.

A loud knock on the door startled her.

'What are you two doing?' somebody shouted from the other side.

Peter raised his eyebrows at Kaisa. He got up and opened it. Jeff and Tuuli burst through the door, arm in arm.

'This is strictly *veerbooteen*,' Jeff said.

He was wagging his finger at Peter. Tuuli was giggling.

Jeff turned to her and said, 'Isn't that what you say in Finnish?' He was drunk, slurring his words.

Jeff winked at Peter. 'And you two can't be having sex – you're not even married yet.'

Kaisa glared at him. He was under strict instructions not to breathe a word about the registry office wedding to anyone.

Tuuli stopped giggling. '*Förbjuden*', she corrected. 'And it's Swedish, not Finnish.'

She removed her arm from Jeff's grip.

'What's up?' Tuuli switched to Swedish on her way over to Kaisa. She was dressed in cotton trousers and a short-sleeved top. Her arms were tanned and she seemed even taller than usual. Kaisa looked into her glassy eyes – she'd had a drink too.

She touched Tuuli's arm and replied, 'It's OK, we just need to talk for a bit.'

Tuuli nodded, turned on her heels and walked to the door. Along the way she grabbed Jeff, and pulled him with her.

'Come along, you Englishman, there are beers to be drunk.'

When Peter shut the door behind their friends, he said, 'They seem to be getting on very well.'

'Yes,' was all she could say.

Kaisa turned away from him. She needed to stay strong, not give in to the happiness she felt. Not now she'd finally dared to talk to Peter about the 'accident'.

She sat down on the bed. The thick heat in the room felt oppressive.

'I need to know,' she said quietly.

'OK,' Peter said and sighed again.

He sat next to Kaisa and she looked at him. His eyes were serious and wide. He opened his mouth to say something, but then seemed to change his mind.

'Why did she come to our wedding?' Kaisa asked.

Peter stood up and went to the window. His arms were hanging either side of him.

'I don't know. She must have heard the rumour about our quickie wedding.'

He turned and gave her a boyish grin. Then he continued, more serious. 'You know what the Navy is like...I couldn't believe it when I saw her outside the registry office.'

'She said she'd gone out with your mate when you were at Dartmouth.'

'Did she? I didn't know.'

Peter returned to Kaisa and knelt in front of her. His eyes were so wide and his expression was so sad, she knew she'd forgive him anything.

'Darling, you've got to believe me when I tell you it didn't mean anything. I was drunk, she was drunk. If I could rewrite history, I'd give anything to wipe the whole, sad incident from my life. Our lives.'

Peter buried his head in Kaisa's lap. She stroked his short, black hair. Kaisa pulled his face up and kissed him. His harsh stubble grazed her cheek.

'I love you,' she said. She decided to forget about Samantha and forgive Peter.

After she'd left for Tampere, two hours north of Helsinki, the English party spent a few days sightseeing in the capital. Sirkka had organised a trip out to the archipelago, as well as getting train tickets to Tampere for all of them later on that week. Peter kissed Kaisa long and hard at the station.

'I can't wait to be married to you again,' he whispered in her ear.

In the evenings in Tampere, a slight sea breeze, coming from the two vast lakes bordering the city, offered some relief from the day's heat, but during the day the sun burnt the tops of Kaisa's shoulders as she, her mother and Sirkka sat in the garden of her grandmother's house and worked on their tans.

Kaisa hadn't visited the place of her birth in years. Being here brought back happier memories of her childhood, and she had to stop herself from giving in to a maudlin self pity. Not only was she marrying Peter for a second time but she was also leaving her home, for good this time. Kaisa's unease about her departure grew, during a last-minute wedding shopping trip into town with Sirkka. They passed by the old Finlayson cotton mill;

the sombre stone statues guarding the Hämeensilta bridge; the people, whose faces were more familiar to her than those in England, or even Helsinki. They all seemed to point a finger at her and ask, 'Why are you leaving your homeland?'

Even her unconventional grandmother, a large woman with short, grey hair and a tight perm and who always wore bright red lipstick, made her feel guilty. Turning away from kneading dough for sweet buns in the kitchen, she pulled Kaisa into a close embrace.

'I'm glad you're finally leaving, but will I ever see you again?' she asked Kaisa.

'Don't be silly, Mummu. Of course you will.' Kaisa inhaled her scent of rose water, so familiar from her childhood, and cried.

Several times over the three days spent in her grandmother's house, Kaisa had nearly spilled her secret about her English wedding to her mother and sister. But each time she started to tell them, she drew back, deciding it would be better for them not to know. Even the Finnish pastor had assured her that no one would notice the difference between an actual ceremony and a blessing. The padre in England had said the same thing.

On the morning of her second wedding Kaisa woke early. The sun was already high in the sky, shining brightly through the thin curtains. She left her sister sleeping on the bed next to her, tiptoed to her grandmother's kitchen and made herself a strong cup of coffee. By ten o'clock the house was buzzing with people. Her mother emerged from the guest bedroom on the second floor and hugged Kaisa hard. Her grandmother had made them all a lavish buffet breakfast with various cheeses, hams and lots of rye bread.

Heli, Kaisa's schoolfriend and the maker of her dress, arrived just after they'd finished eating, and everyone began getting dressed for the ceremony.

They were standing in front of the hall mirror. When Heli zipped up the bodice of Kaisa's white silk-tulle wedding gown, Kaisa felt a flush heat her body, even though she was naked underneath the dress.

'You've lost weight,' Heli said. Her gaze was sharp under her straight-cut fringe.

Specks of dust floated in the stagnant air inside the old house. Kaisa's throat tightened from the lack of air. She looked around for someone to open a window.

'Have you been starving yourself or what?' Heli tutted.

Kaisa looked at her reflection. Her friend was right; the top was a little loose.

'I didn't think I had,' she said.

After assessing Kaisa's reflection, Heli pulled the bodice down and the dress fell to the floor.

'The bodice needs an extra seam,' she said.

Kaisa crossed her arms over her naked chest. When Heli took the dress into the other room Kaisa reached for the T-shirt she'd been wearing.

She turned her gaze back to her reflection, trying to shake off her nerves. Heli returned with the dress and, with the needle and thread between her teeth, asked Kaisa to step inside it again.

'There!' she said triumphantly as she zipped up the gown.

Kaisa admired her work. The bodice fit perfectly.

Carefully, Heli arranged the veil on Kaisa's head and pulled it down over her face.

She heard a gasp behind her. Turning, Kaisa noticed a small group of women had gathered behind her.

Her mother, Pirjo stood there with her grandmother who was dressed in a leopard-print outfit. Pirjo wore a pale-blue suit and a straw-coloured wide-brimmed hat with a few matching blue silk flowers pinned to it. The week before the English party's arrival, Kaisa had helped her choose the outfit in Helsinki.

She smiled at her mother in the mirror, noticing she had tears in her eyes. There was a black-and-white photograph of her parents on their wedding day, displayed on the bookshelf in her grandmother's living room. Her mother, too, had worn a simple, white dress and a long veil. She'd been the most beautiful bride.

Sirkka was also there, wearing a stylish black-and-blue dress and matching hat.

'What time is it?' Kaisa asked.

'Goodness,' Pirjo said in alarm. She rushed to the kitchen window and shouted back, 'The cars are here already!'

Kaisa's grandmother and Sirkka were set to travel in the first car with Heli. Sirkka looked more nervous than Kaisa. Kaisa guessed that the most difficult part for her was yet to come. She'd arranged the entire wedding reception, and Kaisa knew how much she wanted it to be a success.

Sirkka took Kaisa's hands into hers and said, 'See you after the ceremony!'

'It'll be wonderful, I know it will,' Kaisa said.

'Are you ready to go?' Pirjo said her eyes glassy with tears.

Kaisa nodded and her mother gathered up the veil and placed it in Kaisa's arms.

Pirjo held her hand in the car. They were both quiet, looking out of the window as they passed familiar streets and buildings. When the car crossed the bridge over Tammerkoski, Kaisa watched the fast-flowing water of the steep rapid below. She remembered how, as a child, she'd been afraid she might fall into the foam the strong current created and be lost forever. The driver drove slowly along the edge of Tampere centre, turning on to Satakunnankatu, and then driving up the hill to the cathedral. When the car stopped, Pirjo squeezed Kaisa's hand smiling at her reassuringly and hurried inside the church.

Kaisa's uncle was waiting for her at the steps of the church. He was a tall, slim man with slightly thinning, fair hair. Kaisa hadn't seen him for years and it felt strange that it was him, not her father, who was waiting for her.

She swallowed back tears and nodded to him.

'Well, this is an honour indeed,' he said and offered Kaisa his arm.

Slowly, they made their way up the steps. At the entrance, when she saw all the people inside turn towards her, Kaisa had to pause for a moment. She took a few breaths, in and out, to calm her rapidly beating heart. As soon as she stepped inside, the organist started playing Mendelssohn's wedding march. Beginning the long walk down the aisle, Kaisa saw Peter at the top, looking smart in his dark suit. Their eyes met and he smiled at her.

An hour later, Kaisa and Peter walked back down the aisle, now properly man and wife in the eyes of God.

Peter whispered in her ear, 'You've made me the happiest man alive – twice.'

When they both stepped out into the bright sunshine, Kaisa spotted her father. He was standing alone and off to one side of the path leading up to the church. He wore a light-grey suit and was carrying a camera case.

His presence didn't surprise her; it was as if she'd known he couldn't possibly keep away. Had he known the time of the wedding? Had he waited there all day?

He smiled at Kaisa and lifted his hand as if to wave, then lowered it, like he'd changed his mind. Kaisa and Peter walked down the steps, followed by the wedding guests. Her father met them halfway. He stood two steps below the couple, squinting against the sun.

'I brought you a wedding gift. It's just money but I thought you might find it useful.'

He gave Kaisa a boyish grin and moved closer, a white envelope in his outstretched hand. Kaisa gazed down at him.

He took another step up, turned to Peter and said, in English, 'For you.'

Peter took the envelope. He shook hands with him.

'Thank you very much.'

Her father nodded to Peter and turned to look at Kaisa again. She loosened herself from Peter's grip and stepped down until she and her father were on the same level.

He hugged Kaisa, squeezing hard.

'Congratulations,' he said quietly, his voice wavering.

Kaisa could hardly hear him. She pulled back. His blue eyes looked paler than usual, almost grey.

Something soft hit her bare shoulders. She looked around at the combination of rice and confetti the guests had thrown. The noise from the crowd behind them deepened. Kaisa smiled, wiped a tear away from her eye and put her hand through Peter's arm.

When Kaisa turned back to her father, he was gone.

THE FAITHFUL HEART

BOOK 2

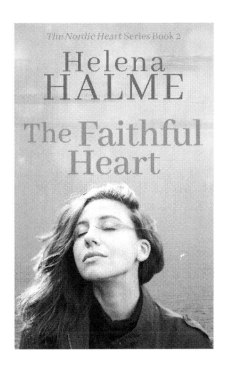

1

Duncan took hold of Kaisa's hand and shook it, grinning
'This is very formal. Don't I get a kiss?'
His palm was warm, as his hand enveloped Kaisa's fingers. She pushed her face closer to Duncan and kissed his cheek. Her lips grazed against the harsh stubble on his chin, and she smelled his aftershave. He was wearing something fresh and fragrant.

During the drive from Helensburgh station to the married quarter at Smuggler's Way, Duncan kept glancing at Kaisa. She was a little nervous about driving him – she'd only passed her test a matter of days earlier. At the same time she enjoyed the warm glow of his intense gaze on her.

She wished it was Peter sitting next to her, but it felt good to be wanted, even if it was by the wrong person. Why couldn't she have an admirer or two in addition to her husband? As long as nothing happened, there was no harm in a little flirtation, was there? She was a woman of the world, not some inexperienced little naval wife who'd only lived in one village all her life.

As Kaisa drove along the Gareloch seafront towards the married quarter, she felt in control. Duncan might fancy her as much as he liked, and he might even come onto her again, but she knew she could brush him off. Kaisa relaxed, and decided she'd enjoy the evening ahead.

. . .

When they got inside the damp, cold house, Duncan brought out a bottle of champagne from his holdall, and insisted they open it before Kaisa began preparing dinner. Kaisa laughed; the thought of drinking champagne in the rented house filled with ugly Ministry of Defense furniture with someone else but her husband seemed so unreal.

She dug out a pair of crystal flutes they'd had as a wedding present from Peter's old flame, Samantha. Kaisa kept them in their original box at the back of the sideboard, because they didn't often drink champagne, but also so that she wouldn't have to look at them. Peter and Kaisa had agreed not to talk about Samantha, or about what they both got up to before they married, and she tried hard not to be jealous. Still, she didn't like using the glasses, but they were the only champagne flutes she owned.

While they sipped the drink, Duncan and Kaisa talked about people they knew. Duncan told her that he was buying a house in Southsea, very near the seafront. Kaisa was jealous; what she would give for the chance to live in Portsmouth again!

Kaisa had pre-prepared a vegetarian lasagne with lentils, and while they ate, she opened a bottle of red wine she'd bought from the off-licence in Helensburgh that morning. They polished the wine off while they ate. Kaisa didn't have an appetite, but Duncan had seconds and even ice-cream afterwards. When Kaisa asked if he'd like something with his pudding, Duncan said, 'What have you got?'

While giggling, because she felt a bit wobbly getting up from the table after all the alcohol she'd consumed, Kaisa went through their cabinet of drinks, which included cloudberry liquor, Finnish *Koskenkorva* vodka, Baileys, and a half-bottle of port. For some reason the contents of the bar made them both laugh uncontrollably, but eventually Duncan chose the port and Kaisa had a glass of Baileys.

As they tasted their drinks, they both fell silent. Duncan was staring at Kaisa, while she sipped the sweet tasting liquid. Her head was spinning, and she smiled at him. Suddenly he reached across the table and took hold of her hand.

'You're so lovely,' he said and kissed her palm.

Kaisa let him hold her for a moment. He really was such a nice man, she thought. And it felt good to have some male company.

She hadn't realised how much she missed just cooking for two, or to have someone else to talk to.

She sighed and thought how lonely she had been for the past month when Peter had been away at sea. Is this what her life would be from now on? Months of loneliness interspersed with a few weeks of happiness? Not that they were always happy when Peter was at home, she thought. They had terrible rows too.

Duncan gazed at Kaisa and continued, 'It's wonderful to be alone with you.'

Kaisa looked at Duncan's face. His eyes were full of desire. She removed her hand.

'You mustn't say that.'

Duncan got up and sank to his knees in front of Kaisa.

'But I must. Besides, you know it. Why did you invite me over if you don't feel the same way about me?'

Duncan's eyes were burning into hers, and his hands were gripping hers. Kaisa was paralysed by his show of emotion. His arms rested on her thighs, and the back of his hands holding hers were close, too close, to the place between her legs.

'Oh Kaisa, I need you,' he said and rested his head on her lap, moving his hands so that they were holding her waist.

Kaisa could feel his hot breath on her, and an image of having Duncan touch her there, of him tasting her, flashed across her eyes.

Kaisa's heart was beating hard. Oh God, how good it felt to be wanted! But she knew this was wrong, and she must stop it.

She took hold of Duncan's face, to make him stand up, but as soon as she touched him, Duncan moved his head upwards and put his lips on hers.

Kaisa couldn't stop kissing him back, it felt so good. When Duncan pulled away, he whispered breathlessly into her ear, 'I want you so much. I have to have you!'

She didn't reply and he kissed her again. Pulling away once more, he said, 'Please Kaisa, I beg you, take me to your bed. No-one will ever know.'

2

SOUTHSEA, PORTSMOUTH – SIX MONTHS EARLIER

K aisa woke to the sounds of the seagulls calling to each other in the distance. She opened her eyes and felt the empty space next to her. An involuntary smile spread over her face when she remembered the night before, and where she was. After two weeks of married life, she still couldn't quite believe that she was finally living with Peter as his wife in a married quarter in Portsmouth. She looked at the radio alarm clock, a wedding present from a distant aunt of Peter's, and saw it was past 9am. Although Peter had gone back to work after their honeymoon in Finland, Kaisa still felt as if she was on a long holiday. Poor Peter had to wake up early, and although he didn't seem to mind, Kaisa felt guilty that she was able to lie in bed all morning.

Again Kaisa smiled as she remembered Peter's first day back at work. On the Monday – Peter was on a training course at the submarine base in Gosport – she'd got up at the same time as Peter and made him bacon and eggs for breakfast while he showered. She'd struggled to operate the gas hob, even though Peter had shown her how to turn on the hissing gas and light the ring the night before. It all seemed so dangerous to Kaisa, who was used to an electric cooker, especially when Peter stressed how important it was to make sure the gas was properly turned off. 'Leaking gas will cause an explosion,' he'd told her. Kaisa was horrified. How did people in England manage?

'This is the life,' Peter had said, grinning at her from the other side of the small kitchen table. Kaisa had still been wearing her dressing gown, shivering in the bleak, unheated kitchen. It had all felt so romantic; Kaisa the young Navy wife cooking breakfast for her husband. But as she'd lifted her head for Peter to give her a kiss goodbye at the door, Kaisa had felt like a 1950s housewife from a black-and-white film. Kaisa went back to bed and thought, 'This is not why I got married – to serve my husband breakfast before he goes off to work.' So on the Tuesday, she stayed in bed. Peter thought it funny that it had taken Kaisa only one day to get over the sentimental notion of making him breakfast in the morning, and joked about it in the pub the following weekend.

'If you wanted a conventional Navy wife, you should have married one of the many English girls with a crush on you,' she'd said when they were back in their new flat.

'Shh …' When Peter had placed his lips on hers, Kaisa had abandoned her mouth to Peter's kisses and let herself be led upstairs to bed.

Kaisa sighed and forced herself out of bed. She pulled on her bright blue satin sports shorts and a heavy cotton T-shirt with a boat neck, and tied her hair back with a satin ribbon. It was a beautiful sunny day, the seagulls were still calling to each other in the distance, and she was going to clean the flat. As she began clearing the living room of a couple of weeks' worth of detritus, she thought how wonderful it was to be living in a huge married quarter, right in the centre of Portsmouth. King's Terrace, a large red-brick Victorian building, where each married quarter occupied two floors, had one of the best situations in the city. The shops at Palmerston Road were within walking distance, as was the seafront at Southsea.

When they'd found out where they would be living, Peter had said they were lucky to be in Southsea – many of the junior submarine officers' families lived on the other side of the water, in Gosport. That would have been difficult for Kaisa. As well as the job interviews she anticipated attending, all of Peter's friends lived on the Southsea side, and, as Kaisa didn't drive, it would have been costly and tedious to take a bus and a ferry across the Solent every day. And the maisonette was huge: there were three bedrooms, two bathrooms, a large (but cold) kitchen and a separate lounge. But the Navy issue furniture didn't please Kaisa's Finnish eye. Every piece was – in one word – awful. She hadn't told Peter how she felt about this, of course. And she had to admit, the ugly solid teak sideboard, dining table and chairs, the moss-green flower-patterned curtains, the red-and-yellow three-piece suite, were better than having no furniture at all. It was just that so many of the wedding gifts from her Finnish friends and family didn't go with the decoration. The straight lines of the Aalto vase that her friend Tuuli had given her looked completely out of sync with the teak dining table and the old-fashioned, intricately carved chairs. If only they'd been able to afford new pine furniture. Then Kaisa could imagine how to arrange their things.

Still, she knew she was lucky. Living like this, together in Pompey – the Navy's nickname for the city – was what she'd been dreaming about during the many painful years she'd been apart from Peter, when she was living in Finland trying to finish her studies and he was in the UK pursuing his naval career. This is what she had wanted: to be Peter's wife – a Navy wife. She looked around the messy living room, and began cleaning it with renewed vigour.

'Isn't it nice that we have one more week together, with me coming home every night?' Peter had said as they had walked home from the pub the night before. The routine they'd got into during the first two weeks of their married life seemed like a dream to Kaisa. When Peter got home, hot from a day spent in a stuffy classroom, they'd drive down to the quieter part of the seafront in Eastney, swim in the sea, come back home, make love, and go to the pub. Because Jeff, Peter's best friend and best man, was still away in the Falklands, they didn't often go to Jeff's father's pub in Old Portsmouth, preferring instead to go to places like the India Arms, or King's in Southsea. Wherever they went, Peter bumped into people he knew. Often he would make arrangements for them to meet up with friends from the naval base in the evening. Kaisa didn't usually know the people, but they were all outgoing young men like Peter: carefree, good-looking, and full of jokes. Kaisa's old life in Finland seemed dull in comparison to the sunny days and jolly evenings in Pompey.

Although Kaisa didn't always understand everything that was being said, she didn't mind sitting next to Peter, holding his hand under the table and soaking up her new life. Occasionally they met other young couples like themselves. During their first week of marriage, Peter introduced Kaisa to Mary and Justin. They'd been married for less than a year and Justin was a submariner, just like Peter. Kaisa liked Mary straight away. She was a tall, lanky girl, with a black, even bob, and a fringe that just touched her eyelashes. She didn't look like any of the other Navy wives Kaisa knew, and she certainly didn't act like one. Even though she was pregnant, she always had a pint of beer, and wore high-waisted jeans.

'I've been wanting to meet you,' she said to Kaisa.

'Oh,' Kaisa said. She didn't know how Mary knew about her, but guessed Peter had told Justin all about his new Finnish wife.

Mary laughed at Kaisa's confusion, and added, 'I hope you wanted to meet me, too, right?'

Mary told Kaisa that she'd known Justin since school, and that her father had been in the Navy too. Kaisa could hear from the conversation between the men and Mary that she knew a lot of technical details about the course Justin and Peter were on, and about the various submarines and ships. Kaisa tried to listen and learn, but she invariably switched off when the Navy talk started in the pub. It wasn't that she was uninterested in Peter's career; she did want to know about these things, but felt stupid asking questions, because she knew so little.

'Sorry, Peanut, we're boring you.' Peter had his arm around her waist and squeezed her closer to him so that he could give her a quick peck on the forehead.

'No, not at all,' Kaisa replied and lent into his embrace. She smiled at the silly nickname Peter had coined for her during their honeymoon. When she asked him where it came from, he'd just kissed her and said, 'You just are my little Peanut.'

'We'll miss them and their boring submarine talk when they're away, won't we,' Mary said.

Mary didn't need to remind Kaisa that soon she was going to be on her own. She knew this blissful state wasn't going to last – and that she should make the most of Peter's presence. But she didn't want to think about his impending absence. They didn't as yet know which submarine he was going to be appointed to, nor where he was going to be based. Because Kaisa knew Portsmouth, and some of Peter's friends, from her many visits to the city, they'd decided she'd stay in their married quarter on King's Terrace wherever he went. Now that she had her degree from Hanken, the school of economics in Finland, Kaisa planned to apply for jobs. But she hadn't yet filled in one application. There'd be plenty of time for that when Peter was away.

Kaisa viewed the mess in the large lounge, which had two tall sash windows facing the road. An ironing board was out, on top of which teetered an insurmountable pile of washing. Most of it consisted of Peter's heavy cotton uniform shirts, which took Kaisa an age to iron. She spotted the bone china mug her mother-in-law had given her on her first Christmas together with Peter in Wiltshire. She could see only half of the beautiful italic text on the flower-patterned mug, but she knew it read, '*Oh to be in England, now April is here!*' She remembered how tearful she'd felt when she opened the present and saw those words. And how surprised she'd been that her mother-in-law, who barely knew her, could understand exactly how she felt. To be living in England, with her beloved Englishman, was barely a dream then, nearly four years ago. Now the mug was half-empty of cold, milky tea, left there by Peter, as he'd hurried out of the door that morning.

As well as the dirty tea mug, on the table were leftovers of their evening meal – a takeaway burger and chips from the new American-style restaurant a few doors down from the flat. This was fighting for space with opened letters, most of which were bills, old recipes, and a few job applications, which Kaisa had planned to fill in. Kaisa speeded up her cleaning and felt good when after an hour the place looked spotless. Peter would be so pleased with her.

She made herself a cup of coffee, sat on the uncomfortable sofa and began sifting through the job applications. She wanted to start earning money – even though Peter had a good salary, it would make their life easier if they had two pay packets coming in. But Kaisa didn't want to take any job – she was a graduate after all, with a Master's degree from a reputable school of economics, not just any three-year qualification in business administration from a polytechnic, or a diploma from a secretarial college. She wanted a job that would lead to a career, just like Peter's Navy career. Kaisa thought about Peter and how handsome he looked in his white shirt, tie, black trousers, shiny black shoes, and naval officer's cap, as he bent over her on the bed each morning to give her a long kiss goodbye. His black hair was often wet from the shower, and he smelled of the coconut shaving foam she so adored. More than once, if she was fully awake, she'd pull him into bed and they'd make love hurriedly. Peter had told her how on those mornings he could hardly concentrate during his first lectures for thinking about her, still warm and naked in their bed. Kaisa smiled and sighed. She hadn't realised that anyone could ever be this happy.

3

The following Sunday Peter took Kaisa to a breakfast party in London. 'What's a breakfast party?' Kaisa asked. She only knew about *sillis*, herring and vodka breakfasts that the rich kids at her university in Helsinki used to organise after the annual students' ball and the 1st of May celebrations.

'I expect there'll be drinking involved, but perhaps not schnapps,' Peter said and grinned. They were driving up the A3 in Peter's grey Ford Fiesta, listening to Radio One and singing along to hits like 'Wake Me Up Before You Go Go,' by Wham! and 'Two Tribes' by Frankie Goes to Hollywood.

Kaisa had never met Jackie, whose party it was, but Peter knew her through some of his Navy friends. Kaisa wondered if she was another one of Peter's old girlfriends, but didn't want to ask. Peter was married to her now.

Kaisa wore a new sky-blue silk skirt and a matching strappy vest. She was a little nervous, because she was not wearing a bra. Peter had said it would be 'absolutely fine' when Kaisa had shown him the outfit, with and without a bra. The straps looked ugly under the thin cloth bands at the top, so Kaisa preferred not to wear one. Luckily it was a very sunny and warm day, the last day of June, and Kaisa took a cardigan that she could always slip on if she became too self-conscious. Her breasts were so tiny anyway that no one, she was sure, would take any notice. Peter had kissed her as they were getting into the car on King's Terrace and told her she looked gorgeous.

'And very Scandinavian,' he added. Kaisa smiled and said, 'You know Finland is not part of the Scandinavian Peninsula, and therefore I can't look Scandinavian!'

'Yeah, yeah,' Peter said and squeezed her bottom. 'Miss Geography, no one cares.'

'On the way up to London, Peter told Kaisa that Jackie's parents were very well to do, and had bought her a flat in a posh area of central London called Chelsea. 'You know, where the yuppies live,' he said and looked sideways at Kaisa.

'You know her well, then?' Kaisa asked.

Peter shot her a quick look, and said, 'No, not really. She's a friend of a friend.'

Kaisa smiled to herself. She now loved teasing Peter about his old girl-friends, just as he liked to pull her leg about her old fiancé in Finland, Matti. Neither of them was jealous of the other anymore, not since they'd sorted out their pre-wedding nerves. Since being married, Kaisa couldn't imagine even looking at another man, and she knew Peter felt the same way about her. Peter looked over at Kaisa and squeezed her knee. 'Fancy a quickie in the car before we get there?'

'Where? On the road while you're driving?' Kaisa laughed, and brushed aside his hand.

The car in front stopped; they'd reached the traffic lights in Petersfield, a small, pretty town between Portsmouth and London. Peter took hold of Kaisa's arm and placed her hand over his crotch. 'I'm ready!'

Kaisa felt his hardness and squeezed it lightly. 'You're crazy.' The traffic had moved and there was the sound of a horn being pressed from behind. 'Go on, concentrate on the road and stop thinking about sex for one second.' Kaisa shook her head in mock disapproval.

When Jackie opened the heavy door, she gave a little shriek of pleasure at seeing Peter and Kaisa. She kissed them on both cheeks and said, 'Come up, please, darlings! You simply must meet everyone!' She was wearing a pink, flower-patterned dress and holding a cigarette. She darted up a light-coloured staircase and, with the hand holding the cigarette, waved to them to follow her. Kaisa worried about the ash falling onto the carpet, but Jackie didn't seem to care. On her feet she had very high-heeled gold sandals that sank into the plush pile.

The flat was decorated with old-fashioned furniture; against one wall was a polished teak sideboard filled with family pictures framed in silver, and in the far corner of the large room stood a beautiful piano, on top of which was a large vase filled with long-stemmed pink roses. The place reeked of money. In the centre of the room was a table laden with glasses, bottles of wine and a large bowl of punch filled with cucumber slices and mint leaves. A man wearing a striped jacket over a cotton shirt and light-coloured slacks, with bare feet, was pouring Pimm's and lemonade into the bowl when Peter and Kaisa walked in. He turned around and looked straight at Kaisa. She adjusted the straps of her top and tried to take hold of Peter's hand, but he moved away from her towards the man.

'Duncan, how the hell are you?' The two men shook hands. Peter turned around and said, 'This is my wife, Kaisa.'

For a moment, which felt like an age, Duncan said nothing but just gazed at Kaisa. He was slightly shorter than Peter, with fine, fair hair and light-blue eyes. 'I've heard a lot about you,' Duncan bent down and kissed Kaisa's hand. His lips felt soft. Fearing she'd blushed, she moved her eyes down to the floor.

There were a lot of people squeezed into the one room, talking and laughing loudly in small groups. As Peter and Kaisa approached each group, faces lit up in smiles. Peter kept pushing Kaisa forward, introducing her as 'My wife, Kaisa.' Her heart filled with pride each time she heard those words and greeted each person with a handshake, apart from a couple of men who seemed to know Peter well and pulled her towards them for a kiss on both cheeks. No one else kissed her hand like Duncan had done. As much as Kaisa tried to remember at least one other name, she couldn't retain any of them. She couldn't really follow the conversation very well, either. The loud music and everyone talking at the same time made it impossible for her to catch all the English words.

Towards the end of the party Kaisa was sitting alone on the bay window ledge admiring the view below. She'd had several glasses of Pimm's, and was glad of a reprieve from trying to make sense of people's stories and jokes. She'd left Peter talking to a slightly older man about the Navy and his course. Jackie's flat was on the second floor and overlooked a cobbled yard where flowers grew in pots and hanging baskets. In Finland people grew far fewer flowers than they did in Britain, and Kaisa still marvelled at a display such as the one below. There were pinks, blues and violets. Small white flowers overflowed the baskets, some of them nearly reaching the ground. Kaisa lazily wondered how such displays of loveliness could be achieved, and jumped when she heard a voice behind her, 'Here you are!' Jackie was holding another cigarette, but had taken off her high-heeled shoes. She looked very short in her stockinged feet. She came to sit next to Kaisa, and

Kaisa noticed that Jackie was wearing a pink nail varnish that exactly matched her dress. 'So what else do you do apart from being Mrs Williams?'

Kaisa told her she was looking for a job. She said she had an economics degree from Finland, to which Jackie lifted her eyebrows and said, 'I didn't think a foreign qualification would be recognised here in England.'

Kaisa didn't know what to say. Jackie inhaled deeply on her cigarette, with her cold blue eyes fixed on Kaisa's face. She removed the now pink-stained cigarette from her lips.

'Oh,' Kaisa eventually said and turned her face down to the floor. It hadn't crossed Kaisa's mind that her degree from Hanken would be ignored by prospective employers. Her mind whirled with questions, but she couldn't think how to put them to Jackie without appearing stupid.

'So how is it being married to Peter?' Jackie asked.

'Fine,' Kaisa couldn't think how else to reply. She didn't want to tell this girl whom she hardly knew that she was the happiest woman alive. That after their four-year long-distance love affair, to be finally married to Peter was a dream come true. Why was Jackie so interested anyway? Perhaps she really was an old girlfriend of Peter's?

'Fine, you say!' Jackie gave a little short laugh and tapped the end of her cigarette onto a small silver ashtray that she was holding in her other hand.

It was gone three o'clock when they set off for home. But when Peter drove along the A3, Kaisa didn't even notice the scenery. During the rest of the party, she had experienced a growing sense of betrayal. She felt as if she'd been cheated. To work so hard for a degree and then not get anything for it. Or not even that. Kaisa felt cheated that she hadn't known about this; it hadn't even occurred to her that the degree for which she had reluctantly studied would not be recognised in Britain. Why hadn't Peter told her about this before? Why hadn't he said anything during the long years they'd been apart because Kaisa wanted to finish her studies? She thought it important to get a degree before she got married, so that she could forge the worth-while career she longed for. If that same degree was a worthless piece of paper after all, what had been the point?

That evening Kaisa went to bed early. When she heard Peter come up the stairs, she wondered if she should ask him about her degree, but decided against it. She'd promised herself never to go to bed on a disagreement, something her mother had taught her not to do, so she decided to pretend everything was fine. When Peter leaned over to kiss her goodnight, Kaisa returned the kiss, but turned over quickly to stop Peter doing anything more.

There was no way she could make love to Peter now, not until she had had it out with him.

'What's up?' Peter said, nuzzling his face into the back of her neck.

'I'm really tired, sorry darling.'

Next day, in search of some facts, Kaisa phoned and asked about the validity of her foreign degree at the Job Centre in Portsmouth. When they eventually found someone who knew about foreign qualifications, the so-called expert just said, 'It's worth putting everything on your job application, dear, you never know what they're looking for.' In other words, Kaisa's degree was more or less worthless. Four long years studying Political Science and Economics, a long summer course in book-keeping, years of trying to study for her exams, while pining for Peter and dreaming of living in England – were for nothing. So, when the ten o'clock news had finished and Peter turned the telly off, the frustration just flowed out of Kaisa. Why hadn't he told her that there was no need to finish her degree if it wasn't worth anything in England? Why did she have to find out from someone like Jackie, a stranger? Or perhaps she wasn't such a stranger to Peter? Kaisa demanded to know, 'Was she or, was she not, an old girlfriend?'

The row went back and forth, with Kaisa accusing Peter of keeping her in the dark about her degree and not being straight about how well he knew Jackie, to Peter swearing he had no idea of the validity of her qualifications in the UK, and denying there had ever been any kind of relationship, apart from a friendly one, with Jackie. And why was Kaisa blaming Peter. 'I'm no bloody expert on the British job market!' he shouted. The pinnacle of the row occurred when Peter admitted that perhaps, 'Jackie did once – a long time ago – have a bit of a crush on me.' Kaisa stormed out of the room and locked herself in the toilet, crying loudly. It took Peter a full ten minutes to coax her out again.

Of course, in the end they made up, and Peter said that he really hadn't had any idea that Kaisa's degree from Finland would be 'worthless' as she put it.

'Are you sure Jackie knows what she's talking about?' Peter said.

'I don't know.' Kaisa was leaning on Peter. She felt silly for having worked herself up into such a state.

Peter lifted Kaisa's chin up with his thumb and forefinger. 'You're a clever woman. And what's more you are very good-looking, funny and I love you very much. You will get a job, but you know there's no rush. Let's just enjoy our time together while I'm still at home?'

. . .

During that last week before Peter went away, Kaisa asked if they could get a sewing machine. She could run up new curtains for their married quarter, making it a little more homely. It was an expensive purchase, but Kaisa promised Peter they'd save money in the long run.

'Alright then, Mrs Williams, let's get you a sewing machine,' Peter smiled and squeezed Kaisa close to himself. Kaisa was surprised when, at the Knight and Lee store on Palmerston Road, she knew quite a lot about the different models they were shown. Glancing at Peter, she saw how her knowledge impressed him, too.

The following day Peter was again impressed when Kaisa made simple, light drapes for the lounge from cheap fabric she'd bought in town. She took down the awful net curtains in their bedroom and hung the new ones in place. 'You should go into business making curtains!' Peter said. Kaisa smiled; impressing Peter made her feel so wonderful. She was acting like a 1950s housewife again, but she couldn't help herself. She promised herself that she'd start applying for proper jobs as soon as Peter went away. Kaisa sighed; they only had two more days together.

4

'I should be back by September,' Peter squeezed Kaisa's body hard against himself. It was only the 8th of July, and he said he'd be away 'for about eight weeks.' The nuclear submarine, HMS *Tempest*, to which Peter had been assigned, was based in Scotland, and he was catching a flight up to Glasgow that morning. Even though Peter was now officially working up in Scotland, Kaisa would stay in the King's Terrace married quarter, just as they had agreed. Kaisa was glad; it meant she could meet up with friends, and begin looking for jobs. Peter told Kaisa the submarine would undergo trials in Scotland for 'about two weeks' first, then be at sea for an undefined time. Kaisa knew better than to ask anything more. Peter's standard, joking reply was: 'If I tell you, I'd have to kill you.'

'But don't forget we'll see each other in Liverpool.'

The submarine was going on an official visit to Morecambe in mid-August, but that too seemed a long time away.

Kaisa thought how much taller Peter always looked when he was about to leave her. They were standing in the hall, saying goodbye. It was early on a Sunday morning, only 5am, and Kaisa was in her nightie, while Peter wore his ribbed Navy jumper over his white uniform shirt. The night before, he'd packed his 'Pusser's grip' – a Navy issue brown canvas holdall with his initials on the side – and was holding his white cap with its gold-embossed officer's badge under his arm. His eyes looked dark and intense. Squeezing Kaisa tightly, he said, 'When I'm with you nothing can hurt me.' Kaisa knew he was nervous about meeting his new captain, and the crew, and she hugged him hard and said, 'You'll be fine.' She was trying not to cry, but a single tear fell down her cheek.

I'll be home before you know it,' Peter said and wiped Kaisa's tear away with his thumb.

Kaisa went back to bed and tried to sleep, but she couldn't. She stretched herself across the bed and felt the empty space next to her. It was still warm from Peter's body. She hugged his pillow, inhaling his scent. She already longed for his touch. Kaisa managed to sleep for a couple of hours and then woke up with a start to the loud screech of seagulls. As she got up and dressed, she thought how tired she felt. Listening to the horns of the ferries and ships (she couldn't tell the difference, even though Peter had told her many times), she wondered how she was going to manage all the weeks without him.

Kaisa spent the next few days cleaning the flat top to bottom, and unpacked the last two boxes they'd brought over from Devonshire Road, where Peter and Kaisa had briefly stayed before they were married. The place was owned by Jeff's parents and had been home for Jeff and Peter when they were both based in Pompey. She bought the *Guardian* newspaper and the *Portsmouth Evening News* and sent out ten applications for jobs. She got an appointment with an employment agency called Bayleys on Commercial Road and, after an interview with a friendly woman, felt more optimistic about her chances. The woman had even looked at her degree certificate and asked a few questions about the courses she'd taken. On the way back home she bumped into Jeff's sister. Maggie was an odd sort of girl. A few years younger than Kaisa, she'd already been married and divorced from a sailor. She played at being much wiser and more experienced, yet when she spoke she sounded more like a teenager.

'You on your own now, yeah?' she said, chewing gum. She was wearing a short ra-ra skirt over a pair of leggings, and a ripped top, with her thin blonde hair up in a messy ponytail. She was very thin, and her skin was pale, almost translucent. She stood with one hand on her hip, while holding a cigarette in the other.

'Yes, Peter is in Scotland and they'll sail in a week or two.'

'You miss him?' Maggie delivered this question without displaying any emotion, neither in her thin voice, or in a change in her demeanour. She took a drag on her cigarette while gazing steadily at Kaisa.

'Yeah, I miss him …' Kaisa said.

'Listen, I'm in a bit of a hurry now, but why don't you come over to the pub tonight, yeah? I'm working there now and I think Jeff's home later.'

Kaisa thanked her and said she would go. It'd be good to get away from the flat and the TV. After Peter left she'd got into the habit of watching all the soaps, including the new *Brookside*, set in Liverpool. The actors' accents were so strong that Kaisa treated it as an English-language lesson, and was glad if she got the whole of the plot at the end of the episode.

Jeff gave Kaisa a big hug when she entered The Palmerston Arms in Old Portsmouth that evening. He'd been away for weeks, and she hadn't seen him since the wedding in Finland.

'How's my favourite married woman?' he joked, and Kaisa smiled. Having Jeff at home was a little like having Peter around, so she relaxed and told him about Peter's new job in HMS *Tempest*.

'I'm a skimmer, you know, so I don't know a thing about subs.'

'Neither do I,' Kaisa admitted and laughed.

The Palmerston Arms was a small pub along the Old Portsmouth High Street, with a dark mahogany bar and a few round tables and stools scattered around the small space. In the corner, where Jeff and his friends liked to sit, there was a fish tank, and a corner sofa with a slightly larger, rectangular table. As with everything, The Palmerston Arms was just a walk away from Kaisa and Peter's flat. It was a warm, beautiful evening, with just a slight sea breeze that had made Kaisa's hair stick out in all directions during the short walk. She'd really need to have it cut, but hadn't yet dared to use a local hairdresser.

'Anyway, you're looking good, Mrs Williams!' Jeff grinned at her and Kaisa smiled back at him. She'd felt such relief at seeing him there – it was never easy to walk into a pub alone as a woman, even if the pub belonged to the parents of your husband's best friend, and best man. Jeff looked exactly as before. He was more heavily built than Peter, and had thinner, light-brown hair that he constantly tried to keep in place by brushing it away from his face. He reminded Kaisa of a friendly bear, and she was very fond of him.

'Hiya, Kaisa,' Maggie waved from the bar, and Jeff's much larger-framed, beer-smelling dad, the pub landlord, came over and nearly squeezed the life out of her. Kaisa tried to turn her head, but he planted a kiss straight on her mouth. His thick beard tickled Kaisa's lips, and for a moment Kaisa relaxed in his fatherly embrace. Before she could make her way to the bar, where Maggie was pulling a pint, Jeff brought out a short, dark-haired girl and said, 'Meet Catherine!'

Not another girlfriend, Kaisa thought, giving Catherine a quick peck on her cheek. Jeff went to get their drinks and motioned towards the corner table. The pub was small, and everyone knew each other. As Kaisa and Catherine made their way past the bar, the other customers said hello. Kaisa couldn't remember anyone's names, so she just smiled and nodded to the familiar faces.

When she got to Jeff's mum, a grey-haired woman with rimless glasses and a pinny over her dress, Kaisa gave her a kiss on the cheek and asked how she was. 'Can't complain,' she said. It was her responsibility to cook the bar meals in the pub, and she was often flustered. Kaisa could see she was glad to have Jeff back, because her eyes were following his every move. She now laughed at something Jeff said. He'd been to the Falklands, and even though the war was long won, and the danger over, everyone knew the Argentinians could mount another surprise attack. Jeff was now telling a long-winded tale about his trip to everyone at the bar. Kaisa couldn't make out what it was about, nor did she understand the punchline, but she laughed at the end anyway, along with Catherine.

It was a typical night in the pub. She and Peter had spent many evenings like this when they lived for a short while in Jeff's house on Devonshire Road before their marriage. The laughter and drink, and the way Jeff and his dad entertained everyone with their stories, made Kaisa suddenly feel Peter's absence more acutely. She realised how often, during their pub evenings, he had to explain stories to her, or translate the naval terms people used. Jeff did some of this for her now, but he was also looking after his new girlfriend, who had a bubbly, overflowing way of laughing at his jokes.

As the night went on, Kaisa and Catherine struck up a conversation. Usually Jeff's dates didn't have anything to say to Kaisa, and Kaisa had nothing to say to them, but this girl had studied politics at Portsmouth Polytechnic, and they began discussing the British electoral system, the subject of Kaisa's theses back in Finland. She loved debating the subject.

'Will you listen to these intellectuals?' Jeff laughed when Kaisa and Catherine had got onto arguing about the merits of first-past-the-post as opposed to proportional representation. Catherine was a strong opponent of coalition government, but their discussion was far from hostile, and until Jeff made them stop by asking Kaisa about Peter, she enjoyed talking about something other than her job prospects or the Navy. She'd have to tell Peter about the new girlfriend when he phoned. As yet she'd not heard from him. She was disappointed he'd not called to say he had got up to Scotland alright, but she presumed he'd not had the time because of 'the trials', whatever they were. As usual with evenings at The Palmerston, there was a lock-in and they carried on drinking after closing time. Kaisa felt herself getting drunker and drunker, but didn't care. She didn't have a job to go to the next day, nor did she have an interview lined up. All she had was time, so why not use it to nurse a hangover?

The next day Kaisa slept in until late in the morning. When she came down the stairs, she hoped there'd be a letter from Peter, but there were just a few fliers and that day's edition of the *Guardian* on the mat. She'd not heard from Peter since she kissed him goodbye on the doorstep five days previously. She knew he would be busy, getting to grips with a new job and a new crew. He said he knew a couple of the other officers on the new submarine, but admitted that he was a little nervous about meeting the Captain, an older officer who'd been in charge of HMS *Tempest* for two years. But since they were still alongside in port (Kaisa presumed, based on what Peter had told her), and not at sea, surely he would have been able to get in touch? Of course, Peter might have contacted her the night before, when she was in the pub with Jeff and his new girlfriend. Although she was desperate to talk to Peter, a part of her felt a sense of triumph at not always being available to him. That is, if he did try to call.

All that evening she waited for the phone to ring, and by ten o'clock she was feeling desperately confused and worried. How could Peter be so busy that he couldn't find time to talk to her? Had something happened to him? Or didn't he miss her at all? Kaisa's heart ached at not being close to Peter – she couldn't sleep at night for missing his shape next to her in their bed.

Peter finally called at 11pm, when Kaisa was about to go upstairs to bed. Just hearing his voice made Kaisa feel wonderful again. She forgot all about her desperation when he told her the news: he'd be back at the weekend.

'That's why I didn't call before,' he said, 'because I didn't want to tell you before it was confirmed – we've all got leave because the sea trials went so well.'

Kaisa hugged the telephone. At that moment she felt so happy she could hardly breathe. It was Friday night and Kaisa would see Peter the next day. She spent the next few hours tidying up the flat, late into the night, and in bed she dreamed about their first kiss.

The next morning there was more news: a letter from the employment agency was waiting for Kaisa on the doormat when she got up. They had a job for her! Kaisa was so happy, she nearly phoned her mum, but decided against it. Telephone calls home were so expensive; besides, she needed to get herself and the flat ready for Peter.

5

P eter looked weathered – all tanned and grinning widely – when Kaisa met him off the train at Southsea Harbour. It was early Saturday evening, and Kaisa had been awake since 9am because she had so much to organise. She wanted the maisonette to look as tidy and homely as she could make it. She'd even ironed one of the linen tablecloths from Finlayson, a wedding present from her grandmother, and spread it over the dining room table. The pattern of pink roses badly clashed with the sofa, but Kaisa decided not to care. She didn't think Peter would notice. She laid the table for a dinner of steak and salad, which she'd half prepared. She'd put the steak in a red wine marinade – a Finnish recipe – ready to fry later. She wanted the stage set for the news she was going to deliver that evening. She dressed carefully, in a skirt and blouse, and wore her lacy French knickers and suspenders. Looking at herself in the mirror, before leaving for the station, she'd been pleased; the sun and sea in Southsea had bleached her hair and made it curlier than it was in Finland, a look that suited her. She'd put on some pink lip gloss and hurried out of the door.

When Peter first stepped off the train he didn't see her, but when she waved like a madwoman he waved back and walked briskly towards her. He scooped Kaisa up in his arms and kissed her for so long that she felt embarrassed. Peter kept grabbing her bottom, and kissing her fully on the lips as they walked towards the station exit. Other sailors, recognisable for their short, smart haircuts and the Pusser's grips they, too, were carrying, grinned at them, but an elderly couple, descending from the first-class compartment on the same train, viewed Kaisa and Peter with disdain.

'We're married,' Kaisa wanted to shout out to them, but instead she smiled in their direction. The man nodded, but the woman looked pointedly away. Peter and Kaisa giggled and ran out of the station.

'Do you want to go to the pub?' Kaisa asked once they were outside. It was Saturday, and they were passing Jeff's parents' pub. Peter kissed her again and whispered in her ear, 'No, I want to go home and take you to bed.'

It wasn't until later that evening, after they'd finished their steak and salad, that Kaisa was able to tell Peter her news.

'I've got a job!'

'That's great news!' Peter gave Kaisa a peck on her cheek.

Kaisa told him about how nice the woman at Bayleys had been, and how she'd been offered a temporary job at Information Data Services, or IDS as everyone called the large American company. Peter hugged her. 'I said you'd get a job, didn't I?' Then he yawned. 'God, I'm tired! We had a few beers last night, with an early start today and no sleep at all on that bloody train from Helensburgh to Glasgow. It was full of matelots, home for the weekend, and already plastered.' He'd changed into his jeans and a blue T-shirt after they'd been to bed. Kaisa looked at his slim torso, and went over and put her hands around his neck.

The next morning when Peter woke up early, Kaisa stayed in bed. She could hear him opening and slamming doors downstairs in the kitchen, and soon he was coming up again with a cup of black coffee for her. Kaisa sat up, yawned, and looked out of their bedroom window. Like the kitchen below, the bedroom overlooked the back of the houses opposite. There was also a nursery school with a playground, where Kaisa had seen mothers drop off their children. The sky was bright blue and the sun was shining into the bedroom.

'It's fantastic to be back home with you,' Peter planted a kiss on her mouth. He slipped back in between the sheets and they made love again, more slowly this time. Afterwards, when they were lying in bed, with the covers off because the heat of the day had made the room stuffy and their exertions made them hot, Kaisa placed her head in the crook of Peter's arm and said, 'I've got a good feeling about this job.' She told Peter that she was going to be working at the Purchase Ledger Department of the new IDS headquarters in Cosham. 'I feel that I'm on my way to a proper career!'

'That's great, but right now, unless you want me to devour you again, I need some food!' Peter stood up and pulled on his jeans and a T-shirt.

He took the stairs down two, three at a time and while Kaisa was getting dressed shouted up to her, 'I think we need to go shopping!' Kaisa started hurrying. As she brushed her teeth, she looked at herself in the mirror. Her face was aglow; she was even happier than before, if that was possible: happy to be married, happy to be in Portsmouth, happy to be a Navy wife.

That lunchtime they went out with Jeff and his new girlfriend, Catherine, who Peter said was a 'bloody Welshie'.

'I like her,' Kaisa told him when they were walking home. Peter put his arm around Kaisa and said, 'Well, I'm glad. Let's just hope he sticks to this one. With his past record, I'm not sure he will.'

When Peter left on the Sunday afternoon, Kaisa decided not to go and see him off at the station. Waving goodbye again would make her tearful, and she'd decided that this time she was going to act like a grown-up. She was a career woman now and career women didn't shed tears over men!

On the Monday morning Kaisa was due to attend the Cosham office at 10am. There she would meet her manager, who would allocate her a job. On Sunday evening, she went to bed early, and put the radio alarm clock on the highest possible setting, a whole two hours before she needed to leave the flat.

The IDS building was a large modern complex with green hanging plants suspended from wide balconies. The bus Kaisa had been told to take was staff transport and everyone on board knew each other and chatted loudly. She was given the occasional glance, but there was one other girl who sat by herself, so Kaisa didn't feel that much out of place. In the large reception area, with glass walls and long pine reception desks, she was greeted by a thin woman in a suit jacket, wearing a tight skirt and flat pointy shoes. She introduced herself as Kerry, Account Manager in the UK Purchase Ledger Department. They were joined by the other girl, called Susan, who'd sat on her own in the bus, and they all took a lift to the fourth floor and a vast room filled with desks and people either busy on the phones or shuffling papers.

'Where are you from?' Kerry asked Kaisa as she led the three of them past several desks towards an office separated from the large room by a glass partition.

'Oh, me?' Kaisa was taken by surprise, since during the ride in the lift Kerry had mostly ignored her, and instead chatted to Susan, who'd been recruited by the same agency as Kaisa. Susan had told Kerry she was from Yorkshire. She spoke loudly, but was very slight with pale skin and long, black hair swept off her face in a tight ponytail.

Kerry stopped by the open door to the glass-framed office, where a man in shirtsleeves sat behind a large desk.

'Richard, this is Susan and Kaisa. They've come to help us from Bayleys.'

Richard's handshake was firm, and while he held Kaisa's hand his pale blue eyes ran briefly over her body, making Kaisa wish she'd worn her interview suit instead of the summery skirt she'd made while working at Stockmann's in Helsinki. She'd fallen in love with the fabric, which had an Alpine landscape drawn across the hem, and had bought two metres to make a gathered skirt to wear in summer. Her top was home-made, too, a design she'd invented by simply sewing two squares together, leaving holes for arms and a larger boat neck for the head. That fabric, too, had been a favourite of hers when she worked at the haberdashery department in Stockmann's. The only problem was that the opening at her neck was a bit larger than she'd intended and occasionally the top slid off to one side, revealing a bare shoulder. Kaisa knew it was a fashionable look, but suddenly, under the gaze of this important man at her new workplace, it didn't seem appropriate wear at all.

Richard asked Kaisa and Susan to take a seat and, while Kerry scurried out of the office, he perched on the front of his desk. The ankle of one of Richard's legs, which he'd pulled up to the desk, was level with Kaisa's eyes and she noticed there was a mass of dark hairs showing in between the hem of his trousers and a pair of bright red socks. Kaisa forced her eyes away and replied to the question that Kerry had asked, which her new boss was now repeating.

'I'm from Finland.'

'Ah, that's interesting. I think we've had one girl from Finland here before. She was very good, efficient and a hard worker.' Richard smiled briefly, letting his gaze linger on Kaisa. 'And what brings you to England?'

Kaisa told him about Peter, and about being married. 'I don't need a work permit,' she said.

'Oh, don't worry about that. The agency sorts out that, thank goodness, so we don't have to.' Richard turned his face to Susan and then, with a serious face, spoke to Kaisa again. 'I must stress that you do not work for IDS. You will be paid by the agency, and told how long you have to work with us, and so on. Of course, you will take your instructions on what to do from us, or Kerry in this case, but there is no contract between IDS and you. Is that understood?'

Both Susan and Kaisa nodded and, as if by magic, as if she'd known when the conversation with Richard had come to a point that could be interrupted, Kerry appeared at the door and ushered the two of them out of the office.

That same evening Kaisa phoned her mum and told her the good news about the job. She didn't tell her it was temporary; she'd been so busy on her first day that she was hopeful they would keep her on longer than the four weeks that had been agreed. Although she was tired, Kaisa felt she'd got to grips with what Kerry wanted her to do right away. She was checking a list of figures on a printed report from the ledgers against statements that had been sent from the suppliers. Some of the sums didn't match, and that's when she needed to look at old records on microfilms. It was easy work, and really beneath her, but it was a start.

That first weekend when she was alone again, Jeff and Catherine took Kaisa out shopping on Saturday. In the evening she went on a pub crawl with them, ending up in an 'Officers only' club called Pomme d'Or. Kaisa had heard Peter and Jeff talk about the place, but she'd never been inside. Whenever she'd suggested it, Peter had always said she wouldn't like it there. Kaisa secretly thought that the reason he didn't want to go was because there were girls there that he didn't want Kaisa to meet. The door was painted black and Jeff had to show his Navy ID at the entrance. A set of stairs led to a dirty-looking cellar with red walls and carpet, and a bar at one end. There was a haze of cigarette smoke hanging in the air, and the music was so loud they had to shout to each other.

'What do you want to drink?' Jeff shouted in Catherine's ear. She opted for half a pint of lager. Kaisa decided to have the same and when Jeff turned around to give the drink to her, she heard a voice close to her say, 'Jeff, my man!' As she turned around she saw a tallish man, with light blond hair and friendly eyes smiling at her.

'Your taste in women has improved,' he said to Jeff, still looking at Kaisa.

Jeff coughed and, brushing his hair back from his eyes, said, 'Kaisa, this is Duncan Lofthouse. This is Kaisa Williams, Peter's new wife.'

Duncan took Kaisa's hand and kissed it, 'Oh yes, the Scandinavian beauty Peter landed himself. But we have met, at Jackie's party, up in town. Don't you remember me, Keesi?' Duncan continued to look deeply into Kaisa's eyes, and, to say something, she leant over and spoke into his ear, 'It's K-a-i-s-a.'

Duncan smiled and said into her ear, 'Well, K-a-i-s-a, would you like to dance?'

The four of them ended up spending the evening together and the next day they all met up for lunch at The Still and West in Old Portsmouth. The pub had a roof terrace that overlooked the Solent, and it was the place to be on a sunny summer's day. They were sitting at a table with a weatherworn wooden bench against the wall, with two chairs opposite. Catherine and Jeff shared the bench, while Kaisa and Duncan settled themselves on the chairs. Kaisa pulled her chair slightly away from Duncan, to avoid the sun in her eyes, but also because she'd spent nearly all the previous evening dancing with him, and didn't want him to get the wrong idea. During a slow piece, 'Careless Whisper', by George Michael, he'd pulled her a little too close, and Kaisa had had to push him away.

'Look, Peter and I went to Dartmouth together, so you have nothing to worry about with me,' Duncan had told her after the dance.

When she'd woken up that morning, with a slight hangover, Kaisa had immediately regretted that she'd promised to meet the others for lunch. The night before it had seemed such a good idea. As many ideas were when you've drank too much! She'd wanted to celebrate her new job, or feel like a normal person going out with friends, even without Peter. They'd had such a laugh at the club, and when Duncan had hit on the idea of a pub lunch, and both Jeff and Catherine had insisted she should come along, Kaisa had relented. She also knew Peter would want her to enjoy herself.

On the top of Still and West there was a light breeze from the sea. Kaisa began shivering as they waited for Jeff and Catherine, who were queuing up for their drinks and burgers.

'Here, take my jumper,' Duncan said and pulled off his light-yellow sweater, handing it to Kaisa. His polo shirt revealed muscular, strong arms. 'That's alright,' said Kaisa, resisting looking at the veins in his arms as well as the chivalrous gesture. But Duncan wouldn't accept her refusal, so she wrapped the jumper over her shoulders.

'Go on, put it on,' Duncan said.

'No, it's OK,' Kaisa said but couldn't stop herself shivering from the cold.

'Well, in that case ...' Duncan pretended to get up and take hold of Kaisa, 'Shall I?'

'No, I'll put it on.' Kaisa giggled and pulled the soft cashmere sweater over her strappy top.

When Kaisa got home from the pub – alone – she'd refused Duncan's offer to walk her home – she wrote a letter to Peter. Before leaving, Peter had told Kaisa that she should write letters, but that the postal delivery was unreliable on the nuclear subs. 'They bring the letters by a boat, which comes alongside, or sometimes by helicopter. But you know how much I love getting your letters, so you must keep writing, darling, even if you don't hear back from me for a few days – or weeks. And don't forget the perfume, or the 'sports pages'. Kaisa had promised to sprinkle her perfume on the letter before she posted it, as she'd done since he asked her to do it when they were unmarried and living in separate countries. The 'sports pages' was harder for her. Peter had told her that all the wives and girl-friends wrote naughty bits in their letters, basically about sex, but Kaisa worried that their correspondence would go astray, and end up in the wrong hands. But she did write every day without fail, managing to end each letter with some saucy sentences.

This time she first told him about her job, how she was checking a list of numbers against another list, and although the work was tedious, she was enjoying being at work and feeling that she belonged. Her boss, Richard, seemed pleased with her work, and said she could take responsibility for a set of purchase ledger accounts soon. It felt a little like a promotion, and although Kaisa hadn't quite got to know all the other people working in her department, she felt at home at IDS. She described the other girls in the office, including Susan, the other girl from the agency.

When Kaisa had finished writing, she noticed the letter came to six sheets of paper. She'd included a naughty sentence at the end, but mentioned Duncan only fleetingly, deciding not to say how much she'd enjoyed his company.

6

Peter had been away for just two weeks but Kaisa missed him terribly. It was so hard not to know where he was, or be able to talk to him. Peter had explained to Kaisa before he left that now he was on a nuclear powered submarine, he wouldn't be able to get to a port as often as he had in the diesel boats, because the nuclear reactor onboard HMS *Tempest* meant they wouldn't be allowed to dock just anywhere.

'I don't expect I'll be able to call more than once or twice during the time we're away,' he'd said. 'And you know the letters won't be picked up as often as in diesel boats.' Kaisa had nodded, she knew about the letters. She'd been horrified that Peter would be sleeping in a confined space with a reactor, but he'd assured her it was perfectly safe. He'd taken her into his arms and kissed her forehead, 'You have nothing to worry about, my lovely. These boats are safer than the diesel ones by far. My old boat was like a tin can, compared to this one.' So she'd tried not to worry and to prepare herself for the long period of no contact with Peter. She was delighted therefore when she got a surprise letter on Monday.

My darling Kaisa,

It's been raining here non-stop, and I had a terrible journey up. The flight was delayed, and when I eventually got to Glasgow I had to wait two hours for a train to Helensburgh. Of course it was pissing down, and there were no taxis, so I had to phone the base for a lift. (Lucky I had coins in my pocket for the phone!) The provost who had to pick me up wasn't well pleased.

I hope Jeff is looking after you. I hear he's going away again at the end of the month, so I hope you'll be in touch with Sally. She'd love to see you.

Kaisa thought back to Sally, the older woman who had been their neighbour in Devonshire Road, and who'd helped her before their first registry office wedding in Portsmouth. When Peter had found out he couldn't get legally married in Finland without a Certificate of No Impediment, which took six weeks to organise, they had to arrange a hasty wedding in Southsea while Peter was on weekend leave from his post outside Naples. When they went on to have the ceremony in Finland, Kaisa was fortunate that her Finnish guests didn't notice the lack of a full service at the cathedral in Tampere. Even her own mother hadn't been aware of the earlier marriage in England. Kaisa remembered how wonderful Sally had been to her, and decided she would visit her very soon. She continued reading Peter's letter.

I miss you more than I can say, and wish you were here with me in my bunk now. The things I'd do to you ... don't be mad, but you may notice that a pair of your lacy knickers are missing. Your scent is driving me crazy.

All my love,
Peter x

Kaisa blushed at the thought of her dirty underwear being found by the steward in Peter's bunk, but that last sentence had made her go all tingly, and she sat down immediately to pen a reply. The 14 days he'd been away felt like months. Kaisa wasn't sure she'd cope without him for the next (how many, she didn't know) weeks. But she was lucky in that Jeff was at home for now. His new girlfriend worked in London and wasn't around much during the week, so Kaisa took on the role of being Jeff's best mate, drinking pints of beer with him instead of ladylike halves, and paying for her own drinks. Jeff was very good to her and Kaisa felt as if, for the first time in her life, she had a brother. Unlike the soft-spoken Duncan. He was in Portsmouth on some kind of course, and like all of Peter's friends had taken it upon himself to look after Kaisa while her husband was away. It was nice, but it frightened Kaisa, because she didn't trust herself fully with Duncan. She'd thought about it a lot. After their burgers at the Still and West, they'd all gone into Jeff's parents' pub for a final drink of the day. Jeff's dad had told them all that Justin and Mary were rumoured to have an open relationship. Kaisa was shocked; they had looked so happy.

'Poor Mary, she's only been married to him just over a year, and she's pregnant!' Jeff's sister Maggie said, and his mother shook her head.

Kaisa didn't say anything but wondered if that was one solution for a Navy marriage? Still, the rumours about Justin and Mary were just that, talk in a pub, so couldn't be relied upon. But she had to admit Duncan was really charming. Kaisa knew she'd begun to like him as soon she saw he was so openly attracted to her, which was very flattering. She thought, 'Why do women still only "love" the men who "love" us first?' Kaisa liked to think Peter was different, but she kept wondering – if he'd not been all over her when they first met in Helsinki, would Kaisa still find herself here in a foreign country as Peter's wife? She brushed these stupid thoughts away. Peter and Kaisa belonged together; they'd fallen in love at first sight at the British Embassy cocktail party in Helsinki, and they would always be together.

Two days later Kaisa had a letter from her mother with some strange news: she was going to leave Stockholm and move back to Helsinki. She'd had enough of the Swedes and on a recent trip back to Finland she'd been offered her old job back at Neste Oil.

'Your sister is going to come with me – she's been offered a job in the Intercontinental Hotel in Helsinki,' her mother wrote.

Kaisa couldn't quite believe this, because when her mother had moved away, just after she herself had started studying at Hanken, she couldn't wait to leave Finland. Ever since, she'd rarely had anything good to say about her native country, but Kaisa guessed she'd begun to miss home after a few years away. She wondered if the same would happen to her after a while in England.

Later that night Kaisa decided to watch the video of her June wedding in Finland, for the umpteenth time. Of course, it made her miss Peter, her sister and mother, and everybody at home.

On the first Sunday in August, when Peter had been away for 15 days, Kaisa felt her longing for Peter had entered new territory. Perhaps it was because there was no post since that first letter, but it felt as if part of her had been ripped out. If only she could talk to him just once and tell him about how well she was doing at IDS, about Jeff and his new girlfriend Billy (Catherine never came back. When Kaisa asked Jeff about her, he just shrugged his shoulders and changed the subject).

Kaisa decided to go for a jog mid-morning, running around the Common and fairground into Old Portsmouth. The weather in Pompey at the beginning of August was glorious, and the seafront was full of sunbathers and couples holding hands. Families with small children had taken over the grassy field at Southsea Common. At the seafront, Kaisa climbed on top of Southsea Castle, with the old battlements overlooking the harbour and the Dolphin submarine base across the water in Gosport. The sun glittered on the sea, and the waterfront was busy with small sailing boats. A large car ferry returning from France tooted its horn to warn the sailors. When the large vessel had passed, Kaisa could make out a few officers having drinks on the Wardroom balcony of HMS *Dolphin*. She thought about the first Ladies' Night with Peter there, more than a year ago now, when she had found out that her nationality was a problem for the Navy. She was from a 'country friendly with the Soviet Union' they'd said, a fact that would prevent Peter marrying her. But here she was, out of breath, but feeling strong and healthy, living in Portsmouth and married to Peter. How her life had changed in such a short time.

And she had a job, even if it was temporary. When she spoke to the other girls in the vast staff cafe at the IDS headquarters, she realised that, with her Master's degree in economics, she was more qualified than the others. Still, she was on a contract via an agency, and not one of the permanently employed staff. Most of the permanent girls had a Bachelor's degree from an English or Scottish university, or just A-levels, which Kaisa knew were equivalent to her baccalaureate exam from Finland.

'This is only a stepping stone,' she told herself.

But thinking back to what Jackie had said at the party in London that time made Kaisa realise how little people around her understood, or rather valued, her Finnish degree. Oh well, Kaisa had a job, which she was being paid for, permanent or not.

That evening Kaisa wrote Peter another long letter. She exaggerated, just a little, the importance of her position at IDS. She wanted him to feel proud of her.

Another day passed without a letter. When Kaisa got home from work, she scanned the pile of post on her doormat, but it was mostly bills and advertising leaflets. She sighed. Kaisa had no idea where Peter was. She remembered that he'd said they might sail soon after he got back to Scotland. At least, now he'd been home for his weekend leave, the time away was shorter.

'I'll be home before you know it,' Peter had said when he'd left.

The next day at work, Kaisa got a phone call from Bayleys; IDS wanted her for another two weeks. Working with figures at IDS gave Kaisa a kind of satisfaction, but she wanted to go so much further. She'd found out there were jobs at IDS that she could apply for, and she now felt certain her career belonged there. But she'd made the stupid mistake of telling Kerry, her manager, that she'd seen an ad in the *Portsmouth News* for 'Credit Controllers for IDS'. Kerry had just shrugged her shoulders and hadn't even commented on Kaisa's remark. Kaisa and her stupid pride. The same pride had made her tell Ann, a permanent member of staff, in the canteen that morning that she hoped to get a better job soon, because of her Master's degree.

'You're still a temp,' Ann had replied. She was the only girl in the department who'd been hostile to Kaisa from the first moment that they'd met. Kaisa didn't know why, but Ann obviously couldn't stand her and now the feeling was mutual. She talked really fast and often used slang words that Kaisa didn't understand. Ann was about the same age as her, or perhaps a little bit older, but the way she made up her hair and face aged her. She wore a cake of foundation, glossy lipstick and so much mascara that her eyelashes stuck together in black clumps. She had this Alexis from *Dynasty* type hair, all piled up on top of her head, with so much Elnett spray that it overpowered the senses of anyone standing next to her. And she wore really high heels, while all the other girls looked professional in their flat Princess Diana style courts. But Ann was a permanent employee, a Purchase Ledger Clerk and, in theory, could tell Kaisa what to do. Kaisa had soon realised she knew more about the job than Ann did, and started asking Kerry if there was a problem, because Ann was never able to help her.

When the manager at the agency had interviewed Kaisa, he'd promised that she could apply for something better as long as she did well in this job first. At least that's something Kaisa had, an assurance that, even though she wasn't English, her intelligence, qualifications and language skills would eventually get her a better job than that stupid girl had.

Apart from Ann and Kerry, all the girls in the department, including Susan who had started at the same time as Kaisa, were interested to find out why Kaisa had come to England. When she told them the story of the

British Embassy party and the long-distance love affair that ensued, they all sighed, 'Oh, how romantic!'

Telling the story made Kaisa miss Peter even more. She was concerned that she'd not heard from him, either by letter or a phone call from some port or other, but tried not to worry that something had happened to the sub.

7

Peter had been away for 19 days, and Kaisa's longing worsened, if that was possible, as the days stretched on and on. Especially when she was stupid enough to watch an old American film on TV. Ronald Reagan played the lead and it was so romantic it made her miserable. While sitting on the ugly sofa, watching the stupid film, she even lit a cigarette, thinking that would help, but it just made her head spin, so she gave up and slumped down in front of the TV again.

After work that day Kaisa had gone into Allders on Commercial Road and bought a beige mac, which, when she put it on at home, she didn't like anymore. She'd wanted something to wear to a job interview on Monday. She'd finally been given a chance to make a career at IDS. On the previous day, after the other girls had gone home, Kerry had come to tell her that Richard wanted to see her in his office. Richard told Kaisa they were looking for a graduate for the Finance Section, and she may want to apply. When he'd given Kaisa the application form she'd been so glad she nearly kissed him. As she left the office, she saw Kerry looking at her. Kaisa was sure it had not been Kerry's idea to tell her about the new post. Now she worried about what to wear. In England, she never knew if a trouser suit or a dress was best. Jeff had told her that if a woman wore a trouser suit, men would think she was a 'lesbo' – 'or radical in some other way,' he'd said and grinned. Peter told her that she looked good in anything she wore, and that was the most important thing. But Kaisa doubted that looking sexy was right; she wanted to look professional, but still stylish and slim.

If only she had more self-control – Kaisa ate far too much when alone. The suit would be too tight on her, she knew it, but what else could she wear? She had no skirts that were professional enough. But she just couldn't resist the English white bread and jam. At home in Finland she ate rye bread, which she was certain was healthier, but she hadn't found any in the shops here. She was sure the white bread was the reason she was putting on weight. Since Peter had gone away, Kaisa had spent nearly every night after work watching telly and eating – all unhealthy and miserable. At least when she stayed at home in the evenings, she wasn't spending any money.

Now she wished she hadn't agreed to have Sunday lunch with Jeff and Billy. She knew what would happen. She'd lay about in bed, getting up far too late to get any laundry, ironing or cleaning done, and leaving just enough time to get dressed and hurry to the pub. Jeff's parents would have a lock-in until 5pm, after which she'd loll about on the sofa reading the Sunday papers for the rest of the afternoon and then watch TV all evening. She'd feel too drunk to do any housework, and she would have spent far too much money on booze and food in the pub. But it was too late to cancel now. Besides, Jeff always made her laugh. And Billy was good fun, too, if she was in a good mood. Perhaps Billy would be able to tell her what to wear to her interview on Monday.

Because she'd promised, Kaisa did go to the pub. As well as Jeff and Billy there was another Navy couple there called Maureen and Matthew. He'd been to Dartmouth at the same time as Peter (and Jeff and Duncan), and Maureen and Billy were old friends. Kaisa wondered briefly if Jeff had met Billy through Maureen, but didn't have the chance to ask, because after they'd had their first drink, the door opened and Duncan walked in, with a wide grin on his face. 'I knew I'd find you lot here.' He planted a kiss next to Kaisa's mouth, and squeezed her tightly. Kaisa avoided sitting next to him, and moved right to the end of the table next to Billy. She excused herself after the first drink, 'I've got an interview tomorrow,' she said and fled before Duncan came close to her and planted another kiss. But later, after she'd eaten cheese on toast instead of the lunch she'd planned to have at the pub, the intercom sounded and she heard Duncan's voice.

'Kaisa, I'm really sorry, but I've got a huge favour to ask you.'

Kaisa considered changing out of her saggy tracksuit and back into her jeans and fake suede boatneck top she'd worn to the pub, but decided she shouldn't worry if she looked a mess in front of Duncan. She'd not had the time in any case, because she'd hardly put the intercom phone down when Duncan was at the door.

'I know this is really cheeky, but could you help an old bachelor out?'

Duncan looked so helpless, and genuinely in need of her expertise in sewing, that Kaisa softened. She took his Navy jumper and promised to mend it. Duncan was so pleased he gave Kaisa a huge hug, lifting her off the floor. When he was about to let go of her, their eyes locked and for an awful moment Kaisa wondered what Duncan's full lips would taste like. But she managed to take control of herself in time and moved away from temptation. 'I should have it back to you tomorrow,' she said. 'Don't worry.'

Peter had been away for 21 days when it was Kaisa's big interview at IDS. The interview was conducted by Richard, together with Kerry and a quiet, older man called Matthew from the Personnel Department. Kaisa couldn't be happier with how it went. She played the efficient, Nordic ice-queen. The macho-female. Afterwards, Kaisa felt as if this Nordic queen had betrayed Peter. When Richard asked if Peter's career would affect her ability to stay on in Portsmouth, she'd said, 'Absolutely not. I will live where my work is.'

'Really?' Richard said, crossing his legs and revealing a hairy calf above his stripy socks. 'We've had a lot of Navy wives working here at IDS, and the majority of them follow their husbands.'

'I'm not the majority,' Kaisa said and returned Richard's stern look.

'So if, as I understand, this is a distinct possibility, Peter – your husband's name is Peter, isn't it?'

'Yes.'

'... let's say Peter gets posted to Scotland. That's quite possible, isn't it?'

Kaisa nodded, keeping her expression neutral. She didn't dare to say anything in case she betrayed her feelings for Peter.

'And you would stay in Portsmouth and not move with him?'

'Yes,' Kaisa said firmly. She didn't want to tell Richard that Peter had already been posted to Scotland – somehow she felt that would make her chances of getting the job smaller.

There was a short silence while Richard looked down at his papers.

'I believe you are living in a married quarter?'

'Yes,' Kaisa said again. This she managed a bit more firmly now. She also moved her upper body slightly forward to show how keen she was. She was glad the suit she wore was black and didn't show the large sweat patches in the armpits of her blouse.

'Are you able to stay in a married quarter if your husband is posted to another location?'

Kaisa stared at Richard and then looked at Kerry. This was a question she hadn't thought of. When they'd discussed Peter's latest posting to HMS *Tempest* and decided it would be best for Kaisa to stay put in Pompey for now, she'd assumed she could stay there forever. Now she made a snap decision and said, 'Yes, I can stay here.'

'And you'd be happy if you saw your husband, say, once in three months or so?'

'Absolutely. I know I moved to England to marry him, but work and a career are more important to me.'

Kaisa watched as Richard and Kerry exchanged glances with Matthew.

Richard smiled and got up. 'OK, thank you very much, Kaisa, we'll let you know after we've interviewed a few more candidates.'

Kaisa closed the glass door to Richard's office, and walked back to her desk. She wondered if it was because Peter was away, that she could lie so effectively. At the end she almost believed it herself – her career was of utmost importance, more important than her marriage, or her husband.

On her way home, thinking about the interview and how she had to lie and pretend to be someone else, Kaisa wished she could have been herself. She wished she could have shown Richard and Kerry the person, the individual, as she really was, and not try to fit into a predetermined mould. Or perhaps it was progress that Kaisa had now learned to fit into that mould?

When Kaisa got to King's Terrace, Jeff was waiting outside her door, wanting to find out how the interview went. While they were drinking coffee in Kaisa's untidy kitchen, and she began telling him about Richard and Kerry, and the questions they'd asked her, the intercom went. She opened the door to a grinning Duncan.

'Hi,' Kaisa said and Duncan took hold of her arms and planted gentle kisses on both of her cheeks before she had a chance to say Jeff was with her. Kaisa didn't want Jeff to think she'd prearranged Duncan's visit. She asked Duncan to go into the lounge and brought him a cup of coffee. She felt terrible thinking it, but Duncan looked very handsome, and even with Jeff in the room, he kept his pale blue eyes on Kaisa. She was still wearing her Nordic ice-queen trouser suit, and she had to hide her blush when Duncan commented on how good she looked.

'If she doesn't get a job looking like that, then whoever interviewed her must be gay,' Duncan said to Jeff, while smiling at Kaisa.

'Actually there was one woman there, too,' Kaisa laughed.

'Oh well, in that case, you're in. Isn't it true that most women fancy other women anyway?' Duncan said.

Kaisa had to bury her face in the steaming cup of coffee to hide another potential bout of blushing. She began to explain to Jeff that Duncan had asked her to mend his Navy jumper, which was true. As she went up the stairs to fetch the jumper, she thought how strange it was that instead of just mending it, sewing up a bit of the sleeve that had come away at the shoulder, she'd also washed the jumper. To her shame, Kaisa had actually liked touching the material that had been close to Duncan – but it made her feel terribly guilty.

Back in the lounge, Kaisa handed the jumper over. Jeff swallowed the remains of the coffee and said to Duncan, 'Time we left Mrs Peter Williams to relax after her busy day in the office, eh?' Duncan got up and gave Kaisa a kiss on both cheeks – not close to her mouth this time, thank goodness. He smelled of aftershave and the wool of the jumper that he was holding with one hand. 'Thank you so much for this. You have no idea what a treat it is for a bachelor like me to have their jumper mended by a lovely girl like you.' Kaisa laughed nervously and tried to ignore the effect his closeness and scent had on her body. If Jeff hadn't been there, she wasn't sure she wouldn't have just fallen into Duncan's arms there and then. What was wrong with her?

When she shut the door and heard the two men talking about some Navy gossip or other on their way down the staircase, she thought how utterly different Jeff and Duncan were from each other. Jeff was so straightforward – he spoke with a Pompey accent, got frequently drunk and had an endless string of girlfriends. On the other hand, she'd never seen the well-spoken Duncan with another girl. Another girl, Kaisa thought. What do I mean by 'another' girl? She went upstairs to change into her tracksuit bottoms and a T-shirt and thought how she must stop thinking about Duncan.

Later that night, as she watched the latest episode of *Das Boot*, a German drama about life aboard a U-boat during the war, Kaisa realised she was projecting Duncan's face, and not Peter's as she usually did, onto the young submarine officer's character. What was happening to her? She needed Peter to come home very soon.

The letter arrived a lot sooner than she thought. It was put into her pigeon-hole at work and she discovered it first thing in the morning. Kaisa's hands trembled when she opened the brown envelope, and when she read the few lines, at first she couldn't comprehend them.

Kaisa suppressed the tears that tried to force their way out, put the letter in her handbag and rushed into the ladies. She read the letter again, now fully understanding its implications.

Mrs Kaisa Williams,

I'm sorry to have to inform you that you have not been successful in obtaining employment with IDS as Account Administrator for the Finance Department.

Thank you for taking the time to attend the interview and for your interest in IDS.

Yours sincerely,

Richard Fairburn

So she wasn't wanted at IDS.

Kaisa tried so hard, what more could she do? Disappointment, anger and shame enveloped her whole being as she sat on top of the loo seat, listening to the mundane chatter of those more fortunate girls with permanent jobs at IDS. They were getting ready for another day behind their desks, applying lipstick and gossiping about their bosses. Kaisa now knew she wasn't as good as them. Even though she had a Master's degree in economics, and she already had good experience in finance from working long summer months as an intern in the bank in Finland, she wasn't good enough for IDS.

Then it hit her. The difference between her and the girls now beginning to leave the loos one by one, was that they were all English. Perhaps Kaisa's English wasn't good enough, or she wasn't modest enough? Perhaps she was too straightforward, or perhaps she was rude without realising it? The English and their sensibilities were difficult to understand sometimes.

Kaisa glanced at her watch when she realised it was quiet outside in the corridor, and saw it was well past nine, the time she should be at her temporary desk. She took a deep breath, buried the letter in her handbag and checked herself in the mirror. The tears she'd feared hadn't materialised, and she looked OK, if a little sad. She lifted the corners of her mouth up, and left the ladies.

All through the day she managed to avoid Richard. She wouldn't be able to take his kindness and pity today. But, towards the end of the day, he surprised her by coming up and tapping her on the shoulder.

'Kaisa, would you pop into my office for a minute?'

Kaisa looked up at him and nodded, 'Yes, of course.'

Once again, Kaisa was sitting inside the large glass cubicle. As she walked behind Richard, Kaisa felt the eyes of the other girls in the open plan office on her back. She was glad she'd worn her favourite white shirt and black cotton jumper combo, so if she got nervous and started sweating again, the dark patches wouldn't show.

'Sit down, please, Kaisa,' Richard said when Kaisa had closed the glass door. 'You had the letter and I'm sure you must be disappointed.'

Kaisa looked down at her hands. Richard was sitting on the edge of his desk, closer to Kaisa than he had been during the interview.

She now looked up and said, 'Yes, I don't understand …'

'You see, Kaisa, we just couldn't risk employing you,' Richard interrupted her, 'I just want to let you know that's all it was.'

'You mean my English isn't good enough?'

Richard laughed, 'Oh God, no. Your English is better than mine, I'm sure of that.'

'So what did I do wrong?'

Richard got up from his perching position, stretched his back briefly, and went to sit behind his desk. He put his hands together and rested his chin on his fingers. 'You see, Kaisa, as I said during the interview, we've had a few girls here who are married to the Navy and we know you ladies like to follow your husbands. You've only been married,' here Richard consulted a piece of paper on his desk, 'just a few months. If your husband is posted away next month, say, I cannot believe you'd stay behind in Portsmouth. That would leave us in the lurch, and we'd have to start the whole recruitment process again.'

'But I said I wouldn't move!' Kaisa said, again feeling a pang of guilt for the lie.

Richard smiled. 'I know that's what you say, but from experience … listen, don't take this to heart, I'm sure you'll find a good job soon.' He got up and went to open the door – a signal for Kaisa to leave the office.

Next day, when Kaisa went to have lunch at the canteen, she saw a group of girls gathered around Susan. As she approached, she heard Ann say to Susan, 'Well done, I knew you were IDS material.' Kaisa rushed out of the canteen and ducked into the loos. Why hadn't Richard mentioned that Susan had applied for the job and got it? Or why hadn't Susan said anything? Kaisa took deep breaths. She was at work, so she couldn't cry her eyes out; she had to control herself. Of course, she understood why they'd chosen her over Kaisa; Susan was single, without a Navy husband who would make her up sticks and leave at the drop of a hat. Kaisa made a fist out of her hands and squeezed hard until her nails dug into her palms. The pain made her feel better and she got up, flushed the loo and walked into the canteen once more. The other girls had now gone, and Kaisa bought a sandwich and a cup of weak coffee. She ate quickly and on her way past Susan's desk, said, 'Congratulations,' and walked briskly back to her own desk.

8

After a few days Kaisa became a little less depressed about her failed job interview. The agency had given her another two weeks at IDS and, since their conversation about the new job, Richard had been very friendly with Kaisa. She thought he felt sorry for her, but Kaisa didn't care – she'd show him when she became the most celebrated businesswoman in the country. In any case, if the reason she didn't get the job was because she loved Peter too much, so what. Wasn't love more important than work? Susan didn't have Peter – as far as Kaisa knew she didn't even have a boyfriend.

Kaisa was missing Peter every second of the day, and seeing Jeff every weekend wasn't helping – somehow he made her miss her husband even more. Besides, Jeff had his own problems. He'd broken up with Billy and said he had no one to love. As usual for a Friday, Jeff phoned Kaisa up and asked if she'd go out to the pub that evening. Even though she was tired, Kaisa couldn't say no to Jeff. Over their first drinks, she asked him what had happened with Billy.

'Dunno,' Jeff said.

Kaisa gave him a friendly hug, and said she wished nothing more than that he'd find someone. Jeff looked depressed and stared into his half-drunk pint for a long time. When Kaisa glanced around the pub, she saw that Jeff's mother was looking at them. Kaisa smiled, but the friendly gesture wasn't reciprocated. Kaisa wondered if she'd done or said something bad to the pub landlady. Both Peter and Jeff often told her that things she had said, or most often hadn't said, were unfriendly or bad manners. She was constantly or tenterhooks and watching what she said and did to make sure she wasn't offending anyone. She'd learned that the English got upset very easily.

'Heard from Peter?' Jeff asked and gulped down his drink.

Kaisa just shook her head. She hadn't had a letter for weeks. When she did get a letter she was elated and skipped up the stairs to their top-floor flat to read it. But once she'd reread Peter's words three or four times, the longing for him became worse again. So in a way not getting letters, although worrying, was less unsettling.

Jeff must have read her mind, because he nudged her. They were sitting side by side on their favourite seat, in the back corner of the pub. Kaisa thought they must have looked a sad pair: one pining for her sailor husband, the other for yet another failed relationship.

'He's alright, you know,' Jeff said and looked at Kaisa from under his blond eyebrows. 'He's probably just too bloody lazy to write.'

Kaisa laughed.

'Go on, drink up, it's my round.'

While Jeff was getting the drinks Kaisa wondered why girls kept leaving him. He was quite good looking in a completely opposite way to Peter. His hair was fair and not very thick, and he was a lot heavier built than Peter, but not in an unattractive way. Was he unfaithful to the girls? That wouldn't surprise Kaisa, but why would he do that if he really wanted a steady girlfriend?

Suddenly Kaisa remembered what had happened in the office earlier that day.

'Listen,' she said to Jeff when he came back with two pints. 'A girl in the office is having a fancy dress party tomorrow and they asked me if I knew any single guys, so I said of course I did, loads!'

Talking about the party cheered them both up, and they started planning how they would get there, because it was just outside Portsmouth, on Hayling Island. Jeff decided that he'd invite three or four guys from the warfare course he was on. One of them could give the others a lift, but that left Kaisa stranded.

'How about if you invite Duncan? His car is in a garage being repaired, but he could drive Peter's car, couldn't he?' Duncan was renting a house on the other side of the water in Gosport.

Kaisa looked at Jeff's face. He looked normal, there was no sign of mischief there. Had he not noticed the tension between Duncan and her the other night?

Duncan was delighted to be invited to Kaisa's IDS party, and agreed happily to the plan. Kaisa spent a long time deciding what she should wear. The theme of the party was Club Tropicana, after the Wham! hit, but Kaisa didn't have any suitable fancy dress clothes, and as it was the weekend before payday had no money to go and buy anything new. She decided to wear the light-blue silk skirt and top she wore to the breakfast party in London in the summer. She knew it suited her and it was summery. On top, she could wear a blue jumper and jazz up her hair with a large pink flower slide that she'd brought on a whim before she left Finland. It was a massive paper orchid, and totally over the top, but it suited her, and the theme of the party.

Duncan was standing outside the row of garages at exactly 7.30pm, as agreed. After kissing Kaisa on both cheeks and telling her she looked beautiful, he helped to open the awkward steel door. Kaisa was wearing high-heeled shoes and was worried she'd make her clothes dirty, so in the end Duncan took the key out of her hand and pulled the door over and open. When Kaisa saw the Ford Fiesta, she immediately felt guilty; what would Peter say if he knew she was getting Duncan to drive her to a party in his car? Jeff didn't think it was a problem at all, but he didn't know what (if anything?) was going on between her and Duncan.

As Duncan drove the car out of the garage, Kaisa managed to close the door. She really should get a driving licence; it was ridiculous that she didn't have one yet. Last night, after their third round of drinks, she and Jeff had promised each other that they'd start taking lessons together. When she turned around she could hear the purr of the engine, but Duncan was now standing beside the car.

'What's wrong?'

'Look at the wheels!' Duncan said.

Kaisa walked around the little grey car and immediately noticed the familiar, faint shape of a heart on the bonnet. Another pang of guilt hit her; Peter had asked her to wash the car after their shotgun English wedding, but she'd postponed doing so, and now the shape Jeff had sprayed onto their car with shaving cream, was a permanent feature of the Fiesta. Jeff thought it funny, and even Peter laughed every time his friend pointed it out, but she knew that really Peter was annoyed at her for not washing it off immediately after he went away on their first day of marriage. It seemed like an age ago now, yet it was only three months.

Duncan was walking around the car. 'Three of the tyres are flat.'

'Oh,' Kaisa said.

'And there's no petrol either.'

Duncan and Kaisa looked at each other. Both were serious for a moment, then burst out laughing. 'What are we going to do?' Kaisa said.

'Get a cab?'

'Well …' Kaisa had only a fiver in her purse. She'd spent more than she had planned in the pub the night before.

'It's OK, I've got cash,' Duncan said and smiled. 'You go and open the garage again and I'll try to reverse it back.'

Luckily, Kaisa hadn't locked the garage. She went over and twisted the handle. This time the door opened easily — it was as if the runners had been oiled from opening it up for the first time in weeks, just minutes earlier.

On the way to the party Duncan and Kaisa laughed about the state of Peter's car, and Kaisa silently promised herself to take those driving lessons. They had a car, and she should drive it and look after it. Her father was an engineer after all; it couldn't be so hard.

The IDS party was in a small flat on Hayling Island, and it took Duncan and Kaisa over twenty minutes to get there. Jeff and his friends had arrived earlier, and Jeff was grinning at her, drinking a can of beer. He was wearing a short-sleeved Hawaiian shirt, open to his navel and revealing a mop of light chest hair. He had flip flops on his feet, exposing equally hairy feet under his frayed jeans. Kaisa thought he looked more like a tramp than one of the Wham! boys in the 'Club Tropicana' video, but as usual there was something charmingly boyish about him, and Kaisa hugged him hard. He really was a good friend, and without him Kaisa would be very lonely indeed in her new home country.

The place was full to bursting with people from work – some Kaisa knew and had talked to, others she knew only by sight. To her surprise, Ann was there too, and complimented her on bringing so many single men. Everyone seemed to know that she was the reason there were several naval officers at the party. When Jeff introduced his four mates to Kaisa, she was reminded of the high value women placed on Peter's profession, and thought how lucky she was. She recalled the times at the Harlequin Club, the Navy's disco, when she'd been eyed suspiciously by the other (English) women there. 'They're just jealous you've bagged a Navy officer,' Peter had once said to her while drunk. They'd been walking home from the pub after another lock-in and she'd asked why the other girls seemed so unfriendly at the Harlequin Club. But these IDS girls seemed to be happy with her rather than jealous.

One of Jeff's friends, whose name Kaisa had forgotten as soon as she'd been introduced, asked her if she wanted a drink, and as soon as he'd said it,

Duncan, too, asked, as did Jeff and his other two friends. 'Can I get you a drink, Kaisa?', 'Kaisa would you like me to get you a drink?' they said in turn. It became a joke and, surrounding her, they all made a show of eagerly waiting to hear which one of them she'd choose. Kaisa just laughed and said, to Jeff, because he was the safest option, 'I'd love a G&T, or white wine, whichever they have.'

The next morning, Kaisa ignored her hangover and decided to check out the Fiesta. She'd decided to sort it out before Peter came home and wanted to see which tyres were flat, and take some details from inside the car so that she could get a garage to come and look at it. As she went to open the garage door, she thought how heavy it seemed again. With some effort, she finally got the door up and over. She stared at the space in front of her.

There was no car in the garage.

It took Kaisa a long while to understand what had happened. Their beautiful little Ford Fiesta, with the permanent mark of a heart on the bonnet, the most romantic reminder of their love, had been stolen.

Upstairs in the flat, Kaisa paced up and down the lounge. What should she do? What could she do? Phone the police? Instead, Kaisa decided to phone Jeff. He sounded sleepy on the phone and when she began to tell him about the car, she could feel her voice breaking.

'Look, Kaisa, I'd phone the police. They'll come and take a statement from you and then you can come to the pub. You'll need a drink after all this.'

One female and one male police officer soon appeared at the door to the married quarter. The male officer was the one who spoke and asked Kaisa questions. Kaisa had told them the whole story, from taking the car out and noting the flat tyres and the empty tank, to how she and Duncan had taken the taxi to the party after reversing the car into the garage.

'So, let me get this straight,' the policeman said. He had a notebook open and a pen poised. 'You, Mrs Williams, don't have a licence to drive?'

'No,'

'And this car belongs to your husband, who is where?'

'He's away – he's in the Navy.' Kaisa said and added, 'A lieutenant in the Royal Navy.' She wanted to make the police understand that she and Peter were a respectable couple.

'And the friend who drove the car away, where is he now?' The policeman gave Kaisa a serious look, as if to ensure Kaisa wasn't lying.

'He is at home. We took a cab to the party and then one back. He dropped me off here first.'

'Right.'

There was a silence.

'And you discovered the car had gone this morning?'

Kaisa nodded and added, 'It had three flat tyres and no petrol. And a shape of a heart on the bonnet.' Suddenly Kaisa felt tearful. 'Sorry,' she said to the policeman. The policewoman smiled at Kaisa and said, 'It's OK, Mrs Williams. We'll take a look downstairs and file the report. I'm sure your husband's car will turn up soon.'

After Kaisa had shown the empty garage to the police, and they'd left her, she phoned Jeff again.

'Meet me at one o'clock in the pub. You need cheering up and I've got some news. I spent the night with a lovely lady from last night.' Kaisa could hear giggling in the background.

Kaisa was shocked to see Jeff's new girlfriend was Susan from IDS. Kaisa had told Jeff about the job, and how they'd both applied for the same position and Susan had won. But Kaisa greeted Susan with a kiss on her cheek, and tried very hard to pretend there was no reason why she shouldn't like her. And, of course, there wasn't; she'd liked Susan as soon as they'd met. Trying to forget about her failed job application, and IDS, made her at least forget about the car. Perhaps it was best that it had gone; surely Peter could use the insurance money to buy a new one? She did worry about telling him, but she put that to the back of her mind and enjoyed the chicken roast that Jeff's parents cooked for Sunday lunch. This time Jeff's mum was all smiles and said she was sorry about the theft of the car.

After lunch and feeling slightly drunk, Kaisa decided to walk home. It was a lovely sunny day. She took in the scent of the sea and listened to the seagulls calling to each other at the seafront, and thought how lucky she was. This is what she had dreamed about during all of those years when she and Peter had been girlfriend and boyfriend, living in separate countries, always yearning to be together. Although they were still separated, at least they were man and wife and shared a home together. Kaisa would just have to get her own career going, so that she could concentrate on work during the times when Peter was away. Then she might not miss him so much, or spend so much time pining for him. Or be tempted by other men, like Duncan.

As soon as Kaisa had stepped inside the flat, the doorbell rang. Outside stood a man she vaguely recognised as living two flats below, in the garden apartment.

'Kaisa, isn't it?' he said and introduced himself as Jack Drummond.

'How do you do,' Kaisa replied as she'd been taught to do by Peter.

'You have a grey Ford Fiesta, don't you?' Jack said.

'Oh, you've found it?' Kaisa wanted to kiss this Jack, who was a little older than Peter and had thinning hair with wisps of grey left on his temples. She was over the moon; the thieves hadn't got far after all.

'Yes, the car is in my garage …'

'What?'

'Yes, it's in my garage, but it's got flat tyres and I'm not quite sure how it could have got there?'

Kaisa went down to the row of garages and helped Jack push the car back into its correct parking spot. Her face was pink from embarrassment. In a gentlemanly fashion, Jack had tried hard not to laugh when Kaisa told him that Duncan wanted to drive them to a party on Hayling Island with the Fiesta, and how he must have backed it into the next-door garage by mistake, after finding that the car had three flat tyres and no petrol in the tank. Kaisa now regretted having told Jack that she'd reported the missing vehicle to the police. He'd asked Kaisa if she'd like him to phone the police on her behalf, and now she saw that it had been a mistake to agree. After recounting the whole sorry tale on her telephone upstairs in the flat, he was quiet for a moment, then turned to Kaisa and asked, with such a wide grin on his face that she thought he'd slit his face open, 'The policeman wants to know if the heart is still intact on the bonnet?'

Kaisa just nodded and Jack thanked whoever was at the end of the line. He hurried out of the flat and Kaisa just knew he and his wife would spend the rest of the evening laughing at her.

9

A fter the car debacle, Kaisa didn't expect to hear from Duncan. It was just as well, Kaisa thought, since Jack, the neighbour, had most probably told the whole world about the car 'with a heart on the bonnet'. That meant that everyone in the Navy would also know that she'd gone out with Duncan. Not that it was unusual in itself; the officers who were ashore often looked after their friends' wives, but for some reason Kaisa felt this was different. It was a little too familiar for Duncan to be driving Peter's car. She wished she'd never agreed to Jeff's plan. Jeff, too, had been busy with Susan. Luckily, Kaisa didn't have to work with her anymore, because the temp contract at IDS had finally come to an end.

On the positive side, it was only eight days until Kaisa would see Peter in Liverpool. HMS *Tempest* would be there on an official visit, and Kaisa couldn't wait to see Peter and feel his lips on hers. She needed to lose some weight before the visit, so she was on a strict diet. No more bread and jam sandwiches.

Now she had too much time on her hands again, Kaisa had started reading *Landlocked* by Doris Lessing. It made her remember how much she agreed with Lessing's view of the world. Especially on the subject of men and women. That women were as independent as men, and had no predetermined duty to marry and have children. But what if she was different and truly loved a man? Love in itself would surely be alright, but what about being really in love and wanting to please your husband? A husband who is a naval officer to boot? Kaisa's need to pamper and please Peter was more acute when he was away. She longed to make him dinner, ready for when he got back from work. She wondered why she'd been so selfish to refuse to make him breakfast in the mornings? She wanted him to need her and her to need him. That didn't sound like a feminist speaking, now did it? Life just wasn't black and white. Still, Kaisa felt as if she betrayed some kind of female code if she acted like a normal Navy wife. But she missed Peter so much. And worrying about him and the submarine kept her awake at night. Peter always played down the dangers the crew faced when underwater, but other people had told Kaisa what could happen. Only the night before, when Kaisa had met Justin's wife, Mary, in the pub, she'd talked to Kaisa about what could happen. Mary's father had been in the Navy too, so she knew all the details of how things worked. Justin had just gone away and Mary said she always worried about him.

'You know it'll be at least two weeks before anyone even starts to look for a missing boat. So if they're sunk, that's it, game over.'

Kaisa shuddered, but said nothing. She didn't want to think about the danger Peter was in; she worried enough as it was. Peter had said HMS *Tempest* was safe, and Kaisa wanted to believe him.

Peter had been away for 35 days when she received a call. She was sitting in front of the TV, with a tray on her lap, when the phone rang in the hall. She spent most weekday evenings like this, watching every programme until it was time for bed. Unless, of course, she was in the pub with Jeff.

As soon as she heard the buzzing noise at the other end of the line, she knew it was her husband.

'Peter?' she said and then the line became clear. It was so good to hear Peter's voice. She'd forgotten its softness. She felt as if he was in the room with her, close to her, and not several kilometres away. Peter told her that they were back in Faslane, in Scotland – or Faslavatory as he called it – and that during their time at sea he'd gained his nuclear submarine qualification. Truthfully, Kaisa didn't really know what that meant, but he sounded so relieved and happy that she was happy for him too. Peter was a winner, which was more than could be said about Kaisa. Perhaps she should put his job first, as was expected of her as a Navy wife, and forget about IDS, and her career? No one would bat an eyelid if she did. But, as she listened to Peter talk about the submarine's forthcoming visit to Liverpool, Kaisa decided to fight against all and everything. That's what she'd done before – or they'd done before. It was what characterised them most: they were fighters against all odds.

'Well, I didn't get the IDS job,' she said, trying to hold back tears. Telling Peter made her remember her disappointment again.

'Never mind, darling, it's probably just meant to be.'

'What do you mean?'

'I've got some not so good news, too,' Peter said.

The tone of Peter's voice made Kaisa grab the receiver with both hands.

'I've got a bit of a pierhead jump to a bomber.'

'What does that mean?'

Peter told Kaisa that he'd been told to join a Polaris nuclear missile sub crew in Faslane in September. 'Someone's got the sack – it's all a bit hush hush, but they've asked me to replace him.'

Kaisa didn't know what to say or think. She knew Peter didn't like it up in Scotland – he said the Scots were unfriendly, and that it was cold and forever raining.

'Does this mean I have to move up?' How would she be able to find a job there? She'd heard the unemployment was worse.

'We'll talk about it in Liverpool, Peanut,' Peter said, and added, 'I can't wait to see you.' He told Kaisa more about HMS *Tempest*'s official visit to Liverpool. 'It's really important that you're there, too,' Peter said. 'All the officers' wives come along, and it's actually quite good fun,' Peter added when Kaisa didn't say anything in reply. Kaisa would have gone to the moon and back if it meant she could see Peter, but she'd been contracted to work at IDS again the following week, and didn't know if she could take Friday off.

'Oh,' Peter said when Kaisa told him about her problem.

He sounded so disappointed that Kaisa immediately said, 'But since they don't want me to work for them permanently, I can't see any harm in taking a sickie.'

Peter laughed at the other end of the line.

Kaisa had learned the term from Ann when she'd told all the girls in the canteen about being hungover one Monday and calling in to say she had a tummy bug. Kaisa had felt sick herself at the time; Ann didn't deserve the job she had, whereas she, Kaisa, would never have lied to her employer if they'd given her a permanent contract.

So they planned what to do in Liverpool and Peter said, 'I don't mind what we do as long as I can take you to bed first.' That made Kaisa's body tingle.

Kaisa told Peter about the car and he laughed so much that, in the end, she got a bit annoyed but let it be. Then he had to ring off because he said there was a queue of guys wanting to use the one and only phone in the

Officers' Mess. Kaisa was relieved he'd not once mentioned Duncan, or wondered why he'd been driving the car. But that was Peter; he was never jealous of her.

Even though the thought of a future move was unsettling, Kaisa felt at peace after Peter's call. Of course she'd been worried about him, or them, because you never knew with submarines, but this peace had another quality to it – she felt just calm and good. Peter had sounded so warm, gentle and caring; full of concern and love for Kaisa. Afterwards Kaisa couldn't concentrate on anything. The trouble was, she just loved Peter too much to care about anything else. She felt so stupid, but she couldn't change that.

The next day, Sunday, Kaisa was about to settle in front of a pile of ironing when the intercom went and Mary came up the stairs.

'I thought you could do with some company,' she said. Mary had brought some biscuits, which meant Kaisa was supposed to make them coffee. While Kaisa stood by the door, Mary moved into the lounge and sat down. She had a visible bump now, although she still had slim legs and small features. Seeing the state of her lounge with a stranger's eyes, Kaisa wished she'd had a tidy up, and was ashamed. But there was nothing she could do now. She poured coffee into the cafetiere and took it into the lounge.

'So how long has Peter been away now?' Mary asked as they sat down on the red-and-yellow sofa.

'36 days.'

'A month and a week …'

'Yes,' Kaisa sipped her coffee. 'But he phoned yesterday evening and I'm going to see him in Liverpool next weekend.'

'Oh, that's lovely.' Mary looked down at her cup. She'd been all smiles at the door, but now she looked sad. Kaisa didn't feel she knew her well enough to ask what the matter was. She wondered if it was true that she and her husband had an open marriage, and if Mary was regretting it. Kaisa said nothing and for a while they both sat there eating biscuits and drinking the coffee. Or rather, Kaisa was drinking the coffee; she noticed Mary was just sipping hers.

'Is it too strong for you?' Kaisa asked nodding at Mary's nearly untouched cup.

'Well …' Mary said.

Kaisa stood up rapidly and knocked her cup over.

'Oh, my God, it's on the carpet!' Mary said and went into Kaisa's kitchen. She returned with a cloth and began to rub at the floor. 'You must get the stain off, otherwise you'll have to pay a fine at handover when you leave.' After several goes with a nailbrush Kaisa got from the downstairs loo, and sheets and sheets of paper towelling, the stain had nearly gone, and they sat back down on the sofa. Kaisa made them both another cup of coffee, a little less strong this time, and they began to laugh about the incident.

'I was just going to get the kettle to water down your coffee,' Kaisa said between giggles.

'Your coffee is a bit …' Mary hesitated, 'powerful, I've got to admit.' They both giggled again. 'But I was so worried about the carpet. With you moving to Scotland soon, you don't want to have to worry about things like that!'

Kaisa stared at Mary, 'How do you know about Scotland?'

'Peter's going to join a bomber, isn't he?'

'Yes, but Peter only told me last night on the phone, so how do you …?'

'Oh, news travels fast in the Navy! Of course he could have had his pick of the jobs, but this one is really good for his career. I know they call them Bomber Queens, because they get the best married quarters and there's so much more room on the Polaris subs, but so what?'

Kaisa stared at Mary. Was she trying to make trouble for her and Peter? She looked friendly and was still smiling from the fit of giggles they'd had earlier.

'He didn't tell you? You know what they're like, especially when they've been away.' Mary's brown eyes were on Kaisa and she looked sincere.

'What do you mean, his pick of the jobs?' Did that mean he could have got a job ashore in Portsmouth, or on a submarine based in Pompey, Kaisa wondered.

'He's doing really well, from what I've heard. He could have said, "no" to the appointer, but this is a really good promotion for him. Unheard of, to move to bombers so quickly. He'll be on Perisher before you know it, and a qualified submarine captain. I bet you'd like to be the captain's wife?' Mary grinned and raised her cup of coffee in a salute to Kaisa.

Kaisa didn't say anything. She thought about all the jobs she'd been applying for in Portsmouth. The effort seemed worthless now. She wondered if Peter knew that Scotland was the most likely place for him if he wanted to get ahead in the Navy? If so, surely he should have told Kaisa this?

Mary went into a long speech about how difficult it was being married to the Navy. She said the wife always loses out because of the moving about. 'It's difficult to keep a career going when you don't know where you are going to be living from one year to the next,' she said and fiddled with her wedding ring.

Kaisa didn't know what to say. Even though she felt closer to Mary after all the fuss with the coffee, she didn't think she should pry into Mary and Justin's relationship. But it was obvious something wasn't quite right. Or was she just the same as Kaisa, wanting a career and not able to have one? 'What would you do if you weren't married to Justin?' Kaisa asked.

Mary looked at her. She didn't say anything for a whole minute or more and Kaisa regretted speaking out. 'I mean, what kind of career would you like to have?' she said.

Mary gave out a short, strained laugh. She stroked her small, round belly and said, 'Oh, I'm not as clever as you, with a degree and all that. I didn't even get very good A-levels, so I guess I'd just work in a shop or something.'

When Mary had gone, it was nearly 1pm. Kaisa decided to make herself a cheese sandwich and, while she was buttering the slice of wholemeal bread and looking out at the empty nursery school opposite, she supposed her life would be easier in Faslane, where Peter would be home more. Mary had told her that there were two bomber crews, and that while one was on patrol with the Polaris submarine, the other was ashore. 'You'll have a lot more time with your hubby,' she'd said. Mary was happier talking about Peter and Kaisa, than she was talking about her own marriage. Thinking back, Kaisa realised she hadn't asked Mary any questions about Justin. She'd been too shocked to hear how much Mary knew about Peter's career. She wondered how much she knew about them?

Watching the empty children's swings opposite, Kaisa remembered that during their honeymoon in Finland, Peter had told her he didn't want children for a few years yet, but that when they did have kids, he wanted them to go to private school. He'd told her that the Navy would pay the fees, but only if she was prepared to move with the Navy, wherever he was serving. But Kaisa didn't want to think about that yet. Children and their schooling was far in the future; she couldn't worry about it now. What she needed to do was get a good permanent job, and look forward to Liverpool and being with Peter. In a few days she'd be able to hold him and tell him how much she loved him.

That was all that was important now.

10

Peter was carrying a red rose when Kaisa saw him on the platform at Liverpool station. There wasn't a happier woman in the world at the moment she felt his arms around her again. He took her to a plush hotel in the centre of the city, and they made love quickly and urgently. Peter had told her that they were going to have 'tea' at the British Legion in Morecombe, so they had to be quick. 'But I can't wait until the evening,' he'd whispered into her ear in the hotel lobby. Afterwards, as she hurried to put on her black-and-white Austin Reed dress and her new mac, she said, 'Will I have to drink tea?' Peter squeezed her bottom and said, 'It's not tea as such; it's what they call dinner. And here they have it earlier. We're up North now!' Kaisa thought, 'Just like in Finland.' It had taken her a long time to get used to the lateness of the evening meal in the UK, and now she found out that having dinner around 5pm was done here, too.

While they waited in the hotel lobby for the minibus to collect the officers of HMS *Tempest*, Peter introduced her to his best friend onboard, an engineer called Tom, and his wife Stephanie, or Stef, as she asked Kaisa to call her. Both Tom and Stef were the kind of couple who were constantly joking with each other, or having mock fights. To Kaisa, they looked as if they were a particularly close brother and younger sister, always teasing each other. Both were also very loud; Kaisa had heard Stef's laugh from the corridor as she entered the hotel lobby. Stef had her long brown hair pinned up on either side of her face, and her eyes heavily made up. Kaisa felt demure next to her.

The meal was hosted by Morecambe's mayor, a large man with a roaring laugh. He wore a uniform with full regalia and was accompanied by a small woman in a lacy dress with pitch-black hair done up in a fragile-looking bouffant. When the mayor spoke, welcoming the officers of HMS *Tempest* to Morecambe, Kaisa realised the reason for the visit was that the submarine was twinned with the small seaside town. Just as her hometown of Tampere was twinned with Norrköping in Sweden, she thought. The guests also included a small group of old submariners, who had fought in the Second World War. They were old men, with wisps of grey hair, and bent-over bodies. Their suits, which looked far too large for their fragile bodies, sagged under the weight of their medals. Peter introduced Kaisa to one of the 'old fellows' as 'a Finn who fought on the other side in the war,' and Kaisa kicked his shins with one of her high-heeled courts. Luckily, the retired submariner hadn't heard the comment and Kaisa could introduce herself as coming from Finland without the sly remark about her country's historical allegiances.

The small, plain hall was dominated by a long wooden table, laid out for dinner with white plates and paper napkins. They were served beef, roast potatoes and bright green peas, with sliced white bread and butter. There was only tea to drink, and Kaisa was too timid to ask for water, or coffee. Trying not to gag, she sipped the sweet milky drink, which two women in housecoats had poured out of tall, two-handed teapots. She decided that she'd never drink tea again; she just couldn't stand the bitter, fatty flavour. The gravy, too, tasted too meaty for Kaisa, and she left most of her food, just managing to pop a few peas into her mouth. After he'd finished his generous serving, Peter glanced over at her full plate and, when no one was looking, switched the plates over and quickly consumed a second dinner. Afterwards, he took hold of Kaisa's hand under the table, and whispered in her ear, 'You look gorgeous.'

Stef and Tom's teasing wasn't reserved for themselves; they began to call Peter and Kaisa 'the young lovebirds' and made heavy hints about their sex life. They were all desperate for a drink after the 'dry' dinner, and went to a number of pubs in Liverpool. Over drinks, when Kaisa tried to stifle a yawn, Tom said, 'Want to take your husband to bed, Mrs Williams?' It was already after midnight, and earlier in the evening they'd also had a drink in the hotel bar with the Captain, his wife and the other officers of the boat. Kaisa had spoken to the Captain's wife, Mercier, an air hostess for British Airways. For some reason, Kaisa had been able to talk to Mercier about finding a career while still being a good Navy wife to Peter in a way she'd not managed with any of the female friends she'd made, or the wives of Peter and Jeff's friends. Mercier was slim, tall, blonde and beautiful and she told Kaisa she'd had similar worries when she and her husband married. 'But you know, it's important that you, too, live your life and do what you want to do with it. If you want a career, then have one. The men can always look after themselves,' she said. At that moment, the Captain, a weathered-looking man with a mop of black hair, had caught Mercier's eye across the room, and the two had exchanged a private smile. Kaisa knew the pair had no children, but that didn't seem to make them less happy. Perhaps that was the way she and Peter should live their lives? Happy when together; concentrating on their own careers when not?

The next morning after making love, in a tangle of sheets, they talked about Scotland, and Peter said that he'd already been allocated a married quarter in Smuggler's Way, just outside Helensburgh. 'We'll have a whole house to ourselves,' he said proudly. Kaisa wondered if he knew how strange all this was for her.

'Are there any jobs up there for me, do you think?'

Kaisa was lying in the crook of Peter's arm and couldn't properly see his face, but she could hear him hesitate. He squeezed her harder to himself, placed a kiss on her head, and said, choosing his words carefully, 'Darling, it may be a bit difficult. But, don't forget, I will be home for six weeks at a time. And if you're working, then we can't do things together during those weeks off, can we?'

The rest of the day they walked around Liverpool, a city Kaisa only vaguely knew as the birthplace of the Beatles. Even though it was the middle of August, the skies were grey with a constant, cold drizzle clinging to the stone-clad buildings and magnificent statues, but Kaisa didn't care about the weather. She was on cloud nine, wrapping herself against Peter for warmth as they ducked into a dimly-lit pub for a lunch of scampi and chips. Peter seemed to be constantly hungry; not only for food but also for her. He had kissed Kaisa's lips over and over while they walked along the rain-soaked streets. Now, in the pub, he squeezed her body close to his and whispered, 'I've missed you,' in her ear. He didn't seem to care that people stared at the two of them. Peter's new job and the threat of a move up to Scotland hung in the air between them, and eventually Peter said, 'The appointment to a bomber is a lot sooner than I expected. But I think the Old Man must have given me a good report,' he added and squeezed Kaisa's hands in his. They were sitting opposite each other.

'The Old Man?' Kaisa asked.

'Oh, that's what we call the Captain.' Peter leaned over and brushed

Kaisa's cheek with his hand. 'I keep forgetting that you don't know these things.'

Kaisa smiled. Peter was so kind to her; she knew he just wanted what was best for both of them. In the evening they went out to an expensive restaurant and had steak and a bottle of French red. For Kaisa, it was wonderful to do something like that; neither of them cared how much it cost.

That evening Stef and Tom caught them in the hotel bar, just as they'd collected the key to their room and were about to enter the lift. Peter gave Kaisa a look of apology but Kaisa shrugged her shoulder and squeezed his hand in agreement.

After Tom bought them both drinks, he, Stef and Peter began gossiping about people from Peter's previous submarine. Kaisa sank into her own thoughts, about the Captain and his wife, and how they seemed so very happy. Suddenly, she realised the others were laughing and looking at her.

'What?' she said.

Tom laughed and said, 'I was just asking if he's keeping you up – or rather – you're keeping him up?' Tom winked at Peter and clinked his beer glass with Peter's.

Kaisa could feel the heat on her face and knew her cheeks had gone a deep red. She'd never been able to talk about sex even with her closest friends in Finland. There'd just been a few hints about the fact that she and Peter had a good time in bed and that, to her, seemed enough. What they did there was too private, too sacred to be shared with others. Peter, too, seemed reserved on the subject, but now he grinned from ear to ear and, smiling at Kaisa, said, 'Can you blame me?'

Stef put her arm on Kaisa's shoulders and said to Tom, 'Don't tease her. They're newly married, Of course they spend every minute in bed, if they can. Just like we used to. Do you still remember that?' She looked at her husband, then smiled at Kaisa, but the group grew quiet.

'Do you need the ladies?' Stef said to Kaisa, breaking the silence. 'Excuse us, gentlemen,' she said to Tom and Peter and got up.

In the loos, Stef added more red colour to her lips and smoothed down imperceptible wrinkles around her eyes. 'I'm pregnant!' she said to Kaisa, watching her through the mirror, 'Did you think I was a bit fat?'

'No, no.' Kaisa was astonished. She'd seen Stef drink G&Ts all evening. Wasn't that harmful to a baby?

'We've been trying for a while and I'm so relieved. When you have to do it, it's not so much fun anymore, you know.'

'Yeah,' Kaisa said.

'And when they're away so much, you just can't fit in all the fucking you need to!' Stef laughed loudly and Kaisa was glad there were no other women in the bathroom to hear Stef's crude language. 'You'll see when it's your turn to get pregnant – it's bloody hard work!' Stef said.

'But, you've been drinking all evening?'

'Oh, don't take any notice of that Old Wives' tale.'

During the three days they were together Kaisa realised how much she'd been worrying about her and Peter's future together. How strange that of all people, it had been the Captain's wife who'd come to Kaisa's rescue, and made her see sense. The conversation made Kaisa understand that what she wanted was a fulfilling career with a good salary, job satisfaction and something that would earn her a good reputation. At the same time she didn't want to give up marriage, children or her love for Peter. If she was forced to choose between the three, she'd choose Peter, although the career would be a very good second. The question of children was something Kaisa didn't think she could handle yet; and if she became pregnant accidentally, she'd have to worry about that when it happened. Peter's Navy career made everything more difficult, she knew that. A Navy wife with a career had to leave the husband in various bases around the country, so not only were you apart during the husband's sea time, but also when the boat was back at base. But there was nothing she could do about that either. Besides, at the moment it was just Peter who had a career, so his work would have to determine where they lived and what they did.

Kaisa waved the boat goodbye at Liverpool docks early Monday morning. She cried a little when they parted, rubbing her face against the rough woollen fabric of Peter's uniform jumper. But she had promised herself she would be smiling when she waved goodbye, a promise she was just about able to keep. There was mist on the horizon, into which the half-submerged black shape silently slipped. HMS *Tempest*, with her husband onboard, disappeared so quickly, that for a moment Kaisa felt as if her weekend with Peter had been a dream. The few wives who'd stayed on in Liverpool to say goodbye turned around, gave each other hugs and went to their various homes. Stef and Kaisa stood there a while longer, shivering in the cold wind. Stef was driving up to Faslane; she was already living in a married quarter in Scotland, because Tom's previous submarine had also been based there. 'You'll get used to the place,' Stef said and kissed Kaisa on the cheek.

11

S he'd only been back from Liverpool for ten days, when Kaisa wondered if it was the time of the month that was making her so moody. Or perhaps it was because her contract at IDS had finished and she'd had nothing to do for the past four days. Either way, she just couldn't lift her spirits. Even watching the children come and go from the nursery opposite, and the happy mothers chatting to each other, didn't make her feel any better. Watching the morning drop-off and the noon pick-up from the kitchen window had become a habit for Kaisa. She wondered what the women spoke about – was it all nappies and tantrums, or did they discuss real things like the women's protest at Greenham Common?

The TV news the night before had included a long report on the American nuclear warheads at the base at Greenham, and how the women there had given up the comforts of their homes to camp outside and try to bring about change. There were several interviews with unkempt, but defiant-looking women, who said they were protecting the children and the future of the world by trying to stop the deployment. There were pictures of the women being dragged away from the fence surrounding the military establishment. The women seemed to think that by protesting against the nuclear facility, they could change the country's defence policy. At the end of the report there was a picture of another peace camp in Scotland, outside the Faslane base. Kaisa pricked up her ears; she wondered if the camp would still be up in Scotland when she and Peter moved there? Kaisa wondered if she'd have been brave enough to have done something similar, if she hadn't fallen in love and married Peter. Of course, she needed to apply for more jobs, but with the impending move to Scotland, was there any point? She concentrated on keeping the flat clean and tidy, and making sure all the clothes were washed and ironed for when Peter came home.

One evening towards the end of the second week after Liverpool, Kaisa's phone rang. She jumped off the sofa and ran into the hall. She hadn't heard from Peter since they'd seen each other; there'd been no letters or phone calls.

'Peter?' she said

'Hello Kaisa.'

'Oh, hello Duncan,' Kaisa was unable to keep the disappointment from her voice.

Duncan didn't seem to notice, and after asking how she was, began talking about the party in Hayling Island and the 'stolen' car. Kaisa couldn't help but laugh when she told Duncan how funny Peter had found the whole affair.

'But listen, Mrs Williams, I didn't phone to talk about our previous exploits.' Kaisa could hear the smile in Duncan's voice and thought how nice it was to talk to him.

'I was phoning to ask if you'd like to come to a Ladies' Night at the base next weekend.'

Kaisa thought for a moment. What would Peter say?

'I'm sorry it's such last minute, but I didn't think I was going to be here, and now I am, and it seems a shame to waste such a good party ...' Duncan paused for a second. 'And I thought you could do with cheering up.'

On the spur of a moment, Kaisa said she'd love to go.

'That's fantastic, Kaisa. I promise we'll have a good time,' Duncan said in a husky voice.

Kaisa noticed she became breathless and her English faltered. 'Good,' was all she managed to say. As she put the receiver down, she wondered why she'd said yes. Had she been flattered by Duncan's invitation?

How Kaisa wished it had been Peter on the phone instead. She loved him so much, and while she'd been at home and not working she'd been wondering about the feeling. No one knew why anyone felt it, or what love was. For Kaisa it was more like an obsession, and she hoped it was the same for Peter. They were so obsessed with having each other and being together, that they had to marry. Or perhaps it wasn't that either. What exactly had happened at the Embassy cocktail party in Helsinki?

At first, there was the nervousness, because Tuuli and Kaisa had arrived so early and had to stand in the corner drinking that sickly sweet sherry.

Then there was the arrival of the English officers and Peter appearing out of nowhere. His dark eyes looking deeply into Kaisa's, asking her name over and over, and standing close to her, shutting everybody else out while he asked questions about who she was, what she did, how come she was there? Kaisa remembered how tall, good-looking and enthusiastic about life he seemed to her, smiling all the time. Kaisa had been brought up to think that if you enjoyed yourself too much, life would hit you in the face in due course. No one got away with enjoying life to the full in Finland. Of course, Kaisa had been engaged to be married to another man, and shouldn't have been looking deeply into the eyes of any foreign sailor. As the evening went on, Kaisa told Peter as much. But he insisted, and now here Kaisa was, married to him.

A few days after the phone call, when Duncan picked her up from the flat, he complimented her on how she looked, but Kaisa kept her eyes down on the floor and couldn't even thank him. The only other people she knew at the Ladies' Night were Maureen and her husband Matthew, and the blonde girl, Jeff's ex-girlfriend, Billy, who was partnered with some old friend of Matthew's. Kaisa felt a bit odd when she had to introduce Duncan to the two couples. Kaisa felt Maureen's eyes on the cleavage of her dress, and knew that she should have chosen the burgundy one that was less revealing and frumpier. Kaisa knew she looked quite good, but the black-and-white dress was too body skimming. Not eating for a couple of days had got rid of the little toast-and-jam tummy she'd acquired in the past few weeks. Luckily, Maureen and Matthew didn't sit at their table, but she could see Maureen keeping a close eye on her and Duncan, who was being his usual attentive self. She talked about Peter, his promotion to the bomber and their impending move up to Scotland. But Duncan didn't seem interested in her future in Scotland. Instead he made her laugh with stories of his three cousins and half-deaf uncle. The uncle was desperate for the daughters to marry well, while the girls were anything but willing. They all wanted to work in London, rather than live in a Dorset farmhouse and become farmers' wives. As she listened to him, Kaisa thought Peter would call Duncan 'posh'. She felt out of place sitting next to him at the table, laid out in the usual linen tablecloths and napkins and heavy silverware. Duncan had eyes only for her all evening, but this made Kaisa feel like an imposter. Of course, it was flattering, to be admired by another man, but it was also very wrong. She knew she was using him to massage her own ego while Peter was away. Even then, when he tried to kiss Kaisa goodnight on the lips, she was taken by surprise. 'No,' she said and pulled herself away. They were standing in the doorway to the King's Terrace flat and she was worried he expected to be asked in for a night cap. But Duncan acted like a gentleman. He held onto Kaisa for just a second longer than he should have done, so that Kaisa could feel the strength of his grip on her bare arms. Then he let go, stepped back and apologised, 'Sorry, Kaisa, I didn't mean to ...' Without looking at her, he turned away and walked down the stairs. Kaisa listened to the clatter of his footsteps, followed by the heavy slam of the door, before going in. She was sure she'd not see Duncan again very soon.

The next day at midday the doorbell rang and there was a boy with a huge bouquet of flowers. Kaisa immediately thought they must be from Peter, but when she read the card it said, 'Thank you for a wonderful evening and sorry if I upset you, Duncan.'

That same evening, Kaisa got a phone call from Peter. The submarine had arrived in Faslane. Peter was tired.

'I've missed you so much,' Kaisa said.

'Me too, but soon you'll be up here and we can be together every night when I am ashore!' Peter said and yawned.

Kaisa told him about Ladies' Night with Duncan. 'That was nice of him,' Peter said.

But when she told him about the flowers (she left out the bit about being sorry when she read out the card), Peter sounded a bit miffed. 'So he's sending you flowers, now, is he?'

Was Peter jealous? Kaisa said she thought that was the done thing after a lady had accompanied an officer to a ball. Peter had to agree this was true, and he also agreed that it was not unusual for bachelor officers to take naval wives whose husbands were away at sea. Kaisa didn't tell him what a fantastic arrangement it was – she'd never seen more beautiful flowers in her life.

When the telephone rang again the next evening, Kaisa felt sure it was Peter, and was disappointed to hear a woman's voice at the other end.

'It's Maureen here, Matthew's wife.'

'Hi,' Kaisa said, wondering why on earth she'd be phoning her.

'I just wanted to call you to let you know that people are talking about you.'

Kaisa gasped. She immediately thought the woman was talking about Duncan. She prepared to defend herself against all allegations when Maureen continued, 'You and Jeff are seen out together a lot these days. Especially now that Peter is going to be a Bomber Queen (she spat out the two words); you've really got to be careful that stories about the two of you aren't doing the rounds. It could be very damaging to Peter's career.' Maureen's voice was thin, almost quivering, as if she was trying to stop herself from shouting her allegations into Kaisa's ear.

It turned out that Maureen, Matthew's wife, had been a close friend of Jeff's ex-girlfriend Billy since school. Billy was a funny sort of girl with long, blonde hair that seemed out of proportion to her short, slight frame. Kaisa never really got to become her friend properly – besides Jeff was only with her for a matter of weeks.

Maureen's words rendered Kaisa speechless. For a while neither of them spoke. Kaisa felt Maureen's heavy silence at the other end of the line, as if she was holding her breath. Kaisa couldn't understand how anyone could think that something was going on between her and Jeff. It was ridiculous. After a while, Kaisa said, as coolly as she could manage, 'Peter and Jeff are best friends. He was our best man, for goodness sake.'

'Oh, I know,' Maureen said with fake kindness in her voice, 'I know it's innocent, I'm just saying that other people …'

'What other people?' Kaisa asked.

'Oh, you know, when Jeff ended it with Billy so abruptly, a lot of people were coming to me and asking what was going on between you and Jeff. If perhaps, he and you were, you know, and that's why he broke it off with Billy …'

Now Kaisa felt like laughing. The woman was blaming the break-up between Jeff and Billy on her! So it was Billy who'd got her friend to make the call. Kaisa wondered if Jeff's old girlfriend was standing next to Maureen now, listening to Kaisa's answers. They were acting like school-girls! Making her voice firm and as 'posh' as she could manage, Kaisa said, 'Well, you can tell Billy and those other people that they needn't worry. And you don't have to worry about me either. I'm absolutely fine.' Kaisa was very tempted to slam the phone down on Maureen (and Billy), but she knew it was important to stay cool, so they exchanged a few more words on the Navy, and Peter's time on HMS *Tempest*. Matthew was a skimmer, serving in the Navy's surface ships, so Kaisa knew he'd know nothing at all about submarines, and it made her laugh that Maureen asked about Peter's sub. Kaisa said she was in the middle of ironing (which she actually was), and that at last got Maureen off the line. 'Yes, of course, I mustn't keep you,' she said and hung up.

Later that evening, when she'd calmed down, Kaisa phoned Jeff. He thought the whole situation was very funny, but after she'd put the phone down Kaisa suddenly felt a little scared. What if the bitch started spreading rumours about her around the Navy? Maureen was right, rumours about a wayward wife could damage a naval officer's opportunities for promotion. Kaisa decided not to mention the call to Peter, but by the time he phoned, gone eleven o'clock, she couldn't stop herself. Kaisa even shed a few tears, thinking about how awful the call had been.

'Don't worry about Maureen, she's just jealous of you!' said Peter.

Kaisa hugged the phone close and smiled into the receiver. This was her Peter, her defender, her hero!

12

Kaisa had a call from Duncan on the Tuesday night after the ball. She'd just put her feet up with her supper on a tray, ready to watch *Brookside* on TV. She'd had jacket potato with cheese and tinned tuna for two nights in a row now because she kept forgetting to buy food. When the telephone went, she thought it would be Peter. Hearing Duncan's voice was quite a shock. He asked how she was, and made some other nonsensical small talk, which made Kaisa wonder if he'd ever get to the point. Eventually he said he was on some kind of course up in London.

'You remember I told you about my cousin Rose who works up here?'

'Yes.'

'She'd love to meet you. I can't promise anything, but she may know of a job that would suit you, and since you're not working at the moment, I thought you might want to come up and see her?'

When Kaisa didn't say anything, he added, 'I thought this would serve as an apology for my behaviour the other night.'

Kaisa wanted to ask what kind of a job, but instead she told Duncan she'd think about it. After she put the receiver down, she wondered what Peter would think if she met up with Duncan on her own. Luckily, he didn't know about the attempted kiss, but he had been jealous over the flowers. Jeff had said they knew each other because Duncan had been at Dartmouth Naval College with him, and had joined the submarine service at the same time.

'Have they been on the same boat?' Kaisa had asked Jeff, but Jeff said he didn't think so. Jeff was a 'skimmer' after all, Kaisa thought, and as an officer serving on surface ships, moved in completely different Navy circles from Peter and Duncan.

Kaisa desperately wanted a job, and a job in London would be a dream. If Peter was ashore for six weeks in his new job, surely he could come down and stay with Kaisa in London instead? She'd be like Mercier, the Captain's wife, with a career of her own. Why couldn't they have a home in London instead? All they would need was a small flat.

The next day, Kaisa called Duncan and told him she'd come up to London. He gave her an address somewhere in Chelsea. She decided she'd go up on Saturday and come back on Sunday morning. Duncan sounded elated on the telephone and after the fairly brief conversation, Kaisa dug out her old *A-Z* and looked up the address. He wasn't far from Sloane Square Tube station, which was great, because Kaisa knew the area well from the year before, when she'd taken her exams at the Finnish Embassy. She looked at an old timetable for the trains and hoped it was still valid. If so, she'd travel from Portsmouth Harbour on the 3.12pm and be in London at 5.25pm. Duncan assured her that she'd have a room of her own in his house.

But what would Kaisa tell Peter? That she was going on a wild goose chase after a job in London? Or should she tell him at all? She thought about writing it in her letter later (she wrote to him nearly every day). But then she thought, he'd just worry about her being in London on her own.

Still, she was nervous on the train. It was guilt, mixed with excitement and worry about finding Duncan's house. As the train pulled into London and the view of fields out of the window were replaced by rows and rows of houses, with long gardens in between, she'd decided to keep her cool with Duncan, and avoid any tension building up between them by talking about Peter. About how happy she was to be married, and how proud she was of his new appointment. She'd paint a chocolate-box picture of her life. By the time she'd got into Waterloo and made her way to Sloane Square she felt a little calmer.

Duncan met Kaisa at Sloane Square station (he sweetly said he didn't want her to be wandering around the streets of London trying to find his home). They dropped off her bag in his house and Duncan took her to a wine bar near Charing Cross. It was a dark-looking cellar that made Kaisa feel a bit worried at first. But inside there were men in suits and women in sleek-cut jackets and skirts, drinking, smoking and laughing together.

Duncan led her to a table at the back, where a woman in a beige ruffle blouse and pointed low-heeled shoes sat drinking a glass of wine. Her blonde hairstyle reminded Kaisa of Princess Diana. The woman got up as soon as they came in. Duncan and the woman kissed each other's cheeks and the woman offered Kaisa her hand.

'I'm Rose, how do you do?

Kaisa replied in the way Peter had taught her, 'I am Kaisa, how do you do?', even though it seemed rather silly to her to repeat what the other had just said. Kaisa tried to smile when Rose asked her to sit down. Duncan told Kaisa that Rose was one of his cousins and an editor at a magazine called *Sonia*. Rose looked down at her hands for a moment, as if to feign embarrassment. From her gesture, Kaisa guessed this magazine was quite a big publication. Duncan went to get some drinks, while Rose started talking. She asked Kaisa a lot of questions about her degree, about where she'd worked and how she'd enjoyed working for IDS. Kaisa told Rose she had considered a career at IDS, but that she also really liked writing.

'I did some translation work when I lived in Finland,' Kaisa said.

Rose kept nodding and listening to Kaisa intently, and when Duncan came back with the drinks said, 'Great find,' to him, and raised her glass. Kaisa took a sip of her spritzer and smiled at Rose as she carried on talking. Rose asked her more and more questions, which Kaisa was able to answer quickly and fluently. Afterwards Kaisa felt as if she'd told Rose her whole life story; all about how she'd met Peter and moved to King's Terrace in Southsea. All through their conversation Rose kept glancing over to Duncan, who was sitting next to Kaisa on the same wooden bench.

'And your husband, what does he think about these ambitions you have for a brilliant career?' Rose said towards the end of their conversation.

Kaisa looked over to Duncan. What had he said about Peter? 'He wants you to have a career, doesn't he,' Duncan said.

Kaisa turned back to Rose, 'Of course he does.'

There was a brief silence. Rose was looking at Kaisa, as if to assess her, while she took another sip of her wine.

Kaisa didn't understand what they were both getting at until Rose said, 'So he's not after babies, then?'

Kaisa felt her cheeks redden and was sure she'd blushed, but managed to blurt out, 'Actually, not at all. He wants to wait ten years, at least.' Kaisa laughed nervously at her lie, but Rose seemed to accept her words, and said she was looking for an editorial assistant. She said they'd had a Swedish girl working in the office, and that she'd been very good, but had to go back to Sweden because she had no work permit.

'Your English is even better than hers, so I have no problem on that score. And Jannica was so smart and efficient, that we miss her already! I have great hopes for you. And no problems with a work permit, eh?' she said and emptied her glass. 'I must dash, see you next week – what day can you make it for an interview?'

Kaisa was so shocked she couldn't say anything for a while. 'I can come at any time,' was all she could say.

'How about Wednesday at 10am?' Kaisa nodded; she was speechless. 'Don't be late,' Rose said. She shook Kaisa's hand, kissed Duncan on both cheeks, and left.

'Well done!' Duncan said and clinked his glass with Kaisa's. She was so delighted that instead of drinking, she put the glass down and hugged Duncan. 'Thank you so much!'

Duncan took hold of Kaisa willingly. Feeling his chest muscles underneath his shirt tighten against her breasts, she froze with the pressure of his strong arms around her. Kaisa quickly checked herself and pulled back from Duncan's embrace. His face was now very close to hers and she could see he was leaning towards her mouth. She moved away from him on the seat and took a sip out of her glass.

'Is that what this is about?' Kaisa said, not looking at him, but down at the table. Kaisa tried to keep her voice level. Suddenly she felt cheap; this is how the world goes around, she thought. Duncan organises a job for her and as thanks for that she has to sleep with him.

Duncan touched her arm, 'Kaisa, please.'

Once again Kaisa pulled herself away so that his hand fell back on the table.

'I'm a married woman and I am not going to sleep with you even if I get this job!' she said and lifted her eyes to his face.

Kaisa was surprised by what she saw. Duncan had gone entirely pink; the whole of his face and his neck were blushing. 'I'm so sorry, Kaisa, I didn't mean to …'

'Well, don't then,' she said and got up. 'I'm going to take the next train home back to Pompey.'

'Please, Kaisa, sit down.'

Kaisa looked around the bar. The dark cellar was filling up and a few people were eyeing up the potentially free table, while watching their apparent argument with mounting curiosity. She saw Duncan was embarrassed, his face was a little less red, but everyone could see he had upset her for some reason. Now Kaisa felt sorry for him, and thought staying another ten minutes wouldn't hurt. She sat down opposite Duncan, on the chair Rose had vacated. 'Go on, I'm listening.'

'Kaisa, I care for you. You know I do.'

Kaisa could tell he was going to take hold of her hands at that point, but at the last minute decided against it. 'Peter is a friend, and I know how happy you two are, so you must trust me, I would never come between you two. But I am a red-blooded man, you know, so if you insist on putting your arms around me, I cannot help but respond.' Duncan smiled at her, and his eyes had a friendly expression.

Kaisa relaxed, of course Duncan was a gentleman, and returned his smile.

'Another drink to celebrate?' he said and got up.

'OK!' Kaisa replied.

They stayed in the wine bar until it closed. Duncan bought a bottle of something called Cava, a really lovely bubbly wine. 'Spanish champagne,' Duncan said. He seemed to have no money worries, and he wouldn't hear of letting Kaisa pay for a thing.

After the wine bar closed, Kaisa and Duncan staggered back to his place, which was a charming old terraced house with white-framed sash windows. Duncan offered Kaisa a nightcap, but she said, 'No, thank you.'

'Oh,' he said and swayed a little.

Kaisa realised he was drunk. They both were. 'I'm quite hungry, though,' she said and giggled.

Duncan made some scrambled eggs, sausages and baked beans.

'The only thing I can cook is breakfast,' he said and gave Kaisa a boyish smile. His blond hair flopped over his eyes when he was spooning the beans onto her plate. They took the food to the front room and watched Hitchcock's *The Birds*, balancing the plates on their laps. When the film was over, Duncan said, 'Time for Bedfordshire!' He showed Kaisa upstairs to a little room overlooking the dark street, lit up by a single yellow lamp. 'The loo is at the end of the corridor,' he said and put her bag on the top of a double bed. The room was furnished in the same way as Jackie's flat, and fleetingly Kaisa wondered how well Duncan knew her. Had they been lovers? The flower-pattered curtains tied with a satin bow on either side of the sash window matched a frilly cover on the bed. Two bedside tables had lamps with shades bearing the same flower pattern. The room looked very feminine. Kaisa felt her shoes sink into the thick, light-coloured carpet. She felt as if she'd stepped inside a doll's house; all satin and frills.

Suddenly Kaisa could feel Duncan's arms around her, and his lips on her. For a brief moment, Kaisa's reflexes took over and she kissed him back. But she remembered who and where she was and pulled herself away.

This time Duncan didn't seem to be at all embarrassed to be rejected. He just took one step back and, waving his hand, said, 'Good night, Kaisa. If there's anything at all you need, I'm next door.'

After he'd gone, Kaisa stared at the door he'd closed behind him. As if in a trance, she took off her shoes, tiptoed onto the landing and listened for movements. It was all quiet in his room. What was going on? Suddenly Duncan had seemed a different person again. Would Kaisa be safe here after all? She tiptoed back into her room and noticed there was a lock on her door. She turned the wrought-iron key as gently as she could, and when she could feel there was a click, she feigned a cough to cover the sound.

In the morning, Kaisa woke late after a night of fitful sleep during which she'd dreamed of being found in bed with Duncan by the reproachful Peter. She woke with a start and decided that she'd take the first train home to Portsmouth. After she fell asleep again, it was Rose who entered her dreams. She was holding both Kaisa and Duncan's hands and they were in a church somewhere, with frilly curtains and flowers everywhere. Rose was giving them her blessing, but after a priest in a vast white robe had married them, Rose lifted her finger and, wagging it at Kaisa, said, 'No babies, Kaisa, remember, no babies.'

The upstairs was empty when Kaisa tiptoed to the bathroom. She decided against a shower and did what Peter called 'a submarine dhoby'. She washed her face, armpits and between her legs, the latter requiring some gentle gymnastics, as the basin in Duncan's house was much higher up than in the flat in Portsmouth. But Kaisa didn't care, she just wanted to go home.

Kaisa found Duncan frying bacon and eggs downstairs in the kitchen. 'Sleep well?' he said, turning around to smile at her. She looked into his pale blue eyes, and his expression changed. He took the pan off the heat and sat down at the small kitchen table. 'Look,' he said, running his hand through the mop of blond hair. 'I'm so sorry about last night.'

'It's not OK,' Kaisa said.

As if surprised by her words, Duncan now really took Kaisa in. She stood in the doorframe, holding her bag, which she'd packed, ready to leave.

'Look, Kaisa, I promise it won't happen again.' Duncan went to touch his hair once more, rubbing his scalp with both hands. When Kaisa didn't reply, he gave her another glance and pleaded, 'Please don't go before you have breakfast.' He motioned his hand to the pan on the stove. 'I know it's almost the same thing as last night, but, I'm only good at one thing.' He gave her a lopsided grin.

Kaisa sighed and put down her bag.

This seemed to spur Duncan into action and he served Kaisa a plateful of food. He put a fancy new gold coloured cafetiere in front of her, 'I know you don't like tea,' and pushed a smoky glass cup and saucer towards her. The smell of coffee was irresistible and even though Kaisa hardly ever ate bacon (it was so greasy and meaty tasting), she was famished that morning. Perhaps it was the tiredness after the sleepless night, and the vivid dreams she'd had; or all the wine in the cellar bar the night before.

'Help yourself. I hope the coffee is strong enough?' Duncan sat opposite her and gave her a boyish smile, and even though she was still angry with him, Kaisa couldn't help but return it. 'I knew a Swedish girl once, and she liked very, very strong coffee,' Duncan said and smiled. Kaisa wondered if he was talking about Jannica, but decided it was none of her business. She didn't want to make small talk; instead she ate in silence, thinking about everything that had happened the night before – the arrival in London, finding her way from Waterloo to Sloane Square, meeting up with Duncan and Rose. The interview and a possible job offer.

Duncan coughed and pointed at the kitchen window that overlooked a small garden. 'It's started raining.'

'Oh,' Kaisa replied, still deep in thought.

'What shall we do today?' Duncan asked.

Kaisa looked up from her plate. She was holding the coffee cup, about to take a sip. 'I have to go,' she said, surprised that he didn't know this. Hadn't he heard her before?

Duncan sighed and said, 'Of course.'

After a brief silence he added, 'It's just that I was going to take you to a pub for lunch, there's a really nice place close to here.' Now Duncan wasn't looking at Kaisa, but moving a piece of bacon around on his plate. 'We could go to a new art gallery that has just opened, or would you prefer the British Museum? It would be a shame to come all way up to London and not see anything.' He now lifted his eyes to Kaisa. There he was again, the nice Duncan, full of friendly concern for her welfare. 'Or there's St Paul's Cathedral, have you been there?'

Kaisa didn't say anything.

'Or Westminster Abbey? Or the Tower of London? I have my car, so we could drive over really quickly; heck we could see all of them!'

'I've been to St Paul's,' she said quietly. She was looking at her hands, trying very hard not to return Duncan's smile.

'Oh,' he said. Duncan looked so disappointed that she added, 'Where's this new gallery?'

'Oh, it's not too far, near the Lord's Cricket Ground in NW.' When Kaisa didn't react, he said, 'You follow cricket?'

'No, Peter likes all sports, but I just like ice hockey.'

'I don't like sports, not really, only cricket.' Duncan said. He told Kaisa about the new gallery. 'Do you like art?'

'Yes, I suppose so,' Kaisa said uncertainly and thought back to the Picasso sketch Tuuli had in her apartment in Helsinki. Tuuli loved modern art, but Kaisa was fond of the traditional Finnish artists who'd painted dark canvases of pine trees, or scenes of farm workers making hay bales.

'That's settled then,' Duncan said.

Duncan drove Kaisa in his little blue sports car. As he opened the door for her, and asked if she minded the roof being down now that the rain had changed into bright sunshine, Kaisa wondered if all unmarried officers in the Royal Navy owned a sports car. Driving through the city, with her hair flopping over her face and swirling around, reminded Kaisa of the first time she visited Britain, when Peter took her to London. She'd never been there, and he wanted to show her all the sights, just like Duncan. Kaisa felt a pang of guilt sitting next to Duncan and decided that as soon as she got home she'd write a long letter to her husband and tell him all about the weekend. Although perhaps not Duncan's attempts to kiss her.

Kaisa got home on Sunday evening, after they'd been to the pub for lunch, which Duncan insisted on buying. 'It's the least I can do after the way I've behaved,' he said. Afterwards he drove to Westminster Bridge and they had coffee and ice cream on the banks of the Thames, overlooking the Houses of Parliament.

Back home, Kaisa tried to piece together what had happened; she would have an interview in a women's magazine on Wednesday. Although she'd rather work on a serious publication, this was still a huge opportunity. It could lead to other more important jobs, and though she'd never even dared to say it out loud, she'd dreamed of being a journalist ever since she was little girl. She put Scotland out of her mind; if the Captain's wife could live in London and work as an air hostess, why couldn't she live in Pompey and work in London? Surely there was no reason why they couldn't get a small place in London in due course?

How she wished she was still working at IDS, and could tell both Kerry and Ann about her brilliant new job opportunity. But that was just her pride talking; she hadn't got the job yet. How awful it would be, if she told them about the interview only to fail it? More importantly, she needed to consider what to wear. It was late August and the weather was still very warm; it might be too hot for her trouser suit. On the other hand, it was the smartest thing she owned and she guessed she could leave the jacket off until the last minute. The interview seemed like a dream come true! Having decided on her outfit, Kaisa sat down and wrote to tell Peter all about her weekend in London. She hoped he'd be proud of her and wish her luck.

13

On Monday when Kaisa came back from a shopping trip to Commercial Road, where she'd bought a new shirt to wear with her trouser suit, she found a letter from Peter waiting for her. It was such a joy to read his words and to hear how the trip was going. He couldn't tell her any details of his work, of course. Kaisa wasn't sure she'd understand all the engineering terms anyway but, reading between the lines, it looked as if they were testing the boat, and it was going well. How she wished she could speak to Peter and tell him about London and the interview on Wednesday, instead of just writing to him about it. In the worst-case scenario, Peter wouldn't get any of Kaisa's letters until he was back. Often their correspondence was out of sync, so it was hopeless to discuss anything properly. She'd just have to tell him in person when he came back.

Kaisa was missing Peter intensely. She tried to understand why it was suddenly so much harder to be without him, and thought it must be because of the trip to London and Duncan's unwanted approaches. Kaisa missed just hearing Peter's voice. After a while the silence became unbearable. Of course, she worried, too, but like any good Navy wife, she'd trained herself not to think of the worst. Still, thoughts of him drowning inside that metal tube in the chilly depths of the Atlantic (or the Arctic, or even the Baltic – she had no idea where he and the submarine were at any given moment) made her want to curl up in a ball on the floor and weep. But then she'd brush these thoughts of a disaster aside and imagine that everyone was safe onboard and wonder what he was doing at that very moment. Was he on or off duty? Was he thinking of Kaisa? Probably he was, if he was bored. Peter once told Kaisa that 95 percent of his time at sea was spent waiting for something to happen, and the remaining 5 percent was very exciting, when something did happen. Kaisa knew better than to ask what that 'something' was.

The weather in London was awful in the end. In Pompey, when Kaisa woke up at 6am to catch the 7.15 train, it was warm and dry, but as soon as the train pulled out of Guildford, it started to rain. It was also a lot colder than in Portsmouth, and Kaisa wished she'd taken her mac. She got absolutely drenched while looking for the *Sonia* offices in Soho, and got lost so many times, that when she eventually found the dark building opposite a busy sandwich shop, she was fifteen minutes late. When she saw how the girl at the reception desk looked at her, Kaisa felt ashamed. Her jacket was soaking wet and her light-coloured leather shoes had dirty-looking damp patches at the toes. She pushed strands of hair that had fallen over her face behind her ears, and tried to smile confidently when she asked for Miss Rosalind Cummings.

The offices were quite different from what Kaisa had imagined. The hallway was dark, but the first floor, to which the girl escorted her, was flooded in light, even on such a rainy day. There were desks and typewriters and wastepaper baskets everywhere. Mostly female faces turned up to look at Kaisa when she passed each desk, but no one seemed to take much notice of her or her shabby appearance. When the girl got to the end of the room, she knocked on a half-glazed door and a woman's voice replied, 'Come in!'

Rose looked far more intimidating in her own surroundings than she'd done in the dark wine bar. She was sitting at a vast desk, covered with photographs and papers, with two telephones. There was a floor-to-ceiling window behind her, overlooking the sandwich shop, where there was still a queue of people waiting to be served.

'I'm sorry I'm late, I got lost.' Kaisa said after the girl had shown her to a seat opposite Miss Cumming's desk.

Rose, as she still insisted Kaisa should call her, was wearing a brown-checked skirt and a cream jumper. 'Don't worry about it. Soho can be a very confusing place if you don't know it.' She looked Kaisa up and down and then glanced over her shoulder at the window behind her. 'Raining, is it?'

'Yes,' Kaisa said and looked at her wet shoes.

'For goodness sake, take that jacket off!' Rose started laughing and, despite feeling like a drowned rat, Kaisa joined in and giggled nervously.

Even though she was shivering from the cold, she felt sure there'd be sweat patches showing under the arms of her blouse. Clutching her old *London A-Z*, which Peter had given her on that first visit to London, Kaisa had been running up and down streets for the best part of an hour. But she felt forced to take the jacket off, damp patches, or no damp patches, and as she did so Rose handed her what looked like a striped woollen shawl. 'That's a Jaeger poncho – from their autumn collection.'

After she'd collected herself a bit and felt warm and cosy underneath the soft wool, Kaisa dug out a CV from her handbag and handed it to Rose. She smiled at Kaisa, took the piece of paper and studied it in silence.

Those few minutes, while Kaisa waited for (what she hoped would be) her new boss to examine the one sheet of text, seemed to take forever. It was as if she was reading the story of Kaisa's life. She shifted on the wooden chair and tucked her feet underneath the seat. Eventually Rose looked up from the desk and said simply, 'When can you start?'

'You mean …?'

Rose smiled again, 'I told you this would be a mere formality.' She got up and said, 'I'll show you around. You can type, I presume?'

Kaisa walked behind Rose into the main office, where she was introduced to three women who were sitting at a cluster of desks divided by head-height screens. There was Molly, 'the fashion editor', who complimented Kaisa on the poncho. She was about Kaisa's age, with long dark hair and bright red lipstick. 'Thank you, but it's actually …' Kaisa began, but was interrupted by Rose, who took her arm and said, 'And here's Laura. She writes the Aunt Betty column.' Laura was an older woman, perhaps Kaisa's mother's age. She had a short bob, wore half-moon glasses and a cardigan over her shoulders. 'And this is Jacquie, she's Features.' Kaisa had no idea what that was, but thought she'd ask later, because now Rose was heading back to her office, shouting behind her, 'Molly, can you get a typing test set up for Mrs Williams?'

On the train back to Portsmouth Kaisa could hardly believe what had taken place. Had she really been for an interview at the glamorous London offices of a fashion magazine? Rose had said that Kaisa should come up for a typing test the following week and that she'd start at the beginning of October. She gave Kaisa a sheet of paper with the working conditions and the salary. On the train, Kaisa worked out that this would not be that much more than she was getting at IDS, but at least it was a proper, permanent job. And in London.

Before Kaisa had left *Sonia*, and shaken hands with Rose, her boss-to-be asked what Kaisa's husband thought of her new job. Kaisa replied truthfully, 'He's away, so he doesn't know yet.' Rose gave her another quizzical look, just as she had when they'd discussed Kaisa's husband in the wine bar with Duncan. Kaisa wondered now, as the grey London landscape turned into green rolling fields, whether she was just puzzled about husbands in general. She must be at least ten years older than her, and still unmarried, so perhaps she wanted to find out how it all worked between a husband and a wife? Oh well, Kaisa could tell Rose all about it when she started working for her.

And Peter would soon be home, just before they were due to fly to Helsinki to see her mother and sister. She'd do the typing test on the 2nd of September (she hoped that wasn't the day Peter came home!), and on the morning of the 3rd they'd be flying into Finland, and she'd be home. Kaisa could not wait to see her sister Sirkka and her mum; she missed them so much.

Duncan phoned Kaisa about two hours after she got home from London. He'd heard the good news from Rose and wanted to congratulate her.

'It's you I need to thank!' Kaisa said.

She didn't tell him, but she was still a bit worried about the typing test. Kaisa knew she could type in Finnish and in Swedish, but wasn't sure if she'd be quick enough in English. Oh well, Rose kept saying it was just a formality.

But what Peter would say when he found out that Kaisa was going to be working in London, and with a cousin of Duncan's, worried her a lot more than the test. Plus there was the money. When Kaisa worked out how much it would cost to travel to London and back every day, she realised that she would actually be earning less than she had at IDS.

14

There was only 24 hours to go until Peter would be home. It was about a week earlier than Kaisa had expected. He had phoned Kaisa first thing in the morning and told her he'd be flying from Glasgow the following day and should be back in Pompey by midday. It was so wonderful to hear his voice that Kaisa couldn't really speak.

'Are you alright?' he asked, and she nodded, swallowing hard and trying to find a voice.

'Kaisa, are you there?' he said after a while.

'I miss you,' was all she could manage.

'You'll see me tomorrow!' Peter said. He sounded a bit annoyed, and Kaisa had to take a deep breath to stop getting upset. She thought she was being over-emotional, and he was most probably very tired after all that time at sea. Eventually Kaisa managed to say she would meet him off the train and Peter promised to phone from the airport, or the station if he had time. If not, Kaisa was to wait at home. As soon as the phone call was over, Kaisa studied the timetable. She saw that if the flight from Glasgow was on time, Peter should be able to catch the 10.34 from Reading, which meant he'd be at Portsmouth Harbour station at 12.45. Kaisa could not wait to feel his arms around her.

Now Kaisa's biggest decision was what to wear to meet Peter off the train. He liked Kaisa in a skirt, so she considered wearing a new Liberty one she'd bought in London after the interview at *Sonia* magazine. She'd had a couple of hours to kill, and had suddenly found herself at the store on Regent Street. They had the most fantastic stuff there, and Kaisa found the self-assemble skirts in different Liberty prints in the haberdashery department. With her new sewing machine, she thought, it would be no job at all to sew the skirt together – just a few minutes' work. It had taken her a long time to choose the right fabric, but finally she'd decided on a dark-blue paisley pattern, because it reminded Kaisa of a dress worn by her first teacher in Tampere. Now she decided to match it up with a long navy-blue jumper bought from Allders with her first salary from IDS, a tan belt and her blue court shoes. Kaisa looked at her watch; she had just time to run into Knight and Lee on Palmerston Road to get a pair of stockings. Peter so liked her in French knickers and suspenders. A few weeks ago, after she'd come back from Liverpool, Kaisa had bought a matching bra, suspender belt and knickers set in Marks & Spencer, since when the new satin underwear had been sitting in her drawer untouched. She had very nearly worn it on her trips up to London, but it felt wrong somehow. As if she'd expected someone (Duncan!) to see her in her underwear. Kaisa hoped the lingerie would help her tell Peter about the new job in London.

When Kaisa saw Peter get off the train, wearing his smart cords and Navy mac, her heart nearly stopped. He kissed Kaisa long and hard. 'Let's get a cab home. I need to have you now.'

His voice was so hoarse and sexy that Kaisa nearly fainted. In the back seat of the grubby taxi, with the driver sending backward glances at them, Kaisa told Peter how much she'd missed him. They couldn't keep their hands off each other and when Peter realised what she was wearing, he kept stroking the top of Kaisa's stockings through the thin fabric, or sneaking his hand inside her skirt. Kaisa was so happy.

After they'd been to bed he told Kaisa about his next job. The appointer had written to say that he was to serve in HMS *Restless,* the Polaris submarine, for a minimum of two years. 'I will join the port crew on 19th of September.' He sounded very proud. 'We'll have the house in Scotland, and I'll be home for long periods of time,' Peter said and kissed the top of Kaisa's head. How was she going to tell him about the London job?

To buy time, Kaisa said, 'You hungry?'

'I'm starving,' Peter said and jumped out of bed.

Kaisa got up too, and together they put out bread, cheese and a ham salad Kaisa had bought from Waitrose before walking to the station.

While they were sitting across from each other at the small table, Kaisa told him about the job offer in London. She blurted it out quickly, as if to minimise the effect.

'The interview went really well, Rose wants me to start as soon as possible after I've taken a typing test. I'm a bit worried about that.'

Peter was quiet and wasn't looking at Kaisa.

She stretched her arms across the table to take his hands into hers. 'It's such a huge opportunity for me. Just imagine it – a fashion magazine in London!'

'And Duncan organised all this for you?' Peter said and pulled his hands away from hers. He got up to get a glass of water.

'It's fine, he's just helping me out.'

'I bet,' Peter said.

'But the job, what do you think about the job?' Kaisa held her breath while she waited for Peter's reply.

'So what are you going to be then? A secretary?' Peter turned around and leaned against the sink, drinking the glass of water. His voice was dry and he had a non-committal, almost cold expression on his face. He was avoiding her eyes. Nothing like the man she'd made love to earlier, Kaisa thought.

'No,' Kaisa said and hesitated. She thought back to the interview with Rose. She'd used the word assistant; surely, that wasn't the same as secretary? 'Rose wants me to be her assistant,' she said.

He turned away from Kaisa again and put the kettle on, 'Same thing, I think you'll find.'

Kaisa suddenly wasn't hungry anymore. She looked at the half-eaten sandwich she'd prepared from the thickly sliced brown bread Peter had cut for them.

He liked his bread that way rather than ready sliced. The ham sticking out of the side looked ugly to Kaisa now – why hadn't she taken away the disgusting rind of fat from the piece?

Peter turned around and crossed his arms over his chest. Looking at Kaisa with cold eyes, he said, 'But if you'd rather work as a secretary in town for Duncan's cousin than be with me in Faslane, I'm not going to stop you.'

'But Mercier, the Captain's wife, works as an air hostess, and they live in London. She never lives where her husband is based; she stays put and they seem to be very happy.'

Peter sat down opposite Kaisa and took her hands in his, 'But darling, they are rich. They inherited money from a relative and I think that's how they can afford to live in London and fly out to meet each other wherever they are based. I wouldn't be able to do that.'

Suddenly the noise of the kettle boiling filled the small kitchen.

. . .

Later that same night, when Peter was fast asleep, Kaisa got up quietly. Downstairs in the kitchen she saw it was 1am. She couldn't sleep, and rather than toss and turn in bed she decided she'd go and make a cup of hot water and lemon. Now she was sitting at the kitchen table, unable to get up even to put the kettle on. The city around her was quiet; there wasn't even the noise of the seagulls or the horns of ships navigating through the mist to disturb her thoughts.

After their late lunch, Peter and Kaisa had gone for walk along the seafront and then popped into Jeff's parents' pub. Jeff was away but his sister Maggie was working behind the bar, as were Jeff's father and mother. They greeted Peter and Kaisa warmly and Peter told everyone about his new appointment. Apparently, it was very much a promotion (as Mary had told her) and he would get more money. Kaisa looked at Peter as he stood there talking to Jeff's parents about the sub he was about to leave, HMS *Tempest*, about the refit and the testing they'd done. He was holding Kaisa's hand but she felt more distant from him than she'd felt in all the years since they first met in Helsinki. Why hadn't Peter told Kaisa any of these details before, when they'd sat at the kitchen table not talking or eating? Or later, when they'd walked along the Southsea seafront, looking at the sun glimmering on the sea. He should have at least told her about the money. And the promotion. Didn't he think she would have understood?

In the pub, Kaisa tried to smile, and only jokingly said, 'He never told me about the better pay,' to which Jeff's dad nudged Peter and said, winking, 'Keep it that way, son, her indoors doesn't need to know everything!' He was stroking his grey beard, and Kaisa felt tiny next to Jeff's father's large shape. His beard seemed to have got greyer and his eyebrows bushier since she last saw him.

Peter just laughed and squeezed Kaisa's waist and kissed her lightly on her lips. 'She's alright,' he said.

'You think that now,' Jeff's dad said, and puffed on his pipe.

They made love again when they got back home. Afterwards, Kaisa lay awake while Peter fell asleep immediately, his warm body enfolding her into his. For a while, she didn't know how long, Kaisa closed her eyes and listened to his steady breathing. When he turned away from her, she tried to sleep, but gave up and slid out of bed and tiptoed into the kitchen.

Now, sitting in the dark, her mind was perfectly clear. With Peter's raise, her small salary from *Sonia* would pale into insignificance. If she didn't move up to Scotland, Peter would have to live in the Wardroom, which was another expense they could do without. With the travel costs, and the expense of lunch and other things in London, she would not be able to cover the extra charge of the Wardroom with her salary. Besides, Peter had said he'd rather come home to Kaisa in the evenings.

'I wouldn't be able to fly down to Pompey more than a couple of times a year, so we would really see very little of each other.' Peter said later on in the pub. They'd finally been able to speak a few words alone, settled in the corner, their usual seat in the pub. He'd added, 'But of course it's your decision.'

Kaisa had wondered how it was possible that he could do this. He knew how much a career meant to her. But Kaisa hadn't said anything, not wishing to spoil Peter's first day at home. When he'd noticed that she was quiet, Peter had held onto Kaisa's hand and looked into her eyes. He said he had no choice, and that the new job was a really good one, 'A huge step up in my career.' The appointer had been very complimentary about his time in HMS *Tempest*.

Kaisa didn't understand why Peter hadn't told her what a huge change the move up to Scotland was. He must have known for weeks now what his future for the next few years ('minimum of two years') would be. Why didn't he mention it in his latest letter, or in Liverpool? Kaisa rushed to the drawer where she kept Peter's letters and noticed the last one was dated about a week ago. She hadn't told him about the London job either, but that was because of Duncan. Duncan! Was this all to do with Duncan after all? No it couldn't be, Peter just wasn't jealous like that.

But really, Duncan didn't matter; he wasn't the problem here. The problem was that Kaisa needed to decide whether to go after a job in London or move to Scotland. She might have more luck with jobs in Scotland – who knew? Perhaps she could look into working in Edinburgh. And how could she be sure that the job Rose had offered her wasn't just making coffee and typing letters? Why else would she have asked her to do a typing test? Perhaps Peter was right. She was too highly qualified for the job on the magazine. Although he hadn't said it outright, Kaisa was sure that's what he meant.

15

K aisa took an early train up to London, leaving Peter asleep in their bed. For once, Peter had wanted to lie in rather than get up at the crack of dawn. Strangely, it had been Peter who convinced her to keep the appointment with Rose and the magazine. The train journey back and forth was an extra cost they could do without, so Kaisa was pleased that Peter approved of her making the trip. London was sunny and warm and, now that Kaisa knew exactly how to get to the *Sonia* offices in Soho, she was 20 minutes early. The girl at reception (whose name she'd forgotten) smiled at her as if she was already a member of staff, and showed her up to a room with several large daisywheel typewriters arranged on small tables. There was a large clock on the wall opposite, and a desk below it. The room looked like a small classroom. From the open windows to the left, Kaisa could hear traffic noises and shouts from deliverymen and sand-wich boys. A moment after she'd sat down, and the girl from reception had disappeared, a woman she didn't recognise from her previous visit came in and introduced herself as Mrs Rodgers.

'I'm going to give you a sheet of written text and I'd like you to type it up, just as it is, with paragraphs and spaces where they are on the original. I will tell you when to start and when to stop.'

Kaisa was quite nervous, but not as much as she had thought she would be. Partly, she guessed, because she'd decided not to take the job. If she failed the test, it didn't really matter. As it was, she managed to type most of the text on the page before Mrs Rodgers told her to stop, making only minor mistakes, which she was able to correct with the daisy wheel correction tape. Kaisa breathed a sigh of relief and thought how lucky she was that she'd been used to this new kind of typewriter at Hanken. Plus, having to use her grandmother's old typewriter, without any correction facility, to write her theses meant that she was used to typing accurately.

'Miss Cummings would like to see you before you go,' Mrs Rodgers said. She led Kaisa once more through the busy office, where the people she'd met before nodded or said hello. Mrs Rodgers asked Kaisa to wait on a chair outside the office, while she went in. She had with her the typed sheet of paper that Kaisa had completed earlier and Kaisa felt her palms dampen as she thought about her test result. Would it be enough to get the job? She tried not to think about Peter and Scotland, because now she was here, she wanted to come back and work. She had the impression of everyone talking at the same time, some into telephones resting between their shoulder and ear while they typed fast, others standing around in groups discussing an idea or article. The office seemed even busier than before, but once Kaisa was shown into Rose's office, all the hustle and bustle of the outer office faded away.

'So, it seems your typing skills are even better than Jannica's!' Rose said and smiled. She'd waited for Mrs Rodgers to depart and close the door behind her, and for Kaisa to sit down on the chair opposite her. Unlike all the people who worked for her, Rose seemed to be calmness itself. 'Are you looking forward to working with us?' Rose asked and smiled broadly at Kaisa. She was wearing a bright red-and-blue checked jumper and a matching pair of bright blue harem pants, cinched at her narrow waist with a black belt.

Kaisa had been incredibly relieved and pleased to hear that the test had gone well, but now she shifted her eyes down to her hands. She was suddenly aware that she'd have to let Rose down. Of course there was no possibility of her taking this job! What an earth had she been imagining?

Rose had seen her face, 'What's wrong?' she asked.

Afterwards, when Kaisa thought about that day in Rose's office, she felt ashamed at how childishly she'd behaved. But she'd been so confused, not knowing what she should do, and Rose had been so kind. But to burst into tears in front of that powerful magazine editor! Rose had brought her tissues and after she'd calmed down a little, Kaisa told her about Scotland, Peter's promotion, the better pay, and how if she did take the job, she and Peter would be worse off, not better off, financially. On top of that she wouldn't be able to see her husband more than a couple of times per year.

'I see,' Rose said. She was now perching on the edge of her desk, 'I was afraid something like this would happen.' Rose thought for a moment. She reached out to her desk and took out a card. 'Here's my business card. Take it and if you ever come back to England again, give me a call.' Rose showed Kaisa out of the office and, as if in a daze, Kaisa walked past the busy desks, down the stairs, past the girl at reception and out onto the street. It was barely twelve o'clock, and she'd only been inside the office of *Sonia* magazine for less than two hours, but it felt as if a lifetime had passed. It was her career and her life that she'd given up in that office, Kaisa thought. With tears of anger and frustration running down her cheeks, she made her way through the busy streets of Soho into the Underground station at Leicester Square. If she hurried, she could catch a train before 1pm, and be back in Pompey with Peter by early afternoon.

But already on the train back to Pompey, as the dirty-looking rows of houses were replaced by golden fields, she was looking forward to being in Peter's arms, and put the job at *Sonia* magazine out of her mind. She'd come to England to be with her Englishman, and if that meant living in Scotland, so be it. Besides, she had a week in Finland with her mother and sister to look forward to.

Helsinki was colder than Southsea, but it was sunny and Kaisa enjoyed eating all the pickled herring and new potatoes her mother cooked for them, and the cinnamon buns she'd baked just for her. On the second night they were in Finland, Sirkka took Peter and Kaisa out on the town, but they were shocked by how expensive it was, especially alcohol, and didn't really enjoy themselves, knowing how much they were spending. Kaisa kept thinking about Scotland, and how she'd manage there when Peter was away. They'd discussed the future only once more, on the afternoon Kaisa came back from London. When she told him she'd turned down the job and that Rose had been very nice about it, Peter took her into his arms and said, 'You're a star, she could see that. I'm sure you'll find something up in Scotland.'

Her mother and Sirkka were delighted to see the two of them so happy, and even though Kaisa told them about the move up to Scotland, and how she'd had to turn down a job on a fashion magazine in London, the women just nodded noncommittally. They didn't seem to understand the significance of this, or else were preoccupied by their own problems. Kaisa told Sirkka in more detail about the dilemma she had faced, but her sister, too, just shrugged her shoulders. Sirkka seemed distant, and Kaisa never really got to talk to her properly, or alone, during the week they stayed in her flat.

Sirkka was again working in a hotel on Mannerheim Street, and she was off for only two days – besides, she was yearning to go back to Lapland where her boyfriend was. 'If they offer me a job up there for the skiing season, I think I'll take it,' she said to Kaisa. Kaisa thought her sister looked happy for once and didn't want to disturb her with her own troubles.

Back in Southsea, Kaisa wished she'd been more patient with her mother and Sirkka. There had been no rows, but Kaisa had been short with both of them more than once. And she'd not really talked to them about her worries – or listened to theirs. It was more difficult when Peter was there with her; they had to speak English, and there was no time for long chats over coffee and cinnamon buns. The Finnish word for mother, *äiti*, brought tears to her eyes when she wrote it on a 'thank you' letter a few days after they'd got back to the flat in King's Terrace. Why was Kaisa's life always so complicated? Why couldn't she have stayed in Finland, perhaps married a Finnish man (not Matti, though!), who would have been used to women having careers of their own. In Finland, she could have got a good job eventually (she had to admit it to herself, it wasn't easy there either, but at least her degree would be recognised). Or she could have moved to Stockholm. Hanken was very well thought of in Sweden, as were Finns, these days recognised for their hard-working characteristics rather than the heavy drinking they'd been known for when she was a child. Her mother had hinted at how well she'd be regarded in Sweden, but had stopped talking about it when she'd seen Kaisa's face.

'I just thought that one day you two might move to Sweden,' she'd said.

'And what would Peter do?' Kaisa had replied impatiently. 'He can't speak Swedish and he's in the Navy! Who would employ him here?' Kaisa got up from the table where they were having coffee, and went over to Peter who was reading a two-day old issue of *The Times*. Why was her mother now trying to sell Sweden to them when she herself had just moved back to Helsinki? But Kaisa had not asked; she'd been far too occupied with her own problems. She now regretted her impatience and wondered if she'd really listened to her mother – or Sirkka – they might have been able to help each other. But now it was too late; Kaisa didn't know when the opportunity would arise to talk properly to either of them again. Phone calls were so expensive, it was difficult to discuss anything too deeply.

Now, alone again in the flat on King's Terrace, and with nothing else to do but plan for the move to Faslane, Kaisa wished she could relive her short time in Helsinki. She hadn't even had time to see her friends. Tuuli had

taken three months off from the bank where she'd been working since grad-
uating, and was travelling around Europe, and Kaisa had never even told
her school friends she was in town. When Peter was getting ready to depart
the day after their return from Finland, she'd cried and said she missed her
mother.

'Darling,' Peter had said, looking at her with alarm. They were standing
at the railway station, waiting for the platform number to be announced.
Peter was on his way back to Scotland. 'Soon you'll be with me in Faslane,
and when I'm not away, I can come home every night.'

The words, 'When I'm not away,' rang in Kaisa's ears as she walked
home from the station. It had started raining while they'd waited for Peter's
train, and Kaisa had no umbrella, so she was soaked through by the time she
ducked inside the block of flats.

This time Kaisa missed Peter dreadfully from the first night she was on
her own, and during the first week the feeling of loneliness seemed to only
get worse. She thought it was because she'd got used to his presence in her
bed, and to discussing everything from their future together to what they
should have for dinner. It was so lonely in the flat without him.

Perhaps when she was in Scotland with him, she might try to find out
more about what he actually did every day at work, and how the nuclear
submarines worked. How she had changed. She didn't recognise herself in
that sentence. How did she end up being a Navy wife, only concerned with
her husband's career and not her own? On the TV there'd been another
report from Greenham Common and Kaisa wondered how she'd ended up
being married to a naval officer who'd soon be working in a submarine with
nuclear warheads onboard? She was now a willing part of the vast
machinery that wages war – or if it didn't wage war, it certainly increased
the arms race. When Kaisa mentioned these things to Peter he always
answered, 'We keep the peace more like!'

For something to do, Kaisa had phoned Sally and they agreed to meet
up. It was the first time since her marriage in Finland that Kaisa had seen
the older woman. Sally was as small and thin as ever, but her dark hair had
more grey strands. Kaisa thought it weird that she could talk to Sally about
anything at all, as her life was so different from her own. But she made her
laugh when she said Kaisa had gone all 'posh' with her accent.

'Oh, sorry,' Kaisa said, but Sally replied, 'No, it's good, girl, that's what
you need to do when you're with those other officers' wives.'

They sat in Sally's kitchen drinking instant coffee out of flower-
patterned mugs. Although Kaisa couldn't stand the stuff, because it tasted
more like muddy water, she didn't say anything because it was so lovely to

see her old friend and neighbour. Sally and her husband and their son still lived on Devonshire Road, opposite number 23, where Kaisa had spent such happy times with Peter and Jeff and the rest of the gang when she first came to live in Britain.

The street hadn't changed at all. While walking along the road from the bus stop Kaisa had fully expected to meet Jeff coming out of number 23, and was startled when a total stranger suddenly stopped outside the house and walked inside.

It seemed not much had changed in Sally's life – her guitar-playing, country music-loving husband still went to the pub at the end of the street each night for a pint, and occasionally Sally would join him for a vodka and tonic. Their son, Jamie, was now at school, so Sally had started a 'little' part-time job in a hairdressers at the bottom of the road.

'Hey, I could see if I could get you a job there too?' she said, but then she must have seen something in Kaisa's eyes, because she immediately added, 'Of course, you're married now and won't be wanting work in a salon!'

Kaisa explained that she'd only been working as a dogsbody at IDS, but that she'd not applied for any more jobs because of the pending move to Scotland.

'Oh, but you just moved here!'

Kaisa had to look down to her half-full cup of coffee to hold back the tears.

'You know Peter is in one of these nuclear subs,' she said, swallowing hard.

'And they go away for months and months and then they have a long time at home. If I don't move up there we'll never see each other.'

'I know, lovey,' Sally said and touched Kaisa's hand.

'I can't quite believe I'm actually married to someone who does that.' Kaisa added, and bit her lip.

'I know, it's wonderful!' Sally said and gave Kaisa the broadest of smiles. 'I always knew he'd ask you eventually!'

'No, I don't mean that.'

'Oh?'

'No, I mean, he is part of this huge war machinery, when I'm ...' Kaisa looked at Sally to see if she understood what Kaisa meant. Sally's eyes were wide and her head was tilted to one side. Kaisa took a deep breath and continued, 'You know the women at Greenham Common?'

'Hmm, you mean the hippies at the peace camp?' Sally said after a while.

'Yes, the thing is, I sort of understand what they are protesting about ...'
Kaisa looked to see what Sally's reaction was. Kaisa didn't know why all
this had come into her mind again. Perhaps it was triggered by the scenes on
the news the night before, of women linking arms and blocking the whole
of the entrance of the base with their physical presence, while all the time
singing protest songs. They wanted to stop another delivery of nuclear
warheads to the base. Policemen in black uniforms with batons were trying
to wrench the women apart, and eventually they succeeded. Many of the
protestors were taken away in a black police van and arrested, the news-
reader said. Still, watching the women fight the policemen with nothing but
their bodies and the support of their friends, made Kaisa wish, for a brief
moment, that she'd been one of them instead of married to Peter. Then she
remembered how much she loved him and missed him and thought what a
stupid girl she was. How could Kaisa ever do something like that? She
didn't even have the courage to voice her opinions in front of Peter's friends
or their wives. And she couldn't even remember the last time she'd really
discussed the arms race with Peter. It must have been well before they were
married.

When Kaisa saw Sally's startled face, she said, 'Anyway, thinking of
him sleeping on top of those weapons makes me so scared.' There Kaisa
was again, losing her nerve when it came to saying what she really thought.

'Oh, yes, I understand, but they do know what they're doing. The subs
are incredibly safe. And I'm sure he doesn't sleep right on top of them!'
Sally laughed. She hugged Kaisa so hard when they parted, as if she wasn't
going to see her ever again.

16

HELENSBURGH, SCOTLAND

I n mid-September 1984, Kaisa and Peter moved up to Faslane. It rained on the day the removal van arrived at Smuggler's Way, and it had rained every day since. 'If it's not raining, it's about to,' Peter laughed and said that's what the officers at the mess said to him. Kaisa hated rain, but laughed all the same.

Their new house, or married quarter, was in Rhu, on a hillside about ten minutes' drive from both Helensburgh and the base at Faslane. Kaisa could see the steel-grey loch in the distance between two other pebbledash houses exactly like theirs. The view was fantastic; it took in the Gareloch out into the east, where Kaisa could see the autumn colours in full glory on the opposite banks. Kaisa hadn't known how beautiful the scenery was. It reminded her of Finland, and Kaisa felt an acute pang of homesickness when she looked at the grey loch and the auburn and red leaves on the trees. But the houses on the hill with the stunning view were ugly. They were two- or three-storey square blocks, made out of grey concrete. The cold wind and rain brought in from the loch found its way between the buildings, creating a chilly wind tunnel.

The house itself was quite small; it had a tiny garden with a lawn and a two-seater swing at the back. The first night Kaisa and Peter slept there, they were kept awake by the empty, rusty swings swaying in the breeze. Next morning, Peter got up and, finding an old can of oil under the sink, went out in his dressing gown and oiled the joints of the frame. Kaisa watched the fabric of his gown flap in the wind and wondered how he didn't feel the cold. His annoyance was keeping him warm, Kaisa thought. He hated being kept awake at night, especially if he had to go to work the next morning.

A single paved path divided the lawn in half in the garden. There were no flowerbeds. ('Because nothing will grow here,' Peter said laughingly when Kaisa pointed out the lack of plants.) Their neighbour's house almost touched theirs, and some evenings Kaisa could hear their TV through an open window.

As in their King's Terrace married quarter, all the furniture was ugly, and all the curtains drab. Kaisa planned to take them down and replace them with the ones they'd had in the flat in Portsmouth, but she soon found that the windows here were a lot smaller than in Pompey. Peter said it would be a waste of money and fabric to make new curtains because they were not going to be in Faslane for more than three years. 'Three years!' Kaisa thought and her heart sank. Is that what a 'minimum of two years' meant?

This time the colour scheme of the ugly Navy issue furniture and the whole house was blue, if that's what you could call it. It was really a dark blue-grey-green. Like a baby's first poo, thought Kaisa. She knew this because in their first week in Scotland, they'd been invited to visit one of the naval wives in the Wardroom who'd just given birth. Peter knew the husband from a course they'd been on together. Phoebe, the new mother, was holding the baby when it suddenly produced so much poo that the blue-green stuff leaked out of the nappy. All Kaisa could think was that it was exactly the same colour as their sofa in their new married quarter. Phoebe must have seen Kaisa staring because she laughed and said, 'That's the first poo. They all produce it.' The new baby girl was Phoebe's third daughter.

'We submariners only make girls,' Peter's friend, Bernie, laughed. He nudged Peter and said, 'Isn't it time you started your own netball team?'

Kaisa didn't understand what Bernie meant at the time, but Peter told her in the car on their way home that in England only girls play netball at school.

'So?' she still didn't understand what he'd meant.

Peter sighed. 'Because submariners tend to only produce girls – it must be something to do with the nuclear radiation onboard – and because Bernie and Phoebe now have three girls, guys in the Wardroom keep teasing him that he'll soon have a netball team of his own.

'Oh,' Kaisa said. She didn't want to bring up the subject of babies, but since they'd been in Faslane, she'd noticed that almost all the other wives were either pregnant or had kids.

When they got back to their house, it was cold and damp inside. Peter quickly put the heating back on and tinkered with the boiler for a long time, so that it would come on early in the morning and just before he was due home from work. 'If you want to have hot water during the day, you press this red button,' he showed Kaisa what to do. In the King's Terrace flat, the heating had not been a problem, because they were in between floors, and enjoyed the heat of the flats below and above them. 'And if you are cold, I mean really cold, during the day, you press this button.' Kaisa looked at the complicated panel, and decided she'd just wear more jumpers. As if he'd read her mind, Peter added, 'I think it's quite expensive to heat this house, so we must be careful.'

'When do you think we'll have the phone?' Kaisa asked. They'd been promised a phone and that the connection would be there the same day as they moved in, but there'd been no sign of the telecom engineers.

'I'll ring them again tomorrow,' Peter said, and Kaisa was reminded how lovely it was to have him at home to organise things. She still found all the arrangements with house movers, electricity and phone companies difficult; she just didn't seem to possess the right words to speak to them.

When they at last got a telephone connection, Peter and Kaisa spent nearly the whole of the following weekend writing letters to friends and family telling everyone their new address and phone number. Peter said that when they had more money they would get cards printed with their details, but for now they used the same kind of blue Basildon Bond paper that Peter had used to write to her when she was in Finland. It seemed so strange to Kaisa to be writing to her mother and Sirkka, and Tuuli, on that particular paper. It was as if her life had been flipped upside down since she left Finland. When she thought about it, perhaps it had.

It seemed Peter was determined to make Kaisa feel happy in their new home in Scotland, so he took her down to the base to show her the swimming pool and tennis courts. Kaisa was not at all good at tennis, but Peter tried to teach her, and they had fun messing about. It was one of the rare mornings when the sun was out, and the wind was mild. Afterwards they swam in the vast pool on the base. The water was nice and warm, not cold like in Finland, and it was like stepping into a warm bath. Peter laughed when Kaisa told him about the chilly pools at home. 'You like to punish yourselves, don't you!' Peter said. He told Kaisa she could use all the facilities at the base, which pleased her. There was even a sauna in the ladies' changing rooms, though there was no water to throw on the coals and everyone wore a swimming costume. Noticing this, Kaisa was glad she'd taken a towel in with her and noted this strange British habit of wearing clothes inside a hot sauna for future visits. Not that this sauna was warm enough. When she asked where the bucket for throwing water onto the coals was kept, a slim older woman with short grey hair next to Kaisa looked horrified and said, 'Oh goodness, you're not allowed to do that. That's dangerous!' Kaisa didn't want to tell her that she was from Finland and that, as this was a Finnish sauna (she'd seen 'Kota', the manufacturer's name, on the stove), throwing water on the stove was exactly what you were supposed to do to create steam. Kaisa decided to speak to one of the staff next time she was there. All the same, it was nice to have a sauna, even if it wasn't as hot as she would have liked.

Afterwards, when she met up with Peter in the reception area, he asked one of the staff to write up a temporary card for Kaisa so that she could come into the centre whenever she liked while he was away. The man at the reception told Kaisa in heavily accented Scottish that her proper pass would be in the post in a few days' time. The only problem was that the base was a fair walking distance from the new married quarter. Being on the hill meant even the awful little shop was a long walk away. 'I'm sure you could get a lift from one of the other wives,' Peter said during the drive back. Kaisa said nothing and he looked sideways at her. She was sure he knew by now how difficult she found it to ask favours. 'If you babysit the girls, I'm sure Phoebe would give you a few lifts,' he added, and he put his hand on Kaisa's knee, 'All you have to do is ask.'

'Yeah,' she said and looked at the steel-grey loch beyond the base and the wire fence. The road ran along the hillside with woods to one side and the inlet on the other. It suddenly occurred to Kaisa how beautiful the place would have been without the unsightly base with its ugly dockyard buildings and the menacing black shapes of the submarines rising from the grey water.

'There'd be no jobs in this area, and Helensburgh would be a ghost town if the Navy wasn't here.' Peter said, as if once again he could read her thoughts. They were just passing the even more unsightly peace camp on the other side of the road.

'What these people don't understand is that the Navy brings jobs and prosperity to this forsaken land.' Peter added.

As the car came to a halt, Kaisa saw a girl with matted hair, wearing a colourful stripy woollen poncho, stoking a fire in the middle of a circle of run-down caravans, all in different states of disrepair. One of them was painted bright red, but the rest looked dirty and old. The whole site was a mess. When they'd been to see the new baby, Phoebe said that the women on the campsite wrapped old T-shirts or ripped pieces of cloth between their legs when they had their periods. 'They don't believe in consumerism and sanitary towels are a capitalist invention, it seems!' Everyone around the room had laughed, but Kaisa had shuddered. Now, looking at the woman crouching next to the fire, Kaisa imagined that under the layers of skirts she had just a dirty cloth to stem the flow of her period.

'This is all we need!' Peter said and suddenly Kaisa noticed that beyond their vehicle two cars had been stopped by a group of demonstrators. 'I'd forgotten it was Wednesday!'

'What do you mean?'

'Oh, the silly campers hold a demonstration every Wednesday.'

A dozen or so women and men in colourful baggy clothes were using pots and pans and large spoons to make as much noise as they could. They held a large canvas 'Peace' sign between them and advanced slowly along the road. On both sides of the road cars had stopped to let the demonstrators pass. Two policemen in uniform looked on, joking and laughing with each other. When the group came closer to their car, Kaisa caught sight of a girl with big dark-green eyes. She was visibly pregnant and gave Kaisa the peace sign and the sweetest of smiles. Kaisa couldn't help but smile back.

'They look friendly,' she said to Peter.

'They're a nuisance, is what they are,' he said and revved up the engine.

During the first few days in their new house, while Peter was at work, Kaisa was mesmerised by the view from their married quarter. She sat in the lounge and watched the submarines come and go, and the yachts sail in and out of view. The loch looked beautiful in all weathers, although Kaisa loved the stormy days best. Of course, watching the view meant that she didn't get any unpacking done, or send any job applications, so eventually Kaisa had to stop gazing out of the window all day long.

Because it was too far to walk to the shops from the new place, Peter decided he should teach Kaisa to drive, but after two attempts, it wasn't going very well. Peter got exasperated when she stalled the car or used the wrong gear, and Kaisa just got angry and eventually refused to go out with him. 'Darling, it'll be so much easier for you if you can drive when I am away,' Peter said and squeezed Kaisa tightly after the second failed attempt. Kaisa just nodded and tried to hold back the tears. Of course, she could walk into town, but it took nearly an hour there and an hour back. And it was often raining, or at least drizzly, so it wasn't very pleasant. There was a small shop at the bottom of the hill, but the mouldy vegetables she'd spotted when she first went in put her off going there again. Kaisa thought back to Southsea and how much easier life was when she could just walk to Waitrose, or Commercial Road for clothes shopping.

Luckily, Peter was ashore until HMS *Restless* got back, and working at the nearby Faslane base, so he was home every night. They went out to the pub with Peter's new friends from *Restless*, and once they went to visit Stef in Dumbarton, where she and Tom had bought a house. Tom was away, but Stef greeted them full of smiles. She was huge now, and complained bitterly about how uncomfortable pregnancy was. Kaisa looked at her large shape, while Stef sat and drank a mug of tea and smoked a cigarette in the little semi-detached house. Her living room was still full of boxes, but Stef didn't make any excuses for the mess.

'Tom left me with all this,' she laughed and held onto her back. 'That's what they're like,' she said and nudged Kaisa.

Peter and Kaisa exchanged looks when Stef went to make them coffee in the kitchen at the other end of the house. It was bitterly cold inside the place, and Peter blew on his fingers and rubbed his hands together. Kaisa stifled a laugh.

'How long is Tom away?' Peter shouted into the kitchen.

'I wish I knew, but I think he'll be back for the birth in December – I bloody well hope he will anyway.' Stef reappeared at the door carrying a tray with a pot of tea and some mugs. She'd emptied a packet of chocolate Hobnobs that Peter and Kaisa had bought with them into a blue bowl. Peter sprung up to take the tray from her and urged Stef to sit down.

'What a gentleman he is,' Stef said and laughed again.

Driving back towards Helensburgh, along the Gareloch, which was veiled in a wall of rain, Peter said, 'When you can drive, you can go and see Stef any time you like.'

Kaisa was quiet. Stef hadn't been talking about anything else but the forthcoming birth; about what kind of painkillers she would demand, and laughing at the 'natural birth brigade', as she called women who attended antenatal classes with the National Childbirth Trust. 'I know how to breathe, thank you very much,' she'd said.

Peter looked across at Kaisa and said, 'Too much baby talk?'

Kaisa smiled. 'Yeah.' She needed to get a job fast.

Every day she scanned the papers (they got *The Telegraph*, and even the *Helensburgh Advertiser*), and applied for a lot of jobs. But she never heard anything back. Kaisa didn't know if it was her foreign degree, or what, but no one seemed to want to employ her.

Perhaps it was all the pregnant women, or the new mothers, or the lack of a job offer, but since they'd been up in Scotland Peter and Kaisa argued a lot, and then made up in bed. They didn't talk properly any more, or clear the air after a fight. Sometimes Kaisa thought she loved Peter more when he was away and that he'd noticed she loved him less. Kaisa wouldn't take any criticism from him, and got mad straight away. The driving lessons didn't help. Peter said they had to get used to each other again, and laughed and hugged Kaisa when she got angry. Even though Kaisa wanted to be happy, she couldn't feel content. It was so much more difficult to do anything while Peter was at work; she couldn't just walk down to the seafront or to the shops like she could in Pompey. And the weather was always bad.

Peter greeted Kaisa's outbursts with silence, and she wished she knew what he thought. When she said she wasn't good enough for a job, he said, 'Of course you are,' but it didn't sound as though he meant it anymore. Kaisa often thought he simply said what he imagined she wanted to hear, as if she herself had put the words into his mouth.

'My God, I wish you would come up with something original for once!' she'd shouted after he'd thrown yet another platitude at her, about how she'd soon find a good job. His hurt silence made her even more angry, but desperate at the same time. She wanted to burst into tears when she thought about their marriage. Why hadn't she thought about how life would be with him before she got herself into this mess?

Kaisa was sitting on the ugly sofa, watching the darkening sky above the Gareloch. It was just after three o'clock and she'd finished another job application, so she allowed herself an hour or so to rest her eyes on the sea view before Peter came home. It had been drizzly all day, and she hadn't managed to get to the shops. They'd have to have tinned soup for supper.

When Peter came home, he told Kaisa the bad news: HMS *Restless* was going to be on patrol over Christmas. Kaisa looked at Peter, but said nothing. It was their first Christmas together as a married couple.

'Couldn't you go and see your mum and Sirkka?' Peter was holding onto her hands. They were sitting on the uncomfortable sofa, facing each other. Peter told her that he'd suspected this, but had received the confirmation that day.

'I'm so sorry, darling.'

Kaisa thought about what Christmas would be like in her mother's small flat in Helsinki. It would most likely be just her mother and Sirkka, just like when they'd been teenagers, after their parents' divorce. Those Christmases had been for the most part happy, but also a little sad. They had all missed father, even though no one had voiced it out loud. Kaisa didn't really want to relive those times, and she also felt she was too grown-up to spend Christmas with her mother. Besides, the flights would be expensive, and since she wasn't earning any money, they could ill afford the fare. 'No, I'll stay here.' Kaisa said.

'Or, you could go and stay with my parents. They'd be delighted to see you.' Peter's face was full of concern.

Kaisa thought this was possibly worse; she really didn't feel she knew Peter's parents well enough to be spending the holidays with them. 'I'll think about it,' she said. 'But don't go telling your mum anything yet, until I've decided what I'm going to do.'

Peter also brought home a 'Next of Kin Form', which Kaisa had to sign. They had to decide whether they wanted any bad news to be delivered during the patrol.

'If something happens to you, I wouldn't want to know while I'm away, because I couldn't come back anyway.' Peter was still sitting next to Kaisa on the sofa, looking intently at her face. 'And same for you. If something were to happen to me – which it's obviously not going to – would you want to know? Because the boat would not come back under any circumstances.'

'Not even if you ... or me ... died?' Kaisa asked. She was speaking very quietly, and was fighting back tears. It wasn't enough that Peter was soon going to sail away for months in a submarine full of nuclear missiles; she would now have to sign a form giving away her right to know if he was even alive. And vice versa, if she was deadly ill, or dead, he'd not know until the boat was back in Faslane.

'Darling, I know I have the strangest job, but this is what I do.' Peter hung his head.

Kaisa put his arms around Peter, and hugged him. 'It's OK, it's best to not know, I agree.' She picked up the form, ticked the 'no news' box and gave it to Peter.

Peter kissed her and then, sounding a lot more cheerful, said, 'There is the Familygram, where you can tell me your news each week.' Peter said that all the wives could write up to 50 words. 'No sports pages though, because the Captain or Jimmy, you know the 1st Lieutenant, will read them before they pass them onto us.'

'OK,' Kaisa said.

'I'm going to leave you a Christmas present, though, and I already know exactly what I'm going to get you!' Apparently, the other officers had told him they left presents for their families, and took their own away to sea. They would have a Christmas dinner onboard, and open their presents on the morning of the 25th as if they were at home. Kaisa felt a little tearful again, thinking about Christmas on her own, but decided not to dwell on it now. There were a few more weeks until Peter's departure, so she had time to think.

fter the many arguments during the driving lessons with Peter, they decided Kaisa should get a proper instructor. Peter was going away soon, and the thought of having to ask someone like Phoebe, or be dependent on Stef, or any of the other wives, made her more determined to try to learn as quickly as possible. Kaisa needed to be independent. Her first lesson with a small Scottish man went well. He even told her that she'd probably only need a few sessions with him and she'd pass easily. Peter promised to take Kaisa out in the little Ford Fiesta at the weekends.

'As long as you don't shout at me,' Kaisa said.

Peter sighed and said, 'I never shout at you.'

Kaisa didn't point out that when he'd tried to teach her to drive every session had ended with an argument. He would shout at her about not looking in the mirror, or being in the wrong gear or going too fast. Kaisa also didn't remind him that her last so-called lesson with him ended in them not talking to each other for a whole day.

Someone from the boat had recommended the driving instructor, and although his Scottish accent was so strong that Kaisa couldn't always understand what he said, he was very nice, especially after she told him she was from Finland. 'A fellow Viking, eh?' he said and laughed.

He was a very patient man and didn't bat an eyelid when Kaisa stalled on the first corner they came to. He had glasses that hung on his chest by a long strap, and which he would occasionally put on his head to look at a map or some kind of handbook kept in a pocket on the side of the door. His hair was wispy and grey, and he had pale blue eyes that looked at Kaisa from under bushy grey eyebrows. His car was a bright red Ford Fiesta, a newer model than the one Peter had, but he said it would be easier for her to learn with the same type of car. After driving up to the shops in Helensburgh and back, he said Kaisa was a natural. She stalled only once more and loved the feeling of speed.

'We need to be careful with her, I can see that,' the instructor said to Peter on their return. Peter stood at the doorway with the money for the lesson.

'Finns are great rally drivers and I think we have another one here!' the instructor said as he waved goodbye.

'Yes, I know,' Peter said and sighed.

After the successful driving lesson, Kaisa decided she'd take the train into Glasgow and register with an employment agency in the city centre. She got up early and Peter dropped her off at the station. She wore her black trouser suit and the beige mac (it was raining again), and felt a little like a businesswoman going to a meeting in the city. Glasgow seemed a very large and busy city, and it took her a while to find the office in West George Street, but she'd allowed enough time and was ten minutes early. The lady at the agency was friendly. Her Scottish accent was a bit difficult for Kaisa to understand, but once Kaisa showed her the certificate she'd got from Hanken and told her about working in the bank in Helsinki, plus her time at IDS in Portsmouth, and the job offer from *Sonia* magazine in London, the woman became much more interested. 'Aye, I'm sure we'll find you something,' she said.

On the way home, Kaisa was overjoyed. In Glasgow, she'd killed time before catching her train back by shopping on Buchanan Street. Peter was going to pick her up from the station at 5.30pm, so she had a few hours to spare. On the spur of the moment, she'd bought herself a new dress from the House of Fraser to wear to work, even though they couldn't really afford it, and she didn't even have an interview yet. But the woman at the agency had been so efficient and professional, and hopeful. She stuffed the shopping bag into her almost empty briefcase, which she'd taken to portray a professional attitude. She didn't want the agency people to think she'd be happy with a job in a pub or a department store.

When Peter met Kaisa at the station, he kissed her lightly on the lips. Before he could ask, Kaisa told him everything about the agency, the woman, and how hopeful she'd been that Kaisa would get work.

'Is this an actual job in Glasgow?' Peter asked.

Kaisa looked at his profile; he was waiting to cross the street into West Clyde Street, which ran along the waterfront. 'I don't know, they didn't have one for me at the moment, but she was hopeful.' Kaisa said.

'Oh, that's good.' Peter said nothing more.

Kaisa was suddenly furious; he hadn't listened to her at all. She'd told him she'd seen a woman at an agency, and that they would now start to match her details with employers. She sighed and looked out over the water. The morning rain had cleared and the Gareloch looked calm and blue for once. You could clearly see the opposite bank. There were some lush green and red colours of autumn still visible, even though it was early October. It was truly beautiful, but Kaisa could not enjoy the view. Why was it, she thought, that Peter didn't seem to understand her at all? Why wasn't he interested when Kaisa talked about her career? Or perhaps it wasn't his lack of response, but the language he used. She wondered if he even knew what kind of job she was after? He didn't really know what she did in the bank, or at IDS, nor did he ever ask. Perhaps it was the same with him; Kaisa didn't understand Peter's job. Besides, he wasn't allowed to tell her (or didn't want to tell her, she didn't know which). All Kaisa knew was that he was good at his job on the submarine, because people, like the Captain on Peter's previous sub, HMS *Tempest*, kept telling her so. Even Duncan had told Kaisa that Peter was very clever.

Still, Peter and Kaisa were arguing a lot less now. They'd settled down to married life in Smuggler's Way, and Kaisa had unpacked most of the boxes. In the past few weeks there'd been many parties and Kaisa had met some of the other wives of officers serving as port crew in HMS *Restless*. Peter had told Kaisa that there were two crews, one called starboard and the other port. Peter was part of the latter. Peter had even been given a few days off and they'd been to stay with Jeff in his parents' pub in Southsea. Kaisa had no idea they had so much room upstairs on the third floor. Peter and Kaisa had their own bedroom while Jeff stayed in a room opposite, with his girlfriend, Susan.

On the night of their visit, as they sat with their first drinks in their usual seat in the far corner of the pub, Jeff glanced at Susan and, grinning at Kaisa and Peter, said, 'We've got some news!'

'You won the pools?' Peter said.

'Very funny,' Jeff said and took hold of Susan's hand, 'We're engaged!'

'Oh, congratulations,' Kaisa said, and Peter added, 'Well done, mate,' and stood up to kiss Susan.

Although Kaisa knew Peter didn't like Susan much, Jeff seemed a lot happier and more serious about Susan than Kaisa had ever seen him before.

After they'd done the usual hugs and kisses, Jeff's mum and dad had come over to talk about the engagement party they were planning, which Peter and Kaisa wouldn't be able to attend, since Peter would most probably be away.

Jeff and Peter then started discussing their respective careers. Jeff was about to serve on a ship, which would be based in Northern Ireland. Kaisa listened to the men's conversation with half an ear, because she knew about the political situation there, and knew Jeff would be in danger. It was his second time there and Kaisa worried about him. But she didn't want to say anything, and instead listened to Susan talking about the people she and Kaisa both knew at IDS. Kaisa wondered if she'd forgotten that they'd both applied for the same job, and whether she knew that she'd been employed in Kaisa's stead, merely because of Kaisa's marriage to an officer in the Royal Navy. How would they react to the news that she, too, would now be married to the Navy? But Susan seemed to enjoy gossiping about the girls, Richard and Kerry and couldn't wait to tell her that Ann had been sacked; she'd had too many days off sick, Susan said. There was some justice then, Kaisa thought. Susan said that Kerry was as tight-lipped as before and Richard as vague and smiley as he always was. Listening to Susan, Kaisa was transported back to that painful day when she'd found out that IDS hadn't wanted her, and realised she'd not completely gotten over it. She'd thought that the job offer from Rose at *Sonia* magazine had wiped away any previous disappointments, but listening to Susan going on and on about IDS and how fantastic her job was, made Kaisa feel inadequate again. Nobody wanted to employ her now. She realised all she was good at was satisfying Peter in bed, and that was it. When he went away again, Kaisa wouldn't even have that.

In the morning, Jeff's mum served them all cooked breakfast in the upstairs dining room where Peter and Kaisa had held their first wedding reception. It seemed like such a long time ago, even though it was actually less than six months. Kaisa wondered if Susan and Jeff would also marry in Portsmouth. They hadn't set a date yet, but they were all smiles and couldn't take their eyes off each other. Watching them, Kaisa felt bad for resenting Jeff's bride-to-be, so she hugged them both warmly when Peter and Kaisa left for the long drive back up to Scotland.

18

B y mid-October the rain seemed constant in Helensburgh, but Kaisa was looking forward to seeing her sister Sirkka. She was finally coming to see Kaisa in her new life as Peter's wife. Sirkka had already left Helsinki and was at that moment crossing the North Sea. If everything went well, she'd be arriving at Helensburgh station at 9.30pm the following day, and she'd stay for nearly two weeks. Kaisa couldn't wait to see her sister, and was planning a trip to Glasgow and a dinner party with some of Peter's bachelor friends. Peter laughed when he heard Kaisa's plan; he didn't think Sirkka was the marrying kind. 'Who said anything about marriage?' Kaisa replied and that shut Peter up.

Sirkka arrived smiling at the train station in Helensburgh. It was a dark, cold night, but Kaisa saw her sister straight away as she stepped off the train. She'd had her hair highlighted very blonde, and had lost some weight. She looked very stylish in her tight blue jeans and yellow jumper, with wooden, dangly earrings. Kaisa thought she'd want to go home and sleep – her mammoth journey included a ferry from Helsinki to Stockholm, a train to Gothenburg, followed by a ferry across the North Sea to Newcastle, and another long train journey with two changes in Edinburgh and Glasgow, to Helensburgh. But as soon as they'd put her suitcase in the back of the car, Sirkka asked if they were going to the pub. Peter was very puzzled, Kaisa could see that, but he drove to The Commodore, which was on the water-front and on the way home to Smuggler's Way. They arrived just before closing time and quickly ordered a pint each. Sirkka wanted cider, even though Peter tried to explain that cider was drunk more in England and wouldn't be very good in Scotland.

The pub was full of Navy people and locals – it was a Friday night – and they all stared at Kaisa and Sirkka when they spoke Finnish. A bunch of sailors from Peter's old submarine, HMS *Tempest* sat in the opposite corner. Peter nodded to them and raised his glass in a greeting, but after that tried to ignore their obvious comments about Kaisa and Sirkka. Kaisa, too, smiled at the few faces she recognised from the visit to Liverpool and Morecambe. Because it was so late on a Friday evening, everyone was very drunk, and a young sailor suddenly came over to their table and introduced himself.

'Dear Mrs Williams, Able Seaman Rick Stannard at your service.' The boy saluted Kaisa and turned to Sirkka, but lost his balance and spilled some of the pint he was carrying over Peter's trousers. 'That's enough, Stannard,' Peter said and got up. The rest of the sailors who'd been sniggering in the corner of the pub grew silent and Stannard, visibly shocked by his own drunken actions, walked backwards and, bowing his head, said, 'Sorry, Sir, sorry.'

'C'mon, let's go home,' Peter said.

Sirkka looked at her half-full pint of cider and raised her eyebrows at Kaisa. 'Can we just finish our drinks first?' she said to no one in particular.

Peter turned his head sharply in Sirkka's direction, looked at her half-full glass and said, 'Of course, apologies.' He then drowned the last drops of his own pint of beer and got up. 'Excuse me, ladies.'

'What's up with him?' Sirkka asked Kaisa in Finnish.

The group of sailors in the corner had been talking in low voices among themselves, but hearing Kaisa and Sirkka speak Finnish again, their attention turned to the two women once more. Kaisa felt sorry for Stannard, and smiled at him. She soon regretted her kindness, as her reaction produced an immediate wave of laughter and whoops from the other men. To make matters worse, before Kaisa could stop her, Sirkka lifted her glass towards the group, creating even more commotion in the pub. Now all the other customers were looking at Sirkka and Kaisa, and Kaisa could feel her cheeks reddening. She was glad when Peter reappeared and the sailors in the pub grew silent once more.

'C'mon Sirkka, drink up,' Kaisa said and gulped down her own beer. I've got some food for us at home, I bet you haven't eaten much all day?'

Later in bed Kaisa told Peter she was sorry about the commotion in the pub. 'That's alright.' Peter said, 'Don't worry about it.'

Next day, when Sirkka and Kaisa went into Helensburgh (Peter was on duty), people seemed to know who they were. The lady in the butcher's shop, which Kaisa had been to only once before, asked how long her 'friend from Finland' would be staying.

'This is my sister, Sirkka,' Kaisa said and Sirkka smiled broadly and began asking about different cuts of meat. Sirkka wanted to make Sailor's Stew, a traditional Finnish dish that required very thinly cut steaks. Even though Sirkka's English wasn't as good as Kaisa's, she seemed to be able to communicate with the shop lady much better than Kaisa. The two laughed together at the lack of correct words, and when Sirkka had chosen the meat, the lady gave her a discount on the final sum. That was so unlike any Scot Kaisa had yet met, and she was happy that her sister was with her.

In the evenings, after a dinner that Sirkka usually cooked and Peter praised to high heaven, the two sisters would sit on the sofa and empty a bottle of wine. They talked about everything, about their childhood, their mother and father, about Sirkka's move to Helsinki, about Kaisa's career and the magazine job, and the lack of any work for her in Scotland.

'I'm sure you'll get something soon, just don't give up,' Sirkka advised her younger sister, and Kaisa's eyes filled with tears. How she had missed her sister, and her friend. Sometimes Kaisa looked over at Peter, who, having to work early the next morning, didn't join them, but sat alone at the table reading a paper or went to bed early. She knew he wouldn't have been able to understand them in any case, but couldn't help wonder if he minded that Kaisa was so occupied by Sirkka's extended stay with them.

On Sunday evening, when Sirkka had been with Kaisa and Peter for over a week, Peter came down in his dressing gown and asked the sisters to be quiet.

'Unlike you, I've got to go to work tomorrow!' he said, when Kaisa giggled and said she was sorry. It was past 1am, and they'd opened a second bottle of wine. Kaisa knew she was quite drunk, but Peter's words hurt her.

'Well, I am so sorry that I am talking to my sister who I haven't seen for months! And I'm sorry I'm not going to work tomorrow, because I don't have a job. Thank you for pointing that out to me!' Kaisa got up and ran to the bathroom and began crying. Sirkka ran after her, and Kaisa could hear that she said something to Peter and that the two of them began shouting at each other outside the bathroom door. Kaisa looked at herself in the mirror. Her make-up had run and she looked like a drunken old woman. Is this what her life had come to?

When Kaisa came out of the bathroom, Peter had gone to bed and Sirkka was sitting on the sofa, sipping wine.

'Are you alright?' she asked Kaisa. 'He is such a brute, Peter. I had no idea ...' Sirkka started, but Kaisa shook her head and Sirkka had the good sense to be quiet. She should never have got into the middle of it.

'Are you happy? I worry about you.' Sirkka said and that started Kaisa off again. She put her head on her sister's shoulder and had a cry. But she didn't have many tears left. She wiped her eyes and blew her nose on a tissue Sirkka handed her. Looking into her sister's dark-green eyes, she said, 'I'm fine. It's just not having a job, you know, that gets me down.'

Sirkka was quiet for a moment and then looked down at her hands, 'You know if you and Peter aren't suited to each other after all, there's no shame in admitting it. You could always come and live with me in Helsinki ...'

Kaisa was shocked that her sister would think her marriage a failure, and looked up at her sister's grave face, 'No, we love each other!' she said. Kaisa moved away from her sister and straightened her back, 'You've got it completely wrong.'

'Kaisa, please. I've heard you row in the evenings.' Sirkka put her hand on Kaisa's shoulder, but she shook it off, leaned back on the sofa and closed her eyes. 'I'm going to bed,' she said and walked slowly up the stairs. It was true, Sirkka's presence had made things worse between her and Peter. In bed the night before (where they usually rowed, then made up with sex), Peter said he had thought Sirkka would cheer her up, and Kaisa told him she did. Peter had not replied, but had turned over and gone to sleep. That night they didn't make love and Kaisa wondered if Sirkka was the problem after all. Talking to her sister had made Kaisa realise how dependent she was on Peter and it made her furious. She began to blame her joblessness on Peter, and in a way it was his fault she was now in Scotland, where it seemed job prospects were even worse than in Portsmouth. She hadn't heard a peep out of the friendly agency lady and she hadn't dared to phone her again after the first time, when she was unexpectedly dismissive.

There also seemed to be a power struggle between Sirkka and Peter. They both wanted to decide what to eat, where to go, even what kind of wine they should buy in the off-licence. Sirkka annoyed Peter, Kaisa could see that, whereas Sirkka just didn't take into account what Peter thought at all. Kaisa felt it was really about money with Peter; she knew having Sirkka over for such a long time cost them a lot more in food and drink. And with Kaisa not working, money was tight. What's more, Peter kept insisting on buying the rounds in The Commodore, which had become their habitual drinking place. But in bed at night, they didn't discuss any of this, they just argued about how Peter had not wanted to stay for another pint in the pub, or how Kaisa had insisted on buying expensive strawberries in the supermarket when Sirkka wanted them for a complicated dessert recipe. As usual, the thing that was really wrong was never talked about.

19

Towards the end of her visit, Sirkka told Kaisa she was deeply in love with the man in Lapland, the boyfriend she'd been seeing on and off for the past year. They were sitting having breakfast after Peter had gone off to work, watching the weak winter sun glitter on the surface of the Gareloch. It was a cold day, but unusually clear, and they could make out the line of trees on the other side of the loch. Kaisa replied that she was so glad her sister had found someone, but Sirkka looked back at her sadly and said, 'He doesn't love me, though.'

Kaisa suddenly felt very sorry for her sister, and felt guilty that in the last few days, Sirkka had begun to annoy her. After the incident with Peter, the relationship between her husband and her sister had been strained, and Sirkka kept asking Kaisa if she was happy in her marriage.

'Peter is very controlling, you know,' Sirkka had said to Kaisa, and she could only agree. But when she thought back to her life in Finland, she remembered that her former fiancé, Matti, had been much more controlling than Peter. Kaisa knew Peter only wanted Kaisa to be happy and to learn how to cope with life in England – and now in Scotland. Besides, Kaisa had married this man and she loved him. On the other hand, Peter had told Kaisa that he could always hear Sirkka in the house because she slammed the doors so loudly that the whole place shook. Kaisa had said that she didn't think her sister appreciated the effort she and Peter were putting into making her comfortable, taking her to pubs and even organising a dinner party for her (which was disastrous; Sirkka refused to speak to anyone and just sat at the table drinking her wine). She felt like a traitor talking to Peter about Sirkka like that, but Peter was her husband. Why, wondered Kaisa, could they not all get along?

Sirkka made both Kaisa and Peter feel as if they were always doing something wrong. Even when Kaisa had finally got a job interview in a clothes shop in Helensburgh, and the manager had told Kaisa she was probably too well educated for the job and would leave as soon as she got a better offer, which was a risk the shop just couldn't take, she saw in Sirkka's eyes that her sister felt she should have acted differently to get the job. It was on the tip of Kaisa's tongue to ask her sister what she should have said but Kaisa didn't think she could confide in her sister anymore, and had decided not to mention her worries.

But now, when she heard about this man in Lapland, Kaisa's heart melted. 'Oh, sis,' she said and hugged Sirkka. Perhaps it was this failed love affair that was making her sister miserable and judgemental about her and Peter's life?

When Sirkka left with all her bags and a full-to-bursting suitcase, Kaisa cried all evening. But after five full days, when her sister hadn't phoned to let her know she'd got home safely, Kaisa began first to worry and then feel annoyed. They'd spent a whole two weeks together, talking and laughing and trying to make sense of life. Even so, Kaisa wasn't sure Sirkka could understand her situation and her new life, and at times the concern she saw in her sister's eyes was unbearable. But now Sirkka couldn't even be bothered to phone and thank Kaisa and Peter for their hospitality. The annoyance with her sister turned into anger and one night Kaisa had a dream in which she hit her sister, only to regret it when she saw the red slap mark on Sirkka's face. Kaisa couldn't understand what had happened to her. She couldn't live with her husband without constant arguments, and now she couldn't get on with her sister either. It was almost funny how she spent most of her time trying to convince others that she was OK and not depressed. Still, within herself, she didn't have much hope for the future. Yet, on the other hand, she had a vision of herself one day being really BIG at something. But that was immediately followed by a huge wave of despair, ready to engulf her any minute. Why couldn't Sirkka help? Perhaps Kaisa didn't let her. By now Kaisa was afraid of the wave; she felt close to sinking into it.

20

K aisa wondered if there was any hope. She'd stood still for so long that she couldn't remember when she last did something useful.

Each morning she got up exhausted after a bad night, but full of willpower, trying to believe there was some good in people, and when she saw there wasn't, her mood changed suddenly, and she started crying and shouting at poor Peter, believing everything was his fault. Or his country's fault.

Perhaps Kaisa simply hadn't settled in Scotland yet. Everything seemed wrong to her, and she couldn't accept the way things were. The coffee was awful, watery and tasteless. The sickly tea everyone offered instead was even worse. The obsession with the words 'please' and 'thank you' when most of the time people saying those words didn't even mean them made Kaisa angry. The false smiles and the Scottish rain. The rain! Would it ever stop raining? At least in Finland at this time of year, there was beautiful white snow on the ground.

Reading Doris Lessing, Kaisa kept thinking she should be brave and never accept things as they are, but try to change the world. But how could she make an impact when no one gave her a job or a chance to do something? And what about children? Was having children a way out? A way of making an impact on the world? Perhaps being a mother would be the only thing Kaisa would accomplish in life, like most of the other Navy wives she'd met.

But the very next day there was good news at last. The agency in Glasgow got in touch about a job with a magazine called *Anglo-Nordic News*. It was a new glossy publication for businesses with connections to Nordic countries, but the job was selling advertising, some of which she would have to do from home. It seemed Kaisa was not deemed to be good at anything else. But, she thought, this would be a start, another stepping stone. The woman at the agency had been very impressed by the job offer from *Sonia* magazine in London, which is why she thought Kaisa would be perfect for this job. The *Anglo-Nordic News* had only just been set up, but this time next year the magazine could be a well-known publication and Kaisa could be an important lady in publishing. There was hope, after all.

But when Kaisa told Peter about the possible job, and about the salary, which was commission-based, he said, 'And what happens if you don't sell any advertising?'

Peter had just come home from work and, because Kaisa had only got the phone call about an hour before, she'd entirely forgotten about dinner. Peter had not even had time to take off his coat, which was dripping from the horizontal rain falling outside, when Kaisa told him about the job.

'Well done, darling,' Peter said absentmindedly, and added, 'I'm starving.'

There was another row, during which Peter made them some cheese on toast with beans. They sat down at the kitchen table opposite each other, still arguing.

'It's alright for you and your brilliant career. When it comes to my career, you don't care,' Kaisa said and glanced at her hot plateful of food. Peter was now taking large forkful after large forkful of beans in quick succession and ladling them into his mouth. Kaisa wasn't at all hungry, and suddenly she had an unreal sense that this wasn't her, arguing with her Navy husband (Peter was still wearing his uniform shirt and jumper) about who said what when, and what they meant or didn't mean by a comment. She felt dizzy, and rested her head in her hand.

Peter looked up at her, 'Are you OK?'

Kaisa didn't say anything, she was too angry to speak normally to Peter. But she was light-headed, and sick with it. She rushed out of the room and ran into the small cloakroom off the hall. It was freezing cold in there, because it was next to an outside wall and had no heating. Shivering over the loo, Kaisa threw up. Peter knocked on the door, 'Darling, I'm sorry!' Kaisa washed her face and let Peter take her upstairs to bed. He tucked her in and kissed her forehead, 'I love you very much, Kaisa. I hate arguing with you.'

'Me too,' Kaisa said.

Kaisa's sickness passed overnight, and she put it down to a tummy bug she'd picked up in the pool at the submarine base. She stopped going for a few days and instead, while waiting to hear from the *Anglo-Nordic News*, began reading novel after novel. She'd now read all of the books Doris Lessing had written and began reading one of Peter's books called *Couples* by John Updike. Kaisa was terrified of his view of marriage. Were love affairs really inevitable in a marriage? It seemed other couples didn't talk to each other about anything either. Or was it that they only discovered new dimensions in each other through sex and infidelity? What really happened to the love Kaisa originally felt for her old fiancé in Finland? Would she also stop loving Peter at some point? It scared Kaisa and she talked about the book to Peter. They were in bed and the rain was beating down on the windows outside.

'What if we, too, stop loving each other?' Kaisa said.

'It's just a book,' Peter said and turned over.

When Kaisa woke, Peter told her he'd had a dream in which she'd left him and gone back to Finland. Kaisa looked at Peter and saw he still had sleep in his eyes. She hugged him and told him that she too had had a vivid dream, in which Peter had disappeared into a secret building wearing his uniform. No foreigners were allowed inside. They laughed about their absurd dreams together and made love. Then Peter had to get dressed and go to work.

21

K aisa wasn't going to be anything big at the *Anglo-Nordic News*. They didn't want her. They didn't even want to interview her. The lady at the agency had been very apologetic on the phone, but after she'd heard she wasn't wanted, Kaisa stopped listening to her. She put the phone down and cried a little.

Kaisa felt she was being left out of the life going on outside their damp, cold house in Smuggler's Way. She needed to be occupied. Her mind wandered to Rose and the job in London and for a while she allowed herself to daydream about a typical day in the Soho office. Suddenly in the scenario, Duncan popped up, taking her to lunch in some swanky London place. For a crazy moment, Kaisa wondered what it would be like if she'd said yes to Duncan's advances in London and they'd become lovers. Perhaps that's what she needed to do, have an affair with Duncan? She brushed the mad, and bad, idea aside. What she really needed was a job. Why wouldn't anybody employ her? She knew there were thousands of reasons; there were always explanations. It wasn't personal, it wasn't that Kaisa was useless, worthless. But she felt unwanted, oh, so unwanted. And alone. She missed Sirkka, and her mum. Only yesterday she'd called her mother and had only just managed to hold back the tears. They hadn't even talked about anything in particular, only about their dog, Jerry. He was getting very old and her mother was worried about his hearing. That had set Kaisa off immediately, and she had to end the conversation abruptly. Luckily, Peter had been on late duty and was not there to witness Kaisa weeping over a dog.

When Peter came home on Friday, he was full of smiles. He flung open the door, and threw his cap on the sofa. 'Fancy going out for a drink with Stef and Tom? He's just come back and I saw him in the Wardroom today; we agreed to meet up. Isn't that nice?' Tom was still on HMS *Tempest*, and Kaisa knew Peter liked going out with him and gossiping about his old boat. It would be nice to see Stef, too. Hopefully with Tom home, there'd be less baby talk.

Kaisa had done nothing of any importance all day, and was so bored she just wanted something to happen. As usual, she took her frustration out on Peter, but he was very quiet and hardly said a word to Kaisa.

'Let's just go out and meet Stef and Tom, Kaisa,' he pleaded with her. His eyes were dark, and he looked tired. Was that all it was, or was he punishing her for some reason by not arguing with her. His silence and conciliatory tone made Kaisa even angrier. Because it was alright for him, wasn't it? He was pursuing his chosen career, he was doing well, and he kept telling Kaisa that. Whereas Kaisa wasn't wanted; she was an outcast. Earlier that same day when she'd gone for a walk, just for something to do, not one person had said hello or spoken to her. The only wife on the estate she knew was Phoebe, but she wasn't part of a group she'd seen chatting together at the bottom of the hill. The women had looked at Kaisa sideways, and had grown quiet when she passed. She suspected their husbands were senior rates, and somehow they knew Kaisa was an officer's wife. Or perhaps they knew she was foreign and didn't want anything to do with her?

'Did you say hello to the women?' Peter asked, when she told him about the incident.

'Of course I didn't!' Kaisa said sharply. Too sharply. Peter always made everything to be her fault. 'They looked at me and didn't say a word. Actually they looked away from me as if I was a leper!' she shouted.

Peter was quiet. He was getting undressed, pulling his uniform trousers off and revealing his white boxers with the tight buttocks that Kaisa so loved. When he took his socks off, he sniffed them before flinging them into the bin. Kaisa couldn't help smiling at the absurd gesture. 'Are you smelling them to see if you could re-use them?' she said. It was a common submarine joke that, when at sea, the sailors used their underwear at least twice, wearing socks and pants inside out the second time around. Peter spun around quickly and, sensing her mood change, scooped her up and tumbled onto the bed with her. 'My cheeky little Peanut!' He started kissing her, but

Kaisa protested, 'We've got to go, there's only half an hour until we need to be in the pub.' But she soon gave in to him, and afterwards they had to hurry so as not to be late to meet Stef and Tom.

In the car, as they drove along the rainy seafront towards The Arden-caple, Kaisa thought what a good man Peter was. She knew she was a drain on him, but sometimes it was so difficult to reach him. The only way to force him to react was a row. Kaisa tried to remember that the reason she was argumentative was because she had nothing to do in Scotland, and because of her unhappiness there was no room for Peter's feelings. But he was the only person Kaisa had to talk to. All the same, she didn't think they talked enough. Certainly they went to bed enough, and it could well be that sex would save them. But Kaisa often felt separate from Peter and preoccupied when he was with her; sometimes, she had to admit to herself, she just went through the motions in bed. Lately, when Peter said, 'Promise me you will never leave me,' she couldn't reply. She couldn't make a promise like that.

Perhaps Kaisa wanted Peter to go away again, so that she could dream and long for him? Was that how their relationship would work? Was that what their love was made of – missing each other? Kaisa looked at Peter's profile, as he concentrated on parking the car in front of the white-clad pub. He was a handsome man and she loved him, but she knew both of them kept pretending that all was well, and knew it wasn't. Kaisa was unhappy. There, she'd said it. To herself, silently, at least.

Stef and Tom were full of smiles, and Stef, who by Kaisa's calculations must have been more than eight months gone, had a big bump underneath her mohair jumper. 'I don't fit into any of my ball gowns, so goodness knows what I'll wear for the Christmas Ball next week,' she said. Kaisa had already decided she was going to wear her burgundy dress, which she hadn't worn in Scotland before. She had only two evening gowns, and really she needed a third one, so that she could ring the changes. You couldn't wear the same dress every time.

Seeing how happy Stef and Tom were made Kaisa wonder about children again. Would it really be so bad if she got pregnant now? On the way back in the car, she mentioned a baby to Peter, but he said, 'Look darling, you must believe me, you will get a good job one day. Something will turn up, I promise.'

'You think so?'

'Yes, I really do.' They'd arrived outside the house, and Peter took Kaisa's face between his hands and, looking deep into her eyes, added, 'And you know I will support you, whatever you decide to do, don't you?'

Kaisa nodded. Peter took her into his arms and squeezed her tightly. If only Kaisa could believe what Peter had told her.

22

HMS *Restless* was home. Peter had told Kaisa that morning in the car, on their way to the base for a swim. Once they got through the gates, Kaisa noticed how busy Faslane was. There were uniformed men milling around, walking briskly from one low building to another.

'And don't forget the Christmas Ball next week,' Peter continued. 'It's strange that it's in November, but it'll be great because both the port and starboard crews will be able to attend for once. Oh, and your admirer will be here, too!' Peter said, and squeezed Kaisa's knee.

Even though Kaisa knew exactly who Peter meant, she had to know for sure. 'Who?'

'Duncan!' Peter turned his head towards Kaisa and grinned. 'He's coming up tonight for the attack teacher course – so he'll be staying on for the ball.'

Kaisa's heart was beating hard, and she didn't want to say anything in case her voice betrayed her feelings. She told herself not to be so silly, and just said, 'Oh,' trying to sound non-committal.

Duncan said he'd stay on the base, but he'd already told Peter he was looking forward to seeing Kaisa. Peter smiled wickedly. 'I'll have to keep a tight hold on you so that he doesn't steal you away from me.' He tried to kiss her on the mouth while driving the car but Kaisa brushed him away. 'Watch out, you're a dangerous driver!'

'Oh, so after a few lessons, you're the expert,' Peter laughed.

When they arrived at the base, Peter stopped the car outside the sports centre to let Kaisa out. 'Really, please don't say anything to Duncan about me. It'll be embarrassing,' she said.

Peter nodded and kissed Kaisa on the mouth, 'Scout's honour.'

Kaisa got a lift back from the base with Phoebe, who was a lot slimmer in her jeans and Barbour jacket than when Kaisa had seen her with the baby. At home, Kaisa looked at her wardrobe and thought the burgundy ball gown looked a bit shabby. She couldn't wear her old black-and-white one again, because she had worn it to the Ladies' Night in Pompey with Duncan. Besides, it was far too summery with its thin straps and light fabric. But where could she go to buy a new one? But more than the gown, the prospect of seeing Duncan kept playing on her mind. She was looking forward to it and dreading it in equal measure.

The ball was at the base, in a massive room decorated with red flowers and satin drapes. There was a large window with a beautiful view over the hill leading to the Gareloch and, even though it was dark, bitterly cold and rainy, with a threat of snow in the air, the water looked enticing in its blackness against the harbour lights below. Kaisa and Peter bumped into Duncan almost straight away, in the back bar, and discovered they were sitting at the same table as him, along with Stef and Tom.

'You are looking lovely, as always,' Duncan said and kissed Kaisa's hand. Kaisa blushed and looked down in an attempt to hide her face. The wet mark left by his lips caused a burning sensation on Kaisa's hand, and she put it through Peter's arm to try to get rid of it. Duncan didn't have anyone with him, so he placed himself on the other side of Kaisa and they stepped into the dining room together. Stef and Tom were already sitting down and Stef was glowing in her green taffeta dress. Her breasts were larger than before and she was showing a large tummy underneath the folds of her gown. She whispered to Kaisa, 'Got this yesterday in Glasgow. I couldn't resist it when I saw how my boobs looked in it.' Kaisa had not felt she could spend money on a new gown. Once she'd tried the burgundy one on, she realised she'd lost weight with all the swimming. Her slimmer figure made the dress fall nicely off her hips, and she was happy with the way she looked.

After the meal, which was a lavish buffet set along one long wall of the room, Duncan put his arm over Kaisa's chair, and bent his head down, close to her ear, 'How about a dance?'

Kaisa could feel his hot breath on her neck and her heart skipped a beat. She looked over to her other side, where Peter was in deep discussion with a fellow officer from his new boat. 'I'm going to have a dance with Duncan,' she whispered to him and, after giving her a quick glance, Peter waved his hand, 'I'll see you down there.'

A disco was set up in the Wardroom downstairs. Luckily they were playing fast songs, so Kaisa didn't have to dance close to Duncan's body. She giggled while dancing to 'Come On Eileen' by Dexys Midnight Runners, remembering the first-ever submarine dance she'd been to with Peter. It was for the whole of the ship's company, and when they'd played the same song, the sailors had gone wild for it. A couple of the young sailors had bought Kaisa drinks, and when Kaisa had asked why they kept bringing her gin and tonics, Peter had replied that they wanted to get her drunk. 'They think they might have a chance with you.'

'But you're here,' she'd replied and Peter had squeezed her hard and kissed her on the lips in full view of everybody and replied, 'Indeed I am.'

She was conscious of Duncan's pale blue eyes on her, but whenever she looked up, his smile was just friendly – there were none of the passionate looks he'd given her during the Ladies' Night in Portsmouth, or when she'd stayed with him in London. Soon they were joined by the others, and their group – Stef, Tom, Peter, Kaisa and Duncan – danced and laughed together late into the night. Even Stef and Tom stayed till late. Although Stef didn't get on the dance floor, she sat at the table, sipping her drink, and grinning at the rest of them. They were one of the last groups to leave the party. Peter and Kaisa said goodnight outside the base and stepped into one of the taxis waiting to take the party-goers home.

On the way, Kaisa thought how relieved she was that Duncan had acted normally. She also thought of Stef, who'd asked her to come and visit once Peter had gone away. Kaisa couldn't help but be a bit jealous of Stef's house and her pregnancy; at the same time, the thought of being pregnant now, when she still hadn't taken the first step on a career ladder, made her shudder. Or perhaps it was the inevitable rain beating down on the windows of their minicab?

The next morning, Kaisa spent most of the day watching the swell on the loch and trying to read another novel by John Updike. She was more than a little hungover, and couldn't concentrate on anything else, like applying for jobs. She wondered how Peter could go to work after so much to drink and so little sleep, but he'd got up at the usual time and, careful not to wake Kaisa, had left for work at 8am. Kaisa's thoughts kept going to Duncan. Neither he, nor Peter, had said whether he was staying another night in the Wardroom, or whether he was going back to Portsmouth today. She knew he was based in Pompey, appointed to a sub that was in refit there, but she hadn't asked him what his schedule was. She hardly knew what her own husband's movements were, so it would have seemed odd if she'd started asking questions about Duncan's. It had been nice to see him in any case, she thought, but she decided to stop obsessing about him. They were all good friends, and it was obvious that Duncan had got over whatever fixation he'd had on her.

The weather had changed dramatically while she'd been sitting in front of the loch, reading John Updike's *Marry Me* on the awful blue-green sofa that you couldn't get comfortable on. Unlike the characters in Updike's novel, Kaisa had never felt that marrying somebody should be compulsory, quite the contrary. Her parents didn't manage to stay together, so she'd been determined never to marry. Yet, somehow she'd got herself engaged to be married at sixteen, to a man seven years older than her. Matti, the dependable Matti, had given her security and been a father figure, she could see that now. After her parents' awful divorce, she had been numbed and afraid and needed someone to care for her. Looking back, she and Matti had shared a strange relationship. Kaisa was so young, and he was so much older that he was like a teacher to her. And Kaisa had craved that. Matti was such a traditionalist. He and his strong mother wanted Kaisa to be prim and proper. That didn't last long – it was so against everything Kaisa believed in.

Even though she really was too young to know better (and Matti old enough to understand that Kaisa couldn't possibly know her own mind), Kaisa was ashamed to have let Matti down so badly. He'd been convinced they would marry as soon as she'd finished her studies at Hanken, have children and grow old together. If she was honest, even before she'd met her handsome Englishman, and fallen head over heels in love with him, Kaisa had known the relationship with Matti wasn't honest on her part. She'd been ready to leave, but she'd made a promise she didn't want to break. She was now ashamed that it took another man to make her see sense. Sometimes it felt as if she was just a pawn, a prize being passed from one man to another, or like a pet going from one owner to another.

After Kaisa left Matti and Helsinki, she'd gone to live with her mother and sister in Stockholm for six weeks. There she'd felt as if she had regained her independence. When Kaisa had returned to Helsinki to finish her studies, she was a new person intent on removing all pain and distractions from her life. She'd decided to finish with Peter, for a while at least, so that she could rethink her life in peace. But Peter had convinced her, during a long phone call, of his love. He pleaded with her to give him another chance. So she had. It had been flattering and she sometimes wondered if that was why she'd stayed with the long-distance relationship. Because Peter seemed to love her so much?

Now Kaisa just felt too tied to him, to his career, and to his world. There was nothing of Kaisa here, nothing of her own. There was just Peter and his job, which always came first. Without work, Kaisa would have no chance of surviving on her own in Scotland. At least when she was working at IDS in Portsmouth, she had a life, and a job. Here in Scotland she lived in Peter's shadow and it didn't suit her. However much Matti had tried, he'd never turned Kaisa into a 'little housewife', who lived her life through her husband, so how would Peter think she'd be content with that? Kaisa remembered their visit to Lucy and Roger in Edinburgh, before she married Peter, and how afterwards she'd told Peter she'd never be a Navy wife like Lucy. Peter had replied, 'I bloody well hope not.' But now, it was as if Peter had forgotten about those few days they'd spent in Lucy and Roger's married quarter.

Kaisa kept apologising to Peter for complaining all the time. He was so happy and it hurt her that he couldn't see Kaisa's unhappiness. Every time she as much as hinted that she was less than blissfully content, she felt like she'd cut him with a sharp knife. So, in the end, she acted stupid and irritable, to avoid telling him the truth about how she felt. It always led to an inconclusive argument that only ended when they made passionate and exhausting love. They repeated this spiral about once a week. Sex seemed to counterbalance the process, but for Kaisa it acted like a drug. The more they made love, the more Kaisa was sinking into a dream world and wanted to forget all of her real worries.

23

Kaisa passed her driving test on the first attempt. It was a Friday, and the small town of Helensburgh was busy with traffic, but Kaisa kept a cool head and managed all the hill starts, did a near-perfect three-point-turn, and even parallel parked the car on the seafront. She was so pleased and relieved that, after her delighted driving instructor had dropped her off, Kaisa couldn't wait for Peter to come home. She knew the submarine was going to sail any day now, so the timing couldn't be better. Now she could drive to the shop or even go to the cinema in town. Peter hugged her and said she should drive out to the shops in Helensburgh the next day. With Peter about to sail, they'd planned to fill the larder and the fridge full of food, so that Kaisa wouldn't have to worry about doing a big food shop. In case she'd failed her test, Phoebe had offered to drive her to the base and to the shops, but with her new baby and her two small girls, Kaisa really didn't want to trouble her.

When Peter sailed, only two days later, there was a dusting of snow on the hills on the opposite side of the Gareloch. Peter had told Kaisa there was no point in coming to the base to say goodbye, because they didn't know the exact time they'd be leaving. 'Stay here in the warm bed,' Peter said, and gave Kaisa a long, lingering kiss. So, with her dressing gown wrapped tightly around her body, she watched Peter get dressed and pack his Pusser's grip at 5am on a cold November morning. After Peter had gone, Kaisa tried to sleep, but couldn't, and sat in the lounge, waiting for HMS *Restless* to come into view. At a few minutes past seven, she was rewarded with a magnificent view of the submarine making its way slowly past her window. It was flanked by two tugs to keep other boats away. Kaisa thought that it truly looked like a 'sleek black messenger of death', an expression she'd read in the papers. Her husband, her love, was inside that vessel, and tears began to run down her face. Of all jobs, why did Peter have to be a submariner, and a submariner in a Polaris sub to boot? In vain, Kaisa waved, even though she knew nobody, certainly not Peter, would see her. She wished she'd gone down to the base after all, to see Peter one more time. What if he never came back? What if there was some kind of incident, and they had to fire the missile? They'd all be dead by then, Kaisa thought, and decided to pull herself together. Nothing would happen, as Peter had said over and over. Still, how would Kaisa manage on her own for two months – or more – without him?

Peter had told Kaisa that Phoebe would find it too difficult to manage with the baby and her other two children when the submarine sailed, and Kaisa had promised to help her look after the bigger girls on some afternoons. After the submarine had disappeared from view, Kaisa decided to get dressed and go and see Phoebe – she needed to get out of the empty house, and thought Phoebe might want some company too.

'Ah, Kaisa, come in,' Phoebe said, balancing the baby on her hip. Phoebe's girls, aged just two and three and a half, were sitting in front of the TV, still in their pyjamas. They were nice children, but Kaisa didn't really know what to say to them. Luckily, they totally ignored her, and were engrossed in a Disney cartoon on the telly. There were two other women in the lounge, sitting next to the girls. Kaisa had met both of the Navy wives, whose husbands were on the same crew as Peter, fleetingly at the Christmas Ball. 'Hi, Kaisa,' they both said, as if it was the most natural thing in the world to be gathered at Phoebe's house early on a cold Scottish morning.

'You know Pammy and Judith?' Phoebe asked. Kaisa nodded.

'The first day of patrol is the worst, believe me,' Phoebe said, and added, 'Tea?'

'Sorry, I don't drink tea,' Kaisa said.

'Oh, OK … what would you like instead, water?'

'Coffee if you have it, please,' Kaisa said and felt awkward with the two other women looking quizzically at her.

'Did you see them sail?' Phoebe asked her, and Kaisa was glad of the change of subject.

'Yes, Peter told me not to go to the base, but I saw the boat on the Gareloch.'

Phoebe lifted her face up from the baby on her lap. 'Oh.' The other two women also lifted their faces, away from the children's programme on TV.

'I always used to go and wave them off before the children. But now, with baby Millie, it's just too cold,' Phoebe gave Kaisa a curious look, and Kaisa felt that she'd broken another kind of English – or possibly Navy – code.

Phoebe told Kaisa that her husband, Bernie, was an engineer on HMS *Restless*, and that they couldn't wait to move back down to England. Phoebe was a nurse before she met Bernie, but she didn't think she'd ever get back to nursing now.

'Perhaps I'll go back to work, but to something else, when the girls start boarding school,' she told Kaisa now. Kaisa didn't say anything but wondered how on earth she could even think about being parted from her lovely daughters.

'There are no private schools in Finland,' she said instead, and in case Phoebe and the other two wives wondered why she was being so quiet all of a sudden.

Pammy, who had very dark hair cut in a bob, was very friendly, in an English way; distant but polite. She told Kaisa that her husband was new on HMS *Restless*, just like Peter. 'They're the same rank, aren't they?' said Kaisa.

'Yes,' Phoebe said.

'There are no jobs for the English here,' Pammy sighed. She was really slim, and Kaisa didn't even realise she was pregnant until Phoebe gave baby Millie to her.

'Here you go Pammy, you might as well start practising now!'

Pammy must have seen Kaisa's surprise, because she touched her flat tummy underneath her tweed skirt. 'I'm just six weeks along.'

'Oh,' Kaisa said. She was thinking that she hadn't met any other wife on the Rhu estate who worked, didn't have children or wasn't pregnant.

'So congratulations are in order,' Phoebe said and lifted her tea mug. She was also holding onto the wriggling body of her two-year-old, Sarah, whose chocolatey face Kaisa was dying to wipe clean.

'Yes, well done you!' said the third Navy wife, Judith. She'd brought her one-year-old baby, Sophie, a fat little thing with wispy blonde hair, who sat sturdily on the floor alternately eating a pink plastic toy and banging it on the floor. Kaisa worried about the bacteria she must be transmitting into her body, but the mothers around her didn't seem too concerned.

Kaisa noticed there was a sudden silence and everyone was looking at her, as if she should be saying something, 'Oh, yes, congratulations, sorry.' Kaisa muttered, and cursed the straightjacket of English manners.

The women around Kaisa began a steady chatter. They talked about nappies, how difficult something called Pampers were to get from the one shop that sold them in Helensburgh, and how much more expensive the nappies were in Scotland than in England. Pammy complained about the lack of lettuce, or fresh vegetables, and this Kaisa agreed on. She told them how she and Peter had been trying to get some courgettes for one of her vegetarian recipes, but had given up when the only thing they found was a box of large, hollow-sounding marrows.

'Oh how sweet young love is. Did you hear that girls? He goes food shopping with her!' said Phoebe, and they all laughed. Kaisa could feel her cheeks grow red and was sure she'd blushed.

'We mustn't tease her,' Pammy said, and Kaisa shot her a grateful look.

'More tea, anyone?' Phoebe said and began to heave herself up. She'd already told them she was still sore from the birth.

'Never again, ladies, never again,' she'd said laughingly. 'I don't care how much Bernie craves a son, 'this shop is well and truly shut.'

'So how was it, Phoebes?' Pammy asked.

Phoebe shot Kaisa an enquiring look, as if to ask, 'Can she take this?' Kaisa said nothing, but wondered if they wanted her to leave. Instead, she sat still and began to think about Peter and how soft his lips had been and how badly she'd slept the night before, because she was already treading the empty space in their bed, while half listening to Phoebe tell the tale of the birth. Her waters had broken at home, after which they'd rushed to hospital. 'It was fast, but my God it was painful,' she said. 'And a new record for the hospital, the midwife told me – 33 minutes from me getting into the hospital and this little beauty arriving.' She touched her daughter's cheek. Baby Millie had fallen asleep on Pammy's lap, and responded to her mother's touch with a soft gurgle and faint movement of her fat little legs and arms. Kaisa was surprised how much she wanted to hold her, and for the umpteenth time she wondered why it would be so wrong to have a baby now. Peter and she loved each other; he had a good job and career and could support a family; whereas Kaisa didn't even have a job.

But now, with a driving licence, the world would be Kaisa's! She remembered that she hadn't even told Phoebe. 'Oh that's nice,' Phoebe said absentmindedly. The baby had started crying, while one of the older girls was whingeing about something and pulling at her mother's sleeve. Pammy stood up, gave Millie to her mother and began talking to the little girl about the cartoons. She was a natural mother, Kaisa saw, and thought how alien motherhood seemed to her. Perhaps it was just as well that Kaisa planned to concentrate on trying to find work – any work – rather than rush into the world of nappies and babies.

When, after endless cups of tea and coffee, the women began to leave Phoebe's, with promises to keep in touch, Kaisa returned home and phoned her sister in Helsinki to tell her she'd passed her driving test.

'Wow, that's fantastic! Have you told mum yet?'

'No, I just got back, you can tell her, can't you?'

There was a silence at the other end. Sirkka knew Kaisa hadn't spoken to her mother for a few weeks now. There just hadn't been time with the ball and Peter's impending departure. But really Kaisa was afraid of the emotions that calls to her mother stirred in her. 'Go on, just ring her,' Sirkka said.

'OK,' Kaisa said.

They didn't speak for long because international telephone calls were even more expensive from Scotland. Kaisa had wanted to talk to Sirkka about having a baby, but she didn't seem to be in the mood to talk. So Kaisa lifted the receiver again and started dialling her mother's number, but at the last minute she lost her nerve. Kaisa was afraid her mother would start asking what jobs she'd applied for and what the prospects were like in Scotland. Her mother had the idea that there were many opportunities for her in Scotland and if she knew Kaisa could now drive, she would think she could take a job further afield. But Kaisa was tired of applying for jobs and getting only rejections. Besides, Kaisa couldn't even pretend she'd stay here if Peter was posted back down South. Everyone knew the score, and no company in Helensburgh, or even Glasgow, was stupid enough to employ Navy wives.

It was midnight and Kaisa was already in bed. She must have just fallen asleep when she heard the phone. Stumbling in the dark to get down the stairs and reach it reminded her of the night calls Peter used to make when she was in Helsinki. This time, however, she immediately thought something must be wrong.

'Hello, Kaisa!'

'Hello,' she replied, but couldn't place the voice. She was still half asleep. It wasn't Peter.

'What's happened?' Kaisa said, the feeling of dread rising inside her.

'Nothing, you silly thing.' The voice laughed at the other end of the phone.

'Duncan!'

'Yes, I thought I'd see how you are settling in up there in the dark North.'

Duncan and Kaisa hadn't spoken since the ball at the base.

Duncan told Kaisa he was coming up to Faslane again. She told him Peter was away at sea. 'Oh, that's a shame, I really wanted to see him, too, but if it's OK by you, I'll pop in for one night with you?'

He told Kaisa that he was doing a week-long course on the base in Faslane, and he'd be sharing a married quarter with some of the other guys, but because of a 'Royal Navy cock-up' the place wasn't available until the day after they started. 'I could stay in the Wardroom, but …' he said.

'Of course you must stay with us, or me.' Kaisa said. 'I'll come and get you from the station.' Those words sounded so good.

'What, you've passed?' Duncan said, 'Congratulations!'

'Thank you,' Kaisa said, trying to sound bright and charming, although she felt groggy and sleepy. She brushed aside what Peter might think about Duncan staying in the married quarter alone with her. She wanted to see Duncan, and as long as she was careful, it would be alright, she was sure of it. Besides, if he was the way he'd been during the ball, she would have nothing to worry about.

A couple of days after Duncan's phone call, and less than a month after she'd passed her test, Kaisa dared to drive all the way to Glasgow. Each week she'd driven a little more each day, reaching Dumbarton the week before, and now Glasgow. Her new friend Pammy, whom she'd invited for coffee after they met at Phoebe's place, came with Kaisa and showed her how to park in a multi-storey car park just off Buchanan Street, the main shopping street in the city.

'You've got to be a bit careful where you go in Glasgow,' she said, 'especially if you are English.'

'But I'm not,' Kaisa said.

Pammy laughed and replied, 'By the way you sound, you may as well be!' She told Kaisa that there were very rough areas in Glasgow, where women on their own shouldn't go, and that the Scots could be aggressive, particularly to the English.

'They hate us,' she said, and Kaisa was again glad she was born in a country that hadn't gone around conquering and pillaging other nations.

They had lunch in the top-floor restaurant of the House of Fraser department store.

'You did really well today,' Pammy said. 'It took me months to pluck up the courage to drive into London and park in a multi-storey.' Pammy told Kaisa she'd grown up in Surrey, which was close to London. She'd met her husband Nigel while they were both still at school. When Nigel had gone to Dartmouth, she'd started secretarial college and had briefly worked for a fashion designer before marrying Nigel. She had worked in various part-time jobs since, but preferred to move around the country with her husband. They'd been married for two years and Smuggler's Way was their third married quarter. 'Now, with this little one on the way, I'll have my hands full,' she said and smiled.

Pammy was small and slim, and during the past month, when Kaisa had

got to know her better, her little tummy had expanded slowly. Kaisa hoped
that when she got pregnant she'd look as pretty and slim as Pammy did. In
the car on the way back from Glasgow Kaisa told her so, to which Pammy
just laughed and said, 'Oh God no, I'm huge!' But Kaisa could tell she was
pleased, because she said, 'You know, Nigel really likes his girls to be slim,
so I've started to measure my ribcage just below my boobs, and my thighs,
to make sure I'm not going to be vast afterwards.'

Kaisa looked down at her sturdy legs. Although she was a lot taller than
Pammy, she knew her thighs were like tree trunks compared to Pammy's
thin pins under her checked pinafore dress.

That evening Kaisa wrote her first Familygram to Peter.

*I drove to Glasgow with Pammy today and parked in a multi-storey car
park. We had lunch in the city and drove home. I feel so proud of myself and
Pammy said I did well too. I miss you terribly. Lots of love Kaisa x*

Kaisa looked at the brief note and hoped it would pass the Captain's inspec-
tion. She sighed and folded the thin blue paper, and glued the sides together.
She'd drop it off on the base the next morning, before her usual swim.

25

After Duncan's phone call, Kaisa had put his forthcoming visit out of her mind. With the excitement of having passed her driving test and being able to get into town and to the swimming pool at the Faslane naval base on her own, it'd been easy.

But now, an hour or so before his train was due to arrive at Helensburgh Central, Kaisa's thoughts kept going back to the kiss Duncan had planted on her lips after the Ladies Night ball in Portsmouth. Because he had been so normal when he'd accompanied Peter and her to the Christmas party only a few weeks later, she was convinced that he'd got over his little infatuation.

So why was she suddenly so nervous?

She couldn't even decide what to wear. The weather was cold, but for once it wasn't raining, so she could have worn a skirt, but immediately decided against that. She always wore a skirt when welcoming Peter home, so that would give a completely wrong impression to Duncan. Of course he wouldn't know about Kaisa and Peter's little games, but she was sure he'd notice if she made too much of an effort. On the other hand, she didn't want to be too scruffy. Her usual 'boy clothes', as Peter called them, the jeans and checked shirt she often wore, were far too informal. Eventually Kaisa settled on a newly washed pair of black cords and a black jumper, with a scarf in animal print tied around her neck to give the outfit a little colour. She made up her face with black eyeliner to match her clothes. Looking at herself in the mirror before she set off, she was pleased with the way she looked.

But by the time she stood at the station watching the passengers come out of the train, looking at the faces, trying to find Duncan, her palms felt all clammy. She fiddled with the wedding rings on her left hand, turning them around her finger. Was she too made up? What if she saw someone from the married patch? Would they get the wrong idea?

When Kaisa finally spotted Duncan, she saw he'd seen her first. He was walking up to her, his eyes taking in her whole body. When he got close to her, he stood still, looking deeply into her eyes. Kaisa let out a short, nervous laugh, and stretched out her hand. Her cheeks were burning under Duncan's direct gaze, but she couldn't help but respond, and sink deep into those pale blue eyes. She knew it was wrong, but she had butterflies in her tummy.

Later, after a boozy meal, Duncan knelt in front of her and somehow they started kissing. Kaisa wanted to stop, but she couldn't. Duncan's desire for her felt so good, it filled a void she'd had inside her for what seemed like forever.

Kaisa gazed at Duncan when he pulled her up from the chair and led her upstairs. As if in a trance, she let herself be undressed, while Duncan kissed her neck, her breasts and climbed on top of her. His touch on her was rough, rougher than Peter, but her body responded and she let out a moan.

Duncan entered her and suddenly, as if she'd woken up, she looked up at the ceiling, and knew she wanted him off her. She needed to tell him to stop, but she couldn't get the words out. She felt utterly ashamed. She'd led him on, she'd let him do this, and now it was too late.

26

The day after Duncan's overnight stay, Kaisa stayed in bed. She was very hungover after all the wine they'd drunk, and she wanted to stay in bed in the hope that she'd wake up into a different world, a world in which the night before hadn't happened. She feigned sleep when she heard Duncan lean over her, to see if she was awake. She didn't get up when she heard him in the bathroom, or when he put the kettle on and made himself a cup of tea. She wished he would just go, disappear, and that she'd never have to see him again. When he finally shut the front door behind him, Kaisa crawled out of bed and saw the note he'd left on the kitchen table.

'Thank you for last night, love Duncan x'

Kaisa ran into the bathroom and emptied the contents of her stomach.

She was a bad, bad person.

Kaisa didn't go out at all that day, but the next day, when Peter had been away for exactly three weeks, Kaisa drove the short distance to Phoebe's house. She didn't want to go to the base for a swim, because she feared she might bump into Duncan. She would normally have walked up the hill to Phoebe's house, but it was pouring with rain.

Phoebe greeted her with a smile, and almost immediately gave baby Millie to her.

'Can you hold her for a moment while I see to the other two.'

When she came back, Phoebe asked how Kaisa was coping.

'Fine,' she lied and rocked the lovely little girl in her arms. She was fast asleep, a dead weight on her lap.

'She sleeps too much during the day and not enough at night,' Phoebe said, and added with a sigh, 'I think I should put her down in the cot.'

Kaisa handed the baby over.

When Phoebe came back downstairs, Kaisa said, 'They've been away exactly three weeks today.'

Phoebe lifted her eyes to Kaisa and regarded her for a moment

'This one will be the shortest one because it's over Christmas.'

'Really?' Kaisa said.

Before he went away, Peter had told Kaisa that this patrol could be as short as six weeks, but that it could also be ten weeks.

'They'll be back right after the New Year.'

'Why?' Kaisa asked.

'Because it's so hard on the families.'

Phoebe tapped the side of her nose and smiled

'I didn't tell you that.'

Kaisa was silent, thinking that now she had less time to prepare herself for facing Peter after what she'd done. She shuddered.

They were sitting in Phoebe's tiny kitchen, which was the same size as Kaisa's even though Phoebe had three daughters, whereas Kaisa only needed room for her and Peter. But Phoebe had five bedrooms to Kaisa's three, because Bernie was a Lieutenant Commander and senior to Peter.

Kaisa was sipping a coffee that Phoebe had just put in front of her, thinking how weird her life had become. She now had no control over where or how she lived anymore. But stranger than that, neither had any of the other Navy wives Kaisa knew. It seemed such a medieval or Victorian way to live. Once again, Kaisa wondered how an earth she'd got herself into living such a life, when Phoebe, sighing, said, 'I almost forgot, I've got to talk to you about something.'

Her friend looked tired and her hair was uncombed and sticking out in all directions. She was wearing a pair of jeans and a roll-neck jumper. She pulled the arms of her jumper over her hands, and put them around her hot mug of coffee in a vain effort to keep warm. All the married quarters the Navy owned were desperately cold; the heating didn't work at all well and Peter had told Kaisa it was very expensive. In Finland, all flats were heated centrally, so Kaisa never had to consider how much her heating bills were. In England, she'd got used to wearing several layers indoors in winter, even in Pompey, so today she wore a thermal vest, a brushed cotton shirt in a light-blue check and a bulky navy-blue jumper over stonewashed jeans. Peter called the clothes her 'dressed like a boy' outfit, but Kaisa didn't care how she looked; just as long she was warm.

'I hear you've been a naughty girl!' Phoebe said, giving Kaisa a serious look.

Kaisa looked up at her friend, but couldn't think what to say.

'You had a man staying with you a couple of nights ago!'

'How did you …?'

'Oh, someone saw him come out of your house,' Phoebe said, and added, 'I hear he's quite handsome, too?'

Kaisa's heart was beating hard and she could feel her cold cheeks redden. Trying to sound nonchalant, she said, 'Oh, he's just an old friend of Peter's. He's on a course up here for a few days and they'd messed up his accommodation, so …'

The sound of the baby alarm interrupted her.

'Right,' Phoebe said and got up.

'Could you keep an eye on the two in there while I fetch Millie?'

'Yes, of course!'

Kaisa was relieved the conversation was over. She shot up so quickly that she spilled some of the coffee on the table. The baby was now crying fully and the noise from the baby alarm filled the kitchen. Kaisa took a dish-cloth from the basin and said, 'Sorry, I'll wipe it up.'

Phoebe stood in the doorway, resting her body against the frame.

'Look Kaisa, this is none of my business, but be careful. The wives get very bored here and for some of them the best thing since sliced bread is gossiping. Innocent or not, another man leaving your house in the morning after obviously spending the night alone with you while your hubby is away is manna to their bored minds. And don't mention it in the Familygram will you? It'll only worry Peter.'

The 6th of December was the coldest day Kaisa had yet experienced in Faslane. It was a week since Duncan had stayed the night, so Kaisa braved the swimming pool at the base. The pool was almost empty; only one other woman was swimming slowly up and down the lanes. Kaisa lowered herself into the water and started swimming. She loved the feeling of her powerful body in the water. For once, her long limbs and strong legs seemed to have a purpose as they propelled her from one end of the pool to the other.

At school, Kaisa used to win swimming competitions, even in the sixth form, when most of the girls in her class shunned the pool because they didn't want to show off their bodies. Kaisa wasn't good at gymnastics, so the pool was the only place where she felt she could excel. Kaisa had all but forgotten her love of swimming during her studies at Hanken and since marrying Peter, but here up in Helensburgh she came for a swim every day but Sunday – missing a whole week had been difficult.

After twenty lengths, Kaisa decided to go to the sauna. When she was getting out of the pool, she saw a pair of feet planted squarely in front of the ladder. Kaisa looked up and saw Duncan, wearing a pair of navy-blue swimming shorts, bending down to give her a hand out of the water. As if she needed it! He had a wide smile on his face when he said, 'I thought it was you! Some of the chaps said that a Nordic beauty was swimming here and I thought it could only be you.'

Ignoring his stretched-out arm, Kaisa stepped nimbly onto the tiled surface surrounding the pool. She bent down to retrieve her towel from a bench by the wall, and quickly covered herself up.

'Hello, Duncan.'

'I'm not going to get a kiss?' he said and bent his head towards Kaisa.

'You know I can't …'

She moved away from him and hit the cold steel arm of the steps leading into the water. Duncan took hold of her.

'Watch out, you mustn't slip.'

Kaisa looked at his hand on her wet arm and for a moment they stood still without speaking. The warmth of his fingers burned her skin. Kaisa didn't know what to say, and wished he'd just go away. Eventually she moved her arm and pulled the towel tighter round her body. She lifted her eyes to his face.

'I didn't know you were still up here.'

'I'm taking the sleeper down South tonight,' Duncan said, and added softly, 'unless …?'

There was a long silence again.

Kaisa started shivering.

'You're cold,' Duncan said and stretched out his arms towards Kaisa.

She had nowhere to go; the pool was right behind her. Suddenly she remembered the old lady and wondered if she'd seen them, but the pool was empty. There was just a couple of male lifeguards at the other end, talking to each other. Kaisa couldn't hear what they were saying so she assumed they couldn't hear them either. Kaisa breathed a sigh of relief, took a step to the side and started walking towards the ladies' changing rooms.

'Nice seeing you Duncan,' she shouted behind her and waved to him.

Once safely inside the changing rooms, Kaisa went straight into the sauna and, still shivering in spite of the heat, poured two ladlefuls of water onto the stones. There was no one else inside and she was glad that on one of her visits with Peter she'd convinced the friendlier of the two lifeguards that the sauna needed steam. Slowly Kaisa's body stopped trembling and, feeling brave, she spread her towel on the top bench, took off her swimming costume and let the steam and heat caress her body. Suddenly tears started running down Kaisa's face. What had she done? Why had she been so stupid?

Driving home, Kaisa realised it was Finland's Independence Day. She thought about home and how everyone used to light white and blue candles in their windows at six o'clock as a quiet mark of respect for those who had been killed in the wars against Russia. Or that's what her father had told her when she was little. Flags would have been flying all day all over the country, and in many cities there would be firework displays later that night. She remembered that Sirkka had sent her a pair of traditional white and blue candles as an early Christmas present. She'd light them at exactly 4pm, which was six o'clock in Finland. No one would know why there were two candles alight in a married quarter in Helensburgh, but that didn't matter. Kaisa knew she was marking her country's independence and that was enough for her. How could she almost forget this important day? The candles were tucked away in the house somewhere. At least Kaisa could be patriotic, even if she was a bad person in other ways.

27

Kaisa got a phone call from Pammy late one evening, a couple of days after the incident with Duncan at the Faslane pool. She said she wanted to know how Kaisa was doing.

'I'm just looking out for you,' she said. She'd been to an antenatal class, where Duncan and Kaisa had been mentioned over coffee afterwards. Her heart racing, Kaisa asked, with as calm a voice as she could muster, who was spreading these rumours about her. Pammy's reply shocked her, 'Love, they're not rumours now, are they? Duncan did stay the night with you when he could quite easily have stayed with me, or in the Wardroom.'

Pammy told Kaisa that Nigel knew Duncan. They'd been at RNEC Manadon, the naval engineering college, at the same time. Kaisa had no idea and wished Duncan had told her. Kaisa knew this was the same as being university friends, so it was surprising – and suspicious – that Duncan hadn't contacted Pammy.

'He even came to our wedding,' Pammy said.

'Perhaps he didn't know Nigel was stationed up here?' said Kaisa.

Pammy was silent at the other end of the phone. After a while she said, 'Oh, he knew alright, but ...'

Kaisa had another thought, and interrupted her friend, 'If he had stayed with you, it would be you all these bored women would be gossiping about.'

'Well, I guess so, but you know you are ...'

'I'm what?' Instead of shame, Kaisa began to feel anger welling up inside of her.

'I'm an old pregnant cow and you're a tall Scandinavian beauty!' Pammy was laughing now and Kaisa joined her.

'You're not old!' Kaisa said too quickly, and realised she should also compliment her, so added, 'and you are very attractive, too!'

'Yeah, yeah,' she said, and added, 'but Kaisa, you can tell me, did anything happen with Duncan? Because if it did, you know it will come out …'

Kaisa tightened her grip on the receiver. She considered what she should say to Pammy, and then replied, 'Of course not! What do you take me for?' She hoped her voice was as light as she intended it to be.

'In that case, this'll blow over, before the boys come home, I'm sure of it,' Pammy said and started talking about her pregnancy, which wasn't going so well. She'd had some bleeding, but the midwife had told her she'd be alright as long as she rested and didn't lift anything heavy. 'So now here I am in bed, laid out like a beached whale.'

Kaisa offered to do her shopping and agreed to go over to her house after her swim the next day. Kaisa decided she'd make her something nice to eat, perhaps her vegetable quiche or mushroom soup.

That night Kaisa could not sleep. By midnight she was still lying in bed, wide awake. She couldn't take her mind off what people were saying about her. How soon after the boat was back home would the wives tell their husbands, and how soon would the tale reach Peter's ears? How would Peter react? Would he believe the rumours, or would he think them funny, as he had done before when there were rumours about her and Jeff, and laugh them off? Kaisa put the light on and, sitting up in bed, grabbed her pen and letter-writing pad and began composing a letter to Peter. Although she knew he'd not get the letter until he came home, she wanted to set down her side of the story. She wanted to keep the tone light, just telling him that Duncan came to Faslane and stayed over in their house, and that now there was gossip about it, just as there was gossip in Pompey about her and Jeff. She started three times, but gave up. She couldn't find the words to tell Peter about Duncan. She knew it was because she'd never lied to Peter before.

The next day Kaisa drove over to Pammy's after a really long swim. When she parked the car outside her house, which was on the road below Kaisa's, towards the Loch, she saw that Pammy's flower-patterned, Navy-issue bedroom curtains on the second floor were still drawn. Kaisa glanced at her watch and noticed it was nearly ten o'clock. Surely she wouldn't still be in bed? Kaisa rang the bell and, when there was no answer, she tried to look through the kitchen window. Kaisa's doorbell was broken, so she thought Pammy's might be, too. There were some dirty dishes in the sink, but the room was empty and dark. Kaisa shivered. It wasn't raining that morning but the clouds were low and threatening and there was a chill wind, which caught her hair, still wet from the pool. Kaisa pulled her Barbour jacket more closely around her body and walked back to the car. While she sat there, wondering what to do, a woman she didn't know ran towards her. Kaisa wound down the window and, before she could ask what was up, the woman said, 'You looking for Pammy?'

She wore a thick cardigan with muddy walking boots and dark-red, woolly tights under a tweed skirt. Her accent was northern, but Kaisa couldn't place it. 'She was taken to hospital first thing this morning,' she said. 'I'm Annabel, by the way,' she added and reached her hand inside the car.

Annabel told Kaisa they'd just moved to Helensburgh, and that her husband had joined the HMS *Restless* starboard crew, and that he, too, was an engineer. 'We asked if she wanted us to go with her, but she said no. She started bleeding heavily last night and called the ambulance herself.'

'Oh, no,' was all Kaisa could think to say.

The woman, Annabel, regarded Kaisa for a while.

'You're married to Peter Williams, aren't you?' she said.

Kaisa nodded. Heavy drops of rain had begun falling onto her windscreen.

'Look, do you want to come in for a cup of coffee?' Annabel said.

Kaisa looked over to her house. A little girl stood at the open front door, hugging the neck of a large black Labrador. The child and the dog were watching Annabel's every move.

'No, no, I think I'll go and see Pammy.'

Again Annabel's eyes were on Kaisa for a long time before she said, 'Look, I think her mother is flying up from London today, so ...'

'OK, coffee would be lovely,' Kaisa said and ran inside Annabel's house out of the now pouring rain.

The house was filled with warmth. Although there were still many card-board boxes stacked in the corner of the large living room, the space itself was so much more homely then Kaisa's house, or any of the other married quarters she'd been inside. Annabel had a large three-piece suite covered in light yellow fabric in the centre of the room (not Navy issue), with blue velvet curtains hanging either side of the large bay window. The Navy issue dark mahogany dining table was replaced by a pine suite, with a beautifully carved pattern on the backs of the chairs, reminding Kaisa of furniture in Finland. Annabel had even hung curtains in the kitchen, made out of yellow-and-navy striped cotton fabric. While she made the coffee and produced chocolate-covered Hobnobs from a yellow biscuit jar, she said, 'Please excuse the mess, we're still unpacking.'

'What mess?' Kaisa thought, following her into the lounge and sitting on the comfortable sofa.

Annabel told Kaisa how her husband had been woken up by the ambulance arriving and how they'd spoken with Pammy, who'd been conscious but upset. It seemed Pammy had phoned her mother in the middle of the night when the bleeding had increased, and her mother had convinced her to phone the duty doctor at the base, who in turn had called the ambulance. Annabel said they hadn't talked about it, but it looked as though she may have lost the baby.

Kaisa wondered how long Annabel had known Pammy. She was beginning to realise what a small world the submarine service was. Peter had told her that most of the officers knew each other, so why wouldn't most of the wives know each other, too?

Kaisa was so sad for Pammy. She'd told Kaisa that she'd had many miscarriages before, and Kaisa knew how much she wanted a baby. During their trip to Glasgow she'd told Kaisa how happy she was to have got past the three-month mark, because she'd lost all the other babies during the early stages of her pregnancy. Pammy's midwife had also told her that it was much less likely that she would lose her baby once her pregnancy had passed three months.

At home, looking at her empty, but cluttered living room, Kaisa slumped on the uncomfortable sofa and looked at the Gareloch veiled in a wall of steel-grey rain. She felt so sad for Pammy, but also for herself, a feeling she knew was selfish and egotistic. She hadn't just lost a baby, but she felt down because she'd done something stupid and unforgivable. Something so bad it could make her lose Peter forever.

She opened a letter she'd found on the doormat as she got in. It was a card from Stef 'announcing a new arrival' – a little girl, born on the 6th of December, 1984. Kaisa decided to mention on her congratulations card that the baby was born on Finland's Independence Day. She found it hard to know what to write on such cards, so she was glad that for once she'd have something unique to say.

Kaisa decided to drive into Helensburgh to buy and post Stef's card – just for something to do. On her way back, having missed a turning, she found herself on the road to the base. There was another peace rally outside the fence. Kaisa's car was the only one to be stopped, and when she peered at the group, Kaisa noticed the same pregnant girl that she and Peter had seen before. It was only her and three other women and two men holding an old piece of sheet with the words, 'Free Scotland of Nuclear Arms – CND'. There were hand-drawn flowers and a round, yellow smiley face surrounding the slogan. The small group stood in the middle of the road and the women sang while the men drummed a slow beat on worn-out looking tambourines. Kaisa remembered Peter's hostility towards the protestors but, looking at the women and men in front of her now, she couldn't understand why he hated them so much. The other wives had exactly the same reaction to the anti-nuclear protestors as Peter.

'Did you know that they have no loos there, and do both their number ones and twos in the forest?' Pammy had said when Kaisa had driven her to the base one time. She shivered when she thought about living like that. As she waited in her car for the protest to end, thinking that the protestors ought to be more afraid of the Navy personnel, and not the other way around, there was a knock on her window. The pregnant girl was standing there, with the slight drizzle falling onto her matted, short blonde hair. 'Sorry we're holding you up,' she said and grinned.

'That's alright, I'm not in a hurry.'

'We don't really like doing this, but it's in the camp rules.' The girl glanced over to one of the men whose expression seemed hostile.

'What do you mean?'

The drizzle had become heavier, and it now looked more like sleet. Kaisa hoped there'd be snow soon. But the girl looked very cold so, surprising herself, Kaisa said, 'Why don't you come inside the car to warm up a bit.'

The girl looked at the group in the middle of the road and, touching her round belly, which was covered with her long, colourful poncho, she swiftly walked around the car, opened the door and sat next to Kaisa. 'Lyn,' she said and offered Kaisa her hand. Kaisa tried to place her accent but couldn't.

'I'm Kaisa. Where are you from?' Kaisa added. Lyn's hand was ice-cold.

'Leeds,' Lyn said and began warming her fingers by rubbing them against the heater in the car.

'You're frozen,' Kaisa said.

Lyn just grinned at her as if to say, 'I know'. Kaisa glanced at the old caravans on the side of the road, which made up the camp. There were a few faded tarpaulins fixed across the vehicles. 'It must be difficult to stay there all year round when it's so cold and damp,' she said.

'It's alright. We light fires most days and the caravans have heaters. The only problem is drying the clothes. Oh, and this. I'm not sure if we'll have enough hot water when it's my time.' Lyn put both of her hands around her belly. 'Oh, he's kicking; do you want to feel?'

Kaisa looked at Lyn's belly, which stretched the fabric of her trousers to its limit. She was about to say, 'No, thank you,' when Lyn took hold of Kaisa's hand and placed it on the lower part of her round tummy. Through her hands Kaisa could feel slight movements, and then a sharp kick, which nearly propelled her hand away from the tummy. Kaisa looked at Lyn, whose smile had grown wider, 'It's quite amazing, isn't it?'

Kaisa was speechless. She kept her hand on Lyn's belly in the hope that there'd be another wonderful kick, but the baby was still. 'Thank you,' Kaisa said quietly. She felt humbled by what this unknown girl had shared with her. Kaisa looked into Lyn's dark-green eyes. Kaisa noticed now that Lyn was very beautiful in spite of her clothes and the short hair that stuck out in all directions. It was her eyes that did it; they were clear and had a glow to them. The two women sat there, inside the car, silently smiling at each other when suddenly the noise outside became louder. They both looked ahead out of the misted-up windscreen. Lyn pulled the sleeve of her jumper up to her hand and wiped the window clean. The small group of women and men were shouting, 'Lyn, come on!' and waving in their direction. They'd rolled the sheet together and were standing by the side of the road.

'I'm off,' Lyn said and leaned over as much as she could to give Kaisa a kiss on the cheek.

28

W hen Kaisa drove down to the base the next day for her daily swim, she tried to see Lyn, but it was raining so hard that there wasn't anybody sitting outside. There were just faint lights in the windows of the run-down caravans, showing that there was someone at home.

After her swim, Kaisa decided to drive into Helensburgh to post a note she'd written to Pammy. She didn't want to intrude on her grief over the lost baby, especially as her mother was with her, but she thought a note might be a good idea. Peter would be proud of her English manners. The thought of Peter gave her a hollow feeling in her tummy, but she tried to ignore it and instead began thinking about what a pregnant mother would need. After the Post Office, she went into the little supermarket and got a pint of milk, some bread and some greens, which Peter's mum cooked to go with her Sunday roasts, carrots and some red lentils, which Kaisa found at the back of the shop. She guessed Lyn would be vegetarian, so she didn't buy any meat or eggs. On a whim, Kaisa also bought a variety of chocolate bars, which the shop displayed on the counter. 'For the kiddies, eh?' the shop owner said. Kaisa just nodded and braced herself for the short walk to the car. It was raining again, and there was a bitter wind blowing, which made it impossible to defend yourself against the heavy drops. The town looked deserted, with only a few men waiting outside The Henry Bell pub. Kaisa looked at her watch; it was a few minutes to twelve, and almost opening time.

The rain was still falling and the wind blowing when Kaisa reached the camp. She parked on the road and, carrying the two bags of shopping, made her way carefully towards the first of the caravans. The ground was wet and muddy and Kaisa cursed herself for not wearing a pair of wellies.

Kaisa could hear laughter from inside when she knocked. Trying to be heard above the sound of the falling rain, she shouted, 'Hello!' There was no reaction. Kaisa's flimsy tennis shoes were caked in mud and her jeans were wet and stuck to the skin from the dripping rain, which now also ran down Kaisa's waxed jacket. Whoever thought that a Barbour was a useful piece of clothing in Scotland, she'd never know. It was favoured by all the Navy wives, and Kaisa had fallen into the trap of thinking it must be perfect for the Scottish climate. But no, the jacket was either insufficiently warm on a cold and rainy day like today, or too hot when temperatures were mild.

Kaisa knocked again and almost immediately the door was flung open and the guy who'd been leading the marches two days previously, surveyed her. His eyes were dark and he was wearing a loosely knitted jumper with faded jeans. He was barefoot and Kaisa averted her eyes from the sight of his dirty toes. Lyn was sitting next to a younger, very slim girl with bright purple hair.

'Hi,' Lyn said, 'come in!'

The guy, still looking intently at Kaisa, took one step sideways, and she squeezed past him.

'It's bloody pissing out there again, isn't it!' Lyn said and laughed with the girl next to her. The curse startled her, but Kaisa was drenched, and glad to step inside the warmth of the caravan. 'I bought some stuff ...' she said.

The guy snatched the bag from her.

'Gerry, for fuck's sake!' Lyn shouted and, with difficulty, heaved herself up from the little couch. 'Thank you,' she said as she peered into the shopping bag. 'I love chocolate,' she said and came over and gave Kaisa a kiss on the cheek. 'Take your coat off,' she said and, looking at her soaked shoes, added, 'and you'd better take your shoes off too and put them next to the wood burner.'

While Kaisa struggled to take her shoes and coat off in the small space without knocking into either Lyn's belly or stepping onto Gerry's hairy toes, Gerry himself was digging into the bag, 'We're not a bloody charity, you know that don't you?' He took out a Lion bar and bit into it. Crumbs of chocolate fell onto his blond, shaggy beard.

Kaisa didn't know what to say, or do, and just stood there, in the middle of the caravan, slowly thawing out. The wood burner gave the room a familiar, almost sauna-like smell. The couch where Lyn and her friend were sitting, Kaisa now saw, was a bed. At the end of the space was a tiny kitchen, filled with pots and pans, and a small table with two chairs either side. Gerry sat down on one of the chairs and, having nowhere else, Kaisa sat down opposite him.

'So who the hell are you?' Gerry said. His face was, she now saw, full of pimples and his arms looked thin and his chest caved in. Kaisa had thought he was older than her but, looking at him closely, she saw that he was just a youngster, perhaps 18 at the most.

'Gerry, why don't you and Lisa go and make sure the log pile is still covered up?' Lyn said.

The purple-haired girl stood up and, taking Gerry by the hand, left the caravan. 'Thanks for the food, that was a nice thing to do,' Lisa said and gave Kaisa a quick hug. She smelled of a damp forest, and Kaisa wondered how the two of them would manage in the rain and wind wearing just thick jumpers. Didn't they have any waterproof clothing here?

'How have you been?' Kaisa asked Lyn when the door had closed behind Gerry and Lisa, making the small caravan shudder again.

Lyn was holding onto her round belly. 'I'm fine,' she smiled. 'Listen, don't worry about Gerry. He's not quite right, but he's got nowhere else to go so we keep him here. And it's better to have him on the demos; the police behave better when there's a man with us.' She was quiet for a moment and began pulling on the fluff covering her colourful poncho. 'It's strange how Gerry sort of scares the police. I think they see he's a bit unpredictable.'

Kaisa's mind was racing, 'But he's not dangerous?'

Lyn gave one of her easy, rippling laughs. It made Kaisa smile, although she was scared on her behalf. She was about to give birth to a baby and there was a madman on the premises. How did she sleep at night?

But instead of discussing Gerry, Lyn tilted her head and, looking at Kaisa with those green eyes of hers, asked, 'Who are you, really?'

And so Kaisa began telling Lyn, this hippy girl everyone else she knew thought was wicked and crazy, her story; how she met Peter five years ago at the British Embassy cocktail party, and how even though she'd been engaged to be married to a Finnish man, she'd fallen head over heels for the Englishman. And how for four years they'd struggled to be together, writing letters, telephoning each other and, when they had the money, travelling back and forth to be with each other. Kaisa even told Lyn about the other girl Peter had fucked (yes, she used that word; inside that tiny caravan it seemed OK to use crude words like that), and about her one-night stand with the tennis player. Kaisa told Lyn about how her father had behaved, about his drunkenness, and his Jekyll-and-Hyde character. She told Lyn about her studies and how just when they were about to be married, she'd had doubts about tying her life with a man who served in the Armed Forces. And about how the Navy didn't seem to want her either, branding Kaisa as a dangerous pro-Soviet woman. Lyn laughed at that.

Kaisa then told her about the job offer in London and even about Duncan, but not about his recent visit. That was too raw to talk about yet.

'Wow, and how old are you?' Lyn asked after Kaisa been speaking for a long time.

'Twenty-four.'

'Same age as me.'

While telling her tale, Kaisa had moved to sit next to Lyn on the sofa, and Lyn had made them some herbal tea. It tasted odd, a bit like hot water mixed with freshly cut grass, but it was warming and made Kaisa feel as if the caravan, and meeting the mad Gerry and Lisa, and talking like they were old friends with Lyn, was a dream.

'How long until you're due?' Kaisa asked.

'Oh, I think it's about a month away.'

'And will you go to hospital?'

Lyn laughed again, 'No, Lisa is a midwife, that's why she's here.'

'How many of you are there?'

'Usually it's about twenty-five, but everyone has gone home for Christmas. Except us, who have nowhere else to go.'

Kaisa was just about to ask why she had no home, when Lyn got up and said, 'Listen, I need to lie down for a bit.'

Kaisa tried to ask her if she needed anything else, but she wouldn't say.

'See ya!' she said and waved Kaisa off.

29

I n the week before Christmas, Kaisa spent a lot of time with Pammy. When her mother went back to London on Sunday, the 15th of December, Kaisa took over the caring for her friend. She'd met Pammy's mother only fleetingly but, during that short time, she'd taken Kaisa to one side and made Kaisa promise that she wouldn't leave her friend alone. They were virtually neighbours, so it was easy for Kaisa to keep an eye on her. Pammy had been prescribed bed rest for at least a fortnight, and told not to lift anything heavier than a bag of sugar. During one of her trips to Helensburgh to buy food and other supplies for Pammy and herself, Kaisa checked how much a bag of sugar weighed. This didn't seem like much. When Kaisa told Pammy about the bag of sugar, she said, with a strangled voice, 'Just as well I don't have a child that I'd need to lift ...' She tried to laugh but began weeping instead. Kaisa hugged her and, although at first her shoulders tensed between Kaisa's arms, eventually Pammy relaxed and let Kaisa comfort her. After a while she wiped her face with the hand-kerchief she seemed to be permanently clutching, and said, 'I'm being silly. I really don't know what the matter is with me this time.'

Even though she was so very sad about the baby, at times Kaisa seemed to be able to make Pammy laugh, mainly with her silly stories about Finland and her family, and about how Peter and she met. The more times Kaisa told the story, the more it became a tale outside herself. As if it had happened to someone else altogether. Pammy said she thought Kaisa should write a book about it, but she didn't think she'd be able to do that. What language would she write in, for a start? Besides, what would Peter say if Kaisa told the world about their 'love story'?

Every time Kaisa now went shopping, she made a habit of buying some bread, butter and chocolate for Lyn, too. She'd sit with her for a few minutes in the stuffy caravan, sometimes a little longer if Gerry wasn't around. Kaisa still felt very wary of him, and worried for Lyn, but the pregnant girl seemed to be fond of the gangly teenager. Kaisa didn't tell Pammy of her 'second patient', as Kaisa had begun to think of the two women. Although, she supposed, the two had really become her best friends. Even though their circumstances could not have been more different, they were actually quite alike, Kaisa thought, as she reversed her car out of the lay-by next to the camp. She hid her face in a hooded sweatshirt she'd taken to wearing, so as not to be recognised by anyone passing in a car. The camp was by the side of the road between Rhu, where the turning to the married quarters was, and the Faslane base, which meant most of the cars passing would be driven by people working for the Royal Navy, either locals at the dockyard or sailors and officers. But there was very little traffic, especially when the submarines were on patrol. Today, the road was deserted, and Kaisa breathed a sigh of relief.

As usual, it was a rainy day. Pammy had given Kaisa a key, and while Kaisa was putting the shopping into the cupboards, and into the almost empty fridge, Pammy came to sit on a kitchen chair. Pammy's mother had made her soups and casseroles and had done a big shop just before leaving, but now the provisions were running low. Kaisa had brought Pammy a quiche and some limp lettuce she'd found at the small vegetable section in the shop. She'd also got some cabbage and some greens, because Kaisa believed Pammy needed to eat more vegetables to get better.

'There's some quiche for lunch, how about it?'

'That'll be nice. Can you stay?' Pammy asked.

'Yes, of course,' said Kaisa.

'You don't have to you, you know,' Pammy said.

Kaisa turned to face her from the sink, where she'd been washing the lettuce leaves. Pammy's voice had sounded tearful again.

'You've been really good to me, shopping for me and making food and keeping me company. But you must have things you need to do yourself?'

Kaisa looked at her friend. Her voice was strained and she was fiddling with a handkerchief, which she was folding into a small square. Kaisa couldn't understand; had she offended Pammy in some way?

'I have nothing else to do,' Kaisa said simply.

'That's alright then,' Pammy said, still in the same hurt voice.

'What's the matter?' Kaisa went over to sit opposite Pammy at the small kitchen table. 'We're friends, aren't we?'

'Yes,' Pammy said and got up. 'Don't mind me, I'm just a sad old girl feeling sorry for herself.'

Kaisa took hold of Pammy's hands and gently pulled her back down. 'Look, Peter is away, I don't have a job, and I like being with you. What else would I do with my time? Since we've been friends, being here in Faslavatory hasn't been so bad. Before you, I had no friends at all, and it was awful. I think I could have gone mad. During the first weeks in this place, I was seriously considering going back South on my own. I was dreading the time when Peter would have to go away. But then I met you and Phoebe and it's been alright.'

Pammy looked at Kaisa with a sad smile on her face, and Kaisa feared she might start crying again, so she added, 'And you showed me how to park in a multi-storey car park in Glasgow! What more could a girl possibly want?'

Pammy laughed and Kaisa got up and started preparing lunch again. As she was cutting up a piece of dried-up cucumber and a tomato with a wrinkly skin, Kaisa thought that what she was really doing here, and with Lyn at the camp, was running away from her own problems. Looking after Pammy and Lyn had given Kaisa a much-needed escape from her own thoughts and the rumour mill, which by now, if Phoebe was to be believed, was churning at full speed.

Time was also speeding ahead, in a way that it had never done when Peter had been away before. Christmas Eve was only four days away, and if Phoebe was to be believed, the boat would be coming home any time after the New Year.

That evening, Kaisa got a phone call from Jeff. She was very surprised to hear from him, because she knew he was in Northern Ireland.

'You alright?' she asked, immediately worried something bad had happened.

'Peter at home?'

'No, he's still on patrol – they're not due home until after Christmas and New Year.'

'Right.'

Kaisa could hardly hear Jeff's voice; the line was very bad and he sounded as though he was at the bottom of a well. 'You alright?' she asked again.

'Listen, the thing is …'

'What is it?' Kaisa was now very worried. She knew this couldn't be anything to do with Peter, but was it about her and Duncan? Had the rumours somehow reached Portsmouth, and so via his parents, or someone else, Jeff in Northern Ireland?

'Susan's broken off the engagement,' Jeff's voice was muffled. Was he crying? Jeff was devastated. He'd received a letter from Susan, telling him that it was over. He'd immediately telephoned his mum, because Susan had got into the habit of going to the pub almost every evening, just to spend time with Jeff's family.

'What did she say?' Kaisa asked.

'Nothing. Susan had just come in the night before last and given the ring to my mum, and told her that she'd written to me. But in the letter she said that …' Jeff inhaled deeply, and continued, 'that it's her job.'

'Oh,' Kaisa didn't know what to say.

'They've refused her a promotion because of me.'

'Oh, Jeff.' What more could Kaisa say? Susan had made her choice, which was the opposite of the one Kaisa had made. But how could she explain to Jeff that he was worth less than a career at IDS?

When Jeff had finally got off the line, Kaisa began feeling angry with Susan. Surely she would have known how they felt about Navy wives at IDS? Surely she would have been told why she got the job instead of Kaisa, or was that really how it was?

30

Three days before Christmas Kaisa had a phone call from her mother, asking her to come and spend Christmas with her in Helsinki. This was the second phone call from her in the last two weeks. They'd usually phone each other about once a month, if that, because of the expense. Kaisa said, again, that she didn't have the money for the flights. 'Look, Mum, even if I drove down to London from here, it would cost more money than we have to either fly or take the various ferries and trains back to Finland,' she said. Her mother accepted the excuse begrudgingly, and then started crying.

'Don't, please, *äiti.*' Kaisa pleaded.

'Oh, it's just that I miss you so very much, and with Christmas coming up ...'

'I know, Mum, but I can't help it. We'll have a long talk on Christmas Eve, yes?'

Her Mother didn't reply, she was still sobbing down the phone and Kaisa guessed this wasn't about her and Christmas. With all the recent phone calls there must be something else.

'What's really the matter?' Kaisa said, trying to keep her voice from breaking.

'Sirkka is moving to Lapland, and she's not spending Christmas with me either,' her mother said between sobs.

'I didn't know that,' Kaisa said and tried hard to keep the chill out of her voice.

'You don't care, I can hear that,' her mother said, her sobs now having subsided. She blew her noise loudly.

'Mum, I just can't afford the flights. What about your friends from work? Couldn't you spend Christmas with them?'

'Well, actually I am. Still, it would've been nice to have at least one of my daughters with me. Goodness knows what my friends will think.'

Now the truth was out, Kaisa thought. It's always about what other people think. Or was she being too harsh? Kaisa decided that she should try to sympathise, she was her mother after all.

'It's hard, I know,' she said, and continued, 'but Peter and I were there in September, and we'll come again soon, I promise.' They chatted some more about her mother's friends and what she was going to do for Christmas Eve, and Kaisa thought she was alright at the end of the call. As soon as she'd put the phone down Kaisa called Sirkka.

'I've just been talking to Mum. She was crying about Christmas,' Kaisa said as soon as she answered. Sirkka was living on a floor below their mother in the same block of flats in Töölö in Helsinki. It was a nice area, with a large park nearby, facing the sea.

'Don't take any notice, you know what she can be like,' Sirkka said. She was mumbling down the phone.

'Are you eating something?'

'Yes, sorry. I'm just packing. Hold on a minute.' Sirkka left the phone and Kaisa counted the minutes, or the money, this holding on was costing her. 'I'm back,' Sirkka eventually said.

'So, Mum told me you're moving to Lapland?'

'Yeah, it's a fantastic opportunity. You know I wanted to work up there for the skiing season and now the hotel in Ylläs, where I worked before, wants me to do the Christmas shift, and then there's a chance of getting the restaurant manager's job in the New Year. It's just what I want.'

'So you're leaving Mum on her own?'

'I told you not to take any notice of her. She's not on her own; she's got masses of friends …'

'I mean for Christmas!'

Sirkka sighed, 'Christmas is really only a couple of days out of the whole of the year. I don't know why people get into such a state about it all.'

'But Mother shouldn't be on her own at Christmas.' Kaisa said quietly.

Sirkka was silent for a moment. 'Kaisa, this is a fantastic opportunity for me. You know how unhappy I've been living here in Helsinki, virtually under my mother's roof, and in a job that I am under-qualified for. As for the people in Helsinki … well, you know what it's like …' Sirkka was again quiet for a while, and then continued. 'If you're worried about her, why don't you come home? Why is it always me who has to hold her bloody hand?'

'You know I can't afford the flights; besides, Peter might be coming home right after the New Year. I haven't seen him for nearly two months …'

Sirkka interrupted her, 'So, you see, you put your life first, why shouldn't I – for once?'

When Kaisa didn't reply, Sirkka said, 'I've got a train tonight and I haven't packed yet, so I've got to go. I'll let you know my address and phone number when I get there. OK?'

Kaisa put the phone down and thought she should have gone to Finland to be with her mother for Christmas. Perhaps the incident with Duncan wouldn't have happened if she'd been busy planning her trip home. She had no idea Sirkka wasn't going to be there and now it was too late. Still, she felt guilty about her mother too. As for her father, she hadn't spoken with him since the wedding. She'd heard from Sirkka that he was slimming down and getting fit. That didn't sound like her father at all, but for Kaisa all the hurt from the time she'd lived with him, and his insistence that her mother couldn't attend the wedding if he paid for it, was fresh in her memory. Peter kept reminding Kaisa that, in spite of their argument, her father did come to the wedding, and that he gave them a large sum of money as a wedding present. 'Which he didn't need to do,' Peter usually added.

'Of course, he needed to give us a present after first agreeing to pay for the wedding, and then making my mother foot the bill!' Kaisa would reply. Peter just shrugged his shoulders at that. He didn't really understand; his family, with a mum and dad still married, and an older sister and brother, was normal compared to Kaisa's close relations. Besides, the reason Kaisa couldn't make up with her father wasn't just because of the wedding; it was also about all the times, while she'd been a student at the Hanken and living under his roof, he'd let Kaisa down or been just plain nasty to her. Sirkka should try life with dad, Kaisa thought now. After that, the experience of staying in a flat that just happens to be in the same block as Mum's, would be a piece of cake! At least their mother didn't get drunk all the time on *Koskenkorva*, or have terrible mood swings. In the two years Kaisa had lived with her father, she'd never known which man would come home – the fun, friendly dad from her early childhood, or the angry, drunken chauvinist, who'd sneer at everything she said. He'd remind Kaisa how much like her mother she was, almost spitting out the statement. Kaisa had heard from Sirkka that he was now living in a large new flat in Espoo with the girlfriend he'd met when Kaisa lived with him. She was a nice, artistic woman, but Kaisa pitied her. Why would anyone want to spend their life with her father? Kaisa had sent her father and the girlfriend a change-of-address card when they'd moved to Smuggler's Way, but she'd had no reply. Perhaps the feeling between father and daughter was mutual.

On the morning of the 22nd of December Kaisa woke up to a snowy view out of her window. The little patch of garden in front of the house was covered in white and all the rooftops sloping down to the Gareloch wore a blanket of freshly fallen snow. The view reminded Kaisa of home, and she suddenly felt tearful. Don't be silly, she thought, and she remembered that the car would need sorting out. Kaisa dressed quickly and found a pair of mittens. She dug out her old snow boots, which she'd bought in Rovaniemi in Finnish Lapland years ago and brought up to Scotland on Peter's advice. Stepping into the unusually bright morning light, Kaisa used an empty music cassette case to scrape ice off the windscreen. A new neighbour, a man a few years older than Peter, wearing a long Navy issue flannel great-coat, came out of his house. The golden stripes on his lapels and shoulders glinted brightly. Kaisa had seen the family move in a few days previously. She'd said hello to the wife, as she'd got into the car with her children one morning, just as Kaisa was leaving for her daily swim. The couple lived one door down from Kaisa and had children of various ages. The man began brushing snow away from the top of his own car, a Volvo Estate, with an un-gloved hand and, glancing towards Kaisa, asked if she needed help, or a lift anywhere. 'The roads will be treacherous, so if you don't have to go out, I'd stay at home today,' he shouted to Kaisa from the top of his car.

'I'm fine,' Kaisa said, 'I'm just going to the base for a swim and then over to a friend's house.' Kaisa looked at the man's hands, now red with the cold, and added,

'You should wear gloves to do that.'

The man, too, glanced at his hands and said, 'You may be right!'

They carried on clearing their respective cars, and Kaisa noticed that every now and then the man's eyes moved towards Kaisa's snow boots and at her waterproof skiing mittens. Kaisa was making a much better job of dealing with the snow and ice than he was.

'You've done that before,' the man said, smiling. When he'd cleared half of his car, he came over to Kaisa and said, 'I'm Max.'

Kaisa introduced herself, too, and Max said, 'I know who you are. I met Peter a few months ago: you're the Scandinavian wife.' With his cold fingers he took hold of Kaisa's bare hand and held it for a long time. His gaze was direct and his lips were curled up in a half-smile. He was very blond. 'My grandmother was Swedish, but I'm afraid I don't speak any of your language.'

Kaisa wanted to tell him that: a) She wasn't Scandinavian but Nordic, and b) Finnish and Swedish were not one language; that in fact they couldn't be further apart, linguistically speaking. But she bit her lip and looked down at her boots.

'You also know Duncan Lofthouse, don't you?' Max said, still holding Kaisa.

Kaisa was too shocked to reply, but pulled her hand from his grip.

'Anyway,' Max said, rubbing his red hands together, 'I think we should drive down to the base in convoy, so that if the hill hasn't been sanded and salted, you'll still have the opportunity to turn back.'

'OK,' Kaisa said. At the same time as wondering what it was about these Englishmen that made them act so chivalrously towards women, her mind was filled with dread. The way Max had held onto her hand, and the way he'd looked at her, made Kaisa fear he knew something. But why would Duncan have told him anything? Or was he just guessing, enjoying talking to the woman at the centre of the rumours? Was there something about Duncan that made the rumours ring true? Had he done this before?

Sometimes the paternal concerns naval officers showed towards their friends' or colleagues' wives made Kaisa more angry than flattered. Why did all the men assume Kaisa was incapable of looking after herself? Or was she just overreacting again, like Peter said, or just an ungrateful cow, as Pammy and Kaisa liked to joke. And was this chivalry only found in the men in the Navy, or were all Englishmen the same? But like a good little woman, Kaisa did indeed follow the more knowledgeable man down the road and made it to the base, safely under his wing. In truth, she felt she had no choice. During the short drive Kaisa decided she'd ring Duncan that same evening, even though that was the last thing she wanted to do. But she had to know who Duncan had been talking to, and what he'd said, before Peter came home.

By the next day, the snow was gone. It had lasted for only half a day and, by the afternoon, when the light was fading, the rain had cleared it from all but the most persistent little areas in the corners of the houses on Smuggler's Way. After her usual morning swim, she made a very short visit to see Lyn, who was just as delighted about the snow as Kaisa.

'How long have you got to go until the baby's due?' Kaisa asked.

'I'm really not sure of the dates, but I think it should be early January.' Kaisa wanted to ask about the father, and to suggest that she should go to an antenatal clinic in Helensburgh, but she knew Lyn would just change the subject on both scores.

Later, when she got to Pammy's, she talked about the snow in Finland, about how it made everything look so much softer and brighter and how it even lit up the landscape at night. They also discussed Christmas, and Kaisa proposed that they should spend it together. She offered to make a Finnish Christmas meal for Christmas Eve. Pammy thought it was a brilliant idea, and even though she couldn't do much, she insisted that she'd cook the turkey. 'It'll be exactly two weeks on the 24th, and I'm getting stronger by the day,' she said, and she squeezed Kaisa's hand. They'd become such close friends during the past two weeks. Although Kaisa wouldn't dream of saying so to Pammy, for Kaisa the terrible thing that happened had brought something good with it: their friendship.

Pammy insisted she should go to Helensburgh with Kaisa and so they drove to the shops together. They managed to get all the vegetables for Pammy's meal, and Kaisa got a swede and a few carrots for the Finnish vegetable bakes. They even found rollmops for the herring course and some small pickled cucumbers and cooked beetroot.

At the butchers, Pammy bought a small turkey, and Kaisa a small piece of cooked ham for the meal on Christmas Eve. She'd also decided to make Karelian stew, for which she bought lambs' kidneys and diced pork.

Pammy said they should go to the off-licence and Kaisa was surprised to find Finlandia vodka there. Pammy bought a bottle of champagne, which was hugely expensive, for Christmas morning. They also got a good bottle of red and one of white wine. They giggled like two teenagers when they looked at all the booze and food bought for just the two of them. 'We'll be fat as pigs and drunk as skunks when the boys come home,' Pammy said. Kaisa looked at her. Even though Pammy was shivering in the chill wind, which sent their hair flying in all directions, her cheeks had a red tinge to them and her eyes were clear and had a spark to them, which Kaisa hadn't seen since they'd driven to Glasgow together weeks ago.

When Kaisa got home from Pammy's, she plucked up enough courage to at last phone Duncan.

'Hello,' he said almost immediately after Kaisa had dialled the last digit.

Kaisa was so taken aback that he was at home in London, that she couldn't speak for a moment.

'Hello,' Duncan said again. Now he sounded a bit annoyed. 'Who is it?' Kaisa heard a woman's voice in the background. Kaisa immediately put down the receiver.

31

After much discussion with Pammy they'd decided that, since Kaisa's dishes for the Finnish Christmas Eve could all be pre-prepared, she would cook them the night before Christmas Eve, then go over on the 24th and stay for two nights at Pammy's house. So at least Kaisa had lots to do to keep her mind occupied and away from Duncan. While she listened to Radio One, which seemed to play the Band Aid song, 'Do they Know It's Christmas?' continuously, Kaisa got the Karelian stew ready for the oven, prepared the Finnish beetroot *rosolli* salad and the vegetable bakes. As she chopped, grated and mixed the vegetables, Kaisa tried to keep thoughts of Duncan out of her mind, but with no luck. She wondered how many people he'd recounted the events of that stupid, drunken night to. And why would he do that? Kaisa didn't understand, and she knew she had to talk to him. As she cooked, she decided to have a glass of wine, but only found an old bottle of red that she and Peter had received as a housewarming present from Pammy and Nigel. Peter had said it was expensive, so Kaisa decided to leave the bottle and make herself a gin and tonic instead. There was no ice, and the tonic was flat, but she emptied the glass quickly, drinking it as if it was medicine. The alcohol only hit her after she'd finished the second tumbler. Taking the third drink with her, Kaisa went over to the telephone in the hall and dialled Duncan's number again. She was alarmed when she noticed it was past ten o'clock, but the ringing had already begun at the other end and, taking a sip out of the glass, Kaisa sat down on the chair and waited.

'Hello?' This time Duncan's voice sounded drowsy, and questioning.

'Hi, it's me … Kaisa.'

After a short while, Duncan replied crisply, 'What a lovely surprise!'

Kaisa could almost hear him straighten himself up. 'How are you?' he asked before she could say anything.

'Um, I'm not OK.'

'Why, what's the matter?'

Kaisa told Duncan what Phoebe had said about seeing him leave the house, and how Max had told her that Kaisa and Duncan knew each other. When she'd finished, there was silence at the other end. 'I am worried about what Peter will think when he hears all the rumours.' Kaisa's heart had started racing and she felt all the fear, and anger, swell up inside her. 'They're coming back right after New Year,' Kaisa said, trying to keep her voice level.

'But Kaisa, all you have to say is that nothing happened,' Duncan said, and added, 'If you want to, that is.'

'What do you mean, if I want to!' Kaisa's voice had gone up, and she feared she sounded hysterical. Kaisa knew how much Englishmen, particularly naval officers, disliked female shows of emotion.

But instead of appearing to be annoyed, Duncan's voice grew low and husky. 'Kaisa, you know how I feel about you. If you want, I can get into the car tonight, or take the next flight tomorrow morning and bring you back to London. You know you have a job here. Rose was here just tonight and she was saying how much she could do with you right now. You could live with me and …'

'Duncan, no, I can't,' Kaisa interrupted him, because she couldn't listen to his fairy tales anymore. For a brief moment, as she'd been listening to his sexy voice, Kaisa had allowed herself to imagine what it would be like to live in London. That dream of working for a swanky magazine, going out to lunches in nice restaurants and being a legitimate part of fashionable and eccentric Soho hadn't yet left her. It had been so close and, like a fool, Kaisa believed that she could have both Peter and that life. But she couldn't. Peter would never leave the Navy and if Kaisa wanted to be married to him, she had to accept life as a Navy wife. That was all there was to it. Now that Kaisa finally understood that, she'd done something that could make her lose him just like that. If Peter found out about Duncan's visit, Kaisa didn't know what he would do. He could do anything. Kaisa felt tears rolling down her face.

'Duncan,' she said, trying to calm down. 'What have you told people?'

'Nothing, I haven't told anyone anything.' His voice sounded hurt.

'What do you think I am? I am a gentleman and a gentleman never tells.' Now Kaisa could hear a smile in Duncan's voice and imagined him sitting by the phone in the hall of his house in Chelsea.

'This is really serious, Duncan,' Kaisa said. 'Do you promise that you haven't said anything to anybody?'

'Cross my heart and hope to die,' Duncan replied.

Kaisa sighed and finished the call. She still wasn't convinced. What if Duncan was lying? What if below that surface of innocence, he was just playing a game? A game where Kaisa was the prize.

It was the morning of Christmas Eve and Kaisa had a headache. After the telephone conversation with Duncan, she'd drunk two more gin and tonics while watching *Just Good Friends* on TV. In the episode, Penny gets a divorce and Vince asks her to marry him. It was supposed to be a comedy, but Kaisa cried herself to sleep afterwards.

She was going over to Pammy's later, but before that she had to phone her mum quickly and then afterwards drive into Helensburgh to get some supplies for Lyn and Lisa – a sort of Christmas parcel for the two of them (and the scary Gerry). Kaisa couldn't buy anything extra when in the shops with Pammy the day before, and, of course, she couldn't have stopped at the camp either. Kaisa wouldn't have time to stay, but she just had to see Lyn to wish her Merry Christmas.

Before she left for town, Kaisa opened the present Peter had left for her. She didn't want to do it in front of Pammy, and Christmas Eve was when presents were given in Finland after all. There was a beautiful card with a picture of reindeer and Father Christmas, and the parcel contained a delicate nightdress and dressing gown in baby-blue satin, wrapped in white silk paper. She wondered where Peter had got such an expensive gift, and guessed he must have gone shopping in Glasgow without her knowing. Kaisa had a little cry as as she touched the wonderful garments.

32

A New Year, a new life. Oh, how Kaisa wished that could be true. For her it was more a New Year, new problems. Christmas with Pammy had been very different from anything Kaisa had ever celebrated. On Christmas Eve, after she'd been to see Lyn at the camp, Kaisa had hurried home to take all the Finnish food over to Pammy's. They had got quite drunk on the vodka schnapps and, as a fool, Kaisa had told Pammy all about Duncan. Pammy hadn't said it, but Kaisa had seen in her eyes that she disapproved. During the rest of the time they spent together, Pammy had been distant. On Christmas morning they'd exchanged small presents while drinking the champagne Pammy had insisted on buying, which had made Pammy a little more friendly. Pammy had cooked the turkey and vegetables, helped by Kaisa, who'd insisted on lifting the bird out of the oven and washing any pots and pans. After the meal, Pammy had put the TV on for the Queen's Speech, after which Kaisa washed up the dishes while Pammy dozed on the sofa during *The Two Ronnies Christmas Special*. They'd spent the rest of the evening in front of the TV and, even though all the programmes were festive, to Kaisa it hadn't seemed like a proper Christmas at all. Kaisa had gone home on Boxing Day and watched more telly in the days leading up to New Year.

On New Year's Eve, Kaisa phoned Pammy to ask if she wanted to go to the New Year's Hogmanay party at the base, but Pammy said she was too tired.

'What's wrong? Aren't you feeling well?' Kaisa asked her. She was worried that all the alcohol and the cooking on Christmas Day had made Pammy worse.

But Pammy replied crisply, 'No, I'm absolutely fine.'

Kaisa sighed and said, 'Look, are you angry with me? After Christmas Eve, when I told you …'

'Kaisa, I really do not wish to discuss it,' Pammy interrupted her, 'it's your life and I have no interest in your sordid affairs.'

Kaisa was stunned, and couldn't speak.

'But don't worry, I am not a gossip, so your secret is safe. Just don't expect me to condone your actions, that's all!'

The line went dead.

Kaisa stood in the hallway, with the cream-coloured receiver in her hand, unable to think straight. What had happened? Kaisa had thought Pammy was her friend and would have understood how lonely and desperate she was when Duncan came to stay with her. And Kaisa had told Pammy she'd been very drunk! Of course Kaisa knew she had done something very wrong, but she didn't need Pammy to tell her that. Kaisa knew she was being stupid, but she thought bitterly how different real life was from the sitcoms on TV. In *Just Friends*, when Penny accidentally slept with Vince while she was still married, nobody batted an eyelid. They just thought it funny that she should feel bad about it. Even so, how could Pammy feel it was an offence against her personally, what Kaisa had done? Wasn't it Kaisa's problem?

Kaisa felt so angry with Pammy after the phone call, she decided to go to the Hogmanay party on her own. She'd accepted the invitation after all and she knew Phoebe and the other wives would be glad to see her and keep her company. The only reason she'd considered not going was that she hadn't wanted to leave Pammy on her own if she didn't feel up to it. Well, that problem was not an issue anymore.

Although the last day of 1984 was bitterly cold, the morning was lovely, with bright sunshine, which almost blinded Kaisa as she stood at the kitchen window watching the rays glimmer on the surface of the Gareloch. The temperature was minus one. As Kaisa admired the view, her mind wandered and she thought about Lyn. She'd looked so pale and cold when Kaisa had seen her on Christmas Eve. She also wondered if the baby had arrived. Deciding to go and see her, Kaisa showered and got dressed. Wearing her old snow boots, she stepped into the sunshine only to be confronted by Phoebe.

'Where are you off to in such a hurry?' she asked while planting a dry kiss on Kaisa's cheek. 'And look at you all suited up for the cold! Honestly, you Scandinavians always have the right gear for this weather.'

Kaisa dismissed the false reference to her being Scandinavian – again. Instead she tried to think of a reason why she could say she was going out. 'It's so beautiful, I thought I'd go for a walk.'

Phoebe looked at Kaisa in horror, 'A walk? In this freezing weather?'

When Kaisa didn't say anything, Phoebe pushed past her into the house. 'Sorry, I was freezing myself silly out there,' she said once inside the hall.

Kaisa sighed and closed the door behind them.

'Don't be like that,' Phoebe said, taking off her leather gloves and her old battered-looking Barbour. She walked into the lounge and Kaisa cringed at the state of it; she'd been in such a hurry to go and see Lyn that she'd forgotten to tidy up. The sofa was littered with books and old papers, and the small coffee table still had the remains of that morning's breakfast on it.

Phoebe lifted a pile of papers and placed them on the floor. After wiping some crumbs off the sofa with the back of her hand, she sat down. Barely perching on the edge of the sofa, with her back straight and her feet neatly adjusted to one side, she said, 'Anyway, I tried to call you this morning. Where were you?'

'I don't know, I've been here all the time.' Kaisa said. Was Phoebe checking up on her?

'Well, I've got good news!' Phoebe said, smiling.

Kaisa sat down opposite Phoebe. She tried to affect a dignified pose similar to the one Phoebe was displaying, but it was difficult to arrange her feet as neatly as Phoebe whilst wearing the clumpy snow boots.

'They're coming back!'

'Who?'

'Oh, for goodness sake, what's the matter with you today? The boys! They are going to be here on the third, or possibly the fourth of January!'

'Oh,' Kaisa said.

'Aren't you happy about seeing Peter again?' Phoebe settled her eyes on her. 'Is it because of …'

Kaisa quickly interrupted her, 'No, sorry, of course I'm glad. It's just been such a long time …'

Phoebe tilted her head sideways. 'Ah, yeah, the first patrol is the worst one. Believe me, once you've done as many as I have, it'll be pure routine.'

'Thanks for letting me know,' Kaisa said and got up. The last thing she needed was one of Phoebe's lectures on how to be the perfect Navy wife. Or her sympathy, for that matter.

'Well, I'll let you go on your walk. You were the last one of my list, so …'

As with everything, even the notification of any news from the bomber submarines had a pecking order in the Navy. Before Peter went away, he'd shown Kaisa the information flow chart of HMS *Restless*. It showed the order in which officers' wives and family would be told about the homecoming of the crew. The Captain's wife would get the first message from the base, and she'd tell the Jimmy's (or First Lieutenant's) wife and the Head Engineering Officer's wife. They, in turn, would phone the next two wives on the list, and so it would go on. Kaisa had noticed that she was near the bottom of the list, just before the families of the 'Part Threes', or trainee Submarine Officers. 'It's because I'm a junior officer on the boat – but not for long,' Peter had said and grinned. 'Don't you worry, soon you'll find yourself on the top of that list!' He had squeezed Kaisa's waist.

Kaisa ushered Phoebe out of the house, but even as she was shutting the door behind herself, Phoebe shouted, 'Don't forget to make an appointment at the hairdresser; they get booked up really quickly after word gets out!'

Kaisa had forgotten. Phoebe had told her how the Polaris submarine wives always got their hair done before the men came home. Peter and the other officers often joked that the Russians didn't need fancy underwater sonar to discover the whereabouts of the British nuclear deterrent. All they needed to do was phone up the two hairdressers in Helensburgh. If they were fully booked, the arrival of one of the subs at its Scottish base was imminent.

Kaisa drove towards the base feeling completely numb. The sun was already low over the horizon and she could hardly see through the dirty windscreen of the car. The water in the washer had frozen solid, so the wipers just made the screen dirtier, smearing it with dried-up mud. When Kaisa parked her car by the camp, she was surprised to see another car at the end of the lay-by. Through the windscreen she could just make out a uniformed man walk out from the camp and get into his car. With horror, Kaisa realised who it was: Max from the married quarter next to hers! Kaisa quickly ducked inside her car. She crouched by the passenger seat and wondered wildly if he'd seen her. Wouldn't he recognise her car? Now she was glad the windscreen and side windows were so dirty from the constantly wet and muddy roads into Helensburgh. Lying down in the car, Kaisa listened as Max started his Volvo estate and drove past her without stopping. Kaisa blew air out of her lungs and waited a few minutes before she dared to look out onto the road. Max had driven off. She gave it another few minutes before getting out of her car. Again, she looked around, but the road was empty as usual.

'Hi,' Lyn said and took the bag of goodies Kaisa had assembled from the leftovers of their Christmas meal, which Pammy had insisted, in her hurt voice, that Kaisa take home with her.

'Why was that guy here?' Kaisa asked her as soon as they'd sat down inside the stuffy caravan.

'He came and issued some kind of warning. Gerry did something to the sign yesterday,' Lyn sighed. She looked so pale and tired that Kaisa decided to make her a quick turkey sandwich. She'd told Kaisa she'd started eating meat during the latter stages of the pregnancy because 'Lisa had gone ballistic' when she'd heard she was a vegetarian. Lyn wolfed down the sandwich and then lay down on the bed and fell a sleep while Kaisa sat and watched her. She looked so peaceful with her messy short hair half-covering her face. Kaisa wondered if she was happy.

On the way back, with the sun now set beyond the horizon, Kaisa could see what Gerry had done. Over the sign 'Her Majesty's Naval Base' he had scratched a line across the word 'Naval' and replaced it with 'Murder'. Kaisa grinned. What would Max and the rest of the officers and their wives think if they knew she'd made friends with one of the peace campers?

The day so far had been difficult enough to put Kaisa off going to any party, but she couldn't face spending New Year's Eve on her own. She thought about Pammy and considered ringing her again, but then remembered her cold tone of voice, and the word 'sordid', and decided not to. Pammy knew many more of the other wives than she did. She could call upon them if she felt lonely. She obviously did not want Kaisa's help, or friendship, anymore. Besides, she'd said herself that her health was almost back to normal, so Kaisa could not be expected to babysit her anymore. She tried not to think about everything she'd done for Pammy, and how unfairly she'd been treated by her. She decided to put the woman at the back of her mind. She was going to go to the party in a cheerful mood, she'd make sure of that.

As Kaisa was getting ready, the doorbell went again. Outside stood Max.

'Hello,' he said. 'We thought you might need a lift tonight. You are going aren't you?' He was smiling with his lips, but his eyes remained serious. This was the last thing Kaisa needed, but the truth was that she hadn't thought about the drinking and driving at all. It also occurred to Kaisa that refusing the offer of a lift would look really strange.

'That's very kind of you,' she said.

'OK, we're leaving in an hour!'

Kaisa shut the door and went to the kitchen window. To her horror she saw Max lingering next to her car, which was parked right outside the door. He lifted his eyes back to the house and, not knowing what else to do, Kaisa raised her hand and waved to him. He didn't wave back, but nodded, and turned away. Had he recognised the number plates from earlier that day? Kaisa was hoping he didn't have a good memory for numbers, but knew she was fooling herself. All the submarine staff had to have a good head for figures, Peter had told her. They needed it to make calculations when looking through the periscope, and everything had to be done in the head. Peter used to practise his mental arithmetic when they went shopping for food together, adding up the prices of the items Kaisa put in the basket and then checking the total at the till.

Luckily, Max's wife Caroline liked to talk so, on the way to the base, she told Kaisa all about their Christmas down South. They'd only come back the day before and had left the children with her parents in Hampshire.

'It was so warm down there, you can't imagine! The sun shone nearly every day!'

Kaisa was glad of her neighbour's chatter. She didn't have to contribute more than nods and the occasional shake of the head, but Max worried her, because he kept glancing at Kaisa through the driver's mirror. She averted her eyes for most of the short journey, and when she caught him looking, smiled at him sweetly, while making inane comments, such as 'Really,' 'I know,' and 'How lovely,' at Caroline's monologue. Finally, when they arrived at the base, Kaisa saw Phoebe and made her way towards her. Phoebe was surrounded by some of the other officers' wives from the boat, but when Kaisa arrived the women grew quiet.

'We were just saying how much we are looking forward to the boys coming home,' Phoebe said to her pointedly.

Kaisa looked at Phoebe and the other women, who were now studying either the floor, their drinks or retrieving something out of their handbags. Kaisa was rescued by a steward, who offered the group pink punch from a silver tray. He was wearing a white waistcoat and gloves that were blackened with dirt on the palms. As Kaisa took a drink, Phoebe leaned into the other women and whispered, 'Did you see the state of those gloves?'

'It's a disgrace,' someone else said.

'The Scots don't know how this should be done!' another piped in.

The scandal over the dirty gloves prompted so much discussion that Kaisa didn't need to contribute. Instead, she quietly sipped the pink-coloured welcome punch. It tasted sickly, but strong; just what she needed.

The long tables were laid out with white cloths and silver cutlery. Kaisa was fortunate enough to be seated well away from Max and Caroline. She didn't quite know how, because there must have been more women then men there, with whole submarine crews away at sea, but they had managed to do a table arrangement of boy, girl, boy. Kaisa was sitting next to a pimply-faced Part Three who, after telling Kaisa his name was Sean, ignored her and just drank pint after pint of bitter, while conducting a lively conversation with another Part Three opposite. Occasionally, he would glance at Kaisa's breasts, but he didn't seem able to look her in the eyes. Kaisa was wearing her black-and-white, low-cut dress, which she knew suited her but which she'd worn at least three times at naval events before. The straps of the dress were so thin that she couldn't wear a bra with it and, judging from the reaction of her table partner, the lack of a brassiere showed. Kaisa cursed her foolishness and vanity – not only did she have the reputation for being a hussy; she now dressed like one. When the meal was over and they all retreated to the Wardroom bar where the dance floor had been set up, her companion offered Kaisa his arm. She'd already forgotten his name, but she was pleased not to have to confront either Max or Phoebe and the gossiping women on her own. Sean (he reminded Kaisa) turned out to be a good dancer. Kaisa and the young officer spent most of the evening on the dance floor, which suited her, because it meant she didn't need to talk to anyone. Kaisa could feel the eyes of the women on her, but by now she was drunk enough after copious amounts of wine, not to care. Kaisa also loved port, and had matched her companion in consuming a few glasses of it when the decanter was passed around the tables after dessert.

At midnight, with crossed hands, Kaisa and Sean and the rest of the large crowd, sang 'Auld Lang Syne' together. Sean fetched Kaisa's coat from the lobby and took her outside to view the fireworks. Watching the flares light up the dark Scottish sky made Kaisa tearful. She missed Peter, and would so much rather have been with him than the pimply youth. But the music started up again, and Sean led Kaisa once more to the dance floor. After a few more tracks, she saw he was getting quite drunk. When 'Every Time You Go Away' by Paul Young came on, he took hold of Kaisa's waist, pushed his crotch against her thigh and began singing into her ear. Kaisa moved her body away and, laughing, said, 'I think it's time for me to go.' As luck would have it, Max and Caroline were just then scanning the dimly lit dance floor for her.

'We were thinking of leaving,' Caroline said. Kaisa gave Sean a light peck on his cheek and thanked him for looking after her all evening. Sean waved his hand and returned to his mates and another pint of beer.

On the way home, Caroline closed her eyes and leaned against the front seat. Kaisa was in the back again and tried to do the same, but she felt Max's dark eyes on her in the rear-view mirror. 'You made quite an impression on the young lad, there,' he said, but didn't smile. Kaisa shuddered, but didn't reply. She was glad it took only ten minutes from the base to reach the married quarters at Smuggler's Way.

33

The 2nd of January was a bank holiday in Scotland, which meant the swimming pool at the base was closed, as were the shops, so Kaisa couldn't even go and buy supplies for Lyn. Of course, she could have driven the small distance to see if the heavily pregnant girl was alright, but Kaisa thought Lyn was used to her bringing something and she had nothing in the house that she could take. And Kaisa felt the need to be more careful. Having thought about it, she was fairly sure either Max recognised her car outside the camp, or remembered the number plate of the car parked there, and noticed that it matched that of Kaisa's Ford Fiesta later that day. Why he didn't say anything was a little puzzling. Kaisa had decided that if he asked, she was going to say the water in the windscreen washer had frozen, so she'd parked on the side of the road to clean the windscreen. (Which was very slightly true, because Lyn had given Kaisa some boiling water to defrost the water container under the bonnet.) Besides, Kaisa was fairly sure Max hadn't actually seen her go into the camp.

But Max, of course, was the least of her worries. The day before, on New Year's Day, while Kaisa was watching the traditional celebratory concert from Vienna, and feeling very homesick, because she used to watch it with her mother or Sirkka, Phoebe phoned. 'Your behaviour at the Hogmanay party was despicable.' Kaisa couldn't quite believe her ears.

'What do you mean?'

'Well, you know perfectly well. I spent the whole evening defending you, telling everyone that you were not that kind of a girl, and then you go and show yourself up like that!'

Kaisa held the receiver away from her ear and closed her eyes. She counted to ten and said slowly, 'Phoebe, there is no need for you to defend me. I can take care of myself.'

'That's apparent!'

When Kaisa didn't reply, she carried on. 'And to think that poor Peter is coming home tomorrow! Goodness knows what he'll think when he hears …'

'And what is he going to hear? And from whom?' Kaisa interrupted her. In spite of trying to stay calm, her voice had risen, and she could hear herself shouting the last words.

'There's no need to …'

'Goodbye, Phoebe,' Kaisa said and slammed down the phone. She put her head in her hands and felt tears roll down her face. Kaisa had less than 24 hours to think of what to say to Peter. Plus she had to clean the house and do a mountain of washing, including Peter's shirts, which had been in the laundry basket since before he went away. How would Kaisa be able to dry and iron it all in time? The married quarters up on Smuggler's Way were all damp; worse in the winter. Laundry could sometime take 48 hours to dry properly. There was no way she'd be able to get everything done. Kaisa was such a crap housewife, a crap Navy wife, a crap wife in general.

34

Peter scanned the jetty for Kaisa, but couldn't see her blonde head among the group of wives and children fighting the horizontal rain and wind blowing from the Gareloch. Eventually he spotted her standing at the other end of the jetty, her arms crossed over her chest, struggling with an umbrella against the strong winds. Peter waved but saw that Kaisa wasn't even looking, or trying to spot him.

When he was finally standing in front of Kaisa, her scent was lovelier and her pale blue eyes even more beautiful than he'd remembered.

'I've missed you,' he said and kissed her fully on the mouth. She tasted as sweet as he'd imagined during the long, boring hours of duty. 'Let's get out of this rain.' Peter ushered Kaisa away from the men and women and children crowding around each other. 'Where's the car?' he said and saw it almost as soon as he'd said the words. Even though it was raining, he could see the Ford Fiesta was covered in mud. Peter strode purposefully towards the driver's side and flung his Pusser's grip onto the back seat. He decided not to say anything, although he found himself wondering what on earth Kaisa had done during all the weeks he'd been away if she hadn't even had time to take the car into a garage for a wash.

'You want to drive?' Kaisa said. She was standing behind him, keys in hand, apparently waiting for him to move to the passenger side. Peter gave her cheek a peck and, taking the keys from her hand, said, 'Yeah, I'll drive.'

Kaisa gave him a blank look, then, without saying a word, walked around the car, closed her umbrella, chucked it inside, and sat down.

They drove the short distance home to Smuggler's Way in an awkward silence. Kaisa kept shifting in her seat, not looking at Peter. Once, after he'd nodded to the guard by the gate of the base, and they were on the straight road running along the Gareloch, Peter squeezed Kaisa's knee and she turned briefly around and returned his smile.

There was so much he wanted to tell her. About the difference between this patrol and his experiences at sea on a diesel boat, or even HMS *Tempest*. How they'd moved slowly and quietly from place to place, unlike the cat-and-mouse game they'd played with Russian subs in his previous appointments. He wanted to tell her how many letters he had written to her when alone in his bunk. They remained unsent, kept safe in his uniform pocket. And he wanted to say how incredibly happy he'd been to spot her on the jetty at last, having been scared that she wouldn't be there to welcome him home. During the long patrol, he'd kept having the same dream about her leaving him and returning to Finland. She's just nervous about having me around again, Peter convinced himself now, as he turned the car into Smuggler's Way and drove up the hill. The ugliness of the pebbledash married quarters took him by surprise again, but he decided not to share this depressing thought with his wife. Peter knew she hated the grey buildings as much as he did, so why make it worse by discussing it?

'So you didn't get time to wash the car?' he said instead, as he turned the engine off outside their house.

Kaisa turned her head towards him and said, as if the thought had never crossed her mind, 'Oh, no, sorry.'

'Never mind, we'll do it together at the weekend, shall we?'

Peter was looking forward to a glorious four weeks' holiday after he'd done the usual couple of days' work to prepare the submarine for the second crew.

'I thought we could drive down to Wiltshire to see my parents?' he said when they were finally inside the house.

'I've got something to tell you,' Kaisa said. Her face was deadly serious and she looked close to tears. Peter stepped nearer and took her into his arms.

'Darling, I've missed you so much!' Peter went to kiss Kaisa but noticed that there were tears running down her face. 'It's OK, I'm home now,' he said and handed her his hankie.

'Oh, Peter,' Kaisa said and began sobbing against his shoulder.

35

Of course, Peter couldn't hear Kaisa out before they'd made love. Kaisa, too, needed the intimacy. What with looking after Pammy, and visiting Lyn, worrying about Duncan and all the rumours, Kaisa had forgotten how much she'd missed Peter. After the submarine had docked, she'd been scanning the jetty, but she must have been looking in the wrong direction, because suddenly he'd been in front of her, looking pale, but handsome.

Now lying in bed, listening to his steady breathing (he'd fallen asleep almost immediately after making love), Kaisa wasn't sure she'd be able to tell him the truth. She looked at the radio alarm clock, lifting herself up gently, so as not to wake Peter. It was coming up to three o'clock. The submarine had docked just after midday, but it had taken an age for the crew to disembark. By the time they'd got home it was already getting a little darker.

Kaisa got out of bed, and tiptoed into the kitchen. She closed the door and went over to her coffee maker. She put the kettle on for Peter's tea and measured coffee into the percolator. The rain had given way to beautiful late afternoon sunshine, which turned the colour of the loch a pale pewter. She could just make out the submarines at the base to the far right. Looking at the sleek, black shapes, she understood why the boats were the colour they were. Kaisa hugged the hot cup of coffee with her hands, and jumped when she heard the door behind her open.

'Any chance of a cup of tea?' Peter said and put his arm around Kaisa's waist. He nuzzled his face into her neck and whispered, 'God, I've missed you.'

Kaisa turned around and gave Peter a kiss. 'Me too,' she said and smiled. She'd decided that she wasn't going to talk to Peter today. Not on his first day at home. That just wasn't fair. But she did have to tell him about Jeff and Susan. She hadn't wanted to tell Peter about their break-up in the weekly Familygram, because she knew it would have upset him.

'Darling, Jeff phoned me before Christmas. Susan broke off the engagement.'

'Oh, no,' Peter sat down at the kitchen table while Kaisa told him about Susan and the missed promotion at IDS.

'So she chose a career over Jeff,' Peter said drily. He wasn't looking at Kaisa, but down at his mug of tea.

'Yeah,' Kaisa said.

There was a silence between them, which neither seemed to want to fill.

'I've missed you,' Kaisa said finally, and bent down to kiss Peter.

'Me too,' he said and pulled her onto his lap.

Peter and Kaisa spent the first weekend of his six weeks ashore in a blissful, private cloud of happiness. Although Kaisa kept worrying about Lyn, she didn't have the courage to tell Peter about her new friend. Each time they drove past the peace camp, she tried to crane her neck to see if Lyn was sitting by the fire outside the caravan, but the campsite looked empty and deserted. She wondered if Lyn had had the baby already and was in hospital. She knew there was a small maternity ward over the hill, near Loch Lomond, but she might have been taken to Glasgow, as Pammy had been. Kaisa couldn't believe Lyn would have the baby in the caravan. She hoped Lisa, the midwife friend, was sensible enough to take her to a hospital. At least Lisa was there, Kaisa thought.

But there was no time for Kaisa to worry about Lyn, or Duncan for that matter, because Peter had planned a full social schedule for them. On the Saturday after he got back, they went to visit Stef outside Dumbarton. Kaisa felt ashamed that she hadn't been to see her, but blamed her own newly acquired driving skills. She said she was still afraid to go further than Helensburgh on her own. That was a blatant lie, she knew it, but she was caught out so quickly with the question, she didn't know what else to say. Tom was away, but Stef had her mother staying with her to look after Jessica, as they'd called the baby. Kaisa was glad she'd at least sent a congratulations card before Christmas, and now they took another card and a present – a pink bear they'd found in a gift shop in town.

Peter and Kaisa spent the Sunday morning in bed, lazing around until midday, when Peter said they should drive to the pretty village of Inveraray, which Peter knew from his time in O-boats.

'There's a castle and a really good pub called The George,' he told Kaisa. 'We'll have a pint and lunch and then have a walk around the castle. Would you like that?' Peter squeezed Kaisa's waist.

They were lucky with the weather. The sun peeked out from under the low clouds as Peter drove up the hill and past the base. Kaisa scanned the peace camp on her right, but again it looked deserted. She decided to put thoughts of Lyn out of her mind – surely she'd understand that now her husband was back, Kaisa wouldn't be able to come around as often – or at all? Kaisa reminded herself that Lyn had Lisa, and the scary Gerry, to look after her.

The landscape changed almost immediately when Peter drove past the base. They climbed higher and higher, and skirted a deep loch on their left.

'That is Loch Long,' Peter said.

'How do you know all these places?' Kaisa asked, but Peter tapped his nose,

'If I tell you, I'd have to kill you.' Peter laughed. Kaisa smiled, but felt shut out; it may have been a joke, but the truth was that so much of Peter's life was secretive. Kaisa couldn't really understand how he could cope with all that confidential information without sometimes wanting to share it with his own wife. Kaisa had one huge secret that she was keeping from Peter, and the pressure of it made her jittery and unhappy.

The scenery became even more impressive as Peter drove around the loch and across a majestic valley with high hills in every direction. Even in the bleakest month of January the colours of the heather against the dark pine woods and the steel-coloured sky took Kaisa's breath away.

'Wouldn't you like to go hiking with me here?' Peter asked.

'Yeah, sure,' Kaisa said, at which Peter laughed. 'Try to sound a bit keener!'

Kaisa couldn't think of anything worse than hiking. It sounded far too close to orienteering, a sport she'd hated at school in Finland, where it had been a compulsory activity in the long autumn term. Kaisa had never been able to understand how a compass worked, or been able to determine direction from just looking at the position of the sun. She couldn't comprehend the point of walking through forests, open to all elements, getting bitten by mosquitoes – or, worse, snakes – when you could just as easily drive to your destination, take a picnic, walk a few metres, eat, enjoy the scenery and leave. Or as they were doing today, drive through the pretty bits and have lunch in a lovely pub. But she didn't say any of this to Peter. Instead she said, 'That'll be nice, as long as it is dry. I hate being cold, you know that.'

Peter just laughed and squeezed her knee. Kaisa was stunned by the beauty of the road leading to Inveraray. Like so much of Scotland, the stark colours, the water and the stillness of the countryside reminded her of Finland. She breathed in the air and stared at the view.

'C'mon, we'll get wet.' It had just started raining as Peter parked the car. They ran along the tiny high street straight into the pub. The George Inn was a hotel, really, and when they walked into the low-ceilinged back bar, the landlady, an older woman with very blonde hair and very red lipstick, welcomed Peter with a hug. 'How are you young lad, then?' she said and began pulling a pint. 'The usual?' she said and gave Peter a wide smile.

'Thanks, Greta. This is my wife, Kaisa.' Kaisa shook Greta's hand, and noticed that she had a firm grip and a direct gaze. She was wearing a colourful jumper, which was a little too low cut for a woman of her age, and revealed too much of her wrinkly décolletage. When they sat down with their drinks, having ordered the food (scampi and chips for Kaisa, ham, egg and chips for Peter), Peter told Kaisa he'd stayed there the year before when his O-boat had been docked in the harbour. Again, Kaisa was disturbed about how much he didn't tell her about his life away from her.

36

'So, I hear Duncan has been in town?' Peter said as soon as he walked into the house.

'Yeah,' Kaisa replied. She put the kettle on, with her back to Peter, playing for time.

It was Tuesday night and Peter had been home for five days. He'd been working for the past two days back at the base, getting the sub ready for the starboard crew, while Kaisa had been washing and ironing clothes, ready for their trip down South to see Peter's parents.

'Did you see him?' Peter asked.

'Yeah, he came to stay when they cocked up his accommodation.' Kaisa said and bit her lip. Had she sounded casual enough?

'When?' Peter's voice was hard now.

Kaisa hadn't been looking at Peter, but she knew she must, otherwise he'd know something wasn't right, so she turned around and faced him, 'Oh early December, I think it was.' Peter's expression was hard, his eyes were dark under his cap, which he'd not taken off yet. He was also still wearing his flannel Navy greatcoat, and his black boots. Kaisa could smell he'd been drinking. The rumour mill has done its trick, Kaisa thought and made an effort to stay calm. 'Take off your coat,' she said, keeping her voice level and busying herself with the kettle, 'A cup of tea?'

Peter had disappeared into the hall and Kaisa heard him fling his boots hard on the stone floor. He sat heavily down at the small kitchen table and, speaking into his hands, which he held in front of him, said, 'Kaisa, you have to tell me the truth. The guys at the bar told me that Duncan had been here overnight and that something had happened between you two. You know I don't easily get jealous, but when I asked Nigel if he knew anything, he told me that you'd confessed it all to Pammy over Christmas, and ...' Peter's voice broke, and he put his head in his hands.

Kaisa froze to the spot. How could Pammy do this to her? After all that she'd done for her? After she'd promised not to say anything? What kind of friend was she?

Peter was staring up at her. 'Kaisa?'

Tears were streaming down Kaisa's face, 'Oh Peter, you know I love you.'

She went to sit opposite her husband and took his hands into hers. 'Darling, it was a stupid, stupid mistake. I was very drunk and I missed you so dreadfully, and then he was here, and ...'

'Oh, my God,' Peter said, flinging himself off the chair and walking into the hall. Kaisa stopped breathing. She could see Peter's back shake, and knew he was crying. She went over to him and said, 'Please darling, please, it meant absolutely nothing. I've felt disgusted with myself since, and I never want to see him again.'

Peter shrugged Kaisa off him. He put his boots back on, took his keys and banged the door shut behind him. Kaisa wanted to run after him, but she knew the neighbours would see her and witness their row, knowing what it was all about. She couldn't let Max have the satisfaction of seeing that. She cursed the fish bowl they lived in, because she knew Peter, too, would have hated the neighbours seeing their domestic drama unfold. But when Kaisa stood by the kitchen window and listened to Peter's car swerve down the hill, she knew she should have stopped him. He'd been drinking; what if he had an accident or drove into a ditch. Worse, he'd lose his licence, which would harm his career, or at the very worst ... that didn't bear thinking about. What had she done? What could she do now? Run after him? Or perhaps she should go next door and ask Max to go after Peter?

At 10pm, when Peter and been gone for four hours, Kaisa telephoned Pammy. She expected her former friend to be as hostile as she had been after Christmas, but instead Pammy said, 'Oh, Kaisa I am so sorry. I told Nigel not to say a word and then he goes and blurts it out. He told me all about their session in the back bar.'

'Have you seen Peter?' Kaisa asked.

'Why, what's happened?'

Kaisa told Pammy about Peter storming out and how she was worried he'd been drinking and could have had an accident.

'I'm sure we'd have been told about an accident by now,' Pammy said. 'I'll get Nigel to go and scan the pubs in town. I'm sure that's where he'll be.'

Kaisa was beside herself with worry. She tried to sit in the living room and watch TV while she waited for Pammy to call back, but she couldn't sit still. She paced up and down the room, stopping every now and then to listen for the sound of their little Ford Fiesta turning into the drive. At last, exactly 28 minutes after she'd put the phone down, it rang again.

'Peter is OK. We found him in The Commodore. He's really out of it, so we thought it best if he sleeps it off here tonight. Is he due at the base tomorrow?'

Kaisa collapsed on the floor. She covered her mouth with her hand, and tried to control her weeping. The relief she felt at the news was overwhelming.

'Kaisa, are you there?'

'Yes,' Kaisa said with a strangled voice.

'Oh, you poor love,' Pammy said. 'He's alright now, but if he's working tomorrow he'll need to get changed before going to the base, so ...'

'Yes, he's working all this week and on Friday we're going to drive down to Wiltshire.'

'OK then, I'll get him to phone you tomorrow morning. Try to sleep Kaisa, and again, please accept my apologies. I've been feeling awful. You've been so good to me, and I know how lonely our lives are when the men are away. At least I have family in the same country, whereas you are all alone. So I really do understand how that thing could have happened, and I'm so sorry I wasn't there for you when you needed me. Will you forgive me?'

'Yes,' Kaisa whispered. She was slumped on the floor of the hall, holding tightly onto the receiver.

'I'm so angry with Nigel. He had no business ...' Pammy continued.

'No, the fault is all mine. And thank you for finding him. You've no idea ...' Kaisa broke down again, and they finished the call, promising each other to meet up the following day. 'We'll help you two to patch things up,' Pammy promised.

When Kaisa had put the phone down, she let the flood of tears overwhelm her for a moment. She sat on the floor in the hall, crying. Suddenly realising she was shivering with the cold, she pushed herself up, wiped her face with an old tissue and went into the living room to turn off the TV. She switched off all the lights and went to bed, setting the radio alarm clock for 6am, so she'd have time to iron one of Peter's uniform shirts and set out clean underwear for him before he got home. She knew he needed to be at the base at eight, so that would give her enough time, she hoped.

But she was woken up by Peter coming up the stairs before her alarm had gone off. He climbed into bed and held onto her, 'I love you,' he said.

'I love you, too,' Kaisa mumbled. She was fuzzy-headed with sleepiness. During the night she'd woken up to several awful dreams about Peter. In one he'd drowned in his car, in another Gerry from the peace camp had strangled him, and in the third, the final dream, she herself had pummelled Peter's chest with her fists so that his body was black and blue. 'I'm so sorry,' she now said.

Peter took Kaisa's face into his hands. 'I've not slept for thinking about you and me.'

Kaisa was suddenly wide awake. She stared at Peter's unshaven face, at his sad-looking eyes and the straight line of his lips. 'And?' she whispered.

'I can't live without you.'

'Oh, Peter,' Kaisa said and buried her head in his chest.

Peter took hold of Kaisa's chin and made her face him, 'But you've got to look after me and be good to me.'

Kaisa's face crumbled, 'Yes, of course I will.' Tears were now streaming down her face, 'Peter, I love you so much, no one else, I promise.'

They held each other for a while and then made gentle, unhurried love.

Afterwards Kaisa ironed a shirt for Peter, made him breakfast and told him she'd drive him to the base. They were running late, but Peter said it wouldn't matter because both the Captain and the Jimmy were busy with the handover and they wouldn't notice if Peter wasn't in the Wardroom. 'We don't have much to do so we spend most of the time just spinning dits. That was naval speak for telling tales, and Kaisa thought bitterly that this time it was she who'd be the butt of the jokes. As if Peter had read her mind, he said, 'I won't let anyone talk badly about you.'

There was steady rain falling from thick cloud as they drove in silence past the dirty-looking houses on the estate. Heavy rain discoloured the concrete and made the walls look as though they were bleeding. When they drew near to the peace camp, Kaisa spotted a few colourful jackets and woolly hats in the distance, followed by the clamour of pots and pans.

'Bloody hell, I forgot it's Wednesday,' Peter muttered beside her. He had his eyes closed. He was wearing his cap on a slant, so that the black, shiny peak covered the top part of his face.

They were the first car to be stopped going north and, keeping the windscreen wipers going, Kaisa scanned the protestors for Lyn. She nearly jumped out of her seat when there was a knock on the car window. It was

Gerry, gesturing madly at her to wind down the window. He was wearing a bright yellow raincoat, which was a couple of sizes too large for him. With his wide eyes, and wispy blond hair and beard poking out from the over-sized hood, he looked like *E.T.* from the Spielberg film.

'Good God, Gerry, you made me jump. Is Lyn OK?' Kaisa said before she remembered Peter was in the car with her.

'What the hell?' Peter was now wide awake, sitting upright. 'Who are you talking to?'

Gerry was standing outside in the rain. Water was dripping into the car from the edge of his hood. 'Oh, so this is your posh Navy husband then? How does it feel being married to a murderer?'

'Wait here,' Kaisa said to Peter and, turning to Gerry said, 'Shut up. Let me get out and we'll talk.' She wound up the window.

'Kaisa,' Peter said and went to grab Kaisa's arm. She turned to him and said, 'I won't be a minute.' Kaisa stepped out of the car, wrapping her Barbour close around her body. The rain was falling in a steady stream, and it forced Kaisa to pull her hood over her head.

'Is Lyn OK?' she asked again.

'Yeah, she's had the baby and it's a boy, called Rory.' Gerry was grinning now, and he had none of the angry craziness about him that Kaisa had become used to. Kaisa wondered, once again, if Gerry was the father of Lyn's child. She hugged Gerry and the two of them began jumping up and down in the rain. Soon they attracted the attention of the police monitoring the demo, as well as the handful of protestors, who began whistling and whooping at them. The two police officers who'd been watching the proceedings from the side of the road, began moving towards Kaisa and Gerry.

'Where is she?' Kaisa asked.

'In Glasgow. We took her in yesterday, and the baby was born last night.' Gerry looked almost harmless now, with his wide grin reaching all the way to his eyes. Perhaps Lyn was right and he wasn't dangerous after all, Kaisa thought.

'Is this man bothering you, ma'am?' one of the police officers now standing next to Gerry asked Kaisa.

'No, I'm fine.' Kaisa told the officer. 'Send my love to her,' Kaisa told Gerry. She gave him another hug and got back into the car.

'What the hell was that all about?' Peter said as soon as she'd closed the door.

'They're moving now,' Kaisa said and restarted the engine. The inside of the windscreen was full of mist, so she wiped it with the sleeve of her jumper. Ignoring Peter and the stares of both policemen, as well as the other protestors, none of whom Kaisa recognised, she drove to the base in silence.

When she'd parked the car, Peter said, 'Are you going to tell me what that was all about?'

Kaisa inhaled deeply and turned to Peter, 'Don't be angry with me, but I've become friendly with one of the women on the peace camp.'

Peter stared at her. He had dark circles around his eyes and his skin looked grey. 'Are you crazy? Do you realise what harm that could do?'

'No,' Kaisa began, but she couldn't carry on, as Peter interrupted her.

'You are something, you are! First you sleep with one of my friends, then when you can't sabotage my career with that, you sleep with the enemy, too! Don't tell me that boy was another one of your conquests?' he added sarcastically.

'No, please, Peter ...' Kaisa tried to interrupt him, but Peter wouldn't listen to Kaisa.

'You know they are the enemy, right? That they are in contact with the Soviets, and that the info they supply to the other side could not only endanger a whole patrol, and the crew of the sub, but MY CAREER!' Peter was shouting now.

'They're not Soviet spies, for goodness sake!' Kaisa said. Even though her heart was beating so hard she thought she might faint, she let out a snort. The thought that the gormless (but admittedly scary) Gerry, or the caring Lisa, or the so recently pregnant Lyn for that matter, had anything to do with espionage was ridiculous.

'You know absolutely nothing about it!' Peter said. He'd raised his voice, so that a passing sailor shot a curious look towards the couple arguing in a misted-up car.

They were both silent for a moment while they waited for the man to pass. Then Peter continued, with a lowered voice full of contained rage, 'It was enough of a test for my future in the Navy that I married a girl from a Soviet-friendly country. How do you think they will react to the fact that you are now fraternising with those Commies?'

Kaisa was stunned. She looked at Peter, who now took hold of her arms and, shaking her, shouted, 'Answer me: what the fucking hell did you think you were doing?'

Kaisa lowered her head. What could she say? It was obvious that Peter's career came first, and the relationship with her was secondary. Kaisa thought about the time before they were married, when Peter hadn't told her about the problem presented by her nationality until she found out about it during a Ladies' Night at the Dolphin base in Portsmouth. And then there was the long wait while Peter asked his appointer whether he'd be allowed to marry a woman from Finland and still be able to serve as a British naval officer. For months Kaisa had no idea where she stood, or whether they'd be able to marry and finally live together in England. She now wondered if Peter had already then been having doubts about their relationship.

Peter let go of Kaisa's arms. 'Right, if you don't have anything to say for yourself, I'm off.' Peter got out of the car and slammed the door shut. Kaisa sat in the car thinking hard. She'd taken her swimming stuff with her, but now she had no desire to get out of the car and into the pool. She felt numb, and had a weird sense that the last twelve hours had happened to someone else and not her. 'A swim will do you good.' She could hear her mother's voice and tears started to run down her face. She sat in the car sobbing, until another man, this time in civilian clothes, passed the car park and gave her a funny look. Kaisa took a deep breath and wiped her face with a threadbare tissue she found in the pocket of her Barbour. Perhaps a swim was exactly what she needed, Kaisa thought, and got out of the car.

37

W hen Kaisa emerged from the changing rooms, she was disappointed to see another shape moving in the water. She usually had the pool to herself during her early morning swims. When the man reached the end of the lane, she saw to her horror it was Duncan.

'We must stop meeting like this,' he said, and grinned at Kaisa. Duncan was dripping with water. He'd got smartly out of the pool, using his strong arms, and was now standing in front of Kaisa in his swimming trunks.

'What are you doing up here?' Kaisa said.

'That's not a very nice welcome,' Duncan grabbed Kaisa's arm and planted a wet kiss on her cheek. 'I hear you've been causing all kinds trouble here.' Again, Duncan smiled widely at Kaisa. 'My offer still stands, if you want to get away from it all.'

Kaisa wriggled free and wiped the spot where Duncan's lips had touched her skin. 'Please don't,' she said.

Duncan's face grew serious, 'Are you OK, Kaisa?'

'No, not really.'

'Look, I'm sorry …' Again, Duncan tried to grab Kaisa's arms, but she stepped away from him. She looked around her, but thankfully the pool was empty. Even the lifeguard had gone somewhere else and, as usual, the viewing gallery was empty.

'I just need you to go. Peter knows and he's, well, he's very angry.'

Duncan stood quietly in front of her for a while. 'Right,' he said eventually. 'I thought it was just the rumours, you know, and that no one would know for certain.'

'No, he knows,' Kaisa said. 'I told him everything.'

'OK, right, well,' Duncan grew silent again. He wasn't looking at her, but down at his hands. They were wrinkled from the water, and his nails looked strangely white.

Suddenly Kaisa saw a door behind Duncan fly open. Peter stormed into the hall, fully clothed in his uniform trousers, boots and jumper. Behind him, the lifeguard was trying to stop him. 'Sir, you can't go in …' But Peter would have none of it, and in a few seconds he'd got hold of Duncan's arm. Peter's fist hit Duncan's face before Kaisa, or Duncan, could react.

'You bastard!' Peter shouted.

'No!' Kaisa shrieked.

Before Duncan could steady himself, Peter punched his stomach. Duncan fell into the pool backwards, making a horrible splash.

'Please, Peter,' Kaisa shouted. She tried to get hold of Peter, but he pushed her away and she lost her balance. As she scrambled to her feet, Peter dived into the pool after Duncan, who was now trying to swim away to the other side. The lifeguard madly blew his whistle and threw a lifebuoy into the water.

The two men ignored the whistle, and the lifebuoy, and began a desperate fight in the water. Duncan managed to push Peter's head under, but Peter surfaced and hit Duncan's shoulder so hard that Duncan fell sideways and for a moment his whole body went under.

'Stop!' Kaisa and the lifeguard shouted at the same time. Kaisa turned to the guard. 'Aren't you going to jump in?' The man gave Kaisa a funny look, but did dive in. At the same time, three other men came running into the pool, and they, too, plunged in. They managed to get Duncan up and dragged him out of the water. He was coughing and spluttering, but seemed to be OK. Peter didn't fight against the men, but swam between them to the side where Kaisa was standing. When Peter got out of the pool, Kaisa saw that he had blood dripping from his mouth.

'Are you alright?' she said, but she was pushed away by two provost ratings, who wrapped a blanket over Peter and led him away.

'Best you clear the pool, ma'am,' one of them said to Kaisa over his shoulder.

Neither Peter nor Duncan resisted the bulky provost ratings. When the large hall was empty, Kaisa realised she was shivering. She held onto herself and wondered what she was supposed to do. She walked towards the door where they had taken Peter and Duncan, but then realised it was the men's changing rooms; besides she was still in her swimming costume. Kaisa ran in the opposite direction and slipped on the wet tiles. When she got up, she realised she'd cut her knee. In the changing rooms, she dressed quickly, put a piece of toilet roll on her bleeding knee, and walked out of the pool. It was still raining, and Kaisa began shivering again. She made her way to the Wardroom lower down the base, but was stopped at the entrance.

'How can I help you?' said the man behind the desk. He had thin dark hair that was combed to one side, covering a bald patch. At that point Nigel walked out of the back bar and came over to Kaisa. He touched Kaisa's arm and said softly, 'Kaisa, would you like me to drive you home?'

'No. Where's Peter?'

'Listen, Kaisa, would you like a cup of tea?'

Kaisa looked at Nigel's hand, which was resting on her arm. 'No, Nigel, I would not like a bloody cup of tea. I want to know where my husband is!' She'd raised her voice. The man behind the desk coughed, and inclined his head towards the Captain, who'd walked into the hallway and was now standing behind Nigel. Nigel turned around and, touching his forehead, said, 'Sir!' Kaisa saw the Captain wore many more gold braids on his jumper than Peter or Nigel did. He nodded to Nigel and stretched his hand towards Kaisa. She had already guessed this was the Captain, although she'd not met him before the submarine sailed. Peter had told her she would meet him after they got back from Wiltshire. The Captain's wife usually had a dinner party for officers and their wives at some point during the men's time ashore.

'How do you do, I'm Kaisa Williams.'

'Now, my dear, Peter is being calmed down and his, hmm, injuries are being looked at. As soon as we think it's safe for him to go, you can take him home. If you like, you can wait here.' The Captain pointed at the table and chairs by the entrance to the Wardroom.

'Thank you,' Kaisa said in the most dignified voice she could muster.

38

Peter was shivering by the time the provost had got him to sit down in the sickbay waiting room. He didn't know if it was the cold, or the rage draining from him. He could hear Duncan in the examining room on the other side of the door answering the nurse's questions with a monosyllabic, 'Yes,' or 'No'. Hearing his voice, Peter balled his hands into fists. He winced with a sharp pain, which came from his right shoulder and hand. Looking down, he saw there were red marks on his knuckles. Suddenly Peter felt exhausted, and nauseous. He shifted a little in his seat, which made the provost sitting opposite him get up.

'It's OK, I'm calm,' he said, and the expressionless man nodded in reply and sat down again.

Peter heard steps along the corridor and, as soon as he spotted the Captain, he got up and saluted him, a gesture that made him flinch with pain again.

The Captain stood in front of him and for a moment just stared at him, saying nothing. His new captain was a fair-haired man with pale eyes. He had an acute sense of right and wrong. At sea, he demanded absolute commitment and didn't tolerate any kind of squabbles between his men onboard. Peter liked him, and after the long patrol they'd just been on, considered him a great leader. He wanted to be just like him one day. And now here Peter was, in front of the Captain, with his head lowered in shame.

'I'm surprised at you, Peter.' The Captain's voice was a low murmur, like thunder before the crash of lightning.

'Sir,' Peter lifted his eyes and looked squarely at him.

Again the Captain just stood there, glaring at Peter. At that moment, the door to the sickbay opened and Duncan stepped out. He had his right arm in a sling.

'You'd better go in. I'll speak with you later.' The Captain marched back down the corridor.

Peter didn't look at Duncan, and passed him without acknowledging his presence. If he never again set eyes on the bastard, he'd be happy.

After the nurse had checked Peter over, and bandaged his hand, he was led by the provost to an office where the Captain stood waiting outside the closed door.

'Sir, I'm very sorry,' Peter said and saluted him.

'I wouldn't expect this from a junior rate, Peter, and you know we cannot tolerate this kind of thing.'

'Yes, Sir.'

The Captain's face softened just a little when he continued, 'I know there may have been extenuating circumstances, but this kind of behaviour is unheard of. You are a good, young officer with a long career ahead of you. Don't let your wife spoil that for you. As it is, you are in deep shit now, and I'm not sure I can get you out.'

'Yes, Sir.' Peter knew he should be angry with Kaisa, but now all the rage had deserted him. All he wanted was to get this over and done with and go home to her. 'Peter, you're a fucking fool,' he thought to himself.

The Captain sighed, and began pacing the corridor outside the office. Peter stood as still as he could, holding onto his cap. He was still cold, but he'd stopped shivering, perhaps it was something to do with the painkillers the nurse had given him for the hand and his sore shoulder.

Soon, a slightly built Wren opened the door. She smiled at Peter, and he thought, fleetingly, that she'd probably not had so much excitement in years. She was a good sort, with a father and a brother in skimmers. She showed Peter and his captain into the office of the Captain of the Base. Peter had never been inside before, and was taken aback by the view out of the wide window. It felt as if they were suspended above the base, with its submarines in dock, and the Gareloch beyond. The office was dominated by a vast desk, behind which sat the Base Captain. He was an older man, with wisps of grey hair slicked back from his forehead. He wore a pair of rimless spectacles, earning him the nickname Himmler among the staff at the naval base.

On their side of the desk stood Duncan. He was motionless, looking ahead of him at Himmler.

'Officers fighting at the base!' Himmler boomed. 'I have a loony bin of a peace camp opposite; I do not need to be sorting out two officers who are behaving like rutting stags!'

'No, Sir,' Duncan and Peter said in unison.

'This kind of thing cannot and will not happen on my base.' Himmler said, now addressing the captain of Peter's sub.

'No, Sir,' he replied, and added. 'There are some circumstances which might explain my junior officer's behaviour ...'

But Himmler cut him short, 'I've got to deal with a senior rate who's been exposing himself in Helensburgh waterfront car park. There's talk of increased demos by the loonies down the road. I don't have time for a spoilt frustrated wife. Get a fucking grip, Williams, and get her stowed away. I'm supposed to be running the country's nuclear deterrent, not a bloody marriage counselling service.'

'Yes, Sir,' Peter said.

Himmler turned to Duncan, 'And you, I want you to understand that I have nothing but contempt for what you did to a fellow officer. They are not the actions of someone who holds a Queen's Commission. And now get the fuck out of my sight. You'd better be off the base by tonight, and make sure I never set eyes on you again.'

'Yes, Sir,' Duncan replied, saluting Himmler and Peter's captain. He gave Peter a brief look and left the room, followed by one of the provosts, who had been sitting on chairs along the back wall of the office. Peter felt a shiver run down his spine, a surge of the anger that had made him seek out Duncan as soon he'd heard the bastard was on the base. Peter concentrated on his breathing and on the view of the Gareloch outside the window. If he didn't keep calm now, he could certainly wave his career goodbye – if it wasn't over already.

'What happens to you both will be decided, but you, Williams, you'll be getting it big time.'

'Understood, Sir.'

'Now fuck off out of my office.' Himmler turned around in his chair to look at the view. Peter glanced at his captain, and said, 'Thank you, Sir.'

The Captain led Peter away from the office and told the provost he'd take care of him now.

'You heard what the Captain said.' Peter's captain's expression was a little softer now. 'I will try to make your case, but I fear the worst.'

'Thank you, Sir,' Peter replied. He was now hanging his head. 'A court martial?' he asked.

The Captain sighed, 'God knows we don't need the publicity. With the campers opposite, and the general mood of the country, the press will love this.' He looked at Peter. 'But, you know it's probably around the base by now, the ratings will all know, so it will be difficult to avoid one.'

'Right, Sir,' Peter said.

For a moment both men stood still in the corridor, looking at their feet.

'Go home now. You're on leave as from now, understood? Your pretty wife is waiting for you in the entrance. And for God's sake, stow her away as the Captain said, eh? Right now she's a bloody liability.'

'Yes, Sir,' Peter replied. He saluted the Captain and walked along the long set of corridors towards the Officers' Mess.

39

K aisa had to wait for nearly two hours before Peter emerged, bandaged up and looking sheepish from a door at the far end of the lobby. During that time she had had three cups of weak coffee, which the man with the greased back hair brought her. The Captain had disappeared almost as soon as Kaisa had sat down, but before he left he'd said to the caretaker, 'Make sure Mrs Williams has everything she needs.'

'Would you like a cup of tea, love?' the man asked as soon as both the Captain and Nigel had left. Kaisa shook her head and said, after some hesitation, 'I don't drink tea.'

'Oh,' the man replied and looked quizzically at Kaisa as if she was somehow deranged. 'I only drink coffee,' she added with a sigh.

'Ay, ay, coffee coming right up!' The man went off to a side room that led to a small kitchen. He seemed relieved that he could bring her something, so perhaps he wasn't as unfriendly as Kaisa had first thought.

When Kaisa saw Peter, she got up and went over to him. He was accompanied by Nigel, who nodded to Kaisa and said to Peter, 'Anything you need, mate, just give me a ring, yeah?'

'Are you OK?' Kaisa asked and Peter nodded, although he didn't look at her. His hand was wrapped up, and he had a cut on his lower lip. He was wearing his greatcoat over his jumper, and with his shoulders hunched and his eyes red, he looked like an old sea dog.

'Just drive me home,' he said and marched out of the door. Kaisa gathered up her coat, and sports bag, and hurried after him.

On the way home, Peter was quiet and, closing his eyes, adopted the same position he had on the way to the base a few hours earlier, with his cap covering half of his face. How their lives had changed in that short time! Kaisa felt so nervous, not knowing what Peter was thinking (was he angry or ashamed?) that she stalled the car twice going up the hill leading away from the base. At the gate, where the guard had to check their papers, Kaisa nearly flooded the engine. As the two military policemen inside the booth opened the gate, they gave Kaisa a long stare, which made her try to start the car in first gear and stall again.

'For goodness sake,' Peter said, and Kaisa nearly burst into tears, but finally she got the car started. The drive to their married quarters at Smuggler's Way was the longest journey she'd ever made. When they passed the peace camp, she didn't dare to look in the direction of the camper vans and colourful banners. She just kept her eyes on the road, occasionally wiping away the tears that were running freely down her face.

When Kaisa parked outside the house, Peter got out and winced as his arm touched the doorframe. Kaisa went over to him and asked if she could help.

'No,' he said and waited for her to open the door to the house. Inside he let her help him get his coat off over the bandaged hand.

'Is your shoulder hurt?' Kaisa asked when he winced again.

'It's fine,' Peter said and laid himself gingerly on the sofa. Kaisa went to take his boots off, which he allowed her to do, but he kept his eyes away from her. She fetched a blanket they'd received as a present but, looking at the blue-and-green tartan, she suddenly remembered the gift had come from Duncan and decided against it. She fetched a single duvet from the guest bedroom instead. By the time she was back downstairs, Peter was fast asleep. Clutching the bulky duvet, she sat down opposite Peter. He looked rugged. Although he'd shaved that morning, already, only a few hours later, he had dark stubble on his chin. His hair was tousled; he'd not had time for a hair cut since coming home, and Kaisa could see the dark hairs curling at the back of his neck. The cut on his lip looked a little swollen, but this only made him look more handsome. Oh, how Kaisa loved him. Why didn't she always remember this, and realise how lucky she was to be married to the man she loved? And such an attractive man, too. Not only was he darkly handsome, with long black eyelashes framing his dark-green eyes, but he was tall and slim, with muscular arms. Everyone else Kaisa knew, including Duncan, paled in comparison to Peter. Not one of the officers on board *Tempest*, or *Restless*, nor anyone else she'd ever met, was as good-looking as her husband. So what if he didn't always understand her need for a career of her own? Or her doubts about his profession? Weren't these things that they, as a newly married couple could, and would, naturally, work on together? Kaisa suddenly felt like laughing when she thought back to the fight in the pool. It had been like a scene from a film! That Peter, who'd never been jealous, would hit another man, was quite a show of emotion. He obviously cared, Kaisa thought, and she immediately felt ashamed of her self-centredness. The last thing she wanted was for her love, Peter, to be hurt, or for anyone to be hurt by him. She tiptoed closer to Peter and gently covered him with the duvet. As she tucked the corners carefully around Peter's face, he opened his eyes. 'I'm sorry,' Kaisa said.

'So am I,' Peter replied. 'C'mon, give me a kiss.'

Kaisa knelt down beside her husband and gently kissed his lips, trying to avoid the cut, but Peter didn't seem to mind. He put his good arm around Kaisa and squeezed her hard towards him. She closed her eyes. She felt safe in Peter's arms.

THE GOOD HEART

BOOK 3

1

HELENSBURGH, SCOTLAND

I t was a cold morning, on 30th January 1985. There was no rain, and Kaisa could just about make out the faint outline of the sun in the distance, low above the Gareloch. The sight of the opaque light behind a thin layer of cloud made Kaisa feel oddly optimistic. She held on tightly to the cup of coffee she'd brewed and inhaled the familiar, comforting smell. She had decided she would drive them to the community centre on the Churchill Estate, on the other side of Helensburgh, where the court martial was to be held. It was only a quarter past eight, and Peter was already wearing his full uniform, with sword; he looked very smart.

'Do you want something else before we go? More tea, or water?' Kaisa asked. She saw Peter's straight back through the open kitchen door. He was standing in front of the mirror in the hall, adjusting his cap. Without turning to look at her, or speaking, he shook his head.

Peter hadn't wanted her to come to the court. But his lawyer, Lawrence, had told them Kaisa needed to be there to show the court that they were a happy couple. Kaisa had recoiled from the phrase. She didn't know what happiness was anymore.

That morning she'd dressed in the black trouser suit that she kept for job interviews, with an off-white roll-neck jumper inside the jacket for warmth. Pammy, her friend on the married patch, and the only Navy wife who still talked to her, had said it was bitterly cold at the community centre, and that they might have to wait around outside for hours before the proceedings started. Kaisa didn't ask how her friend was so knowledgeable. She wondered if the waiting around was part of the punishment, but there'd been very little information about the day; just the one letter summoning Peter to the court martial at 10 am.

'You are not needed as a witness because you're my wife; you just need to be present,' Peter had told her. His eyes were dark, and as usual when he spoke with Kaisa these days, they displayed no emotion whatsoever.

'I'm going to drive,' Kaisa said to Peter's back. She could see his image in the mirror, but couldn't see his eyes under the black peak of his Navy officer's cap. She thought how handsome he still was, even though he'd lost so much weight. The past few weeks, during the awful state of limbo before the court martial, Kaisa had often coaxed Peter to eat. He'd lost his appetite for food, and life, it seemed. She couldn't pinpoint the time when he had changed; at first, when the consequences of all her terrible actions had played out, they'd been able to comfort each other. They were like two survivors, thrown together in a sinking ship, bailing out water, fighting together to remain afloat. But slowly, Peter had drifted away from her, into his own shell, into his own world. He'd grown quieter, and wanted to be with her less. Now when Kaisa tried to touch him, he flinched.

Kaisa knew it was the impending court martial that was playing on Peter's mind, so she let him be. She understood how much his career in the Navy meant to him, and hoped that when the proceedings were over they would find a way to love each other again.

Outside, braving the strong winds whipping up the hill where the grey pebbledash houses of the married quarters stood, Peter looked thin and gaunt. When he removed first his sword and then his cap and placed them carefully on the back seat of the car, Kaisa saw the dark circles around his eyes.

Kaisa parked on the sloping car park, and pulled up the handbrake hard. Peter winced; he just couldn't get used to her driving. Not looking at her, Peter got out and picked up his sword from the back seat. He fixed it onto his belt and walked across the small yard towards the entrance of Drumfork Naval Club, a low-slung, 1960s building. It was used as a social space for naval families, and as everything in Helensburgh, was run-down and grey-looking. Peter noticed the ice on the ground too late and slipped on the steps.

'You OK?' he heard Kaisa say behind him, but he didn't have the energy to reply to her. Instead, he cursed under his breath and took a handkerchief out of his pocket to wipe the palm of his hand. There were a few spots of blood. 'Fuck,' he said out loud. Glancing down, he saw his uniform trousers had escaped the worst of it and still looked crisp and smart; they still had the deep creases he'd ironed into them that morning.

Inside, it was even colder than on the windswept hill. Peter rubbed his hands together, keeping the hankie between them in an attempt to stem the blood, which was dribbling out of the fleshier part of his right palm. He nodded to the same Wren who'd shown him into Himmler's office three weeks before. She didn't smile as she stood up from the grey plastic chair she'd been sitting on, but her eyes had a kindness to them. Peter moved his face away from hers. During the past weeks he'd heard nothing but condolences, people saying how sorry they were. He didn't need their sympathy – he needed this to be over and to get back to work. Even Kaisa had nothing but sorrow in her eyes and Peter couldn't stand it. What he needed was anger; he needed people to understand how angry he was. Angry at Kaisa, angry at Duncan, angry at the Navy for posting him and his new, young, pretty wife to this God-forsaken arsehole of a place, angry at Scotland and the bloody Jocks complaining in their harsh accents, angry at the drab, ugly married quarters on the hillside, overlooking the steely cold Gareloch, angry at himself for being so stupid as to care that his wife had slept with someone else. He put his handkerchief back into his pocket and told himself to calm down.

The door behind him opened and his lawyer, who had been to see Peter at home, shook his and Kaisa's hand. Peter flinched; the stone steps had grazed his palm and even though the bleeding had stopped it still hurt.

'You OK?' The guy, who was probably only a few years older than Peter, asked.

Peter looked at his hand. 'Yeah.'

The lawyer nodded and turned to Kaisa.

'Perhaps, Mrs Williams, you'd like to go in. Sit at the front – they need to see you together.'

Kaisa nodded and went inside.

When they'd met previously, the lawyer had also immediately said how sorry he was about the 'incident' as he called it. Lawrence Currie was a lieutenant like Peter, but he'd studied law in Edinburgh and had a slight Scottish lilt when he spoke. The accent had put Peter off him at first, but he'd warmed to the man when he'd told Peter that the court martial would 'run its course whatever you or I may think.' He'd said that the panel would have decided what the outcome would be even before Peter stepped inside the room. 'So the best thing is to stand there, reply to any questions as quickly and briefly as possible and get out. You can then get on with the rest of your life.'

'Yes and No responses are the best,' he'd added.

Now Lieutenant Currie motioned for Peter to go and sit at the far end of the room. Out of the earshot of the Wren, Peter supposed.

'We've got a little time to go over everything,' the lawyer started.

He told Peter that he should plead guilty to assault. 'I will then bring in the mitigating circumstances of you being back from your first patrol, the wee shite, whom you'd considered to be a friend, taking advantage of your pretty, foreign wife, and so on.'

Peter nodded. He wasn't looking at the lawyer, but was hanging his head. He was trying not to let the anger rise again.

'Are you OK?' the lawyer asked, again, touching Peter's arm.

Peter looked up. 'I'm not pleading guilty.'

The lawyer was silent for a moment, then sighed and said, 'I strongly advise you to throw yourself at the mercy of the court. They will have sympathy for you.'

Peter moved his eyes away from Lawrence.

The lawyer sighed again. 'Now, don't forget they will take your sword from you. It means as an officer, you are placing your rank, status and reputation on hold for the duration of the proceedings.'

Peter nodded. 'When are we going in?'

'Any minute now. But there's something else I need to tell you. There will be reporters outside with cameras. One is from the local rag, *Helensburgh Advertiser*, but there are also the nationals: *Daily Mail*, the *Sun* and the *Telegraph*.'

Peter put his head in his hands. He thought about his parents, his brother in London, and his sister. They'd all read about his stupid actions, and now they would have to explain it to their friends. Until now he'd been something of a local hero in Wiltshire; his achievements in cricket during his school years had often been written about in the *Wiltshire Times*, and when he passed out from Dartmouth, there'd been a long article about it in the same local paper. That was partly because Prince Andrew had graduated at the same time, so the Queen had also been there. Still, it was a picture of Peter in the freshly pressed naval officer's uniform that had appeared inside the paper. Even when he'd married Kaisa, his mother had sent in a wedding picture of them to the paper, which had printed it with the caption 'Local submarine officer, RN, marries a girl from Finland.' Now they would have something far juicier to write about. Would they dig out the picture of him and Kaisa on their wedding day? Suddenly a phrase he'd often heard came to his mind: 'There's a touch of the pirate about every man who wears the Dolphins.' He grinned and recalled when he had caught the Dolphins, the badge of the submarine service, between his teeth from a glass of rum. It was an old Royal Navy right of passage on qualification and proved that submariners were a bit wild. He immediately regretted such thoughts and straightened his face. Then the door opened and he was loudly called in by a Naval Provost.

2

The court martial suite of the Drumfork community centre was a large room at the back of the building. There was a long table at one end, and chairs set out on each side, with a gangway left empty through the middle. Kaisa sat at the front, with her blonde head bent and her hands crossed in her lap as if in prayer. The room was full. Peter recognised Pammy and Nigel but avoided looking at the rest of the crowd. The large table had five empty chairs. Another, smaller desk was set to the side, occupied by a lieutenant, the advocate for the Crown, Lawrence said. Lawrence hurried to the empty seat next to the other lawyer and the Provost indicated for Peter to stand in front of the court. As he passed the crowd, Peter's eyes settled briefly on Nigel, who nodded almost imperceptibly. Moving his eyes away from his friend, Peter saw a colourful round rug in one corner of the room, and on top of it an unruly pile of plastic toys. The room must be used for a play group, Peter thought, and again he felt the urge to smile. 'For fuck's sake, keep it together,' he told himself, and he concentrated on setting his mouth straight.

For a moment the room seemed to sway in front of Peter's eyes, but he managed to steady himself by closing them for a second. A court official nodded for Peter to remove his sword. With shaking hands, he struggled to unclasp it from its scabbard. He thought he'd prepared himself for this naval tradition, but now when it came to it, his hands wouldn't obey his commands. Eventually Peter managed to get the sword free, and he placed the gold-handled weapon on the table in front of him.

The official, a small man with a serious expression, proceeded to tell everyone to stand. There was a hush as five men, also wearing full dress uniforms, their swords awkward in their hands, walked in and settled down in the chairs facing Peter. The Captain, the President of the Board, who wore small half-moon glasses perched at the end of his long nose, sat down in the middle, with the two commanders on either side. A lieutenant, a submariner Peter had once been introduced to, but whose name now escaped him, went to sit at the far end of the table, and a very young looking sub-lieutenant with a pink face, sat nearest to the lawyers. Neither looked at Peter.

That Peter didn't know any of the Board came as a great relief to him. His mouth felt dry and he swallowed hard. The men gazed gravely at him and then the President asked him how he pleaded. Peter said he was 'Not guilty.' He tried to make his voice as steady as possible, but there was a tremble at the last syllable. He heard whispers behind him, and avoided looking at his lawyer. Lying awake the previous night, he'd decided he just couldn't admit to guilt. Even though he'd punched Duncan first, it was his so-called friend who had done the unthinkable. Even Himmler had said so on that awful day of the fight.

Peter was then told to sit down. The lawyer next to Lawrence got up and told the sorry tale of Peter's 'assault' on Duncan. The Naval Provost who'd been at the pool and the two lifeguards then gave their account of the fight that Peter had started. Peter zoned out, trying to keep his nerves steady.

When the prosecution had finished the President said, 'Over to you Lieutenant Curry.'

Just as he'd told Peter outside, Lawrence spoke about the mitigating circumstances and how Peter 'had been pushed to the edge.' He paused and leaned over to his desk to pick up a piece of paper. 'With your permission, Sir, I'd like to read out a short statement from the other party.' There was a collective intake of breath, then a murmur from the crowd.

'Silence, please,' the Captain said, and nodding at Lawrence added, 'Go on.'

With a clear voice, Lawrence read out a statement from Duncan in which he said he was sorry about his indiscretion against 'his fellow naval officer, and friend, Lieutenant Williams,' and that he had not suffered any long-term medical consequences from the incident. He also stated that he was not planning now, nor any time in the future, to seek any kind of compensation for the actions against his person. After Lawrence had finished reading, the courtroom filled with a low chatter, causing the

Captain to raise his head and give the room a stern stare. 'Please, I must insist on silence.'

Looking at Lawrence, he said, 'Is that it?'

'Yes, thank you, Sir,' Lawrence replied. He sat down, giving Peter a glance and a quick nod.

'The court will adjourn to consider its decision,' the President said and everyone got to their feet.

When Peter was called back inside, his eyes shifted to the table, where his sword had been moved so that the tip was pointing towards him. So they'd found him guilty. Peter's feet felt heavy, as if he were in chains, while he walked slowly towards the end of the room. Would they dismiss him from his beloved Navy? He could see Kaisa was again seated at the front, with her head turned towards him, her red-rimmed eyes looking at Peter.

The next part of the proceedings went by in a flash. Peter was told that he could continue to fulfil his duties for Her Majesty's Submarine Service, and keep his rank, but that he'd be fined £500, to be taken from his salary in the next six months. The court was dismissed and the Board, led by the Captain, clattered out of the room; Peter was handed his sword. The court official gave him a long stare as he held the weapon flat in his hands. Peter placed his sword inside the scabbard, attaching it back to the belt smoothly this time. He wanted to smile, but thought better of it. He took hold of the handle, and immediately felt himself stand taller.

Lawrence came up to him and shook his hand. 'You took a chance; that could have been much worse.'

'Thank you,' Peter said. He was a little curious about how the lawyer had got the statement from Duncan, but he didn't ask. He didn't want to know anything about that bastard ever again.

Outside, the reporters ambushed Peter and Kaisa, as they tried to rush to their car. The flash hurt Peter's eyes and he pulled his cap further down.

'Give us a smile, Keese,' one reporter, mispronouncing Kaisa's name, shouted, and Peter could feel Kaisa lean closer to him. He took hold of her hand and pushed past the reporters. He saw Lawrence stay behind to answer their questions.

In the car, Kaisa put her hand on Peter's thigh. She didn't say anything, just stared at the road ahead of them. He looked at her small, slender fingers, with their nails bitten to the quick. When had she started biting her nails? He realised that he felt nothing under her touch. Usually the pressure of her hand so close to his crotch would have caused an immediate reaction; but now there was nothing. She removed her hand to change gears.

'A fine was good, right?' she said and glanced at him.

'Yeah, obviously the best thing is not to be court-martialled at all. It'll be on my record forever,' Peter said drily and watched the still, steel surface of the Gareloch. That should put a stop to her bloody optimism, he thought.

His words had the desired effect, and shut Kaisa up. They drove the rest of the way in silence. Back at the married quarter, Kaisa went immediately upstairs. Peter could hear her crying in the bathroom. He slumped onto the sofa and closed his eyes.

3

In the afternoon after the court martial, Peter had to do something to clear his mind. He decided to go and fetch his things from the base. As luck would have it, the first person he bumped into was his Captain. The old man called him into his office. 'Peter, you're a good young officer, who's had a bit of bad luck. Just do a good job in your next appointment, and this will soon blow over, believe me.'

'Thank you, Sir,' Peter replied.

'Now, there's one more thing. Did you see the reporters in there?'

Peter lifted his head, 'Yes, I did. Lt Currie told me about them,' he said simply. 'And,' Peter felt his voice falter, but paused trying to steady his nerves, 'they took photos,' He looked down at his polished boots and continued, 'to show ...'

Peter couldn't find the words, so the Captain came to his rescue, 'Yes, I understand, to show a happily married couple.'

Peter nodded.

'Well, that's what you two were, and I'm sure will be again.' The Captain went on to tell him to expect some coverage in the local rag. 'There will be something in the national press too,' he said, taking hold of Peter's arm. 'Just hold firm, don't make any comments. If you haven't done so already, it might be best if you tell your family as soon as possible. And take your phone off the hook,' he added.

Peter went home. Kaisa was still upstairs; she had fallen asleep, fully clothed on their bed. Peter didn't want to wake her, so he tiptoed downstairs and dialled the number of his parents' house. It was the most difficult conversation he'd had in his life. His father was quiet, listening to Peter's sorry tale, and when it was over there was a long silence at the end of the line.

'Dad?' Peter said, wondering if the old man had heard any of what Peter had told him.

'I'll get your mother,' his father replied eventually, and Peter heard the phone being placed on the table. He imagined the tidy bungalow his parents lived in now that their three children had grown up and left home. He thought, again, how this scandal would affect the order of their lives. How would their large circle of friends, many of whom were ex-Navy or ex-Army and had fought in the Second World War, take the news? Would they be sympathetic, or would they talk behind his parents' backs and shun their company? He remembered how thrilled his parents and the whole family had been when Peter graduated from Dartmouth Naval College. When the Queen herself attended the passing out parade, they were bursting with pride.

The wait for his mother to come to the telephone felt like an age. He could hear her ask what was up, and the muffled reply from his father, which he couldn't decipher.

'Peter?' his mother said, with a higher pitched voice than usual.

'I'm sorry, mum,' Peter said. He began telling her the whole story, about how Kaisa had been with a friend of his, Duncan, while he was on his first patrol.

'He seemed such a nice young man,' Peter's mum interrupted, and Peter remembered the weekend during their time at Dartmouth when he'd invited Duncan to Wiltshire to stay with his parents. Peter tensed up and formed a fist with the hand not holding the receiver. 'Well, he's not.'

At that moment, he heard a sniffle from the lounge, and saw Kaisa sitting on the sofa, her knees up to her chest, her body balled up tightly. Peter hadn't heard her come down the stairs. She was crying hard now, and Peter wished he could go to her instead of having to finish the conversation with his mother.

But Peter had to continue. He told his mother how he'd found out about the affair on his return, how the bastard had been at the base, talking to Kaisa at the swimming pool, how he hadn't been able to control himself and how he had knocked Duncan into the water.

'I was dismissed my ship,' Peter was hanging his head, the shame of the court martial fully hitting home.

'Oh, Petey,' her mother used a nickname Peter hadn't heard in years, not since he was a small boy. He suddenly yearned to see his mother, to be comforted by her.

'It'll probably be in the papers,' Peter said instead, delivering the final blow.

'Oh,' was all his mother could say. 'What do you mean, in the *Wiltshire Times*?'

'Well, probably not, unless ... it'll be in the national ones, most probably.'

'The *Telegraph*?'

Peter sighed, 'I don't know mum. We'll be down next week, if that's OK?'

There was a pause.

'Mum?' Peter wondered if the line had gone dead.

'Of course, we'd love to see you,' his mother said.

Peter asked her to pass on the news to his sister and brother, and hung up.

That evening, he and Kaisa sat in their cold house at Smuggler's Way and drank half a bottle of vodka. Kaisa cried, on and off all night. Peter wished he could cry too, but he simply wasn't able. All he wanted was to numb his senses. He couldn't help Kaisa, couldn't bring himself to comfort her.

The next day the story appeared in the *Telegraph,* on page three, where the salacious stories were usually found. It felt unreal to see a picture of him and Kaisa, looking solemn but standing close to one another, printed there, with the headline, 'Two Royal Navy Officers Fight Over Pretty Swedish Wife'. The article was short, but his head was pounding and he felt sick when he saw the words, 'The actions of 24-year-old Lieutenant Peter Williams are believed to have been fuelled by jealousy, after it was revealed his wife, Kaisa Williams, also 24 and originally from Sweden, had been having an affair with a fellow Navy officer while Lt Williams was away at sea.' In the *Daily Mail* Peter's court martial and Kaisa's affair with Duncan was a front page headline, 'Two Royal Navy Officers Brawl In Pool Over Sexy Swedish Blonde'. But the *Sun* was the worst, 'Bomber Boys Battle Over Bonking Blonde Bombshell'. Peter read the articles swiftly. The tabloids he merely scanned, but he read the *Telegraph* in full. It gave the verdict and even described Peter as 'a brilliant young officer' and reported on the 'great interest shown in the case' at the court martial.

Peter put the papers in the bin. His head was hurting from the vodka. He found a packet of paracetamols above the sink and swallowed two with a glass of water, while surveying the grey mist over the Gareloch. When he turned around, Kaisa was standing in the doorway to the kitchen, silently watching him. She moved slowly to the bin and pulled out the papers.

'Swedish!' she said, and Peter, surprised at his own reaction, had to suppress a smile. He wanted to hug Kaisa, it was so typical that her incorrect nationality would be the one thing she commented on, but something stopped him. Examining the paper with her head bent, she looked so tired, her face drawn and the blonde hair hanging limp on her shoulders, that Peter felt a strong urge to protect her, to tell her everything would be alright, and that he loved her. But he couldn't move, nor speak. He gazed at her, willing Kaisa to look up and say she was sorry. Instead, she put the papers back in the bin and, not looking at him, said, 'I think I will go to Helsinki to see mum and Sirkka.'

4

HELSINKI, FINLAND

They were sitting side by side at the end of the jetty, with their feet just touching the water. Peter had rolled his uniform trousers up and Kaisa was wearing a summery dress. The sun glittered on the surface of the lake. For once, it wasn't raining. Peter turned his head towards Kaisa and took her hands between his. His dark eyes under his naval cap looked as sparkly as the surface of the water. Kaisa sighed with happiness. She lifted her chin and moved her head closer to Peter's. As his lips approached Kaisa's, she opened her eyes and woke up with a start.

It was dark, and the heavy, stuffy room was silent, apart from the gentle snoring of her sister, Sirkka. Kaisa turned over and tried to get back into the lovely, summery dream, but she was now wide awake, disturbed by the snoring, which was getting louder. She could have gone and adjusted her sister's pillow, which is what she usually did if the snoring got too loud, but Sirkka was working an early shift at the Intercontinental Hotel on Mannerheim Street the next day, whereas Kaisa could lie in — or sleep all day if she wanted. She looked at the clock with the small reflective dots on the windowsill behind her and saw it was nearly 4 am. The events of the last few weeks flooded back to her, and she wanted to howl with misery. The shame of the fight between Peter and Duncan over her, and Peter's immediate sacking from the bomber submarine, HMS *Restless*; the whispers and looks of the other Navy people, even from their so-called friends, in the shops in Helensburgh, when she and Peter had tried to live a normal life before his court martial; and Peter's visible disappointment at the sudden nose dive his career had taken, made worse by its astronomical rise. His appointment to the Polaris submarine in Helensburgh just a few months after passing his nuclear qualification had been such a coup; he'd been one of the youngest officers of his rank — lieutenant — to be appointed to one of the subs that served as Britain's nuclear deterrent. Not being able to take the covert hostility of her fellow Navy wives on the married quarter estate in Rhu, nor Peter's growing indifference to her, Kaisa had decided to flee back to Finland the day after Peter's court martial.

Her mother and Sirkka had welcomed her with open arms. They had decided that she should stay with Sirkka in her one-bedroomed flat in Töölö to begin with. But during the past days Kaisa had detected a slight change in the way her mother treated her; her own failed marriage to Kaisa and Sirkka's father had at least lasted nearly twenty years, whereas Kaisa's relationship seemed to have broken down before she had even celebrated the first wedding anniversary. Of course, Pirjo hadn't pointed this out yet — but Kaisa was sure it was only a matter of time.

Kaisa had been in Helsinki for nearly a week now. She knew she had to forget the past — and Peter — and focus on the future. She couldn't carry on living in her sister's one-bedroom flat, and sleeping on her (admittedly quite comfortable) sofa bed forever. If she was to stay in Helsinki, she needed to find a job, somewhere to live on her own. She needed some purpose in her life. Unless of course, she decided to go back to Peter. They hadn't discussed the future when Peter had dropped her off at the train station in Glasgow to take the train to Heathrow. Officially, she was taking a little break in Finland with her family. Or that was what they had told each other and their friends Pammy and Nigel.

'Write to me when you get there, eh?' Peter had said at the train station, and he had kissed Kaisa lightly on the lips.

Kaisa had nodded, not being able to hold back the tears. They'd rolled down her face, smearing the mascara she'd put on that morning. But Peter hadn't reacted, or wanted to see Kaisa's tears. Unlike the many partings they'd had before they were married, when Kaisa was still a student in Helsinki and Peter was based in Portsmouth. Then Peter would always wipe, or kiss, Kaisa's tears away, and as a parting gift he'd buy her a single red rose. Today Peter just looked away, with his hands in his pockets, indifferent to Kaisa's emotions.

'I'll let you know when the new appointment comes through, and where I'll be living,' he'd said, glancing sideways at Kaisa. His eyes were narrow, and didn't show any emotion when they briefly met hers. He looked quickly away again, towards the empty track, as if he was longing for the train to arrive, impatient to get rid of his troublesome wife. Kaisa knew all he wanted was to get back to work, to get back onboard a new submarine, to rebuild his career. She didn't seem to feature in his plans for the future.

At the chilly station, where they could hear the rain beating down on the Victorian tin roof, they'd stood facing each other, but Kaisa couldn't bear to see the cold expression in her husband's eyes, so she stared at his hands instead. There were a few hairs growing on them, and Kaisa had an over-whelming desire to stroke them and lace her fingers through Peter's. She imagined that he'd look up, surprised, and that his eyes would light up at her touch, like they used to do. He'd pull her hand up to his lips and give her palm a gentle kiss. How she'd longed for him to say he loved her, but instead, when the train pulled into the station, screeching noisily, he'd said, 'Do you want me to help you with the suitcase?'

Kaisa had just shaken her head. She wanted to hold him, to tell him once more how much she loved him, but no words came out. She was so ashamed, and seeing him reminded her of that shame, and of the hurt she'd caused, not only to him, but to his career. Words, which Peter had uttered to her in the dead of night, a few days after the fight with Duncan at the Faslane base swimming pool, rang in her ears: 'You've broken the two things that matter to me most in the whole world. My love for you and my Navy career.' They were probably the most poignant, and perhaps the most honest, words her husband of only seven months had said to her during their marriage.

5

In just a year, Tuuli had grown into a businesswoman. She swept into the café at the top of Stockmann's Department store, wearing a brown woollen overcoat over a smart trouser suit and pointy flats. She still carried the briefcase the two of them had bought at the beginning of their four-year course at the Swedish School of Economics in Helsinki — or Hanken — as everyone called the low-slung university in northeastern Helsinki. Kaisa remembered that particular shopping trip with fondness; they'd ended up buying the exact same briefcase, in different colours. Kaisa's was brown, whereas Tuuli had opted for black. In those early days of their studies at Hanken, they hadn't realised how similar they looked; they both had fair hair, blue eyes and they were both tall — although Tuuli had at least ten centimetres on Kaisa. Everyone, from their fellow students to staff at the famous flirting place, the university's library, mixed them up. Having similar briefcases didn't help. But Hanken was a place where everyone knew everyone by sight at least, so people soon got used to Kaisa and Tuuli looking the same, though some still thought them to be cousins or even sisters when they graduated.

'How are you?' Tuuli said as they sat down with their coffees and cinnamon buns from the self-service counter. There was concern in her eyes and Kaisa had to take a deep intake of breath in order to stop the tears.

'I don't know,' she said instead. A few days after the incident in the pool, Kaisa had written a long letter to Tuuli from Helensburgh, recounting the sorry tale of her unfaithfulness, the fight between Duncan and Peter, and Peter's impending court martial. The letter Kaisa had received in reply was so supportive and kind that Kaisa had cried, and it had played a large part in her decision to 'take a break' in Helsinki. The fact that both Peter and Kaisa had decided on a one-way ticket, bought over the telephone from a bucket flight shop in London, spoke volumes about how long this 'break' in the marriage might last.

'You need to come out with me,' Tuuli said after she'd heard about Kaisa's living arrangements with her sister in Töölö. Sirkka and her mother rented two flats in the same post-war, stone-clad block on Linnankoskenkatu. Both flats had only one bedroom, with a small lounge and a narrow kitchen at the side, but they were in the city, within easy distance from the centre of Helsinki. Sirkka's flat overlooked a busy crossing, while her mother's flat on the floor above had a view of the peaceful inner courtyard. The two women often shared an evening meal together and went walking in the nearby park or, in winter, skiing on the frozen sea near the shores of the president's summer villa. It wasn't a bad place to be based, and Kaisa was grateful to have somewhere to live.

'That'll be fun. Where do you want to go, the KY club?' she said to Tuuli, without much enthusiasm.

Her friend laughed. 'God, no. Haven't been there for ages. That place is for the kids. No, we'll go to a couple of new bars. Unless you want to go to Old Baker's?' Tuuli reached her hand out and squeezed Kaisa's arm.

Kaisa shook her head. The two young women were quiet for a moment as they reflected on the first time Peter had come to see Kaisa in Helsinki, six months after they'd met at the British Embassy cocktail party. Peter had been a young naval officer, and had come to talk to them at the party, just as Kaisa and Tuuli were about to leave. On Peter's second visit to Helsinki, after they'd exchanged increasingly passionate letters, Kaisa had taken him to Old Baker's on Mannerheim Street. The place boasted of being an 'English pub', but Peter had been refused entry because he was wearing a pair of cords — deemed to be 'jeans' by the bouncer. 'Sorry, you need to be smartly dressed to come in,' the bearded man with a huge belly and a gruff voice had told Peter. He'd had his hand on Peter's chest and spoke to him in loud Finnish. Peter had turned to Kaisa and Tuuli for an explanation. Kaisa vividly remembered Peter's disdain at being told he — an Englishman, and an officer of her Majesty's Royal Navy — wasn't smart enough to gain entry to a place calling itself an English pub. Kaisa and Peter later suspected the bouncer had simply not liked the look of the dark-haired foreigner. It was the first of many times Peter had been publicly singled out for being a stranger with a Finnish girl. Kaisa and Peter had mostly laughed at the prejudice, but on that first time, it had hurt Peter deeply. Kaisa now reflected on her own unhappiness in England and in Scotland, where she'd constantly felt discriminated against — whether it was in the workplace or among her fellow Navy wives. She now wondered what would have happened if the tables had been turned and Peter had moved to Finland to be with her. Would he have had an equally tough time of it? Or worse? And how would he have reacted? Kaisa looked at Tuuli. She knew that sleeping with a friend of hers would be the last thing Peter would do. Guilt, which wracked her every moment, raised its ugly head again, and for a second, she wished she'd never gone to the Embassy cocktail party, and never met the handsome Englishman.

'No,' Kaisa said. 'I don't think I want to put my foot in that place ever again.'

'I understand,' Tuuli said, and gave Kaisa's arm another squeeze. 'But we'll still go out tomorrow night, OK?'

Tuuli had a studio flat a few streets south of Sirkka's place. She'd bought a bottle of wine to share before they went out. The price of drinks in bars was so high in Helsinki, it was usual to have a drink or two at home beforehand.

'So where are we going?' Kaisa asked. Tuuli looked very slim and tall in her black satin trousers and glittery gold jumper, with a narrow gold belt tied at the waist, highlighting her perfect figure.

'Oh, definitely start at the Sky Bar, then Happy Days and Helsinki Club. We'll see how long Mrs Williams will last,' she said and lifted her glass in a salute.

'Don't worry about me,' Kaisa grinned. She was wearing trousers too, with boots underneath — it was minus ten outside — but she'd decided on a frilly satin blouse after Sirkka had persuaded her out of the black jumper she'd tried on first. 'You're trying to look like a bloody nun, are you?' Sirkka had said.

Kaisa had acquiesced, though she didn't like the inference that Tuuli was taking her on a night out to find a man. Men had caused her enough trouble as it was. Plus she was still married. But she didn't say any of those things to Sirkka. She suspected her sister all but believed that her marriage to Peter was over.

As planned, Tuuli and Kaisa went to the Helsinki Club after they'd been to three other clubs. In each place, they ordered a *Lonkero*, a bitter lemon and gin drink that they had always drunk in the student's bar, for old times' sake. The place was half-full, and Kaisa wasn't at all surprised to see the old group of rich boys from Hanken there. It was as if time had stopped and her life in England hadn't happened at all.

'C'mon, come and say hello,' Tuuli said and grinned. She walked confidently towards the group of ten or so people, sitting on a dark-blue velvet sofa in the corner of the bar. A few couples were on the dance floor, leaning into each other and moving slowly; others were buying drinks at the bar. The lighting was dim and the music loud. The bar, which was lit from underneath, made the faces of the people standing against it seem unreal and spooky.

Tuuli sat down next to Tom's blond friend, Ricky, and the two kissed each other on the mouth. Kaisa was so amazed that she couldn't move. She stood in front of the group, trying not to gape at her friend.

'You remember Ricky?' Tuuli said nonchalantly — too nonchalantly.

The good-looking blond boy, whom Kaisa knew Tuuli had tried to resist at Hanken, got up and reached out to Kaisa. 'Nice to see you again.' He turned around and pointed at Tom, who was sitting in the middle of the group, next to a dark-haired girl, his arm on the top of the sofa above her shoulders. 'You remember him, don't you?' Ricky's eyes had a mischievous look, which Kaisa could spot even under the dark lighting of the club.

Tom looked up and their eyes locked. He nodded and, removing his hand from the top of the sofa, took a packet of cigarettes and made a gesture of offering one to Kaisa.

'No thanks,' she mouthed and shook her head. She bored her eyes into Tuuli, who was ignoring her.

'Sit down, Kaisa,' Ricky said and he and Tuuli shuffled along the sofa, making a space next to Tuuli.

'Would you two ladies like a drink?' Ricky said.

'Yes, I'd love one. Gin and tonic, please.' Kaisa had decided she was going to have one drink with the group, not wishing to make a fool of herself, and then leave. With Ricky gone to the bar, Kaisa whispered into Tuuli's ear, 'What the hell?' But Tuuli just shrugged her shoulders. 'I'll explain later,' she whispered back.

It was typical of Tuuli to keep something momentous like this under her hat, Kaisa thought, as she sat back against the blue velveteen sofa. A mention that she was seeing Ricky might have been expected, seeing the amount of time the two of them had once spent talking about the group of rich boys. It had been Ricky and Tom who had come onto them in the student's bar during Kaisa's and Tuuli's first week at Hanken, and whose advances they'd repeatedly rejected during their four years there. Or was this a set-up? Kaisa looked along the sofa to where Tom, the lanky boy with a wolfish smile, who'd been interested in Kaisa, sat. His head was bent close to the dark-haired girl's face. No, Tuuli must surely know that Tom, whose only goal in life during his leisurely studies seemed to be to bed as many girls as possible, was the last thing Kaisa needed now? And what was Tuuli doing with Ricky? Was it serious?

The next day was a Sunday, and the weather had turned even colder. The sun, high in the pale blue sky, nearly blinded Kaisa when she opened the venetian blinds in her sister's living room. It was already noon, so the pale winter light flooded the small flat. Kaisa shivered, even though the flat was suffocatingly warm. She felt sorry for her sister who'd left the flat at 6 am, when it was still pitch black, for an early shift at the hotel. She watched a green tram trundle past on the road below, and a woman, holding the hand of a small child, walk briskly over the road. The toddler wore a pink and white snow suit and a stripey woollen balaclava, with strands of blonde hair escaping over her pale blue eyes. Being dressed in layers of clothing made her shape round and her struggle to keep up with her mother seem impossible. She tried to brush away the hair with one fat mitten. Kaisa's mind wandered to children, and she thought about how different it would be to have them here in Finland. The winter clothing must be a pain, but childcare was easier, she guessed. Plus it was a safer society in which to bring up a child, surely? She shrugged herself free of baby thoughts – she couldn't even keep a marriage alive, how did she think she could look after a baby?

Kaisa was drinking coffee and eating a rye and cheese sandwich for breakfast when the telephone in the hall rang out.

'You want to meet up for coffee later?' Tuuli's voice sounded a bit hoarse, and Kaisa wondered how long she'd stayed on at the Helsinki Club after Kaisa had left, having had her one drink.

The two friends met up at the Fazer café in the centre of Helsinki. Tuuli was wearing jeans and a long mohair jumper under her camel coat. She wore a scarf wrapped around her head to keep the cold out. The sun had gone behind a thin layer of cloud and there were a few sporadic flakes of snow falling. Looking at the glass display of cakes, Kaisa couldn't resist a Berlin bun – a deep-fried jam doughnut covered in pink icing.

'Do you remember how we could just afford one of these for our lunch at Hanken?' Kaisa asked Tuuli when they'd sat down. They both laughed.

They'd found a table by the large windows overlooking Kluuvikatu, a road linking the main Helsinki shopping streets of Aleksi and South Esplanade. Kaisa hadn't yet dared to walk along the Esplanade park, where she and Peter had kissed properly for the first time. She could hardly believe it was nearly five years ago.

'So, what's the score with Ricky?' Kaisa said after her friend had been silently munching on her Berlin bun for a while. She'd decided that instead of mooning over her own disastrous love life, she was going to go straight to the point with Tuuli.

Tuuli lifted her blue eyes at Kaisa. 'I'm sorry about last night, but I'd agreed to meet him there and I couldn't say no, and then you turned up and I wanted to go out with you too, and …'

'That's alright, but you could have told me!'

Tuuli put down her half-eaten bun and looked down at her hands. 'Yeah, I know.'

'So, what's the score; how did you meet up again? Or did you have something going on with him at Hanken?' Kaisa was leaning towards her friend, who was still looking down at her hands. 'Oh my God, he stayed over last night didn't he?'

Tuuli lifted her head up, looking sheepish. 'OK, I've been seeing him for about a month, on and off.'

Kaisa's friend told her how she'd seen Ricky outside Stockmann's department store during her lunch hour one day and how he'd seemed so nice, so much nicer than he had at Hanken. He'd asked for her telephone number and she'd given it to him there and then. He'd called her the next evening, and that same Friday night they'd gone out to eat at a small Italian restaurant near where she lived in Töölö Square. 'One thing led to another and he came home with me,' Tuuli said.

Kaisa was quiet. She wondered how much her own tumultuous time in England had been the reason for the lack of letters between her and Tuuli, and how it had made her blind to the lives of others around her.

'We're not seeing each other, though,' Tuuli now said. 'It's casual, and that's how I want to keep it.' Kaisa's friend closed her mouth and leaned back in her chair. Her face told Kaisa that was the end of the matter; there was no more to be said. But Kaisa couldn't help asking about the other rich boy.

'What about Tom, is he seeing the short black-haired girl?'

'No, I don't think he's attached. He's only just back from Italy. I was as surprised to see him there as you were. You still fancy him?'

'God, no!' Kaisa said and laughed. 'He's the last person on my mind. Can you imagine what trouble he'd cause?'

Kaisa felt her friend's piercing eyes on her. Tuuli's demeanour had changed and she was far more relaxed now the conversation had turned away from her own life. 'You could use him for a bit of fun, though, couldn't you?' she said.

6

Kaisa was having breakfast alone at the small table in Sirkka's narrow kitchen when she heard the post thump onto the doormat in the hall. It had become a self-imposed routine of hers to try to get up before the postman began his rounds in the block of flats. She'd make herself read the main broadsheet paper, *Helsingin Sanomat*, to see if there might be some jobs she could apply for. Usually, there was nothing she could even imagine doing. She had her degree from Hanken, that was true, but no work experience to speak of. She got up with a sigh. Three of the letters were for Sirkka, but one, with a postmark from Dorset, was for her. The original address on the thick envelope was for the married quarter in Helensburgh. Just seeing 'Smuggler's Way' written, and then crossed out, on the blue paper made Kaisa shiver. She turned the thing over in her hand, but there was no return address on the back of the envelope. She examined the handwriting and suddenly knew who the letter was from.

Kaisa dropped the envelope onto the table and stared at it. She went to pour herself more coffee, to buy time. To let her think more clearly, and consider her options.

Why would he write to her? And was she sure the handwriting was his? The upright style was very similar to Peter's; in fact it seemed to be a kind of style most people in England had. But Kaisa knew for sure the letter wasn't from Peter; she'd recognise his handwriting anywhere. So, what did he want with her? Wild thoughts began circulating in her mind. Perhaps he was deadly ill? Or what if the letter wasn't from him, and was from one of Peter's fellow officers? What if something had happened to Peter?

Kaisa tore open the envelope. There were two pieces of paper. She began to read. Kaisa snorted at the words she was reading. She dropped the sheet onto the kitchen table, but curiosity soon got the better of her and she continued reading.

'Dear Kaisa,

I hope this letter finds you well.

I wasn't sure if I should write to you at all, but felt I needed to contact you this last time to tell you how sorry I am about everything that has happened. I now understand that, however much I wish it were otherwise, you love your husband, and I wanted to reassure you that I respect your decision.

You may not be aware that knowing you has changed my life beyond recognition. But I wouldn't have it any other way. I still love you, Kaisa, and keep the fond memories of our short, but intense, liaison close to my heart. I have now left the Navy, and am living with my uncle, trying to make a go of it as a farmer. (Address below.) Surprisingly, I'm enjoying life in the country rather better than anticipated. Of course, there is a distinct lack of female company, but I have been assured next month's Young Farmers Spring Ball should rectify that problem! Not that I will ever feel the way I feel about you, Kaisa, for anyone else. But, we must all move on, and rest assured, unless you approach me, this will be my last communication with you.

Of course, I very much hope we can remain friends. I understand if right now, so soon after the terrible events in Faslane, you would find it difficult, but you know, time is a great healer. As an aside, I must admit, I feel a little wronged by the powers that be in the Navy. It was your husband who attacked me after all! But I shall keep to my word and not pursue the matter – if only for your sake, and for the sake of our continued friendship, Kaisa.

It is late here on the farm, and I have to be up early to supervise the milking. We have a herd of 50 cattle, and a few acres of land, and I have grown quite fond of the cows. I call them my 'girls'! So if you are ever in the neighbourhood, you must come and visit me and my girls. It is rather beautiful here, and very peaceful. You know I would welcome you with open arms as a dear friend.

I've rambled on long enough. Please write to me and tell me your news. I cannot wait to hear back from you.

Yours always,

Duncan x'

Kaisa stared at the few pieces of paper for a long time. She examined the handwriting on the envelope again. Was that Peter's hand that had crossed out the address at Smuggler's Way, and replaced it with Sirkka's in Helsinki? If so, had he recognised Duncan's handwriting? Oh, that man! Why would he continue to pursue her even after everything that had happened? If Peter was still in Helensburgh, and had seen that Duncan was writing to her, would he think they were still in touch? Her hand holding the envelope began to shake, and her breathing became shallow. She tried to calm down, to take long breaths in and out, but her heart was racing. This was so bad, so bad. If only she knew where Peter was, but she hadn't heard from him since they parted at Glasgow train station. He hadn't replied to the letter she'd sent the day after she arrived in Helsinki.

When she'd first seen the envelope with the British postage stamp on the mat, she'd thought it was from Peter. Even the thickness of the envelope had made her hopeful that he'd written a proper letter, telling her his news, and perhaps that he missed her.

But as soon as she'd seen the crossed-over address, she'd known it wasn't from Peter. Tears began welling up inside of her, but she resisted them. She really must stop crying all the time. She put the letter in the bin, throwing the wet coffee grains over it. She refilled the percolator and stood listening to the dripping water, trying to forget about Duncan. But thoughts of the two of them in bed in the dank, cold flat in Helensburgh filled her mind. She remembered how terrible she'd felt afterwards, and how Duncan had still pursued her even after he'd had his way with her and she'd made it clear she wanted nothing more to do with him. Or had she made it perfectly clear? Perhaps she'd still flirted with him, pleased to have his attention? Kaisa felt her head ache. She needed to forget about Duncan, about that awful night and about all the terrible consequences on her life. When the second pot of coffee was ready, Kaisa poured a cup and, determined to find a job and forget all men, sat down at the table and began reading that morning's *Helsingin Sanomat*.

7

Kaisa woke up late. She'd heard her sister get up and go to work, but had fallen asleep again, only to have another wonderful dream about Peter. But after that she'd had a nightmare in which Matti rose from his grave, walked into the chapel in a black suit and was met by the sixteen-year-old girl in a white gown. Auntie Bea had smiled at Kaisa, who was one of the guests, and said, 'Isn't it wonderful that they can still get married even though Matti is dead?'

Kaisa shook her head and tried to tell herself it was just a dream. She stretched her neck to look out of the window. It was Sunday and she'd promised to go for a jog with her mother. She saw it was a sunny and relatively warm April day. The winter was finally giving way to spring. Couples were walking hand in hand, or with their children between them, wearing light overcoats or macs. It had rained heavily the night before – probably why she'd had such an awful night's sleep, Kaisa thought – and the side of the road was running with water. The temperature on the side of Sirkka's living room window showed 10 degrees Celsius; Kaisa decided she'd wear a padded jacket over her jogging clothes.

She walked up to the next floor of the block of flats and, using the key her mother had given her the day she'd arrived in Helsinki, opened the door.

'Hello,' she called out. Kaisa was still not used to the emptiness of her mother's flat. Each time she stepped through the door, she expected to be greeted by Jerry, the cocker spaniel they'd got after their parents' divorce. He'd died just before Kaisa had left Faslane and Peter. If she was truthful, the dog's death had touched Kaisa deeply, and was one of the reasons she wanted to come home.

Neither Sirkka's small flat below, or her mother's roomier apartment on the third floor of the five-storey block, felt like home to Kaisa. After two months on her sister's sofa bed, Kaisa was desperate to find a place of her own.

'I'm not ready yet,' her mother called from the bathroom, and Kaisa stepped into the kitchen. Seeing there was freshly brewed coffee in the percolator, she took off the padded coat she'd borrowed from her sister, placed her scarf and gloves on the kitchen table, and poured herself a cup of strong black coffee. She ran a little bit of cold water from the tap over the cup. While she'd lived in Britain, she'd got used to weaker coffee, a fact that neither Sirkka or her mother let her forget. 'You've become an English-woman,' they'd laugh, but Kaisa knew behind the joking there was hurt. They didn't want her to change, nor lose her to England. Well, they've got me back now, Kaisa thought. She sighed and sat down to gaze at the view of the inner courtyard while she waited for her mother to get dressed.

'It's still cold out there. Are you sure you have enough on?'

Kaisa nodded, 'I've got Sirkka's jacket.' She surveyed her mother, who sat down opposite her at the kitchen table. People said Kaisa looked just like her, and there was no denying it. Often, especially recently, in Helsinki, the face looking back at Kaisa from Sirkka's bathroom mirror was a younger version of her mother. It was a more modern version of the woman who smiled happily from the framed black-and-white wedding day portrait that her mother still displayed on her dresser in the living room. Pirjo had always looked younger than her age. Now, at 49, she sported curly, mid-length, blonde hair. Today (for a jog!), she'd made her face up with light blue eyeshadow that went with her shiny jacket and pale pink lipstick that matched her nails. She looked good, and the only difference in their appear-ance, apart from the make-up, was that Kaisa's mother was a couple of kilos heavier and a few centimetres shorter. People often – no, always – thought they were sisters when they were out and about, a compliment her mother revelled in. However, such comments made Kaisa feel invisible; the thought of her mother appearing to be in her twenties rendered Kaisa's existence insignificant, or even impossible.

The two women jogged along the now quiet Linnankoskenkatu towards the sea. In that morning's *Helsingin Sanomat* there had been an article about the ice no longer being thick enough to support people's weight. The two women therefore decided to run on the path along the shore. You could make out dark patches in the middle of the sea where the ice was melting.

'It's very late for the sea to be iced over, isn't it?'

'Hmm,' Pirjo said.

Kaisa looked at her mother. The sun was high up in the piercing blue sky, but there was a harsh wind, which made running more difficult than usual.

Instead of replying to Kaisa's comment, Pirjo lifted her eyes to her daughter. 'So, Kaisa, have you come to a decision about what you are going to do?'

Kaisa had anticipated this question, and thought it to be the reason she'd been invited on this Sunday jog.

'No, not yet.' She didn't want to tell her mother about the meeting with the bank manager, nor her lunch and failed date with Tom. Both of these things were just what her mother wanted to hear. She wanted Kaisa to make a life for herself in Helsinki, near to her and Sirkka, but Kaisa still wasn't sure she wanted to stay in Helsinki. After Vappu's visit, and the revelation that Matti had taken his own life, all Kaisa could think about was fleeing the city. But where to? England? Where would she live?

At least she now knew the awful pictures that Matti took would never be seen by anybody. Right after Vappu's visit, she'd cut the negatives into tiny pieces and put them in the bin. When she'd dropped the plastic bag into the large container in the courtyard she'd felt a huge weight lift off her chest. Her life with Matti was history, and her marriage with Peter was history. She knew she shouldn't care about Peter anymore, but she couldn't stop loving him. She was still his wife – for now at least – and obviously Peter thought that too. Even though the letter had been cold, or positively chilly, it was a letter. With money. The cash had angered and saddened Kaisa at first, but afterwards she wondered if that was Peter's way of saying that he still loved her?

'Oh,' Pirjo said.

'It's difficult, because I don't really know what Peter is planning, or thinking.'

'I know, darling, but it's been two months now, and ...'

Kaisa said nothing. It was upsetting to say the word, 'divorce', even though she needed to face it. Really, she thought it was too soon, but how could she explain this to her mother?

'Did Sirkka tell you her news?'

Kaisa stopped and turned to face her mother, 'No.' She was panting, suddenly feeling very out of breath.

Her mother took hold of Kaisa's arms, and said, 'You know that man in Lapland? Jussi?'

'Yes, but I thought that was over?'

'No, it isn't. He's coming to see her for a weekend.'

Kaisa stared at her mother. 'Did she ask you to tell me this?'

'Er, no, not really, but …'

'So why did you?'

'Well, I thought you needed to know. I mean, the flat isn't big enough for two, really, so when Jussi is there …'

Kaisa began jogging again. Her mind was in disarray; why hadn't her sister said anything about this development in her on-off relationship with Jussi?

The next morning Sirkka was fast asleep when Kaisa heard the post fall onto the mat in the small hall. She got quietly out of bed, listening to her sister's gentle snores coming from the open door to her bedroom.

There was the morning paper, *Helsingin Sanomat,* which Kaisa usually read cover to cover, soaking in the news and studying the job adverts, although there weren't many positions advertised in the Monday edition. But on the mat, together with the newspaper, was a letter. It was a large brown envelope, addressed to her in Smuggler's Way, but someone had crossed out the address and put Sirkka's address on the side. She scanned the writing, but it wasn't Peter's hand. Kaisa tore open the letter. There was a magazine inside, and a single sheet of handwritten text.

'Dear Kaisa,

I wanted to write to you to tell you how sorry I am about all that has happened. I feel responsible for some of my cousin's behaviour, and feel that my involvement encouraged him. You must believe me that I had no idea of his true intentions towards you. Had I known, I wouldn't have met up with you in London. Duncan merely told me that you were the wife of a good friend, smart and talented, and looking for a job. Of course, as soon as I met you, I realised he was right, and purely because of that I offered you the job. Please believe me, I had no ulterior motive, other than wanting to employ a talented person.

You must also know that I am not speaking to Duncan, and will not do so until he apologises to you fully.'

. . .

Kaisa thought back to the letter she'd received from Duncan, in which he'd apologised for his behaviour but in the same breath invited her to see him in the country, so she didn't really think his apology was sincere.

'But I am also writing to let you know that I have left Sonia *magazine to work in an exciting venture that I have known about for some time. Your situation did, I admit, play a part in my decision to leave commercial magazine publishing and enter more serious journalism. I am proud to tell you that I am now Chief Editor of* Adam's Apple, *a feminist publication, produced since 1973 by a women's commune whose work I admire. We carry stories of oppression against women from around the world, but also give advice to women on how to be a feminist today.*

I am writing to ask you if you'd consider coming to help us in this cause? I cannot promise a large salary, but it will be a worthwhile job, a chance to play a role in an important publication. The Scandinavian countries are so much further ahead in the cause for equality, and we would be delighted to have you onboard to share your knowledge and enthusiasm. I know you are a fellow feminist; I remember our discussions. And I remember you telling me that you wanted a job where you could make a difference. Well, here I am offering you one. I've enclosed the latest issue of Adam's Apple, *so you can see what kind of magazine it is.*

Please think about my proposal and write to me.

Yours sincerely,

Rose'

Kaisa reread the letter three times before she could quite comprehend what it meant. She began leafing through the copy of the magazine, which to her looked very left-wing. The cover had a picture of three women against the backdrop of a coal mine, with the caption 'Women Winning the Strike'. So they were pro the miners. As a Finn, having lived all her life in the shadow of the Soviet Union, she was naturally sceptical about communism, but as a student of Political Science, she knew that the left-wing in the UK had about the same ideologies as the Coalition Party in Finland, which was the right-wing party. And Rose was right, she wanted to make a difference, and she was passionate about women's rights. She felt the familiar butterflies in the stomach: a *real* job in London! A job where she could make a difference to women's lives. Rose had said in her letter the magazine was produced by a women's commune. What, she wondered, was it like working in a women's commune in London? Did they all live where they worked, and was it a squat? She imagined a derelict old Victorian house without plumbing, cold and damp, with a garden full of faeces. No, she couldn't imagine Rose in an environment like that. They must have proper offices if Rose was part of the organisation. Kaisa looked at the magazine again, and found that the address was Clerkenwell Close, London EC1R. Kaisa tiptoed back into the lounge, aware of her sister's gentle snoring as she passed her bedroom. She found the *London A-Z*, which she'd sentimentally packed in her suitcase when leaving the married quarter at Smuggler's Way. She found Clerkenwell Close and saw it was just a little north of Fleet Street, the area where all the newspapers were produced. Surely that was respectable enough?

8

When Kaisa had spent three weeks sleeping on her sister's sofa, Sirkka came home from work one evening and asked to speak to her. It was just past seven and Kaisa was watching *Coronation Street*. There seemed to be nothing but English programmes on Finnish TV, which reminded Kaisa of her old life in Portsmouth and Helensburgh. It seemed utterly unfair to her, but at the same time she thought it was a punishment she deserved.

'Have you thought about what you're going to do?' Sirkka asked after Kaisa had made coffee for them both. They were sitting facing each other at the small table in the kitchenette. Her sister looked tired; she'd just finished a week-long shift of ten-hour days, two of which had begun at 6.30 am.

'About what?' Kaisa asked.

Sirkka sighed. 'About your future!'

Kaisa stared at her sister.

'It's really lovely to have you here, but you can't stay here forever, watching English soap operas.'

Kaisa tried but couldn't stop the tears that began running down her face.

'Oh, Little Sis, what are we going to do with you?'

'I'm sorry, I just can't seem to …'

Sirkka stood up and hugged her sister. 'Look, I'm doing this for your own good. I know it's hard, but I think it's time to decide what you are going to do.'

Kaisa cried a little more against her sister's shoulder and then, taking the piece of tissue Sirkka offered, wiped her tears away and blew her nose. 'I've been looking at the job adverts in *Helsingin Sanomat*, but they all want you to have work experience, and I don't have any.'

Sirkka sat down again and took Kaisa's hands in hers. 'Look. You have a good degree from a good university – something a lot of a people would kill for – but you do need to take the job search seriously if you want to stay here.'

Kaisa nodded.

'Mum and I've been talking. There is a chance she could find you a job at Neste. They're growing and need staff, especially graduates.'

Kaisa shook her head, 'Working in the same office as mum? You must be joking.'

Sirkka returned her smile, 'It's vast, their HQ in Espoo. You might never see her!'

'All the same. I think I'll find something myself.'

'There's a girl.' Sirkka yawned again and looked down at her hands.

They were quiet for a moment. The noise from a tram trundling past the block of flats broke the silence between them. Kaisa noticed for the first time that there were faint lines around her sister's eyes and mouth. We are getting older, she thought. We're no longer the youngest girls in the disco, the most fresh-faced and fashionable in a bar.

'There is something else.' Sirkka sighed and lifted her blue eyes to Kaisa.

'What?' Suddenly Kaisa thought about money. Of course, her sister needs her to pay rent! 'Look, as soon as I get a job, I'll pay you …'

Sirkka smiled down at her hands and shook her head. 'No, you can stay here as long as you like, it's not that!'

'So …'

Sirkka took a deep breath in, and lifted her eyes to Kaisa once more. 'Matti has been asking after you.'

'What?' Kaisa couldn't help but raise her voice.

Sirkka took Kaisa's hand into hers once more. 'Look, he comes into the hotel from time to time. I can't stop him now, can I?' she said quickly, and added, 'and tonight, he asked me about you.'

'How …?'

Sirkka leaned closer to Kaisa. 'It's a small town, and you know he lives quite nearby.'

Kaisa's sister told her how on one night months ago, Matti, Kaisa's ex-fiancé, had turned up at the hotel where Sirkka was working. She'd been helping out in the bar because one of the waitresses had been ill, when she had suddenly been faced with Matti.

'You can imagine, I nearly had a bloody heart attack!' Sirkka said and smiled, but seeing Kaisa's straight face, she continued to tell her that they'd exchanged a few words. Sirkka had told him how she and Pirjo had moved back to Helsinki.

'He's still as annoying as ever,' Sirkka said, 'telling me that he was glad we'd come to our senses and returned to the motherland. He sounded like our father.'

Kaisa couldn't believe her ears, or rather she struggled to hear Sirkka's words.

'Anyway, since then he's been in a few more times, and he always makes a point of saying hello, whether I'm in reception, the restaurant, the bar or wherever. He comes by on his way home from work.'

Kaisa had a terrible thought. She looked at her sister's face, 'Surely you're not?'

Sirkka laughed, 'Oh God, no! Kaisa, for goodness sake, I'm not that desperate!'

Kaisa felt bad, and took hold of her sister's hand. 'Sorry, I'm being impossible. Tell, me what did he say about me?'

Sirkka sighed. 'Well … he'd seen you on the street, I don't know when. As I said, it's a small town and he must drive past our block of flats every day. He just wanted to know how you were. He seemed genuinely concerned.'

Kaisa gazed at her sister's face. 'What did you tell him?' she asked even though she knew the answer.

Sirkka looked down at her hands again, 'I'm sorry, I blurted it out before I knew what I was doing. I get so busy at the hotel, you know, and …'

'It's OK,' Kaisa said.

'Anyway, he says he's got something of yours he wants to give back.'

In bed that night Kaisa couldn't sleep. She tried not to think about what Sirkka had told her about Matti. It was just too much.

But after the chat with her sister, Kaisa knew she had to work harder to take charge of her life. It was funny how their roles had changed, she thought. Whilst studying in Hanken, and being engaged to be married to Matti, Kaisa had seemed the one who had a plan in place for the rest of her life. Sirkka, after a string of unsuitable boyfriends, and even after getting her qualification as Maitre d'Hotel, hadn't settled in one job, or one place, but had flitted between Lapland, Helsinki and Stockholm, never wanting to set down roots anywhere. Apart from the mysterious man in Lapland, whom Sirkka rarely spoke of, there didn't seem to be any other boyfriends, unsuitable or not, on the horizon. Again, Kaisa felt a pang of guilt; her preoccupation with her new life in England had made her selfish and ignorant of the lives of her family and friends. Now both her friend Tuuli and her sister Sirkka were getting on with their careers and appeared to be so much more in control of their love lives, too. To think she'd been the one with a clear head about what she wanted out of life!

Just look at her now. She had no idea if there still was a marriage to be saved with Peter. She had no idea what he was thinking. She had fled Scotland and left Peter to fend for himself, when it was her who had caused his present troubles. And now Matti wanted to meet her. Tossing and turning in bed, Kaisa thought how she had used Peter to disentangle herself from Matti, and how she had never really explained to Matti why she couldn't be with him anymore. Kaisa thought back to her behaviour after she'd met and fallen head-over-heels in love with Peter. Had she even told Matti that it hadn't merely been Peter, or meeting another man, that had made her relationship with him impossible? Had she ever told him that she'd been doubting their engagement even before she met Peter, worried about their seven-year age gap, and how young she had been, only fifteen, when they'd first made love? She knew she'd never told him how his domineering mother had made her feel trapped and inadequate. She shuddered when she remembered those long weekends in the cottage by the lake, when she had spent hours standing in the hot, stuffy kitchen preparing food and washing up, while Matti sat reading a newspaper or one of his firearms magazines in the shade of the porch outside. Whatever the rights and wrongs of their relationship, surely Matti deserved to know why she had ended it so abruptly? She decided to phone the number her sister had given her and agree to meet him. But as Kaisa thought about what she would say to him, she realised she couldn't imagine facing her ex-fiancé now. Now that she had another failed relationship behind her. Now that she had abandoned another man. Betrayed another man with someone else. Oh God, it was as if there was a string of men lying in Kaisa's wake, men whom she had betrayed and stopped loving. Perhaps there was something wrong with her?

Matti was already sitting at a table at the far end of the café when Kaisa arrived. It was a smallish place on Runeberg Street where, Kaisa remembered, they would sometimes have coffee and cake after a film in the Adlon cinema next door. As she walked past the small movie theatre, Kaisa saw it was closing down and felt a surge of melancholy. She remembered the last film they'd seen there – *Autumn Sonata* by Ingmar Bergman. It was about a complicated relationship between a mother and daughter, and Kaisa recalled that while she had loved the film, Matti hadn't liked it at all. Afterwards they'd sat in this same café, not talking, after Kaisa had – in vain, as it turned out – tried to convey the brilliance of Ingrid Bergman's performance as the famous concert pianist mother, and how good Liv Ullman had been as the long-suffering daughter.

The café hadn't changed; it was still a dark room, starkly furnished with small black round tables and French-style chairs with curved backs. There was a large window overlooking the street, and Matti must have been watching her walk up to the door, because he was looking straight at Kaisa when she entered. He was standing by a table in the far corner, and when Kaisa reached him, she was surprised to find he was a lot shorter than Peter. She knew he was only slightly taller than her, but the difference seemed significant now. He still had the dark hair, though she noticed it was thinning a little at the top. Kaisa couldn't believe she had spent so many years with this man. He seemed like a stranger to her now. And he was so much older. Kaisa did a quick calculation and realised he would be 31. The age her mother had been when they all moved to Sweden! It seemed inconceivable to her that she'd kissed and made love to him. Kaisa shuddered at the memory of their life together.

Matti and Kaisa stood awkwardly for a moment, not knowing how to greet each other. Eventually Matti reached out his hand. 'Hello Kaisa,' he said and indicated for her to sit down.

Matti's grip on her hand was firm, and warm, but Kaisa removed her fingers from his as soon as politely possible.

'I haven't ordered anything yet,' Matti said. 'Would you like a cake, or a cinnamon bun?' His unsmiling eyes were steady on Kaisa and she wondered if he was still angry at her. Suddenly she remembered that you could never tell with him unless he was really enraged, when his brown pupils would expand and his cheeks would get a slightly flustered pink hue.

Kaisa looked at the counter a few tables away, and spotted some *Aleksanterinleivos,* her favourite jam-filled cake with pink icing, in the glass cabinet.

Matti offered to go and get the cakes and coffees, and while he was safely out of the way, Kaisa removed her coat. She'd thought long and hard about what to wear to this awful meeting that she didn't really want to have, and had eventually decided on a cream jumper and jeans. She certainly didn't want to wear anything sexy, or feminine. Now she remembered that Matti hated jeans, but it was too late. Besides, she could wear what she liked. Her heart raced and she felt dampness in her armpits under the jumper. She sat down and tried to calm herself. She suddenly remembered that Sirkka had said Matti had something for her. What could it be? She tried to smile when she saw Matti walk towards her with the tray of coffees and cakes. He, too, had chosen an *Aleksanterinleivos.*

'So, you're back in Finland,' Matti said while he was munching on the sweet cake. He glanced pointedly at her left hand where she still wore her engagement and wedding rings.

'Yes, but I'll be going back soon.' Kaisa was surprised at her own lie, but she didn't want to give Matti the satisfaction of thinking her marriage was over. She began fiddling with her rings, turning the diamonds the right way up. 'Peter is away at sea, so I thought I might as well come over and stay with my sister and mother for a while.'

Matti had stopped eating. Another thing Kaisa had forgotten was how straight he held his back, even when sitting down. Even here in a café, enjoying a cake, he was behaving as though he was on some army parade ground. He now looked at Kaisa and said, 'That's not what your sister told me.'

'Really?' Kaisa tried to keep her voice level, but she heard the shrill tone. She couldn't look at Matti.

'Sirkka thinks you're getting a divorce,' Matti said and touched Kaisa's hand.

9

That night in bed Kaisa cried, silently without waking Sirkka. Her sister had been working late, and when she came in around midnight Kaisa had pretended to be asleep. She couldn't believe Sirkka had actually told Matti about her troubles. She had no right!

But Matti knowing about her separation, however temporary, hadn't been the worst of it.

Kaisa couldn't believe how stupid she had been. She thought of how in love – or lust – she must have been to have done what Matti had asked her. And how even more stupid to have forgotten, or pretended to have forgotten, about the existence of the photographs. A cold wave had run through her body when Matti had brought out the worn-out yellow folder and handed it to her.

'I have a new girl now, so I thought you'd like to have these back,' he'd said, grinning. 'She's sixteen. Innocent and pure just like you were.'

Kaisa hadn't listened to Matti as he told her about this new conquest. As if in a dream, she saw him lift the flap and look at the first photo in a stack of some ten, fifteen prints. In the photo, Kaisa was lying on a bed, in her old room in the small flat in Lauttasaari that Pirjo had rented after the divorce from Kaisa's father. Kaisa was naked, apart from a pink silk scarf tied around her small waist, and lying on her tummy. Her upper body was lifted, with her arm supporting her head, revealing her small, pert breasts, her pink nipples echoing the colour of the scarf. Her expression, looking straight at the camera, was the same she'd seen on the sex magazines she'd so eagerly, but with a huge feeling of shame, studied while working at the R-Kiosk the summer she'd been seduced by Matti. Her face showed pure lust. But that wasn't the worst of it. The worst of it was what was showing in the lower half of her body. Her bottom was slightly lifted, and with her left knee pulled towards her tummy, Matti behind the camera had had an uninterrupted view of her most private parts from behind.

In the café, Kaisa had quickly put the photos away, and buried the packet deep inside her handbag. Soon after this she'd left, trying to stop the tears of shame just behind her eye sockets.

She now remembered vividly the day Matti had convinced her to pose for the photos. He'd been telling her how beautiful she was, like a model, and during a weekend when both her sister and mother were away, they had spent the whole two days in bed. Matti had taught Kaisa things she'd never heard of, how she could satisfy him, but also herself. Something inside of her had flipped; she'd been a different person, she'd imagined herself as one of the women in those magazines, full of lust, just thinking about how best to be fucked, how best to suck, lick and bite to arouse Matti, her new grown-up boyfriend. All she had wanted to do was to please him, and pleasing him had felt good. When Matti had brought out the camera, she had felt even more aroused, and had done everything he had asked of her; posed in every way he had wanted her to. Even the scarf had been his idea.

Afterwards, during the four years they spent together, Kaisa had felt embarrassed each time Matti had shown her the photos, which he kept in a locked drawer in his bedroom. Once, as a joke, he'd said, 'You shouldn't be ashamed, they're so good they should be in a magazine.'

Kaisa had been horrified and had made him promise never to show them to anyone.

How could she have forgotten about their existence?

Now, lying in bed she knew that if she was honest with herself, she hadn't forgotten, but with the love she felt for Peter, the love that was so different from anything she'd ever felt for Matti, she'd stopped thinking about them. The idea of asking Matti to give the photos back, or even of discussing them with him, was so repulsive that she'd let it be, hoping he – in his rage – would have destroyed them himself.

That was obviously not what had happened. Kaisa felt sick thinking that he would have been looking at them during all the years she'd been with Peter. She felt violated by Matti. Thinking back, she had been so young, barely sixteen when the photos had been taken. Whereas Matti had seemed like a grown-up, at 23. He'd certainly been more experienced, in sex, as in everything else. Had he taken the photos as some kind of insurance, to have something hanging over her if she changed her mind and didn't marry him after all? Kaisa shook her head. No, if nothing else Matti was honourable. Besides, surely he would have used them against her when she fell for Peter? And why give them back to her now? Suddenly Kaisa thought of something. He had given her the prints, but what about the negatives? Were they tucked inside the sleeve of the packet as they sometimes were? With her heart thumping, Kaisa got out of bed, picked up her handbag, and tiptoed into the kitchen.

She found the packet, took out the photos, and not wishing to look at them, turned them face down on the kitchen table. She spread the photos, feeling between them, but there was nothing there. Next her fingers searched through the paper sleeve, looking for a strip of black film, but there was nothing inside the envelope, and the see-through pocket on the side of the packet was empty. The negatives had been taken out.

After the discovery of the missing negatives, Kaisa hardly slept. She lay awake, trying to make herself have sweet dreams by thinking of other things, of Peter, and how wonderful their love-making had been. But it seemed he no longer loved her. Rather than cry, again, and feel helpless, she suddenly realised, in the dead of night, that she must take charge of her own life. Never again would she be taken advantage of in the way Matti had, and even Peter had, not understanding how difficult life as a Navy wife would be for her. Hadn't he just left her to it, expecting her to cope with his absences, and the different language, culture and people in Britain, on her own? Always just worrying about his own career, not taking into account her ambitions for a meaningful job of her own?

Kaisa still loved Peter, she knew that, and she also knew she'd do almost anything for him, but she also needed to live her own life. She decided she'd start applying for jobs in earnest, and find a place to live. She'd stop waiting for a letter from Peter, and ask Tuuli if there were any jobs in the bank where she worked. She needed to get out of Sirkka's flat, and out of this area, where she might bump into Matti any day. Kaisa turned over and punched her pillow hard. She had wanted to scream at Sirkka for talking to him; for telling him anything about her present life. She wanted to go back in time and not be so stupid as to agree to be photographed naked and full of lust. But she couldn't. What would Sirkka have done in a similar situation? Not that she could imagine her in a similar situation. Apart from one boyfriend, who always drank too much, Sirkka kept in touch with all her exes. For Kaisa, just seeing Matti in the flesh was repulsive. Besides, her current situation would bring nothing but pleasure to her ex-fiancé. Hadn't he predicted as much when she'd left him for the Englishman?

'It won't last,' he'd said when he'd phoned her the last time. She'd still been living in the flat in Lauttasaari, the small apartment belonging to Matti's aunt, which Kaisa had eventually been unable to afford. She'd spent all her small student loan on expensive telephone calls to England, mooning over Peter's letters and failing her exams, so much so that the university had stopped her grant.

Kaisa opened her eyes and looked at the shadows the streetlights painted on the wall of the darkened room. This had to stop. She would have to stop running her life according to the men in her life. The thought sent a current through her body. She flung off the duvet and sat bolt upright in bed. She listened to see if Sirkka was asleep in the room next door, and heard the faint sounds of steady, sleepy breathing. Slowly, so as not to wake Sirkka, she got out of bed again and tiptoed into the kitchen. She shut the door gently behind her and in the light coming from the streetlamp outside wrote on the notepad that her sister kept for shopping lists:

TO DO:
    1. Find a job
    2. Find a flat
    3. Forget about men

Kaisa stared at the piece of paper and immediately did the opposite of the last item on the list: she thought about Peter. She could almost feel his strong arms around her, and hear his husky voice murmuring 'I love you,' just before falling asleep after making love with her, his arm heavy on her waist. The last time they'd made love was on the day of the fight between Peter and Duncan. Their bodies fitted so well together, it was almost mechanical, had it not been so wonderful and awful at the same time. Kaisa had wanted to hold onto Peter tightly, wishing the love-making would last forever, wishing they could shut out the rest of the world and stay in bed, entwined in each other's arms. Afterwards Kaisa had cried silently into her pillow, while Peter turned over and fell sleep. She hadn't been able to settle and had marvelled at Peter's capacity to go into a deep slumber so quickly, so effortlessly. Now, after four weeks of not hearing from him, she began to wonder if her initial worries, long before they married, were justified after all. Perhaps he couldn't *really* commit, couldn't *really* care about her.

Kaisa looked at the note again and shook her head. What had she just written? 'Forget about men!' She tiptoed back to bed and willed herself to sleep.

The next day Kaisa received another letter. This time she recognised the handwriting straight away.

'Dear Kaisa,

I hope you are keeping well and enjoying having some time with your mother and sister. Life here in Helensburgh hasn't changed much; spring is on its way, they say, but the slightly warmer temperatures seem to have brought us even more rain! There is the odd daffodil out in our garden, bravely fighting the wind and rain, but otherwise the landscape is as miserably grey as ever. Nigel is away again – you perhaps know that the boat is on patrol now until who knows when? I have been told that we might see the boys sometime early summer in June, but you know how it is, 'I have to kill you if I tell you' and all that. My pregnancy seems to be going well, the due date is June 22, by which time Nigel should be back. Wish me luck that everything goes well this time! Especially as I don't have you to look after me and lean on if the worst happens again.

A new family has moved into your old married quarter, but the wife, Phyllis, is utterly dull. She has a little girl of three and a boy who's just about to start school. All she talks about is which public school is best and how her son is allergic to nuts. Oh, how I miss you, Kaisa!

I hear Peter is doing alright in Plymouth. I hear he's living on the base, which I presume is a temporary solution until he finds you two a married quarter down there. Nigel and I had a very happy few years down south – Plymouth beats Helensburgh hands down, I tell you.

But the reason I wanted to write to you – apart from to ask how you are – is that I have heard some disturbing news. Now, this may just be gossip, and most probably is, but I really felt that as your good friend I ought to tell you. Before he went away, Nigel heard a chap say in the wardroom that Peter is seeing someone. Of course, he told the guy off, and said not to spread silly gossip like that, but the fellow was quite certain. You see, he is a distant cousin of this girl, Jackie, and he said he'd heard straight from her at a party in London that she and Peter were an item. I've been really disturbed by this piece of stupid gossip, and didn't know what to do, but felt that you should know. I'm not sure who this Jackie person is, and if there is

any truth in it (which there most probably isn't!), but if I were you, I'd get
myself back to Plymouth sharpish.
　　Sorry to bring you such silly gossip, and I hope I haven't done the wrong
thing by telling you.
　　Your friend,
　　Pammy xx'

Kaisa looked at the heavy yellow Basildon Bond paper, where Pammy had,
with a neat hand, written the deadly words. Had Kaisa understood the
English correctly? To be sure, she reread the letter three times, and each
time she scanned the paper her chest grew tighter. At the end of the final
read she was struggling to breathe, and got up to get a glass of water. She
was on her own in her sister's flat. Sirkka had gone to see a friend – it was
her day off.

　　Kaisa sat down at the kitchen table and put her head in her hands. Peter
with Jackie? It couldn't be true. But she was reminded of the time early on
in their marriage when Peter had taken her to a party at Jackie's beautiful
apartment in London. She'd asked Kaisa how it was to be married to Peter
in a way that had made Kaisa suspicious and jealous. She'd also told Kaisa
that her hard-won degree from Finland would be worthless in England. It
was obvious the girl didn't like Kaisa, and thought Peter had made a
mistake by marrying her. Of course, Jackie didn't say as much, but as her
cold eyes peered at Kaisa, her manicured red nails holding a cigarette, Kaisa
knew immediately that Jackie had history with Peter. Peter and Kaisa had
had a fight later, during which Peter admitted that Jackie used to have a
crush on him. He'd not admitted to a relationship, but now Kaisa wondered
if he'd lied to her then? Had Jackie and Peter been together before he'd got
to know Kaisa – or even when they'd decided to be 'free to see other
people' while Kaisa was finishing her studies in Helsinki? To have an open
relationship, Kaisa reminded herself, had been Peter's idea, and his suggestion had nearly broken her heart.

　　Kaisa looked at her sister's wall calendar, pinned above the kitchen
table. She'd been in Helsinki just over four weeks. In just one month Peter
had already found himself a girlfriend.

　　It was also news to Kaisa that Peter was in Plymouth – he hadn't even
bothered to write to tell her where he was living.

　　Kaisa slumped down at the table and cried. She was sobbing when she
heard the doorbell.

　　Outside stood her mother.

'What's the matter?' She walked through the door and past Kaisa.

'Why aren't you at work?' Kaisa managed to blurt out between sobs.

'I have the day off, you know, because of the conference this weekend.'

Kaisa nodded. She'd forgotten. Her mother had said she'd be at home on Thursday and then travel to some work-related weekend in Eastern Finland on Friday. She was wearing smart white running pants and a matching jacket with red and blue stripes on the side of the trousers and top.

'I came down to see if you fancied going for a jog.' Pirjo's clear blue eyes were on Kaisa, 'But what's happened?'

Kaisa made some more coffee, sat down and translated the letter for Pirjo.

'And this Pammy, who is she?'

Kaisa glanced at her mother. She noticed that Pirjo was wearing make-up to go for a run, and in spite of the hollow feeling she had in her stomach, and the utter despair she was feeling, her lips lifted into a smile.

'She's a friend, a good friend.'

'You sure about that?'

'Yes!' Kaisa said impatiently.

Her mother straightened her back. 'No need to be so irritable. I'm just saying that good friends don't usually ...'

'She's a really, really good friend!' Kaisa tried to keep her voice level, 'that's not the issue here. Peter has found someone else!'

Pirjo was quiet, and put her arms around Kaisa.

Kaisa allowed herself to be hugged and comforted by her mother for a while.

'The worst thing is, I think they've been together before,' she whispered.

Her mother let go of Kaisa. 'What?'

Kaisa told Pirjo about the breakfast party, and about Peter's confession that she'd had a thing for him.

'That doesn't mean that they've been together,' Pirjo said. Her eyes were kind, and she took the tissue from Kaisa's hand and wiped away her tears.

Kaisa let herself be comforted by her mother. She put her head on her shoulder and Pirjo hugged her hard. 'I know Peter. He is a very good boy and he would most certainly write and tell you this himself.'

Kaisa didn't say anything. She wanted to believe her, but she also knew Peter. Hadn't he left the girl he was seeing when they'd first met simply by ignoring her letters? And that girlfriend hadn't committed the ultimate sin and been unfaithful to him.

10

Since being in Helsinki Kaisa had avoided the bank on the corner of South Esplanade and Erottaja, where the ladies had followed the long-distance romance between Kaisa and Peter closely. It'd been one of her former colleagues who'd organised the invitation to the British Embassy party where Kaisa had met her Englishman. But now that she was looking for a job, a natural place to start was the KOP bank. She'd telephoned her old bank manager and he'd agreed to see her.

'So when did you come back?' Mr Heinola's handshake was firm. Kaisa felt her resolve to appear confident and ambitious about a career in the bank melt under her old boss's direct gaze. Kari Heinola wore clear-framed glasses over a round face. He was slightly shorter than Kaisa, and she noticed his fair hair was thinning on top. He asked her to sit down on the opposite side of his large desk.

'About a month ago.' Kaisa looked at her hands.

'And you're settling back here?'

'Yes.' Kaisa's voice broke, even though she'd tried hard to keep it level.

The bank manager leaned back in his leather chair and placed his hands in front of his face, fingers tapping against each other.

Kaisa kept her eyes on Mr Heinola, and waited.

'It was hard going in England, was it?'

Kaisa found herself telling her old boss how difficult it was to get a job, not just as a foreigner, with a foreign qualification, but also as a Navy wife. She poured out the frustration she'd felt during the long six months she'd spent, bored and frustrated, looking for jobs, first in Portsmouth and then in Scotland, where her career prospects were even worse. She told him about the job at DMS, and how her duties had increased there, but how she had then been refused a permanent job merely on the grounds of her marriage to a Navy officer. She also told him about the job offer on a magazine in London, and how she'd had to turn that down due to Peter's job on a nuclear missile-carrying submarine.

'Leave it with me, Kaisa.' Mr Heinola got up and reached out his hand. 'I'll see if there are any opportunities within our bank. You've always been a smart girl, and a good worker, so although I can't promise anything, I will try my best.'

Kaisa left her old boss's office the same way she'd entered, by the staff door on the side of the building, which led straight onto Erottaja. She'd not been brave enough to go downstairs to the banking hall to meet her old colleagues. Explaining how she'd ended up back in Helsinki to her old boss had been demanding enough for one day; she couldn't go through it all again with the friendly ladies.

Still, Kaisa felt jubilant that she'd managed that much. For the first time since her short-lived marriage ended on the day of the fight in Faslane, Kaisa felt in charge of her own life. This was, after all, what she had envisaged she'd do before she met Peter. Kaisa decided to celebrate with a coffee at the nearby Fazer café. She walked briskly across the Esplanade Park, not looking at the statue of Eino Leino, where Peter had given her sweet kisses and she had fallen firmly in love with him. Peter was now history; whatever her feelings towards him were, they could not be together, Kaisa could see that clearly. She needed to sort her life out, move on, get a job. Besides, she was fast running out of money. She was ashamed when she thought of the £100 Peter had insisted she take with her when he left her at Glasgow station. At first, Kaisa wouldn't hear of it, but Peter had insisted, saying, 'It's my duty to look after you. You're still my wife.' But everything in Helsinki was much more expensive than in Helensburgh. She'd calculated that if she continued to spend at the same rate she'd run out of money completely in a matter of days. Luckily, Sirkka had refused to take any money for rent, but Kaisa felt she needed to buy the odd bag of groceries, even though Sirkka often brought food home from the hotel.

Inside the Fazer café, while waiting to be seated, she stopped to dig out her purse from her handbag, to make sure she had enough money to pay. When she looked up, she saw the smiling face of a man looking down at her.

'Hello,' Tom said, 'lost something?'

Kaisa had forgotten how tall Tom was. The guy was positively towering over her. His eyes were dark and his light brown hair was a little shorter, and tidier, than she remembered. He was wearing an expensive-looking dark grey overcoat, which was open, revealing a suit underneath.

'No,' Kaisa felt suddenly as flustered as she had at Hanken when the two of them had played their cat and mouse game. 'This is ridiculous, pull yourself together,' Kaisa thought, straightening up.

For a moment neither said anything. Kaisa had turned away from Tom to watch a waitress clearing a table that had just been vacated by an older lady in a fur coat. The waitress was wearing a black dress and a frilly white cotton pinafore with a matching head band. The Fazer uniform. The whole place looked as if it was from the 1930s, which is why it was popular with the Helsinki upper classes. It made sense that Tom would come here for his lunch; it was one of the most expensive places in town. Kaisa cursed her frivolity; really, she couldn't even afford a coffee at the cheaper Happy Days Café opposite. There was, after all, no guarantee that her old boss would find a job for her. She should have gone straight home to Sirkka's flat after the interview and raided the fridge there. Now she was stuck here, having to deal with this rich boy. Although he looked like a man now, Kaisa still thought of him as a spoiled brat. He'd only ever been interested in her because he couldn't have her. But she couldn't leave now; behind Tom the queue had increased; if she left, it would look as if she was running away from him. She didn't want him to think he had such an effect on her.

'Here you are, a table for two,' the waitress said, looking at Tom and Kaisa.

'Er, we're not …' Kaisa began, but Tom said, 'Thank you,' and indicated with his stretched arm for Kaisa to go first.

'So, you're back,' he said after they'd given their overcoats to the waitress and been handed menus in exchange. They were sitting opposite each other in a corner table. Kaisa had been looking down at the small card, but now lifted her eyes and replied, 'Yes.' Kaisa examined Tom's face. She wondered how much he knew of her situation. Surely Tuuli wouldn't have told Ricky anything? This must just be the rich boy fishing.

Tom smiled, 'Well it's nice to see you.'

Kaisa didn't have time to reply before the waitress was back, with her pad and pen poised for their order. Kaisa hadn't even had time to read the menu properly, but Tom said confidently, 'I'll have today's special.'

'Same for me, please,' Kaisa said and hoped the bill wouldn't come to more than she had in her purse.

'And we'll have two glasses of the Chablis,' Tom added.

Kaisa didn't have time to protest. The waitress had taken the order and disappeared.

'Aren't you working?' she said simply, but Tom just laughed. Reaching into his pocket, he took out a packet of cigarettes and offered her one. As he brought the lighter – silver and engraved – close to her face, she saw something surprising in his eyes. A kind of gentleness that she'd not noticed before.

'What are you up to in Helsinki? Visiting?' Tom leaned back in his chair, and took a long drag from his cigarette.

'Well, yes, I suppose, a long visit.'

'Good, I'm in luck then,' he said and smiled. 'I'm just back myself.'

'Really?'

Tom told Kaisa that he'd been living in Milan with his parents for the last few months. 'My dad got me a job in a bank there, but it didn't work out.' He said, giving her one of his infectious smiles.

Kaisa couldn't help but smile back at him. These were more words than the two of them had exchanged during the whole of the four years they'd known each other in Hanken. Yet now it felt as if they were old friends.

The waitress came back with their wine, and Tom lifted his glass to hers. 'To you and me in Helsinki!'

Kaisa raised her glass too and they laughed. When the food came, they chatted some more. Tom said he wasn't working at the moment, but was 'meeting someone later, hence the suit.' Kaisa told Tom she'd probably be staying in Helsinki for a while. 'Perfect,' said Tom.

Kaisa grew serious at that remark, and a for a while both of them were quiet.

'Let's have another glass, my treat.' Tom said when the waitress came to collect their empty plates. The mystery dish of the day had turned out to be rather wonderful arctic pike with a parsley sauce. Kaisa just smiled. She couldn't resist this friendly rich boy. Her grin widened.

'What's so funny?'

'You know what we called your lot in Hanken?'

'No?'

'Oh, I don't think I should say.'

'But you have to now! You can't just give me that gorgeous smile of yours and then not say what brought it on.' Tom stretched over the table. His face was so close to Kaisa's she could have kissed those full lips.

Kaisa grew serious and leaned back in her chair, away from Tom. 'Rich boys,' she said quietly.

. . .

When Kaisa got to Sirkka's flat, there was a letter on the mat. This time she recognised the writing immediately. She picked up the blue Basildon Bond envelope and rubbed her hands together. She was frozen. She'd taken the wrong tram from Mannerheim Street, which meant she had to walk two blocks to Linnankoskenkatu. She'd been so confused after the lunch with Tom, which he'd insisted on paying for.

'I am the rich boy, after all,' he'd said and grinned.

His comment and the whole of the situation had made Kaisa feel very embarrassed, and she'd laughed nervously. All the same, it was a relief, because she wasn't sure she would have been able to pay the astronomical prices the place charged for food, or the fine wine. When Tom had asked for her telephone number while they waited for his change, she wrote down her sister's number. Tom then gave Kaisa his number. He was living in a flat in Ullanlinna, he told her. It was in the southern part of Helsinki, where the beautiful Jugend houses from the turn of the century were. It was Kaisa's favourite area of the city, and naturally the most expensive. Not a surprise that Tom would be living there, she thought.

She turned the envelope over in her hands. It was very thick and she wondered what that meant. Was he writing her a long letter of goodbye, or a long love letter? Perhaps the stories of Peter and Jackie were just rumours after all. Suddenly Kaisa was afraid to open the envelope. She gazed down at the cold street below. It was two degrees below zero, she read on the little thermometer attached to the outside of the kitchenette window. While she'd been walking from the tram stop, it had started snowing, the light white flakes falling gently onto the ground. An opaque carpet of snow was now covering everything outside, the tops of the street lights, the sand box by the side of the road, even part of the roof of a tram trundling past. It was getting darker, even though it was barely three o'clock, and the snow glimmered here and there against the steel grey sky. Kaisa sighed, sat down at the small table and tore open the blue envelope. Out fell British bank notes, and one sheet of written paper.

'Kaisa,

Hope you are keeping well. Please find enclosed £200. I will send you this each month after I get paid.

Send my regards to your mother and sister,
Peter'

. . .

Kaisa stared at the ten pound notes, scattered on the table in front of her, then re-read the letter. At the station in Glasgow Peter had promised to send her his new address, but week after week, there had been no correspondence from him.

After Pammy's letter, Kaisa understood why; he'd moved on. She didn't want to be the one to ask him about Jackie, because that would make it official in some way, so she hadn't written to him either. She still hoped it was mere gossip; she knew how easily stories like that began in the Navy. With bitterness, she remembered how Maureen had phoned to accuse her of having an affair with Jeff, Peter's best friend and best man. Remembering that ridiculous telephone conversation with one of the other Navy wives in Portsmouth had given her hope in the last few days.

But now this – just three cold sentences and money. The ten pound notes looked dirty to Kaisa. In addition to the detached tone of the letter, they added an extra layer of hurt to the lack of warmth, or love, in Peter's words. Kaisa looked at the handwritten lines that Peter's favourite fountain pen had made. At least he had taken that much care, to use his good pen, the one he saved for official Royal Navy correspondence and his love letters to her – when she had deserved them. But this time there were no kisses. How she now missed that little cross, which had been so puzzling when Peter first wrote to her, after their romantic meeting at the British Embassy in Helsinki. After he had explained the tradition to her, that little 'x' gained so much importance. She would often kiss the letters on that spot, hoping Peter had done the same before putting the sheet of paper in the envelope and posting it. But now, only eight months after their dream wedding, the kisses had disappeared from Peter's letters. Kaisa put her head in her hands. What had she done? How could she have been so stupid to spoil their love for each other? It was obvious now that she had lost him forever.

She examined the letter again. The address in the top right-hand corner was new: 'HMS *Orion, BFPO Ships, London.*' That must mean Pammy was right; he was living in the wardroom, on the base in Plymouth. Poor Peter, he didn't even have a home to go to. But then, she thought, he would have all his mates around him, drinking beer every night, not having to worry about a home, or a wife — a foreign, troublesome wife, who was always unhappy with something or other. And he could go and see Jackie whenever he was free.

Suddenly Kaisa felt anger. He could have written a few words to say where he was, and how he was. He could have said he was seeing someone else and made their split official. They were still married after all, and what had happened wasn't all her fault. Kaisa had entered the marriage not understanding that she would have to give up her career and follow her husband from one port to another, often at very short notice. Or that even if she'd chosen to stay put in Portsmouth, to pursue a career, and not move up to the isolation of Faslane, she'd have to accept that she would see her new husband only a few times a year. Or that most employers didn't understand — or value — her Finnish degree. And even if they had, many employees still didn't want to give jobs to Navy wives, because they knew they'd up and leave as soon as their husbands were posted elsewhere, whatever the wives said in job interviews.

Kaisa sighed. She did need the money, however. She counted the notes, picked up her coat and took the tram to the centre of town again. She walked up to a different bank on Alexi, and changed the Sterling notes to Finnish Marks. At least she had money again, she thought, as she slipped into Stockmann's department store and found a pay phone. She took out her diary and dialled a number.

'Hello,' the man at the end of the phone said.

'Hi, it's Kaisa. I just wanted to call and thank you for the lunch.'

11

P eter sat on his bunk and looked at the letter he'd just picked up from his pigeon hole in the cold and deserted hall outside the wardroom. Without thinking, he did what he always did when he saw Kaisa's handwriting on top of the envelope: he held it up to his face and breathed in the scent. A long time ago, it must have been their second or third meeting after the Embassy cocktail party in Helsinki, he'd asked her to put a little bit of her perfume on the sheets of paper before slipping them into the envelope. He remembered how Kaisa had been puzzled by his request but had promised to comply. After that, all her letters were soaked in perfume, so much so that he'd been teased about it as a young sub-lieutenant onboard his first submarine.

How long ago those heady and carefree days were now. But as he became aware of Kaisa's fragrance once again, he breathed it in all the same and carefully opened the seal.

'Dear Peter,

Thank you for your letter and the money. I will pay you back every penny once I have a job. There may be one in my old bank here in Helsinki. I went to see the manager yesterday and he seemed hopeful.

It's still very cold here. It snowed yesterday and overnight, and the ground is covered in a white blanket, making everything look pretty and clean.

Kaisa'

Peter reread the letter and stuffed it into a drawer of the desk by the window of his cabin. He sighed, picked up a thin but clean towel, and headed for the showers.

An hour later, he was drinking a pint in The Bank, a pub in the centre of Plymouth. It was Friday night and, as had become his custom, he was going for a few beers with the young, single, Part Three. The term used for a trainee officer onboard a submarine suited Simon particularly well, because he was a round-faced, pimply 19-year-old, and prone to taking things too seriously. He'd fallen for all but one of the practical jokes the others had played on him, including the old favourite 'Spar Lash'. Peter, too, had fallen for it on his first ship. In the joke, the Part Three is sent to look for a piece of wood and when he finds it, is asked to throw it overboard, at which point the Senior Officer says, 'Here you go, Spar...lash.' Of course the whole of the ship's company is in on the joke, and in the course of looking for the 'Spar Lash' the Part Three is sent around the boat several times, before someone hands him a piece of wood suitable for throwing overboard.

Peter would have preferred to spend his weekends with an officer more his age and rank onboard HMS *Orion*, the diesel boat he'd been demoted to after the disastrous events in Faslane, but apart from Peter, Simon was the only one who wasn't going home to a wife or girlfriend at the weekend. Peter liked Simon well enough and had become a bit like an older brother for him, dragging him home when he'd had too much beer, and making sure he wasn't picked up by any of the working girls along Union Street. And to be fair, Simon was good fun. For one thing, he didn't want to talk about Peter's court martial, a subject the other officers onboard never forgot to mention.

As usual, The Bank was heaving on a Friday night. There were a few sailors from HMS *Orion* there, too, and Peter lifted his pint in a greeting to the group of men standing and drinking a few feet away from him, their tight T-shirts displaying impressive sets of tattoos. Peter often wondered what made sailors think it a good idea to go through the pain of carving the name of a sweetheart on their flesh. Just as well he hadn't had the crazy idea of carving Kaisa's name on his biceps, he thought, and immediately decided to pull himself together.

He saw Simon emerge from the gents. 'Another round?' Peter asked. He'd have to cheer up before going to the Plymouth Yacht Club, a disco down The Barbican otherwise known as the 'Groin Exchange' (or 'the GX' for short).

By the time Peter and Simon had finished at The Bank there was a small queue outside the glass doors leading to the Yacht Club. The GX was downstairs, and as usual there was a fair number of local Plymouth girls there, but this time Peter also noticed a group of Wrens standing by the bar at one end of the dimly lit room. He recognised a shortish blonde girl who worked in the office at the base. She'd smiled at him when they'd passed each other in the corridor, and he seemed to remember talking to her on one occasion. But he couldn't remember her name. Did he even know it? She was wearing a pair of jeans and a light blue satin blouse, revealing the contour of her full breasts. Not bad for a split-arse. He lifted the glass of beer that Simon had given him towards the Wrens. 'You really that lazy?' Simon shouted into his ear, and Peter grinned. Yes, tonight he really did feel that lazy, he thought, and walked towards the group of girls.

Sam, or Samantha, had a rippling laugh, or a giggle really, and this was her reaction to almost everything Peter managed to shout into her ear in the loud club. Soon he took her to the dance floor, and during Alison Moyet's *All Cried Out*, he pulled her close and moved with her to the music. He kissed her and found she tasted of bubble gum. She let him put his hand on her round, firm buttocks, and then move it up to her back, feeling for her bra buckle. It was the traditional kind, not a front fastener, with just one hook. 'That'll be easy to deal with,' he thought. Removing his lips from the girl's mouth, he pressed himself harder against her. She responded by pushing her soft breasts against his chest. 'You're lovely,' he whispered in her ear. He moved his hand to her neck and she let out an involuntary sigh into his ear. Peter could feel himself harden, but he knew he must be patient. When the track finished, he pulled himself away from Sam and gave her a smile. 'Would you like a drink?' He went to join the crowd trying to attract the attention of the barman, who'd now been joined by a thin, pretty girl, with dangly earrings and short black hair. When she looked up from pulling a pint for a guy standing next to Peter, her eyes met his, and for a moment the two looked at each other. She had bright blue eyes, which contrasted with her black hair. Not her real colouring, Peter thought, and found himself wondering what hue her pubes might be.

'So, what will it be?' she eventually said and Peter gave her his order: 'A pint of Bass and a G&T.'

Peter couldn't take his eyes off the barmaid. When she bent down to get the small bottle of tonic from the other side of the bar, Peter noticed she had a tattoo of a swallow on the small of her back. Her arse was the shape of a heart, 'What's your name?'

The girl looked up. 'For me to know and you to find out. Two pounds, please.' She had a London accent.

'Daylight robbery,' Peter grinned and gave the girl the money.

She shrugged and moved to the next punter. Peter stood for a moment and watched her, but he was pushed away by other men trying to get to the bar.

Peter danced with Sam for the rest of the evening, and Simon got together with one of Sam's friends. At 1 am, he paid for a cab to the base, having made sure that Simon and his Wren were safely in a taxi of their own. Sam and Peter kissed in the back seat and when they arrived at the residential quarters they tiptoed across the linoleum floor towards the officers' cabins. It was obvious the Wren had done this before. As soon as they entered the hall leading up to the new wing of the Victorian building, where one corridor led to his quarters and another to that of the Wrens, she removed her shoes, grinned at him, and took his hand. But Peter didn't mind; it was better that way. As soon as they were inside his cabin, Sam removed her top and began kissing him. He took off his shirt and kicked off his trousers. As they kissed, Peter undid the clasp of her bra and, taking a step back, admired her large round breasts. He cupped them in his hands, noticing the unusually large areolas, before removing her jeans. She was wearing small, pink, lacy knickers. Sam took hold of him, and Peter groaned. She moved her hand up and down, and Peter had to think about Mrs Thatcher to stop himself from an embarrassing early loss of control. It had been too long. Sam wasn't a true blonde after all, Peter found, when she pulled down her own pants, but she wasn't too hairy. Peter pushed her gently onto the bunk and parted her legs. She made the right noises when he touched her between the legs, and when a few moments later Peter came on top of her, she responded with soft moans of pleasure.

Afterwards, when Peter was lying on his bunk watching Sam getting dressed, he reached out and took her hand. 'Come and sit down for a minute.'

'I've got to be off, I'm on duty tomorrow am.'

'Yeah, I know, but I just wanted to say ...'

'What?' Sam had brown eyes, Peter noticed and felt bad he hadn't seen them properly before.

'I'm married, you know.'

Sam looked down at her hands. She was buttoning up her now wrinkled satin blouse, 'Yeah, I'd heard.'

'And you know about the court martial, right?'

'Yep.'

'So, my life is pretty complicated at the moment.'

Sam didn't say anything.

'I'm sorry, but this can't go any further.'

She stood up and said, 'Sure. We had fun.'

'Definitely,' Peter said and kissed Sam quickly on the lips.

That morning at breakfast, Sam was in her uniform, sitting in the middle of the wardroom with three other Wrens. She gave Peter a quick look, and he heard some muffled giggles when he walked past their table. Peter nodded to the group and went to sit on his own in the corner of the large dining hall.

The Devonport wardroom was a large space in the old part of the Victorian building. When Peter had first entered the room after his appointment to HMS *Orion*, and seen the oil paintings of famous sea battles on the walls and models of ancient sailing ships hanging from its ceiling, he immediately wanted to show the place to Kaisa. But that wasn't to be.

The steward brought him a cup of tea and he ordered a full English. Opening that morning's copy of the *Telegraph*, he began reading an article about the housing market when two older officers from HMS *Orion* joined him. It was Saturday, and Peter wasn't on duty, and not in uniform, but the engineer and his oppo were wearing their ribbed Navy jumpers with the Lieutenant Commander's rank visible from the golden braid on the shoulders.

'Trapped last night?' James, the engineer grinned, nodding at the corner table where the Wrens were still making a show of Peter by nodding and grinning in his direction.

'Wouldn't you like to know,' Peter said. He turned back to his paper. James Sanders (his nickname was Sandy onboard, but Peter never used it to his face because he thought the guy was a complete prat) and his best mate onboard, Malcolm 'Mac' Rowbottom, sniggered. Peter knew both men had unattractive wives. He had met them at a 'families day' during the half-term holiday. Peter remembered how he'd walked into lunch that day and was faced with a noisy room full of wives and kids. He'd thought of Kaisa then, knowing how much she would have hated a 'families day' had she been with him, which, of course, she wasn't.

'You went to the GX last night, the Part Three told us.' Sandy wouldn't let it go.

Peter nodded. Luckily his breakfast had arrived and he began eating as quickly as he could.

'No water sports this time, eh Bonkie?'

Peter lifted his head up and looked at the man. Mac was sniggering next to his oppo, trying to hide the laughter in his linen napkin. James Sanders was the one officer onboard who kept reminding Peter of his sordid past. Every few days he came up with a new joke about it. This week's jibe was 'water sports', a reference to Peter's fight with Duncan at the Faslane base swimming pool. Peter suspected the engineer was bored with his own life, and jealous of Peter's (if only he knew). Still, he was becoming a nuisance. Once Peter had been appointed to *Orion*, and knew his career in the Navy wasn't over, that he'd been given another chance, he'd decided to put up with the inevitable jokes and jibes. Black humour was the life blood of the Navy, after all. If you couldn't joke, you shouldn't have joined. And he deserved it; he'd messed up. He'd even thought the nickname, 'Bonking Boy', shortened to 'Bonkie', was quite funny. But after a couple of months most of his fellow officers had let it be. (Although he was still known as 'Bonkie'.) Everyone except Sandy, that is. Peter wondered whether he lay in bed at night, thinking of new ways to torment Peter?

Now Peter gave Sandy a grin. 'Very funny.'

As Peter walked back to his cabin, his thoughts once again turned back to the events of the last few months. How he'd been standing in the cold community club in Helensburgh, in front of the Captain of the base at Faslane, and the President and the Sub-Lieutenant. How he'd been taken aback by the similarity of the court martial to court room dramas he'd watched on TV. And how he'd felt as if he was watching the proceedings rather than being part of them. In the end, he'd been found guilty of causing grievous bodily harm to a fellow officer and fined. Of course, even before the court martial he'd been dismissed his ship. And as Lawrence, his lawyer, had said outside the office afterwards, he'd been 'bloody lucky'.

Peter didn't see the dark-haired barmaid at the GX again until several weeks after he'd first spoken to her. He and the Part Three had been to the club a few more times, and Sam had been there too. Peter had taken her back to his cabin twice since the first time. He had to watch it, he told himself now, as he scanned the dark room at the Plymouth Yacht Club for the group of Wrens. It seems they'd given the club a miss this Saturday. Suddenly Peter remembered that Sam was going to see her parents in Yorkshire for the weekend. As his eyes moved along the room, he spotted the dark-haired girl smoking a cigarette on the other side of the bar.

'Back in a minute,' Peter said to Simon, and he made his way smartly towards the girl.

'Do you come here often?' he said, leaning towards the girl. He noticed she was a fair bit shorter than him. She was wearing a dark top, off one shoulder, revealing creamy white skin. 'No bra,' Peter thought and gazed at her small, perky breasts, which were visible under the thin fabric. Her skirt was short, and she was wearing thigh-length cream boots.

He'd taken her by surprise. She turned her face towards Peter, and smiled, getting the joke.

'I'm Peter,' he gave her his hand, taking advantage of the smile.

The girl considered the outstretched hand for a moment, and eventually slipped hers into it. Peter held onto her a moment longer than necessary, enjoying the feeling of the slender fingers in his grip. 'And you are?'

She told him her name was Valerie, 'Val for short.'

'Can I have my hand back now,' she said. Her face was unsmiling but there was a flicker in her dark eyes that Peter liked.

'And what do you do?' Peter said. She'd found the formal style funny, so Peter decided to carry on with the same tone.

Val told him she was down from London, 'Helping my uncle with this place.'

'And what do you do in London?'

'You are a nosy beggar, aren't you?' Val said and took a long drag on her cigarette. But she was smiling.

'So if you don't want to talk, how about a dance?'

Val displayed great style on the dance floor. Her slim body moved slowly, but rhythmically, with the music. Peter wondered if she was a dancer. When a slower piece by Phil Collins came on, she took Peter's hand and moved away from the dance floor. She leaned against the bar, where Peter had first seen her.

'You're a great dancer,' Peter said into her ear.

Val grinned and lit another cigarette.

'Would you like a drink?'

Val eventually told Peter that she was studying History of Art at Saint Martin's College in London. Her family was from Plymouth, and she'd come down for the weekend.

'You've got a real Cockney accent going on there,' he said.

Val laughed for the first time, 'Yeah, I share a house with a couple of Cockney rebels, and it's catching. But I can do Plymouth too.' Val launched into a West Country accent, and Peter replied in his best Wiltshire drawl.

'Got to get tis straw out of mi mouth and get mi tracktoor,' he said, and again Val laughed.

At the end of an evening spent dancing and talking, Peter asked Val if he could see her again.

'Sure,' she replied and they agreed to meet up the next day. Knowing everything would be shut in Plymouth centre, he suggested they drive out to one of the village pubs for Sunday lunch.

'Ok,' Val said and they exchanged telephone numbers.

Peter scooped up Simon and they took a taxi back to the base. Peter wondered why Val had asked so little about him. He'd said he was in the Navy, which virtually went without saying at the GX. When he'd mentioned he was in submarines, she hadn't seemed interested. He supposed that, as a Plymouth girl born and raised, Val knew all there was to know about the Navy and its officers. The locals had a name for the Navy – 'fish heads' – and most of the Union Street working girls were supported by the Navy. The Navy's reputation could certainly have been better with local girls. At least the GX only admitted officers; still, as Peter knew full well, that was no guarantee of good behaviour.

12

HELSINKI, FINLAND

'I need to see you,' Kaisa said, trying to sound as matter-of-fact as she could.

'Hello, Kaisa,' Matti said. Kaisa could hear him purring like a satisfied cat at the other end of the line. So this *was* a game to him, she thought.

'You know why. Same place today at 5 pm?' she said.

'If you insist.' Matti said.

Kaisa had discussed the photos with her sister, who had laughed at first. Obviously she hadn't shown them to her, but she'd told her the worst of it with as little detail as possible.

'Well little Sis, I didn't think you'd get up to something like that!' They'd been sitting in Happy Days Café, having a beer after Sirkka's shift. Sirkka was smoking, taking a deep drag out of her cigarette and making rings out of the smoke.

'I thought you'd stopped,' Kaisa said, picking up the packet of Marlboro Lights, and taking one for herself. 'Can I?'

Sirkka nodded, watching her sister carefully. 'So he gave you the photos, but kept the negatives.'

Kaisa nodded.

'Bastard,' Sirkka said. Kaisa looked at her and smiled; Sirkka had cut her hair short and the new style made her look younger. Sirkka's short blonde curls and make-up tonight reminded Kaisa of the times they used to go out together in Helsinki, after their parents had taken them back to Finland from Stockholm in the seventies. She wanted to talk to Sirkka about those times. How they had used fake IDs to go to nightclubs like TF and Botta, where the lower age limit was at least four years older than they were. How had they managed to keep their fake IDs and nights out at grown-up discos a secret from their parents, Kaisa wondered. Then she remembered how their mother and father had been too busy fighting, eventually leading to a second separation and divorce.

'I'm following in my parents' footsteps,' Kaisa thought bitterly. Their parents had always been too preoccupied with their own unhappiness to notice that their daughters were running wild. Their father had tried, she guessed. He'd constantly nagged Sirkka to do her homework, and he'd have fits of rage when she came home with a poor school report, or discovered that they'd stayed out far longer than they should have done. He never told Kaisa off, which Sirkka felt was a complete injustice. This had make Sirkka even more determined to do as she pleased.

'He might have destroyed them, of course,' Kaisa said, forcing herself to think of her present, much more pressing problem. Hearing herself utter these words, she knew she was being naïve, deluding herself once again. She was too preoccupied with what Peter was doing. For the past two nights she'd not slept for dreaming about Peter and Jackie entangled between white sheets.

'Yeah, right.' Sirkka said, and with her face serious, added, 'You need to see him. I'm sure he's still in love with you, so use that to get them back.'

Kaisa had stared at her sister, 'I'm not ...'

Sirkka placed her hand on Kaisa's arm. 'No, silly. I'm not telling you to go to bed with him. I mean, just charm him a little, you know, with your look of pure innocence. Flutter your eyelashes and tell him you want the negatives.'

'You make it sound so simple.'

Sirkka put out her cigarette and took a swig of beer. 'It is simple. I'm sure if you really try, he'll do anything for you.'

Kaisa laughed.

'And what about Peter,' said Sirkka. 'Do you really think he is seeing this Jackie person?'

Kaisa nodded. She didn't dare look at the kind expression on her sister's face. She was so tired, she knew she'd begin crying again.

'Well, it might just be a revenge fuck.' Sirkka took another drag of her cigarette. Her eyelashes looked very dark and long, and Kaisa absentmindedly wondered if she'd changed her mascara. 'It's what men do; it makes them feel better,' Sirkka added and smiled.

This time Kaisa made sure she was the first to arrive in the café, so she got there a full fifteen minutes early, got herself a coffee and sat down at a table by the window. She wanted to see Matti on the street before he came in.

Kaisa had taken the photos with her, to make her case more forcefully, she guessed. But she kept the envelope in her handbag, planning to bring it out at the right moment. While waiting, she looked around: only two other tables were occupied in the small room. Of course, it was a Monday, and the weather had turned that morning, with cold rain, occasionally changing into sleet, falling steadily. Everyone apart from a crazy person like Kaisa would be rushing home after work, not stopping for a coffee with an ex-fiancé. Kaisa let out an involuntary snort. Once again in her life, she wondered how she'd got herself into such a bloody mess.

A man sitting at a table on the opposite side of the café looked up at Kaisa. When Kaisa responded to his stare, he averted his eyes and went back to reading the evening paper, *Iltasanomat*. That's what she should have done, to distract herself, picked up a newspaper from an R-Kiosk on her way down from Sirkka's flat. But she'd been too preoccupied with trying to keep dry. The rain had been so heavy that her winter boots were soaked. As she sat and waited to confront Matti, she realised that the other customers would be able to hear what she had to say. Of course, she should have suggested somewhere like The Happy Days Café, which was always bustling whatever the time of day – or weather.

As planned, Kaisa saw Matti as he parked his car on the other side of the street. He had no umbrella and the rain, which had now turned into hail, was settling on Matti's fur hat. He hadn't worn the hat the last time they met, though Kaisa remembered him often wearing it when they were together. It was nicknamed the Russian, because all the Soviet leaders wore one in winter, and the Finnish politicians copied them. It had become a popular hat in Finland. After her year in Britain, seeing so many men wearing them made Helsinki look like a Soviet bloc country in Kaisa's eyes. She remembered with fondness how Peter had made that same comment to her the first time he'd visited Helsinki. Kaisa had been very upset with him because of it. Of course, she'd not been angry with him for long; they were so in love then.

Kaisa sighed and watched Matti as he made his way towards the café. In spite of the weather, he didn't seem to rush. After patiently waiting for the traffic lights to turn green, he walked with a steady pace across the wide road, which the tramlines divided into two. Kaisa's mouth felt dry and she fought an urge to leave unnoticed before he got to the other side.

It took a while for Matti to get himself out of his coat and hat, both of which were covered in hail, which seemed to melt as soon as you saw it, leaving a puddle on the floor of the café. But all the while, as he shook himself like a wet dog, his eyes were on Kaisa.

'Nice to see you again,' he said. He was beaming, as if this was a meeting of two old friends. 'I'm getting a coffee and a Berlin bun. Can I get you anything?'

Kaisa shook her head and waited for Matti to go up to the counter and order.

'I want the negatives too,' Kaisa said as soon as Matti returned with his coffee and the large bun topped with pink icing. While he was getting his coffee, she'd taken the photographs out of her bag and placed them on the table between them.

Matti was quiet for a while, studying his hands, but not looking at Kaisa or the photos.

Kaisa glanced around the café to see if the man with the newspaper was listening. To her relief, he seemed to be engrossed in his reading. The girl serving at the counter had disappeared, and the café was now almost empty except for Kaisa and Matti, and the man behind his evening paper.

'The photographs are mine, so it's only fair I should have the negatives,' Matti eventually said.

'Why?' Kaisa said, and when Matti didn't reply, she leaned across the table and whispered, 'So that you can develop another set and ogle at them while you're ...' Kaisa glanced in the direction of Matti's crotch.

'Don't be so crude,' Matti spat out the words. His eyes had a look of pure hatred, just as they had when she'd told him about Peter, in her bedroom in Lauttasaari. She'd found Matti waiting for her when she got back from her secret meeting with Peter the day before he sailed back to Britain aboard HMS *Newcastle*. Kaisa had been in a trance from the Englishman's kisses and his promises to write and see her again. And then, bang, a confrontation with Matti had brought her back down to earth. His eyes had had the same dark threat to them then as they did now.

Kaisa lowered her gaze and said, 'But it's not fair. These pictures, they're of me. Me before ...'

'Not fair!' Matti had raised his voice, and both Kaisa and Matti glanced briefly around the café in embarrassment. But the place was empty. The man with the newspaper had disappeared without Kaisa noticing.

'Is it fair that you left me for some foreign sailor, who has now, by all accounts, left you. As predicted by me. I was good to you, Kaisa, as was my mother.'

'Don't talk to me about your mother!' Now it was Kaisa's turn to raise her voice. 'You should have heard the names she called me after I broke up with you.'

'Well, didn't you deserve those names, the way you cheated on me?'

'I didn't …' Kaisa began, but a sudden sense of hopelessness over-whelmed her and she felt tears well up inside. She must not cry, whatever happens, she told herself. Snatching the photographs, she placed them back in her handbag and got up.

She put her coat on, not looking at Matti, who had also got up and now took hold of Kaisa's arm. 'Please Kaisa.'

Kaisa lifted her eyes to him and said, as calmly as she could, 'I think you are being horrible. Those pictures are of me, and you should not have them anymore. We were engaged to be married, that's true, but you know as well as I know that I was only 15 and you were 22 when you seduced me. By the way, I believe that is illegal now.' Kaisa held her gaze steady on Matti. His eyes were still dark, but his mouth twitched at the word 'illegal'. 'With that in mind, I had every right to change my mind as I did.' Kaisa paused and was about to leave it at that, but added, 'And you know full well that I was never unfaithful to you. On the contrary, after we broke up I still slept with you for months, out of pity, even though I had already promised myself to another man. And that, as well as falling for you when I was only 15, I regret bitterly.'

Matti opened his mouth, but nothing came out.

'You can post the negatives to Sirkka's address, or even give them to her at the hotel. When I get them, and only then, will I reconsider my decision to report you to the authorities.'

Kaisa left the café, and not caring about the rain outside, ran along the street towards Sirkka's flat.

13

Tom's flat on the top floor of a Jugend-style house on Neitsytpolku, had a sea view towards the small islands in the Gulf of Finland. The name of his street, 'Virgin Walk', wasn't lost on Kaisa, especially later in the evening, when she walked along it to the nearest tram stop, on her way home.

The meal Tom was preparing as Kaisa stepped into his beautiful apartment, with its bay widow overlooking the sea, was pasta bolognese (his mother was Italian). He'd brought some cured bacon back from Milan.

'It's called pancetta,' Tom said, and smiled at Kaisa. In Italian, he sounded even more charming, and Kaisa was tempted to ask him to speak Italian to her, but felt silly. She didn't know him well enough, yet.

The wine, too, was from Italy, a deep red that warmed Kaisa's throat as she drank it. The first kiss happened in the kitchen, when Tom was cooking. He'd asked Kaisa to come and taste the sauce. They stood very close to one another by the stove, gazing at the boiling red mass of the meaty sauce, and Kaisa could feel his taut body tense as her thigh touched his. She felt Tom's eyes on her when she licked a small spoon clean of the sauce.

'It's good,' she smiled, and when she gave the spoon back to him, he grabbed hold of her hand. She felt his hot breath on her.

'Come here,' Tom said. He pulled her towards him and bent down to kiss her mouth.

His lips were fuller than Peter's and he squeezed Kaisa tightly, while he pushed his tongue into her mouth. Kaisa was tense, but she tried to relax, tried to feel something. Tom didn't seem to notice her lack of commitment, and pulled away only in order to see to the cooking. He gave Kaisa one of his wolfish grins and put a little of the pasta water into the sauce. 'This thickens it,' he said.

The food Tom had prepared was delicious, although Kaisa had no appetite. She had great difficulty eating the long strands of the special pasta – also brought back from Italy, and Tom, laughing, showed her how to twist the pasta in a spoon with her fork. But she didn't mind not being able to eat; she didn't want her tummy to be bloated. They finished the bottle of wine while talking about music, about their respective friends in Hanken and what they were doing now. Kaisa skipped most of the story of her short marriage. She simply said, 'It didn't work out.' Tom didn't ask her to explain further. He told Kaisa just as little about what he had been doing in Italy for best part of a year, and Kaisa in turn didn't ask him to elaborate.

When the wine was finished, Tom asked if she'd like to move to the sofa in the large main living area. He locked his eyes with Kaisa's and she nodded. She knew what was about to happen, as did he.

Tom put some music on his brand-new record player. The steely stack of equipment stood alone in one corner of the room. When Kaisa saw him open up the cover of *Faces*, by Earth, Wind and Fire, her heart beat faster. The first track transported her back five years to the first time Peter had come back to Helsinki to see her, and they'd listened to almost nothing else. Perhaps if Kaisa had said something then, had told Tom to choose another record, things could have been different.

While the first track played, Tom came to sit next to Kaisa and started to kiss her again. Trying to push the music and memories of Peter away, she pressed her lips against Tom's. He slid his hand underneath her mohair jumper, and started to fondle her breasts. Kaisa hadn't worn a bra on purpose. She wanted Tom to see that she was prepared to go to bed with him. Under her jeans, she was wearing a pair of lacy French knickers. Earlier, getting dressed in Sirkka's flat, she'd considered wearing a skirt with stockings and suspenders, but thought that would be over the top. She didn't want to appear too prepared, or too easy. Besides, the weather had been awful all day, with a combination of rain and sleet beating down the windows in the small flat in Töölö. Kaisa couldn't afford a taxi all the way to Ullanlinna, and would have frozen to death waiting for the tram in such skimpy underwear.

She felt a pleasant excitement from Tom's hands exploring her body, and for a moment, Kaisa relaxed. Tom pulled away, gazed at her eyes and silently led her to his bed – a mezzanine built into one end of the large room. Not letting go of her hand, he coaxed her gently up the wooden ladder. Once there, he pulled his T-shirt over his head and took his jeans and pants off.

Kaisa gazed at Tom's muscular torso, not daring to look down. Not yet. Instead, she too pulled off her jumper and jeans.

'Nice,' Tom said when he saw her knickers.

But when Kaisa moved her eyes down from Tom's handsome face and broad chest, she was surprised to see that he wasn't ready.

'Just play with me for a bit,' Tom said in a hoarse voice, and Kaisa did, but there was no change. She kissed him on his lips, moving to his neck and chest, but Tom pulled her up again and hugged her, 'I'm sorry,' he said.

While Kaisa had been up in Tom's flat, the temperature in Helsinki had dropped again and a blanket of fresh snow covered the city. It muffled all sound and made the streets artificially quiet. As Kaisa waited for the tram on Tehtaankatu, she felt as if she was in a magical place. This was in such contrast to the embarrassing events of just a moment before, adding to the weird times she felt she was living through. In the tram, her sense of being an actor in a surrealist play continued. The streetlights along South Harbour cast a magical glow against the white landscape as the tram trundled past the now empty market square and towards the imposing view of Helsinki Cathedral. Sitting in the empty tram on the way home, viewing the impossibly beautiful snowy scene, she wondered what had gone wrong with Tom. They had both vowed not to breathe a word to anyone about what had happened, but she now thought she must have done something wrong. Perhaps if she'd asked him to speak Italian to her, things would have gone differently. With everything that had happened to her in the past few weeks, she knew she'd been tense, and perhaps Tom had sensed that.

In a way Kaisa was relieved. She realised going to bed with Tom wouldn't have helped. It would only have made her more confused, would only have complicated her life further. What on earth had she been thinking?

'Oh, my God!' Tuuli exclaimed. 'But good for you for facing up to him. Let's just hope he is as honourable as he always made out and gives you back the negatives.' She clinked her glass with Kaisa's and they both laughed. Although Kaisa had no desire to laugh.

Kaisa had decided to tell Tuuli about the photographs. Or rather, the words just tumbled out of her while they shared a bottle of wine in Tuuli's minimalist apartment in Töölö. Her friend asked how she was and what she'd been up to. It was almost too good a story not to share, although Kaisa still felt the shame of her behaviour. How had she been so stupid to let Matti take those images?

'It was terrible. He was so smug with his Russian fur hat and army posture.' Kaisa said.

They both laughed again, and Tuuli poured Kaisa more wine.

'It's good to have you back,' she said, and examining her friend's face, added, 'I always wondered what you saw in him.'

'Yeah, well, I was young and with my parents' divorce, I guess he was a father figure.'

Tuuli nodded and grew serious. Again they were quiet for a while. Kaisa looked around the small flat. It was a studio, with one large room, a separate kitchenette and an alcove, which was entirely taken up by Tuuli's bed. In the hall, there was a small bathroom. It was exactly the kind of place Kaisa wanted. It had high ceilings, and the window in the living room overlooked an internal courtyard, formed by two L-shaped 1950s stone buildings. Although the flat was close to the tram, and the main Helsinki thoroughfare, Mannerheim Street, none of the traffic noise reached this side of the block. Tuuli had bought the place six months earlier, and she'd told Kaisa the mortgage was killing her. That was the reason for the sparse decoration, Kaisa supposed, but she loved the simple style; there was a standard lamp, a small desk and one print hanging above the sofa – the same sofa Tuuli had in the flat she'd rented during her studies at Hanken. Her old apartment was just a few streets away. Kaisa remembered the place – and the sofa – where she'd crashed so many times after missing the last bus to her own place in Lauttasaari, or later Espoo, the commuter town West of Helsinki, when she was living with her father. The walls were white and a single piece of light fabric hung on one side of the window. Venetian blinds fitted inside the triple-glazed windows, a standard feature in all flats and houses in Finland. Curtains were just for decoration here – unlike in Britain, Kaisa thought, where you needed heavy drapes to keep out the light and noise, not to mention the chill from drafty windows.

'I'm pleased to see you still have the same sofa,' she said and smiled at Tuuli.

The two friends began to talk about 'the good old times' when they were studying at Hanken, before Kaisa married Peter and left Helsinki for Portsmouth.

'So what's really going on with you and Ricky,' Kaisa said. Tuuli was a very private person and although they told each other everything, Kaisa always felt Tuuli was more reticent than she was. Kaisa felt another pang of guilt; she hadn't written to Tuuli many times during her short marriage. Again, she'd been too self-obsessed to think about her friends. That must stop now, Kaisa thought as she waited for her friend to open up.

'I told you, we have occasional sex!' Now Tuuli giggled.

'And you aren't hooked on him?'

Tuuli took a large gulp of wine, 'No!' she exclaimed, but Kaisa wasn't convinced. She knew that Tuuli had been hurt badly by a boy in their second year at Hanken, just when Kaisa's relationship with Peter had got more serious and he'd asked her to marry him. Although they never discussed it, Kaisa knew Tuuli was afraid the same thing would happen to her again.

'He looks pretty smitten with you,' Kaisa now said.

Tuuli grew serious, 'You think so?'

Kaisa nodded.

'Hmm,' Tuuli said and added, 'No more talk of old flames, what about we go out this weekend and *don't* go to the Helsinki Club afterwards?'

Kaisa smiled and agreed; nothing would convince Tuuli that men were trustworthy. Perhaps she was right.

'But before we drop the old flames altogether; what about you. How did your date with Tom go?' Tuuli said, and nudged Kaisa's knee with her toe.

Again Kaisa found it impossible to keep a secret from Tuuli. And so, making her friend swear to secrecy, she recounted her disastrous attempt to have sex with Tom.

'Wow, that's a surprise!' Tuuli said, but now she wasn't laughing.

'Remember you mustn't tell anyone, especially Ricky!' Kaisa said.

Tuuli grew even more serious, 'Of course I won't!'

'It was so embarrassing,' Kaisa said. 'It seems he doesn't fancy me after all, if he can't even get it up.'

Tuuli looked at her friend, and leaned over to touch her arm. 'Kaisa, you must know that had nothing to do with you! It's his problem. Probably just all that drinking they did in Hanken.'

'Yeah,' Kaisa said, but she knew she didn't sound convincing, because she wasn't even convincing herself.

14

S irkka and Kaisa got off the bus near a cluster of newly built high-rise houses. To get to the suburb of Soukka in Espoo, they'd taken the tram to the bus station in the centre of town, and then a coach. Sitting in the bus, Kaisa had been flooded with painful memories of the time she lived with her father. Not that it'd all been unhappy, but for the most part she'd been desperate to finish her studies. She'd longed for Peter, and had been fearful of her father's sudden mood changes. Her father could be pleasant to be with, or a drunken bear with a sore head. She'd never know which version of him she'd find at home.

'I can't believe he's still living in Espoo,' Kaisa said, as they made their way past a children's playground, a covered cycle store, rubbish bins and the traditional carpet airing stand common to all blocks of flats in Finland. The developers had left a rocky mound in the middle of the utilitarian looking houses, where a couple of boys were climbing up and down a slippery rock. Kaisa was transported back to her own childhood; she remembered how she often played alone in the small courtyard outside their block of flats in Tampere.

This was Sirkka's second visit to the four-bedroomed flat that their father had bought with his girlfriend, Marja, a few months back.

'And I can't believe Marja is still with him,' Kaisa added.

Sirkka said nothing. Inside the block of flats, they entered the lift and Sirkka pressed 10 for the top floor.

But as they waited for the lift to make its way up the many floors, she looked gravely at Kaisa. 'He's very keen to see you.'

'Really?' Kaisa said. Sirkka had changed her tune, she thought. She'd always been the one to be the most critical of their father. For many years the two hadn't seen each other, so Kaisa had been surprised when Sirkka had not only suggested going to see their father and his girlfriend on Sunday but also admitted that she'd been there once before.

'He just called on me at work one day and asked me to come over the following Sunday,' Sirkka had told Kaisa.

'And you just went?' Kaisa had asked.

'Yes, well, I like Marja, besides, I was curious.' Sirkka had regarded Kaisa for a while. 'He was OK, you know. Since the accident he's been a lot more … I don't know, softer somehow.'

Kaisa remembered being told about the accident the previous winter. His car had veered off the icy Lauttasaari Bridge. She'd not even contacted him afterwards. Again, Kaisa felt she'd been selfish. But she'd still been angry with him for trying to stop her mother from attending her wedding to Peter. In the end, Kaisa's refusal to bar Pirjo had led to her mother paying for the wedding instead. The person absent from the reception had been her father. He'd come to the church, but her uncle had given Kaisa away, not him. How could one forgive a father that?

Kaisa's heart was beating hard and she noticed that her palms were damp when she and Sirkka rang the bell outside her father's flat. The hall smelled of fresh paint. The bell didn't make any sound, so after a few minutes, Sirkka knocked on the door instead. Almost immediately, Marja opened the door. She flung her arms open and hugged the two girls hard. Kaisa was unprepared for the gesture and could feel her body tense.

'Come in, step in,' Marja said. She was wearing one of Kaisa's old jumpers. When she saw Kaisa looking at it, she said, 'Oh, you remember this?' She pulled at the picture of a deer, rendered with old-fashioned stitching on the front. Kaisa remembered that she'd bought the jumper at Hennes and Mauritz in Stockholm during one of the trips Sirkka and Kaisa had made to their old home town when they were first living in Finland. That was at least ten years ago. Before she left for Britain, she'd filled a bag with old clothes for the Salvation Army, which Marja had promised to deliver to the charity.

'This was such a great jumper, I couldn't give it away. I decided to keep it for myself. So many of the clothes that you discarded were perfectly fine! Waste not, want not,' she said and opened a door into a large living room.

Kaisa was so surprised by this thinly veiled criticism of her spendthrift ways that she said nothing. She turned to face Sirkka, raising her eyebrows. Her sister made a face, crossing her eyes and pursing her lips. Kaisa stifled a giggle, and followed Marja.

Her father was sitting in one of the large comfy chairs she remembered from their old house. He was wearing dark navy cords and a navy jumper with a light blue Marimekko shirt underneath. These were the clothes Kaisa had helped him choose when she was still living in Lauttasaari. Kaisa could see he had lost weight. He looked tanned, and combined with the colour of the shirt, his eyes seemed bluer. There was a healthy glow about him. He opened his arms and Kaisa rushed to hug him. Swallowed by her father's bear hug, Kaisa let her body relax. She fought back tears, sensing the old feeling of security that her father's embraces had given her as a child. When he eventually released her and hugged Sirkka in turn, Kaisa stepped aside and, turning her head so that Marja's beady eyes couldn't see, wiped the corners of her eyes with her fingers.

Marja had prepared coffee with bread, cheese, gravad lax and ham for them. But before they were allowed to tuck into the spread, proudly presented by Marja, their father showed his daughters the various rooms in the large apartment. The rectangular lounge overlooked a wooded landscape and had a glimpse of the sea on the far horizon. The rays of the early spring sun glittered on the steel-blue surface. The ice had all but gone, but the sea still looked cold and uninviting.

'Not bad, eh, for your old man?' Their father grinned.

Sirkka nodded and Kaisa made a show of looking at the view, 'That's wonderful.'

'The flat is on the top floor and occupies one whole corner of the building, with two aspects. This is the biggest flat in the whole of the block!' their father continued. Kaisa could see his chest fill with pride. As he took them from room to room, she made the 'ooh,' and 'aah' sounds she knew he expected. Sirkka, however, remained impassive, seemingly unimpressed by the place. Kaisa nudged her, as their father led them to each bedroom in turn. Having been so keen on this visit, Sirkka now appeared to be bored by the flat and their father. But Sirkka gave Kaisa a quick smile.

'Enough room for grandchildren to come and stay!' their father said, turning around to face his daughters.

This last comment at least made her sister react. She said, laughing, 'You've got a long wait for that!'

'On a sunny day you can see all the way to Björkö island!' their father continued, as he brought them back through the lounge and ushered them onto the wide balcony. It was a sunny but cold day, and at this height the wind was stronger, making their father's thin hair stand up. He looked a bit like a friendly professor rather then the Jekyll-and-Hyde character Kaisa had lived with a year ago. He offered Kaisa a pair of binoculars that he kept on the windowsill. Not knowing what she was looking for, but seeing the contrast of colours between the dark wooded forest, the pale blue sky with fluffy white clouds, and the cold grey colour of the sea on the horizon, she nodded appreciatively. She saw no island, and had no idea what, or where, the place he was talking about could be. She assumed the island was much further away, towards the Gulf of Finland.

'Can we go inside, it's too cold out here,' Sirkka said and rolled her eyes at Kaisa. It was a look Kaisa remembered vividly from her childhood and it sent her into a fit of giggles that this time she couldn't contain.

Her father gave Kaisa and Sirkka a look of impatience, a carbon copy of the encounters between Sirkka and their father when the sisters were growing up.

'Oh well, you girls are too young to appreciate a good property deal. But there will come a time when you do. Let's have something to eat – and more to the point something to drink!' he said, seemingly determined not to spoil the good mood of the occasion.

Marja, who hadn't joined them on the tour around the flat, was sitting at the round kitchen table, looking very satisfied with herself, wearing Kaisa's discarded, ten-year-old jumper. Suddenly Kaisa wondered whether there had been any underwear in those bags of old clothes, and if her father's girl-friend was at that very moment wearing her old knickers. She wracked her brains, fighting off another fit of unexplained laughter, but decided such things had probably gone straight out with the rubbish. She hoped so.

When they opened the *Lonkero*, which Marja said they'd bought 'specially for you, Kaisa', a comment that caused Sirkka to snort, and Kaisa to kick her shins under the table, Marja suddenly said, 'So, Kaisa have you left the Englishman?'

On the way back to the city, Kaisa was fuming.

'She's unbelievable!' she said to Sirkka as soon as they'd sat down in the empty bus. The bus driver, who seemed to be in a hurry, had not bothered to wait for Sirkka and Kaisa to sit down before pulling away from the bus stop, making both girls lurch along the gangway. The smell of the bus reminded Kaisa of Peter's visits to Espoo when she was living with her father, and those happy memories somehow made her even angrier.

'Who?' Sirkka said.

'Marja, of course. First she takes my stuff, and then wears my jumper in front of me. Can you believe that!'

Sirkka sighed, 'Well, she's very tight with money.'

'And then that comment about Peter and our marriage. Where did she get the idea that I'd left him?'

Sirkka looked out of the window. Kaisa stared at the back of her sister's head.

'Sirkka?'

Her sister looked at Kaisa. 'What should I have told them? You've been living with me for over a month. Marja asked me how long you'd been in Helsinki, and I told her, so she must have put one and one together.'

Kaisa examined her sister's face. Was she lying? But why?

'You didn't say anything about me leaving Peter, did you?'

'No,' Sirkka exclaimed loudly. The bus stopped at a set of traffic lights. Hearing Sirkka's raised voice, the driver gave the two young women a cursory glance through the rear-view mirror.

Trying to keep her voice low, Kaisa said, 'So what did you tell her exactly?'

'That you've been here for over a month. She asked me when are you going back to England and I said I didn't know.'

'Oh, Sirkka!'

Her sister straightened herself up in the seat. 'You wanted me to lie to her?'

Kaisa looked at her sister, but didn't reply. She was still angry, but she realised how difficult her situation was for Sirkka too.

'Look, I didn't know what to say. You know how Marja is, she is so bloody nosy. I was only phoning them to say you were here, since you hadn't done that yourself. You know Helsinki isn't such a big place. What would have happened if you'd bumped into one of them in town? I didn't expect her to give me the third degree on the phone!' Sirkka looked upset. Her eyes were pleading with Kaisa.

Kaisa took hold of her sister's hand, and said, 'Sorry, I'm being a bitch, aren't I?'

Sirkka squeezed Kaisa's fingers. 'No, I know it's difficult for you, but it's not easy for me either. The amount of times even people at work ask how long you're going to stay, what your plans are ...'

'I know, I know. And I will sort myself out, I promise,' Kaisa said, interrupting her sister. 'I'm going to phone Mr Heinola tomorrow to see if they've got anything for me in the KOP bank. And if he doesn't have anything, I'll go around to Stockmann's. You never know, they might have something for me. Then I can start looking for a flat for myself.'

'That's not what I mean. You can stay with me as long as you like,' Sirkka said, holding Kaisa's hand as if she was ill.

Kaisa smiled at her sister. 'I know, you've been incredibly kind and patient. It's time I moved on with my life.'

15

Kaisa had been in Helsinki for six weeks, and still didn't have a job. Every day, including Sundays, when *Helsingin Sanomat* was full of job advertisements, she'd look through the pages and think about applying for something. Despite her promise to Sirkka, another week had passed without her plucking up the courage to phone Mr Heinola at the bank. She kept putting it off, thinking she shouldn't appear too keen. But none of the jobs advertised in the paper seemed right for her either. On a Sunday in late March, when the snow had all but melted from the little patch of grass at the edge of the block of flats, Kaisa was sitting alone in the kitchen, nursing a hot cup of coffee. When the announcement caught her eye, she dropped her cup on the floor. Absentmindedly, as if it was happening to someone else, she saw the black-brown liquid spread in mid-air then fall to the tiled floor, followed by the shards of the broken china cup. She felt the coffee burn her toes and the lower part of her right calf, and yet she was numb; her senses seemed to be suspended.

Beloved
Matti Johannes Rinne
B 10.02.1953
D 20.03.1985
Taken away from us too soon.
Service and burial 27 March 1985
at Hietaniemi Chapel.

Sirkka rushed into the kitchen, her short blonde hair standing up, and her eyes large and wide.

'What are you doing?'

Kaisa looked at her sister but she seemed to have lost the ability to speak. She was still holding the newspaper in her hands, open on the first page, where the death notices were prominently displayed. What had made her look at them, she wondered? She felt as if she wasn't really in the room. Even her sister's dishevelled form, with her dressing gown open and her hair looking as though she was in a wind tunnel, seemed to be far away. She moved her eyes back to the notice, and with great difficulty, because her limbs seemed to have lost their ability to move, lifted one heavy hand and pointed at Matti's name.

'Oh, my God,' Sirkka said. She put her arm around Kaisa, and gently took the paper from Kaisa's hands to reread the notice.

Kaisa looked down at the floor. Seeing the mess of the broken coffee cup, she thought she ought to get up and clear it away. She tried to move, but couldn't. Instead she felt something wet on her cheeks, and realised she was making muffled noises.

'Oh, Kaisa, I'm so sorry.' Sirkka pulled Kaisa towards her and suddenly Kaisa felt a piercing pain reach inside her chest. She leaned against her sister's shoulder, trying to breathe, so that the pressure would go away. Sirkka rocked her back and forth, making soothing sounds, but nothing, nothing stopped her sensation of being suffocated.

'I'm coming with you,' Sirkka said.

'Really?' Kaisa glanced at her sister. She was standing in the doorway to the kitchen wearing a pair of black trousers and a black shirt. 'I thought you were at work today.'

'I've taken the day off.' Sirkka stepped inside the kitchen and put a hand on Kaisa's shoulder. 'I don't think you should go on your own. You never know what that mad old cow will get up to.'

'Please, Sirkka, don't say that. She's just lost her only son.' Kaisa bit the inside of her cheeks and took a slow breath in and out. She didn't want to start crying again.

It was two days after Kaisa had found out about Matti's death. After crying for so long that she no longer could, she'd decided she would be brave and phone Matti's mother. She remembered their last conversation vividly. Mrs Rinne had accused her of being a common whore because she had left her son and fallen in love with the Englishman. Kaisa had been upset at the time, but now she understood. Kaisa had broken a promise made to her son and Mrs Rinne had only been protecting him. Besides, none of that mattered now. But instead of Mrs Rinne, the telephone had been answered by a young-sounding girl.

'Just a moment,' she'd said and then Kaisa recognised the voice of Aunt Bea, Mrs Rinne's sister.

'Ah, Kaisa,' she'd said and her voice had sounded deep, and serious, but normal under the circumstances.

After Kaisa had expressed her condolences, Aunt Bea told Kaisa that Matti had been killed in a hunting accident. She said that Mrs Rinne wasn't taking any calls.

'Of course,' Kaisa had replied.

'Are you coming to the funeral?' she had then asked, taking Kaisa by surprise. 'Yes, of course I am,' Kaisa said.

Now, getting ready, she was regretting her rash promise.

'Thank you,' she said to her sister and hugged her. 'I thought I'd be OK to go on my own, but I don't think I am.'

The day of Matti's funeral was bitterly cold, but sunny. Sirkka and Kaisa walked slowly inside the walls of Hietaniemi cemetery, where bare trees flanked the paths between the headstones. The ground under their feet was sanded, but it was hard and Kaisa could still spot traces of snow here and there in front of the headstones. Some of the graves either side of the main thoroughfare leading up to a chapel were large, important-looking plots, separated from the others by chains. Some had just a small stone at the head of the plot. They passed a beautiful statue of an angel, set on a tall plinth, and Kaisa glanced away, trying to keep her mind on getting through the day. Against another large headstone, there was a statue of a mother and a child. The child had her head on the mother's lap, while the mother caressed the child's head. Kaisa swallowed hard; she must control herself and not cry. She took a handkerchief out of the pocket of a black overcoat her mother had lent her, and dabbed at the corners of her eyes.

'Are you OK,' Sirkka whispered, and squeezed Kaisa's arm.

She nodded. When they approached the pale yellow chapel built on a small hill, they saw a group of people, all dressed in black talking in hushed tones, outside the large wooden doors. Kaisa took hold of Sirkka's arm, and as they got closer she saw there was a woman with white hair, looking frail, but wearing bright pink lipstick, in the middle of the group. She was sitting in a wheelchair. Kaisa looked at Sirkka and said, 'I have to go and say hello.'

Sirkka nodded and let go of her sister. She remained still, standing a little away from the group, while Kaisa moved forward. She recognised Matti's Aunt Bea straight away, but she didn't know any of the other mourners standing around Mrs Rinne. She nodded to Bea, and went up to Mrs Rinne. She'd decided to just say, 'My condolences,' and then step back and wait for Sirkka to accompany her inside the chapel. But when she got up to the wheelchair, Mrs Rinne lifted her eyes towards Kaisa.

'You!' she said. Her eyes were dark and surprisingly clear.

Kaisa took her gloves off and reached out her hand: 'My condolences.'

Mrs Rinne took Kaisa's hand. Her bare fingers felt fragile; thin and bony. Kaisa squeezed her hand gently, and then went to pull away, but Mrs Rinne, her dark eyes boring into Kaisa, kept a firm grip on her. The old woman's nails dug into Kaisa's hand, hurting her. Kaisa tried to pull away again, but in vain.

'You bitch,' Mrs Rinne said under her breath and pushed her nails deeper into Kaisa's flesh. Then, as suddenly as she'd set her eyes on Kaisa, she let go of her hand, and turned her dark gaze away from her.

A young girl with long, straw-blonde hair took hold of the wheelchair. Whispering something to Mrs Rinne while glancing disapprovingly at Kaisa, she pushed her into the chapel. The rest of the mourners, without so much as a look in Kaisa's direction, followed Mrs Rinne and the girl inside.

Sirkka appeared at Kaisa's side.

'Are we going in?' she said, looking at Kaisa's face.

'Yes, we must.' Kaisa replied. As they walked into the dark and cold interior of the church, Kaisa glanced down at her hand. Mrs Rinne had drawn blood from her palm.

Inside, the chapel was half full. Kaisa followed Sirkka, who chose an empty pew at the back. Kaisa was glad. They were two rows behind the others mourners, so if she needed to cry, she could do so unnoticed. The service was short; only three hymns, and apart from the pastor only the young girl with blonde hair spoke. To Kaisa, she didn't look any older than sixteen, and until she began reading from the single sheet, her small, thin hands trembling, and her hair covering half her face, Kaisa had no idea who she was. She presumed it was one of Matti's cousins, one of Aunt Bea's daughters.

'I wanted to say a few words,' the girl began.

Before continuing, she lifted her head and looked straight at Kaisa. Her pale blue eyes had such coldness in them that Kaisa forgot the burning sensation in her right palm. Kaisa quickly lowered her eyes. It had been a mistake to come to the funeral.

'Matti and I were engaged to be married,' the girl said.

Kaisa lifted her head and stared at the girl. So Matti hadn't been lying; he had found someone else. Another young woman to control. Involuntarily, Kaisa's hands formed into fists, but she winced when she noticed the pain in her right palm.

While the girl spoke, saying how little time they'd had together, and how Matti had 'been taken away far too soon', Sirkka held firmly onto Kaisa's left hand. Kaisa wanted to get up and tell the girl how wrong this was, how a 32-year-old man, tragically dead or not, shouldn't be engaged to a 16-year-old girl. But as the blonde girl stepped down from the pew and sat next to Mrs Rinne, Kaisa thought it really didn't matter any more. Matti was gone, gone with the help of his own gun. The guns, which Kaisa had always felt uneasy about, and even afraid of, had been his own undoing in the end. For the umpteenth time Kaisa wondered how he could have accidentally shot himself. After Kaisa had got over the initial shock of his death, she had stayed awake wondering how it had happened. Of course, there was no one she could ask, and really, it had nothing to do with her.

Still, the night before, Kaisa had had the awful realisation that Matti had deliberately shot himself. That he'd committed suicide and that it was Kaisa's sudden appearance in Helsinki that was the reason. Or the confrontation about the negatives, about their relationship and how she'd been only 15 when he'd seduced her. Had he believed her when she threatened him with the police? In the morning, getting ready for the funeral, she'd chided herself for being too melodramatic, for imagining she was the centre of everyone's universe. After all, Matti and Kaisa had met just twice since she'd returned to Helsinki, and to Kaisa her old fiancé had seemed perfectly happy, perfectly normal, perfectly himself. Kaisa wanting some old photographs back couldn't have upset him that much, could it? She'd decided not to breathe a word of her mad theory to anyone, not Sirkka, not her mother, not even Tuuli.

And now? With all that hostility shown to her by Matti's new girlfriend, and Matti's mother? Kaisa shook her head, and whispered to Sirkka, 'I can't go to the grave.'

Sirkka nodded and when the pallbearers had taken the coffin out of the chapel, followed by the family, with Mrs Rinne, Aunt Bea and the girl in the lead, Sirkka and Kaisa, the last to leave the church, walked in the opposite direction to the other mourners. Passing the beautiful headstones, they walked quickly out of the cemetery, towards the tram stop.

'Wait, Kaisa!'

Kaisa and Sirkka stopped when they saw a woman, heavily pregnant and wearing a black fur hat and a short swing coat, running towards them.

As the figure moved closer, Kaisa saw who it was. 'Vappu?' she said.

The woman was out of breath when she reached them. Kaisa supported her arm with her hand, 'Are you OK?'

'Yes,' Vappu said between pants, 'I just didn't want to miss you! I thought I saw you come into the church but only knew for sure it was you just now.'

Kaisa regarded her old friend for a while, 'Congratulations!'

Vappu smiled up at Kaisa, 'Thank you.' Then her eyes moved back toward the slow-moving cortège on the other side of the church. 'I have to go, but ring me. I want to see you before you disappear again.'

Vappu pressed a piece of paper firmly into Kaisa's palm, 'Promise to call me.' Vappu's pale blue eyes were serious, and although the pressure of the hand made Kaisa wince, she closed her fingers around the piece of paper and nodded, 'I promise.'

Vappu turned on her heels. Not looking back, she began walking at a fast pace towards the far end of the cemetery.

'What was that all about?' Sirkka asked as they began making their way toward the tram stop again.

'Don't you remember my old friend from Lauttasaari?' Kaisa said. 'I didn't think she'd be at the funeral, but of course she would. It was at her family home that I first met Matti.'

'Of course. I'd forgotten all about that.'

Both Sirkka and Kaisa were quiet as they walked along the hard sanded path towards the entrance of the cemetery. Kaisa was thinking back to when she was 14, and a new girl at Lauttasaari school. She'd made friends with Vappu on her first day and had spent more time in her large house than she did at home.

'What really happened to him?' Sirkka said once they were sitting inside the tram and moving north towards Linnankoskenkatu.

Kaisa shook her head. She was too upset to speak. The tears that she'd managed to hold back inside the chapel, were now flowing freely.

'Oh Kaisa,' Sirkka said and put her arm around her sister's shoulders.

16

For nearly two weeks after the funeral Kaisa hardly went out. She saw Tuuli for lunch at Stockmann's but refused to go on a night out. She wore black, or dark clothes, as if she was in mourning for a close relative. Sirkka didn't comment on her outfits, neither did her mother, even though Kaisa could see they both glanced at her black jeans and T-shirt, when, two Sundays after the funeral, they sat down for a traditional Easter lunch in Pirjo's smartly decorated flat.

'They have no right to be angry with you,' Pirjo said and patted Kaisa's arm.

Kaisa fought tears; she'd done so much crying, not knowing for whom or for what.

'I know,' she said. In her mind, she was aware that she wasn't to blame for Matti's death. And she knew how impulsive and vindictive Matti's mother could be. Besides, Mrs Rinne had looked ill, and losing an only son must be completely devastating. Whether she deserved her wrath or not, Kaisa didn't blame Mrs Rinne for any of her feelings of hostility, or her actions. Instead, Matti's death, and the awful funeral with the young girl in tears and Mrs Rinne scratching Kaisa's hand, had made her realise how much damage she had inflicted on the people around her. In a way, she was mourning her own life so far.

Even before the funeral, she'd felt helpless and insignificant after Scotland, her failed marriage, and her infidelity. Now that Peter had found a new life without her, and Matti had gone, Kaisa thought she might as well be dead herself.

This was partly why she hadn't phoned Vappu even though she had promised. The crumpled piece of paper was still in her handbag, where she had placed it after the funeral. How could she see her old friend, whom she had more or less abandoned after she'd got together with Matti? Besides, Kaisa couldn't even remember when she'd last seen Vappu before the funeral. Seeing her open face, the same vibrancy in her pale blue eyes that she remembered from their school days, had made her long to talk to Vappu, but what would she say? How would she be able to explain why she was back in Finland? Kaisa assumed Vappu had heard all about her affair with the Englishman from Matti, or from her brother Petteri, whose best friend Matti had been. Kaisa wondered if the whole family had been at the funeral and seen her skulk away. How ashamed of her behaviour she now was! She should have faced up to them all, and gone to the graveside to do her duty as Matti's long-term girlfriend and former fiancé. Suddenly she felt a great urgency to leave Helsinki again. There were too many skeletons here.

Kaisa heard the telephone ring in the hall before she was awake. It was eight o'clock on a Monday morning and Sirkka had already left for work.

'Hello,' Kaisa said trying not to sound sleepy. She hoped it might be Mr Heinola from the bank.

'Kaisa, I found you!'

For a moment Kaisa wanted to put the receiver back on its base, or pretend she was Sirkka, a game the sisters had played as teenagers, but she couldn't do it.

'Vappu?' she said.

'Listen, I'm in the telephone box outside your flat. Can I come up?'

'Now?' Kaisa looked at the clutter in the small flat. Her bed was unmade in the lounge, and from the hall Kaisa could see the plates and cutlery from last night's dinner, as well as her sister's breakfast dishes, piled up in the sink. Her own clothes were scattered around the lounge, on chairs and at the foot of the bed.

'It's bloody cold in this phone box and it stinks of wee,' Vappu said.

'OK, I'll buzz you up,' Kaisa said.

She put the phone down and pulled on a pair of jeans and a jumper. She made the bed as best she could and rammed her clothes inside her suitcase, which she pushed into a hall cupboard. She opened the venetian blinds and the room flooded with light. 'That's a bit better,' Kaisa thought, but she didn't have time to assess the state of the kitchen before Vappu was ringing the doorbell.

Her friend's belly was even larger than Kaisa remembered, and it was hard to hug her. Vappu smiled and said, 'I know, I look like a bloody beached whale!'

'When is it due?'

'Oh, today, actually,' Vappu said and, added, 'but don't worry, I'm sure I'll be late.'

Kaisa couldn't help but smile at her old friend. Her shape was completely different, with the pregnancy, and Kaisa spotted a few lines around her eyes, but otherwise she was the same lanky 14-year-old that Kaisa had met at her new school in Lauttaaari all those years ago. As she made the coffee, Vappu looked up at Kaisa from the small kitchen table. With a serious tone of voice, she said: 'I wanted to see you before I get busy with this little one.'

Kaisa nodded. She had no idea what her friend was talking about, or why it was so urgent for them to see each other.

Vappu gazed at Kaisa, 'You know that I'm married, right?'

Kaisa shook her head, 'No, but I sort of guessed …'

'Well, while I've been with Risto, I've come to realise that what happened to you with Matti, when you were so young, it wasn't right.'

Kaisa stared at her friend.

'The thing is, Risto is a policeman. That's how I found you, just as well I remembered your maiden name and that your sister is called Sirkka.' A quick grin passed over Vappu's face.

Kaisa nodded, but couldn't return her friend's smile.

'Anyway, he's worked on an underage sex case before.' Vappu's blue eyes were steadily gazing at Kaisa. She was wearing a colourful long blouse over a pair of black pants. Her legs were spread wide and she was leaning onto the kitchen table for support. Kaisa realised it must be very uncomfortable sitting with a large belly like that on the small kitchen chair.

'Do you want to go and sit in the lounge? There's a comfy chair there.' Kaisa held her hand out and helped Vappu up to her feet. Once they were both settled in the room next door, Kaisa asked, 'When you say cases like these, what do you mean?'

'Well, you were underage, weren't you, when Matti and you ..?'

'Yes, but he's gone now, so …'

'But he has – had – photographs, didn't he?'

Kaisa was stunned; how did Vappu know about the awful pictures Matti had taken of her? 'Yes, but what, how?' Kaisa stammered. She put her head into her hands in shame. Had Vappu seen the images of her wanton and smiling like a whore into the camera? To calm herself, she slowed her breathing. Looking down at the floor, she continued, trying to steady her voice. 'How do you know about the photos and what do they have to do with anything?'

'Matti gave me the negatives before he – before the so-called accident.'

Kaisa found herself staring at Vappu's face again. She was thinking hard. Was her awful fear that he'd taken his life true after all? 'You mean he?' Kaisa couldn't bring herself to say the words, 'Did he?'

Vappu nodded. Her face was serious, and her gaze was steady. 'He gave them to me for safekeeping, and so that I could give them to you.'

'Oh, my God.'

'He couldn't live with himself. He asked Risto if you were right to say it was illegal. And,' Vappu eased herself out of the low-slung chair with difficulty and put her hand on Kaisa's knee. 'You know that girl, Satu, he was about to marry. She was just fourteen when they met two years ago. He told Risto he had no idea it was against the law. But Risto said he must have known.'

Kaisa couldn't speak. Why hadn't she kept her big mouth shut? Why had she gone and stirred up everything? Again ruining other people's lives.

'Risto blames himself,' Vappu said.

Kaisa pressed her hands together, trying to hold herself still. She had a great desire to stand up and howl. She was feeling dizzy.

'But we've only been together two years ourselves, and Risto had no idea how young Satu was. She is like you used to be; she acts a lot older than she is.' Vappu took a white envelope out of her handbag and handed it to Kaisa.

'Anyway here you go. Do whatever you want with them.'

Kaisa opened the flap of the white envelope and saw a set of dark films inside. She got up and hugged her friend.

'Look Kaisa, this is not your fault. Remember that.'

17

LONDON

L ondon was drizzly, but Kaisa was surprised by how much warmer it was by the end of April than Helsinki. She was too hot in her new thickly-lined winter coat, which her mother had bought for her at Stockmann's after hearing about the job in London. It was camel wool, and far too warm, plus the rain made a special pattern on it, as if it was made out of leopard skin. For her mother, Kaisa had put a slightly more glamorous spin on the job offer than was the truth, and hadn't shown her the copy of the magazine that Rose had sent. Pirjo hated communists: something to do with Kaisa's grandparents and the Winter War when Finns fought the Russians. Kaisa didn't want her to think she was going to be working for a left-wing publication.

The offices of *Adam's Apple* were on a side street a few minutes' walk from Farringdon tube station. Kaisa spotted the office instantly, because there were piles of magazine stacked on the pavement, and people milling outside talking and smoking. She was greeted with waves and smiles when she asked for Rose, 'She's upstairs, third floor.'

'Kaisa, how lovely to see you!' Rose gave Kaisa a hug, and added, 'I am so glad you could come.'

The first thing that hit Kaisa when she stepped inside the office was the smell of printed paper. It was a strange combination of a Finnish forest, chopped wood and glue. The inside of *Adam's Apple* looked a lot more chaotic than *Sonia* magazine, where Rose had worked before, but the chaos seemed friendly. The business of producing the magazine seemed to take place in one large room, lined with desks. Rose had got up from her position at the back of the room, where she'd been sitting typing. Behind her was a tall bookcase crammed with books with different coloured spines.

Rose took her hand and smiled, 'Welcome to London!' she said.

Kaisa saw a completely different woman in front of her. Instead of the Princess Di-like, upper-class, well-spoken, carefully put together woman, she now saw a carefree, passionate Rose who was almost make-up free. She'd let her highlights grow out, and Kaisa saw her hair was greying at the roots.

Rose introduced her to the other three women in the office. Rachel was sitting on a table, scribbling something on a notepad. She was a dark-haired girl, about Kaisa's height and build, with a long back and long legs. She had short, choppy hair, and wore a white shirt buttoned up at the neck and loose-fitting black trousers. 'Hi' she said to Kaisa and went back to her writing. On the other side, two women were reading. They smiled and nodded briefly when Rose introduced them as Barbara and Jenny.

Kaisa suddenly felt overdressed. Most of the other women were wearing casual jumpers and trousers, or even jeans, whereas Kaisa wore her black trouser suit under the warm camel coat. She'd have to remember to wear something more suitable for the next day.

"You might have seen Jack, our driver, and the others outside? We've just got delivery of this month's issue, so it's an exciting day for us!' Rose immediately took one copy of the latest issue and gave it to Kaisa. On the cover it said, 'Sex, Drugs And Rock and Roll' in red ink over a black and white picture of a woman.

'Looks great,' Kaisa said.

Rose began talking about the articles, what socio-political issues were covered by the latest magazine (which was Rose's first) and what they were planning for the next. She was so enthusiastic, her face shone.

But Kaisa was worried about money. She was excited by Rose, and about the prospect of working on a magazine in London. She couldn't believe she'd have an opportunity to further the feminist cause, but she was concerned about how she was going to support herself in London. In her letter, or in the expensive phone calls Kaisa had made from her mother's telephone to agree a start date, Rose hadn't made any mention of Kaisa's pay.

Rose had, though, arranged a cheap bed-sit for her in Notting Hill, in a large white-clad house on a road called Colville Terrace, a few streets away from the tube station. She'd left Kaisa some bedding, a kettle and even an ironing board and an iron, set neatly on the single bed of the large room.

She had a small kitchenette arranged against one wall of the room, with a large bay window overlooking the street. But the night before, Kaisa's first night back in England, she had slept badly. The street had been noisy around 11 o'clock, with people spilling out of the nearby pubs. It was also cold, and by the time the street had grown quiet, Kaisa had needed the loo. The carpet on the wide wooden stairs was so threadbare, that when Kaisa climbed the stairs to the bathroom on the floor above, her footsteps echoed through the house. Now, as she listened to Rose, Kaisa wondered if she'd been foolish to take a job without knowing any of the details. She'd been too keen to leave Helsinki, what with all that had happened with Matti, her mother's constant queries on what she was going to next, and the visit from her sister's boyfriend from Lapland looming on the horizon. Kaisa had missed his arrival by two days, something she was sure had been carefully arranged by Sirkka. Still, both her mother and sister had shed a few tears when they'd said goodbye at Helsinki airport. There was no going back to Helsinki now.

Her old bank manager in Helsinki had let her down too; he said jobs were hard to come by, even with Kaisa's degree. The job in London was her only chance to move on, to make something of her life. Plus being in England meant she was closer to Peter, even though she knew she was a fool to think they'd patch things up again. Kaisa was still getting money from Peter, but she knew it was wrong of her to keep taking it, and besides, there were no guarantees that this would continue. Especially if he heard she was working for a publication like *Adam's Apple*. Kaisa didn't even have to ask if the magazine was against the Polaris missiles – it was written all over the women's faces.

'Take it, and read it later.' Rose added, 'Listen we're all going to the pub, you wanna come?'

'Sure,' Kaisa said. 'But, I need to know about the job …'

Rose looked at her, and laughed. 'Oh my, of course.' She pulled out a sheet of paper which had a carbon copy behind it and handed it to Kaisa. 'There's a café around the corner. Go there and read this through, and if it's all OK, come back and sign it, and we'll be all set.'

Kaisa found the café. It was empty apart from an older woman wearing a coat tied up with a piece of string and surrounded by plastic bags, all filled to the brim. The place smelt of fried food and had heavily steamed up windows. Kaisa ordered a cup of black coffee and sat down at a table covered with a red-and-blue checked cloth. She began reading her contract.

. . .

Rose had insisted Kaisa should come to the party, which was being held in a disused warehouse near the offices of *Adam's Apple*. Kaisa knew she was worried about her.

'You spend all your time just working and sleeping. You're a young woman, you need a sex life!'

Kaisa had blushed; even after six weeks at the magazine, where sex was talked about as if it was as normal as eating bread, she still hadn't got used to discussing freely what people got up to in their bedrooms. Or in public toilets, or parks, or stationery cupboards, or wherever. (In London in summer, anything went). Two of the women working at the magazine were lesbians, and due to the lack of a boyfriend, she assumed, she'd been asked many times if she was one too. Kaisa always vehemently denied it, but the truth was that she really didn't have any appetite for sex at all. With either a man or a woman.

Whenever she thought about sex, her mind wandered back to her last two meetings with Matti, and the photographs, then his death, and the awful funeral. Then she thought of Tom, and his flaccid manhood, and she wanted to cry. If she couldn't have Peter, she didn't want anyone, she decided. She'd been surprised by how little she'd cried since being in London. She'd got herself a little portable TV in the bedsit, and spent most evenings watching English TV, which was so much better than the programmes they showed in Finland. Only on her two wedding anniversaries had she shed a little tear. On the first one, a year after their shot-gun wedding in Portsmouth – hastily arranged after Peter failed to get a certificate in time for their planned marriage in Finland a month later – Kaisa had bought herself a red rose and a bottle of white wine. She'd finished the whole bottle watching *Coronation Street*, followed by *Brookside*. It had only been a problem because the day fell on the Saturday of a Bank Holiday weekend, when she had little to do but wander around Portobello Market buying vegetables for the week ahead. On the anniversary of the 'proper' wedding, 2 June, a Sunday four weeks later, she'd hoped in vain Peter would remember and send her a card. For days afterwards, Kaisa had scanned the post, but nothing came. And why should it, she'd scolded herself. Her sister and mother remembered the date, and had phoned her, taking turns to speak. But it was difficult to talk in private in the hall downstairs, where the land-lady and her slimy boyfriend could hear every word. Knowing how she'd felt on the anniversary in May, she had decided to go out for the day, and had walked from her bedsit in Notting Hill to Hyde Park. It had been a beautiful sunny day and she'd bought an ice cream and watched boys play football on the grass. She remembered how Peter had broken her heart in

Hyde Park by telling her they should be free to see other people while Kaisa was finishing her studies and unable – and unwilling, it has to be said – to move to England to be with him.

She felt as if she'd seized up since Matti's death, as if everything had closed up down there. With those awful pictures, and what Vappu had told her about Matti's life after Kaisa had left him, she felt that she'd had too much sex in her life already. Thoughts of Duncan entered her mind, and she brushed his memory away. Men were bad news, all of them. This was her new life, working on a worthwhile feminist cause in London. Why was it so important to be sleeping with someone as well?

But in the end Kaisa agreed to go to Rose's party. She knew she would need to talk to other people eventually, people other than her colleagues, all of whom were women, except for the magazine delivery boy, Jack, who appeared once a month on the doorstep of the offices in Clerkenwell. He was an overconfident young lad, who joked with the women about lesbians and 'giving them all one'. Rose and the rest of the editorial staff put up with him, calling him a prat to his face, to which the boy laughed and said, 'You're gagging for it, admit it.'

The warehouse party was to celebrate someone's birthday. It was a friend of Rose's but Kaisa didn't know her. She was turning 30 and had a rich daddy, who was paying for it, Rose told Kaisa. 'Free booze, lots of good-looking men and women,' Rose said and grinned. 'Let your hair down for once, Kaisa.'

At home in her bedsit, which was damp and cold even in June, Kaisa spent a stupid amount of time deciding what to wear. Finally, after trying on several trousers, jeans and top combinations, she decided on a cotton dress, which she'd bought from Miss Selfridge, a heady moment after the last issue of *Adam's Apple* had come out. She'd written an article on the benefits of proportional representation, and how it would help women be better represented in parliament. It was her first long piece in the magazine, and she'd felt on such a high, she'd gone to Oxford Street and bought the dress and a pair of high-heeled shoes to go with it. For weeks, the dress and the shoes had stayed unworn in the small wardrobe in her bedsit. There didn't ever seem to be an occasion to wear them. Kaisa's daily uniform was what Peter would have called her 'boy clothes', jeans and checked shirt with a jumper if it was cold. The dress, in contrast, was very feminine; it had a gypsy-style ruched skirt and an off-the-shoulder top. The summer had arrived in London and the weather was warm. She couldn't wear a bra with the dress, but she'd lost nearly five kilos during her time in London, so that wouldn't be a problem. She just didn't have an appetite, and often skipped having an evening meal altogether. It wasn't so easy to cook in her small bedsit, especially when she had to sleep in the same room, with the smells of the cooking lingering into the night. Kaisa added a narrow gold belt to the outfit, pulling it tightly across her waist. She put on some make-up, including eyeliner, and even wore lip gloss for once. When she gazed at herself in the mirror that she'd put against one wall of the bedsit, she approved of the way she looked. Perhaps it was time she trapped, she thought, and smiled at the memory of an expression Peter often used. Don't think about him, she reproached herself, and closed the door behind her.

18

'C'mon it'll be fun,' Val said and pulled Peter's hand. They were in London, walking from Farringdon tube station towards an address that Val had written on a piece of paper. Peter had asked to see the address, so that he could plan their journey on the tube, but Val had pulled the piece of paper from his hand and laughed. 'I live here!' Peter had got hold of her tiny waist and tried to wrestle the paper out of her hand, but she'd not given it up. Instead, they'd ended up on her bed, making love for the second time that morning.

Peter had weekend leave and had come up to London to stay with Val in the house she shared with five other people in Earl's Court. It was a massive Victorian townhouse with the bedrooms arranged over four floors. Val's bedroom was on the top floor, in a former attic space, which had been turned into a room with two dormer windows overlooking the rooftops of West London. Val said she knew the girl whose party it was, and she insisted on going. Peter didn't like parties anymore, not since the court martial. There was just too much to explain when people asked him what he did. When they found out he was in the Navy, they wanted to know all about his career to date. He hadn't learned to lie properly yet, and often left a silence in the air, revealing that there was more to his past than he was saying.

Peter now felt almost equally uncomfortable walking along the London streets, not knowing where he was, or where they were going. He wasn't sure if Val deliberately put him in situations where he felt uneasy. Earlier that day, when he'd arrived on her doorstep, Val had introduced him to two of her fellow housemates as 'My bit on the side — or, no sorry, I'm his bit on the side!' When Peter had shaken hands with a lanky boy with long blond Duran Duran-style hair, and what Peter could have sworn was make-up around his eyes, she'd added, 'And he's in the Navy.' The inevitable questions had followed, which Peter had tried to put a stop to by saying he was a submariner, based in Plymouth.

'So you're not firing nukes as your job then,' the boy, who'd introduced himself as Josh, had said, giving Peter a hard stare. 'One of them,' Peter had thought and decided he needed to be careful about what he said.

The second person sitting at a long pine table in the dark kitchen accessed through a long corridor on the ground floor of the house, was a girl with spiky, mousey-coloured hair. She wore trousers that were too large, bunched up around the waist. Her oversized T-shirt was tucked into the trousers, making her look a bit like a clown. She was wearing no make-up, apart from very red lipstick. 'I'm Jenny, she said and shook Peter's hand, holding onto it for a bit longer than was comfortable. Peter thought the girl was a little older than Val or Josh, and it turned out she was the owner of the place, and occupied the entire first floor. 'I'm a nurse,' she informed Peter. Later, up in her room, Val told Peter Jenny had inherited the house from her parents, who'd been killed in a car accident a few years back. She was their only child and didn't know what to do with herself now she was on her own, so she put an ad in the paper to share her house with students.

Peter could hear the loud music of the party a few streets away before he saw the disused warehouse. The open windows on the second floor were flung open to the warm June evening, and the flickering lights of a disco ball gave the street below an unreal feel.

19

The party was packed with people, all talking, laughing and dancing. Waiters carrying trays of drinks and canapés moved through the large space, which doubled as the dance floor, although many people swayed along to the music in small groups wherever they stood. There were fairy lights and pink balloons emblazoned with the number 30, and Kaisa wondered which one of the many women in expensive-looking satin dresses was the birthday girl.

Kaisa sought out Rose, who stood next to an older man with a huge moustache.

'You look lovely,' Rose said into Kaisa's ear. Smiling, she added, 'This is Roger.'

Roger took Kaisa by surprise by kissing her quickly on the mouth. The brittle blond hairs on his upper lip tickled Kaisa, and she laughed to hide her embarrassment.

The music was so loud, even at the far end of the room that you couldn't talk normally. Frankie Goes to Hollywood was playing, and Kaisa noticed how the space looked exactly like the one in the *Two Tribes* video. All that was needed was a boxing ring and sawdust on the floor. They were joined by staff from *Adam's Apple,* and Rose began a shouted-out conversation with them about the next issue. They were in disagreement about the cover, a discussion that had started in the office on Friday afternoon. Kaisa didn't want to take part, because she saw both sides of the argument. Besides, she was the newest member of the team, and didn't feel she had enough experience to know what would be best – a commercial cover that might pull in more readers, or a punchier one, conveying the message of feminism to readers and non-readers alike. On Friday, there'd been a lot of heated talk about what *Adam's Apple* really stood for versus concerns about the falling readership. Rose was in the latter camp; she'd been brought in to revive the magazine, Kaisa had learned, and wanted a more mainstream feel. Some of the older members of the editorial team felt she was going too far. Kaisa knew Rose would be looking for her support, but late on Friday afternoon Kaisa hadn't been able to decide which course was best. She'd said nothing and kept her head down, preparing her latest article.

Kaisa moved away from the group, and lit a cigarette. It was a warm June night, and she was glad she'd worn the new gypsy dress that left her shoulders bare. Still, she felt hot, so she moved towards the large windows to get some air and cool down. It was when she looked out onto the street below that she saw them. Or him.

It couldn't be him, surely. Kaisa's eyes must be playing tricks on her. Or could it? Kaisa leaned further over the open window and stretched her neck for a better view of the two people who stood in the spot below the street-light. Kaisa froze when she saw it really was Peter. He was holding the hand of a slight, dark-haired girl. 'Jackie?' Kaisa thought with mounting horror. Peter was wearing jeans and a cotton shirt, and the girl wore a pretty little flower-patterned dress. It wasn't Jackie after all. My, the man moves fast, Kaisa thought, but she immediately reproached herself – hadn't she tried to have sex with Tom? And tonight, she was on the lookout, whether she admitted it or not. On her feet, the unknown girl wore cowboy boots. The look suited her. Although she couldn't fully see their faces, Kaisa could hear Peter and the girl laughing as they stepped inside the door.

What was Peter, a naval officer, doing in an artsy party in London? Kaisa panicked, and wanted to flee. But she knew Peter and the girl must now be coming up the stairs. Kaisa scanned the vast space for an exit sign, or another entrance. Suddenly she heard a group coming through a door behind her. She put her cigarette out, slipped past them and climbed a steel staircase onto the roof of the building. She was out of breath when she reached the roof. She'd been so flustered, she hadn't counted the number of floors. When she reached the roof, she noticed that someone had put cushions on the ledges to make temporary seats. Kaisa scanned the area, but couldn't see anyone there. The noise of traffic and the hum of people standing outside a pub a few streets away drifted towards Kaisa. Sighing with relief, she sat down on the nearest seat. She needed to think. For whatever reason, Peter was at the party, and whoever that pretty girl was, Kaisa didn't want to see either of them. At least it wasn't Jackie, Kaisa thought; still, she fought back tears when she thought about Peter and this new girl. Really she shouldn't have been surprised. Even before they were married, Kaisa had to fight off the girls vying for Peter's attention. She'd known that he'd moved on as Pammy's letter had indicated. His letters containing her allowance were as short as ever. Kaisa felt bad about continuing to accept Peter's money, but her salary was so small she needed the extra cash to survive in London. When she'd told Rose about Peter's allowance, Rose had said, 'You're still married, he has a duty to support you.' Kaisa felt that was a little hypocritical, but didn't want to say so to Rose; besides, she was sure her boss would come up with a perfectly well thought-out reason for Kaisa still being entitled to some of Peter's money. Something to do with the inequality in wages, Kaisa supposed. To her surprise, when Kaisa had told Peter about her new address, he hadn't commented on her move to London. She hadn't told him about *Adam's Apple,* just that she'd got a job working on a magazine. Peter hadn't even asked if she was working for *Sonia,* so he was obviously utterly uninterested in Kaisa's life. Kaisa realised she'd been hoping that he was simply still angry, and that with time he'd come around. How foolish she'd been! It was obvious he wasn't in the least bit concerned about Kaisa; as long as he paid her off each month, his conscience was clear. Kaisa could feel the familiar anger surge inside her. How was it possible even after all these months of not seeing him, and having a new, meaningful career (in London!), and after all they'd been through, that Peter could still ignite such emotion in her?

Kaisa shivered in the balmy air of the June night. She needed to think rationally. She would have to leave the party soon, but she needed to be sure she could slip out without being seen by Peter and his new girlfriend. Just thinking that thought made Kaisa feel short of breath. As she gasped for air, she told herself to calm down.

'What are you doing here?'

Kaisa hadn't noticed that the door to the roof space had opened, but she recognised his voice immediately. She got up and looked at Peter. He had put on some weight, she saw, but it suited him. His arms looked more muscular under his striped cotton shirt, and his face even more angular. He stood in the doorway, which made his hair and eyes look darker against the light coming from the stairwell below. He moved towards Kaisa and got a packet of cigarettes out of his jeans pocket.

'I could ask you the same thing,' Kaisa managed to say. With shaking hands, she took a Marlboro Light out of the packet Peter offered her, and waited for him to find his zippo lighter. As if in a dream, she put the cigarette to her lips and bent down to catch the flame from the lighter between Peter's cupped hands. She saw the zippo had a ship's crest on it and guessed it must be that of HMS *Orion*. Kaisa pulled a drag and watched Peter light his own cigarette.

'How are you,' Peter asked, his face showing no emotion.

Suddenly Kaisa's knees felt weak, and she sat back down on the raised bit of the roof. 'I'm fine.'

Now Peter grinned at her, 'Fancy seeing you here.'

Kaisa looked at him in surprise; it was as if the old Peter was back. 'Yeah, I wasn't expecting you either.'

Peter took a seat next to Kaisa, and for a moment they sat side by side, smoking their cigarettes.

'So how is life in the big city?' Peter asked, turning his face towards Kaisa.

She told him about *Adam's Apple,* and about her bedsit in Notting Hill.

'A feminist magazine, eh? That must suit you down to the ground.' Kaisa could hear the bitterness in his voice.

Kaisa took a deep drag on the cigarette. 'Yeah, Rose got me the job. She's invested a lot of money in it and wanted me to help her.'

Peter's mouth was a straight line. 'That's cosy.' He got up and, with his back to her, gazed across the London skyline. Kaisa spoke to his back, 'Really, Peter, you must believe me, he's the last person in the world I want to see. And Rose has been very good to me. I haven't seen him and Rose isn't speaking to him either. She thinks what he did was despicable.'

Peter gazed down at her, and Kaisa noticed his eyes looked sad. 'He still writes to you, though, doesn't he?'

Kaisa's heart raced. So it had been Peter who had forwarded Duncan's letter to her in Helsinki. She could feel tears well up inside, but she controlled herself. 'I had nothing to do with that.'

Peter turned around and sat next to her again. 'Really?'

'Really. I tore it up, and wouldn't dream of writing back to him. I have no feelings – apart from anger – towards him.' Kaisa had placed her hand on Peter's arm. Looking down at it, Peter said, 'You and me both.' She quickly took her hand away and the two sat side by side, watching the view over nighttime London in silence. There was an office building opposite, all its windows dark apart from one.

'Someone's working overtime,' Kaisa said, and stubbed out her cigarette on the lead roof.

'Or having it off with the boss,' Peter said, flicking his cigarette over the edge of the roof.

Kaisa turned her head towards Peter. 'Sorry, bad joke, in the circumstances,' he said. He was smiling, and nudged Kaisa. She also laughed and they sat quietly for a few moments more, then spoke at the same time.

'I wanted to …' said Kaisa. 'Perhaps I should …' said Peter.

'You go first,' Kaisa laughed.

They argued for a while about who should speak first, and Kaisa felt the awkwardness diminish by the second. 'No, you go, no you …' Eventually Peter spoke. 'Look Kaisa, I was wondering if we should talk about the future.'

'Yes, I was thinking the same.'

'Go on.' Peter's voice was soft and kind, and his eyes had the familiar tender look in them. She wanted to lean across and put her head on his shoulder and ask for his forgiveness. But the image of Peter with the unknown girl laughing on the street below reminded her that he was no longer hers.

'I am not earning as much as I'd like. The magazine isn't really making money yet, so,' she began.

'It's OK, you're still my wife. I'll carry on helping you as long as you want.'

'Thank you,' Kaisa said.

'It's OK.' Peter put his hand on Kaisa's knee. Kaisa looked up at him and before she could say anything, Peter had put his lips on hers. His kiss was urgent, and he placed his arms around Kaisa. She relaxed into his embrace. Her heart was pounding.

Kaisa wasn't sure if she saw the girl first, or felt her punch Peter in the back.

'What the hell is going on here?'

The dark-haired girl was standing in front of them, with her hands on her hips, staring at Peter and Kaisa, who'd detached herself from Peter and was staring back at the girl. Peter quickly stood up, 'Look Val, this is,'

'I don't care who the hell she is! I leave you alone for a minute, and you sneak up here and make out with a bloody …' The girl gave Kaisa a look up and down, and continued, 'a bloody blonde bimbo!'

Kaisa couldn't help herself, and let out a short laugh, or more like a snort. A bimbo, her? She looked at Peter to see what he would say, or do. Surely he would tell the girl to F off? Surely the kiss meant they were back together, or at least they'd try to patch things up again? Or?

Peter took the girl into his arms, and even though she resisted at first, she soon gave in and listened to Peter's words: 'Look, it meant nothing. Kaisa is my ex, and one thing led to another …'

Kaisa stared at the pair in front of her. Did she hear Peter correctly? It meant nothing! Kaisa got up and ran through the open door and down the stairs. When she reached the floor where the party was, she heard Peter's voice call out behind her, but she ignored it and ran through the room and down the stairs again. It wasn't until she was sitting at the back of a black cab that she let herself cry.

20

P eter got a first class ticket back to Plymouth because he just didn't have the patience to share a compartment with sailors he knew, as he had on the way up to London. He wanted to read the *Telegraph* and think how he could untangle himself from the web of women he'd become caught up in.

First there was Sam. Sex with the soft-skinned Wren was very satisfying, and she was always available. She was also kind, and cared for him, as he'd found out during an awful night when Peter had come back to the base from the GX alone. They'd bumped into each other in the corridor. He was very drunk, could hardly stand up, but Sam put his arm around her slender shoulders and quietly guided him into the correct cabin, undressed him and even brought him a glass of water and a bucket from the bathrooms, in case he was sick later. To be truthful, Peter didn't remember all that was said, but the next morning, when he woke up with the most awful hangover and tried to piece together the events of the previous night, he knew he'd poured his heart out to her. He remembered how he'd tried to take her clothes off for a quickie, and she'd just laughed and said, 'Another time, darling Peter.'

It was that word, 'Darling' that had unsettled him. Following that drunken night, he'd only been with her once or twice. He'd tried to play it cool with Sam, to show her that it wasn't serious. He'd told her from the start that his life was too complicated for a relationship, so she must know. But she was there, always around at the base. They still greeted each other in the wardroom, but he saw the yearning in her eyes, and as much as he liked the girl, he couldn't cope with that. It was difficult because the refit on HMS *Orion* kept overrunning; they should have sailed weeks ago. Now he was single again, he relished the time away at sea. It was different before, when it had meant leaving Kaisa.

Kaisa.

Thinking about Kaisa turned his thoughts immediately to Val. For some reason, he felt guilty about his affair with the young student. He was a little older than her, that was true, but only by a couple of years. It wasn't as if he was cradle snatching!

Sex with Val was a different thing altogether. Once, when they'd managed to sneak into her room at her parents' place in Plymouth (Peter hadn't met them and had no intention of doing so), Val had bitten his nipple during sex. Because they'd needed to be quiet, Peter couldn't cry out, even though the pain had seared through him, taking him by surprise. Somehow, that had made it better, though. There was plenty of passion with Val, and just thinking about her in the empty carriage, with the motion of the train gently rocking his body, Peter felt himself harden.

But she'd not let him back into her bed since she'd surprised him with Kaisa on the roof. Peter had to plead with her just to let him back into the house in Earl's Court, and then she'd made him sleep on the sofa in the lounge on the second floor. He'd had a disturbed night, with various residents of the house coming in at different times. Waking early, he had tried to call Kaisa on the number she'd given him in one of her long letters. He wanted to hear her voice, and was surprised to find she wasn't at home. Did she have someone else too? Someone she'd run to after kissing him? Peter waited for half an hour for her to ring back, but when the telephone in the hall remained silent, he snuck back into Val's bedroom upstairs and gathered his things. She was sprawled on her bed, wearing just her T-shirt. Her feet were protruding from under the blanket that covered the lower part of her body. From the contour of the thin covering, Peter could make out her feminine shape and remembered the small patch of dark hair between her legs. He could see her small breasts poking out from underneath her T-shirt. It took all his willpower to control himself and not take her into his arms. When he was at the door, he went back and kissed her forehead. Her lips were pink, and her eyelashes dark against her pale skin. He touched her cheek, but Val just murmured and turned her head away. He left the room on tiptoe and made his way to Paddington.

21

On the Sunday after the party, Kaisa stayed in bed as long as she could. By twelve o'clock she couldn't read anymore, and decided to go and get a newspaper and then telephone Rose to explain why she'd left without saying goodbye. There was a telephone fixed to the wall on the ground floor of the house, and as she lifted the heavy black receiver she saw her name, or a version of it, written on a folded piece of paper, stuck with a red pin on the noticeboard. It was the custom at the house, which contained five bedsits, to leave telephone messages on the board. Once again, whoever had taken the message hadn't bothered to come up the stairs to find her, nor could they spell her name correctly. Kaisa sighed and read the message.

'Keesi, someone posh called Peter left a message to call him back.' There was a London number below. On the spur of the moment, Kaisa lifted the receiver and dialled the number.

She had to wait five or six rings before anyone answered. 'Hello?'

Kaisa recognised the voice straight away. Surprising herself with her gumption, she said, 'Can I speak with Peter, please?'

There was a short silence at the other end. 'Who's calling?' Val said.

'It's Peter's wife.'

'Just a minute.'

Kaisa held the receiver with both hands and waited.

After a while, Val came back to the telephone and said, 'Sorry, he's not in.'

'But …' Kaisa began, but Val had already put the phone down at the other end, and all Kaisa could hear was the long tone of an empty line. He hadn't wanted to speak to her after all! Kaisa sat down on the rickety chair that the landlady had placed next to the phone, and thought for a moment. Had Peter's kiss been a reflex, a habit he'd not been able to shake off? Didn't it mean anything after all? Had it been a mistake, just as he'd told the girl, Val? Kaisa imagined the scene at the other end of the line: Val going to tell Peter that his wife was calling, and Peter shaking his head. Perhaps they were now in bed, laughing at Kaisa's eagerness to get back together with him? Kaisa shook her head. If that was the case, why had he phoned her in the first place?

Kaisa went back up to her bedsit and dug out a picture she had of Peter. She regretted she had no wedding photos of them together. In Finland, where they'd had the big wedding after the hasty registry office affair in Portsmouth, wedding photos were traditionally taken in a studio just before the ceremony. But Peter had said that was crazy; the groom wasn't supposed to see the bride in her wedding dress until she walked up the aisle. Instead, he wanted photos outside the church with all the guests and confetti flying above their heads. But the Finnish photographer wasn't used to taking wedding photos in the open air, and the resulting portraits were dark and terrible. They'd decided not to develop many of the pictures, and had ended up just giving one to Peter's parents and another to her mother and Sirkka. The photo of Peter that Kaisa kept in her purse was taken a few months before they were married. It showed him sitting on the casing of a submarine, wearing a white uniform shirt, with the cuffs rolled up, and resting his arms on his knees. Wearing a cap, he looked relaxed, with his head turned towards the camera, laughing at whoever was taking the photo. The sun was behind him, and in the background you could see the dock-yard, with a large crane just to the left of Peter. Kaisa always wondered who had taken the picture, and who Peter had been smiling at? When she'd asked him he said he couldn't remember.

On Monday morning, Kaisa came into the office of *Adam's Apple* early. She wanted to get a head start on the article she was preparing. She wasn't yet as confident in her English as a native speaker would have been, so it took her a lot longer to write the pieces Rose was now asking her to produce for every issue. This one was about what it was like to come and live in the UK as a foreign woman. Kaisa had interviewed three different people for the piece. In Brixton, in a council flat that smelled of strange spices, she'd interviewed Suni, an Indian lady, who wore a colourful sari and offered her home-made almond sweets. A lady from Jamaica had come into the offices, and spoken so heartrendingly about her first weeks in Britain, nearly twenty years ago, that the whole office had been in tears. Apart from Jenny, who'd balled her hands into fists and said, 'Those bastard skinheads, I could cut their fucking balls off.' But to Kaisa the tragedy of her story was the reaction – or lack of it – of ordinary people in England.

Imagining she'd be first in the office, Kaisa was surprised to see Rose sitting at her desk at the end of the room.

'Hi, Kaisa,' Rose said and looked up from the pile of papers in front of her. She'd recently started wearing a pair of reading glasses, with a golden string, which hung on her chest when she removed them, as she did now.

Leaving her handbag at her desk, Kaisa headed for the little kitchenette off the main office. She was holding a packet of her special coffee. Good coffee was the one thing she missed about Finland – the instant variety that everyone seemed to drink in England was more like muddy water – but about a month ago she'd made a discovery. In the streets around the office, she'd found several good coffee houses, mostly run by Italians, and she had recently found a new way to have proper coffee in the office, without having to buy an expensive percolator. Packets of single-cup ground coffee were stocked by a nearby shop. Every Monday she bought a packet of ten on her way to work and they just about lasted the five days. She could ill afford to offer them to others, but as everything was shared in the office she always asked around just in case.

'Would you like a cup of coffee?' she asked Rose from the doorway.

'Yes, please, but instant will do for me,' Rose said and smiled.

When Kaisa came back with two cups of hot, steaming coffee, Rose said, 'What happened to you on Saturday?'

Kaisa felt pang of guilt; after the unsettling call with Peter's girlfriend (just thinking about those two words made her chest fill with pain), she had completely forgotten to telephone Rose. She slumped down at her desk. 'Peter was there.'

'What?' Rose got up from her desk at the other end of the room and came to sit in front of Kaisa. She took Kaisa's hands in hers and said, 'Are you alright? What happened?'

Kaisa told Rose about seeing Peter, fleeing to the roof, how they'd talked and how it had seemed like old times. As if the past few months and the awful business with Duncan and Peter's court martial hadn't happened. 'And then he kissed me.'

'Oh, Kaisa,' Rose said.

From her face, Kaisa couldn't determine whether she thought this was a good thing or a catastrophe.

'And then his girlfriend saw us and punched Peter.'

'Oh, my God, was he alright?'

Suddenly Kaisa began to giggle; the whole thing seemed like a scene from a very bad film. But Rose regarded her with a serious face. 'What happened then?'

Kaisa told Rose what Peter had said to the girl, that the kiss hadn't meant anything. 'Peter told the girl I was just his ex.' Kaisa said. 'And then I missed his call on Saturday morning. When I called the number he'd left, the girl said he wasn't there.'

'Oh, Kaisa,' Rose said again. She rubbed Kaisa's hands, and cocking her head, gazed at her face. 'You still want to get back together with him, don't you?'

Kaisa looked down at her lap. 'I do still love him, but I don't know if we can ever get back together. I love my job here, and I'd never be able to give that up.' Tears were running down Kaisa's face. 'So I don't think our marriage was ever going to work.'

Rose hugged Kaisa. 'Oh you poor, poor love.'

When they heard the door open at the bottom of the stairs, and the voices of the other women, Rose quickly fetched a small packet of tissues from her desk and handed them to Kaisa, who fled to the cold bathroom next to the kitchenette. There, looking at her puffy red eyes, she decided enough was enough. She needed to face facts. Peter had moved on, that was probably why he'd called her on Saturday morning. To tell her the kiss was a mistake, and that she should forget about it. And Kaisa decided she would. She, too, would move on. She would make an effort to find somebody too. She'd say 'Yes' to the after-work drinks at the pub, she'd even go to the clubs Jenny and Barbara were forever talking about. She would at last have some fun.

22

Three weeks after she'd seen Peter at the party, and the kiss, Kaisa still hadn't heard anything further from him. There was no letter, no phone call. Kaisa hadn't told Peter where the offices of *Adam's Apple* were, so the only phone number and address he had for her was the Notting Hill bedsit. After she'd missed the call on the Saturday, Kaisa had stuck a note next to the telephone asking everyone to PLEASE let her know about any calls. Of course, this was what was supposed to happen anyway, but the others in the house seemed to have nocturnal lives; Kaisa very rarely saw anyone else.

Kaisa knew Peter could have gone off to sea. Still, serving in a diesel boat, he'd have the opportunity to write and post a letter even at sea, unlike when he served on the nuclear subs, or the Polaris ones. Kaisa shivered when she thought about the awful, long weeks she'd spent alone in Helensburgh. It felt as if all of it, the friendship with Lyn at the peace camp outside the Faslane naval base, the brief, but life-changing affair with Duncan, the disapproval of the other Navy wives, which she'd felt so acutely during the whole of their time in Scotland, had happened to someone else. Out of all the other wives she'd got to know in Scotland, she'd only been in touch with Pammy since leaving Helensburgh for Helsinki. Pammy and Nigel now had a little baby girl. Kaisa had sent a long letter of congratulations and a parcel containing a pale pink teddy bear with the softest fur and a friendly face, which she'd found and fallen in love with at Hamley's on Regent

Street. Pammy wrote back and begged Kaisa to visit; Nigel had gone on patrol the day after the baby was born and Pammy was desperate for company. She wrote to say how she still felt responsible for all that had happened between Kaisa and Peter, and for the fight with Duncan. Of course, it was true that had Pammy not told Kaisa's secret to Nigel, and he in turn hadn't told Peter, perhaps the fight in the pool at the base might never have happened. But Kaisa knew it was really nothing to do with Pammy; it was all her fault, and hers alone. She was the one who had let Duncan into her bed, and then gone and told Pammy about it. So it seemed strange how so many people around her felt guilty about the affair. Even Rose, her boss, felt bad about it, because she had encouraged the friendship between Duncan and Kaisa, not realising that her cousin had designs on her. But Kaisa had benefited from Rose's guilt, she was sure of it. Why else would Rose have invited her to London and given her such a crucial role in the magazine? It was true that *Adam's Apple* had no formal management structure, but everyone recognised that Rose was their editor, and Kaisa, as the newcomer, was the junior member of the team. Kaisa had also learned that when Rose had joined the magazine, she'd brought a substantial amount of money with her. It was these funds that had kept the magazine going, and before Rose had stepped in, there'd been talk of closing down the press. This made Kaisa feel even worse; in effect, Rose was funding her career. So Kaisa worked as hard as she could, helping Rose with research, writing articles whenever she was asked, even making cups of tea and coffee for everyone.

But the salary from *Adam's Apple* wasn't enough to sustain Kaisa, so she – to her shame – continued to accept the £200 from Peter, which he now paid directly into her bank account once a month. When Kaisa talked to Rose about taking the money, her boss was still adamant that she deserved it and she shouldn't feel bad.

After the party, Kaisa got into the habit of going to the pub with the rest of the girls after work. She'd have one pint of beer with them (all the women drank pints unlike the lady-like halves that the Navy wives ordered) in The Horseshoe pub at the end of Farringdon Close. The Horseshoe reminded Kaisa of The Palmerston Arms in Portsmouth; it had the same black paint outside, beneath a white-clad upper storey where she presumed the landlord lived, just like the publican parents of Jeff, Peter's best man. The bar filled half the pub, and there was even a snug at the back, around the far corner, just as there was at The Palmerston. There were no bunkettes, however, only round tables and chairs, in mock mahogany. The crowd in the pub mostly consisted of staff from other small publications around the area, and the team from *Adam's Apple* was often viewed with something alternating between fear and mockery. The other crowd, the working men, who came in their dirty overalls, splattered with paint, would nudge each other, make jokes under their breath, and grin in the women's direction. On occasion, the women, tired of the jibes, would go to the Three Kings at the other end of Clerkenwell Close. Or if they were celebrating a new issue, or a large donation, they'd cross the railway tracks and go into the Coach and Horses, which was frequented by reporters from the *Observer* or the *Guardian*, whose well-known offices were a few paces away from the large public house.

On a Thursday in late August, the staff of *Adam's Apple* were celebrating their best distribution figures since Rose took over the editorial team. They'd sold over 1,500 copies of the summer issue, and Rose's latest cover, for which she'd again had to fight hard, was deemed a great success. When Rose had opened the envelope containing the sales report, she'd thrown the sheet of paper up in the air and declared that the drinks would be on her after work. They had their first pints at The Horseshoe and then made their way to the Coach and Horses. Usually nights at this larger, and a lot posher pub, where the lounge and the rowdier bar were separated by a half-glazed wall, would go on until closing time. Alternatively, they'd move south to the bars around Fleet Street. As it was a Thursday, when the women entered the bar it was already full to bursting. Rose knew many of the *Guardian* reporters who drank there, so there were a few whistles and loud clapping when they entered. Everyone there had read the same sales reports and knew of the success of Rose's new venture. Most of the men in the pubs of Clerkenwell were a lot older than Kaisa, but on this night her eyes met a tall man, leaning on the bar, next to a greying man in a waistcoat who was talking animatedly with Rose. Kaisa recognised Roger from the warehouse party; she wondered if Rose was having a relationship with him.

Kaisa was handed her drink – she'd switched to a G&T because too much beer made her feel bloated – and was standing alone, separated from her colleagues by the general commotion their entrance had caused. The man next to Roger was watching Kaisa, and when their eyes met, he lifted his pint to her in a greeting, his smile revealing the whitest teeth Kaisa had ever seen. Kaisa smiled back, feeling a warmth in her body, and a flutter in her stomach. The man wore a white shirt, the sleeves rolled up on account of a heatwave in London, and a waistcoat and matching trousers in dark grey stripes, which were obviously part of a suit. He had very dark features, a black, almost shiny, mop of hair, and brown eyes. Kaisa hadn't felt a flutter like this in months, even years. The man leaned over to say something to his shorter friend, and walked over to Kaisa.

'Hello, I'm Ravi.' He offered his hand and for a moment she just stood there, holding onto his warm, firm handshake and sinking deep into those dark eyes. Ravi had thick, almost feminine eyelashes, making it look as if he'd applied eyeliner under and above his eyes. 'What's your name?' he continued when Kaisa didn't say anything.

'Kaisa,' she breathed. She hardly had any air left in her lungs.

'And you are part of this women's magazine?'

'Yes,' Kaisa said, and managed to move her gaze away from the man's eyes.

'Well, for an *Adam's Apple* reporter, you don't have much to say for yourself!' Ravi laughed.

Kaisa laughed and took a sip of her G&T. The laughter had managed to break the spell, and she asked, 'Are you from the *Guardian*?'

'Oh, lord, no. I work in the City.' Kaisa now realised, listening to the man's voice, that he was a posh boy.

It transpired that Ravi's parents were Indian. They'd come over to Britain during the partition, and Ravi, the youngest of five had been born in the UK. He'd been a clever boy at school and had gone to Cambridge, where he'd studied law. He worked for a Swiss bank.

'What are you doing here on a Thursday night?'

'Oh, one of my friends from Cambridge works for the *Observer*, so we often meet after work.'

Kaisa and Ravi talked all evening about everything and anything. Ravi told her about his traditional Indian family, about how his mother cooked the best dahl and chapatis in the world. Kaisa knew nothing about Indian culture – she'd been to an Indian restaurant while in London, of course, but Ravi said that food in those places was nothing like his mother's. He said how different life had been in Cambridge after his grammar school just outside Birmingham, where he'd grown up.

'I was the only Indian boy at my college in Cambridge, and although everyone was friendly, I knew I wasn't one of them,' Ravi said. Kaisa was mesmerized and wanted to lean over and kiss those full lips. She realised she was a little tipsy.

Kaisa knew exactly what he meant. She told Ravi about her studies at Hanken, where the others had come from wealthy Swedish-speaking families, and she'd felt like an outsider. She also told him about her move from Finland to the UK, and about her failed marriage.

'You're married?' Ravi asked, his face displaying surprise. 'You seem hardly old enough to be out of school!'

Kaisa looked down at her hands. If only he knew the whole sorry story, she thought. They talked until last orders were announced at 11 pm, and then Ravi told Kaisa he was going home.

'But I've enjoyed talking to you,' he said and looked deeply into Kaisa's eyes.

'Me too,' she smiled.

Kaisa gave Ravi her telephone number, and he thanked her, bowing his head. Kaisa realised the reason she was attracted to him, apart from his looks, was his polite and attentive manner. In London, men were different, much more direct with their advances. Kaisa had got so used to the politeness and chivalry displayed by naval officers that she was shocked by British men's rowdy and leery manners in the pubs around the office. Jenny had laughed when Kaisa had mentioned this to her.

'Why should men open doors and let women go first?' She laughed, but growing serious, added, 'It's patronising and sexist.'

Kaisa could only agree; still in her unvoiced opinion it was equally sexist to shout out lewd remarks at a woman passing a building site, or to bother a woman in a pub when she obviously didn't want to talk, or to shut a door in a woman's face if she didn't reciprocate a man's advances. In Finland, men had to be quite drunk before they approached you in such a forthright manner.

Ravi telephoned her in the office the next day. 'I didn't give you this number,' she laughed.

'No,' he said, 'but I knew I'd get hold of you here. I wondered if I could take you out tonight?'

Kaisa was so surprised, that she didn't immediately reply.

'If you're free, that is?'

'I'd love to.'

Ravi said he'd pick her up from work, and Kaisa panicked; she was wearing her 'boy clothes' to work again, and remembering how smart Ravi had looked the previous evening, she wanted to wear something more feminine.

When Kaisa told Rose about her date, and asked if she could take a long lunch hour, Rose gave Kaisa a £50 note and said, 'Treat yourself.' Kaisa tried to refuse the money, but Rose was so insistent, it suddenly seemed impolite to say no. She ran down the stairs from the office and made her way to Miss Selfridge on Oxford Street. It was still hot in London, so Kaisa looked for a summer dress in the sales. She found a floaty Laura Ashley-type cotton dress. It fitted her nicely, making her look slim, with a small waist. She found a pair of strappy wedge sandals, too, and then took the tube home to make a quick change and collect some make-up to apply later. When she got inside the house, and picked up the pile of post on the mat, she saw a blue airmail envelope addressed to her in familiar handwriting. She tore open the letter and read the words inside.

'*Kaisa,*

I hope you are keeping well. I'm away at sea, but will be back end of August. I wonder if we could talk? I will be in London on 28th. Meet me at Café des Amis, 11 Hanover Place, Covent Garden at 7 o'clock.

Peter'

Kaisa sat down on the thinly carpeted stairs, and reread the short letter. What did this mean? After the kiss, and the missed phone call, she hadn't heard from Peter for two whole months; no nearly three months, because it was now nearly the end of August and the party had been in mid-June. The letter was dated two weeks earlier, and the postmark was somewhere in Scotland, so he must have posted it from one of the small villages they occasionally docked at. But why did he want to meet? To talk about what? And today! Kaisa thought for a moment, but she knew, had known as soon as she read the letter, that she had to meet up with Peter. There was no getting around it. But she didn't have Ravi's number.

Kaisa got up and dialled the office number, 'Rose, I've had a letter from Peter. He's in London tonight and wants to meet up.'

'You must go,' Rose sighed, 'What will you tell Ravi?'

'That I've taken ill. A tummy bug? Is it alright if I stay at home this afternoon? Just in case he comes early or something. And can you talk to him, please?'

'OK,' Rose said, adding, 'Look, if you want to meet afterwards, we'll be in The Horseshoe until closing time.'

The Café des Amis was on a side street off St Martin's Lane. Kaisa didn't know Covent Garden very well, and got lost before she saw the red neon lights of the restaurant. When she got inside, she was led down a set of stairs into a cellar, which was lit by dimmed lights and candles on red-check tablecloths. Peter was already there, sitting at a table in the far corner of the room. He looked tanned, and his hair was a little longer, touching the collar of his shirt. He stood up when Kaisa approached, and kissed her lightly on the cheek.

'You look good,' he said as they both sat down, and then seeming to regret his words, he coughed and added, 'I mean, that's a nice dress.'

'Thank you, so do you.' Kaisa had decided to wear her new purchase. She needed to have the confidence of looking her best when seeing Peter. She now gazed up at Peter's face and saw he was smiling. 'I mean you look good, too, not that your dress is nice.'

They both laughed.

'You got my letter,' Peter said after the waiter had given them menus and Peter had ordered a bottle of red wine.

'Yes, today!' Kaisa told him how she'd gone home during her lunch hour (she didn't say why), and had she not happened to do that she would not be sitting opposite him now.

'Well that's lucky then,' Peter said, but he wasn't smiling. His eyes were sad, as if he wished Kaisa hadn't got the letter in time. 'What will you have?' he added quickly before Kaisa could say anything. 'My treat.'

Kaisa ordered *moules marinieres* to start and a steak for mains. She felt like eating meat tonight, even though during her time in London she'd become almost vegetarian. Most of the girls in the office were fierce non-meat eaters, so it was just easier not to bring in ham sandwiches. Besides, Kaisa liked the lentil stews and bean salads they ate, and it was cheaper. Her new diet must have been why she'd lost so much weight. She was a size 10 now, whereas when she was married she'd sometimes had to go up to 14 in jeans and trousers.

'You've lost weight,' Peter said and lifted his glass.

Kaisa wondered if he was reading her mind.

They tasted the wine, which was very good, and again neither spoke for a while.

Kaisa could sense that there was something Peter wanted to say, but he didn't know how to get around to it. Kaisa was surprised by her own reaction to him. She had been very nervous on the tube, which was probably why she had got so hopelessly lost, but now, facing him, her feelings had settled. It was nice to see him looking so well. The gaunt look he'd had in June had disappeared. Perhaps he'd put on some more weight, or perhaps it was the sea air. 'You've been away?' she asked.

'Yes, got back on Wednesday. I've been in Pompey with Jeff.'

'Oh, how is he?'

'He's getting married.'

"Finally!' Kaisa laughed, 'is this one going to go through with it?'

'I think so, she's a Wren, so there should be no problem career-wise.'

'That's good. Send him my love.'

Peter's eyes met Kaisa's and he nodded. 'The wedding's tomorrow.'

'And you're not out with him? Shouldn't he be having his stag night now?'

'No, Milly, that's his wife-to-be, forbade it.'

'Well, miracles never cease,' Kaisa said.

They both laughed again. Kaisa wondered if he was going to take Val to the wedding, but stopped herself before formulating the question. Who Peter decided to date was nothing to do with her.

With the wine, their conversation grew warmer, and they began reminiscing about Jeff's various girlfriends, which led to talk about their married quarter in King's Terrace and the incident of the lost car. Although it was Duncan who had driven the car into next door's garage, making Kaisa believe that the vehicle had been stolen, his name was studiously avoided by both of them.

'I'm sure the policeman and woman had a good laugh afterwards. I can't believe I told them the car had a heart on its bonnet!' Kaisa said, giggling, remembering how Jeff had drawn the shape of a heart on their small Ford Fiesta after the registry office marriage in Portsmouth. Because Kaisa had neglected to wash the car for weeks afterwards, the heart remained a special feature of the car.

'Bloody Jeff. I got less money for it because of the corrosion that shaving foam caused!'

'You sold the Fiesta!' Kaisa exclaimed and they both laughed again at the sentimental associations of that car.

Towards the end of the meal, when they were both tucking into their puddings – they'd both asked for a *creme brûlée*, almost simultaneously – Peter grew quiet.

'I've missed you,' Kaisa said. She was surprised by her boldness, but suddenly thought this was her chance, and if Peter was here to talk about a reconciliation, why shouldn't she help him out a little? She reached across the table and touched his fingers. 'You know I regret everything that happened.'

'Everything?' Peter said, and hearing the hostility in his voice, the coldness that had made her flee Helensburgh for Helsinki, she removed her hand and looked down at her dessert. The waiter appeared with coffee, and they both thanked him. Kaisa was grateful for the interruption, and when the waiter had gone, she lifted her eyes once more to gauge if Peter's mood had permanently changed.

'I am sorry,' Peter said, 'and of course I've missed you too.' Peter now took hold of Kaisa's hand and she had to fight back tears. 'But we have to make a decision about the future.'

'What do you mean?'

Peter gave Kaisa a long, kind look, as if to warn her, 'I want a divorce.'

23

'How did it go?' Jackie asked as soon as Peter walked through the entrance at the bottom of the stairs.

'Fine' he replied and gave her a light kiss on her mouth.

'C'mon, did she make a fuss?'

'Let me have a drink first.'

Jackie was wearing a very short leather skirt, and when she bent down to pick up a glass from the sideboard, Peter could see the tops of her stockings. 'Gin and tonic OK?'

'Sure.'

Jackie disappeared into the kitchen, which was just off the large living room in her Chelsea flat. Smiling, she brought in two drinks in heavy cut glass tumblers. Peter took one and swirled the ice cubes and the slice of lemon in the glass to buy some time. He was sitting on a dark burgundy Chesterfield sofa, and Jackie settled herself next to him. She pulled her legs up and curled herself like an attention-seeking cat in the crook of Peter's arm. Peter could see inside her bra, and enjoyed the view of a pink areola. Now the straps of her suspenders were visible too. Peter put his glass down and ran his fingers along Jackie's thigh.

'Not until you tell me everything,' Jackie said and gently brushed Peter's hand away. 'You naughty boy,' she purred and placed her hand on his groin. He felt himself harden even more.

They had sex on the sofa, fast, and afterwards Jackie said, 'Really, now you have to tell me.'

She'd been to her bedroom to change into a dressing gown, but she'd kept her stockings on. She knew exactly how to play him, Peter thought, and relaxed back into the sofa. 'Another drink?'

While Jackie went to fix them a second round of G&Ts, Peter thought how perfect she was for him. Their 'romance', as Jackie insisted on calling it, whenever she described their two-month old relationship, began at the Drake Summer Ball. Peter had just come back from London, where Val had practically thrown him out of her house, and he was in no mood for a party. He'd forgotten all about the event, and on the morning of the ball, he had to beg the laundry to clean and iron his Mess Undress shirt in double quick time. When he'd signed up for the ball, he'd decided not to ask Sam to accompany him, although she'd sent him woeful glances right up until the day of the ball. He'd had enough of women for one weekend, so he was going to fly solo for once. Besides, the taste of Kaisa's mouth was still lingering on his lips.

But he soon changed his mind. He'd spotted Jackie as he sat down at one of the long tables of the wardroom, below the wooden models of 17th-century sailing ships. She was sitting diagonally opposite him, wearing a low-cut dress with a pearl choker around her neck and long black gloves. The dress had no straps, and she was not wearing a bra. When she leaned over, Peter (and every other officer around the table with a view of her chest) could make out the loose, untethered shape of her breasts. When Peter caught her eye, she smiled and held his gaze for a moment longer than necessary. 'Game on,' Peter had thought and sought her out as soon she got up.

'Fancy seeing you here,' Jackie had said, taking his arm when he reached her at the end of the long table. Peter kissed her lightly on the cheek, and walked her to the ladies. He'd gone to pee himself quickly, and then waited outside the ladies for her. He'd been rewarded with a wide smile, and when they were back in the wardroom, Jackie had organised for Peter to sit next to her for the coffee and port. They'd talked all night, occasionally going for a dance in the disco set up downstairs. They were old friends, after all, Peter thought, but he knew he was really fooling himself. Jackie and he had had a short dalliance when he'd been at Dartmouth, well before Kaisa. She was a catch, everyone kept telling Peter then, but he wasn't interested. He wanted to be single and free of any ties. His career in the Navy was just beginning, and the stories older naval officers kept telling him about the 'runs ashore' when the ship docked at different ports, and skirt was easy to come by, excited him. His future didn't feature a wife sitting at home, waiting for him to come back from sea. Luckily, he'd already been appointed to his first ship at the time, and had sailed the next day. Jackie and Peter had exchanged a few letters, and had kept in touch even after he'd met Kaisa, but there had never again been more to it than friendship. Peter recalled the breakfast party Jackie had invited Peter and Kaisa to the year before. They'd been so happy and Kaisa had looked gorgeous in her strappy top, which she'd worn without a bra, showing off her lovely figure. All the men at the party had been jealous of him, and that bastard Ducan had been all over Kaisa. Peter brushed away any thoughts of *him*, and instead thought of how Jackie too had congratulated him on his beautiful new bride. She'd seemed genuinely happy for him then. But, of course, Kaisa had smelled a rat; she knew Peter too well, and on the way home they'd had another argument, this time about Jackie. Peter shook his head when he remembered all their bitter rows, then recalled the way they used to make up in bed afterwards, and sighed. It was no use thinking of Kaisa, she was history now.

At the ball, Jackie had initiated a kiss goodnight with Peter, and he held tightly onto her tiny waist. The trouble was, even though she was short, had dark hair and a large, wide breasts so different from Kaisa's blonde locks and small pointy breasts, there was something about the curve of her bottom and the smooth skin of her thighs that made Peter think of Kaisa. When they were doing it, he'd close his eyes and pretend he was with his soon-to-be ex-wife.

'So,' Jackie now said, handing Peter his second drink, 'please tell me how it went.'

'Actually, it was alright.' Peter said, taking a sip of out of the glass.

'Yeah?' Jackie narrowed her dark eyes, which were smudged with makeup, making her look more dirty, and sexy. Her hair was short and wavy, a sort of auburn version of Princess Di's. She had a very long, slender neck, and she held herself well, displaying her posh background, Peter supposed. It was her class that turned Peter on. For now, although she was from a very different world from his, she was only wearing stockings, suspenders, and expensive French knickers underneath her silk dressing gown, just for his benefit. He knew this posh girl was all his.

'So she agreed to the divorce?'

'Well …'

Jackie moved herself away from him. 'Peter, you did tell her?'

Jackie had been the one to insist on the conversation with Kaisa. Her father was an admiral, and she knew a thing or two about how the Navy worked. She'd said that for his career, the best thing he could do was to get a divorce as soon as possible. 'You won't get anywhere if you don't deal

with her,' she now said. 'You know that. I talked to Daddy only yesterday
…'

Peter sat up on the sofa. 'What, you talked to your father about me?'

Jackie was playing with the belt of her dressing gown, rolling it up to a
tight ball. She wasn't looking at Peter. 'I just wanted to hear it from him,
you know, to see what his advice would be.' Jackie lifted her eyes to Peter.
'He has a lot of experience and has chaired a lot of court martials. He really
knows what's best, so why wouldn't I ask him?'

Peter slumped back down on the sofa and took a long pull out of his
glass. He didn't want to think back to the court martial, to that awful chilly
morning last January. To how unhappy Kaisa had been, to her hopeless
tears, to his inability to comfort her. He lit a cigarette and offered
Jackie one.

'No thanks,' she said.

Peter took a few drags out of his cigarette before he spoke. 'So, go on,
tell me what he said.'

Jackie's dad had confirmed what Peter already knew. Everyone felt that,
though Duncan had behaved despicably in seducing another officer's wife
(here Jackie looked down at her hands, and not at Peter. She knew Peter
didn't like talking about the detail of the events in Helensburgh), Kaisa had
also been to blame. There had also been talk in Faslane about Kaisa
befriending one of the peace campers, but these rumours were just that,
rumours. 'Still, rumours can bring down a career,' Jackie's father had said.
He'd concluded that if, as his daughter had told him, Peter was already
estranged from his foreign wife, the best thing he could do was to make the
state permanent. 'Forget all about her, put the whole saga down to the hot-
headedness of youth and move on,' was his advice.

When Jackie had finished, the two were silent. Peter lit another
cigarette, and listened to the distant noises of the city. Jackie's flat was in a
cul-de-sac of mews houses, and the main thoroughfare was several streets
away, so the far-away sound of police sirens reached the flat only occasionally. But now, some poor bugger must be in trouble, Peter thought, as he
listened to the wail of sirens disappear into the London night.

'Well, I told her I want a divorce and she seemed OK about it,' Peter
finally said. He got up and yawned. 'Bed?' he said and Jackie nodded.

24

Ravi telephoned Kaisa the next day. She was still in bed when she heard the knock on the door. An older man, Colin, who Kaisa knew lived in the ground floor flat with the landlady, Mrs Carter, stood in his pyjamas and a stripey dressing gown outside her door. 'Phone for you.' He seemed angry in his worn out slippers, his grey hair sticking out in all directions. Kaisa suspected it was Colin who hadn't told her about Peter's phone call earlier in the summer, and was now annoyed with her because he'd seen her note on the pinboard. She thanked him, put on a jumper over her pyjamas and flip-flops that she wore to go to the bathroom, and hurried down the two floors to the entrance hall.

'Hello.' Kaisa was a little out of breath, but she was afraid Peter would give up if she made him wait for too long.

'Hi, Kaisa. It's Ravi, I just wanted to phone and see if you are feeling better.'

Kaisa held on to the receiver, trying to think what to say. 'Hi, Ravi.'

'Rose told me you weren't very well?'

'I'm fine now, feeling a bit weak, that's all.'

'I'm glad.'

Kaisa cleared her throat. 'Thank you for calling,' she found it difficult to lie, so she said simply, 'and I'm sorry I couldn't make it yesterday.'

'That's alright. But, I really wanted to see if you'd be up to doing something tonight. Or perhaps on Sunday?'

Kaisa sighed.

'But don't worry, if ...'

'Ravi, I'm not feeling quite up to going out yet,' she said, interrupting him. Now she wasn't lying. She'd not had a tummy bug, but she wasn't feeling well after last night.

'Oh, OK. Take my telephone number in case you change your mind.'

Kaisa hung up and stood in the hall for a moment. Should she have bucked herself up and agreed to see Ravi after all? But she just couldn't. She needed to be on her own and think. Kaisa walked slowly up the stairs and, once in her room, flung herself on the bed and let the tears flow.

She spent the rest of Saturday morning in Notting Hill Gate Library, a large white-clad stucco building just off Portobello Road, where the market was in full swing. She was helped with her research by an older woman wearing half-moon glasses. 'I think you might need to consult a lawyer, dear,' she said to Kaisa after they'd spent more than an hour going through various government information papers.

Kaisa walked home through the throng of people wandering slowly along Portobello Road, browsing the rickety stalls that sold anything from silverware to fresh vegetables. They looked happy and free, talking and laughing with each other. Kaisa couldn't concentrate on the colourful scene. She felt as if she was in a trance. Just as she had got herself a job, almost a new boyfriend, and had finally accepted during the hour or so spent crying her eyes out that her marriage to Peter was over, her life in London was to be served a final, fatal blow by the British government.

It had occurred to her, as she had lingered in bed that morning, trying to get used to the idea of a divorce from Peter, that if he really wanted to sever their relationship for good, she probably could live with it. She had a new life now, living in London with a job that was worthwhile. Isn't that what she'd always wanted? The job may not pay as well as it should, but Kaisa was sure she could ask Rose for a pay rise to cover at least some of the money she'd lose from Peter's monthly allowance. She'd felt bad about taking the money for so long, and it would be a sort of relief for it to stop. They hadn't discussed money at the restaurant the night before, but it was obvious to her that a divorce meant the allowance would end. She was certain that wasn't the reason for Peter's wanting a divorce, but she'd been too shocked to ask him. If she was truthful to herself, she hadn't wanted to be told he was going to marry the leggy dark-haired girl from the party. But now, thinking about their marriage and how it all came about, Kaisa had remembered that the only reason she had 'leave to stay in the United Kingdom', as the stamp on her passport said, was because she was married to an Englishman. What if they divorced? Would her 'leave to stay' be removed?

The answer from her research at the library was that this was most probably the case.

Kaisa cursed herself. She should have been braver. If this was true, she needed to stay married for at least seven years to be able to say and work in England. Otherwise she'd have to apply for a work permit, which she knew she wouldn't get for her job at *Adam's Apple*. Every week they got a letter or two asking if there were any jobs going at the magazine from school leavers, and even graduates in journalism. Most of the letters were written in terrible English, but some of them were good, and these were kept in a special file on the shelf behind Rose's desk. Any one of those girls could replace Kaisa in the blink of an eye.

When she got back to Colville Terrace, Kaisa took out the scrap of paper on which she'd written Ravi's number.

'Hi Ravi, I'm feeling better.'

Kaisa didn't come clean to Ravi about why she wanted to see him until they were sitting opposite each other in a Chinese restaurant. She'd planned to tell him on the phone, but he had sounded so elated about her change of heart that she couldn't bring herself to spoil it. When she saw his wide smile outside Tottenham Court Road tube station, she walked up to him and let him kiss her on the cheek. He suggested going to see a film, *Letter to Brezhnev*, at nearby Leicester Square Odeon. When they were out of the cinema, sitting in a restaurant in China Town, Ravi said, 'That wasn't very diplomatic of me, was it?'

Kaisa smiled, 'Actually, the theme sort of touched upon the reason I wanted to see you.'

'Oh?'

'Yes, finding, and, in my case, losing love during the Cold War. My husband wants a divorce.'

Ravi's beautiful face was suddenly serious. There was also a look of disappointment in the line of his mouth. Kaisa wanted to tell him that she also really liked his company, but that she just wasn't ready for a relationship yet. She might have been, had she not seen Peter again. But she couldn't tell him the truth about last night, not yet. 'I'm sorry, but I've come out with you under false pretences. I need your help,' Kaisa said.

Ravi gazed at Kaisa for a long time. 'I'm not a divorce lawyer,' he said finally.

'I know, and that's not what I meant.' Kaisa told Ravi about what she'd found out in the library. The man sat opposite her and listened. The restaurant was a large room, where round tables, covered in crisp white linen, were set out in the middle of the room. Small Chinese women walked in and out of a set of swing door at the far end, pushing a trolley filled with bamboo steamers and bowls covered with small silver domes. Each time they moved through the doors, smells of cooking wafted into the dining room. Ravi had ordered for them both, because Kaisa had never been to a Chinese restaurant before, and the menu didn't have an English translation. They'd been given bowls of rice and a sticky vegetable dish, but they hadn't touched them yet. Kaisa hoped Ravi wouldn't be angry with her. She didn't know him at all, but she was desperate. Ravi was the only lawyer she knew.

When Kaisa had finished speaking, Ravi picked up a set of chopsticks and smartly moved a piece of courgette from the dish into his mouth. Kaisa watched him and waited.

'OK,' Ravi said and carefully set down his chopsticks on a side plate. Absentmindedly, Kaisa noticed how slender his fingers were.

'This is not my area of expertise. I'm a commercial lawyer, but I have dealt with a few work permits for Swiss residents in the bank.' He lifted his eyes up to Kaisa and continued. 'You are correct in that you will lose your right to stay in Britain, and your work permit, if you divorce. If you had had a child with your husband, that would be a different matter. In that case, you'd be able to stay as you are now. Another issue is the length of marriage. Here there are two problems. Firstly, since the marriage has been so short, less than seven years, as you correctly found out, you will simply lose your leave to stay. Secondly, and here I need to give a word of caution, if it is deemed that your marriage was a sham, in other words, you married under false pretences, both of you could be charged with an offence against the Immigration Act. It will normally only result in a fine, so there's no danger of a custodial sentence. However, if you were to stay after your divorce, then you may be detained under the Immigration Act, until you are deported back to Finland.'

Kaisa noticed how he avoided saying Peter's name and couldn't help but smile, which she suppressed as soon as she saw Ravi's serious expression. 'I see,' she said, and added, 'What do you think I should do?'

Their conversation was interrupted by the delivery of more food. A smiling lady placed a steaming bamboo dish from her trolley in front of them and bowed. 'Please,' she said and carried on towards the next table.

Kaisa picked up a hot dumpling. 'This is delicious!' she said, and now Ravi smiled.

'Look, you really need to go and see a family lawyer, or someone who specialises in immigration law. You could try the Citizens Advice Bureau.' Ravi lifted his dark eyes at Kaisa. 'But I think the best option is to stay married.'

On Monday, when Kaisa got to the office, Rose was already there.

'So, how did it go on Friday?'

Kaisa slumped down in her chair and said, 'He wants a divorce.'

Rose came over and perched herself on Kaisa's desk, 'Oh, my dearest. But, you know, this might be for the best.'

'Yes,' Kaisa said and added, 'so I went out with Ravi on Saturday.'

Rose smiled, 'Good girl!'

Kaisa didn't tell Rose why she'd met up with Ravi. She didn't want Rose to think she might lose her permit to stay in England, so she just smiled and picked up the list of companies Rose had given her the previous week. With the increased reader figures, the magazine was writing to as many potential advertisers as possible. Rose had told Kaisa that the magazine was still losing money. The letters all said the same, but Rose didn't want to send photocopies. 'Not personal enough,' she said, so Kaisa's job was to write fifty letters that were identical apart from the person's name and address. It was boring work, but Kaisa didn't mind it. As long as she could stay in London and work for *Adam's Apple*, she'd be happy. The idea of asking Peter to forget about a divorce and stay married to her for another six years so that she'd be able to stay in the UK sent a chill down her spine. How would she be able to ask Peter that? She decided she'd just have to get in touch with him and explain the situation. At the end of their unusually unromantic evening, Ravi had asked her if she wanted to see him again. His eyes were so very brown and his mouth so very full that Kaisa couldn't resist him and had said, 'Yes, but I am a bit confused, so ...'

Ravi had taken her hands into his over the table and said, 'I understand.'

He was such a gentleman, and so good-looking, but Kaisa had noticed how they'd received sideways glances by people on the street. When they'd queued up to buy their tickets at Tottenham Court Road tube station, an older man had stared at them so intently that Kaisa thought he would say something. Not letting go of Kaisa, Ravi had straightened himself up and looked back at the man. Eventually the man had muttered something under his breath and turned towards the woman behind the glass. Ravi lived in north London, so they'd parted ways at the bottom of the escalator. 'May I kiss you,' Ravi had said, causing Kaisa to smile. After a moment's hesitation she replied, 'Yes.'

Ravi took hold of Kaisa's waist, and pulled her close to him. His lips were soft, and when they met Kaisa's mouth, she relaxed into Ravi's arms. The kiss lasted just for a few seconds, but it was so gentle that Kaisa had an odd dreamy sensation all the way to Notting Hill Gate. In bed that night, she half wished she'd asked Ravi to come home with her, but she knew she couldn't have gone through with anything. It was just lovely to be kissed by a man after such a long time. Kaisa tried to brush away the memory of Peter's lips against hers in June. She must forget all romantic ideas she had of their continued relationship and move on. It was obvious he had. All she needed was for him to postpone the divorce. She hoped he'd agree to stay married for the sake of her work permit – and career.

During her lunch hour, Kaisa used the telephone box on the street corner and telephoned the wardroom at Devonport. 'Can I speak with Lieutenant Peter Williams, please?'

'Just a moment, madam,' came the reply from a man at the other end. Kaisa had half expected them to tell her he wasn't available. Still, he probably didn't know and had to check. Kaisa hoped that Peter hadn't sailed yet; at the same time, she was nervous about having to speak with him. But she couldn't risk him talking to a lawyer, and starting the divorce proceedings, before she'd told him what the consequences would be for her. Or perhaps he knew? No, that couldn't be. Kaisa remembered how friendly their dinner had been – or more than friendly. It had been like old times until he'd dropped the bombshell.

'Yes,' the voice at the other end of the line said.

'Peter?' Kaisa found she was suddenly breathless.

'Kaisa?' Peter's voice was full of surprise. 'Is something wrong?'

'No, no,' Kaisa heard the concern in his voice. She was touched; he still cared for her! 'But I need to speak to you about what we discussed on Friday.'

'Oh?'

'Yes, it's a bit difficult on the phone. I'm in a telephone box outside my office, and, well, there's a guy waiting to use the phone.' Kaisa looked at the man through the dirty glass of the phone box. He was wearing a suit, watching her every move and listening to her every word. 'It's not very private,' she added, giving the man a look, but he continued to stand there, close to the door.

'Right,' Peter said. He was quiet for a moment, thinking.

Kaisa didn't dare say anything, and just waited.

'Look, we're sailing on Friday, and I don't have any leave before that.'

'I see.'

'But, if you can get yourself here, I'm off till tomorrow evening.'

'To Plymouth?'

'Yes, unless it can wait six weeks?'

Kaisa was thinking hard. A return ticket to Plymouth would be expensive, but she could manage it. She'd have to leave work early, and come back with the last train of the day. Or perhaps with the milk train that ran through the night.

'Ok,' she said and Peter told her the train she needed to catch. He'd come and meet her at the station.

It took nearly four hours to get to Plymouth, so on the long journey she practised what she would say to Peter. She first thought she'd ask him why he wanted a divorce, but then realised that she didn't want to hear his reasons. No, the best thing was just to come out and say it. Explain how much she loved working for *Adam's Apple,* and that she needed to be married to continue working in the UK.

25

eter was standing on the platform in Plymouth, wearing a pair of
cords and a light blue cotton shirt. He'd tied a jumper around his
shoulders. It was early September, but the weather was still warm,
even with the sun just setting behind the drab-looking 1960s railway building. Kaisa walked nervously towards him, but couldn't help but smile and
quicken her step when she saw the grin on his face. For a moment, she felt
as if everything that had happened during the past year was forgotten. As if
any moment now, Peter would open up his arms and welcome her into his
embrace. But when she got close to him, he continued to stand motionless,
looking at her. She was conscious of the clothes she'd chosen for the journey. She was wearing a skirt for once, instead of her 'boy clothes', and her
beige boots that she knew Peter liked. She wore a mohair jumper over a
strappy vest, and had taken a small overnight case with make-up and a
change of underwear in case she needed to go straight to the office from the
train the next morning.

'Hi,' Kaisa said and stopped in front of him.

'Am I allowed to hug you?' Peter said, after they'd stood facing each
other for a while. The train had emptied of people, most of whom had
walked past them, some giving them odd looks for standing in the middle of
the concourse, in their way. Now the platform was empty.

Kaisa didn't say anything but nodded and moved closer to Peter. He put
his arms around her, first tentatively, then firmly, and hugged her hard.

Kaisa breathed in Peter's scent. He'd used his familiar coconut scented aftershave, and the smell of it made Kaisa feel faint. She'd dropped her bag on the platform, and now lifted her hands and wrapped them around him. His body felt taut, as he squeezed her hard. Quickly, he let go of her and took hold of her bag. 'This way,' Peter said and guided her through the low-slung building towards the car park. His new car was another sports model, but this time it was red and a lot bigger than the Fiesta, or the yellow Spitfire he'd had when Kaisa first visited him in Portsmouth five years ago.

'Nice car,' she said while Peter busied himself with getting the roof down. 'A Golf GTI,' he said with some pride. 'Get in,' he added and put on a pair of aviator sunglasses.

They drove through the city, which was a combination of old white-clad buildings and new high-rises. After the crowded streets of London, Plymouth seemed to be deserted. With the roof down, Kaisa could sense the presence of the sea, even though she hadn't yet glimpsed it. There were the familiar calls of the seagulls and the unmistakable smell of seaweed. The place reminded Kaisa of Portsmouth, and also of Helensburgh. They drove through a street that had grey cement buildings set onto a hillside, just like the Scottish naval quarter estate. Kaisa looked away – she didn't want to be reminded of that place. The sounds and smells of the sea did make her miss Portsmouth, however, and she wanted to share this with Peter, but she remained quiet. She didn't want to start an argument, which reminiscing about old times might bring about. But she could still feel his strong arms around her, and if that wasn't going back to old times, what was? She glanced at Peter's profile. His mouth was set into a half-smile, as it always used to be, before Helensburgh. She couldn't make out the expression in his eyes because of the sunglasses. She suddenly remembered that they hadn't really argued properly since before Peter's fight with Duncan.

Peter parked the car near the seafront, in an area he said was called the Barbican. 'There's a decent French restaurant here.' They walked side by side down a narrow street, with stone-clad houses on either side and the dark blue sea beyond. The restaurant was called Chez Marie and Peter and Kaisa were shown to a table in the corner of a small room. It was covered with pink linen and set with long candles. Peter ordered himself a beer and Kaisa a G&T.

'You look good,' Peter said and grinned.

'Thank you,' Kaisa replied, and added, 'so do you.' Peter's eyes looked intensely dark. He continued to smile at Kaisa, and she wondered if he knew what she was about to ask him. Or had he had a change of heart? The place was nearly full; only one other table was unoccupied, and there was a pleasant low murmur of other people's conversations, which made Kaisa feel more comfortable about what she needed to talk to Peter about.

Kaisa turned her eyes towards the menu and asked if Peter had been there before.

'Yes,' he said.

Kaisa tried to look at his face, but he too had his head bent over the menu, a black folder in which the first two pages listed the choice of wines. Kaisa looked around the room. All the other tables were occupied by couples; this restaurant was obviously where you took a girlfriend, or your wife. So, who had Peter brought here? The dark-haired girl from the party?

'I think I'll have the Dover sole,' Kaisa said.

'You not having a starter?'

Kaisa glanced back at the menu and made a snap decision. 'OK, I'll have the moules marinieres.'

Peter looked up at her and grinned. 'Good girl, I'll have it too, and the steak with chips.'

As soon as they'd put down their menus, the waiter came to the table and took their order in heavily accented English. He nodded at Kaisa when she told him her choices, and looked deeply in her eyes when he said, 'Very good, madam, the Dover sole is delicious.' Peter placed his order and asked for a bottle of white wine and a glass of red to have with his steak later.

When they were alone, Peter lifted his beer glass. 'The food is very good here, so I hope you like it.'

'I'm sure I will.' Kaisa felt dizzy, the way Peter had told her she was a good girl reminded her of all the other times they'd eaten out. He knew she didn't usually have starters, and only ordered one so that Peter could have one too. Peter was always hungry, whereas Kaisa's appetite was much smaller. It was as if, since meeting at the station, they'd gone back in time, and were back in Portsmouth having a celebratory meal in one of the French places there.

The waiter brought the wine and there was the silly tasting bit, when Peter smiled at Kaisa as he sipped the wine and nodded his approval.

'I have no idea if it's any good or not!' he said when the waiter had disappeared, and they both laughed.

'We came here to celebrate one of the guys getting his Dolphins,' Peter said, as if he'd known she was wondering about the girl.

'Oh,' Kaisa said.

'Yes, he's become a mate. Looks up to me a bit. Not that there's much to look up to.'

'Of course there is!' Kaisa said. 'Everyone was always telling me how good you are at your job,' she added, before she could help herself.

Peter looked at her, and now his eyes had grown sad and serious. Kaisa knew she'd upset him with talk of the past. They were quiet for a while, both draining their glasses.

'How's Jeff?' Kaisa said after another awkward silence.

Peter told Kaisa about Jeff's wedding in Portsmouth Cathedral, and about the reception afterwards. 'He asks after you,' Peter said, and he lifted his eyes towards Kaisa.

'Really?' Kaisa wondered again if Peter had gone alone to the wedding. 'Tell him I miss him.'

Peter opened his mouth to say something, but changed his mind. After a while, having fiddled with the stem of his wine glass, he said, 'I will.'

Kaisa asked Peter about Jeff's new wife, and Peter told her how practical Milly was, 'a no-nonsense kind of girl'. Kaisa laughed; they both agreed this was exactly what Jeff needed. Peter said how much in love with her he seemed, and how she could wrap his parents around her little finger. 'Milly lost both of her parents when she was young, so she's had to look after herself from an early age,' Peter said, and added, 'Saying that, she's really, really lovely.'

'What's she going to do now?' Kaisa knew that Wrens had to resign their commission once they became married, something that seemed Victorian to her. At the same time, how could two Navy careers ever be compatible with children? It would be worse than having a civilian wife who worked in one place. Wrens didn't go to sea but they got sent to different bases and even abroad if they were appointed to work for Nato.

'I'm not sure, but no doubt she'll think of something practical that'll fall in line with Jeff's career.'

'That's good,' Kaisa said. 'Unlike me,' she thought but didn't say anything. Anyway, it was different for an English girl, she thought. And Milly was in the Navy herself, so she knew the drill better than anyone.

26

The sight of Kaisa stepping off the train took Peter's breath away. When he'd suggested she came down to Plymouth, he hadn't for a second thought that she would. He knew, of course, she wanted to talk about the divorce, but he didn't know why she was so against it, because that's what her trip down to him must have meant, surely? But here she now was, wearing those boots that looked so good on her, with a skirt pulled tightly around her small waist. She'd lost weight and a slimmer frame suited her. It made her legs look even longer and her face more slender and fragile-looking. The outline of her small, perky breasts was visible underneath her thin jumper and Peter couldn't take his eyes off her as she walked towards him. She was so stunning, that all the men leaving the train couldn't help but give her a glance. It made Peter wonder how many men in London had asked her out.

When Peter had booked the French place, which was the only decent restaurant in Plymouth, he hadn't realised it was so obviously the number one romantic spot. When he'd been there for Simon's celebration dinner, after he'd finally got his Dolphins, and become a submariner, there was a group of twenty officers, some with their wives or girlfriends, and they nearly filled the small dining room. But tonight, when he stepped inside the restaurant with Kaisa, Peter felt a little embarrassed when he saw all the other tables occupied by couples leaning in and whispering sweet nothings in each other's ears. He glanced at her, and hoped she wasn't getting the wrong idea. 'This is the best restaurant in Plymouth,' he said, but immediately regretted his words. That, too, sounded as if he'd planned to make a special occasion out of this evening.

But everything was so easy with Kaisa; the ordering of drinks, wine, food. They knew each other so well, and talking about old times, about Jeff and his new wife, made the evening go quickly. It wasn't until Peter noticed it was past ten, and the tall dark-haired waiter, who couldn't take his eyes of Kaisa either, had brought them coffees that she eventually told him why she was there.

'Look, Peter, I know you want to move on.' Kaisa leaned closer to him and her piercing blue eyes fixed their beautiful gaze on him. Whether it was all the wine he'd drunk, or whether it was the false naturalness of the situation (him out with his pretty wife; what could be more normal than that?), or whether it was the candlelight that made Kaisa's face glow and her lips look soft and inviting, he wasn't listening to what she had to say. Instead, Peter put his hand on hers, picked it up and kissed her palm.

'I love you,' he said.

Kaisa pulled her hand away and stared at him. Peter, too, was shocked at what he had said. 'I mean, I still love you,' he muttered. 'You're still my wife.'

'Yes, yes, of course,' Kaisa said. 'But you said you wanted a divorce.' She leaned over and whispered the last words. While they'd eaten, drank, talked and laughed, the place had emptied, and they were now the last people sitting down at a table. They'd suddenly both become aware that the two waiters standing at the back of the room, seemingly waiting for them to leave, were now intently listening to their every word.

Peter looked up and nodded towards their waiter, to show he wanted the bill. 'We can't talk here,' he said to Kaisa.

Outside, it had started raining. Large drops were rapidly falling down, as if someone was emptying a bucket of water over them. Kaisa had no coat, so Peter gave her his jumper. They ran to Peter's car and once inside, started giggling. They were both absolutely drenched. Peter's shirt was sticking to his chest and when Kaisa pulled his jumper over her head, Peter could see her hard nipples poking through her thin jumper. He leaned across the gearbox and took Kaisa into his arms. They kissed with an urgency he couldn't remember ever feeling with anyone. Peter slipped his hand under Kaisa's jumper, and she gave a moan when his fingers touched her breasts. He was so hard he thought he might pass out.

When Kaisa put her hand on Peter's crotch, he whispered, 'Back seat?' The carpark was deserted and with the torrential rain outside, the streets around the Barbican were empty. Kaisa nodded her assent and climbed between the seats. Peter dashed in and out of the car, locked the doors and joined Kaisa on the back seat. As soon as the light inside the car went out, Peter reached underneath Kaisa's skirt. He pulled her tights and knickers down and hurriedly undid his fly.

They held each other's gaze, and when Peter entered her, Kaisa moaned softly and arched her back. He could feel her grip on him and kissed her small, pink nipples, her mouth and finally her slender neck as, with a loud groan, they both climaxed.

Afterwards they held each other and listened to the rain pelting onto the roof of the car. Peter stroked Kaisa's blonde hair, which had gone curly in the rain during their passionate lovemaking. She was half-sitting, half-lying down in the crook of his arm, with her legs across the back seat of the car. Peter thought he'd never forget this moment, and stared at the snowy mountain scene that formed the pattern of her skirt. Had she worn the outfit, which she'd often worn when she met him off the train during their marriage, to trap him, he wondered briefly, but brushed aside such thoughts. That was what Jackie or Sam might do, but not Kaisa.

'You OK?' he now asked her.

The head underneath his hand moved and Kaisa sat up. Her make-up was smeared and she looked as if she'd been sobbing. Peter was shocked, he hadn't realised she was crying. 'What are the tears for?'

Kaisa put her head in her hands, 'Oh Peter, what are we going to do?'

27

Peter drove Kaisa to the train station and waited with her until the night train pulled up to the platform. He'd held her all evening after the love-making in the car, and had told her over and over how much he loved her. She too, had told Peter how much she loved him, and promised to write to him. Peter was going to go away in two days' time, but this time he'd be on a diesel submarine, which meant correspondence would be easier, as the boat would be docking at several ports during its time at sea.

'As long as you write to me too,' Kaisa had said to Peter, looking into his dark eyes.

After Peter had climbed back into the driver's seat, with Kaisa next to him, they hadn't discussed the future any more. Peter told Kaisa, 'We'll work something out,' and at the time Kaisa had believed him. He held her hand and only removed it to change gears, grabbing hold of her again when they were driving along the main thoroughfare towards the station. It felt so good, this familiar feeling of his fingers around hers. She wanted the drive to go on forever, and very nearly asked Peter to drive her all the way to London, just so she could carry on being close, inhaling his scent and feeling his warm hand around hers.

When the train pulled up Peter found Kaisa an empty compartment, where she could lie down across three seats. They hugged and kissed each other for so long, he nearly missed the whistle and got stranded on the train. Hurrying out, he took hold of Kaisa's hands once more, and said, 'We'll be together again, I promise.' He stayed on the platform to wave goodbye. As she stared at his diminishing figure, she let the tears run freely down her face. No one was there to see her smudged make-up or hear her sniffling.

Kaisa had a fitful night's sleep on the train. She was restless because of everything that had happened during the evening, but she was also disturbed by the train stopping at each and every station on the journey to London. When she arrived at Paddington at just past 5.30 am, she could still feel Peter's kisses on her lips. But then she found out she had to wait for the tube to start running at 6am. Sitting at the end of a bench, just a few centimetres away from a drunk fast asleep and covered with old newspapers, she shivered in her skirt and thin jumper and began to think about the future with Peter. How would they be able to make things work? And how could Peter go from wanting a divorce to wanting them to try again in the space of three days? What was the real reason for the final separation, and his desire for a divorce? Another woman? That girl from the party? Kaisa put her head in her hands, but that made the man next to her shift, and an awful smell of sweat, combined with urine, hit Kaisa's nostrils. She stood up and began walking along the empty platforms, thinking.

Even if Peter really did want to make a go of things and wasn't just 'thinking with his dick' as he sometimes said of the sailors and their love lives (or 'lust lives' as he put it too), what was he going to do about the woman he was seeing? Supposing there was another woman. A huge problem with a future life together was money. Peter's salary was just enough to live on if they were in a married quarter, and Kaisa's salary hardly covered her living costs. Even together they wouldn't be able to afford to rent a flat in London. Besides, what would be the point if Peter couldn't afford train fares back and forth to London each time he was ashore and on leave? Then there was Kaisa's career, which she'd fought so hard to get off the ground. The problems that had always existed between them would still be there. Unless Kaisa gave up her job in London, and moved down to a married quarter in Plymouth, they'd never see each other. But there was no telling how long Peter's appointment in HMS *Orion* would last; Kaisa knew that it was highly likely his next sub would be based in Helensburgh. And Kaisa just couldn't go back to that life. Perhaps she really didn't love Peter enough? Kaisa fought tears. When a thin man with long, dirty blond hair approached her for money she quickly wiped her tears away and began walking up the road from the station. She found an open café with steamed up windows opposite the station. It was full of construction workers in overalls, but a girl in a pink apron showed her to an empty table at the back.

'What can I get you?' she said, looking Kaisa up and down. There were a few sneers from the men, and one shouted, 'Walk of shame, is it love?'

The waitress turned around and said, 'Shut up or I'll throw you out.' Returning to Kaisa, her pen still poised over her notebook, she said in a hushed voice, 'Don't mind the animals here.'

Kaisa smiled a 'thank you' to the girl and ordered a coffee and a cheese roll. The watery liquid warmed her a little, and although she had to scrape a thick layer of butter from inside the bun, eating it made her feel better. How she wished Peter was with her to protect her from the men, who were still leering and shouting the occasional comment on her appearance in spite of the telling off from the waitress. It felt as if they knew she'd been fucked in the backseat of a car only hours before, and she felt dirty and vulnerable. Kaisa nodded to the waitress, who was leaning across a small bar at the back of the café, smoking a cigarette. Kaisa paid and returned to the station, where the early morning rush-hour had begun. Kaisa took the tube to Ladbroke Grove, and tried not to think about Peter or the future.

After a quick shower and a change of clothing in her bedsit, Kaisa got to work just after eight. Rose, as usual, was already there.

'Hi Kaisa,' she said but only looked up from her desk quickly. Kaisa was glad Rose had forgotten about her trip down to Plymouth; she didn't have the energy, or desire, to tell her about her wonderful but confusing evening.

About an hour later, when all the other women had settled themselves behind their desks, Rose stood up and said, 'I need to talk to you all. I'm afraid I have some very bad, and sad, news.'

Kaisa and the other members of *Adam's Apple* editorial office listened in quiet shock as Rose told them that the paper was folding. 'We have enough funds to complete this forthcoming issue, but after that, I'm afraid it's over.' Her voice trembled and Kaisa could tell her boss was fighting tears. 'So let's make this issue the best yet!' she said and left the room.

The women looked at each other in shock, then their gazes turned to Rachel, who had been at the magazine the longest and often accompanied Rose to meetings with 'the money men'.

'But I thought the increased sales figures this summer meant we were OK,' Jenny said. She wore her usual uniform of a white shirt, buttoned up to her neck, and high-waisted black trousers. She had her hands buried deep inside her pockets.

Rachel shook her head. 'They've been telling Rose to put up the price, but she won't because she says it's vital all women, especially those struggling with money, can afford to buy a copy.'

Everyone around the room nodded. 'What are we going to do?' Jenny said.

'We'll make the next issue the best yet!' Rachel said, and at that moment Rose came in. The little make-up she wore had gone, and Kaisa suspected she'd been crying. Kaisa had never seen her face look so white and gaunt.

She moved her gaze from one face to the next and said, 'You have been, are, all amazing women, and I am so grateful for all your support over the last six months. But we have to face facts. I have sunk all my money into this project because I firmly believe women need a voice, a sensible voice amongst the glossy magazines advocating traditional values. But there is no more, and it seems my last backers have had enough. But I believe *Adam's Apple* has made a difference both in the past, and during my short stewardship, and it has influenced the rest of the women's press to cover stories that are relevant to the woman of today. All we can now do is make this last issue of *Adam's Apple* count, make it into something that will be looked upon as a shining example of modern, feminist journalism.'

Kaisa and the rest of the staff clapped.

'So, my good women, let's get back to work!' Rose said.

Kaisa went back to her desk, following the example of the others. She tried not to think about the future, because she believed in the magazine and its power to change the lives of women in Britain for the better. And she wanted to do just as Rose had said: help make the last issue the best yet. But she couldn't help but think about her own situation. She looked around the room. All the other women were seasoned journalists, or editors. They would get work without any problems. Although *Adam's Apple* was a radical paper, sneered at by some of the other (male) journalists in the Coach and Horses, she understood from the way the women talked in the office that most people in the industry had a secret admiration for the magazine. It was progressive, left-wing and often challenged the status quo of British society. 'It's what every reporter dreams of doing when they're at journalism school,' Jenny had once told Kaisa.

Kaisa sighed. She hadn't been to journalism school. She looked down at the list of companies she was asking to advertise in the magazine, and saw she was about halfway through. She got up from her desk and went over to Rose.

'Are we still sending these out,' she asked, holding up one of the letters.

Rose leaned back in her chair and thought for a moment. 'Why not, send them all as usual. We might as well try up till the very last.' She smiled at Kaisa and then her expression changed. 'Oh my God, I'd forgotten, how did it go yesterday?'

Kaisa shrugged her shoulders. 'Fine, a bit confusing, but fine.' She couldn't help herself. A wide, happy smile spread over her face.

Rose's eyes were on Kaisa, 'Oh yes?' she said. Her voice was full of meaning, and she was grinning.

Kaisa looked down at her hands. How could Rose know what had happened in Plymouth between her and Peter. Suddenly she felt angry at her boss. It was her life, not Rose's. If she wanted to sleep with her ex, that was her business.

'I'll finish these today,' she said, not looking at Rose. 'I'm sorry it's taken so long.' Kaisa turned on her heels and returned to her desk. She could feel her face redden and knew Rose was still looking at her.

At one o'clock Kaisa got up and said she was going to get a sandwich. Rose looked up from her papers. 'Wait, I'll come with you.' The other women around the office were still hard at work, with their heads bent over typewriters, but Rachel glanced up and gave Rose a questioning look. She shook her head, as if to answer an unposed question. Kaisa wondered what the two women had said about her. Rachel knew Kaisa was the only one in the office who wouldn't be able to get a job when the magazine folded, or had Rose told Rachel about her private life? As far as Kaisa knew, Rose hadn't told anyone about how they'd met, that Kaisa knew Duncan, her cousin, or what had happened between Kaisa and Duncan. The anger surged again; Rose had no right to tell anyone about her life!

'OK,' Kaisa said, but she gathered her things and walked quickly out of the office and onto the street without waiting for Rose.

'Wait Kaisa!' Rose shouted.

Kaisa sighed. Perhaps it was the sleepless night after such an incredibly wonderful, but unsettling evening that was making Kaisa so ratty and sensitive. Or maybe it was the knowledge that she'd be jobless soon. She had a month's notice on the bedsit, but she could pay the rent with Peter's allowance, which he was still paying into her account every month. She had no idea how he could afford to do it, but presumed living in the wardroom was cheaper. But without any other income, that left no money whatsoever for food. At worst, she'd have to go back home, to Helsinki, and sleep on her sister's sofa bed again, but after everything that had happened, with Matti's death, the disastrous date with Tom, and her sister's new relationship, she didn't even know if the sofa bed was still available to her. Besides, she had no money for the journey. She'd have to call her mother and ask her for the fare.

'Let's go to Terroni's – I'll buy you a proper coffee and a sarni. I know how much you like your coffee!' Rose took hold of Kaisa's arm, and Kaisa couldn't help but smile at her.

'Hello, Toni,' Rose said. A tall dark-haired man came out from behind a counter laden with Italian meats, fresh salads and cheese. At a further section, Kaisa saw cream filled cones and small cakes. Behind the counter were two large coffee-making machines, where another man pulled leavers amid plumes of steam.

'How is my favourite lady?' the Italian man said as soon as Kaisa and Rose walked in. 'Please, please sit down and tell me what you want.'

'Thank you, Toni, we'll have two caffe americanos – yes?' Rose looked over to Kaisa. 'Black coffee, that's right, isn't it? No milk?'

Kaisa nodded. Rose had never taken her to this place before; it was like being abroad with the hustle and bustle of diners, staff hurrying between tables, and the steam rising from the coffee machines. The sweet scent of real coffee made Kaisa's spirit rise. Kaisa remembered the Italian restaurants in Stockholm; they'd had the same aromas of cooking and coffee.

'And who is your beautiful young friend, Rosa?'

'This is Kaisa. She's come all the way from Finland to work with me.'

The man took Kaisa's hand and kissed the back of it. Kaisa was reminded of how Duncan had done the same when she'd first met him at Jackie's party. 'Finland! A beautiful woman from a beautiful country.' Toni was a slim man, with a mop of dark hair, a little older than her, Kaisa supposed. His eyes were dark and he was shamelessly flirtatious. Kaisa noticed a ring on his left finger.

An older, shorter man, with a round belly, shouted something in Italian to Toni, and he sighed theatrically. Letting go of Kaisa's hand, he went back to the counter. 'I will bring you coffee.'

'I keep telling him my name is Rose, but he says that Rosa is the same name in Italian, so he insists on calling me that.'

Toni made a fuss of the two women, bringing them toasted bread called bruschetta, topped with tomatoes, olive paste and strong smelling cheese.

As soon as they had a moment to themselves, Rose looked at her. 'I know you must be worried about your job.'

'I am,' Kaisa said.

'Which is why I brought you here.'

'Oh?'

'I know it may be difficult for you to find something similar to *Adam's*

Apple, but I will recommend you to a couple of people. However, I've been thinking about it, and I think it would best if you enrol on a journalism course. I can write you a letter of recommendation, and it'll just be for one year, but it'll open doors for you.'

'But, I haven't got the money,' Kaisa said. Suddenly she felt huge affection towards Rose. How wrong she'd been; instead of gossiping about Kaisa's love life, Rose had been worrying about her future.

'Yes, this is why I brought you here.'

Kaisa said nothing; she was confused.

'I know it's not what you want, but hear me out.' Rose took a deep intake of breath and continued. 'Toni here is always looking for someone to help out, and I know if I ask him, he'll give you a job as a waitress. I know it shouldn't count, but your looks will bring in customers.'

Kaisa stared at Rose. This was completely against what they both believed in.

'Don't look at me like that. Sometimes when the chips are down, we have to take advantage of what we have.' Rose grinned. 'While working, I think you should enrol on the journalism course. There's an evening programme, so you can work during the day here, and attend lessons afterwards. It'll be very hard work for a year, but I know you'll manage.'

Kaisa looked around the café. It was busy with men in suits. Some were queuing up at the counter, and some were sitting at tables eating their lunch and drinking coffee. Toni smiled at her from the other side of the counter. Even though he'd been flirty before, his smile now was friendly. Had Rose already spoken to him about her? To her surprise, Kaisa could imagine working here. She nodded to Rose.

The older woman put her hand on Kaisa's and said, 'Think about it.'

28

The phone began ringing when Kaisa was still outside, looking for the keys to the front door. She hurried to open up and ran down the few steps to the back of the hall.

'Hello?'

'Hi, it's me,' Peter's voice sounded low.

Kaisa hugged the receiver. 'Hello.'

'You got back OK?'

'Yes, the train stopped at every station, so I didn't get much sleep.' Kaisa said.

'I couldn't sleep because I was thinking of you,' Peter said. 'I miss you,' he added.

Kaisa didn't know what to reply to Peter. Did his words mean that they were back together now? But surely he didn't think that she would come back to him, and the life of a Navy wife, after everything that had happened? 'Peter,' she began.

'Yes, I know, Kaisa. I'm going away tomorrow, and you're up in London with your career. But I just wanted to tell you how much I love you.' Peter paused for a short moment. 'I wanted to tell you that before we sail.'

Kaisa could hardly breathe. Did he know how she'd longed to hear those words? All those months in Helensburgh, first when the bomber was on its long patrol, then after the fight, when they'd both been so unhappy and Peter had drifted further and further away from her. And all the time in

Helsinki, when she'd written to Peter and he'd replied in short, official-sounding communications. But what, she suddenly thought, about that girl he was seeing?

'Kaisa, are you there?'

'Yes,' Kaisa tried to disguise her sniffles.

'Please don't cry. I promise I will sort something out. If we love each other, we can make this work, I promise.'

'The magazine is folding,' Kaisa managed to say between sobs.

'Oh.'

'Yes, we have about six weeks until we are out of the office and I'm out of a job. I don't know what I'm going to do.' Kaisa found a tissue in her handbag. She heard a door open and the man who lived with the landlady passed her on his way to the kitchen in the back of the house. He gave her a look of utter disapproval. Was crying against some sort of house rule? Kaisa turned her head towards the wall and away from the man's gaze.

'Kaisa, you know you can always go and stay with my parents, don't you?' Peter said. 'I'll write to them tonight and tell them you'll be in touch.'

'No, Peter.' The thought of having to face Peter's mum's disapproving gaze, or worse still a sad one, filled her with dread. And his father, who'd been so kind to Kaisa, how would she ever be able to meet him after everything that had happened? Having to see Peter's family again hadn't crossed her mind before. She knew for certain she couldn't face them alone.

'What will you do then?'

'Rose has organised a job for me in an Italian café, and she thinks I should go to night school to take a journalism qualification.'

'I see,' Peter's voice was dry. Kaisa remembered how Peter had reacted when she told him about working for Rose, Duncan's cousin. He hadn't believed that Kaisa no longer had anything to do with Duncan. 'It's one alternative. She has also recommended me to other magazines, but without a journalism qualification, she thinks it'll be difficult.'

Peter was quiet at the other end of the line.

'I haven't decided what I'm going to do yet, but if nothing works out, I might go back to Helsinki.' Kaisa was surprised at her own words, at her confidence. Suddenly, she knew what her options were after the most confusing twenty-four hours of her life. She realised she couldn't go back to being dependent on Peter again. And the thought of seeing Peter's parents scared her. Her only alternative was to go back home to Finland. Her hands holding the receiver became clammy just at the thought of facing Peter's parents, let alone his brother and sister-in-law, or lovely Nancy, his sister. She felt sure that his family would think everything that had happened was her fault. And they were right, of course. It was all her doing. She had ruined Peter's career and she had no right to him, she saw that clearly now. She didn't want to spoil his life any further.

'Well, I just wanted to hear you'd got back to London, OK,' Peter now said. His voice had cooled.

'Thank you, that was very kind of you.' After a short pause, she added, 'I really enjoyed last night.' She wanted to tell him how much she loved him, but she knew that by doing so she would give him false hope.

'Yes, so did I.' Peter's voice was dry. 'I've got to go,' he said and put down the receiver.

Kaisa listened to the long tone on the line. She was rooted to the spot, looking at the scribbled notes on the wall before her. Half-covered by another, newer communication to someone called Tracy was a piece of paper in Kaisa's own handwriting asking to be told of any phone calls for her. How long ago it seemed since she'd missed Peter's call. And now, today, after the most wonderful reunion, she was the one who'd decided there was no future for them.

29

K aisa fell in love with Italian food and culture. Had she not been on her feet all day long, she was sure she would have put on tons of weight and become the shape of the 'Mama' who cooked in the kitchen. Mama was as tall as she was wide, but as soon as Kaisa started at the café, two months previously, Mama had taken Kaisa under her wing. She even taught Kaisa Italian, though in truth all the family members who worked at the Farringdon Road café corrected her pronunciation of the dishes and words like 'prego', which meant please, and 'grazie', which meant thank you. Kaisa found it easy to pick up the language, and she began to feel like one of the family.

When she'd phoned her mother to tell her she was working in an Italian café, her mother had said, 'You have Italian blood, of course you like it. And you'll learn the language fast.' Kaisa had laughed She didn't quite believe the stories about her Italian roots. There was no evidence, just some tale, told by an old aunt, that the family name, Flori, on her maternal grand-mother's side, hailed from a small village in Northern Italy. Kaisa didn't think her mother would have approved of her graduate daughter working in a café if it hadn't been Italian.

Kaisa still lived in the bedsit in Notting Hill and took the tube to Farringdon each day, but instead of turning right towards Clerkenwell Close, she walked for ten or so minutes to the café on Farringdon Road.

She'd even started calling Rose, 'Rosa', during her daily visits to

Terroni's. Kaisa knew the older woman was checking up on her, making sure she was OK. She also helped Kaisa with her English. The course at London School of Journalism was demanding, and her assignments were becoming more and more difficult, so Kaisa needed all the help she could get. Rose was now working for the *Observer* where she'd become the editor of a supplement aimed at women. 'Back to fashion, make-up and trouble with men,' Rose had laughed, but Kaisa had heard from Ravi, whose friend worked at the paper, that Rose had been taken on to revamp the supplement and make it 'more current and relevant to women of today'. He also told her that Rose was doing a brilliant job and that she was highly regarded by everyone in the industry.

'You're lucky to have such a prestigious woman as your friend,' Ravi said.

Something good had come out of all the bad that her affair with Duncan had caused, Kaisa thought, but she didn't say anything to Ravi. Although she was seeing him regularly, she didn't consider that she was in a relationship with him. They'd had sex a few times, but she didn't feel the same about him as she had about Peter. She'd discussed Ravi at length with Rose; in fact, she'd discussed her whole life at length with Rose. They'd become firm friends in spite of their ten-year age difference. Kaisa felt much older than her 25 years, because of all that had happened to her.

'It's OK to have sex with someone who you're not madly in love with,' Rose had advised her. 'It's a lot easier, and less painful. Just enjoy it! Men don't worry about being in love with women they fuck!'

Kaisa had laughed nervously and looked around to see if anyone had heard what they were talking about, or Rose's language. They'd been sitting at a restaurant in Maida Vale, where Rose often took Kaisa after her course finished in the evening. She refused to let Kaisa pay for anything. She said she still felt responsible for what Duncan had done, however much Kaisa protested that she'd been a willing partner. In the early days of Kaisa's course, which had started in September, Rose had surprised Kaisa by waiting outside the Victorian red-brick building where her classes were held. She'd hugged Kaisa warmly and suggested they go and eat something. When they'd sat down, she'd put her hand on Kaisa's arm and said, 'Let me treat you. I don't have any children of my own to look after.'

'I'm too old to be your child!' Kaisa had protested, but Rose had just laughed and said, 'OK, a younger sister then!'

Soon it had become a regular event, that once a week, on a Thursday, Rose would turn up at the school and they'd walk arm in arm to their favourite place by the canal in Little Venice, where the Maitre D' knew Rose and Kaisa and gave them their favourite table at the end of the glass-walled room.

It was now late November. Terroni's café in Farringdon was filled with elaborate Christmas chocolates, beautiful glacé fruits and piles and piles of tall Italian cakes called *panettone* in cardboard boxes. Kaisa was desperately home-sick and really wanted to go home to Helsinki for the holidays – she had three weeks off from the School of Journalism – but she couldn't afford the airfare. So she'd decided to work in the café on the days it was open, but she still had the whole of Christmas week to fill, when Terroni's would be shut. Rose had asked her to come to the family farm in Dorset, but Kaisa didn't want to risk seeing Duncan, nor did she wish to meet any of Rose's other cousins. They were bound to know about the affair and how it had caused Duncan's dismissal from the Navy, and the break-up of Kaisa's marriage.

'Duncan would behave, you know that, don't you?' Rose said with concern in her eyes.

But Kaisa shook her head, and Rose didn't mention the matter again.

Even Ravi, who didn't celebrate Christmas because he was a Hindu, was going to his parents' home outside Birmingham. He hadn't invited Kaisa to come with him, and she suspected his mother wouldn't approve of their relationship.

On the last Thursday in November, two weeks before her classes were due to finish for the year, Rose and Kaisa were sitting at their favourite table in the restaurant in Maida Vale when, smiling widely, Rose said, 'I've got some great news!' She brought a newspaper cutting out of her handbag. 'Look at this!'

Kaisa read the notice: 'Finnish radio journalist for BBC World Service.'

'But I've never worked for radio, and I'm not even a journalist yet.'

'Yes, but read on, they say they can train you! How many Finnish speakers do you think there are in London?' Rose said. 'Holding a valid work permit, that is!'

Kaisa hung her head; the work permit and her marriage to Peter were still unsolved issues. She hadn't spoken to him since that awful telephone conversation after returning from Plymouth. He hadn't contacted her about a divorce, so in theory she was still married to him and had the right to work in England. And the monthly allowance was still going into her bank account. But a national broadcaster like the BBC would surely check her living arrangements and see that she was separated from her husband? She looked at Rose.

'You know, Rose, if I'm separated from Peter, I am not entitled to a work permit, so I'm actually illegally employed by Terroni's at the moment.'

'Who says?'

'Ravi.'

Rose leaned back in her chair and said, 'I see.'

'Sorry, I didn't want to tell you before.'

'Oh, I'm sure no one will check,' Rose said. She was quiet and suddenly Kaisa got the feeling that something else was worrying her.

'Are you OK?' Kaisa asked.

Rose looked up, startled. 'Yes, I'm just thinking about Christmas.'

'What about it?'

Rose gazed at Kaisa and hesitated, 'Oh, it's nothing.'

Kaisa leaned over and took hold of the older woman's hand, 'Something's bothering you, I can tell.'

Rose lifted her pale eyes to Kaisa's. 'Roger's asked me to marry him!'

'That's wonderful news!' Kaisa got up and went to hug Rose, but before she could put her arms around her friend, Rose said, 'I haven't said yes yet.'

Kaisa sat back down. 'Why not? Don't you love him?'

Rose sighed, 'Well, I just never thought I'd marry. You know, with my career, there's just not been time for a serious relationship.' And then she smiled, 'But I really, really like being with Roger. He has his own career at the *Guardian,* and we are quite grown-up, both of us, so …'

'So, why not marry him?'

'He's coming to the country with me for Christmas, to meet my uncle and the rest of the family.'

Kaisa smiled. Tactfully, Rose hadn't mentioned Duncan. 'That'll be nice.'

'Yeah,' Rose replied.

'So, did he give you a ring?' Kaisa asked.

Rose smiled and dug out a small container from her handbag. Inside was a huge emerald ring, the kind that Princess Diana had.

'It's beautiful!' Kaisa said. She knew Roger was quite high up at the newspaper, but she had no idea he was rich enough to afford a ring like that.

Rose gazed down at the ring, but didn't put it on. 'Isn't it a bit too much?' she said, but her smile had grown so wide that Kaisa knew she'd say yes to Roger.

'It's perfect. I'm so happy for you.' Kaisa got up again and hugged her friend. Rose's body seemed slight in her embrace and Kaisa felt quite protective towards her. 'Why don't we all go out and celebrate in the New

Year?' Kaisa said. Although she'd met Roger several times in the pub, she didn't know what kind of man he was. Kaisa suddenly felt responsible for her friend and wanted to make sure she wasn't making a mistake.

Rose nodded and put the ring back inside its tiny box.

30

Peter got off the train in Westbury and saw his sister standing beside her car outside the small station. It was the day before Christmas Eve and it was raining when he emerged from the station building. Peter's mum had begged him to come home for the holidays, now he wasn't at sea, and Peter had eventually agreed. Christmas on the deserted base would have been depressing, and the alternative, to go and stay with Jackie in London, didn't appeal to him. He was trying to cool things with her after she'd thrown a strop about Kaisa. He knew she thought he would propose to her as soon as he divorced Kaisa, but that was the last thing on his mind. And he couldn't bring himself to send Kaisa the papers a lawyer had prepared for him, not yet.

Nancy looked flustered, something he wasn't used to seeing in his older sister. As he sat down in the passenger seat of her her brand-new silver Volvo Estate, he glanced behind at the two Moses baskets strapped head to head in the back seat. While he'd been away at sea, Nancy had given birth to twins, a boy and a girl. They were now about two months old, and both had the Williams' hallmark mop of dark hair. One of them, the boy, Peter assumed, judging by his powder-blue romper suit, began crying as soon as his sister sat down in the driver's seat.

'Shh, Oliver,' Nancy said and quickly started the engine.

His sister lived in a large Bath stone house in Trowbridge, only a couple of streets from where Peter and Nancy had grown up with their older brother, who now lived in London. Her sister's magnificent, detached house was a lot grander than their old family terraced house, but that was explained by the man his sister lived with (scandalously unmarried, even though Nigel kept asking Nancy to tie the knot). Nigel owned his own estate agency, which took on properties over a certain price. Nancy had known Nigel since school, and they'd been going out forever, so neither Peter, nor his mother, understood why she wouldn't marry. Nancy just smiled, and said, 'There's no hurry, is there?' The twins had obviously made it more urgent, as Peter's mother had pointed out in one of her many letters to Peter, but Nancy had simply said that she wasn't going to walk down the aisle with a huge bump under her dress.

When she parked the car outside a green garage door, Nancy asked Peter to carry one of the babies inside. As soon as Peter lifted Oliver's basket, he opened his large blue eyes, lifted his little arms up and began to whinge.

'Just let him cry,' Nancy said in an exasperated voice as she led the way into the house. She placed Beth, the baby girl, on the kitchen table and told Peter to place the other basket next to it. The kitchen, like the hall they'd walked through, was wide and filled with light from the French windows overlooking the garden. Everything looked new; since Peter's last visit they'd fitted out the kitchen with light-coloured cabinets and a breakfast bar with dark leather stools.

'Do you want me to do anything?' Peter asked over the noise of the babies. Beth had joined Oliver in his protests.

Nancy looked at Peter, as if considering whether he could be trusted to carry out any kind of task relating to the twins. 'Sit down at the table and hold Beth while I give Oliver his bottle. 'Wash your hands first,' she ordered, and Peter visited the small cloakroom off the hall. When he came back, Nancy had both babies in her arms. The scene was so unfamiliar to Peter that he stood in the doorway, unseen, for a moment. Without realising it, in his mind he replaced his sister's face with Kaisa's, and the over-whelming sensation of tenderness and pride he suddenly felt towards the crying babies took him by surprise. He had to swallow a lump in his throat.

Holding Beth was even worse. Her little fingers were perfect, and her little feet, moving anxiously in the arms of a total stranger, melted Peter's heart. 'She's beautiful,' he said and smiled at his sister, who was feeding the now quiet Oliver from a bottle half-filled with milk.

'Do you want to feed her?' Nancy asked and showed Peter how to tip the bottle so that Beth could drink without getting air inside her tummy. The little sucking noises Beth made, while still eyeing him suspiciously, brought a smile to Peter's lips. 'You've done well,' he said to Nancy, and her sister returned his smile. Gazing down at this little wonder suddenly made all his problems with the court martial and Kaisa's rejection fade away. Peter realised he was an uncle now, an uncle to these wonderful, new human beings. They were his flesh and blood, if only by a fraction. Inhaling the new baby scent, he vowed to be there for the twins, his little niece and nephew. He would look after them if need be.

Nigel found the sister and brother feeding the babies in the kitchen. 'You've got a job there if you want it,' Nigel joked. He was wearing a smart business suit and was carrying a large leather briefcase, which he plonked onto the breakfast bar. He gave Nancy a peck on her cheek and said, 'Fix me a G&T while I make a couple of calls.'

Nancy just nodded, but Peter said, 'I'll do that while you see to these two.' Beth had fallen asleep in his arms, so Nancy placed her back into the Moses basket.

'So, how's the life of a sailor?' Nigel said when Peter handed him the drink. He was sitting, still in his suit, in an armchair in the corner of the lounge, next to a green pot plant. His round face was a little flustered, as if the effort of walking from his car to the house was taking a toll on him. Peter noticed he'd put on weight; the striped shirt underneath his suit jacket was straining at the buttons. His fair hair was thinning, and he looked every bit the prosperous estate agent he was.

'OK,' Peter replied. He dreaded these moments with Nigel because, unlike his sister, Nigel didn't evade any subject. Peter suddenly realised that Nigel completely lacked tact. That must be why he was so successful in business, Peter thought, and took a large gulp of his own G&T. The embodiment of Thatcher's Britain, Nigel made money out of the rich who wanted bigger and better homes. His company, Hammond's, didn't let anyone who wasn't wearing designer clothes, or at least a smart suit, even walk into their office. 'I wouldn't know, we don't sell council flats,' Nigel had once sniffed when Peter had asked if there was any money to be made in Thatcher's new policy of letting council residents buy up their properties.

'You've got over that thing, the court martial, now?'

Peter lifted his eyes to Nigel. He was looking at Peter squarely, inquisitively. Peter saw no malice in his plump face, and wondered how he'd convey to his common-law brother-in-law that this was one subject he really didn't want to discuss.

'Yeah,' he said, hoping that would do the trick.

'Saw it in the papers. Not too bad, as far as I'm concerned, brought a lot of interest and even a few house sales my way. People love a scandal, and as far as I could see you were well within your rights to give him what's for.' Nigel lifted his glass towards Peter. 'So, well done, I say.'

'Thanks,' Peter said and downed the rest of his drink.

'And that Scandinavian girl, you still married to her?' Nigel continued.

There he goes, Peter thought, the second subject he'd rather not talk about. Classic Nigel.

Peter was rescued by his sister, who'd changed out of the tracksuit she'd been wearing earlier and into a neat little dress that suited her slight frame. 'Is he boring you with talk of his house deals?' she said, sitting on the arm of Peter's chair.

'No, not at all,' Peter said, and gave Nigel a look that he hoped conveyed his unwillingness to discuss things any further. 'You look nice,' he added.

'Well, we thought we'd take you out. One of Nigel's friends has taken over a pub in Hilperton, and the food's really good, so we thought we'd go there if that's OK with you? Nigel's niece is babysitting. Do you want to have a shower and change before we go?'

During the meal, when the nice-looking barmaid, who kept giving Peter the eye, took their plates away, Nigel leaned back in his chair. Sending Nancy a quick glance, he said, 'The reason we wanted to see you before you go to your parents is that I have a proposition for you.'

Lying in bed in Nancy's pink guest bedroom later that evening, Peter thought about what Nigel had said to him. 'My customers would love you, ex-naval officer, good manners, looks and charming personality.' Peter knew the job would be that of a salesman, but the starting salary Nigel had suggested (without commission) was more than he was earning. But was he ready for the civvy lifestyle? If he was truthful, his last time away with HMS *Orion* had been the most boring yet. Nothing had happened. They hadn't got a sniff of a Russian sub, or a destroyer, and the only thing they'd done was endlessly repeat the workouts they'd already completed before going away. And the cramped quarters onboard the diesel submarine had got on his nerves too; as had the jibes about being a 'Bomber Queen', the Navy's slur for the submariners who'd served on the much more spacious Polaris vessels, if he even hinted that he didn't enjoy living in someone else's armpit. He hadn't dared complain about the way they had to sleep and eat their meals in the minuscule wardroom.

But could he cope with civilian life back in Wiltshire so soon after articles about him had appeared in the local and national newspapers?

'Everyone will have forgotten about it already, the papers will be fish and chip wrappers by now,' Nancy had said, taking his arm between her hands. 'We just want you to be happy, Peter,' she'd added, and it made him realise that she worried about him. Had Nancy and her mother put Nigel up to this?

Peter promised he'd think about it. Nigel shook his hand as if he'd already agreed to the whole deal.

The next day, Christmas Eve, Nancy drove Peter and the babies, plus a great deal of baby equipment, to his parents' house.

For a while Peter stood outside his parents' house. He'd only been to see his family once since the court martial, a short visit mainly spent holed up in the blue bedroom. The same bedroom in which he'd spent many nights making love to Kaisa, trying not to be noisy. Once he had to hold his hand over her mouth for the duration, and they'd giggled afterwards, realising too late that his parents would hear and think they were still doing it. During his last visit, only days after the court martial, he had cried for the first time since his childhood, remembering how happy he'd been there with Kaisa. He couldn't remember ever feeling more sorry for himself. It just wasn't the way he was made.

His mother and father had been gentle with him, not mentioning the fight, Kaisa's infidelity, or the court martial. But Peter had seen the disappointment in his father's eyes. His father had said, without looking at him, 'You'll put this behind you. Just work hard, lad, and they'll forget all about it.' His father had been in the Navy himself during the war, and although Peter didn't know much about his time at sea, he could guess that his father had seen and heard far worse than the tale of his pathetic fight with Duncan. His parents had even hidden the papers in which the story appeared, placing them underneath a pile of magazines next to the fireplace in the lounge. Of course, on the second morning in his parents' house, when they'd been at work, he'd found the papers. Disgusted by what they said, he had fled Wiltshire, leaving a note to his mother. 'Sorry, Mum, couldn't stay. I'll write to you. Love Peter.'

He'd travelled back to Helensburgh and found the flat in Smuggler's Way cold and empty. There was a letter from Kaisa on the mat, in which she said she'd arrived in Helsinki OK.' There'd been no mention of when she was going to return. That night Peter had gone to the Ardencaple with Nigel and drunk himself silly.

Now, as he opened the door to the pink painted bungalow, Peter could still see pain around his mother's eyes. She hugged him, 'I am so glad you are home and safe.'

Peter returned the hug. He was reminded that here were the people who truly loved him. His long and boring time at sea had given him time to think and to put his misadventure into perspective. He had come to realise that he wanted to work hard and make something of himself. He'd thought that something would be his career in the Navy, and that, as his father had told him, he just needed to get his head down and work hard. Which he had. His Captain on HMS *Orion* had told him he'd done well just before he set off on leave. 'I had misgivings about you Peter, I can't lie. But you've worked hard and I'm glad to have you as one of my officers.' That had meant a lot to Peter. He had crossed his fingers and hoped that he'd soon get a call from the Appointer with a better job. But now, for the first time since he'd applied for the Royal Navy at the age of seventeen, he was thinking that perhaps a civilian life might be a better option after all.

Peter, Nancy and his mother sat around the small kitchen table while the twins slept. 'We all worry about you, you know,' his mother said. She placed her wrinkly warm hand over Peter's on the table and squeezed it hard.

'I know mum, but I'm OK now.'

'Glad to hear it, son.'

'Nigel offered him a job last night,' Nancy said, and their mother immediately, too soon, replied, 'Oh really, well that's something, isn't it, Peter?'

Peter smiled but didn't tell the two women that he'd realised their ruse. He went along with it. 'I have to think about it, mum. I can't just leave the Navy like that anyway. I have to give at least one year's notice, or longer, if they can't replace me in HMS *Orion*.' Peter looked from his sister to his mum, and they both nodded.

'Of course, dear, of course. But it's worth thinking about, don't you agree? Nigel is doing very well, and he needs help from someone he can trust. Family, that is.'

Nancy gave her mother a look of warning, and she got up and put the kettle on. Peter nearly laughed. How did his mother know so much about it if she'd just heard about the job offer now? It was so evident that the two women had plotted this. If he was going to consider the job, he'd need to get Nigel on his own. Peter resolved to swing by his agency on his way back to Plymouth during one of the days between Christmas and New Year.

31

K aisa's Christmas was saved at the last minute by Toni, her boss at Terroni's. The day before Christmas Eve, he asked what she was doing for the holidays and when he heard she would be alone, he invited her to the restaurant for both Christmas Eve and Christmas Day. At first, Kaisa refused, but Toni roped in Mama, who in the end convinced Kaisa she was 'part of the family' anyway, so she must join them. They had a tradition to close the restaurant and have a big family party, setting all the tables together and closing the curtains to the outside world.

In the end, Kaisa spent Christmas Eve with her friends from the *Adam's Apple* – Rachel, who was now working for the *Guardian* together with Rose, called in at the café and invited her for drinks at the Coach and Horses. Rose had already left for Dorset, but both Jenny and Rachel were there. Kaisa enjoyed the evening; in London, everyone seemed to be up for a party on Christmas Eve, and Kaisa met and flirted with several good-looking men.

On Christmas Day, Kaisa was treated to the best food she'd ever had at Terroni's. There were fresh griddled fish, delicious salads, ham, pasta and the most fantastic cakes, moistened with coffee and filled with Italian cream cheese and fruits. It wasn't quite like the quiet Christmases in Finland, but it was better than the one she'd shared with Pammy in Helensburgh, which ended in Kaisa confessing to her affair with Duncan, and led to all that followed. With the Terroni family on Christmas morning, when her glass was refilled over and over again, first with Prosecco then with white and red wines, those dark days in Scotland felt like light years away.

Kaisa spent New Year with Ravi, again in the Coach and Horses, and then on the morning of 2nd January she got a letter from the BBC asking her to attend an interview. She was so delighted she told Mama and Toni about it. They both looked sad, and made her promise to come back and see them often when she was 'a famous BBC reporter'.

'I haven't got the job yet,' Kaisa had laughed.

'But you will, Bella,' Toni had replied and hugged her.

Bush House, the headquarters of BBC World Service, was on Aldwych. Kaisa took the tube to Holborn and, because she was early, took a slight detour through the gardens of Lincoln's Inn Fields. The trees were bare and sad-looking, but the grass behind the iron fence was green, unlike in Finland, where, according to her sister, there was still snow on the ground. When she came to the impressive-looking building, which dominated Aldwych with its tall pillars and inscription reading BVSH HOVSE, Kaisa felt intimidated. Was the incomprehensible lettering Latin? The lobby, too, was high-ceilinged and clad in cream marble. Kaisa had never been inside a place like it. Her voice shook when she asked the lady behind a round desk where she should go. After scanning a list, she gave Kaisa a name badge and told her to wait on a leather sofa.

An older Finnish woman, who introduced herself as Annikki Sands and had a very stern manner, came to fetch her. When they were going up in the lift, Kaisa could make out at least three languages being spoken around her. At Terroni's she'd become used to hearing Italian, but this was different; it was as if she'd suddenly stepped into the most international and sophisticated world. These people even dressed differently; one man in the lift had a dark moustache and wore a spotted bowtie with a matching handkerchief in his jacket pocket. When he saw Kaisa looking at his attire, he made a slight nod and smiled. Kaisa turned her head towards Annikki, who luckily had her back to Kaisa and so hadn't seen her fraternising with the locals already. Somehow Kaisa knew the older Finnish woman wouldn't approve. When they reached the fourth floor, Annikki Sands walked in front of her, past a vast central lobby, where five different red clocks displayed the time in different parts of the world. People were milling around and Kaisa saw two doors surmounted by red lights saying, 'Quiet: Recording.'

The interview was conducted in a small, messy office, with piles of Finnish newspapers and magazines stacked high against the walls. The smell of newspaper ink made Kaisa recall her days at *Adam's Apple*, but otherwise it couldn't have been more different. For one thing, everyone spoke Finnish. Kaisa had been in London for such a long time that her Finnish faltered at first and she had to look for words, but she soon got used to it and spoke fluently. The woman, Annikki, didn't smile once for the duration of the interview. Kaisa assumed she was about the same age as her mother, in her late forties. The man next to her was a little younger and had a very quiet voice and manner. When Kaisa shook his hand, their palms barely touched before he pulled away. 'My name is Juha Helin,' he said. Juha was short, with soft sandy coloured hair. He looked kindly, and Kaisa was glad she had had at least one friendly face in the room, especially when Juha seemed impressed by Kaisa's degree from Hanken, as well as her short career in journalism.

'And you are taking a diploma at the moment in London?' Annikki Sands asked. Her tone was so level, that it almost dipped at the end of the question.

'Yes,' Kaisa replied, and when her words were followed by a silence, she realised she should elaborate. She described the subjects she'd covered to date, and told them how much she enjoyed studying at the School of Journalism. Kaisa had noticed that, once again, she was the most highly qualified on her course; none of the others in her class of about twenty people even had a university degree, let alone a Masters from a school of economics. Still, she was studying in a foreign language, which meant that she wasn't any faster at learning the techniques than her classmates.

After she'd finished, they both nodded, and then looked at each other.

'Your CV is very impressive. Have you applied for other jobs?' Annikki Sands asked.

Kaisa was quiet for a moment, then said, truthfully, 'No, but my previous employer at *Adam's Apple* has suggested a few places, such as the *Guardian* or the *Observer*, where she works.'

Annikki and Juha exchanged glances.

'You'll need to do a voice test,' Annikki Sands said. 'We all broadcast as well as write the programmes, so you will need a voice that is strong enough. I'll organise that, and send the appointment date and time to you.' She looked down at her notes and Kaisa confirmed that they had the correct address.

When Kaisa was walking back to Holborn tube station, she realised she'd not even asked how many other applicants there were. The advert had given the salary, which was far more than she'd ever earned, twice what Rose had been able to pay her at *Adam's Apple*. The start date, too, was stated in the newspaper – 3 February 1986 – though Annikki had hinted that they might have to move that forward. Kaisa cursed her nerves; it had taken all her concentration during the interview not to let her voice quiver, or her hands shake, but she should have been more inquisitive; she feared she might have come across as someone who didn't care whether she got the job or not. That said, when she'd left, the man, Juha, had smiled at her and nodded as if to say that she'd done well. But then, he might have done the same to everyone they interviewed. Plus, she had only nodded when they'd asked if she was married to an Englishman. There had been no mention of their living arrangements, or what her husband's profession was, so Kaisa didn't volunteer the information.

The BBC letter offering her a job as a 'Junior Reporter, World Service, Finnish Section' arrived exactly two weeks after Kaisa had attended the interview at Bush House. It appeared that the voice test had just been a formality; they told her that her pronunciation needed to be worked on, that her 's' was a little too soft, but that with training she could become better. Even the interview with a slim, carefully made-up lady from the Personnel Department, who told Kaisa she was a former air hostess with British Airways, hadn't brought up Peter's profession. When Kaisa had told the woman her address she hadn't asked if she lived alone or with her husband. Kaisa decided she'd assumed they lived together, and Kaisa hadn't volunteered any other information. She had spoken with Rose on the telephone the night before the interview, and she had been adamant that she was within her right to work in the UK.

'Besides, once you're there, even if the divorce comes through, they'll have to get you a work permit, because by then I bet they'll be counting on you, my dear,' she'd said.

Rose was staying with her uncle for an extra two days, in addition to the two weeks she'd taken off for Christmas and New Year. 'I've not taken a long holiday like this for ages,' she'd said on the phone. Rose had seemed very relaxed and Kaisa wondered if this was a long celebration of the engagement, because she kept postponing her return.

As it was, the personnel manager, who, with her slim figure and blonde hair pulled into a chignon, had reminded Kaisa of the wife of one of Peter's former captains (who had also worked as an air hostess for the national airline), hadn't asked a thing about Peter, apart from his name.

32

On Kaisa's first day, in early February, she found out that she'd been the only applicant with the relevant qualifications and a work permit. They had interviewed a couple of reporters from Finland but 'their English language skills weren't as good as yours,' Annikki told her. 'Besides, it's easier with someone who already lives here in London. And your Swedish language knowledge will come in useful too,' she added. Her face was still stern, but Kaisa could see a smile hovering at the corners of her eyes. Kaisa decided not to worry about her work permit, but reminded herself that she needed to let Peter know about her new status, just in case some eager civil servant somewhere in the great machinery of the Royal Navy and the British Broadcasting Corporation decided to check her credentials. She'd have to contact Peter, but she had no time to worry about that while Annikki showed her around her new workplace and introduced her to the new work colleagues.

That same evening, after an exhausting day spent meeting the Finnish team and being told she'd start a course in radio broadcasting on 10th February, she decided to try to call Peter. She had no idea if he was still based in Plymouth, nor if he was away at sea. But she wanted to tell him the good news about the new job at the BBC. The magnitude of this hadn't really hit Kaisa yet. She'd been so worried about the work permit, and then about her ability to do the job. Now she just needed to make sure Peter wouldn't do anything, such as file for a divorce, for the next few months.

Kaisa dialled the number for the Devonport wardroom. She was nervous; what would she say to him? How would she formulate what she needed to ask him? She was standing in the hallway of the house at Colville Terrace, and prayed that the slovenly boyfriend of her landlady wouldn't suddenly decide he needed something from the kitchen. That had happened more and more often, but tonight the whole house seemed empty; keeping her fingers crossed, Kaisa listened to the rings on the other end of the line.

'Hello, I wonder if I could speak with Lieutenant Peter Williams.'

The gruff voice at the other end said, 'Who's calling?'

'It's Kaisa Williams,' Kaisa hesitated for a moment and added, 'his wife.'

'Just one moment, please,' the man said. He betrayed no emotion, or recognition of the name. Perhaps Peter's court martial and the events leading up to it had already been forgotten, Kaisa thought. Or perhaps this man was new and didn't know Peter's infamous history.

Kaisa could hear the echo of steps, then a door being closed at the other end, and then more steps. The receiver was picked up.

'Hello?'

Hearing Peter's voice took Kaisa's breath away. She was reminded of all those times when they'd been apart, her still living in Finland and him in Britain, when phone calls had been so precious. And then when they were living in the married quarter in Portsmouth, and he'd been away. She remembered the delight she'd taken in listening to him say he missed her, and the relief in realising he was safe, that the submarine hadn't sunk somewhere in the middle of the ocean, only to be reported missing weeks later. The horror of what the men onboard would have gone through would play on Kaisa's mind when she couldn't get to sleep. She always imagined the worst.

'Hello,' Peter said again. This time his voice displayed irritation.

'Hi, it's me,' Kaisa said quickly. She didn't want to lose him now. She held tightly onto the heavy black receiver.

'Kaisa,' Peter's voice was warm. 'How are you?'

'I'm well, and you?'

'Good.' There was a brief silence. 'We came back a few hours ago.'

Kaisa could hear that Peter had had a beer (or two) and she smiled without thinking. The crew wouldn't have had a drop to drink during all their weeks away, so sometimes just one beer could make them sound drunk. 'Really?'

'You didn't know?' Peter said.

How could she have known, Kaisa thought. 'No.'

'Oh.'

'Listen, I have a bit of news: I've got a job with the BBC!'

'Really,' Peter said. 'Congratulations.'

But Kaisa could hear disappointment in his voice, and she suddenly felt annoyed. This is what it always came down to with Peter. He didn't care what kind of job she had. All he wanted was to have sex with her, to have her at home when he came back from sea. She realised he must think she was calling to arrange a date. He thought nothing had changed; that she was desperate to see him again and to have him in her bed. But surely Kaisa had made it clear how she felt during their last conversation? Besides, the lack of letters over the months when they hadn't seen each other must have told him it was over? Of course, Kaisa had thought about him. Each time she was with Ravi, she thought about Peter. But she forced herself to forget all about him, for the sake of her career. However, it was evident from his reaction now, that to him, her career didn't matter.

'I'm only letting you know so that you needn't pay me any more money,' she said, trying to sound matter-of-fact. But she could hear the note of irritation in her voice. So what, she thought, serves him right.

'Oh, right,' Peter began, then stopped and said nothing more.

'We also need to decide about the divorce,' Kaisa continued. She was now so angry, she thought to hell with everything. She was the best candidate for the BBC job after all, and the others would have needed work permits anyway, so the BBC must be prepared to apply for one. Besides, now she had a contract, she was sure the BBC wouldn't get rid of her that easily. She had skills that no one else had, so she was sure she'd get a work permit now. She didn't need this selfish, arrogant, naval officer of an ex-husband anymore!

Again Peter started to say something, but then the doorbell to the house rang. Kaisa listened for a moment, but there was no movement in the whole place. The doorbell rang again and she said, 'Hold on a minute.'

Kaisa placed the receiver on the small table, and went to open the door. She was glad of the distraction, to control her temper. How was it possible that Peter could make her so angry so quickly when she didn't even live with him anymore, and hadn't talked to him since the brief phone call after that stupid, stupid, loss of self-control she'd had in Plymouth?

On the doorstep stood Ravi, holding a vast bunch of flowers in one hand, and in the other a bottle of champagne. He was grinning widely, showing his incredible white teeth. 'I thought we should celebrate your brilliant new career!' Ravi looked more handsome to Kaisa than he had for a long time. He was wearing a pair of smart trousers and a striped shirt under a double-breasted jacket with gold buttons. His pitch-black hair was just touching the collar of his shirt and his lips looked full and inviting. Kaisa smelled the flowers and in a loud voice said, 'Thank you, darling, come in, I just need to finish this telephone call.' She took hold of Ravi's arm, and pulled him inside.

Ravi stepped in and, looking puzzled, gave Kaisa a quick kiss on her lips. 'Who is it?' he whispered.

'Oh, it's no one important,' Kaisa said, again loud enough for Peter to hear, and she picked up the receiver.

'Sorry, I need to go. I just wanted to let you know about the money,' Kaisa took a deep breath, and continued, 'and the divorce. You can go ahead with it now.'

'Right,' Peter said. Kaisa could hear emotion in his voice now. Was it anger, or something else? She hesitated for a moment, but then thought, I'm glad I've upset him. Bloody man!

'Good,' she said.

'Yes, good.' Peter said.

'Bye,' Kaisa said and put down the receiver.

Ravi was standing in the hall, looking uncomfortable. They didn't often meet in the house, and if they did, they tried to sneak upstairs unnoticed. Kaisa's landlady, or the unpleasant boyfriend, didn't approve of Ravi. The landlady had once asked Kaisa, when Ravi had been waiting for her outside the house, what she was doing with a 'Paki'. Surely Kaisa, a good-looking girl, even if she was foreign, could do better than that? At the time, Kaisa had been going through a bit of a crisis of conscience with Ravi and had decided to finish it with him, perhaps because it was only a week after she'd slept with Peter, or because she realised she didn't love him and never would. They hadn't yet had sex, and Kaisa knew that she would have to let it happen soon, so it was only fair to end it. But the landlady's racism had made Kaisa defiant. She'd got drunk that evening and had invited Ravi to her bed. At the same time, Kaisa couldn't afford to be thrown out of the bedsit, so they'd been careful not to be seen in the house together again.

'Come on, let's go upstairs and open this!' Kaisa said. 'The house is empty!' she grinned, taking the flowers from him. She led him up the stairs and into her room. She didn't have any proper champagne glasses and they had to drink it out of water tumblers.

When they'd settled on the bed, sitting side by side, Kaisa began kissing Ravi, and undoing his buttons. Ravi put his hand on Kaisa's fingers, stopping her midway. 'Was that your husband on the phone?'

Kaisa looked at Ravi's dark eyes. 'Yes, why?'

Ravi stood up, and placing his glass on the small kitchen worktop opposite Kaisa's bed, said, 'Look, I like you a lot.' He rubbed the dark stubble on his chin and gazed at Kaisa for a while. 'As a matter of fact, I think I might be falling for you.'

Kaisa sat on the bed, looking at her hands. She didn't dare to look at Ravi.

'But I cannot be part of a game you are playing with your husband.'

Kaisa looked up, 'What do you mean, a game?'

Ravi came over to her, crouching opposite her, and took her hands in his. 'Our relationship is not an easy one. Already we have to sneak around this place.'

'But I don't care about them!' Kaisa looked at his sad eyes.

'I know you don't, and believe me, I don't give a shit about people like that either. I meet them every day, so I'm used to it. But my community, they would be, and are, the same. I'm constantly fighting a battle against my mother.' Ravi lifted Kaisa's chin up and looked deep into her eyes. 'She wants to find a suitable wife for me. She's relentless.' Ravi gave a small laugh. 'So, what I'm saying is that if we were to get more serious, it will be difficult and we will need to be sure of our feelings for each other.'

Kaisa nodded. She moved away from Ravi, and went to stand by the sink. She couldn't face him.

'And I'm not sure you are over Peter,' Ravi said to her back.

Tears began running down Kaisa's face. The whole awfulness of the conversation with Peter just dawned on her, at the same time as the realisation that she was also losing Ravi. He stood up and put his arms round her. He rocked her back and forth for a while. Kaisa turned around in his arms, and put her head on his shoulder. 'I'm getting make-up on your smart shirt,' she said.

'That's alright.'

They stood there for a moment, until Kaisa finished crying. Ravi let go, and gave Kaisa a peck on her wet cheek. 'If you need any help with anything, call me, eh?'

Kaisa nodded. When the door closed behind Ravi, Kaisa sat down on the bed, sipping the champagne. She sat like that for at least an hour, watching the lights of the houses opposite go out and the street quieten. The room grew darker, and Kaisa got up. She put the half-full bottle of champagne in her little fridge and found the pint glass Ravi had once stolen for her from the Horse and Coaches, when she'd told him she only owned a pair of tumblers to put his flowers in. Kaisa sighed. Ravi was right, she knew. She cared for him. But she still had feelings for Peter. What kind of feelings, apart from the anger and annoyance she felt for him, she didn't know. But because she felt those emotions so strongly, it was obvious she needed more time to get over him. Had she been selfish to have sex with Ravi? Had she led him on? Not according to Rose, but then Rose wouldn't have predicted that Ravi would leave her. Suddenly Kaisa laughed; she'd been dumped! This was how it felt. Served her right for everything she'd done to the men in her life; still, she couldn't help but feel sorry for herself. She pulled her legs up on the small comfy chair in her room, poured some more champagne, and settled down to watch an old American black-and-white film on TV.

33

Peter put the phone down and stood gazing at the door to the wardroom for a moment. Then he turned back to the phone and dialled a number. 'Are you doing anything this weekend?'

Jackie shrieked. 'You're back! No, what are you planning?'

Peter made a date to go up to London on Friday evening. Jackie's delight at the other end of the phone was palpable; Peter almost felt embarrassed on her behalf.

Peter hadn't seen Jackie since Kaisa's visit to Plymouth. They had sailed a few days later, and had not got back until just before Christmas. The next trip had come as a surprise; they'd sailed immediately after Peter got back to Plymouth after the New Year. Jackie had written to Peter, and he'd even managed to reply, but he'd kept his letters cool on purpose. He didn't want a repetition of the discussion – or rather argument – about his divorce and the possibility of marrying Jackie. Peter shook his head; she must be completely mad to think he would enter headlong into another serious relationship like that. 'Women!' he thought a few days later as he drove along the motorway towards London. He decided that if Jackie started that kind of talk again, this would be the last time he'd see her.

But when Jackie opened the door to her flat in Chelsea, and flung herself around his neck, he regretted his decision to drive all the way up to London to see her. He felt bad, because he knew he was taking all his anger for Kaisa, all his jealousy, out on Jackie. He was using her.

'Darling Peter, I knew you'd come around!' Jackie cooed.

'Look, this was a mistake,' Peter said, forcing Jackie's hands from his neck. He was holding onto her wrists, and realised too late that he was squeezing them a lot harder than he'd intended.

'Kinky!' Jackie laughed, 'You want to tie me up?' she said and wriggled her bum. She was wearing just a thin dress and high-heeled shoes. It was a cold evening, and he could see her hard nipples through the gathered material of the dress. Peter could guess what, if anything, was underneath, and felt himself harden. 'Come in!' Jackie said and pulled him inside.

Why the hell not, Peter thought, but afterwards when they were lying on Jackie's satin sheets, smoking cigarettes, Peter said, 'Look, we can't do this anymore.'

'What?' Jackie sat up in bed, revealing her full, naked breasts.

Peter sighed, 'Sorry, Jackie, but I ...'

'Shh,' Jackie said and kissed Peter. 'Don't worry, I'm not going to mention the 'M' word,' she gave Peter a grin, 'or the 'D' word for that matter. Let's just have fun, eh?'

'OK,' Peter said, but he knew that wouldn't be the end of it with Jackie. However, if she didn't want to spell it out, if she said she wanted just to have fun, that meant no ties, right? But this woman scared him and Peter resolved that this was the last weekend he would spend with her.

On Sunday, when it was time for Peter to return to Plymouth, he told Jackie at the door, 'I'm sorry, but this is it.'

Jackie's face fell, 'What do you mean?'

'I'm not going to be back.'

Jackie stared at Peter. She tried to pull her mouth up into a smile, but managed just a lopsided grin. Peter shifted his weight from one foot to another. He wanted to be away, but he also wanted to make sure Jackie was clear on his decision. Her father was an Admiral after all, and goodness knew what weight he still carried in the Navy.

'Look, I'm sorry. I just can't.' He took Jackie's hand in his. 'It's my career, and who knows what my next appointment is going to be.'

'But I do!' Jackie said.

'What?'

'But if you don't want me ...'

Peter gazed down at Jackie. She was standing in her stockinged feet, shivering inside her dressing gown. Was she bluffing? 'Have you done something, organised something to do with my career?'

'Oh, Peter,' Jackie came and put her hands around his waist. 'I just asked Daddy if there was any chance you might get a job nearer London, you know a shore job for a change, and he said he'd see what he could do.'

. . .

Peter drove back to Plymouth with his head whirling with different ideas. A shore job in London would change everything. But, of course, nothing was certain yet; Jackie's dad could be bluffing; why would he want his daughter anywhere near Peter? Perhaps once upon a time, but not now when his career was doing a nose dive. 'A submariner in a nose dive is never a good thing,' Peter thought and grinned at his own joke. All the same, if he was given this fantastic opportunity to be ashore for a while, he'd make use of it. Poor Jackie, she'd well and truly shot herself in the foot this time.

34

When she got home to her bedsit, there was a cream-coloured letter waiting for Kaisa. Even before she turned the envelope in her hands, she guessed who it was from. She could recognise Peter's handwriting in a darkened room by touch alone, she was sure of it. She smelled the envelope before opening it, but there was no hint of his coconut aftershave. It wasn't what he normally did, anyway, it was the other way around; Kaisa was the one who was supposed to drown her correspondence in perfume.

'Dear Kaisa,

I hope you are well, and still living in the same address in London and that this letter reaches you.

I wasn't sure if you wanted to hear from me, but after so many weeks at sea, I felt I should at least let you know I'm back in port and not likely to go away again soon. And I have some news.

I am visiting my family in Wiltshire at the moment, and this is one of the reasons I wanted to write. I thought you'd like to know that Nancy and Nigel have had two little babies, twins, Oliver and Beth. They're now three months old, and very beautiful, although the boy, Oliver, cries a lot, especially at night. Nancy is very well too, as is Nigel. My mum and dad send their regards, and wish you well.

Love,

Peter x'

Kaisa reread the letter three times, standing in the hall. She was rooted to the spot, mulling over what Peter's words might mean. The tone of the letter was like old times; he'd even put an x after his name. Suddenly a door opened and Mrs Carter peered at her.

'Everything alright?'

Her landlady was wearing a faded housecoat and had rollers in her artificially bleached hair. She looked annoyed.

'Yes, sorry, I just got a letter and ...'

'The hall's not for lounging in,' Mrs Carter said.

'Who is it?' Kaisa heard Colin's shout from inside the room.

'No one,' Mrs Carter said and banged the door shut. Kaisa put the letter back into the envelope and fled upstairs. Kaisa's landlady had been particularly unfriendly to her in the past few weeks. She'd told Kaisa that she was going to marry the brute Colin, who'd been staying there ever since Kaisa moved in. He didn't seem to get dressed, and was always wearing his long johns, or boxer shorts in summer, whenever Kaisa saw him in the stairwell. Mrs Carter had told her that they were going to be making changes to the house. 'Colin thinks we should turn this place into luxury flats,' she'd said. There was no timetable for this, of course, and Kaisa doubted the two of them would ever get round to it, but it seemed obvious they wanted her out. In any case, Kaisa didn't want to rock the boat by making a nuisance of herself and give Mrs Carter and the horrible boyfriend any cause to ask her to leave sooner than they were planning. Although, with her new BBC job, she'd be able to rent a whole flat, Kaisa didn't want to count her chickens. Not yet.

Thinking about her living arrangements calmed Kaisa and she could now go back to wondering what the letter meant. She looked at the envelope. It was dated more than a month ago, 2nd January 1986. Why had it taken so long to reach her? And why had Peter written to her in the first place? Before he went away in November, she thought they'd made it clear to each other that they had no future together. Perhaps he had suddenly felt nostalgic for her, and the happy times they'd had in his parents' house in Wiltshire. Kaisa looked at the postmark on the envelope, it had 'BFPO Ships' on it, which meant he'd sent it while away at sea, or from the wardroom before he went away. Still, that meant it had taken a month to reach her. Another thought entered her mind. Because she'd had no communication from Peter, she'd assumed he was away at sea for Christmas. Although she'd not wanted to spend the holiday with Peter, in her desperation during the days leading up to the holidays, when she was facing a long weekend alone in the bedsit, she might have considered meeting up with him if she'd known he was ashore.

Kaisa looked at Peter's letter again. She thought about those mysterious words, *'not likely to go away again soon'*. What did they mean? Kaisa's heart skipped a beat when she thought the unthinkable. No, that could not be what he meant? Peter would never even think about leaving the Navy – or would he?

Then there were the babies, twins! Kaisa wondered if the gene ran in Nigel's family. She'd certainly never heard of any twins in the Williams family. Finally, the mention of Peter's parents made her shiver. Even after all these months, and after everything she'd done, the life she'd forged for herself in London (with the help of Rose, of course), she still feared seeing Peter's parents the most. Of course, there was no chance she'd suddenly bump into them in Terroni's in Farringdon, or at the BBC in Aldwych, or on the street in Notting Hill. Still, just the thought of facing them after what she had done to their son made her palms damp. No, she would never be able to see his mother or father ever again.

Kaisa put the letter away and went to make herself a cup of coffee. While she sipped it, she thought how nice it would be to see Nancy and the twins. Then she imagined herself holding hands with Peter, looking down at two babies in their separate cots. There was no stopping her mind now. She immediately imagined herself in Peter's arms, kissing his lips, held firmly in his embrace, running her fingers through his thick black hair. 'Stop,' she told herself. 'Stop. That'll never happen, so just stop it now.' But she couldn't help herself, and she reread Peter's letter. She realised the sentence about not going away soon could mean anything. It could be that the submarine was in refit, that he'd joined another submarine that was being built, or that he was on a lengthy course in Portsmouth, or even London. The most unlikely alternative, that he'd decided to leave the Navy, was ludicrous. It wasn't even worth thinking about.

The rest of her first week at the BBC, Kaisa existed in a haze of learning new things and meeting new people. She'd even been invited to the pub on Friday night, and she'd got to know the other Finns who worked at Bush House. She realised that the work was going to be hard, because it involved a lot of translation. News stories from the main bulletins at the BBC needed to be translated quickly into Finnish, edited into a suitably short bulletin, and broadcast, often on the same day. Her Finnish language skills had suffered during her time in the UK, but Juha, who had been assigned as her supervisor, told Kaisa she'd soon learn the ropes.

'There are people working here who've lived in England for ten, twenty years. It was much harder for them to relearn Finnish. You'll be fine,' he said in his understated way as they were queuing up for food in the canteen.

On Saturday evening, after her first weekend duty at the BBC, Kaisa sat down and wrote a letter to Peter. She'd learned that they would work four days on and then have four days off, but that would include any day of the week. Bank holidays were treated as any other day of the week. 'But we have Christmas off,' Juha had told her. She'd been to the pub with Juha after they'd completed that day's short weekend bulletin (Kaisa helped, but Juha did most of the work and read out the news in Finnish). There they'd met a couple of male reporters from Italy who'd been impressed by the little Italian Kaisa had learned at Terroni's. They also knew the café, and Mama Terroni, and said they recognised Kaisa from their visits there. It felt strange to have her different lives collide, but no one seemed to think it odd that a woman with her qualifications should have worked as a waitress for a time. London was truly different, Kaisa thought, and she smiled at the handsome Italians.

'Dear Peter,

When we spoke I didn't get to say how happy I am for Nancy and Nigel. (I only got your letter last week.) They must be delighted with the new additions to their family, as must you and your parents be. And you are now an uncle! Please send my congratulations to Nancy and Nigel.

I'm sorry our conversation on Wednesday was cut short, it is difficult to talk when living in somebody else's house. This bedsit living is a bit like the wardroom, I'm sure. You can never be alone on the telephone without someone listening in.

The reason I phoned, was that I wanted to tell you that you can go ahead with the divorce. As you, I am sure, understand, my issue has been with a work permit. I found out some time ago that if you divorced me, as a foreign subject I wouldn't be allowed to stay in the UK. Now, however, with my new job at the BBC, I think I might be able to get a work permit after all. Also, as I said on the telephone, you don't need to support me financially any more. So you can be rid of me at last.

Best,

Kaisa'

.   .   .

Kaisa reread what she had written and sighed. She'd decided not to put an 'x' for a kiss at the end of her name. That decision had taken at least ten minutes. She thought back to that crazy night in Plymouth and how wonderful it had felt to once again be held in Peter's arms. And the act of sex, how wonderful it had been, how good it had felt with Peter. She shivered when she thought about it now. She couldn't help it, but she longed for his touch, for the taste of his lips. But it could, would, never work, so Kaisa folded the paper, put it inside an envelope and, licking the glue, sealed it. She now had four days off, and on Monday she resolved to go and look for a flat of her own. Then she could give notice to her landlady and be able to have a bit of privacy at last. Perhaps then she could meet someone new.

35

A week and a bit later, after Kaisa had done two four-hour shifts at the BBC, and had started her formal BBC journalism course, held in the top floor conference rooms at Bush House, she was getting ready to go out. She'd had to pull out of the course at the School of Journalism, but the lady in the personnel department had told Kaisa that BBC training was more prestigious. 'This will stand you in good stead worldwide,' she'd said smiling. Kaisa had been sad not to finish her course in Maida Vale, but the tutor had given her a letter, explaining to any prospective employer why she had dropped out. 'A job at the BBC!' he'd said. 'That's a job for life! Well done!'

Some of the other students had looked at her differently when they heard her news. Kaisa hadn't told them that she'd been the only proper applicant, or at least the only one with relevant education, experience, and language skills living in the UK.

Not working at Terroni's and dropping out of the course meant that she saw less of Rose, and so they'd decided to meet up on the Monday evening after her second four-day shift at the BBC. On the phone, Rose had told her that she'd accepted Roger's offer of marriage, and Kaisa had congratulated her. Rose had invited Kaisa to an engagement party at Roger's place in a couple of weeks' time. Kaisa hadn't been to the Coach and Horses since Ravi had broken up with her, and sitting on the tube on her way to Farringdon, she wondered if he'd be there. When she dug into her handbag to reapply her lip gloss, she noticed at the bottom of the bag the unsent letter to Peter. She'd been meaning to send it every day, but hadn't had time even to buy a stamp. She felt the thin envelope in her hands, and wondered if she should rip it up, when the train pulled into Farringdon.

The Coach and Horses wasn't full on a Monday evening in late February, and Kaisa quickly realised that she was about fifteen minutes early. The first person she set eyes on was Ravi. He was talking to a man, whom Kaisa recognised as one of his friends from the *Observer*. It was too late for Kaisa to back away – they had both seen her, and Ravi's friend had even waved. Kaisa took a deep intake of breath and walked towards the two men.

Ravi gave her a kiss on her cheek, and asked if she wanted a drink. Kaisa looked around; there was no sign of Rose.

'OK, she said, I'll have a glass of white wine.'

She suddenly thought Ravi must be thinking she was here to look for him. 'I'm meeting Rose later,' she said as he handed her the drink.

'Oh, OK.' Ravi said. Exchanging some silent message, with Ravi, his friend excused himself to Kaisa, saying he needed to read through something, and went to sit at a table in the corner of the pub. With his head bent, he started shifting through a pile of papers. Both Kaisa and Ravi looked at him for a while. Kaisa wished Rose would turn up soon; she didn't know what to say to Ravi.

'How have you been?' Ravi looked at Kaisa, his black eyes full of emotion.

'Good, the new job is tiring, but I like it there.' Kaisa moved her eyes away from his; she didn't want to sink into those deep pools of liquid black.

'Good, good,' Ravi said.

They stood quietly for a moment, sipping their drinks. Kaisa thought what a good-looking man Ravi was, and wondered if he'd succumbed to seeing any of the girls his mother had suggested for him. But those dark eyes, and the floppy black hair, and his muscular build didn't have any effect on her anymore. She was now glad he'd broken it off; he'd been right, she had no romantic feelings for him.

'Look, Kaisa,' Ravi looked around him to make sure their conversation remained private. He put his hand on Kaisa's arm and said, 'I've missed you.'

'Oh, Ravi,' Kaisa said. She didn't want to lead him on, but didn't know what to say.

At that moment she saw from the corner of her eye the door to the pub open and a man walk in. Afterwards, Kaisa was sure she'd felt his presence even before she'd turned to face him.

'Peter,' she said. Ravi still had his hand on Kaisa's arm, and suddenly she realised that anyone seeing the two of them like that would think they were a couple. She quickly pulled her hand away and moved towards Peter, who stood glued to the spot near the door of the pub. When Kaisa got to him, she saw his eyes were dark and serious. She wanted to explain to him that there was nothing going on between her and Ravi; that she kept thinking about the exciting, thrilling and completely mad lovemaking in the car in Plymouth; and that she couldn't forget about him. Instead, she said, 'What are you doing here?'

Peter brushed past her to the bar. 'It's a free country, isn't it?'

He was now standing next to Ravi, who, taken aback at hearing the name, stepped away from Peter, and glanced questioningly at Kaisa. She just shrugged her shoulders and stood next to Peter.

When he'd got his drink, Kaisa said, 'Shall we go and sit down?'

Peter took a long pull out of his pint, and nodded. He gave Ravi a long look, turned away and walked to a table at the other side of the bar. 'Sorry,' Kaisa mouthed to Ravi as she followed Peter.

'So, you've moved on, then?' Peter said as soon as he'd sat down.

His voice was loud, and Kaisa could see he was angry. His tone of voice took her by surprise. She couldn't believe it. What right did he have to lecture her on moving on! She remembered the party in the summer, when they'd only been apart for a few months. He had kissed Kaisa, then immediately told the girl he'd come to the party with that the kiss hadn't meant anything. And when they'd gone out for a meal in Covent Garden a few months later, at the end of a wonderful evening, which had made Kaisa believe they were going to be reconciled, he'd told her that he wanted a divorce. True enough, after Plymouth, he seemed to want to get back together again, but by then Kaisa had known it wouldn't work.

Kaisa tried to suppress her anger. She took a deep breath in and sat down opposite Peter.

'It's not what you think.'

'Really?' Peter said.

'Not that it has anything to do with you.' Kaisa said, looking squarely at him. She was trying to keep her voice level, but she could hear her own words faltering.

Peter stared at Kaisa. He lowered his eyes to his pint, took a swig and said, 'No, I didn't say it was.'

They were quiet for a moment, not looking at each other. Kaisa could feel the eyes of Ravi and his friend, and a few other regulars in the pub, as well as the bar staff, burning holes in her back.

'So, how come you are here?' Kaisa asked, trying to find out if he'd come in search of her, or if it was another of those crazy coincidences that littered their lives.

Peter, who had been drinking his pint in large gulps, put down his empty glass. Finally, he met her eyes. 'You want another one?' he asked and got up.

Kaisa sighed, 'Please.'

He was doing what he did best, buying time and not talking. But Kaisa had got wise to his tactics and would get the reason for his visit out of him. She would have to be firm and brave. But when she glanced over her shoulder, checking that Peter hadn't gone to challenge Ravi, she was shocked to see that was exactly what he was doing. The two men were talking close to one another, seemingly in a civilised manner. When Peter returned to the table, Kaisa gazed at him, trying to gauge what he'd said to her ex-boyfriend. At that moment Rose walked in.

'Hello, darling,' she exclaimed and came to kiss Kaisa on the cheek. Directing her head towards Ravi, and lifting her eyebrows at Kaisa and Peter, whom she'd never met, Rose said, 'Everything alright?'

Kaisa spoke first, 'Rose, this is Peter, my ...' she hesitated and looked from Peter's face to Rose's. But Rose came to her rescue. She stretched her hand towards Peter and said, 'How lovely to meet you at last. I've heard so much about you.'

'I bet,' Peter said drily.

Rose gave a short laugh, 'Well, I should let you talk.'

'Rose,' Kaisa began again, only to be interrupted by Peter. 'Can I get you a drink, Rose?'

'That's very kind of you, Peter.' Rose smiled and said she'd love a gin and tonic.

When Peter had gone back to the bar, Rose sat down next to Kaisa. 'Look, if you want to spend the evening talking things over, we can reschedule.'

Kaisa looked at Rose's kind face. She was so overwhelmed by the situation that she could hardly speak. 'Thank you,' was all she managed to say.

'Just take a breath, darling.' Rose put her hand on Kaisa's arm and glanced at the bar, which had now filled up, forcing Peter to queue. 'Just listen to him, see what he has to say; find out why he's here to see you. Which is why he must be here, right? But don't promise anything. You have the world at your feet now, girl, so be strong and only do what you want to do. OK?' Rose was looking into Kaisa's eyes, and Kaisa nodded. 'OK,' she said.

When Peter came back Rose had managed to lighten the mood by telling Kaisa a story about a talking pig that the *Daily Mail* had carried as their headline that day. 'A slow news day!' She got up and said, 'Thanks for the drink, but I'm afraid I'm here to meet someone else.'

When Rose had gone, Peter said, 'Was that *the* Rose?'

'Yes,' Kaisa replied. 'She's been a very good friend to me, well more than a friend. She found the ad in the paper for this BBC job, and she helped me get the job at the café when *Adam's Apple* folded, and she wrote a letter of recommendation to the School of Journalism.' Kaisa saw Peter's eyebrows lift at the mention of the café and the journalism course. She realised he knew nothing of her life now. Suddenly she remembered the letter, still unposted, in her handbag. She'd thought it best to leave Peter to get on with his life, she now reminded herself.

Peter lifted his eyes to Kaisa, 'Yeah, I went to your old offices today, after Notting Hill.'

'You went to Colville Terrace?' Kaisa interrupted him. She was astonished that he'd tried so hard to find her.

'Yeah,' Peter wasn't looking at her. 'Anyway there was just some caretaker at *Adam's Apple*, a young guy.'

'Jack?' Kaisa said, puzzled. What would the delivery guy be doing in the empty magazine offices?

'Yeah, I think that was his name. He was clearing out the place. Anyway, he knew you, and said there were a couple of pubs you used to go to nearby, so I took my chance and I found you here.' Peter paused for a moment, then added, 'With your boyfriend.'

'He's not my boyfriend.'

Peter gazed at Kaisa with his dark eyes. 'You sure about that?' He shifted in his seat so that he could look over to the bar past Kaisa. 'For a not-boyfriend, he seems to be keeping a very close eye on you.'

Kaisa turned around and saw Ravi looking at them. He lifted his pint at Kaisa and smiled. Kaisa smiled back, and nodded in what she hoped was a reassuring gesture. 'We used to see each other,' she said and faced Peter again. 'But we were never an item as such.'

'*Not an item as such,*' Peter repeated Kaisa's words. 'You've become very English,' he said, again with a kind of dry sarcasm.

Anger surged inside Kaisa and she snorted. 'And you can talk! What about the girl at the warehouse party? The one you told I was your ex, and didn't mean anything?'

Peter leaned back in his chair and said, 'That's over.'

'Oh.'

'That was over before it began. And it had just started when I saw you, so she was the one who didn't mean anything.'

'But you said ...' Kaisa was looking at her hands, trying to make sense of what Peter was telling her.

Peter bent over towards Kaisa and said, 'Look, it's really difficult to talk here with all these people.'

'I know.' Kaisa laughed. 'I suppose this is my local, sort of, so they all know me. Just like in Portsmouth.'

Peter laughed too, 'Yeah, I know.' He shifted in his seat, 'But we could go and have something to eat?'

Kaisa looked up at Peter. His eyes were kind now, and she could see he really did want to sort out their situation. Since starting her job, Kaisa had felt her life shifting, and settling into place, as if something at last was going right. One unsolved matter was Peter. Kaisa knew she needed to move on, so that she could concentrate on her career, and to do that she needed to sort out everything with Peter, once and for all.

'OK.' Kaisa emptied her glass of wine and got up. 'I'm just going to say goodbye.' She left Peter at the table and went over to tell Rose and Ravi, who were now standing next to each other talking at the bar, that she was going to have something to eat with Peter. She nodded to Ravi, whose eyes were still like deep, dark wells, and hugged Rose. 'Take care and remember what I said,' she whispered in Kaisa's ear.

Outside, Peter hailed a taxi and told the driver to take them to Covent Garden. 'You don't mind if we go to the same place as before, do you?'

'No,' Kaisa said. It felt luxurious to just step inside a black cab and be driven straight to one's destination, instead of walking into the dirty tube station. She watched the darkening city flash past as the driver ducked and dived through small streets that Kaisa didn't recognise. She'd sometimes seen Rose expertly hail a cab, and had on occasion accompanied her, but Kaisa couldn't afford to take them on her own. She always used buses and the tube to get around London. Or more often than not, if it wasn't raining, she'd walk. Perhaps now that she was on a much higher salary she could afford a cab or two, but then again, not if she was going to rent a place of her own. She'd been to see an agent, a thin young man in a shiny grey suit, and was surprised at the high cost of renting a one-bedroom flat. 'You'd be better off buying one,' the estate agent had said. He'd told her that she could get a 100 per cent mortgage on a flat. 'Think about it, if you have a steady income, it's worth buying now, mark my words,' he'd said and grinned.

36

Peter was quiet in the taxi, but Kaisa could feel his presence intensely. Their thighs were just touching, and she could feel the tension in his leg muscles through the thin fabric of her dress. He'd been watching the streets flash past on the other side of the cab, but now he turned towards her. 'Look, I've missed you.'

Kaisa was taken aback by Peter's words. It seemed absurd that those same words had been uttered just a few moments before by Ravi. Was she wearing some kind of perfume that attracted men like the rats in that children's tale? Kaisa held her breath when she saw Peter lean towards her, bringing his lips close to hers.

She put her hand on Peter's chest and said, 'Look, we need to talk.' She wasn't going to fall into that same trap of sexual attraction with him again.

'Oh, right.' Peter said, and giving her a searching look, he turned towards the window again. They sat through the rest of the journey in silence, and when they arrived at St Martin's Lane, Peter paid the driver.

'You still want to have dinner with me?' he asked when they were both standing on the pavement outside the Café des Amis. While they'd been in the cab, the sky above London had darkened, and the lights from the passing cars and the neon signs of the restaurant gave Covent Garden a more sinister feel. Against this backdrop, Peter no longer looked so assured.

'We need to talk properly, don't you think?' Kaisa said. She felt like the grown-up, and for the first time in their relationship sensed that she had some control over the situation with Peter.

The restaurant was almost empty; it was Monday night after all. They were shown to a table by the window and ordered their food and wine. Kaisa could tell Peter was a little drunk by now and smiled to herself when he ordered a bottle of water, and then drank a glassful before even touching his wine. He was taking this meeting seriously and wanted to stay clear-headed. For some strange reason, even though she'd had three glasses of wine, Kaisa felt stone cold sober.

Again, she remembered her unsent letter and said, 'Thank you for your letter. And congratulations on becoming an uncle.'

Peter's face lit up, 'Yeah, thanks, I saw them over Christmas, they're beautiful babies. Both have a mop of black hair, and the baby boy, Oliver, he's got a pair of strong lungs on him! Cries a lot. The baby girl is beautiful.'

'Oliver and Beth are lovely names.'

'Yes,' Peter leaned closer to Kaisa and took her hands into his. 'Look, can we start this evening again?'

'Sure,' Kaisa smiled. 'Start by telling me why you wanted to see me?'

Peter sighed and said he'd been worried about her. Not getting a letter in reply to the one he'd sent (again Kaisa felt a pang of guilt over the unsent envelope in her handbag) had made him wonder if she was OK. He said he'd tried to call the house a couple of times, but he'd just been told Kaisa wasn't there. The man at the other end had offered no explanation, refusing to say if Kaisa even lived in the bedsit anymore. Peter had still gone over to the house, but no one had come to the door when he rang the bell.

That bastard landlady's boyfriend can't even be bothered to answer the door anymore, Kaisa thought.

'So, the pub was the final place where I thought I might find you.'

'I'm sorry, I should have replied to your letter.' Kaisa said.

'That's OK, we're here now and you're OK, which I'm glad to see.' Peter told Kaisa that he was now working up in Northwood. 'I'll be up here for a year at least.'

'Where's that?' Kaisa asked.

'Oh, North London, quite a way up. There's a train,' Peter said. He looked at his watch.

'Are you working tomorrow?' Kaisa said, looking at her watch herself. It was only just past 8 pm.

Peter shook his head.

They were both quiet for a moment, and then their food arrived. Kaisa wasn't at all hungry, but she forced herself to pick at the fish that she'd ordered. Peter attacked his steak with his usual enthusiasm; Kaisa smiled when she remembered his constant hunger. Hunger for food, and hunger for her.

While he ate, Kaisa told Peter about her new job, how she'd enjoyed her journalism course, and how she'd had to drop out in order to work for the BBC. She told him about Bush House, and how still, after two weeks, she couldn't quite believe she worked there when she walked through the magnificent pillars flanking the entrance and looked at the oddly spelled name.

'Well, I'm very glad for you. I knew you'd make it,' Peter said between mouthfuls. When he'd finished he put down his knife and fork and said, 'And making it obviously suits you. You look gorgeous.' Peter's face was intense, and his dark eyes made Kaisa's spine tingle. She looked down at her uneaten plateful of food and felt her cheeks redden.

For the rest of the meal they talked about their mutual friends. Kaisa told Peter about Sirkka and her mother in Helsinki, and about her sister's new more serious relationship. Peter told Kaisa about Stef and Tom, how they, too, had had a second baby. And that Pammy was pregnant again. Kaisa felt a quick pang of guilt; she'd not written to her friend since she'd had a 'Thank you' letter back for the pink bear she'd sent. She thought about the letter concerning Peter and Jackie that she'd received in Helsinki. Kaisa now wondered if there'd been any truth in it.

'There's a lot of it about,' Peter laughed, 'must be the water in Helensburgh.'

The mention of that place made them both grow serious and quiet for a while.

'Look, Kaisa,' Peter began, and at the same time Kaisa said, 'What do you want?'

'I want to see you again.'

Kaisa gazed at Peter. He'd stretched his hands out and knitted his fingers with hers. 'Let's start again; let's go out a few times and see how it goes?'

'But, Peter, you're still in the Navy, and one day, in one, or two, or three years' time, you'll be sent back to that awful place.' Kaisa sighed and squeezed Peter's hands, 'And I cannot be a Navy wife, who follows you everywhere you are posted. My life is here in London now. You know that.'

'Yes, I do, but haven't we always made it work, somehow?'

Kaisa laughed, 'Not really!'

Peter also laughed, and Kaisa wanted to touch the small creases that the laughter formed around his eyes.

'No, I know what you mean. But don't we deserve to give each other one last chance?' He squeezed Kaisa's hands. 'Just one more?'

Kaisa looked at Peter. She knew she loved him, but could she afford to take the risk of hurting him again?

'I'm afraid.'

Peter leaned closer to her, 'So am I. But let's not think! Let's just start dating. As if the past hadn't happened and we'd just met each other?' Peter's eyes were playful now, and the pressure of his hands had increased.

Kaisa was thinking hard. 'What if I hurt you again?' she said.

'I'm a big boy, I can take it,' Peter said and he leaned over the table to kiss her. Kaisa's heart filled with such emotion, such love, gentle and passionate at the same time, that she knew he was right.

But she forced herself to pull away from him, and looked deeply into his eyes. 'Are you sure you've forgiven me?'

Peter put his palm on her cheek and replied, 'My darling, there is nothing to forgive. We have no past, remember? We've just met!' He smiled and lowered his voice. 'I want to make love to you for the first time.'

Kaisa returned his smile. It was impossible! This man was impossible! But she knew in her heart that Peter was right.

They deserved to give each other one more chance.

THE TRUE HEART

BOOK 4

Will I spend my life longing for him? Or feeling guilty about a secret I'm keeping from him?

1

LONDON APRIL 1990

K aisa was trying to concentrate on the news bulletin she was preparing for broadcast later that afternoon when the phone on her desk rang.

'Hello, darling!' It was Rose.

Kaisa tried to hide her disappointment. 'How lovely to hear from you,' she said, lifting her voice higher than it normally was. She stifled a sigh in her hand and decided not to think about Peter. He was due home from a long patrol any moment, so when a phone call was put through to her at work, Kaisa immediately thought it must be her husband. He usually called from somewhere in Scotland as soon as he could, to tell her he was safe. Kaisa hadn't spoken to Peter for over six weeks and she was desperate to hear his voice.

'I'm up in town and wondered if I could see you after work?' Rose said, unaware of Kaisa's disappointment.

Rose met Kaisa outside Bush House, the headquarters of the BBC's World Service in Aldwych, central London, where Kaisa had been working for over three years.

'You look good!' Kaisa said, hugging her friend hard. She felt bad for wishing it hadn't been Rose on the phone. She rarely saw her good friend these days, not since she'd retired to the country.

'How's Peter?' Rose asked, letting go of Kaisa.

'On patrol, 'she said, trying not to sound too miserable.

'You poor darling, I don't know how you do it!' Rose suggested they hop into a cab. 'Terroni's, yes?' she said. Kaisa nodded.

Kaisa loved the Italian café where she'd worked a few years ago, even if she had to cross town to visit it. During the months she'd been a waitress there, Kaisa had become one of the family and had even learned some Italian. She'd spent one potentially lonely Christmas Day with the Terroni family, and after that the Farringdon café, with its large steaming coffee machine, small round tables and curved chairs, and the best coffee in London, had been like home to her. Kaisa had got to know Rose, who had introduced her to Toni, the head of the Terroni family, through Duncan, a former friend of Peter's.

Rose had been instrumental in Kaisa's career. She'd first employed Kaisa at the feminist magazine *Adam's Apple,* which she'd run in the mid-eighties, then encouraged her to attend journalism school, and eventually to apply for a job in the BBC's Finnish section. Without Rose, Kaisa was certain she'd still be living in Helsinki, miserable and divorced from Peter, and probably working for a bank like her university friend Tuuli. Not that Tuuli was unhappy, far from it, but work in finance suited her, whereas Kaisa knew it would have made her miserable.

When she'd first met Rose, Duncan's cousin, during a trip to London from Portsmouth, she'd thought her the most glamorous person she'd ever met. Her hair, clothes and manner had reminded Kaisa of Princess Diana.

Kaisa had been newly married and had only lived in the UK for a matter of months, but Rose had offered Kaisa a job as her assistant during a boozy meeting in one of the city's fashionable wine bars.

Peter's career had taken the couple to Scotland, so Kaisa hadn't been able to accept the job in London. Sometimes she wondered what would have happened if she'd refused to move up to Faslane, and had accepted the London job at that point in her life instead of later. At the time, Peter and Kaisa had both thought the idea of living in London impossible; Kaisa's salary wouldn't have covered the living costs, and with Peter serving on a Polaris submarine, going away to sea for weeks on end, they would never have seen each other.

Kaisa grinned as she sat down opposite Rose. It was the life they had now, so why couldn't they have tried it sooner?

'What's so funny?' Rose asked.

'Nothing, just thinking of the past,' Kaisa replied. She gazed at her friend. Rose was quite a few years older than her, and since her move away from London and marriage to Roger, she'd put on a little weight. The added roundness suited her. Her face, framed by dark unruly curls, now mixed with grey, looked softer, and the few lines around her pale eyes just made her look friendlier.

'You look very happy,' Kaisa said and put her hand on Rose's as it rested on the table.

They'd been through the obligatory hugs and kisses from the café owner, Toni, and his wife, and 'Mamma', and were now facing each other at one of the corner tables by the window, their favourite, which Toni – miraculously – was always able to reserve for them.

'No point in dwelling,' Rose said.

'I guess not,' Kaisa said and thought about her own present condition, which wasn't a condition anymore. She was just about to tell Rose about it, when her friend said quickly, as if to get something out of the way, 'But talking of the past, I saw Duncan last weekend.'

'Oh,' Kaisa said and watched her friend as she lowered her eyes and fiddled with her large emerald engagement ring, now next to a gold wedding band on the ring finger of her left hand. Kaisa knew Rose felt guilty and responsible for the affair between Kaisa and her cousin Duncan. Rose believed that Duncan had used her in order to impress Kaisa, and in a way that was right.

On the very night that Duncan had first introduced Kaisa to Rose, who had scheduled a date for a job interview with her, Duncan had tried to seduce Kaisa in his house in Chelsea. That had been the first time. Kaisa had barricaded herself in the guest bedroom, and the next morning had believed Duncan's profuse apologies and promises never to try anything like that with her ever again.

Yet Kaisa knew she had gone to bed with Duncan willingly months later in Faslane; it was her unhappiness at being so far away from home, frustration at not being able to find a job, and her loneliness without her new husband that had contributed to the events of that awful night.

In a way, Kaisa had also benefited from the guilt Rose had felt; she'd done so much for Kaisa that Kaisa herself often felt bad. They had discussed these feelings many times over the years, often without mentioning Duncan's name. Kaisa didn't want to think back to her awful mistake, and she also understood that Rose had severed all ties to him and didn't want to talk about her cousin. Kaisa was surprised that her friend mentioned Duncan now.

Rose lifted her cup of coffee up to her lips and gazed at Kaisa over the rim. 'He's not very well.'

Kaisa swallowed a mouthful of the strong black coffee and put her cup down.

Rose told her that Duncan had been unwell with a severe flu during the winter. A week ago he'd been to see a specialist and been diagnosed with AIDS. Rose whispered the last word, and looked around the café to see if anyone was listening to their conversation.

'AIDS!' Kaisa exclaimed.

'Shh, keep your voice down,' Rose said and leaned over the table to take hold of Kaisa's hand. 'I'm only telling you so that you go and get tested.'

Kaisa stared at her friend, 'Tested, me?'

'And if you have it, Peter may have it too. And all his – and your – sexual partners for the past five years.'

'Oh, my God,' Kaisa felt her heartbeat quicken. The thought of having to tell Peter he had to go for an HIV test was beyond Kaisa. And for Peter to have to tell the two women he'd had affairs with while she and Peter had been separated would be unthinkable.

'And Ravi?' Kaisa gasped.

Rose nodded.

Kaisa felt sick. She took another sip of her coffee, but it suddenly tasted vile. 'But we're trying for a baby.'

'I know, that's why I wanted to tell you so that you can get tested in case …'

Kaisa was quiet. Her mind was full of ifs and buts.

'Look, it's highly unlikely you have it. Duncan, as I understand it, has been more active sexually since you two, were, you know, together. I'm sure he was fine before.'

Kaisa sat with her hand over her mouth. She caught sight of Toni, who was watching the two women from his usual post behind the glass counter. Kaisa took her hand away and attempted to smile at him. The café owner nodded and waved a cup in his hand, asking if they needed a fill-up. Kaisa shook her head vigorously; the last person she wanted to tell Rose's news to was Toni. That would mean half of London would know it by supper time.

'But I thought he was living in the country?' Kaisa remembered a letter she'd received from Duncan, and immediately destroyed, when she was staying in Helsinki after the separation from Peter. He'd complained about the lack of female company in the countryside. Suddenly, Kaisa realised. Duncan must be gay! Or bisexual.

Rose raised her eyebrows. 'It only takes one sexual partner to be infected.'

Kaisa nodded. 'Of course,' then added carefully, 'But I thought you could only get it from gay sex?'

'No, that's not true!' Rose said emphatically. 'Anyone can get it.'

'Oh,' Kaisa said. Suddenly a picture she'd seen of a family somewhere in America, where a father was hugging his dying son with AIDS, came to her mind. In the photo the son had sunken cheeks and eyes, and his father's face was twisted in anguish as he embraced his son. And she thought about Freddie Mercury. There had been reports that he had AIDS. He'd looked thin and gaunt in the pictures Kaisa had seen in the papers.

Kaisa's thoughts returned to Duncan.

'How is he?'

Suddenly, Rose burst into tears, and before Kaisa could do or say anything, Toni and Mamma had come over and were making a scene, talking loudly and asking what the matter was.

Kaisa managed to calm her adoptive Italian family down, and eventually after they had made sure 'Rosa', as Toni insisted on calling Rose, was fine, Rose and Kaisa left the café and walked along the Clerkenwell Road towards Holborn. While they waited to cross the busy Grays Inn Road, walking arm in arm, Rose told Kaisa how Duncan had pneumonia, and the doctors were concerned about him. 'He's just not getting better, Kaisa,' Rose said. Her eyes filled with tears again and Kaisa pulled her into The Yorkshire Grey, a large pub on the corner of Theobalds Road.

'I think we need something a bit stronger than coffee,' Kaisa said.

Rose nodded and settled herself into a corner table. The pub was quickly filling up with post-work drinkers, but it wasn't yet crowded. It was a few minutes past five o'clock on a Friday evening after all, Kaisa thought. The sun streamed into the dark space, making the interior feel stuffy.

Rose took a large gulp of her glass of wine and said, 'Look, I know it's unfair of me to say so, but he's been asking after you.'

'What?'

'Actually, he's been talking about both you and Peter.'

Kaisa looked at Rose. Seeing her friend so upset and the news about AIDS were affecting Kaisa's head. The room began to sway in front of her eyes. Suddenly all the memories of the first year of her marriage came into her mind. After the months she and Peter had spent apart, when Kaisa had forged her own career, finally getting the coveted job as a reporter at the World Service, she had tried to forget about Duncan, and her infidelity. When she and Peter had eventually reunited after several false starts and misunderstandings, they had vowed to forgive each other and forget the past. Since then, they had rarely spoken about the events leading up to their separation, or about the other relationships they both had had during that time.

'He needs to see that you've forgiven him.' Rose said, placing a hand over Kaisa's arm. Her pale blue eyes were pleading with Kaisa.

Kaisa said, with hesitation, 'You can tell him there are no hard feelings.'

Rose tilted her head sideways, and took another large gulp of wine. 'You don't understand.'

It was Kaisa's turn to take hold of Rose's hands, resting on the small, grubby mock teak table. 'What, tell me!'

'He is staying with us, Roger and I, and I wondered, well, we wondered …' Rose began to dig inside her handbag for a tissue. She blew her nose, soliciting sideways glances from a group of men in pinstripe suits who were drinking pints of beer at the bar. When Rose had recovered a little, she finished her wine and Kaisa said, 'Want another?'

'Yes, let me,' Rose went back to her handbag, but Kaisa replied, 'No this is on me. You've bought enough drinks for me in the past.' She smiled, and got a nod from Rose.

Back at the table, when Kaisa was again facing Rose over their glasses of wine, Rose took a deep breath. 'I wondered if you might be able to come and see him.'

Kaisa stared at her friend. 'I, I don't know …' she hadn't set eyes on Duncan since the awful fight between him and Peter in the pool. Duncan hadn't even turned up at Peter's Court Martial a few weeks later. He'd been dismissed his ship immediately after the fight, when his actions, 'unbecoming an officer of Her Majesty's Service' against a fellow naval officer, had come to light, and he'd left Faslane by all accounts that same night.

'Please, do this for me. I know his behaviour has been despicable, but he is a dying man.' Now tears were running down Rose's cheeks.

Kaisa glanced at the men behind her, and put her hands over Rose's on the sticky table.

'Of course I'll come,' she heard herself say, even though she had no idea how she would be able to face Duncan. Or how she would tell Peter any of it: her planned visit to see her former lover, or the AIDS tests they may both have to take. Or the consequences for their plans to start a family. *What a mess she had created.*

2

When Kaisa heard the phone ring as soon as she stepped inside their terraced house in Notting Hill, she knew that this time it must be Peter. She dropped the bag of cheese, ham and a small loaf of sliced bread that she'd picked up from the corner shop onto the floor and hurried to the phone in the hall.

'Hi darling,' Peter's voice sounded tired.

'How are you?' It was wonderful to hear Peter's voice. She'd not seen him for over two months, and hadn't spoken to him for weeks.

'I'm good. Tired. We've had a royal visit so we've literally just docked. It'll take at least two to three days for the debrief.'

Kaisa sat down on the wooden bench that she and Peter had found in a second-hand shop the week they moved into their new home three years ago. It had one wobbly leg, but there never seemed to be enough time to fix it while Peter was at home. She was silent while she waited for what she knew would be the next thing Peter said. He wouldn't be coming home that evening.

To delay the inevitable, and to hide her disappointment, Kaisa said, 'A royal visit! Who?' She tried to sound enthusiastic. She knew how boring life onboard the submarine could be, and how a VIP could boost the crew's morale, including that of the officers.

'Lady Di.'

'What?'

'Yes, it was a surprise to us too,' Kaisa could hear Peter's grin and saw the handsome face of her husband in her mind. How she missed him!

'She came onboard at the Cumbrae Gap and afterwards insisted on visiting the families at the Drumfork Club.'

'Oh.' The name of the place where Peter had suffered the humiliation of a Court Martial put a stop to Kaisa's questions.

'She was so lovely, just natural, talking to all the wives as if she was one of them. You should've been there!'

Kaisa was taken aback a second time. Peter knew full well why she wasn't living up in Faslane with all the other Navy Wives. They'd tried it and it nearly cost them their marriage. Kaisa took a deep breath and decided she wouldn't let her disappointment show.

'What was she wearing?' she asked instead.

Peter's laughter at the other end made her smile. 'You're asking the wrong person!'

'You're hopeless, but I miss you. When do you think you can get home?'

'Perhaps Monday. You'll just have to wait a few more hours to ravish me!'

There was a silence. Kaisa didn't know what to say. She didn't want to tell him her own sad news; nor what she'd just learned from Rose. She also knew she was supposed to go along with Peter's false jolliness. It was the English thing to do, this 'stiff upper lip' that everyone kept going on about. But she hadn't seen her husband, hadn't felt his arms around her for such a long time, and she needed him now more than ever.

'Don't be like that, Kaisa.' Peter now said, correctly interpreting Kaisa's silence. 'Tell me instead how you are feeling? Are you getting enough sleep?'

'But I miss you so much!' Kaisa managed to say. She was swallowing tears, tears of disappointment, but also tears for what she had to tell him. And it just couldn't be done over the phone.

'Me too, my little Peanut. But I'll phone you tomorrow, again. A few more days isn't that bad, is it?'

Kaisa wanted to say, 'Perhaps not for you,' but instead sucked in air through her nostrils and replied, 'I know. But I'm at work Monday till Thursday.'

'Ah, I hadn't thought about that. Couldn't you swap with someone? And work the weekend instead? Or better still, sleep all weekend, so you'll be refreshed when I'm there. You won't get much sleep with me in your bed!'

Kaisa could hear Peter's desire for her in his voice and her longing for him became almost unbearable.

'I'll try,' she whispered.

'There's my girl.' Peter said and added, 'I love you.'

'Me too,' Kaisa said and put the phone down.

She remained on the seat, still in her overcoat, for a while longer and watched as the last rays of the spring sunlight filtered through the back door. The wall of light revealed tiny specs of dust in the long narrow hallway. Kaisa tried to remember when she'd last hoovered. She decided not to swap her shift that weekend, but to work something else out, as Peter had suggested. She was too exhausted after the week she'd had, not least after her meeting with Rose.

She'd been on duty the weekend before, preparing her daily news bulletin on Saturday afternoon, when news of a crowd rioting over the new council charge, dubbed the Poll Tax, had come through.

Kaisa and two male reporters, one from Italy and one from Hungary, had decided to walk down the Strand to take a look. They'd had a sound engineer with them too, and Kaisa had been excited. This could be her big break, getting a live report of an historic event. But even before they'd reached Charing Cross, police had closed the streets leading up to Trafalgar Square. They had heard the crowd, and seen mounted police in the distance, and had even smelled smoke, but they couldn't get close. Kaisa had tried to show her press badge to a WPC, the only one in the wall of uniformed police wearing riot helmets who looked friendly, but the woman had just shaken her head and said, 'You don't want to get into that, love.' It was then that she had slipped.

She didn't know if the fall had contributed to what happened later, and she didn't want to speculate. She'd stayed on the pavement, feeling very dizzy, and the WPC had come over and helped her up. The two other reporters and the sound guy then said it was time to give up and go back to the office, so she'd followed them back to Aldwych.

Late that night, the Tube station at Holborn had been closed, and she'd had to wait nearly an hour in drizzling rain for a cab to drive her home.

The next day, on the Sunday, after reports had revealed how remarkable the protest had been, Kaisa's boss had asked her to write a long piece on the Poll Tax for a feature bulletin. She'd spent most of the night at Bush House. Although she'd been due to take Monday off, she'd gone in to read the special news report herself.

At midday on Monday, she had fallen into bed, and by the next morning her condition wasn't a condition anymore. She'd put the bloody sheets in the washing machine and was back at her desk in Bush House on Wednesday morning even though it felt as if her insides were being pulled off in waves. She swallowed aspirin after aspirin and told her colleagues it was a bad case of the time of the month. Which she guessed it was in a way.

She wasn't looking forward to telling Peter the full details of the riot and her reporting of it, or about the fall. She knew his hopes were up, and that he'd think she'd been careless, which she knew she had been. It was so hard to remember to take care of herself when nothing seemed to have changed in her body.

3

Peter put the phone down and cursed under his breath. When would he learn not to upset Kaisa? She was so sensitive about not living at the base.

Peter loved it that his wife was a news reporter and was very proud of her. Yet at the same time, he knew she worked too hard. And the fact that the job was in London meant that after each patrol he had to wait longer than the other officers and sailors to see his wife.

Most of the crew had wives living nearby, either in the grim married quarters on the hill in Rhu, overlooking the steely grey Gareloch, or in homes they'd bought in the small villages outside Helensburgh. Peter shuddered. He'd never want to buy a property in the cold and rainy West coast of Scotland. When he was ashore, he couldn't wait to fly back down south, not just to see Kaisa, but also to be away from Scotland.

At the same time, he couldn't help but feel that if Kaisa was up in Helensburgh, she wouldn't find it so difficult to have a baby. Her job at the BBC meant early mornings and long days and a lot of weekend working.

Up in Scotland, her life would be quieter, she'd be able to rest, and she could concentrate on having a baby. Peter knew, of course, that it was a pipe dream, but he would have loved to see Kaisa as soon as the submarine docked, and see her enjoy events such as the surprise royal visit.

The rumours of a VIP visit had been doing the rounds in the wardroom, and around the submarine, for a week before they were due back in Faslane. Out of the six patrols Peter had been on, only one other had ended with a

VIP visit of some kind. Usually it was the Secretary of State for Defence, especially if they were newly appointed.

Last year, on his first patrol back at the Polaris submarines since his unfortunate dismissal from the submarine five years previously, he'd met the current incumbent, Tom King, who'd come onboard as they were approaching the Faslane base.

King had been a dull man, shaking hands with each of the officers quickly, and hardly speaking to anyone apart from the captain. Peter and the rest of the Wardroom had felt they were too lowly to interest their new Secretary of State, but King had taken great interest in the equipment, including the war head, asking the senior rates several questions in the engine room and in the weapons compartment.

This time, when the Captain told them over the tannoy on the morning of the visit that 'Her Royal Highness Diana, Princess of Wales' would be coming onboard the submarine, the whole vessel had been buzzing. Even the leading galley hand who'd served him breakfast that morning had said, 'You looking forward to diving with Lady Di, Sir?' He seemed to be talking about the impending royal visit, but Peter knew the reference to diving was a sneaky jibe about his past. There was no way they were going to take the princess on a dive, Peter knew that much.

When the Captain, Stewart Harding, an unusually good-humoured man, with a belly that moved when he laughed (generally at his own jokes), met Peter in the gangway an hour or so later, he said, 'This is a huge honour Peter, so make sure to be on your best behaviour?'

'Yes, Sir,' Peter had replied and wondered as he watched the Old Man make his way to the control room if the Captain doubted Peter's ability to act correctly in front of royal visitors. He'd been at Dartmouth Naval College with Prince Andrew, and had met the Queen, for goodness sake! But he knew what the problem really was. Peter had been found guilty on an assault against a fellow Officer. It was behaviour unbecoming of an officer of Her Majesty's' Royal Navy.

He knew that the joke the rating in the galley had made about his 'diving' was because the fight he'd had with Duncan, his so-called friend, had taken place in the swimming pool at the naval base in Faslane, but why did the Captain have to remind Peter to behave? Would they ever forget about the Court Martial, he wondered, as he tried to distract himself with the tasks he needed to oversee as the Navigating Officer onboard.

. . .

Kaisa fell asleep in front of the TV that night, and was woken up by telephone ringing.

'Hello Kaisa, how are you?'

Kaisa glanced at her watch; it was five to six in the morning.

'Mum.'

'Did I wake you? Why aren't you at work? Did you oversleep?'

'No, it's only just six am here. And it's Saturday. I'm off today.' Kaisa sighed; how could her mother always forget the two-hour difference between Finland and Britain?

'Well, you're awake now. How are you feeling?'

Kaisa was quiet. How had she been so stupid to tell her mother? Suddenly, as she was about to speak, tears welled up inside her. 'Mum,' she began, but couldn't go on.

'Oh darling! Not again?'

'Yes,' Kaisa managed to say.

'You poor love. Is Peter with you?'

'No, he was supposed to be home last night, but they had a VIP onboard, so he couldn't make the last flight.'

'I see.'

'He couldn't help it. It wasn't his fault.'

Why did Kaisa always have to defend Peter to her mother? She supposed it had something to do with the months Kaisa had spent in Helsinki, sleeping on her sister's sofa. She'd fled there after Peter's Court Martial. The fight between the two officers had all been Kaisa's fault and Peter's open hostility towards her, combined with the pressure from the other Navy wives on the married patch, and the reports of the 'incident' in the national press, had made Kaisa finally flee Scotland.

While she was in Helsinki, Peter had hardly contacted Kaisa and she knew her mother thought that had been unfair. There had also been suspicions that Peter was seeing an old flame. At the time, Kaisa believed their marriage was over, so although it was devastating news to her, she'd thought it part of her punishment for what she had done to Peter. But her mother didn't see it that way.

'It was Princess Diana!' Kaisa said, trying to distract her mother.

'Oh, really, did he meet her?'

'Yes, of course he did.'

'What was she wearing?'

Kaisa sighed. 'He didn't notice.'

'Have you been to see the doctor?' Her mother asked next.

That diversion tactic didn't work, Kaisa thought.

'No.'

'Why not?'

Kaisa didn't want to discuss her condition – or lack of it – with her mother. Or why she hadn't had time to see her doctor. Her mother was another person in her life who thought she worked too hard. There was an implication that if she wasn't so skinny and stayed at home more, she wouldn't keep on losing the babies.

'Look, I'm going to see the doctor soon. And I need to talk to Peter first.' Kaisa felt bad that she'd told the sad news to her mother first, before Peter, but she also knew her mother thought it was her lifestyle that was at fault.

'Of course. But you know, you could come over here and see a Finnish specialist? They are world-famous you know. We have zero incidents of ...'

'I know, Mum,' Kaisa said, interrupting the familiar flow of praise for Finnish doctors and the infamous zero infant mortality rates.

'Anyway, the reason I called was to tell you that your sister is engaged to be married!'

Kaisa thought about Sirkka, her older sister, who'd been in love with a man from Lapland for years. Theirs was an on-off relationship that Kaisa thought would never come to anything.

'Haven't they only been back together for a few months!' Kaisa now said and immediately regretted the words.

There was a brief silence at the other end. Then her mother replied, predictably, 'Why do you always have to be so negative about your sister?'

Kaisa sighed. 'I'm not being negative, I just want her to be happy.'

'Well she is! Jussi is a wonderful young man. He is head-over-heels in love with your sister and will make a wonderful husband. He's a business-man, you know, with his own building firm. It's doing very well – he drives a brand-new Mercedes!'

'That's wonderful,' Kaisa replied and spent the next ten minutes convincing her mother that she did indeed think that the marriage between her sister and this Jussi, whom Kaisa had met only once, would be a very happy one.

When she felt her mother had been pacified, and she was able to put the phone down, Kaisa was exhausted. She was happy for her sister, of course, but at the same time she didn't want her to rush into a marriage.

Kaisa thought she knew all about true love, and how rare it was – and how easy it was to walk away from a relationship, but how strong the pull back to the person you really loved was. Did Jussi love Sirkka back? Kaisa thought about her own mistakes, and how close she'd come to losing Peter, the love of her life, because of her isolation and unhappiness in the naval community in Scotland. If their love hadn't been strong, she and Peter would never have survived that crisis.

She shuddered as she thought of what she had to tell Peter now. Would their marriage be strong enough to cope with AIDS too?

Later that same morning, while she stood on the Tube all the way from Notting Hill Gate to Holborn with her nose stuck in a man's stinking armpit, Kaisa daydreamed about being comforted in Peter's arms. But she feared having to tell him everything.

Instead of their usual reunion routine of a candlelit supper, followed by sex, she'd have to tell Peter about her 'condition', or lack of it, and about the deadly virus.

This time the tiny foetus – she tried not to think of it as a baby – had lasted over nine weeks, eight of which Peter had been away. Although she'd already had the familiar metallic taste in her mouth the morning of his departure to Scotland, she had decided not to say anything to him. But when he phoned a few days later, while still on the base in Faslane, waiting for the Starboard crew and the submarine to come back from its patrol, so that the Board crew could take over the submarine and sail, she'd been so convinced she was in the family way again, and so excited, she'd spilled the beans and told him.

Peter had been so happy that he'd gone quiet and Kaisa suspected that if she'd been able to see him, she would have spotted tears welling up in his eyes. She too was beyond elated when her GP, Dr Harris, an old man with grey hair, had confirmed her suspicions a week later.

How she now regretted telling Peter about the pregnancy! She should have known better. This was her third miscarriage – again she tried not to utter that word too often, because she'd only start feeling morose.

It was obvious her body couldn't keep hold of a baby, and now Peter would tell her that she was working too many hours and would insist she get help.

A friend of theirs, Pammy, another Navy wife, had told them at a drinks do up in Faslane that after you had lost three babies, the GP could refer you to a specialist. Kaisa thought back to five years ago, when she'd lived in the married quarters in Helensburgh, and Pammy had miscarried for the second time. She was much further gone with her pregnancy, months rather than weeks, and she'd been taken to the local hospital. Her friend had been confined to bed for a couple of weeks afterwards, but had been determined to try again as soon as her husband was home from sea.

With Kaisa's previous miscarriages (that word again), all that had happened was a heavier and more painful period than usual, making her doubt the pregnancy test the GP had taken. Apart from the metallic taste in her mouth, which she'd had every time, she had hardly felt any different. She'd lost her appetite, gone off coffee, and felt a little nauseous every now and then, but that was it.

And now, on top of the awful news that she's lost yet another baby, she'd have to tell Peter about Duncan. And the possibility that they might both be carrying the virus. She couldn't even say the word in her own mind, let alone picture herself telling Peter about it. She shifted her position in the crowded carriage, turning her head away from the smelly man next to her. Nausea, which she knew had nothing to do with a foetus, overtook her and she stepped off the train one station before her destination and walked the rest of the way.

4

R avi looked as handsome as he always did when Kaisa saw him sitting at a corner table in Terroni's on Saturday. He was wearing a smart pair of trousers, with a jumper over a striped shirt. As usual, in his gentlemanly way, he got up when he saw Kaisa. His old-fashioned chivalry always brought a smile to Kaisa's lips, even today, when the world seemed to be conspiring against her. When she'd emerged onto the street at Holborn, gasping for air, the skies had opened and soaked her during the walk to the café.

'A little bit of rain and the whole of London decides to take the Tube instead of walking a few metres!' Kaisa said, shaking her mac, which was dripping with water.

'Cappuccino, bella?' Toni said. *'Come stai?'* he added, carrying a frothy cup of coffee. He kissed her on both cheeks and nodded to Ravi.

'I'm OK,' Kaisa said and signed. *'Grazie,'* she added.

'What's wrong?'

'Oh, nothing: just everything!'

'He not home again?' Toni said and pulled up a chair and sat next to Kaisa.

'No. This time it's Lady Di's fault!' Kaisa said. She was relieved she could talk to Toni about something other than the two awful things on her mind.

Toni took hold of Kaisa's hands, and kissed them. 'Ooh, Princess Diana! How come?' Kaisa explained about the royal visit and about the delay.

'Bella! And you have to suffer because of this selfish princess!' His eyes, gazing intensely at Kaisa were sad, as if he was about to cry on Kaisa's behalf.

Kaisa managed to laugh. During her time with the Terroni family, she'd got used to their overly emotional reactions to everything. Mamma Terroni would shout as if someone had died when the coffee machine was playing up, or Toni hadn't ordered the right kind of biscotti for the shop.

Toni always flirted with Kaisa, even though she knew he loved his petite, dark-haired wife very much. Adriana was often serving behind the counter and saw Toni's behaviour, but she just smiled and laughed at his silliness. Now Kaisa's eyes searched for Adriana. When she saw her leaning over the counter, with a tea-towel in her hand, Kaisa smiled at her, shrugged her shoulders, and released her hands from Toni's grip. 'Men!' she shouted across the little café.

When at last Toni left them with menus, Ravi leaned across to Kaisa and said, 'So that's why I have the pleasure of your company today?'

Kaisa felt immediately guilty. She looked down at the mock-leather covered menu, fearing her face would betray what she felt.

Over the last few years, Ravi had shown himself to be a very good friend to Kaisa. They met up perhaps once a month, when Kaisa wasn't working weekends and Peter was away at sea. This lunch date was out of the blue, because Kaisa hadn't planned on being on her own this Saturday.

Ravi worked as a lawyer for one of the big banks in the City and lived a typical London bachelor life. He worked and played hard, but always managed to meet up with Kaisa when she got in touch. She knew she was relying too much on Ravi, and she also knew it was unfair on him. How would she be able to tell him about Duncan? And the virus that Ravi, too, might be carrying.

'Did you have plans?' Kaisa shot a quick glance at those dark pools of eyes, fearing they might have a stern look to them.

Instead, however, the corners of Ravi's lips lifted up and turned into a full smile, revealing a perfect set of white teeth, 'Yes, I had to cancel a trip to Birmingham to meet another bridal candidate my mother had lined up. So you saved me!'

'She's still trying then.' Kaisa also smiled, and placed her hand on top of Ravi's.

For the briefest of moments Ravi gazed at Kaisa's fingers, then placed his own over them, covering Kaisa's hand with his, 'You're cold,' he said, looking up at Kaisa.

Quickly Kaisa pulled her hand away and began discussing the menu.

While they waited for the food, Kaisa tried to forget about the lost baby and the virus hanging over her. She'd telephoned the GP that morning, and got an appointment for Monday. She'd decided to take the test as soon as possible.

'What's up?' Ravi asked after Toni had brought them coffee and they'd both ordered an Italian salad.

Kaisa looked up at Ravi's concerned expression, his dark eyes filled with kindness. Ravi took hold of Kaisa's hands, which were hugging her cup of coffee on the red-and-white checked cloth. 'Is it what I think it is?'

Kaisa nodded, lowering her eyes. Tears were welling up inside her and she couldn't look at Ravi any longer.

After their lunch, the sun came out and Ravi and Kaisa decided to walk down to Covent Garden. When she saw a blue dress in the window of Wallis, Ravi pulled her into the shop and convinced her to try it on.

'That shade brings out the beautiful colour of your eyes,' Ravi had said and hugged Kaisa.

It wasn't the first time she'd been shopping with Ravi; he was unusually good at picking clothes for her. So unlike Peter, who would soon get bored and tell her he liked everything she tried. She didn't tell Peter about Ravi's talents in that department, though. In fact Peter only knew about half of the times she spent with Ravi. There was nothing but friendship in their relationship, so her conscience was clear.

During the past few years when Kaisa was living in London and Peter was stationed somewhere on the south coast, or in Scotland, as he was at the moment, Ravi had become her closest confidant. He knew all about the babies she kept losing, about how much she constantly missed Peter, and he never tried anything on with her. That showed what a gentleman he was. He'd been educated at Cambridge, of course, and came across as a posh boy, with his Sloaney accent, but Kaisa knew that was no guarantee of good behaviour. Kaisa shuddered when she though about Duncan, a man who had pretended to be her friend, who had been to Dartmouth Naval College with Peter and been a so-called mate of his, yet had still pursued her. Ravi was nothing like that.

At first, when Kaisa had bumped into Ravi again, in a pub where she was having a drink with her old boss, Rose, she had been apprehensive. Rose, who had been an excellent friend and role model for her during her first years in London, when Peter and Kaisa had been separated and on the brink of a divorce, had moved to the country after her marriage, and was rarely up in town. After Rose had left, Kaisa missed their weekly lunches and felt lonely. When Ravi had telephoned to see how she was, she had agreed to meet him. The first time they met after all that had happened between them, Ravi had gazed at Kaisa with his dark brown eyes and said, 'The reason I wanted to see you is to tell you how happy I am that Peter and you are still together.'

'Oh,' Kaisa had said and looked down at her cup.

'I want you to know that I like you very much.' Ravi hesitated for a moment and added, 'as a friend.'

Kaisa had been so taken aback that she hadn't been able to say anything in reply.

Ravi had reached out his hand and touched Kaisa's fingers. 'Is that OK?'

'Yes, of course. I want to be friends too!' Kaisa had finally exclaimed and they had broken into wide smiles. Kaisa wanted to get up, reach across the table and hug Ravi, but she hadn't dared on that occasion.

That had been four years ago now, and after that first coffee, Ravi and Kaisa been meeting at least once a month, sometimes more often. He also came to the house in Chepstow Place for dinner when Peter was at home.

The three of them had got on so well, that on one drunken night they'd decided to go on holiday together. The week in a *gite* in the South of France had turned out to be a glorious idea. During the sultry evenings, when they'd cooked Indian spiced meats on the barbecue (to Ravi's family recipe), and drank copious amounts of rosé, Ravi had told Peter and Kaisa about his frustrations with his overbearing mother, who was constantly pressurising him to get married. Each time he visited his family up in Birmingham, she would spring suitable girls on him.

'I don't want to get married,' he said, holding a tumbler of red wine in his long, shapely fingers. 'Least of all to a nice Indian virgin,' he said, and they'd all laughed.

'I completely understand,' Peter had said seriously, adding with a grin, 'Not that an Indian virgin wouldn't be tempting …'

'That's nice,' Kaisa kicked his shin under the table.

'Ouch, that hurt,' Peter laughed. 'What I meant to say was, had I not met Kaisa, I wouldn't have wanted to marry either.' Peter took hold of Kaisa's hand and kissed the palm. They were sitting next to each other on a bench outside the beautiful old farm building. Ravi was facing them from the other side of the table, which was covered with the debris of the meal they'd just consumed.

They were all quiet for a moment, listening to the loud chirping of the crickets disturbing the otherwise peaceful night. Ravi had shifted on his seat, and said, 'I am a confirmed bachelor, me. And now I'm going to do the dishes. I think it's my turn.'

After that holiday, they'd taken a few days each year to go somewhere in France together. Kaisa and Peter had grown very fond of their Indian bachelor friend. Still, Kaisa was careful not to rouse any jealousy in Peter; after what had happened early on in their marriage, she knew he must always be looking over his shoulder. However much he told her that he never thought about Duncan, or their brief affair, she knew she needed to be careful.

5

There was bad news. The navigation system on the sub was playing up and Peter couldn't travel down South until it was done. Peter's Captain had been standing next to him when they were doing the handover to the Board Crew and had told him the extent of the problem. Peter's first thought was how he was going to tell Kaisa that he needed to stay on in Faslane for a few days more to make sure the glitches in the sub's navigation system were sorted.

But when Peter was about to leave the onboard wardroom, the Captain asked him to come to his cabin.

'Congratulations are in order, Peter.' The Captain said and put his hands over his belly while he leant back in his chair.

Peter just stared at the man.

'Sit down.'

Peter nodded and seated himself opposite the Old Man. The Captain's cabin was a roomy space, with a wide bunk and a desk with two chairs for visitors. Peter would have felt more comfortable standing up. Somehow being seated opposite the Captain felt as if he was in serious trouble.

'You've been selected to attend the next Submarine Command Course.' A smile was hovering around the Old Man's lips. How long had he known about this, Peter wondered.

'Just got the cable this morning,' the Captain added.

Peter was speechless. This was what he had been dreaming about ever since he signed up to the service in his twenties.

'As long as you don't beat anyone up again,' the Old Man said drily when Peter finally managed to thank him for the news.

'No Sir,' Peter replied. He wasn't sure if the Captain had been joking or not.

Nobody could say Peter's career had been ordinary. When at the age of 20 he'd graduated from Dartmouth Naval College with all the pomp and ceremony demanded by the Queen's presence, he'd been destined to great things. Soon after, he'd decided to apply for the submarine service and had qualified in as short a time as possible.

He thought back to those times. He'd been so in love with Kaisa, and had such a brilliant future in front of him, he didn't think anything could ever touch him. He was on his way up, up to the dizzy heights of a celebrated naval career. How confident he'd been when he'd triumphantly caught his Dolphins, the badge of the underwater service, in his teeth from the bottom of a glass of rum!

After that Royal Navy rite of passage, which all newly qualified submariners had to go through, Peter had passed the nuclear exams that followed and been assigned to serve on a Polaris sub. Even with the Court Martial on his record, he was now the Navigating Officer in the Polaris fleet. It seemed his career was continuing its upwards trajectory.

Peter hurried off the sub and walked towards the wardroom on the base. He wanted to telephone Kaisa in London immediately, but when the phone in their Notting Hill home rang and rang, he was disappointed not to be able to tell her the news. He put down the phone, went into the Back Bar and ordered himself a whisky.

He ignored the surprised looks of some of the junior officers drinking pints in the corner and found himself an empty table. He took a large swig of his drink. The whisky burned his throat – he didn't usually go for spirits but the occasion seemed to warrant it.

The timing was perfect: with Kaisa newly pregnant, the course would be over and done with by the time she'd given birth. He allowed himself to dream how he'd be a fully-fledged submarine captain by the time their first baby was born.

Of course, he was apprehensive about the prospect of Perisher, as one of the toughest leadership courses in the world was known. It had a high failure rate, but he knew his technical ability was good, even excellent. Peter didn't doubt his skills in the mental arithmetic needed to calculate various speeds and courses of vessels, but he worried that Teacher, as the course leader was known, might have a preconception about him. Would he try to use 'the incident', as everyone kept calling the brawl with that coward in the Falsane pool, to test Peter's psychological strength? Is that why the Captain had mentioned the fight with Duncan? Did he think his past could affect his performance on the Perisher course?

Peter didn't know who Teacher would be on this occasion, but he'd heard one or two of them could be real bastards. Peter flinched at the prospect of the terrible nickname he'd been given immediately after the Court Martial, 'Bonking Boy', resurfacing. He'd not heard it for years now, and it seemed most people had forgotten about it, or else lost interest in the fight. It was yesterday's news, helped, of course, by the fact that Duncan was no longer a serving naval officer. He'd done the honourable thing, the rat, leaving after 'the brawl in the pool', as the headline in the *Daily Mail* had put it, and after he'd taken advantage of Kaisa.

Peter shook his head to banish thoughts of those times. He knew Kaisa wouldn't do anything like it again, and he also knew that he was partly to blame for her unhappiness in Faslane that had led to the brief affair. Peter had been walking around with his eyes closed, letting the tosser get close to Kaisa. But it was all done now, long gone and never to be discussed. Besides, he was about to be the father of their child, so even if he still wanted to kill Duncan, or still kept seeing Kaisa being kissed in his arms, and sometimes, in his worst nightmares, being pinned down by him, that didn't matter now.

Peter finished his whisky in one gulp and vowed that during Perisher, which would form the most important months of his career – if not his life – he would control himself, like he had done every day of the past five years.

Peter got up and went to telephone Kaisa again. This time she was at home, but Peter decided he'd keep news of the Perisher course as a surprise for her. Instead, he'd ask her to come up to Helensburgh for a few days.

6

W hen Peter asked Kaisa to come up to see him during a late phone call on Tuesday night, she'd jumped at the chance to see him. She was disappointed when there was a delay with his homecoming (again). Now there was something wrong with the submarine. He would have to stay put in Faslane for a few days longer, but could have Wednesday and Thursday off, as long as he remained nearby and at the end of a phone, in case he was needed.

Why that might be was classified information, and Kaisa didn't ask. She managed to change her shift at the BBC, and on Wednesday morning she got into a cab and set off early to the airport. Kaisa knew there was a good chance she could get a standby ticket on an early morning flight to Glasgow at Gatwick. She was desperate to see Peter, not only because she missed him, but because she wanted to tell him in person about the baby.

Or the lack of it.

On Monday, her kind old GP had confirmed the miscarriage, something that hadn't been a surprise to Kaisa. He'd told her to wait three months before trying again.

On the flight she'd resolved not to tell Peter about Duncan, or the test she'd taken at the GP's surgery, during this short visit. She knew that she should, but she wanted to have the result first.

She didn't know what she would do if it was positive. She just couldn't imagine the conversation with Peter. She knew he would be angry, and also scared. And, this was something Kaisa had tried not to think about as she lay awake in her bed, what if AIDS was the reason she kept losing her babies? It hadn't occurred to her until she'd been travelling home on the Tube. Suddenly, like a bolt of lightning, the thought had entered her fuzzy mind.

She hadn't slept properly since her meeting with Rose. When she had eventually dozed off, images of Duncan's face, with sunken eyes and a pallor so extreme that he looked almost opaque, disappeared into the white walls of her bedroom.

The GP had given Kaisa a leaflet about the virus, called 'AIDS and Women'. In it there was a section about pregnancy:

'If the woman or proposed father is carrying the virus, it is best for the woman to avoid becoming pregnant. Pregnancy increases the likelihood of an infected woman developing full-blown AIDS. There is also a very real risk of passing the virus to the baby.'

There was nothing about miscarriages, but perhaps the virus could prevent the baby from forming correctly?

Kaisa shivered and felt bile rise in her throat when she thought about the leaflet, which was decorated with paper chain figures in black, like deadly shadows of the paper chain elves that Kaisa hung over the fireplace in her living room in December.

TV ads showing the word AIDS carved into a gravestone and the message *'A deadly virus with no known cure'* haunted her too; she kept seeing Peter's name on granite above a mound of freshly dug earth.

She gazed out of the window at the blanket of clouds below. The sun was a pale bright oval in the distance, shining into the opaque layer and making it look like a giant, fluffy bed. She had a sudden urge to lie on the clouds and forget all about having a baby, about Duncan, the virus or Peter.

Instead, she closed her eyes and decided she needed to keep her head; the GP had said it was 'very unlikely' that she would have been carrying the virus for five years. He'd taken blood from her, and she'd signed a form to say she wanted the test to be handled anonymously. He'd raised his eyebrows when Kaisa had told him why she needed the test, but hadn't commented apart from handing her the leaflet and saying it was up to her whether or not she told her husband.

The kind, elderly doctor said that the test results would be back in two weeks' time and added that she should encourage her husband to be tested. Kaisa had nodded. She'd been vague about how she might have contracted the virus, just saying it may have happened five years previously from a man who was now severely ill.

She wondered if the GP had worked out that she'd been married to Peter for six years. Still, he had used the words 'very unlikely', which happened to be the same phrase Rose had used. But what were the odds? Kaisa wished she'd known a percentage; was it a 50 per cent, 20 per cent, or even as little as 1 per cent chance that she had AIDS? Not knowing was driving her crazy, another reason why it was best not to tell Peter. If she could at least save him from the worry, when the results of the test were unknown, surely that was for the best?

As the Captain announced they were about to land, and the air hostess removed Kaisa's tray, on which there was a bacon roll (untouched) and an empty cup of coffee, Kaisa wondered how she could keep the news from Peter.

She knew he would be distracted by whatever was wrong with the sub; that his mind would be on the possibility of being called in any minute rather than on his wife.

Kaisa didn't mind, not really; she knew how all-consuming Peter's job was. When, on occasion, there was a big news story affecting Finland, such as the Chernobyl disaster in Russia, when the Finnish authorities had initially kept silent about the increased levels of radiation in the atmosphere, and Finnish citizens had been evacuated from Ukraine, she'd been asked by the BBC to be on call. She hadn't been able to relax for the whole of May, as news about the accident trickled through to Finland from the Soviet Union and the full horror of the disaster became known.

Besides, to talk about Duncan so close to where it had all happened was unthinkable anyway. Once again, for the thousandth time, she cursed Duncan and her own stupidity. How far-reaching could the consequences of her one mistake be?

7

Glasgow airport was deserted on the Wednesday morning when Peter walked into the arrivals hall. He was early; he'd made sure he left the base in Faslane in good time. The last thing he needed was for Kaisa to have to wait around for him. That would make her irritable, he knew that. To please her even more, he'd also managed to stop off at a garage just outside Dunbarton where they sold flowers; it wasn't quite the customary single red rose, but he'd got a bunch of red tulips instead.

The plane was on time, and when Peter saw Kaisa descend the steps at the other side of the luggage carousel, he waved the flowers in her direction and was rewarded with a wide smile. He walked towards his wife, trying not to run; that would have been too much of a cliché, and would have aroused the interest of the other passengers as well as the Caledonian Airlines crew clad in their customary tartan uniforms.

They kissed for a long time. Kaisa's lips were soft and sweet, and she smelled of her usual musky perfume. Peter had to concentrate to prevent an embarrassing bulge from rising in his trousers.

'I'm so glad you could come. Good flight?' Peter asked. He spotted Kaisa's red holdall and picked it up from the moving luggage carousel.

'Yes, thank you. And nice flowers,' Kaisa added and gave Peter another peck on his lips. Peter placed his hand on her waist and guided her towards the exit.

She was wearing a blue dress, which Peter hadn't seen before. He wondered what underwear she had on and whether she was wearing stockings or tights. Briefly, a memory of Kaisa wearing nothing but silky French knickers, suspenders and stockings flashed in Peter's mind and again he had to remind himself to be patient. He'd take Kaisa into bed as soon as they arrived in Helensburgh. Unfortunately, the place he'd managed to wrangle out of the Housing Officer at short notice for the two days Kaisa was with him was on Smuggler's Way, a few houses away from the married quarter where they'd lived as a newly married couple five years previously. He hoped Kaisa wouldn't mind – it was either that or staying at the base where they would have no privacy at all from the crew and all the other officers he knew so well.

'That dress suits you,' he said and squeezed her close as they made their way towards the airport car park, adjusting their walk so that their steps matched exactly.

Looking out of the window during the drive to Helensburgh, Kaisa fiddled with the buckle of the cloth belt on her new dress. The silky dress, with shoulder pads and a pleated skirt, had been an impulse buy. She hadn't intended to buy anything but Ravi had convinced her she must get it.

She looked across to Peter, who turned his head and smiled at her.

'What's up?' he asked.

Kaisa shifted her eyes away from Peter to look at the view. They'd just turned onto the road that the locals called 'Seafront', which ran along the Gareloch. A few sailing boats were bobbing at the end of a wooden pier, but the wide pavement, meant for strolling beside the water, Kaisa assumed, was deserted. There was light rain falling onto the water and the asphalt.

'Just tired, darling,' she said, and turned to look back at Peter. 'I see it's raining,' she added and smiled. The Navy had a joke for the weather in Faslane, 'If it's not raining it's about to.'

How English I've become, Kaisa thought. *When I don't know what to say, or I am keeping a secret from my husband, I talk about the weather instead.*

Peter drove past their old house on Smuggler's Way quickly, and got Kaisa inside the flat before either of them could mention 'the old times'.

Inside, they stood at the window admiring the view of the Gareloch. The rain had stopped and the sun was now high above the sky, glaring down on them from a sky threaded with grey clouds. The surface of the loch had a low mist hanging over it.

To the right, Peter could see the steel roofs of the base, which reminded him to check that the telephone in the flat was working, as had been promised. Peter hoped the problems with the navigating system would be fixed before there'd be any need for a Board of Inquiry about it. That would mean further delays in him travelling back home to London.

He couldn't reveal any of this to Kaisa, and although they were both used to the secrets Peter had to keep from her, it bothered Peter more and more as the years went by, and Kaisa and he grew closer to each other. He knew it was still difficult for her.

Peter moved away from Kaisa, making her turn her head. When she saw him lift the receiver, she sighed, her shoulders moving up and down. She hadn't yet taken off the mac she'd put on when they'd got out of the car, and the breeze from the Gareloch had hit them. When Peter heard the long dial tone, he returned to Kaisa and put his arms around her.

'Take this off. I want to see you in that lovely new dress.'

But when he went to pull the coat off her, he noticed she was shaking. He turned her around and saw there were tears in her eyes.

'Oh Peter,' she said and buried her head into his neck.

'Shh,' Peter said and stroked Kaisa's back. Over her shoulder, Peter looked at the eerie view of the misty lake. He realised now what a mistake it had been to rent the flat. How stupid and unthinking of him! He took hold of her shoulders and gently pushed Kaisa away from him so that he could see her face.

'Look, we can go somewhere else.'

The past few times Kaisa had come up to see him, they'd either stayed with their good friends Nigel and Pammy, when Nigel was still based in Scotland, or Peter had rented a room in The Ardencaple, one of the hotels in town.

Kaisa sniffled and hung her head. She dug a tissue out of the pocket of her coat and blew her nose. 'It's not that,' she whispered, before a new wave of crying took hold of her again.

Peter took a hankie out of his own pocket and wiped Kaisa's tears away. 'What's the matter, darling?'

Kaisa took a deep breath in and blew her nose once more. 'I had a ...' she hesitated and then brought her teary eyes up towards Peter, 'I lost the baby again.'

.   .   .

Kaisa told Peter about the Poll Tax riot and how she'd tried to get closer to the action. She attempted to gauge his reaction as she carried on, telling him how she'd fallen, and how within 24 hours she'd started to bleed.

'I'm not sure if it was that, or if it's something else,' Kaisa said, fiddling with the belt on her dress again.

But Peter's face was full of concern, and he took Kaisa into his arms.

'Darling, please stop crying. We'll try again, won't we?' he said, pulling her away from him.

Kaisa nodded.

'But they do make you work too hard,' Peter said, his face suddenly grave.

Again Kaisa said nothing. She knew he was right, but what else was there for her to do when Peter was away?

She was proud to be the voice of the BBC in Finland. She knew it was pure snobbery on her part, but she couldn't help the sense of superiority she felt each time she told someone she worked as a news reporter for the BBC's World Service.

It also gave her a strange thrill to think how many people were listening to her in Finland while she read the news. Even more so when she had written the report herself. A combination of keeping up to date with the news from Finland, and keeping Finns informed of the world news and the events in Britain, was both rewarding and interesting. Her job was now almost as important as Peter's. She also worked for a large organisation that was well-respected all over the world.

But she didn't say any of this now; she just looked down at her hands on her lap. She wanted so much to tell Peter about the test, about the horror that was hanging over her head, possibly over both their heads. She looked up at Peter, and opened her mouth, but at that moment, the telephone rang and Peter moved away to pick up the receiver in the hall.

Listening to Peter talk on the phone, promising whoever it was to see him later, Kaisa inhaled deeply and slowly let the air run out of her lungs. Had he been called out to the base? She could hardly be mad at him about it, but she wondered what she'd do in the cold apartment on her own. Alone, her thoughts would drive her crazy.

Later in the afternoon Peter lay in bed, with Kaisa in the crook of his arm. She'd not cried for long, and thank goodness he'd been able to comfort her. It was a bitter disappointment, losing another baby, so he hadn't told Kaisa his good news yet. Instead, after the phone call, they'd climbed into bed, even though it was the middle of the day, just hugging and kissing. When Kaisa had begun unbuckling Peter's trousers, he'd placed his hand on hers and, looking into her eyes, said, 'Are you sure this is OK?'

Kaisa had just nodded and placed her fingers on his lips. 'I have condoms in my bag.'

They made love gently, unhurriedly, even though they hadn't seen each other for weeks. Irrationally, Peter was afraid he would somehow hurt Kaisa, but she kept assuring him it was OK. Afterwards, Peter lit a cigarette and said, 'I've got some news too.'

Kaisa pulled herself half up and rested her head on her elbow. 'A shore job?'

Peter saw how beautiful her bare breasts were, with the pink nipples still hard from the sex they'd just had. 'No, I'm afraid not.'

'What then?' Kaisa took the cigarette from Peter and sat up to take a drag. Seeing Peter's expression, she said, 'One won't hurt.'

Peter also sat up and leaned against the wall. 'I'm going to be on the next Perisher!'

Kaisa got up onto her knees and stared at Peter.

'Aren't you pleased?'

'That's fantastic!' Kaisa put the cigarette on the saucer that Peter had been using as an ashtray and placed her arms around his neck. She kissed him on the mouth and Peter took hold of her tiny waist, pulling her away.

'I didn't want to tell you when you'd been through the mill again with the baby ...'

Kaisa looked down at her hands. Peter could see she was trying to control herself, biting her lower lip.

'I'm not the youngest to be put forward, but considering my career, with the Court Martial, it's quite an achievement. It seems someone has dropped out – one of the Canadian officers – so I got in a bit quicker than I'd anticipated.'

Kaisa was quiet again. Seeing her downcast face, with the beautiful, unruly blonde wisps of her shoulder-length hair half-covering her high cheekbones, Peter thought he was such an idiot. Why did he have to bring up the past just now, after what they'd just done, and after what Kaisa had told him?

But just then, she lifted her head, letting the hair fall off her eyes, and Peter saw to his relief that she was smiling. 'I knew you'd do it! Well, done, darling. A captain, eh?'

'All being well.' Peter said, feeling a wide smile spread over his own face. 'But, there's a lot to do before I get that far. Besides, the failure rate is something like one in four, so …'

Kaisa nuzzled into him again. 'You'll do it, I know you will!'

'But it means I don't get any leave as planned. The course starts on Monday.'

At that, Kaisa got up and looked at him with those large blue eyes of hers. They were more intense now, and he was again worried she'd cry. 'But I get some weekends off.'

'OK,' Kaisa said and laid back down, now a little away from Peter. 'You'd better pass then,' she said, and lifting her head up to face Peter, she kissed him fully on the mouth.

8

L isten, I've got another bit of news.' Peter said.
They were back in the small, cold kitchen of the married quarter. Kaisa shivered from the chill, but also from seeing the stripey curtains, in garish green and yellow, which hung either side of the small window overlooking the steep hill, on which a group of concrete blocks of flats faced the dank waters of Gareloch. The curtains were too short for the window and hung limp on either side, neither blocking the faint light of the wet summer afternoon, nor keeping the drafts away from the kitchen. The horrible decor of the married quarter, the view of the loch, and the damp cold, which seemed to creep into every joint of her body, reminded Kaisa of the terrible few months she'd lived in Helensburgh as a newly married and lonely Navy wife. She shuddered again and tried not to think of the past, or what they might have to face in the future, but to concentrate on how happy she was now, this moment, together with Peter. Their life now was nothing like the first miserable year of their marriage.

'Really? What?' Kaisa said. She turned around, her hands dripping water.

Underneath the window with the awful curtains was a stainless steel sink at which Kaisa was washing a pair of tea mugs. She'd spotted a row of the smoked glass mugs in the cupboard on the left side of the window. She didn't trust the previous occupiers to have washed them properly, so she insisted on giving them a run under the lukewarm water. She now dried the cups, added the tea bags, and Peter poured hot water over them. There was no coffee, and Kaisa had forgotten to bring her one-cup filters, so she settled for a cup of weak black tea. But as soon as she brought the mug up to her face and got the scent of the black liquid, she put the cup back down on the counter.

'No good?' Peter said and took a large gulp of his milky tea.

'Sorry,' Kaisa said and poured the tea down the sink. 'I wonder if they might have my coffee filters in town?'

'Might do. We'll drive down and see,' Peter said. He came over and put his hands on Kaisa's waist. He gave her a peck on her lips and continued, 'Look, I'm sorry but we've been invited out to dinner tonight.'

Kaisa moved away and leaned against the sink, letting Peter's hands drop down. 'Oh yes?'

'Don't be like that, Kaisa.' Peter's voice was soft. He was looking at Kaisa, not smiling. 'It's my Captain. I told him you were coming over yesterday, and his wife, you know her, Costa, phoned just now saying that since you were up here so rarely it would be lovely to have us over for supper. I couldn't say no.'

Kaisa nodded. Oh, how she hated these suppers given by Navy wives. It puzzled her why they did it. No one seemed to enjoy themselves during these dinners, not the hostess, nor the guests, so why go to the trouble?

Peter had often told her it was important for the wives to get to know each other so that when the submarine went on patrol, they could support each other. 'It's easier if the wives have already met,' he'd said. They'd ended the conversation there, because Peter knew how Kaisa felt about that support.

Apart from her friend Pammy, Kaisa hadn't experienced any friendliness from the other wives when she'd lived in the married quarters; in fact, rather the opposite. Besides, she knew everyone at these dinner parties would disapprove of her lifestyle and career.

Apart from Pammy, people in the Navy were the only members of the population who seemed to think wives shouldn't have careers of their own. They gave no recognition of achievement, and seemed to think she was being selfish by pursuing her own interests rather than supporting her husband's Navy career. On the other hand, a dinner party tonight would buy Kaisa more time, and being with others would hopefully stop her from telling Peter about Duncan – and the virus.

'What time?' Kaisa asked.

Peter came closer to Kaisa and took her into his embrace, 'It'll be OK.'

. . .

The Captain, Stewart Harding, and his wife, Costa, short for Constance, lived outside Helensburgh, by Loch Lomond, in a place called Arden. It was a tiny village and their house stood in a small cul-de-sac.

Kaisa remembered that Costa loved horses, and wasn't surprised to see that they had stables as well as a paddock fenced off from the garden. Standing next to the stone-clad fireplace in their vast living room, with a gin and tonic in her hand, Kaisa listened to Peter's Captain, a shortish man with a roundish belly overhanging his brown corduroy trousers, tell them how his wife loved the fillies more than she did him. From the conversation, Kaisa had gathered that Costa had bought a new horse each time one of their three children had been sent away to school. The Captain's laughter filled the room. He directed his pale blue eyes at Kaisa and and nudged Peter's side.

'But I hear you are the brains of this marriage, dear?'

Kaisa smiled and shifted herself a little. The roaring log fire was beginning to burn Kaisa's bum. She gazed at the Captain and wondered if he was about to refer to her as a 'career woman'. In the Navy it seemed, women weren't allowed to have careers unless they were unmarried WRENs. Kaisa opened her mouth to say something, and then saw Peter shoot her a warning look.

'Not at all,' Kaisa replied sweetly, but Stewart didn't hear because at that moment the doorbell chimed. Placing his glass on a low coffee table, he excused himself.

When the Captain had gone into the hall, Peter came to stand next to Kaisa and put his arm around her waist. 'Take a deep breath,' he whispered into her ear and gave her a quick peck on the side of her mouth.

'I'm OK,' she said and smiled.

A younger couple entered the room. A stockily built lieutenant, whom Peter introduced as Gerald, came in with his Scottish girlfriend, Erica. Behind them, laughing loudly at a joke the Captain had made, was Judith, the wife of the First Lieutenant Rob, whom Kaisa had already met at the base during the Christmas ball.

During dinner, talk inevitably turned to Lady Di.

'Did you meet her?' Erica asked.

The quiet Scottish girl, Kaisa had found out, was just 22 and worked as a nanny in Glasgow. She had a very pale face, which contrasted with her coal-black hair, and a sweet smile that made Kaisa glad she was sitting opposite her. Although her accent was at times difficult for Kaisa to understand, she liked her.

'No, I work and live in London.'

Erica opened her mouth to say something but before she had a chance, a voice further down the table addressed her.

'She was so nice, very natural. The way she talked to the children you could tell she's a mother herself,' Judy, the wife of the First Lieutenant, said. 'It's such a shame you missed it, Keesi.'

Kaisa smiled and resisted the urge to correct the woman's pronunciation of her name. Peter, who was sitting on the other side of Erica diagonally opposite Kaisa, gave her a look that said 'Don't', so Kaisa just said, 'She looks very friendly' and added, 'Tell me, what was she wearing? Peter told me about the visit, but couldn't even remember the colour of her outfit!'

There was general laughter before Judy described the outfit in great detail — the Navy-inspired dress with gold buttons, white, low-heeled shoes, a matching white hat with a navy ribbon and a white leather clutch bag. She talked at length about the lady-in-waiting, and how nice she, too, had been, making sure no one person got too much time with the Princess.

'There were some sailor's wives, who had to be told to move away. But that's understandable, really. They don't usually come close to royalty, so they don't know how to behave.'

The Captain cleared his throat and, looking at his wife, said, 'It was a successful visit, and I think even Her Royal Highness enjoyed it.'

There was more discussion about the Princess and her charitable work.

'She's wonderful with the AIDS patients, isn't she? Touching them like that. Very brave,' Judith said.

Everyone nodded, and for a moment no one said anything. But Kaisa couldn't help herself. 'AIDS is only transmitted through sexual intercourse, so there's really no bravery involved in touching a patient,' she said.

There was a tension around the table, and Kaisa could feel Peter's eyes on her. She didn't dare look at him.

'That's certainly the current medical opinion, anyway.' Kaisa spoke into the silence in the room, catching Erica's eye opposite. She nodded and smiled.

The Captain cleared his throat once again, and said, 'I think it's time for some port for the gents and some liqueurs for the ladies? Shall we retire to the lounge?'

'Well done,' Costa whispered to Kaisa when they left the table and she briefly stood alone with the Captain's wife, waiting for others to leave the room. Kaisa turned around, wanting to say something, but Costa moved her along and they were back in the lounge with the others overlooking the now darkened view of Loch Lomond.

When Kaisa had first met Costa, at the Christmas ball on the base, where she'd met most of the officers from Peter's Starboard crew, she'd found her quite cold with little to say to Kaisa. She supposed that, as the Captain's wife, Costa must get fed up with having to be nice to everyone all of the time. But tonight, the petite woman who had short, unkempt brown hair, was very pleasant; she didn't have any airs or graces.

Kaisa wondered what she would have to do if Peter passed Perisher, and she too became a Captain's Wife. If they made it that far, she thought. She shivered and told herself to stop thinking about the test. Surely if she did have AIDS, she would be ill? Wouldn't she find it difficult to shake off any little colds or sniffles?

She thought back and realised she'd only been ill, or away from work, due to her miscarriages and the cramps she'd had afterwards. The last time she'd taken an aspirin and gone to work regardless. She tried to shake off thoughts of the test and wondered instead what she would do if she actually managed to hold onto a baby and give birth.

If Peter got a drive in one of the submarines stationed up in Scotland, would she want to give up work and move up here again? When she and Peter had talked about having a baby, they had decided she would stay in London, and use the crèche that the BBC provided in Covent Garden. She knew the waiting list was long, but she'd hoped that if she put down the baby's name, as soon as she was far enough on in the pregnancy, she'd be able to get a place. But that was before Peter knew about the Perisher and a possible promotion. Although he hadn't said it, Kaisa felt sure that, as a Captain, he'd get less time away from the boat. Would she be able to cope with a baby on her own for most of the time? And how would it be for the child never to see his or her father? Perhaps life up in Scotland wouldn't be so bad after all.

She looked around the sitting room where the eight of them were sitting. She'd definitely keep clear of Judy, but she could see herself becoming friends with both Costa and Erica. Plus, you never know, Nigel and Pammy might have moved up to Scotland by then. Pammy had written in her latest letter that Nigel's commission on a diesel submarine in Plymouth was coming to an end, and they didn't yet know where he was going next. 'The uncertainty is the worst thing, isn't it?' she'd written. In London, Kaisa felt much removed from the Navy circles, but decisions about Peter's career were still a major concern in their marriage. Apart from her inability to keep hold of a baby, that is.

And now the horror of the virus.

Which she wasn't thinking about.

The bare fact was that she was still dependent on Peter's work in so many ways. She missed him constantly, and a six- to eight-week patrol meant two months of not trying for a baby. A shore job would mean she'd have a chance of conceiving each cycle.

And then there was all the talk about the nuclear submariners only producing daughters. It was true that most of the children born to the submariners Kaisa knew were girls, but was it really true that the radiation affected the men's sperm so that only girls survived? Kaisa hadn't dared ask the old GP, who she knew would call it an 'old wives' tale'. Besides, Kaisa didn't really mind a girl; in fact, she secretly wished for one. But since she'd lost this latest baby, she'd begun to worry that it might be the radiation that was causing her to have early miscarriages.

Kaisa was shaken out of her own thoughts by Peter, who came to sit on the arm of the comfy chair allocated to Kaisa by the Captain. He was holding two glasses of port in his hands and handed Kaisa one.

'You OK?' he whispered into her ear and Kaisa nodded.

In spite of the not-so-well veiled criticism of her choice of living arrangements by the First Lieutenant's wife, and the brief blip over AIDS, Kaisa found, to her surprise, that the evening did go smoothly. She even enjoyed herself a little.

It had been a beautiful evening, with the sun up until gone eight o'clock, and now when they were drinking port and eating cheese, Kaisa could still see the shadows of the trees and bushes in the vast garden leading down to the loch.

Earlier, before dinner, when it had still been light, they'd all admired the view of Loch Lomond, which had been as still as a millpond. It had stopped raining, and the sun had briefly come out from behind a thick blanket of cloud. The view had reminded Kaisa of the lakes in Finland.

Aulanko in Southern Finland, where she and Peter had spent one ill-fated Midsummer weekend, had the same majestic fells and deep valleys as Scotland, with lakes connected by narrow fast-flowing rivers. Even the pine trees reflected onto the water on the opposite shore had made Kaisa think of home.

Again she wondered if she could live here. If she didn't have to live in a married quarter, perhaps she would manage it?

There'd been a lot of talk about closing down the Finnish section at the BBC lately. Since her wonderful boss, Annikki Sands, had retired, there hadn't been anyone who could defend the work of the Finnish section at Bush House. The other Nordic countries' foreign services had long since been closed down, so Kaisa guessed it was only a matter of time. She wondered if work was still scarce up here in Scotland, and whether she'd be as miserable here now as she had been five years previously. She supposed now she had journalistic experience, she could do freelance work for other organisations, perhaps even for radio stations in Finland. Kaisa was so deep in her own thoughts that she didn't hear the talk turn to babies. She realised when everyone was looking at her that someone had asked her a question.

'Sorry, miles away,' she said.

Stewart, Peter's Captain, laughed and then said, 'We were just wondering when you and Peter are going to start a family?'

With panic rising in her gut, Kaisa glanced at Peter, who, after giving a short cough into his curled-up hand said, 'Oh, not yet. We're having too much fun for that.'

There was laughter from the men in the company, and looks of disapproval from all the women except Erica, who was studying her hands. Kaisa shot a grateful glance at Peter. He smiled at her and continued, 'In any case, I think for the next few months my priority should be Perisher, Sir,' he added.

'Quite so, quite so.' The Captain nodded. He took a sip of his port and added, 'But we will miss you on the next patrol, make no mistake.'

Kaisa shot Peter another look. Was he going to say he would miss the next patrol too? Kaisa knew how boring the extended period away from any contact with the outside world was for him. Peter had told her that most men onboard spent the first two weeks getting used to being away from their loved ones, and the final two weeks longing to be home.

'That only leaves two weeks, or so, doesn't it?' Kaisa said, and Peter had nodded. At the time she had wanted to ask him why if, as he seemed to be saying, he hated the patrols so much, he remained in the Navy, but before she'd had time to do it, he'd said, 'But someone's got to do it.' He had then taken Kaisa into his arms and added, 'And you like the uniform, don't you?' They'd both laughed and Peter had given her a long, delicious kiss. Kaisa had to struggle not to blush at the memory of what had happened after their long embrace that time.

9

On their way home from the Captain's dinner, Peter put his hand on Kaisa's knee and said, 'It wasn't that bad was it?'

He was driving along the narrow road from Arden towards Helensburgh passing strange Scottish places like Fruin, Daligan and Dumfin.

'No,' Kaisa said and smiled.

When they reached the seafront at Helensburgh, she watched the darkened waters of Gareloch and wished she was back in London, and that they could curl up in their small but lovely bedroom in their terraced house, rather than in the cold rooms in Smuggler's Way.

'My God, that woman!' Kaisa said, suddenly remembering Judith. 'The way she spoke about the poor sailors' wives. I bet Princess Di was glad to get away from her and talk to some ordinary people.'

Peter laughed, then added, 'Although you don't make it easy for yourself.'

Kaisa smiled but didn't say anything. She hoped Peter wouldn't start talking about AIDS, because she couldn't guarantee that she could keep quiet about the test.

Interpreting her silence as sadness, Peter said, 'I'm sorry about the Old Man's comments about a baby. I've not told anyone onboard about the, you know the …'

'That's OK, it's better that way. I wouldn't want them to know.'

They were silent as they passed the peace camp. It looked empty, and

Kaisa wanted to ask Peter if they still did the Wednesday demonstrations on the road, but she didn't want to remind him of Lyn, the peace campaigner she had befriended. Her thoughts went briefly back to her friend. She hadn't heard from her for a while. It must be at least six months, Kaisa thought.

'You'll be able to hold onto the next one,' Peter said as he stopped the car outside the bleak block of flats on the top of Smuggler's Way. He gave Kaisa a peck on the cheek and got out of the car. It had started to drizzle and they ran, hand in hand, across the small patch of lawn into the house and up the stairs to the flat.

As Peter watched his wife getting undressed, he was so sorry there was nothing growing inside her small flat tummy. But he knew he mustn't show his disappointment to Kaisa. She was already sad enough.

He went over and put his hand on Kaisa's narrow waist and pulled her close. She was still wearing a skirt and a bra, which Peter unfastened with one hand. His desire for Kaisa was mixed with a desire for a baby, something that would be theirs, something they'd made together.

Ever since he'd held one of the twins, his little niece, baby Beth, in his arms at Christmas nearly five years ago, he'd been imagining himself holding his own little girl, with a mop of black hair like Beth's, or perhaps with Kaisa's beautiful blonde locks and her striking blue eyes. He just longed to be a dad. He pulled Kaisa into bed and as he kissed her neck she moaned. He undid the zip on her skirt and pulled it down.

Afterwards, when Kaisa had turned over and was gently snoring next to him, Peter thought about Nigel, who was one of his closest Navy friends. He now had two little girls. He'd told Peter, 'Every man needs a daughter.' That was when his second child had just been born, and Peter and Nigel were wetting the baby's head in the Ardencaple in Rhu. At the time, Kaisa and Peter had been separated, and Peter had thought he'd never again be in a relationship with a woman he'd want to be the mother of his children. He'd told Nigel that he wanted a child very badly, but that the only woman he loved was Kaisa, so that was that.

Nigel had touched his shoulder and said, 'You need to forgive her and win her back.'

Peter had looked at his friend and nodded. At that moment, in the middle of a rowdy pub, through the haze of his drunkenness he'd understood clearly that his future was with Kaisa. The next morning, with a severe hangover pounding his temples, he'd dismissed the thought and put it down to sentimental talk brought on by the recent birth and the several pints of beer they'd consumed that night.

Yet after several months, and two other relationships, he'd realised that despite the alcohol, he'd been right. The only woman he loved was Kaisa. After he'd managed to win her over a second time, he knew he'd want children sooner rather than later.

But it had taken Kaisa years to be convinced, and when at last they started trying, she'd lost the baby almost immediately. Another miscarriage followed, and now she had lost a third baby. Peter wondered if it was time to stop trying and be satisfied with a brilliant career in the Navy for him, and another for Kaisa at the BBC?

He knew her job meant the world to her. He remembered how after the first miscarriage they'd decided not to try again, and had gone and bought a white sofa for the living room of their Notting Hill home. It was something they could ill afford, but Kaisa had said that with them both working, and earning full-time, they'd soon pay off the hire purchase agreement. New furniture apart, could they really be happy without children?

Sensing that sleep wasn't far away, Peter curled up next to Kaisa, taking in her scent, and thought that for the next four months at least, he would be busy with Perisher, and afterwards, if he passed, he'd most probably be either a First Lieutenant (or 'The Jimmy' as the second in command in a submarine was called) or get his own drive and become a captain of a diesel submarine. He would be away a lot, so not having a baby would probably be best for both of them. Of course, he may well fail, he knew that, and although he believed he'd pass, he also needed to be prepared for a life out of submarines.

10

On Thursday evening, after Peter had said goodbye to Kaisa at Glasgow airport, he decided to go for a pint in the Back Bar at Faslane base before turning in. The only other person drinking alone was Dick Freely, a friend of Nigel's who'd failed Perisher, but had decided to stay in the Navy anyway.

Peter nodded to the man, who was completely bald, but had dark bushy eyebrows and a beard running from his temples to a point below his chin, framing his face.

Peter knew from the rumours going around at the base that Dick had failed the last sea trial, and had, as was customary, been taken off the submarine immediately. He didn't want to think about that scenario too much and was surprised when Dick came over to him and asked what he wanted to drink.

'That's very kind. I'll have pint of Bass, thank you.'

'I hear you're up for Perisher,' Dick said as a young blonde barmaid Peter hadn't seen before poured their drinks and placed them on the counter in front of the two men.

'Yeah,' Peter said and took a deep swig of his pint. He was surprised the bloke wanted to talk about the course. Strange that he'd dived straight in there. Peter didn't know what to say to him.

'If you want any pointers, I'm here,' Dick added with a short laugh.

'Right.'

'Though I may not help much, seeing that I failed.'

'Hmm,' Peter said, moving his eyes away from Dick, desperately seeking another friendly face in the bar. He should have made an excuse earlier, he thought. He was already feeling awkward talking to the guy. But the Back Bar was almost empty; most officers had gone home to their wives and there were no visiting submarines alongside.

'It's OK, I can talk about it,' Dick said and Peter turned his head towards the older man.

'Must have been tough, though?' Peter said. His curiosity had been piqued.

Dick was quiet for a moment, stoking his beard. This time it was Dick who studied his half-full pint of beer. Eventually, when Peter was about to apologise for being so nosy, he lifted his impressive eyebrows and looked up at Peter, 'A bit like a death in the family to tell you the truth. The Mrs didn't take it very well for a start. The divorce came through a few weeks ago.'

'I'm sorry to hear that.' Peter thought about Kaisa. She would probably be glad if he failed; it might mean that his career in the Navy was over. He knew that, secretly, she wanted him out of the service. But of course, at the same time, she knew how much his Navy career meant to him, so she wished him the best. But to divorce him because he'd failed a commander's course? That she'd never do, Peter was sure of that.

'She had got it into her head that she'd be the Captain's wife, I suppose,' Dick said and emptied his glass.

A group of officers neither men knew entered the bar, and Peter and Dick moved to a table in the corner with another round of drinks that Peter had insisted on.

The older man told Peter how shocked he'd been by the whole procedure after his dismissal from Perisher. He said that by the time he was told he was going, he'd already expected to fail. During his last attack exercises, the Teacher had taken control of the submarine twice, and on the second time, he'd seen how the man had nodded to his steward, who'd disappeared down the gangway and packed Dick's bag. It had been the dead of night, and the other three candidates left on the course had been visibly embarrassed when they'd said goodbye to Dick. He hadn't seen them since.

'All three got a drive,' Dick said drily.

Peter didn't ask which captains Dick was talking about. They didn't seem a particularly supportive bunch.

'Don't get me wrong, I completely understand why they failed me. But not to be able to step onboard a sub again. That's tough.'

Peter nodded. It was Dick's turn to get the beers in and as Peter watched him at the bar, he noticed how he still had the submariner's stoop. Dick was a little taller than even Peter, which was unusual in a submariner. The spaces in diesel boats in particular were so cramped that most taller men either never applied to serve in submarines or developed a crouching stance over the years. Something that was evidently difficult to shake off even after you were out, Peter thought.

Back at the table, Dick sat down with a heavy sigh and continued his monologue, which Peter wasn't about to interrupt.

'The worst is that people are embarrassed to mention it. As if I was a leper or something.'

Peter felt ashamed. As soon as Dick had begun talking to him, his first instinct had also been to flee. Then he thought back to his Court Martial. People had treated him the same way. At first no one had said anything, and went to great lengths to avoid him on the base. It was only after a few months that the jibes and insults started flying. He guessed failing a submarine course wasn't that bad.

'Yeah, I know all about that,' Peter said and gave Dick a sideways smile.

'Of course. Sorry. Had forgotten about your little mishap,' Dick said.

'It's OK. What do you do now?'

'That's the best thing about it; I've now got a shore job.'

Peter gave his new friend a puzzled look. 'Really?'

'Missile Command. I head the unit up in Coulport.'

'Oh.'

'I work office hours, and have the same pay, more or less. Without the sea-time. Couldn't be better.' Dick sighed. 'You'd have thought that would have suited Mary, but it seems she was quite happy, or even happier, when I was away.'

'Marriage isn't easy for us submariners,' Peter commented, before he realised what he'd said. 'Sorry, I mean for us in the Navy.'

Dick leaned back in his chair and gave a short laugh. 'No need to apologise. I know what you mean. You've had your struggles in that department?'

Peter gazed at Dick. His expression was open; there seemed to be no malice there. 'Water under the bridge now.'

Dick nodded, 'Sorry, I didn't mean to have a dig.'

'It's fine. Kaisa ...' again Peter hesitated. Apart from his best man, Jeff, and his best mate Nigel, he hadn't spoken about his marital problems with anyone else. He looked around the bar, which was now half-full. They were sitting in the far corner, and couldn't be overheard.

'Kaisa was young, jobless and lonely. And with me away on a patrol, she was taken advantage of.'

'Heard the bastard was thrown out of the Navy?'

'Yeah, after I'd given him a good hiding. But that cost me a Court Martial and a knock-back on my career. So not something I'd recommend,' Peter said and grinned.

'I'll drink to that,' Dick said and finished his pint. 'One for the road?'

'Go on then,' Peter said.

In bed that night, Peter thought how lucky he was. Even if he failed Perisher he knew he could count on Kaisa. He loved Kaisa more now than he ever had. And they had both calmed down a lot. They rarely argued now, just the occasional row, which usually ended in passionate love-making. So why was it so important to have a baby too? Although he knew they'd be happy without children, Peter knew a baby would cement their relationship. He wanted a family, wanted a daughter or a son to bring up, someone to teach right from wrong, not to lie, or be unkind to others. Peter thought what a wonderful mother Kaisa would make. He could see her with a baby in her arms, and the image made his heart ache. He closed his eyes and told himself to stop being silly. What was the point in brooding over something that might never happen? Instead he thought about Kaisa's beautiful body, and imagined what he'd do to her if she were lying next to him now. He fell asleep dreaming of his wife.

11

Kaisa sat in the doctor's surgery, which was nothing more than an ordinary narrow hallway of a Victorian semi-detached house. Her throat was dry and she kept fidgeting with the strap on her handbag. She'd had a call from the receptionist that morning, 'Your test results are in, Mrs Williams.' Kaisa had wondered about the tone of the woman's voice. Was there disapproval in it? She decided to ignore it even if there was, and made her way to the surgery for a ten o'clock appointment with Doctor Harris.

She'd been waiting for ten minutes, checking her watch every 30 seconds, trying to appear calm. The receptionist glanced over to her every now and then, and Kaisa knew she must be aware of the reason Kaisa was there. Did she also know the result of her test, Kaisa wondered? What if it was positive? She would have to tell Peter straightaway.

That weekend Peter had managed to come down from Faslane. They'd spent the two days cooking, going to their local, The Earl of Lonsdale, for a drink or two, doing some gardening and nothing much else, apart from copious amounts of love-making with a condom. Thank goodness she had the excuse of not being allowed to try for a baby too soon after the miscarriage.

On her own in bed last night, after Peter had flown back up to Scotland, Kaisa had woken up several times worrying about the test and not telling him about it. She kept thinking that it was the right thing to do, and that soon, the very next week, she'd know one way or the other. It was a blessing, really, that the phone call from the surgery had come this very morning, although now, sitting and waiting, she almost wished she had a few more days' grace before she knew the result.

She had discussed it all with Rose during several long conversations, which always began with Kaisa asking after Duncan (who was still poorly), and ended with an in-depth analysis of the options Kaisa had.

They had both agreed that telling Peter before she knew the reality of her situation would be foolish. Even in normal circumstances it would be selfish to worry him over a situation that was completely of Kaisa's own making (this was something Rose refuted, however: she still thought that the whole affair was Duncan's fault), but now that Peter was on the critical Perisher course, he didn't need any distractions.

What she'd do if she did have the virus, Kaisa hadn't decided. That was something she hadn't even dared to discuss with Rose. Her friend was convinced that the test would prove negative, and wouldn't entertain any other option. How Kaisa wished Rose was right! If she did have the virus, the thought of telling Peter was unthinkable. She knew it would ruin everything.

Later that same evening she telephoned Rose.

'I'm clear!' she said.

Kaisa heard her friend let out a long sigh.

'Thank God for that!'

'How is he?' Kaisa asked.

Rose didn't reply, so Kaisa added, 'Rose, is everything OK?'

'Not really, ' Rose sighed. 'He's with us still, sleeping in the Yellow Room.'

Kaisa thought back to her one visit to Rose's large house in Dorset. She and Peter had spent a weekend with Rose and her husband Roger, both of whom had now retired early from the newspaper business. They'd slept in the Yellow Room, which overlooked fields and a small stream in the distance. It was a beautiful place, which had made Peter want to move to the country. He'd even proposed leaving the Navy and moving somewhere near his parents' home in Wiltshire. Kaisa had just laughed; she loved London and had decided never to move to a small place again, or to the countryside, where she'd feel out of touch and landlocked. She didn't think Peter would enjoy it either, even though, as he'd reminded her at the time, he was 'a country boy'.

Now Kaisa imagined Duncan sleeping in that same wrought-iron bed, looking over the same view of the fields and the stream.

'Does he still have pneumonia?' Kaisa had read that AIDS patients couldn't fight off viruses.

'Yes, he's got a lung infection among other things. They're trying out a set of different antibiotics at the moment.'

'Oh,' Kaisa said. She wondered if she should send him her love. No, not love, but perhaps regards? Instead she merely said, 'I hope he gets better soon.'

Rose was quiet at the other end of the phone and Kaisa feared she'd said the wrong thing.

'We wondered when you might be able to come down?'

Kaisa bit her lip. She had immediately regretted her promise to visit and had thought Rose would have forgotten, or rather, given up, on the thought of her going to see Duncan. It hadn't been mentioned during their many conversations about Kaisa's test.

'Look, I'm sorry to do this to you, but there may not be much time,' Rose said.

Kaisa could hear her voice falter. She looked at the wall calendar she kept above the telephone in the hall. In the next few days, there was a great big free space when she was off work. It was the week she and Peter had planned to take a little break, before he'd been selected for Perisher. They'd been planning to go and see his family in Wiltshire, but Peter had telephoned his parents over the weekend and told them the good news about the course, and the bad news about the visit. Kaisa didn't want to go on her own, even though she overheard Peter's mother suggesting she should. Kaisa had shaken her head silently at Peter as he stood in the hall, with the receiver half against his ear so that Kaisa could hear what his mother was saying. After all the years, Kaisa still didn't feel conformable in his parents' company. She felt sure his mother hadn't forgiven what she'd done to her son during their first year of marriage.

Kaisa was now thinking hard. She could tell Peter she was going up to see Rose and Roger; the weather was hotting up and a heatwave was forecast. It would be a natural thing to want to get away from London, since she had the time off and he was busy with Perisher. And it wouldn't be a lie.

'OK, how about I come over tomorrow? I'm off work, so I could stay overnight.'

'Kaisa, that's wonderful! Will you take the first cheap train to Sherborne? I think it leaves at 10.15. I'll come and pick you up from the station.'

That evening when Peter phoned Kaisa, she felt such relief. The threat of the virus had been lifted and now all she had to do was to see Duncan once, and then forget all about it. She no longer needed to feel as though she was lying to Peter.

'How is it going, darling?'

'Well,' Peter said. 'First sea time starts tomorrow.'

'Ah, that's perfect! I'm going to see Rose and Roger in Dorset. It's getting unbearably hot and I'm off work, so I thought I might as well get out of town.'

'That's an excellent idea. I only wish I could have come with you,' Peter said.

Kaisa was quiet, she didn't know how to reply. She couldn't say, 'Me too,' because that would be a blatant lie. How was she getting herself into these horrible situations?

'Rose asked me and I couldn't say no.' That at least was the truth, Kaisa thought.

'Well, have fun and think of me when you're lying in that wonderful bed.'

Peter's words reminded Kaisa of making love in the Yellow Room, and how the old wrought iron bed had squeaked so badly that they worried Rose and her husband would hear them.

'I shan't be putting those springs through the same pressure,' Kaisa said and giggled.

12

K aisa spotted Rose as soon as she stepped off the train. She was wearing a summery dress with small pink flowers on it. Laura Ashley, Kaisa thought, and saw how she blended into the surroundings.

Sherborne station was a pretty, stone-built building, with hanging baskets overflowing with pink and blue flowers swaying in the faint breeze. By the time Kaisa's train had pulled out of Waterloo, the sun had already been high in the sky and she'd had to move seats to get out of the glare. She'd begun the journey with great trepidation. She felt guilty about telling Peter only part of the story; and she feared what she might see when she met Duncan. That image of the father with his dying son kept popping into her brain, however much she tried to shoo it away.

'I'm so glad you came,' Rose said.

She'd flung Kaisa's overnight bag in the back of an old, muddy Land Rover, and was now sitting in the driver's seat, leaning towards the windscreen as she negotiated a small roundabout.

The back of the car bore testament to Rose's two Labradors: there were dog hairs all over old checked throws. Was this really the same woman who used to wear high heels and was so adept at hailing cabs on the London streets? Kaisa marvelled at the change in her friend; here, in the country, she seemed freer somehow, definitely more at home, but also more in control. Rose had always been the strong woman in Kaisa's life, her career role model in many ways, so it still took her by surprise to see how much the country life suited her.

But Rose's words and her grave face reminded Kaisa why she was here. 'How is he?'

'Duncan is strong, so we're hopeful.'

While they were driving along narrow roads, bordered by high hedges with the occasional purple flowers, foxgloves she thought they were called, sticking out of them, Kaisa hoped her image of a dying man was not what she'd find in Rose's Yellow Room.

As soon as she entered the white-clad house, which Rose and Roger referred to as 'The Cottage' even though it was at least twice the size of Kaisa's terraced house in Notting Hill, Kaisa felt there was a different atmosphere.

When she'd visited with Peter, the house had been filled with light and laughter; one of the dogs had been a puppy then and had peed on the floor after Kaisa bent down to stroke and play with it. They had all chuckled and Roger had pulled the poor little puppy out of the house by the scruff of its neck, calling it a 'naughty girl' and putting on a stern face. He'd then made stiff gin and tonics for them all.

Rose had produced a huge salad and Roger had grilled steaks on the barbecue. They'd sat in the garden until dusk fell, watching the birds fly about, listening to their nocturnal singing, drinking wine and talking. When it grew fully dark, they'd moved inside to sit in Rose's large kitchen until the early hours, drinking a bottle of rather good whisky that Roger had pulled out of the drinks cabinet.

Now the kitchen looked cold and gloomy, in spite of the full sunshine outside. Roger sat at the table, drinking coffee out of a large mug. Even the two dogs seemed subdued, greeting Kaisa with a couple of sniffs and lazy wags of their tails. There was a smell of disinfectant, and when Rose's husband stood up to greet Kaisa, his face was serious. 'So good of you to come,' Roger said and kissed Kaisa on both cheeks.

'I wanted to,' Kaisa lied and set down her bag.

'Oh, let me take that. You're in the Pink Room at the back of the cottage.' Roger turned and kissed Rose on the mouth. 'You OK, love?'

'Did he have the soup?'

Roger shook his head. The two stood there for a moment, looking at each other. Then Rose turned towards Kaisa, 'Look, Roger will take you to your room and you can freshen up if you want. Are you hungry? Come down when you're ready and I'll make us a sandwich.'

Kaisa nodded and followed Roger upstairs. On the landing, she saw the door to the Yellow Room was slightly ajar. She glanced at Roger, who took hold of her arm and gently guided her along the landing. The Pink Room was opposite Roger and Rose's bedroom.

'There's your bathroom just next door. I'm sorry this one doesn't have an en suite,' Roger said and left her alone.

Kaisa sat on the bed and looked out of the window. This side of the house overlooked the farmland beyond. Nearest to the back of the building was an overgrown orchard. Ripe plums were hanging from a couple of trees next to a stone wall separating the house from the track that led from the narrow road. The rest of the orchard had apple trees, scattered higgledy-piggledy around an area at least four times the size of Kaisa's garden. Beyond the orchard was a field of rapeseed, its yellow flowers stark against the blue skies. The view was breathtaking and Kaisa wondered how a world that had produced such beauty could also produce an illness like AIDS. She overheard steps on the landing and there was a knock on the door.

'Kaisa, are you OK?' Rose came into the room. She was carrying towels and placed them on the bed. 'Sorry, forgot to give you these.'

'Thank you,' Kaisa said. 'How is he, really?'

Rose sat on the bed next to Kaisa. 'I'm worried because he's just not eating very much. And he needs to, to get better and to take the tablets. Otherwise, his tummy gets upset.'

'Oh,' Kaisa said, not knowing what else to say. She had very little experience of illness. She'd once been to visit her grandfather in Tampere General Hospital in Finland, just before he passed. He'd been very poorly and Kaisa had only been in her early teens, so no one had told her much about his condition. Kaisa and her sister Sirkka had sat on plastic chairs next to their grandfather's bed while he coughed a lot.

Later, their mother had told her he'd died of lung cancer. Would Duncan's skin be as grey and his body as frail as her grandfather's had been? Surely he was a much younger man, and even with his illness … Kaisa's thoughts were interrupted by Rose, who'd taken hold of Kaisa's hand.

'Duncan would like to see you now, but I just wanted to talk to you first. He has lost a lot of weight, and he is particularly poorly with the pneumonia at the moment. I don't want you to be alarmed. It's all part of the disease. But he is young and strong and he wants to get better, so the doctor is hopeful that he'll fight this infection.'

'OK,' Kaisa said and got up. 'I'll just need to visit the loo.'

Rose got up too. She pulled her mouth into a brief smile and said, 'Come in when you're ready.'

Kaisa went into the small bathroom and washed her hands. She looked at herself in the mirror and adjusted her hair, which had gone frizzy with the breeze from the open window of the car. She looked at her face and tried to steady her breathing.

What was she afraid of?

All the literature she'd read emphasised that you could only get infected through blood or sexual intercourse. And she wasn't about to jump into bed with Duncan again.

But she knew it wasn't the fear of infection that was bothering her. It was the enormous guilt she felt about sleeping with Duncan in the first place and now seeing him behind Peter's back. But there was something else too. She could easily explain to Peter that she hadn't wanted to distract him during Perisher. 'Family life must come second,' he'd told her when he'd given her the news about the course in Helensburgh. And she understood that. Peter, she knew, had forgiven her for the affair, knowing it was partly his fault.

No, it wasn't the guilt that was bothering Kaisa. It was the feelings she still had for Duncan. She didn't want to see him suffer.

They had been great friends before – before they'd both spoiled it all. Why, oh why had they got drunk and had sex? It was so stupid. Kaisa knew she had used Duncan as a scapegoat; really, she'd been equally prepared to flirt with him. She had needed him to boost her confidence. She remembered how, when she was driving to the station to pick him up, she'd felt like a woman of the world, pretending to herself that she could have relationships with other men while Peter was away. Pretending that she could control the situation; she'd been looking forward to basking under the heat of Duncan's desire.

The air in the room was stuffy. The smell of medicines hit Kaisa as soon as she opened the door. Next she saw Duncan, half sitting up in the wrought-iron bed, propped up by several pillows. He was wearing a white T-shirt and she could see he had lost a lot of weight. His cheekbones were more prominent and his lips cracked. But his smile was the same, and the intense gaze in his light-blue eyes when he stretched his hand up to her had the same effect on her as before.

Kaisa felt short of breath. She was rooted to the spot, just inside the warm, airless room.

Duncan's voice was quiet, and she could tell he struggled to get the words out when he said, 'Kaisa, you came!'

Kaisa moved towards him and took his hand. His grip was surprisingly strong and Kaisa stood by the side of his bed for what seemed like several minutes, just holding his hand. Eventually Rose, who'd been standing at the foot of the bed said, 'Why don't you sit on the chair, Kaisa, so you two can talk. I'll be downstairs if you need me.'

Duncan's eyes moved away from Kaisa and he nodded to his cousin.

'She's been very good to me,' he said with the same quiet, breathless voice.

'Me too,' Kaisa said.

Duncan smiled, 'I did something right.'

Kaisa looked down at her hands. It was true. Without Duncan she wouldn't have known Rose, and without Rose Kaisa was sure she'd still be in Helsinki and not working for the BBC. She felt ashamed. Had she used Duncan and his attraction to her to advance her own career? She looked up at the man lying on the bed. His breathing came in short rasps. With a further struggle, he said, 'You forgive me?' His blue eyes were steady on Kaisa.

She was taken aback, and hesitated for a moment.

Duncan made a wheezing sound, lifting his upper body away from the bed. Kaisa stood up and tried to slip her hand behind Duncan's back, to help him, but he lifted his hand in a gesture to stop her, so Kaisa just stood there, helplessly watching Duncan slowly regain control of the coughing fit.

She saw him lick his lips.

'Do you want a bit of water?' she asked. She'd spotted a glass and a carafe on a table by the window.

'Mmm,' Duncan made a noise and with a slight movement of his head nodded towards the water.

Kaisa picked up the glass and tried to give it to Duncan, but he was too weak to take hold of it. He made a motion with his lips towards the ridge and Kaisa put the glass to his mouth. At first, she tipped it over too much and the liquid ran down Duncan's jaw and made a wet patch on his T-shirt.

'Sorry,' Kaisa said and tried again.

This time Duncan managed to take a few sips, before putting his hand up.

'Thank you,' he rasped, and leaned back against the pillows, closing his eyes.

'I've forgiven you ages ago,' Kaisa said.

Duncan nodded, without opening his eyes.

'Dear Kaisa,' he whispered.

Kaisa put the glass back on the table and saw there was a box of tissues there too. She took one and went to wipe Duncan's mouth but saw that he had fallen asleep. His breathing was still coming in short, croaky bursts, but it sounded steady, so after standing by the window for a while, Kaisa tiptoed out of the room, leaving the door ajar, as she had found it, and made her way down the stairs to the kitchen.

13

FINLAND JULY 1990

Kaisa had decided to fly Finnair to Helsinki for her sister's wedding, even though the cost of the flight was a lot more than if she'd taken BA. But she was rewarded when she stepped onto the aircraft and the air hostess smiled and said, 'Welcome onboard' to her in Finnish. She already felt at home, looking at the blue and white interior of the aircraft. *I am being very silly,* she thought, but couldn't help feel her throat close up with feeling.

She knew Sirkka's wedding would be an emotional affair, but to start choking up this early, on the plane to Helsinki! That was just plain ridiculous. Kaisa decided to buck up and asked for a white wine when the same friendly air hostess came along the aisle with her drinks trolley.

Kaisa was met at the airport by her mother, who was wearing a pair of white jeans and a frilly blouse.

'You look pale,' she said, but hugged her daughter hard. 'I've missed you.'

Kaisa saw there were tears in her eyes and struggled to keep herself in check.

'Oh, don't mum!'

She'd felt tears prick her eyes again earlier, when the plane was about to land and the beautiful green landscape of her home country had opened up in front of her. She realised how much she missed Finland's empty spaces and the green forests and lakes, the sunshine glimmering on the blue water below.

Her mother led Kaisa to her Volvo in the car park in front of the airport building. Again Kaisa was struck by the contrast with London; Heathrow was dirty, bustling with people, with multistorey car parks towering above the terminal. Here there was just a simple space occupied by a scattering of cars a few steps from the airport building.

They were to spend the first night at her mother's place in Töölö, and then travel up to Tampere the next day. On the way into town, Kaisa's mother chatted about the wedding arrangements, while Whitney Houston sang 'I will always love you' on the radio.

Kaisa watched the dark, tall pine trees lining the road pass by and suddenly realised why she was living away from her home country. It was exactly how she felt about Peter. She would always love him, and with that love came his career in the Royal Navy and their life in England.

Kaisa missed Peter even more intensely when she was standing in the doorway of Tampere Cathedral. The pews were half occupied, with people talking in low tones, but even so, there was a special silence to the place. She hadn't been to Tampere, let alone the Cathedral, since her own wedding six years ago, and was taken aback by the memories of that June day in 1984.

Trying to lift her mood, she walked slowly towards the front of the church, admiring the beautiful murals covering the walls and the ceiling. She nodded to a row of her relatives; her two uncles and their wives, and her several cousins, half of whom she hardly recognised anymore because they'd changed out of gangly teenage shapes into grown-ups.

She went to sit next to her grandmother, who sported a black and white zebra print dress and coat, complete with a hat with an impossibly large brim made out of the same fabric. (It had been leopard print for Kaisa's wedding.) As soon as Kaisa sat down, her grandmother gave her a smile and took hold of her hand, squeezing it gently. That grip around her fingers took Kaisa back to her early childhood, before she'd started school, when Mummu had looked after her.

She remembered the many trips to a park with ducks, and shopping for sweet buns in the covered market in the centre of Tampere. She glanced at her grandmother; she looked older and the grey hairs she'd long been battling against were spilling out from underneath the hat. She looked smaller and more stooped now, and her fingers around Kaisa's hand felt cold and papery rather than safe and strong, as they had when she was a child.

'How are you?' Kaisa whispered.

As she leaned into her grandmother, she got a strong whiff of eucalyptus and something else. Then she remembered, 'You still taking those garlic pills?'

Mummu gave Kaisa a startled look and began to rummage in her large handbag. 'I've got some for you.'

'Don't worry now, I'll have them later,' Kaisa said but her grandmother had already pulled a brown medicine bottle out of her bag and was pushing it into Kaisa's hand.

'They'll give you strength and increase your fertility,' Mummu said, fixing her dark eyes on Kaisa.

'Thank you,' Kaisa murmured, turning her face away from her grandmother and staring at the bottle in her hand. It had a green label on it, with Chinese text and an image of garlic bulbs. She could feel her cheeks burn under the old woman's gaze. How many people had her mother told about her problems in having a baby?

At that moment, the organist began to play and Kaisa looked up and spotted the tall shape of Jussi, Sirkka's husband to be, at the altar. Kaisa popped the bottle of pills into her small clutch, and forced herself to look at Mummu, who was leaning forward in the pew, now fully concentrated on the wedding rather than on Kaisa's problems.

Jussi had a mop of blond hair and the physique of a lumberjack. He was a builder by trade, so Kaisa presumed he'd done his fair share of logging. She smiled to herself. She knew Peter would have enjoyed the joke and would probably have made a better one to make Kaisa giggle.

Kaisa had met Jussi just the once, when Sirkka had organised a skiing trip for the four of them in Lapland. It had been a magical week, with evenings spent around the open fire of their log cabin, and days on the slopes in Ylläs ski centre. They'd even seen the Northern lights again, and Peter had made Kaisa promise that they would make the trip up to Lapland every year. But, of course, because of Peter's career, it hadn't happened. They'd had to give up one set of expensive flights when all leave was cancelled due to an 'operational emergency.' Peter had told Kaisa, in confidence, that 'the emergency' was due to there not being enough submarines, or staff to man them, because of the defence budget cutbacks.

During that skiing trip, Kaisa had seen how in love Sirkka was with Jussi. Sirkka had turned into a puddle of giggles each time Jussi so much as looked at her. She'd wondered then if Jussi, 'the man from Lapland', as they'd all dubbed him during the many years of their on-off relationship, had felt equally strongly about her sister.

But here they were, getting married in the very church where she and Peter had tied the knot. As Kaisa gazed at his strong back, clothed in a dark suit, he suddenly turned around and looked directly at her. How he'd found her among the small crowd in the vast Cathedral unnerved Kaisa, but Jussi just gave her a nervous smile. She nodded and returned the smile with what she hoped was a reassuring grin.

14

'You've grown,' her father said and gave Kaisa one of his bear hugs.

Kaisa laughed in spite of herself. It was an old joke from her childhood, when between the ages of ten and twelve, she'd suddenly shot up and her father had said that he couldn't sleep at night for the noise of Kaisa's growth spurts.

Kaisa hadn't seen her father since she'd visited Helsinki about a year and a half ago. It had been the summer that they'd decided to try for a baby, and during that holiday Kaisa had been off the pill for the first time since the age of 16. At the time, in Helsinki, during a lunch that her father had insisted on buying in an expensive restaurant in town, she'd been so excited, as well as scared, that she'd wanted to tell him too. Of course, she hadn't. Instead, she sipped the wine her father had insisted on buying, and sitting next to Peter in a leather cubicle, leaned into her husband and squeezed his hand under the table. Now, as she felt the warmth of her father's firm, solid body, she wanted to rest her head on his broad shoulder and tell him about her dead babies and cry.

Of course, she couldn't do that; this was a wedding, a joyous occasion. She extracted herself from her father's embrace; she'd already spent far too long hugging him. His eyes were on hers and he said, 'OK?' Kaisa nodded and moved away. She was conscious that her mother was watching them.

It was the first time since their divorce that her parents had been in the same room, as far as Kaisa knew, and even though the room in question wasn't even a room, but the steps to the Cathedral, this was something precious that she, Kaisa, needed to protect.

'Keep them separate, if need be,' her sister had told her the day before, when the sisters had met up for a pre-wedding coffee.

Her parents coming together to celebrate their daughter's wedding was a moment she needed to guard, to gently preserve, like a fragile nest of eggs, she'd once, as a child, tried to save in a tree outside their block of flats in Tampere. The wind had blown it this way and that, and from the vantage point of her bedroom window on the third floor, she'd been able to gaze at the nest from above.

The mother bird had gone in and out at first, but seemed to abandon her family after a gust from the northerly spring wind knocked her off the birch. Although she regained her flight after hitting the pavement below, she hadn't come back to the nest. With the help of her sister Sirkka, Kaisa had climbed the tree and put sticks underneath the nest to make it sturdier. But, of course, the mother bird had known it was a lost cause from the beginning.

One day when Kaisa had come home from school and glanced up at the tree, the nest had gone. None of the eggs were there, just remnants of the twigs Sirkka and she had arranged so carefully underneath. Kaisa had looked down and seen a few shells here and there on the pavement.

'Cats, most probably,' her mother had said.

That night in bed, Kaisa had cried and it was only her father who had been able to comfort her.

'I bet that mummy bird is at this very moment building another nest for another set of eggs,' he'd said and tussled Kaisa's hair. 'If something doesn't work the first time, you just need to try and try again.'

His pale blue eyes had looked at Kaisa and he'd added, 'That's just the way of the world, my little girl.'

Now Kaisa moved aside and watched as her mother and father, after a moment of guardedly gazing at each other, formally shook hands.

'Hello,' her mother said, extending her hand forward. She was wearing a light turquoise dress, with a frilly collar and cuffs, with a cream coloured wide-brimmed hat and gloves. She looked very stylish, and about ten years younger than she was.

Kaisa's father took the proffered hand and said, 'Pirjo.' They stood there as though frozen, until Kaisa, aware that her voice had become shrill, said, 'Look there's the happy couple.'

Sirkka looked radiant in her white wedding dress, and Jussi, whose shape loomed large next to Kaisa's sister, stood smiling widely on the steps of the church.

After the speeches and the champagne in the Grand Hotel Tammer, Kaisa sat with her cousins, trying to make conversation with her suddenly shy relatives. She found that their lives were so different from hers that they no longer seemed to have anything in common. Kaisa tried to ask them what they were up to, but most wanted to know about her life in London, about her career at the BBC and about what it was like to be 'famous'. Kaisa had laughed; her job was to compile and read the news in Finnish for the BBC, and she hardly thought that warranted her being recognised on the streets of her hometown.

One cousin, Raila, who was closest to her in age, had asked – jokingly, Kaisa realised afterwards – if she knew Princess Diana, and Kaisa told them how she had nearly met her. She recounted the story about the royal visit to Peter's submarine. She saw how the group grew quiet when they realised Peter had actually talked to the Princess.

'When I asked him what she was wearing, he couldn't even remember the colour of her dress,' she said, but her laughter was met by a wall of silence.

Kaisa wondered if, in the matter of just a few years, she'd changed so much that she could no longer talk to her family in Finland. She was relieved when she saw her sister approach the table, carrying her veil in the crook of her arm.

Sirkka exchanged a few words with the cousins, then sat down at an empty seat next to Kaisa and leaned over the round table to talk to each member of their extended family in turn.

Kaisa watched in awe as her sister spoke to the cousins about their university courses, or the jobs they were doing. What's happening to me, she thought, but before she could try to join the conversation, her sister whispered in her ear: 'I need the loo, do you want to come with me?'

Normally, this kind of request meant something had happened, but when Kaisa glanced at Sirkka's face, it glowed with happiness. Kaisa stood up and followed her sister down the hotel's long, dark corridor to the lift and up to the *Marski* suite, which, Sirkka had proudly told her, they'd managed to secure for the night. It was where Marshall Mannerheim, the Finnish war hero, the commander of the troops that won the Winter War against Russia, had stayed when visiting Tampere.

'It's the best room in the hotel,' Sirkka had told her over the phone weeks ago when she'd recounted all the plans for the wedding.

Now as they stood in the lift, Sirkka took hold of Kaisa's hand and said,

'I do need to go to the loo, but I also want to get you on your own to tell you something.'

Kaisa gazed at her sister's flushed face and at once knew what it was. Her eyes moved down to Sirkka's middle; did she hold a secret under the folds of the white satin of her wedding dress?

'Have you told mum?' Kaisa asked after she'd given Sirkka a huge hug.

'No, not yet. Only you and Jussi know so far. It's only six weeks, so ...' Sirkka gave her sister a cautious look.

Kaisa went to hug her sister once more. 'I'm fine, you mustn't worry about me.'

Sirkka smiled and, seeing how happy she looked, Kaisa also smiled, 'And congratulations!'

Kaisa wanted to say how incredible it was, how she would be a wonderful mother, but she didn't want to jinx it. She thought about the babies she'd lost and wanted to tell Sirkka to take it easy, not to dance tonight and not to stay up too late.

'Are you feeling OK?' she asked instead.

'Yeah, I was sick this morning but only because I was a bit nervous too, I think.' Sirkka smiled, 'Did you notice that I've been drinking sparking water all day?'

Kaisa gasped, 'No, you sneaky so and so!'

'Well, I've not had a drop since we decided to start trying ...' Sirkka gave Kaisa another careful look.

Kaisa saw her sister's expression and said, once more, 'I'm OK, honestly.'

They were both quiet for a moment. Then Sirkka said, 'Look, I know it's early, but I'd like you and Peter to be godparents.'

Kaisa was staring at her sister. How could she be so confident that everything would be OK? Kaisa had lost her first baby just a day or so after the sixth week of pregnancy, and here was her sister at exactly the same point. She wanted to scream at her to be careful, not to plan anything, because the little thing in her tummy was just that, a tiny fragile thing. It was smaller than the chicks the two them hadn't managed to save.

She touched Sirkka's arm and said, 'We would be honoured!'

Sirkka told Kaisa the due date was next February and that Jussi had bought a plot of land in Rovaniemi.

'You're going to live in Lapland?' Kaisa asked, her eyes wide.

Sirkka smiled and placed her hand on her tummy, as if to protect the foetus from any criticism Kaisa might level at her about their future living arrangements. To Kaisa, Lapland was a bit like Scotland; there were no jobs, and very few people, so what would Sirkka do with her time when Jussi was at work? Suddenly Kaisa realised that the new couple would settle where Jussi had his construction business. For some reason, Kaisa had assumed they'd be living in Helsinki.

'Well, I'm staying in my flat until the end of September, and then we'll rent somewhere in the city centre. The plot of land is fantastic, by the water, and he's planning to build a place with a swimming pool and …'

Sirkka stopped and stared at Kaisa, 'What is it?'

Kaisa felt tears prick her eyelids. Her sister must have noticed and was now hugging Kaisa.

'I'm sorry, sis. I know this must be hard for you.'

Kaisa pulled herself away and swallowed hard.

'It's not that. I'm just thinking how much harder it'll be for me to come and see you if you live all the way up in the North.'

'C'mon! There's an airport and it's only an hour from Helsinki. I managed to come and see you in Scotland, didn't I? Now you live in London, it'll be easy for you to get on a plane!'

Kaisa sighed and nodded. She was feeling so emotional. She apologised to her sister.

'Sorry, I'm being silly. I'm so glad to see you happy, though,' she added, and the two sisters hugged each other hard.

When Kaisa let go of Sirkka, she saw her sister was wiping tears from her eyes with the back of her hand.

'We're hopeless!' she said and gave the hankie back to Sirkka. They both laughed and made their way back to the reception.

15

'I t's such a shame Peter couldn't be here,' Kaisa's mother said to her later when they were standing at the bar in Hotel Tammer, waiting for their drinks.

Kaisa turned towards her mother. 'I know.'

'You two are OK, aren't you?' Pirjo said, and continued, 'I worry about you, darling.' She placed a hand on the sleeve of Kaisa's dress.

Seeing her mother's kind eyes, Kaisa felt a lump in her throat. Several times during the day, she'd been forced to explain to her family – her uncles, cousins and her grandmother – why Peter wasn't with her. But this time, fuelled by too many glasses of champagne and a couple of gin and tonics in the night club where the guests had moved to after waving the happy couple off, Pirjo's sympathy caught Kaisa unawares. She forced herself to breathe slowly. She didn't want to cry now, when she'd managed to keep herself in check while talking to her sister earlier.

Kaisa was saved by the bartender, a tall adolescent with straw-coloured messy hair and a strong Tampere accent.

'What will it be?'

After they'd got their drinks and were walking towards a snug in the vast cellar bar of the old hotel, reserved for the wedding party, Kaisa regretted the decision she and Peter had made to keep his Perisher course a secret for the time being. Because of the high failure rate, Peter had thought it best not to broadcast it far and wide. But now Kaisa wanted to tell Pirjo the good news, and also tell her how important Perisher was. Kaisa was so proud of Peter, and wanted to tell everyone. Now, a little drunk, she decided she was going to tell her mother. She touched Pirjo's back, 'Stop for a minute, will you?'

Pirjo's expression was one of pure surprise. They moved sideways to an empty table.

'What is it, Kaisa? Are you OK? Has something happened between you and Peter again? That's not why you are so emotional, and why he's not here?'

Kaisa put her gin and tonic onto the table.

'No, we're more than fine. It's just,' she hesitated for a moment and added, 'he's on this really important course to become a submarine captain. But you mustn't tell anyone because it's a really difficult course and many people fail.'

Pirjo's eye widened, 'Well, that's wonderful! You are going to be an English Captain's wife!'

Immediately after seeing her mother's face, Kaisa regretted telling her Peter's news. Now she'd be on the phone every week asking if Peter had been made a captain yet.

'Mum, it is really likely that he will not pass.'

'Nonsense, Peter will pass, you'll see!' Pirjo hugged her daughter and added, 'I think I'm going to get some champagne to celebrate!'

After the happy couple had retired to their wedding suite, the party went on until the small hours. Everyone toasted Peter in his absence and told Kaisa how fantastic it was that he was going to be a captain. Kaisa's efforts to say it was by no means a certainty were ignored.

Kaisa was taken onto the dance floor by her uncle, who, holding her tightly, danced a tango with her. Kaisa didn't think she'd remember the steps from her time with her old fiancé Matti, who loved all the old-fashioned Finnish dances, but to her surprise, in the firm grip of her uncle, she managed to relax and move around the floor competently.

'Not bad for an Englishwoman,' her uncle said and tipped his head in appreciation.

Next a cousin of hers, a lanky boy Kaisa hadn't seen since he was a shy teenager, took her into a Humppa, a fast dance that made Kaisa giggle. Back at the table, Kaisa had a long conversation with Raila, who told her she was working for Nokia, a local company that was moving into something called digital telephony. She'd studied engineering at Tampere University and sounded very impressive. Kaisa decided she'd been too fast to judge her cousins, and remembered that in Finland it took people a lot longer to talk about themselves. She felt like she was becoming someone else, more

English than Finnish, and felt a surge of sadness. But she brushed the feeling away when Raila pulled her to the dance floor once again. The whole group, except Mummu, who, Kaisa was surprised to see, was still sitting in the corner of the sofa, drinking a bright green concoction, had got up when Lambada came on. She laughed as the dance-floor filled with Finns dancing salsa. Her family and the whole of the nation were just a bit crazy.

16

When Kaisa finally arrived at the door of their terraced house in Notting Hill, after a long journey on the Tube from Heathrow, she was exhausted.

It was a hot, sticky late July afternoon, and the air over London seemed to stand still, suffocating Kaisa as she struggled to pull her suitcase along the hot pavement from Bayswater Tube station. She cursed her decision not to take a cab; she was covered in a thin layer of sweat and wanted a shower, but of course the hot water would take at least half an hour to heat up. She'd turned it all off before going away to Finland. For a moment, Kaisa wondered if the pipes might be hot enough from the day's sun for the shower to be lukewarm, and she decided to take her chance.

Afterwards, wrapped in a towel, she stretched out on the double bed in the bedroom, enjoying the faint breeze coming in through the open window. She thought about Peter and how much she wanted to be held by him. The longing for him was suddenly intense, almost a physical pain inside her chest.

Of course, he was up in Scotland, somewhere at sea, on the first part of the practical sea exercises of his Perisher course. Kaisa wondered if he was thinking of her at all. Would he, at the end of his turn at the periscope, doing whatever complicated exercises they did, lie down in his bunk and dream of her? She didn't think he did.

From the very first time she'd watched him prepare to go to sea, she'd seen the change in his eyes. They were living as a newly married couple in Portsmouth and he was packing his Pusser's Grip, a tattered light brown canvas holdall he always travelled with. After they'd said goodbye in the hallway, kissing each other for a long time, his expression changed, and he could no longer see Kaisa, his wife, nor feel any longing for her. Kaisa saw that his only thoughts were for his job, about the boat he was about to rejoin, about his fellow officers and crew, about his part in the large puzzle that was the Defence of the Realm. She, Kaisa, his wife, had only a small part to play in the huge machinery of the Navy, and that was to love him and look after him when he was at home, and to boost his morale with letters and the occasional telephone call when he was away. Of course, when he was on the Polaris nuclear subs, there was no contact from him for weeks, apart from the short messages Kaisa was able to send to him. Kaisa had no communication from Peter until they were back in Scotland.

In spite of the heat that was rising up from the garden through the open windows, Kaisa shuddered when she thought about the Familygrams. Even though she was a journalist, she was hopeless at writing the 50 words limit. The messages had to be positive and impersonal, yet give Peter confirmation that she still loved him and would be waiting for him when he got back from his eight-week patrol. The communications went through several hands, and Kaisa knew her words might even be read by the Captain.

During the latest patrol, it had become a little easier to pen the messages, even though Kaisa couldn't talk about the pregnancy – a secret they had decided to keep to themselves. As hard as it was to just write about her daily routines in London and her family, it was nowhere near as difficult as it had been to write the 50 words during those dark days in Helensburgh in the first months of their marriage.

That time, when she'd been so miserable without a job, without any meaning to her life, seemed like a lifetime away. Kaisa turned onto her side and tried to shrug away the guilt she felt about keeping the visit to Duncan and the AIDS test from Peter. She hoped he would forgive her for going to see her former lover. After all, Duncan was very ill. Possibly terminally. Kaisa could see that it was what Rose and Roger feared, and when Kaisa had visited Duncan herself, she understood even he had accepted that he might die. He'd hardly been awake during the two days Kaisa had spent in Dorset, but something in the way he'd thanked her for coming to see him, and asking if she had forgiven him, made Kaisa believe that he had accepted his fate. How awful it must be, Kaisa thought. She was glad, even though she regretted ever sleeping with the man, that she was able to bring him some peace with her visit. But would Peter see it that way?

Kaisa put her head into her hands. During the trip to celebrate Sirkka's wedding, Kaisa had pushed Duncan's illness to the back of her mind.

Kaisa wanted so badly to make Peter happy. That was the reason she wanted to give Peter a child, to show him how much she loved him, but she wasn't even able to do that. Even though she'd been lucky to escape the virus, she was already 30 years old, and soon it would be too late to have a baby. She heard Peter's voice in her head, 'Stop that maudlin.' Kaisa smiled. He said it was the Finn in her that looked at life in a pessimistic and dramatic way.

She knew she felt this way because the trip to Finland to celebrate her sister's wedding had been emotional. She'd enjoyed being in Tampere, but leaving her mother and Helsinki – she'd spent a couple of days after the wedding staying with Pirjo in her Töölö flat – had been even harder than usual.

On the last evening, over a meal of cold smoked salmon and salad, and a good bottle of Chardonnay that Pirjo had saved specially for her, Pirjo had raised the subject of Kaisa's father.

'He was looking quite good, although a little too fat.'

Nowadays Pirjo rarely mentioned her former husband, and although Kaisa had expected the subject to crop up, she was still surprised. She gazed at Pirjo, assessing how much she should say about her father.

'Yeah, he seemed OK. It was nice that you two could be there together.'

Pirjo took a sip of wine and said, 'I'll never forgive him for what he did to you over your wedding.'

Kaisa shrugged, 'I know, but I don't think about it anymore.'

Pirjo swallowed a piece of fish and said, 'To say he'd pay for it only if I wasn't there! That was just an excuse. He was always like that, promising the earth and then not delivering when it came to it. Thankfully I was able to step in.'

Kaisa reached her hand out and placed it on top of her mother's. Her flesh felt warm to the touch, although Kaisa noticed her mother's hand had become plumper as she'd grown older. 'I know and I'm very grateful.'

'No need to thank me, that's not what I meant.' Pirjo's eyes were steady on Kaisa. She turned her hand up and squeezed Kaisa's fingers. 'I know you've forgiven him, but just remember that you can't count on him.'

Kaisa took her hand away. 'Look, I know you didn't like seeing me hug dad outside the church, but it felt like old times. You know?'

'I just don't want him to hurt you again.' Pirjo's blue eyes were also full of tears.

'Oh, mum.'

Pirjo placed her knife and fork on her plate, stood up and walked around the table to hug her daughter. 'It'll be OK, you'll see.'

Kaisa knew she was talking about her lost babies. Neither of them had mentioned Kaisa's latest miscarriage, and Kaisa was grateful to her mother for being so reticent for once. Besides, she didn't want to discuss babies and pregnancies in case she let slip Sirkka's news. Kaisa knew her sister wanted to be the one to tell their mother. Suddenly she remembered something, 'Yes, especially if I take Mummu's garlic pills!'

Pirjo let go and looked down at Kaisa. She put her hand on her mouth and through her fingers said, 'She didn't, did she?'

Kaisa widened her eyes, 'Because you'd told her!'

'Sorry!' Pirjo said and began laughing. The pills Kaisa's grandmother took every day were legendary. She spent all her days pouring over health magazines and sending away for the latest crazy cure for anything.

'She gave me charcoal to reduce gas!' Pirjo said, still laughing. 'She thinks I have a problem!'

Both women were now giggling uncontrollably. After a while, they calmed down and her mother said, looking into Kaisa's eyes, 'I hate that you are so far away from me.' She wiped her eyes, and Kaisa didn't know if they'd become damp from laughing or crying.

'I know mum, but that's my life now. Besides, London isn't that far away,' Kaisa said, putting her arms around her mother and hugging her hard.

Lying on top of her bed, listening to the faraway sounds of the city, but feeling lonely, Kaisa thought of her mother and realised that Pirjo would be on her own in the block of flats in Helsinki after her sister moved away. Sirkka's marriage had probably made her feel a little abandoned.

17

K aisa woke with a start to the sound of the telephone downstairs. She'd fallen asleep on top of the bed, covered only by her towel. The view from the bedroom to the garden below was dark, and she saw it was well past ten o'clock as she hurried to put on her dressing gown while running down the stairs.

'I didn't think you were at home!'

Kaisa heard a hint of annoyance in Peter's voice.

'I was upstairs. I'd fallen asleep.'

'Sorry to wake you, but I wanted to see how your trip went.' Peter sounded a lot softer now.

'Don't be, it's lovely to hear your voice. I missed you in Finland.' Kaisa told Peter about the wedding, about Sirkka's pregnancy, and dancing with her uncles. Peter laughed when he heard how mad they'd gone for the salsa. She even told Peter about her grandmother's garlic pills.

'But what about you, how is it going?' Kaisa said.

Peter told Kaisa the first part of the course, held at the Faslane base, had gone 'OK'.

'Just OK?'

'Yeah. It's difficult to say. I haven't been drafted off the course yet anyway,' Peter said.

Kaisa could hear he was smiling. She knew he couldn't tell her details, but she was relieved he'd passed so far. She also knew she needed to be diplomatic in order to keep Peter's spirits up. There was another two months to go, with two tense times at sea.

'How are the other chaps? Do you know them?'

'Yes, of course. They're fine.' Peter was being deliberately short, so she knew he probably was within a hearing distance of the other Perishers, or other staff. 'Listen, I can come home the weekend after next. We're training ashore all next week, so I can get a late flight out on Friday.'

'Oh, darling, that's wonderful! I've got the weekend off too!'

Kaisa watched Ravi walk up the front garden towards her. They hadn't seen each other for a few weeks. With their work schedules, Kaisa's trip to Finland, and the virus hanging over her (and them), there hadn't been a day when they could get together. If she was truthful, Kaisa had avoided seeing him. The thought of having to tell him he might have AIDS, and talking about her seedy past, hadn't been an attractive proposition. Kaisa realised she'd wanted to deal with the possibility of an infection on her own. But now, with the danger over, she was glad to see her good friend again.

'What have you been up to?' Ravi said, his dark eyes on Kaisa.

Kaisa looked down at her hands, which were hugging a mug of coffee on the kitchen table, where they were sitting. She had never been able to keep anything from Ravi. Even when they had briefly been lovers, he had immediately seen how much she still loved Peter. Ravi had known this even before she had realised that she would never get over Peter. She'd been so close to telling him about the virus when they'd met before Sirkka's wedding, and now she was glad she hadn't worried Ravi in vain.

'Oh, Ravi,' she said, glancing at her friend. 'My past has been catching up with me.'

He laughed. She knew nothing would faze Ravi; he was aware of Duncan and how Kaisa had gone to bed with him, so she felt safe in telling him about the awful deadly virus, about the possibility of her having caught it, and about how ill Duncan was.

But when she'd finished her story, and looked up at Ravi, she saw his face was serious. His large brown eyes had widened, and he'd straightened his back. 'Oh my God,' he said, covering his mouth with his hand. 'Is he, Duncan I mean, OK?'

Kaisa shook her head and sighed, 'No, not really.'

'But you are?' he said with the same serious look in his eyes.

'Yes, the test was negative.' Kaisa gazed at her friend. 'But it was an awful time. All the bloody adverts with gravestones on them, and Freddie

Mercury looking so gaunt and horrible …' Kaisa sighed. 'I didn't tell you, or Peter, because I didn't want to worry you. And it was always very unlikely Peter would have carried the virus for five years without falling ill.'

Ravi was staring at Kaisa. His face looked angry now. 'You don't know that. Many people can carry the HIV virus and be absolutely fine.'

'Oh,' Kaisa said. How did Ravi know so much about it? 'How do you know, I mean …'

But Kaisa didn't have time to finish her sentence before Ravi got up and went to stand by the sink, facing the window, with his back to her. 'You are sometimes so bloody stupid, Kaisa!'

'What?' Kaisa said looking at Ravi's handsome slim frame. He was the perfect shape, with strong shoulders narrowing down into a slim waist, making an exemplary v-shape. He was still wearing his work suit, but he'd taken off his jacket as he sat down, revealing a light-blue striped cotton shirt with double cuffs and gold cufflinks at the wrists. He had a strong physique, and Kaisa could see the muscles in his arms and back tense as he stood holding the sink, leaning onto his arms. Suddenly he turned around and said, 'I'm gay, Kaisa.'

Kaisa could hardly concentrate on the news she had to write up on the Monday, even though there was a terrible story about the Unionist MP Ian Gow being killed by an IRA bomb that same morning. She knew she was being unprofessional, when she merely translated the Reuters' text of the news word for word, and added Mrs Thatcher's reaction, as well as a rather poignant quote from the MP's opponent, Labour Party leader Neil Kinnock on how Gow's only offence was to speak his mind. But she couldn't think about the IRA and terrorism without thinking about Peter and the kind of danger he was in, being part of the British armed forces. Unlike his best man and best friend, Jeff, Peter had never been posted to Northern Ireland, thank goodness. That and Duncan and now Ravi, there was just too much going on in her head to concentrate on her work. Which she knew she must do.

'On air in five,' a young summer intern with a mop of black hair and a lanky, slim body, shouted from the door. His face looked scared and Kaisa remembered that he'd only started the week she'd gone on holiday.

'Ok, got it,' Kaisa replied and forced a smile. The boy disappeared and Kaisa gathered her papers and walked out of the small cubicle that was the Finnish section office and into the recording studio.

As Kaisa waited for the green light of the studio turn red, her thoughts kept going to Ravi. How mad he'd been with her for some reason. He had left soon after their conversation about Duncan and his revelation, and when she'd tried to call him at home later, there had been no reply.

When he had told Kaisa he was gay, she had been so surprised that she'd blurted out, 'But, you and I, we had sex!'

Ravi had replied, drily, 'Well, yes, I have been trying to be 'normal', as some people put it, for years.' His face had been tense, his mouth closed and he had exchanged only a couple of words with Kaisa after that. He'd picked up his briefcase and left saying a simple, 'Goodbye Kaisa.' He hadn't even kissed her on the cheek as he usually did.

Kaisa didn't know what she had done wrong. How was she supposed to know? She decided she had to stop thinking about him, or Duncan, and concentrate on Peter. She'd soon have her husband in her bed again. She missed him so much, but at the same time, she was scared about all the secrets she was keeping from him. She must fix her mind on at least keeping him happy when everything else around her seemed to be falling apart.

18

There was a faint drizzle when Peter and the other three officers were waiting for their transport out to the submarine. It being a Sunday night, the Faslane base was quiet and Peter was the first one on the speedboat, nicknamed 'James Bond'. Another joke that the sailors in the submarine service enjoyed. Making fun of their profession was a way of showing the world how proud the men and women working in the Navy were of the senior service.

There were four of them on Perisher. Peter's old trusted friend, Nigel, had ended up on the same course as him, which had been a total surprise to them both. It was an equally good and bad turn of events. With the failure rate one in four, it meant that one of the men now huddled onboard James Bond would be leaving before it was all over. And failure of Perisher meant you'd never again be allowed onboard a submarine as an officer, or in any professional capacity whatsoever. Peter couldn't imagine life without submarines, so he'd decided not to think about it, but seeing his friend as one of the other Perishers, he realised it was highly likely one of them would receive that fate.

The other two men on the course, whom Peter had met at the start of the first lessons on the base, seemed very confident and knowledgeable.

One was a loud Aussie with a mop of bleached hair and incredible blue eyes, which looked azure against his tan, so unusual for a submariner, the colour of the Pacific. Peter didn't usually take any notice of men's looks, or even their eye colour, but this hunk of a guy stood out like a girl.

Talking over coffee between lessons, Peter and Nigel had decided he must be a pansy, but decided to keep that to themselves. It wasn't the done thing anymore to talk about people's sexuality in that way, which was a good thing, Peter supposed. Not that it had stopped Tony from making a comment on any female he met in the pub of an evening or in the mess during the day. It was his constant, over-eager talk about 'birds' and 'leg-overs' that had made Nigel and Peter suspicious. As long as he didn't hurt anyone, it was none of Peter or Nigel's business, was Peter's take on the guy. It didn't mean that he had to like him, though.

The fourth officer on the Perisher course was Ethan, a serious Canadian with an impressive comb-over. He was about five years older than the rest of them and was the only one of the four who had come through the ranks. Not having gone through the traditional officer training at Dartmouth gave the man a different demeanour; you could hear the Lower Decks in the way he spoke. But Peter liked him – his large shape and direct manner reminded Peter of his best mate, Jeff.

As James Bond cut through the dark water, bumping its way through the Cumbrae Gap, the shape of the sub they were going to join came suddenly into view, just as they arrived alongside.

'We'll be popular,' Nigel remarked to Peter as they waited to disembark. 'I bet the poor bastards would rather be in their warm beds with their wives,' he added, and Peter grinned.

Although an honour, crewing a sub serving as the teaching vessel for the Perishers, as the trainee officers were called, came with real work. And often, to make it harder for the Perishers, the training took place at times when the crew would otherwise be on leave, or they were called in at short notice. The Perisher would not only have to deal with the difficult technical tasks set for them by the course leader, or Teacher, but also with a poten-tially unhappy and tired crew.

Being the first to board James Bond, Peter was the last of the Perishers to jump onboard HMS *Ophelia*. The guy in charge of the submarine casing, called the Scratcher, guided everyone onboard. When it came to Peter he said, smiling, 'Watch your step, Sir, you don't want to take a dip.'

Peter stopped and stared at the Scratcher. Was that a jibe at his past? Since the fight in the pool with Duncan, the bastard who'd taken advantage of Kaisa, he'd heard them all; 'Bonking Boy', 'Giving Swimming Lessons?' and 'Taking a Dip?' or a 'Dive' were the most popular ones. In the darkness, Peter couldn't quite make out the man's face fully. He'd pulled his hand up into a salute, which hid his expression.

'Thank you Scratcher,' Peter said and quickly followed the other officers below.

In his bunk that night, Peter couldn't stop thinking about the next day. The Perisher sea trials were notoriously difficult, but he believed he'd prepared well. He'd revised all that he'd learned in the past few weeks, and he'd taken copious notes during the lectures. There wasn't anything there that he'd not remembered well. He knew his mental arithmetic was as good as the blonde Australian's, and the older Canadian's; only Nigel could just about beat him on that score – on a good day. But he couldn't help worrying that they'd bring up Kaisa and Duncan and the fight in the Faslane pool. Would the 'dit' have done the rounds in the boat when they heard he was one of the Perishers due to come onboard? Of course it would. Would he be taunted by his past in the control room the next day? As Peter stared at the bottom of the bunk on top of his, where he could hear Nigel's gentle snores, he resolved that he would let any remarks wash over him. *Wash over him!* That was an apt expression.

After five days at sea, during which each of the Perishers had done two or three turns at the periscope in the control room, Teacher announced it was time to go to the buoy and have a run-a-shore.

'Let's have a beer or two!' They headed for Brodick on the Isle of Arran, and disembarked the submarine. Teacher had arranged for the Perishers and crew to check into The Douglas Hotel, an impressive sandstone building jutting out behind the ferry port and jetty in the small Scottish island town.

The first beer tasted sweet, and each man downed his pint in seconds.

'Another round?' Nigel said, quicker than was healthy for any of them, Peter thought. He glanced at his friend, smiling.

'It's a run-a-shore, come on! And we're still all here. That's something to celebrate,' Nigel said.

Of course, the other three men nodded their assent.

Peter was tired, but also exhilarated. His trials had gone well; so far he'd made only one mistake in not attacking when he should have done. Instead, he'd taken the sub down to a safe depth, away from the oncoming frigate. But he'd seen all the other Perishers make similar small mistakes, and although he knew attacking was important, the safety of the submarine and crew was imperative. Besides, Teacher had told Peter that he was doing well. What's more, there had not been one comment about his past, and although he knew this was no guarantee it wouldn't come up later, it was a huge relief to him. Peter knew it was bound to come up at some point; he suspected Teacher might even instigate some reference to Peter's past to put pressure on him, but he was glad that at least for now, he wasn't the butt of the jokes in the control room as he'd feared. He'd also managed to phone Kaisa earlier in the evening to confirm the good news that he was coming home at the weekend. Peter leaned back on the wooden seat and allowed himself to think about her beautiful breasts. There were only five more days until he could have her warm body in his arms.

As Peter tipped the glass of his second pint, he was pretty satisfied with himself. He smiled at the barmaid, a blonde girl who had blushed when the four Perishers had entered the bar and Peter had ordered their first round of drinks. The girl was very pretty, and a few years younger than him. That felt good too; there was still some charm left in him.

When it was Tony's turn to get a round in, he persuaded the barmaid, in his loud Australian manner, to serve them the drinks at their table to save him having to go to the small bar. There were a few locals gathered around, with some of the sailors from the sub, but it wasn't exactly busy. Peter wondered if it ever was.

The girl, whose name, Katie, Tony had managed to wrangle out of her, brought four pints over on a tray. But as she bent over to place them on their table, she accidentally spilled a little on Peter's lap.

'Oh no, I'm so sorry,' she exclaimed and blushed.

'Don't worry,' Peter said, laughing. He began to brush his trousers, to get rid of the liquid before it had a chance to soak into his cords, and the girl also began rubbing his thigh with a tea towel.

'Let me,' she said, bending down. Suddenly her cleavage was inches from Peter's face. She was wearing a tight black top, and Peter got a scent of dried flowers – roses. He tried to turn his head away from the soft, milky white skin. He could clearly see the top of the girl's breasts, and thought he even saw the pink shade of her areola. He lifted his eyes and saw she was looking at him. Her eyes were a pale green colour, and he noticed that her hair was really strawberry blonde, almost ginger. A whistle from Tony made him turn around. Quickly, he lifted himself up.

'No harm done,' he said and pulled his lips into a polite smile. What was he doing flirting with a barmaid? Get a grip, he thought and sat down again, not looking at Tony or the girl. The barmaid, Katie, now even more red in the face, moved away, muttering 'Sorry.'

'It's fine,' Peter said, trying to smile in a polite, and not at all flirtatious way.

When the girl had gone back to her station behind the bar, Peter turned to Nigel, 'So, did you get hold of Pammy?'

'Wow, wow, wow!' Tony said instead, ignoring Nigel. He got up and patted Peter on the back, 'You're in there, mate.'

'She's a good-looking lass,' Ethan said. He lifted his pint up, 'Enjoy it while it lasts; you'll soon become invisible to that kind of totty.' Ethan was grinning, stroking the few hairs on top of his head, which were neatly arranged in an attempt to cover the large bald patch.

'Not me, I'm a happily married man,' Peter said, glancing at Nigel, then lifting his pint and smiling at Ethan and Tony in turn. 'So be my guest, Tony,' he added, lifting his eyebrows and nodding at Nigel.

Nigel looked down at his pint and tried to suppress a smile.

For a moment no one spoke. Finally Tony, looking flustered, and addressing Peter, said, 'Not what I heard, mate.'

Peter stared at the Aussie.

'That's enough, Tony,' Nigel said. Peter's friend was speaking while shaking his head, without looking in Tony's direction.

Ethan was sitting still, watching Peter. *He knows too*, Peter thought.

No one spoke for a moment.

'To answer your question, Peter. Yes, I did get hold of Pammy and she sends her love. Can't wait to see her and the girls,' Nigel said, breaking the silent tension.

But the Aussie wouldn't let it be. 'You might as well, don't you think, Bonkie?'

Peter looked at Tony. Then he forced a smile. That nickname had enraged him each time he'd heard it after the Court Martial, and even though he'd got used it, it still hurt. But he needed to keep his head.

'Tony,' Nigel said. There was a warning in Peter's friend's voice.

'I mean, your wife is probably at it as we speak?'

Peter looked down at his beer and tried to concentrate on his breathing. He didn't trust himself to look at Tony or Nigel, or Ethan for that matter.

Suddenly, after what seemed to Peter like several minutes, he felt Nigel's hand on his shoulder. Then he heard a forced laughter from his friend. 'You're not married are you, Tony?'

'No, mate, don't need the trouble!' Tony replied. Peter was newly annoyed by the arrogance in his loud voice.

Peter lifted his head. Keeping his eyes steadily on Tony's, he said, 'So why don't you see if you can have a go at our lovely barmaid yourself then, Tony? I'm sure she'll not be able to resist your Aussie charms.' Peter glanced at Nigel, who was sitting next to him.

Tony shifted in his seat and brushed back his golden locks. 'Nah, I think I'll try to get into my bunk early tonight. It's been a tough week, eh?' His tone was more conciliatory now.

'Perhaps she's not your type?' Peter continued, even though he saw that Nigel gave him a look of warning.

'What do you mean, mate?'

Peter took a swig out of his beer, 'Well, perhaps you fancy a girl who's got a slimmer figure, a flatter chest and perhaps a bit more down there, you know?' Peter pointed towards Tony's crutch.

At these words, Tony got up and slammed his now empty pint onto the table. 'Look here ...'

But he didn't have time to finish his sentence. They saw the large, now all too familiar shape of Teacher approach the far corner of the bar where they were sitting.

'How are we doing? Can I get you a round?' the man, with his bulky, authoritative shape was looking at each Perisher in turn.

Tony had sat back down and now said, 'Yes, thank you, Sir, very kind.'

The others, including Peter, murmured their thanks and as Teacher left them to order the drinks, Nigel spoke. 'Listen you two. I don't need to tell you how stupid you are being, do I? Stuff like that could get you both thrown out in a jiffy, and that's not what either of you want now, is it?'

Peter looked at his friend. It was as if Teacher had just thrown cold water over Peter's head and woken him up to the real world. *I'm being stupid. As stupid as I was when I started that bloody fight with Duncan all those years ago. I'm better than this bloody Aussie.*

Peter emptied his glass and glanced across the table at the Australian. Lifting his empty pint up, he said, 'No hard feelings, eh?'

'Yeah, right,' Tony said and got up. 'Any idea where the heads are?'

Nigel pointed Tony towards the men's loos, took a deep breath, and leaned back onto the sofa.

'Well, I'd better give Teacher a hand at the bar,' Ethan said and got up.

'What the hell?' Nigel said to Peter when the older man was out of hearing distance. His face was inches from Peter's and his eyes black with anger. 'What the fuck did you think you were doing?'

'Yeah, I know, I shouldn't have, but everyone knows he's a poofter and that stuff about Kaisa really got to me.' Peter replied.

'Well don't let it. Calling him out won't do you any good whatsoever. Besides, what does it really matter anymore?' Nigel finished the dregs of his beer, and seeing Teacher and Ethan approach with the refills, said, 'Get your head straight, Peter, or I'll throw you overboard myself.'

.   .   .

When Peter and the other Perishers got back to the base at Faslane, after another gruelling week at sea, they immediately headed for the Back Bar. Peter knew Nigel was expected at home at the Smuggler's Way married patch, where he'd moved his family just days before the start of the Perisher course. But he'd agreed to one pint with Peter, who had to wait until the next morning to fly back to Kaisa in London. While chatting, the two men were approached by an old engineering mate of theirs called Bernie. Peter greeted the man, now almost completely grey, and asked if he would like a refill of his empty pint of beer.

'Sure,' he replied and settled himself between Nigel and Peter.

Peter ordered another round and they toasted each other.

'How's it going?' Bernie asked, presumably meaning Perisher. Peter nodded and Nigel said, 'Haven't sunk a single submarine or ship yet, so that's a positive.'

The all laughed at the joke, and then asked after each other's wives. The women had lived in the married quarters when the three men served in HMS *Restless*. Peter looked down at his glass, thinking Bernie didn't bring back good memories.

'I wanted to tell you before you heard it through the grapevine,' Bernie suddenly said, leaning towards Peter and lowering his voice.

Peter looked at the engineer. His eyes had gone grey too, to match his thinning hair. He had a few years on Peter, perhaps five, and made Peter think, *Do I look that old too?* He'd noticed that his own hair was becoming more salt than pepper. An image of his father, who now had a mop of pure white hair, flashed through Peter's mind.

'Duncan has passed away.'

'Excuse me?' Peter said, thinking he hadn't heard right.

'Oh my God. What happened?' Nigel asked. He placed his pint on the bar and glanced along it to see where the steward serving behind the bar was. Luckily he was wiping glasses at the far end, while watching a small TV set fixed onto the corner of the room.

'Well, he died of pneumonia, but it was really ...' Bernie glanced around and leaned in to whisper to the two men, 'AIDS.'

Peter stared at Bernie, unable to say anything. Duncan had AIDS! Duncan was a shirt-lifter? That couldn't be! Why, in that case, would he have gone after Kaisa? Kaisa! Peter put his hand over his mouth, placed his pint on the bar and steadied himself with his hand.

.   .   .

'What the hell, Kaisa?'

Kaisa took a deep breath. She could hear Peter had been drinking. When he'd first phoned her and told her the terrible news about Duncan, Kaisa had been quiet. She'd had the phone call from Rose the night before and had shed a few tears for poor Duncan over the phone with her friend. Soon Peter had realised that Kaisa already knew, and had known for some time about Duncan's condition.

'I didn't want to tell you because …'

'Yes, now, what would the reason be?' Peter said. 'I am extremely interested to hear it!' He was whispering loudly down the phone. She knew he was worried about being overheard. His strangled whispering sounded so angry that Kaisa didn't know what to say. Not since the aftermath of the fight with Duncan had Peter been so livid with her.

'Because I knew you'd be like this,' Kaisa said quietly.

Peter didn't reply.

'But I told you, I'm not HIV positive, and neither will you be.'

'Well, I'm glad to hear it,' Peter said, now using his normal voice. 'It might have been prudent of you to let me know about this whole affair a bit sooner!' he said drily in a loud voice, no longer caring who in the wardroom might hear him.

'Can we talk about this when you're back at home?' Kaisa said, in what she hoped was a conciliatory tone.

'OK,' Peter said and hung up. He hadn't even told her what flight he was booked on the next morning.

Kaisa went into the lounge, flicked the telly on and tried to calm down. The ten o'clock news was just about to start and the gongs of Big Ben rang in her ears and jangled her nerves.

She stood up, turned the sound down and sat back on the sofa. Kaisa took a deep breath and exhaled slowly. It was as if all the sneaking around, the relief over the negative test result months before and the new grief for Duncan hit her at the same time. She understood why Peter was angry; she'd been angry herself when Rose had told her about the AIDS virus.

Even at the best of times, Kaisa hated these rows they had over the telephone. You could never really hear what the other was saying, let alone thinking. She knew she should have told Peter earlier about Duncan and the possibility of her carrying the virus. She knew it was a big deal, especially as she was trying for a baby, however much Rose had tried to convince her that it was highly unlikely she would have contracted it five years ago. She'd told Kaisa that Duncan hadn't been sleeping around that much when he was in the Navy, not compared with afterwards. Kaisa had no idea you could get AIDS if you weren't gay, which Rose insisted Duncan wasn't.

But she also knew that she'd kept a huge secret from her husband, while he was still on Perisher and needed to concentrate on the course. Just thinking about having to tell the whole sorry story to Peter set her heart pounding. It had been right not to tell Peter about the test and the possibility that Kaisa – and Peter – might be infected with AIDS, but at the same time, keeping such a huge secret had been dishonest.

Kaisa put her head into her hands. And now Duncan had died. At least she had seen him, and even though she hadn't actually spoken to him much, because he had been so poorly and struggling to breathe, let alone have a conversation, she believed those few words, and the fact that she'd told Duncan she'd forgiven him, made him understand that she still cared for him as a friend. If only she could make Peter see that.

But her thoughts quickly returned to Rose. Getting up again, she dialled her friend's number. She waited for several rings, but there was no answer. Then she looked at her watch and realised it was too late to call anyone and replaced the receiver on its hook. Poor Rose would be organising the funeral, she thought, and Kaisa suddenly knew she wanted to go. She decided to write her friend a note. She picked up some blue Basildon Bond paper and the fountain pen Peter always used for official Navy correspondence, and began to write.

19

Peter looked tired when he stepped out of the black cab outside their house on Chepstow Place. He hadn't shaved and his jaw was dark with stubble, making him look like an old sea dog, which Kaisa supposed he was. He was carrying his battered, old Pusser's Grip. The cream coloured canvas of the holdall had dark patches at the corners.

Kaisa wanted to run to him and put her arms around Peter's neck, but she wasn't sure how angry he was. Besides, the neighbours might see her and she knew how he hated that kind of public show of emotion, so she stood at the door and smiled at him while Peter took the few steps along the front garden.

It only took one look, and she was in his warm embrace. She could tell he'd forgiven her and had really missed her, this time by the force of his arms around her and the way he pressed his hips against hers.

'Take your skis off first,' Kaisa joked.

'What?' Peter pulled back and stared down at Kaisa.

Close up, she could see his eyes were bloodshot and the stubble on his chin was older than just one day's growth.

'Oh, an old Finnish joke. The soldiers coming home from the Winter War didn't take their skis off before ...'

Peter closed the door behind him and, taking her hand, pulled her up the stairs.

. . .

Afterwards they lay in each other's arms listening to the evening chorus of the birds in the garden.

Peter took Kaisa's face between his hands and kissed her lips. 'I've missed you.'

'I gathered,' Kaisa smiled and laid her head on Peter's shoulder.

They were both quiet for a moment. Then, because she knew she must broach the subject, Kaisa, choosing her words carefully, said, 'I'm sorry, but I didn't want you to worry while you were on Perisher ...'

Kaisa could feel Peter's body tense underneath her. She wondered if she'd made a mistake talking about it now, so soon after their love-making.

Peter lifted himself up, and sat at the edge of the bed, his back to Kaisa. His shoulder lifted as he inhaled deeply and let the air out slowly.

'OK, let me have the whole story,' he said.

'Can you look at me, Peter, please?'

Her husband turned his head around and Kaisa, grabbing the duvet, climbed over to sit next to him. She wrapped some of it over Peter, and sitting like that, side by side, Kaisa told him the whole sorry tale of how Rose had broken the news of the virus, and how she had taken the test, nervously waited for it, while keeping Peter in the dark. She also told him about Duncan, and how ill he'd been, and how he'd asked to see her.

'And you went,' Peter said, lifting his head and looking directly at Kaisa. His eyes were sad, and his face had a resigned look.

'Yes.'

'Right,' Peter said.

'I'm sorry, but now he's gone, I'm glad I did,' Kaisa said, looking down at her hands.

Peter was quiet and Kaisa was afraid to say anymore. Whatever she had imagined, the many scenarios of how she was going to tell Peter everything, none of it was as bad as his silence was now.

Peter shifted a little and Kaisa imagined he was gong to get up and leave her there, hanging, too angry to speak to her. Instead, he put his arms around Kaisa and said into her ear, 'I agree.'

Kaisa's relief was palpable. It was as if a great weight that had been pressing down on her chest had been lifted off. She searched Peter's mouth and was surprised to find that there were tears running down his face. She'd never seen him cry before.

'Oh, Peter, I'm so sorry.'

'No, I should be sorry. You poor darling, having to keep all of this from me, and then I act like a complete ass.'

They kissed for a long time, and then hugged each other, Kaisa rocking Peter on the edge of the bed.

'It's OK,' she kept saying over and over.

After lying in bed for what seemed like hours, Kaisa put her head on Peter's shoulder and said, 'Are you now going to tell me how it's going?'

Peter got up and began searching for his cigarettes. As he looked in the pockets of his trousers, Kaisa admired his tall, muscular back, but noticed that there was a tiny bit of loose fat around his hips that she hadn't noticed before. *We're both getting older,* she thought. *Soon it'll be too late for us to have a child.*

'So?' she said when Peter had got back into bed, sitting up against the pillows, smoking his cigarette.

'It's hard, but I think I'm doing OK,' Peter said, blowing the smoke away from Kaisa and out of the window he'd cracked open after finding the packet of Marlboros in his Pusser's Grip.

'You'll soon have to give that up when you're with me, if I ...'

Peter put his arm around Kaisa's shoulders and kissed the top of her head. 'I know, Peanut.' He straightened himself up and said, 'Are we trying again? I didn't think ... should I have worn a jacket?'

Kaisa smiled, 'No, that's fine, we can try again. It's been three months.'

Peter stubbed out his cigarette on a saucer he'd found on the bedside table and turned his face towards Kaisa's. He took her hand between his and said, 'Are you sure?'

Kaisa looked down at Peter's hands. His fingers were long, and there were a few dark hairs between the knuckles and on the back of the hand. Her own hands between his looked small and childlike.

'I'm fine; besides, it's been more than three months.' Kaisa smiled at Peter and he grinned back. 'We'll just have to make this weekend count then, won't we?'

He took Kaisa into his arms once again and kissed the back of her neck.

It wasn't until they were having breakfast the next morning that Kaisa felt she could broach the subject of Duncan's funeral.

'I spoke to Rose,' Kaisa said. She'd phoned Kaisa back an hour after she'd finished the letter. Rose had been tearful, and upset, but had told Kaisa that she and Peter would be more than welcome to attend the service, which was to be held at their local church on Saturday.

'The funeral is tomorrow. We might want to go? You don't need to go back until Sunday, and we could drive there and back in a day?'

Peter sat at the table, with the *Telegraph* open on his lap, 'You are serious?' He looked at Kaisa with an expression that she couldn't decipher.

Kaisa looked at her hands, 'You were at Dartmouth together. And friends, until …'

Peter was gazing at her. 'You never told me what he said when you saw him.'

Kaisa lifted her head and looked directly at her husband. 'He was really too ill to speak. He had pneumonia and struggled to breathe, let alone talk.' She felt her voice falter and tears prick her eyes. 'But he asked for my forgiveness and I said that I had forgotten about it long ago.'

Peter got up and put his arms around Kaisa. 'That must have been awful.'

Kaisa let herself cry then, tears that she had been holding back for what seemed like months.

'Rose said we should go, "For a show of absolution all around",' Kaisa said, quoting her friend between sobs.

Peter put his hand on Kaisa's chin and lifted her face up to his. He wiped her tears away with a tissue and said, 'Is that what you really want?'

'I think it's the right thing to do,' Kaisa replied.

20

T he church was a small, ancient building with a lychgate. In the graveyard, the old stone headstones were covered with moss and leaning this way and that.

Kaisa and Peter joined the queue of people making their way slowly along a narrow path leading to the entrance. Kaisa saw Rose standing there, with Roger and another, older man, who looked a little like Duncan. She presumed this was Duncan's uncle. Two women, about the same age as Rose, stood on the opposite side of the door. One had a mop of blonde hair swept back in a stylish chignon, the other a short bob, also blonde. Kaisa guessed these were Duncan's other cousins. The hair and facial features of the two women reminded Kaisa of Duncan, while his uncle had the same tall frame, and hunched his shoulders in the same manner. Kaisa shivered and squeezed closer to Peter, slipping her arm in the crook of his.

'You OK?' Peter said and placed his hand on the sleeve of Kaisa's black blazer.

Kaisa looked up at his face and nodded. She was already fighting tears and the service hadn't even started yet.

When it was their turn to greet Duncan's family, Rose made the introductions, saying Peter and Kaisa were 'friends from Duncan's Navy days.' There was a flicker of recognition at the mention of their surname in the face of the woman with the short bob, but the women both just muttered, 'Thank you for coming,' shaking their hands briefly before moving onto the person behind them.

Kaisa and Peter found a seat at the back of the church. A short while after they'd settled down, Rose came up and whispered to Kaisa, 'There's food and drinks at the pub opposite afterwards. I'd be very glad if you could stay?'

'We'll see,' Kaisa said and glanced sideways at Peter. Rose nodded, and Kaisa squeezed her friend's hand, 'You OK?' Rose pulled her mouth into a smile, but Kaisa could see there were tears forming in her eyes. 'See you later, perhaps?' Rose said and made her way towards the front of the small church.

It was a brief service, and Kaisa was struck how, instead of mourning the recently passed, as was the custom in Finland, the aim seemed to be to celebrate the life of the deceased. Rose spoke beautifully about her 'infuriatingly charming' cousin, something Kaisa could recognise. She was thinking back to when she had seen him a few weeks before, lying in the bed, still smiling at her when she'd said goodbye to him. Had he known he was close to death then?

Duncan's uncle said a few words about how his nephew had become a brilliant farmer, and how he loved the land he'd been raised on. Kaisa tried to remember if his parents were alive, because there wasn't anyone of that age group, apart from his uncle, sitting in the front pews. She presumed they were either too distraught or too old to attend the funeral.

Kaisa's thoughts went back to Matti's funeral, which she now believed she should never have attended. She couldn't comprehend that this was the second funeral of a man she'd been intimate with. Was it something to do with her? Was she the kiss of death? Kaisa shrugged away such stupid thoughts. Today was nothing to do with her. It was all to do with poor Duncan and forgiveness. Thinking of forgiveness, during the last hymn, as the coffin was carried out of the church, she glanced over at Peter. On the way up to the little village outside Sherborne, they hadn't said much and Kaisa wondered how Peter was feeling. She guessed he might have changed his mind about going to the funeral.

When the mourners started to make their way out of the church, Kaisa whispered into Peter's ear. 'Rose said there would be food and drinks at the pub opposite. What do you think?'

Peter moved his head away from Kaisa and lifted his dark eyes towards her. 'Don't think that's appropriate, do you?'

'No,' Kaisa said and lowered her head. They waited until the church was almost empty before making their way to the car, which was parked outside the village shop. As soon as Peter pulled onto the main road, the heavens opened and a sheet of rain hit the road in front of them. Large drops of water bounced off the bonnet of the car and the tarmac, making it difficult to see through the windscreen. Peter flicked the wipers on full and switched the headlights on, but it was no use.

'Pull over there,' Kaisa said, seeing a lay-by ahead.

'Bloody hell,' Peter said as he turned off the engine and they heard the sound of the rain pound like machine-gun fire off the roof of the car.

Kaisa turned on her seat and placed a hand on Peter's knee. 'Thank you for coming today. I know it was difficult.'

'Not the most enjoyable day of my life, that's true,' Peter replied, placing his hand on top of Kaisa's. 'But I'm glad we came.' He leaned over and kissed Kaisa on the mouth.

The rain stopped as suddenly as it had started and Peter pulled back onto the road. After a few moments they could see a rainbow in the distance. Kaisa looked at the profile of her husband, and thought how lucky she was. Then she thought about Ravi, who hadn't called since they'd had their fight, if that's what it could be called.

'Peter,' she began, while he was waiting to enter a roundabout leading to the M3.

'Yes, my Peanut, what is it?' He glanced quickly at Kaisa, and then turned his attention to the traffic again.

Kaisa waited until they were cruising along the motorway.

'Ravi told me something the other day.'

'Oh, yes?' Peter said absentmindedly. He was now fiddling with the radio, trying to find a music station.

'He's gay.'

'Bloody hell!'

'Yeah, I know. I told him about Duncan and he got all funny and then just said, "Kaisa, I'm gay." Just like that.'

'When was this?'

Kaisa bit her lip. She hadn't thought this through.

Peter glanced at her again, this time his eyes had turned dark. 'You told him before you told me, didn't you?'

Kaisa was looking out of the window. The rain had left the road wet, with spray making it look slippery and dangerous. 'Slow down, you're doing nearly 90!' she said.

'Don't change the subject,' Peter said but brought the speed down to nearer 70 miles per hour.

'OK, I did tell him before you, but only by a few weeks.'

'It doesn't matter if it was an hour before! I can't believe you. I thought we'd agreed: no more secrets!'

Kaisa felt close to tears, but tried to keep hold of herself.

'I was so lonely, and I had to tell someone. I didn't want to breathe a word of it at work, naturally, not something you'd talk about there, but when Ravi came over to the house, out of the blue, one evening, well I just couldn't ...'

Kaisa saw how Peter's mouth was in a straight line and he was staring at the road ahead. He put the indicator on and pulled out into the middle lane, overtaking a string of three cars. Spray formed in front of them and for an awful moment they couldn't see out of the windscreen, until the wipers began their sweeping motion across the glass. Again Kaisa noticed Peter was speeding, but she didn't dare say anything. He was taking out his anger on the road, and she hoped to God he'd calm down soon.

They spent the rest of the journey in silence, apart from when Kaisa asked Peter if he wanted to stop off for fish and chips as they got close to home. Peter nodded and soon they were parking the car a few steps away from their front door, carrying the delicious-smelling bag inside.

Kaisa arranged the food on plates and looked at Peter across the kitchen table. 'Look, darling, I didn't do it to spite you, or hurt you. You know I get lonely when you are away. Plus I didn't want to tell you all of this when I knew you needed to concentrate on Perisher.'

Peter lifted his head and sighed. 'I know.'

Kaisa walked around the table and went to hug her husband. 'I love you.'

Peter stroked Kaisa's hair, 'I know and I love you too. I think I'm a bit more stressed about the course than I realise.'

Kaisa pressed herself closer to Peter, nuzzling his neck. 'We'd better eat before it gets cold,' Kaisa said, but Peter had bent down and was kissing Kaisa. She could feel herself melt in his arms and desire rise inside her.

'Let's go upstairs,' Peter said hoarsely and almost carried Kaisa up the bedroom.

He peeled Kaisa's clothes off and pulled her knickers off, kneeling in front of her. Kaisa sighed and before she knew it, Peter was holding her legs and entering her, his eyes fixed on hers.

'You make me wild with desire, Kaisa,' he said and bent down to kiss her neck, breasts and mouth.

Before Peter left the house late on Sunday, they kissed and hugged for a long time. Kaisa was sad to be saying goodbye to him, she'd never get used to it, but it wasn't as bad as when he was about to go on a long patrol.

'I'll get a weekend off again soon,' Peter said, and brushed a strand of hair that had escaped from the ponytail Kaisa had fashioned, out of her face.

Kaisa smiled, 'Be careful, I might just get used to having you around.'

'Wouldn't that be something,' Peter replied. 'But honestly, I know I shouldn't say it, but I do have a good feeling about the future.' He placed his hand on Kaisa's belly.

Kaisa glanced down at his hand, then at Peter's face. 'Oh, darling, don't jinx it.'

Peter gave Kaisa a peck on her cheek and whispered into her ear, 'We've certainly given it a go this weekend. What you did to me this morning, I'm getting hard just thinking about it.'

Kaisa blushed, she'd still not got used to talking openly about what they did in the privacy of their bedroom.

When Peter saw her face reddening, he squeezed her tightly against himself. 'Oh, darling, there's no need to be embarrassed. I love when you're passionate like that. Or didn't you notice?'

'Don't tease me,' Kaisa laughed, trying to shake off her discomfort. She knew it was silly, but she guessed it was the Finn in her. At home, you didn't talk about sex openly, if at all.

In bed that night, Kaisa thought that everything was at last going right. Peter's words had echoed what she herself felt. She also had a good feeling about the future. She wondered if there was a little baby growing inside of her already, but immediately decided to cast such thoughts aside. She didn't want to put an adverse spell on any future pregnancy either.

21

'Well, well, Mrs Williams, it is indeed good news. Congratulations!'

Kaisa gazed at her doctor. His grey wisps of hair were a little longer today, showing off his unusually pale eyes. Kaisa wondered absentmindedly if they'd been blue when he was younger.

'Thank you, Dr Harris,' Kaisa replied and smiled. She'd been smiling to herself for weeks now. Although it was good to have the confirmation from her GP, she'd known before she came into the surgery that she was pregnant. This was the fourth time, so by now she recognised the signs. Exactly ten days after Peter had returned to the base and his Perisher course, Kaisa had gone off coffee. Then, she'd had the familiar metallic taste in her mouth, and a few days later, the final confirmation when she couldn't face breakfast in the morning. Her breasts had been sore right after Peter had gone, but she had thought that might have been because of all the sex they'd had. They'd made love several times a day over the weekend. It was as if the closeness of death had made them want to confirm that they were alive. Besides, she'd had an ulterior motive, which she was sure Peter knew was the reason she kept pulling him – very willingly – into bed. After all they'd discussed, after all the lies she'd confessed to, Peter still looked happier than she'd seen him in a long while when he said goodbye to her on the steps of their home.

Kaisa had taken a pregnancy test as soon as her period was a day late, and the little blue line had been clear on the stick. But she tried not to think about it until she had confirmation from her GP. Still, she couldn't help the utter feeling of happiness and fulfilment she had. She tried to keep fear out of her mind too, and for some reason, she was succeeding in not thinking the worst.

'So, because of your, hmm, history,' the doctor glanced at Kaisa's face, probably expecting her to dissolve into a flood of tears any moment. When he saw Kaisa smiling, he continued, visibly relieved, 'Yes, as I was saying, because of your recent terminations, we are able to offer you a course of treatment to ensure a successful pregnancy, hopefully right up to full term.'

'Oh,' Kaisa said. She'd heard from Pammy, her friend on the naval base in Faslane who had also suffered several miscarriages, that after three 'terminations' as the GP called her miscarriages, the NHS would offer some treatment or other. But she had no idea this treatment was offered automatically, or that is was something old Dr Harris would even know about. She assumed this time they'd just monitor her more closely.

'What do you mean by 'treatment' exactly?'

'Hormones,' the GP said. 'This is quite a new thing, but since you've terminated around the same time each pregnancy, I think it may be caused by a dip in your progesterone level and we can address that.' The man was looking at a brown folder, and not at Kaisa.

Kaisa stared at the doctor. Had he known the reason for the miscarriages all along? At first, she'd been convinced it was the nuclear reactor Peter worked so close to, or the AIDS virus. Almost every waking hour of the past few months, nearly a year, she'd wondered what the reason for her inability to keep hold of a baby could be. And here her doctor was, looking at the answer in her notes.

When there was no reaction from his patient, Dr Harris looked up at Kaisa. 'So we have two options. Either you will proceed with this pregnancy without our intervention and hope for the best, or we begin the treatment immediately.'

'What ... what is the treatment?' Kaisa said, stammering a little. She couldn't take in the news that there was a simple fix for her inability to keep hold of a baby. Just like that! She wished Peter was there with her. She wanted him to hold her hand now and ask sensible questions. In Kaisa's mind, only anger whirled, making her unable to utter a word. How could she ask her old GP why, if he'd already diagnosed the problem she had with losing babies, hadn't he told her before? Without coming across rude. The nights she'd spent wondering why her body had rejected the foetus, while all along this man had known the reason!

She looked out of the bay window of the surgery and saw normal people walking outside, doing their usual, everyday things. She noticed for the first time that the wide, beige-coloured vertical blinds, which were half open, looked shabby and faded. She was jolted back into the room when her GP spoke.

'Right, Mrs Williams, it is a 20-week course of injections. You will need to come to the surgery once a week. A nurse will administer the injection.' Dr Harris leaned forward on his chair and looked in Kaisa's eyes. 'This is a new treatment, and we cannot be sure that it works for each patient.'

Kaisa nodded, although she had a feeling that she wasn't in the room, but floating above it. She put her hands down on the chair, making sure she was sitting down properly, and took a couple of deep breaths in and out.

'Are you alright, Mrs Williams?' The GP's expression was full of concern.

'Could I have a glass of water?'

'Of course.' The old GP got to his feet and poured a glassful from a carafe on his desk. He watched as Kaisa sipped the water and placed the glass back onto the leather-covered surface.

Kaisa blinked and said, 'Yes, I understand. Injections once a week?'

'Is that OK?'

Suddenly Kaisa thought of something, 'I work shifts at the BBC. Does it have to be a certain day of the week?'

Dr Harris gazed at Kaisa. He tilted his head slightly and said, 'If you like we can leave your pregnancy to develop naturally, and, if you lose the baby again, try it next time?'

'No, let's do it now,' Kaisa said firmly and tried to smile. She was finally beginning to feel herself again.

'Excellent, I think that is a good decision. And I'm afraid you will have to have it the same day each week. But I'm sure your employer will understand?'

Kaisa nodded.

'Can I ask you something, Dr Harris?' Kaisa said after the doctor had told her to go back to the reception and wait for the nurse to call her.

'Of course, what is it?'

'Did you know all along that it was this hormone, pro ...' Kaisa struggled with the pronunciation. 'Did you know the lack of it was the reason for all the previous miscarriages?'

Dr Harris hesitated, 'No, not really. I have a colleague, Dr Chishty, who advised me that this may be the problem. She is specialising in women's medicine and has been studying the cause of early miscarriages.'

'I see,' Kaisa said. She stood facing Dr Harris, her hand on the door handle.

'So you're lucky we have Dr Chishty at our disposal here,' Dr Harris said and smiled. Then, becoming serious, he added, 'But don't forget, there's no guarantee that it will work.'

22

Peter was snoozing in his bunk, trying to catch a few zzz's before he was due to have his session with Teacher in the control room, when Nigel came into the wardroom and nudged his shoulder.

'Ethan's off.'

'What?' Peter got up quickly and saw the Canadian standing in the gangway. His shoulders were slumped and he was looking down at his cap, which he held in one hand. Tony was next to him, patting his shoulder.

'Sorry, to see you go, mate,' he said and Peter could hear the genuine feeling in the throaty way his words came out. He realised how close they all had grown during the past couple of months. At that moment, Peter felt he almost liked the loud Australian.

When Peter and Nigel shook Ethan's hand, he could see the man's eyes look watery, and for a moment he wondered if he was going to cry. Then they saw Teacher's steward behind Ethan, carrying his canvas holdall. 'This way, Sir,' he said, nodding to the remaining Perishers to get out of their way. He ushered Ethan towards the conning tower.

Ethan's failure after only three days at sea came as a huge blow to all the other Perishers. All three remaining officers crowded into the small wardroom and sat in silence around the central table. They heard James Bond running empty alongside, but no one commented on its sudden appearance.

Eventually, Tony spoke up. 'He made another mash of his calculations this evening. Teacher had to take charge of the sub, and that was one time too many.'

It seemed the older man hadn't been able to keep up with the mental arithmetic.

Peter shook his head at Tony, but said nothing.

'I'll miss him,' Nigel said, and then added, 'but that's the name of the game, eh, chaps?'

Peter and Tony nodded.

A senior rating popped his head through the door, and addressing Peter said, 'Sir, you are required in the control room.'

'Thank you, I'll be right there.'

Peter got up and fetched his stop-watch from his bunk and put it around his neck. He took a deep breath and focused on what he needed to do. He had to concentrate on the forthcoming exercises and forget about Ethan and his departure. For one thing, it meant that if the statistics were anything to go by, the three remaining Perishers were safe. Wasn't it one in four that generally failed? Peter shook his head; he mustn't think that either. Teacher had made it very clear to them that every Perisher could fail. What mattered was that those who passed had both the aptitude and the leadership skills, as well as the technical ability to captain one of Her Majesty's submarines. If there was any doubt in Teacher's mind that something was amiss with any of them, they'd be escorted off. If the Perisher couldn't ignore jibes about a past event in a naval base pool with a fellow officer, for example. Or jokes about the honour of the candidate's wife.

Peter wondered if Duncan's death had filtered through to the crew. What would they say if they knew he'd attended the funeral? Peter hadn't spotted anyone else from Duncan's Navy days at the church; but he couldn't be sure he'd know everyone anyway.

He'd penned a short letter to Jeff, his best man, who had been at Dartmouth with him and Duncan, but he knew Jeff was in the Falkland Islands and wouldn't be home for months. Peter shuddered and told himself to stop thinking about anything else but what he had been taught. *Concentrate, man!*

After the weekend at home, even after spending Saturday brooding over the sorry affair of his former friend, he'd felt in excellent spirits on his return to the submarine, full of confidence that he'd finish the two weeks sea-time with flying colours.

No one had mentioned his past, or Duncan, and even the Aussie had kept his mouth shut on that score. Peter had told both Ethan and Tony about the sudden death, not mentioning AIDS out of courtesy to his former mate.

Both had been quiet, and Peter had suspected they'd already heard through the grapevine. As well as Ethan, Peter had grown quite fond of Tony. It seemed that the incident in the pub in Brodick was all forgotten.

But the sea-time was challenging. The scenarios Teacher put the Perishers through were more complicated than Peter had imagined. At yesterday's exercise he'd had three frigates coming at the boat at once, and it had got very close to Teacher taking control of the submarine. That had happened to Peter only once towards the end of the first sea-time trials, but he knew that if it happened again, he'd be a gonner. Just like Ethan.

23

K aisa had decided not to tell Peter about her pregnancy until after he'd finished Perisher. Whether he passed or failed, he needed to concentrate on the course without worrying about Kaisa or thinking about a baby. The Duncan affair was distraction enough; he didn't need any more dramas.

The wonderful thing was that Peter was able to telephone her almost every week, and the night before her appointment with Dr Harris, when Peter was on his way out to join the sub, he'd sounded buoyant on the phone. 'It's all going well, just the two weeks at sea and I will be able to come home.'

The week the doctor had confirmed her pregnancy and offered Kaisa the hormone injections, Peter had begun the second, and the final, sea-time.

It was now mid-September and the evenings were getting cooler and the weather worsening. Kaisa had been sitting on the bottom step of the staircase at Chepstow Place, watching the rain beat against the living room windows. She'd come so close to telling Peter the happy news during their conversations. But she'd kept her head, and it was now only a matter of weeks before he'd be done. Or be hoisted off the submarine. It was harsh punishment for failure, but Peter had explained to Kaisa that it was a necessary rule. 'You don't want a bitter, old, failed Perisher breathing down a captain's neck in the control room.' Of course, neither of them had mentioned the possibility of failure since it would only bring bad luck.

But when the phone rang in the hall early on the morning of 30th

September, and Kaisa's bum was still smarting from the injection that she'd had the day before, she had resolved to tell Peter about the baby. She was ten weeks gone now; four weeks further in the pregnancy than she'd ever been before, and she was already beginning to show. She needed to talk to Peter about what to tell people at work. She also wanted to tell her mum and sister, and Ravi, if he ever spoke to her again, as well as Rose.

But not before Peter knew.

Kaisa lifted the receiver and said, 'Hello?' even though she expected it would be Peter at six am on a Sunday. (Although her mother had been known to call early at the weekend too.)

'I'm coming home,' Peter said. His voice was thin and he sounded tense.

The first thought Kaisa had was where she should hide the bottle of champagne she'd bought at Marks & Spencer on Oxford Street the previous day. She had stood in the store, staring at the wine display, and eventually picked up a bottle. Even if Peter failed Perisher, she thought, they could still celebrate the baby, although the prospect of an alcoholic drink made her feel a bit queasy. Now, though, she realised how stupid the purchase had been.

'OK,' she said.

'I'm going to be home late afternoon,' Peter continued in the same serious voice.

'Are you OK, Peter?' Kaisa asked.

There was a silence at the other end.

'Peter?' Kaisa said. She was getting worried now.

'Not really.'

Oh, Peter, I'm so sorry.'

Again Peter was silent.

'Let me know what flight and I'll come and meet you at Heathrow.'

'No need. I'm not sure of the timings yet.'

'OK,' Kaisa said.

'Will you be home?'

'Of course,' Kaisa said. She put her right hand on her extended tummy. She was wearing Peter's old white uniform shirt and his thick submarine socks. She liked to sleep in something that even after several washes smelt faintly of Peter. And the house was permanently cold, so to save on heating bills when the weather got cooler, she wore the woolly socks too.

'Peter, do you know if you passed yet?' Kaisa said while holding tightly onto the receiver.

'No, I don't.'

'But what do you think?'

'Oh Kaisa, I don't know, darling. But it doesn't matter, really, does it?'

Suddenly Kaisa could hear the warmth in Peter's voice. 'I love you,' she said.

'Same,' Peter said. Kaisa knew he was smiling by the way he sounded, and she knew he would have told her he loved he if he could. There were probably several people listening in on their conversation.

'I've got to go, darling,' Peter said, 'I'll be home soon.'

But Kaisa couldn't wait. 'Peter, don't go yet. I have something to tell you.'

'Really?' Again Kaisa could hear the smile in his voice.

'Yes, I'm 10 weeks.'

Kaisa could hear Peter catch his breath, 'That's wonderful news!'

'And, Dr Harris is giving me this new treatment; hormone injections for 20 weeks. They are hopeful that it'll sort out the problem.'

'Kaisa, you've made me the happiest man alive.'

Kaisa swallowed hard. She wanted to cry out of joy. Peter was happy; even if he had failed Perisher, he was still over the moon that he would finally become a father. She hugged the receiver even closer to her ear, as if she was holding onto Peter.

'Hurry home,' she whispered.

'I will,' Peter said and he was gone.

Kaisa sat on the steps for a few minutes more, holding onto the receiver, listening to the empty tone at the other end of the line. *I've made him the happiest man alive.*

24

They'd carried out their final exercises. They'd all been allowed to phone their wives, or family, to say they'd be home that evening. The three men sat in the small wardroom and waited. They knew Teacher would call the three remaining Perishers, one by one, into the Captain's cabin.

Nigel was the first to be summoned by the Coxswain. Tony and Peter didn't speak while they waited. Both were tired from the most challenging days at sea they'd ever faced, and nervous about their fate. No words were needed now; each knew exactly how the other felt.

Peter gazed down at his hands and thought about Kaisa and their future together. He allowed himself to dream about holding his son or daughter in his arms, a small round-bellied thing, smiling up at him. He would be a father after all. He thought about the close call they'd had with AIDS, about Duncan's passing and about the treatment Kaisa was receiving. He knew she'd never gone as far as she was now. His heart was filled with trepidation at the prospect of perhaps having to start a new career just as he was becoming a father. Would he be able to provide for his family if he failed Perisher and decided to leave the Navy? He knew he didn't have to, there would be jobs and possibly a perfectly satisfactory career ahead of him in surface ships, but would he want to stay if he could no longer serve in submarines? His naval career would be marred by two black spots: a Court Martial for striking a now deceased fellow officer, and a failed Perisher course.

Suddenly Nigel stood in the gangway, grinning from ear to ear. The Coxswain was standing next to him, addressing Tony, 'Your turn, Sir.'

'Well done, mate,' Tony said, getting up and shaking Nigel's hand. 'Here goes, wish me luck, boys,' he added, placing his cap on his head, leaving Peter and Nigel behind in the cramped wardroom.

'Congratulations, I knew you'd do it,' Peter said and hugged his friend.

Nigel sat down and leaned back on the wardroom sofa, which also served as his bed. He put his hands over his head and exhaled deeply, letting air out of his lungs. With a wide grin he said, 'Thank you. It feels good!' Then, remembering that Peter had not yet found out his fate, he added, 'You'll be OK.'

Peter looked at his old friend. He wasn't at all sure he'd passed. But he couldn't help but smile.

'Kaisa is pregnant again,' he said.

'That's great news. Congratulations!'

Peter was too nervous to tell his friend about the treatment Kaisa was getting; besides, he knew Nigel wouldn't be able to concentrate on Peter and Kaisa's problems. He'd passed Perisher and Peter was glad for his friend. Would he follow in Nigel's footsteps?

The last three weeks at sea had been taxing, and he knew he wasn't as good technically as his friend, and he also lacked the ability to think as quickly as the Aussie did. Although Tony was sometimes a bit too flamboyant, and could fly off the handle at the crew, a side to him that Peter knew too well, he also knew that it had not been a problem during the last – critical – weeks of the Perisher course. Somehow Tony had been able to control his temper. So he'd probably pass as well.

Which left Peter.

Was it a bad sign that he was the last one to be called into Teacher's cabin?

Everything after Peter's meetings with Teacher was a bit of a blur.

When he'd stepped back into the wardroom and Peter had told the others what the Teacher had said, Tony had got a bottle of Scotch from the small cabinet serving as a bar in the corner of the wardroom and poured them all a large drink.

'It's over boys!' Nigel had said, and they'd all downed the strong liquid in large gulps, while waiting for Teacher's steward to pack their bags. It was the tradition that when the Perishers left the training boat for the last time, the practical things would be handled for them.

'You flying down South straight away?' Nigel asked Peter, and he nodded. He seemed to have lost his ability to speak. Kaisa's news and the meeting with Teacher had made him feel shaky. He leaned against the bulkhead and tried to steady himself. It must be the alcohol that had gone straight to his head.

When, a few minutes later, the three of them were escorted off the submarine, Peter still felt unsteady as he climbed up the conning tower. Outside, the cold, fresh air hit his face and filled his nostrils. He put on his cap and felt a little better. He even allowed himself a slight smile. He'd soon have Kaisa, a pregnant Kaisa, in his arms.

He walked along the casing and noticed it was slippery. He was the last one off the submarine, and saw Tony and Nigel had already climbed onboard James Bond.

It was a dark night. Little wind, no stars, just a faint light in distance marking the horizon. Peter wondered what time it was, and realised he had no idea if the silvery light was fading into night or an indication of the sun coming up. He hadn't recognised he'd stopped walking, gawking at the view, until he heard Teacher's steward, who was behind him, carrying Peter's bag say, 'It's cold, let's get onboard, Sir.' His hand stretched out in front of Peter, guiding him towards the waiting launch.

Peter moved forward towards the vessel. The two-man crew onboard saluted him, and he in turn saluted Teacher, making an effort to stand erect on the casing. The man, who Peter suddenly saw looked weary, nodded, took his hand and said simply, 'Captain.'

Peter replied, 'Sir,' and proceeded to get onboard James Bond. He smiled, turned and stepped out, but somehow his foot missed the edge of the other vessel, and at the same time his back leg slipped on the casing of the submarine. He heard the voices of people shouting, while his brain registered the harsh chill in every part of his body, except his head.

He was in the water, and it was cold. He felt the dampness creep into his clothes and hit his skin. His legs felt heavy, so heavy that they were dragging him under. He thrashed madly with his arms, trying to get hold of something, but the side of the submarine was further away, and the hull of James Bond, bobbing on the water, grew more and more distant.

Suddenly, he realised what was dragging him further away – the propeller. He made an effort to calm himself and began fighting the drag with his legs, pounding the water hard, and for a moment, he thought he was making headway.

All I need to do is keep going and they'll get me out of the water.

Images of Kaisa smiling, holding a baby in her arms, came into his mind, as he felt himself being dragged under.

No, this can't be it, not now. Not now when everything is so good.

His head bobbed underneath the surface of the freezing water, filling his mouth and lungs with cold water. He fought against the strong pull of the sea, sucking him further down, and got his face up. He gulped in air. He could see a flashing light coming from somewhere, but a second later his lungs filled with water again and blackness overtook him.

25

After Kaisa had spoken with Peter, she phoned the newsroom at the BBC and told them to leave a message with the duty editor to say that she was too ill to come into work. She told them she had a tummy bug. She climbed back into bed for an hour, trying to sleep. But she couldn't stop thinking about how wonderful Peter had sounded and how he said she'd made him the happiest man alive. Although she knew that he felt the same way about the baby as she did, it was such a relief to hear him say that the foetus growing inside her was more important to him than his career. Or whether he passed Perisher or not.

Kaisa put her hands across her belly and closed her eyes. She wanted to rest so that she'd look fresh when Peter arrived home later that day. She thought about how he'd touch her tummy, and kiss her lips and gently hold her close.

None of her pregnancies before had gone far enough for him to see a visible bump. At only six weeks each time, she hadn't really felt there was a real baby there, apart from perhaps the first time, when they hadn't realised how easily a baby could be lost.

Kaisa thought back to last year, when she had fallen pregnant for the first time. How joyous and carefree she had felt about it then! They had later realised the baby had been conceived in France during their summer holiday with Ravi.

That autumn, Peter had been serving in a diesel submarine, which was on a refit in Plymouth, so he'd been home every weekend. When, after they had returned home, her period had been a week late, she'd suspected something was up and bought a pregnancy test at the Boots on Kensington High Street. It was a Wednesday, and she'd wanted to wait until Peter was home for the weekend, but in the end she had peed on the stick the very next morning. She had hardly believed her eyes when the blue line appeared. The same day she'd gone and bought another test and got the same result the next morning.

When she told Peter about the baby over the phone the next evening, he'd been pleased, but not as emotional as he had sounded this morning. Now they both knew how easily this one too could be lost.

As Kaisa nodded off, she smiled to herself. For some reason, whether it was to do with the hormone treatment she was having, or Peter's warm voice still ringing in her ears, she had a feeling that this little baby would stick around.

It was late afternoon when Kaisa saw a naval padre, followed by a naval officer she didn't know, standing by her door.

Kaisa was on her way home, carrying her shopping bags out of the car. Although feeling guilty about calling in sick at work, and nervous about bumping into someone she knew, Kaisa had gone into town and bought two steaks and ready-made Dauphinoise potatoes, which she knew Peter particularly loved, from Marks & Spencer. She also got herself a new dress; a loose powder-blue A-line thing that she knew would do her for a few months before the bump became too large for anything but proper maternity wear.

Even though she didn't want to think about it, she'd bought the dress because she'd be able to wear it even when she wasn't pregnant. After the baby, she told herself, feigning a confidence she didn't have. She'd decided she would be positive about this pregnancy. She'd heard somewhere – perhaps it was Rose who had told her – that positive thinking could beat breast cancer. Why wouldn't it help her hold onto this baby she was carrying? She would try everything in her power to hold onto it, even if it meant going all 'New Age' on Peter. She laughed at the thought of Peter on a vegetarian camp somewhere, wearing a colourful kaftan and practising yoga with her.

She didn't notice the two men standing in her front garden until she was passing her neighbour's house. She spotted their backs, as they stood outside her door, ringing the bell. Then the padre turned around, and seeing her standing there, watching them, he said something to the officer next to him. The unknown man was in a uniform, much like Peter's, except that he had thin hair, which she saw when he took off his naval cap. Both men began to walk towards her. Realising she had stopped, she started to make her way down the path.

'Mrs Williams?'

'Yes,' Kaisa said, moving her shopping from her right hand to her left and rummaging in her handbag for the house keys. 'I'm afraid my husband isn't home,' she said.

The two men exchanged looks, and again the older officer spoke, 'Can we go inside, please, Mrs Williams?'

Kaisa nodded, 'Yes, but as I said, Peter isn't at home yet, so ...' she said, finally bringing out the keys. The man interrupted her, 'I am Lieutenant Commander Stephen Crowther and this is Mr William Davies.'

'How do you do,' Kaisa said and shifted her shopping to the crook of her arm. It was heavier than she had realised it would be when she filled her trolley at Marks & Spencer.

'Can I take that and carry it for you?' Lieutenant Commander Stephen Crowther said, and without waiting for her reply he picked up the carrier bags. Kaisa nodded, and while the men took her shopping, she opened the door and ushered the two of them inside.

'Would you like a cup of tea?' she asked as soon as they were in the small hall. As she showed Lieutenant Commander Crowther and Mr Davies into their front room, she let out a sigh of relief that she'd cleaned the house before going into town. But the men wouldn't sit; instead they stood in the room, filling it with their presence and making it look cramped and tiny.

'No thank you,' they both said in unison. Then, exchanging glances once more, the older of the two, Crowther, spoke.

'Mrs Williams, why don't you take a seat.'

Kaisa stared at the men, and realising they wouldn't sit unless she herself did, she smoothed down her cotton skirt and seated herself on the old sofa, the first item of furniture she and Peter had bought when they moved in.

The two men immediately sat down opposite her on the white sofa that Peter and Kaisa had found in Habitat last summer. They'd bought it after Kaisa had lost her first baby, when she'd told Peter that she wouldn't want to try again. The sofa was terribly impractical, and showed every little stain, but at the time it had seemed the perfect buy for a childless couple.

'Mrs Williams, I'm afraid we have some bad news.' Lieutenant Commander Crowther was the first to speak again. He seemed to be in the lead, but even he looked nervous and unsure of himself. Kaisa couldn't think why they would bring a naval Padre along to tell Peter that he'd failed Perisher. If that was what this charade was all about.

'I'm sorry, I don't understand,' Kaisa said. 'My husband, Lieutenant Commander Williams isn't here, so ...'

'It's Lieutenant Commander Williams, Peter, we are here to speak to you about.' Crowther was fiddling with his naval cap.

'Oh?'

The Padre got up and came to sit next to Kaisa. 'Mrs Williams, may I call you Kaisa?'

Kaisa looked at the Padre with suspicion. The last time she'd had a Padre sit next to her on a sofa was when he had told her he couldn't provide Peter with the correct documentation to marry her in Finland. That had resulted in a quickie marriage in the registry office in Portsmouth and a blessing in Finland instead of the full-blown wedding ceremony everyone had been expecting.

She couldn't understand what was going on now. Unless ... fear crept up her spine and circled her tummy. She felt her mouth go dry. She nodded to the Padre.

'I'm sorry to tell you, Mrs Williams, Kaisa, that your husband, Peter, had an accident onboard the submarine early this morning.' It was the officer, Crowther, speaking across from Kaisa.

'An accident?' Kaisa heard herself say. Her voice sounded as if it was coming from a deep well, and not from her own mouth at all. She felt the room and Crowther and the Padre, whose name she had suddenly forgotten, grow more and more distant, as if she was moving backwards into a tunnel.

'Yes, an accident.' The man opposite her, or the Padre, Kaisa wasn't sure which one of the faraway figures was speaking, said, 'It was a terrible accident. Peter slipped on the casing when he was about to step onboard the transport vessel and he fell overboard.'

'Is he OK? Where is he?' Kaisa said. Her speech, as well as her vision, seemed to have worsened. She could hardly get the words out. She got up, knowing she had to go to Peter. She had to see how he was. But she felt dizzy and began swaying.

Kaisa felt the hands of the man on her. Or perhaps it was the Padre with his black clothes who was holding her and pulling her back to the seat?

'Mrs Williams, you must keep calm.'

Kaisa nodded. Then she heard a noise and realised it was coming from her. She put her hand on her mouth. *You must keep calm. They won't tell you anything unless you keep calm.* Kaisa nodded and lifted her eyes to the man opposite her.

'I'm so sorry, so terribly sorry to tell you this, but your husband's accident was fatal.'

There was a silence.

'You mean, he's ..., what do you mean, *fatal*?' Kaisa said. She was still holding onto her mouth, and felt wet tears fall onto her fingers. She couldn't breathe.

Now one of the men was crouching in front of her, touching her shoulder, 'Yes I am so terribly sorry but Lieutenant Commander Williams, Peter, your husband is dead.'

Suddenly the room began spinning in front of Kaisa's eyes, and everything went so bright she had to close her eyes.

26

Pirjo booked the next available flight and turned up at the house in Chepstow Place the day after Peter's death. Her eyes looked swollen and bloodshot and she hugged Kaisa hard.

'How did you know?' Kaisa said when at last she settled down with a cup of coffee Ravi had brewed for them. Pirjo gave Kaisa's Indian friend a long stare, but with his usual charm, Ravi soon won her mother over.

After the Padre and the naval officer had managed to wake Kaisa up after she'd fainted in front of the two men in her own living room, they'd asked if there was anyone, any family, Kaisa could call. The only person, apart from Rose, who Kaisa didn't want to call on so soon after Duncan's passing, was Ravi.

'He's gone,' was all Kaisa could say down the phone when she'd called his office. He'd hurried to the house on Chepstow Place and hadn't left Kaisa's side for 48 hours.

Now Pirjo, sitting opposite her daughter at the pine table, lowered her voice. 'I'm here now so you don't need anyone else.'

Kaisa hadn't had the energy to argue. 'I'm pregnant,' she said instead.

Kaisa's mother stared at her daughter and squeezed her hands even tighter.

'I'm having hormone injections, which the doctor thinks will stop me from losing this one.'

Pirjo nodded. 'Oh my darling girl.' Tears ran down her face again and Kaisa had to look away. She couldn't cope with her mother's grief. Besides, what did she have to be sorry about? *It wasn't her husband who had died, she hadn't lost anyone.* Kaisa was hit by a surge of anger so strong that she had to get up.

'I'm tired,' she said and went up to the bedroom.

Upstairs she hit a pillow, and threw it against the built-in wardrobe that stood at the foot of the bed. The thin panel shook for a while, but didn't have the decency to break, so she threw a pregnancy book she'd got from WH Smith's. Again, the veneer panel vibrated slightly, which made Kaisa even angrier. She took hold of the glass of water she always kept on the bedside table and hurled it at the wardrobe. Water and glass flew in all directions, and for a moment Kaisa felt good, but when the door opened and her mother walked in, with Ravi close behind her, and she saw them staring at her, and at the mess on the carpet, she felt ashamed. She sat down on the floor and blacked out.

Kaisa woke later, fully clothed on top of her bed. Someone had placed a crocheted blanket over her legs. She opened her eyes and sat up in bed. She felt her tummy and smiled, because she'd forgotten. For a few delicious seconds, she was happy about the baby, looking forward to seeing Peter later; wasn't he supposed to be at home already?

And then she remembered.

Slowly the faces of the naval commander and the padre came into focus, the strangers who had come with the most horrible news, and she recalled the words: *I am so terribly sorry but Lieutenant Commander Williams, Peter, your husband, is dead.* Kaisa put her head into her hands and began howling. She wrapped her hands around her body and began rocking back and forth.

'Kaisa, you must calm down,' her mother was by her side and holding down her hands, trying to stop her movement. But Kaisa couldn't stop; the only thing that helped at least a little was being able to move, to be able to shout and cry. When Kaisa brushed her mother away Ravi took her place. The man with the beautiful brown eyes crouched in front of her and said, 'Shh, shh, it's OK.' He put his arms around her and whispered in her ear, 'Think of the baby, Kaisa, think about the baby.'

The baby, the fatherless baby. Kaisa thought and carried on crying.

'You're frightening the baby,' Ravi said and Kaisa put her hands on her tummy. Somehow she'd managed to stop the rocking back and forth. And at that moment, she felt a movement, or not even movement, more like the wings of a butterfly fluttering inside her tummy. She looked up at Ravi and said, 'It kicked, the baby kicked!'

They all laughed; made stupid noises somewhere between weeping and whooping. Ravi and Pirjo put their hands on Kaisa's tummy. She didn't feel any more movements, but it was a sign, a sign for Kaisa.

After that, Kaisa's mother and Ravi agreed that he would leave Kaisa and Pirjo alone in the house and go back to his flat in Holland Park. He promised to check up on Kaisa each afternoon on his way back from work, just in case there was a repeat of her 'attack', she assumed.

During the two weeks Pirjo spent with Kaisa, she cleaned the little house from top to bottom, and made Peter's parents welcome when they arrived two days later, fighting tears and hugging Kaisa hard.

On the third day after Peter's death, when dusk had settled over the house and garden, and they were sitting in the lounge, Peter's parents perching on the white sofa and her own mother sitting on the armrest of the comfy chair that Kaisa had chosen, she told them about the baby.

'I'm getting hormone injections, so this one should stick,' Kaisa added. She was again fighting tears, but it seemed there were none left. She was so very tired, so very tired of it all. The telephone had been going all day, with people wanting to speak to her. But she didn't have the strength to talk to anyone, so while she was trying to sleep upstairs, her mother, with her faltering English, had thanked them for their condolences and tried to explain that Kaisa would not be coming to the phone.

As the news of the baby sank in, Kaisa saw tears in Peter's father's eyes. He got up and touched her knee, saying, 'Well done.' Awkwardly, not knowing what else to do, he backed off and, looking at his wife for help, sat down on the sofa again.

In her turn, Peter's mother said, 'God is merciful,' and got up and kissed Kaisa on the cheek. Kaisa stared at the tall, lanky woman and thought, *No, God is cruel and evil*, but she didn't say anything.

* * *

27

The day of the funeral was a ridiculously sunny, early October morning. The beautiful little house in Notting Hill was swathed in autumn sunshine, as Kaisa, Pirjo, Ravi and Peter's parents all piled into the three black funeral cars.

Seeing the coffin inside the hearse, draped with the White Ensign, Kaisa's knees buckled and she took hold of the doorframe. Her mother was behind her and supported Kaisa as she walked towards the waiting car.

It was just ten days after the visit she'd had from the Padre and Lieutenant Commander Crowther. There were some high-ranking Navy officers, including Peter's best man Jeff, and Peter's former Captain, Stewart, smartly dressed in their gold-braided uniforms in spite of the IRA threat.

Kaisa thought absentmindedly that this must be a special occasion, like a royal wedding or something. She also saw Jeff's parents, looking old and frail next to Peter's friend. Kaisa forced herself to say a few words to all of them.

There were so many people at the funeral, some of whom Kaisa remembered from her days in Portsmouth and Helensburgh. She nodded to those she could remember and tried to keep herself steady. She felt so shaky, as if her body didn't want to enter the Kensal Green Chapel they'd chosen for the funeral. She was grateful to Lieutenant Commander Crowther, or Stephen, as he'd insisted she should call him, who now came to stand by her side with Ravi and her mother. He gently guided them all through the day. He'd helped her so much, and had organised the funeral service with Peter's parents.

The only detail Kaisa had insisted on was that the ceremony would be held in London, close to her. She knew Peter wanted to be either buried at sea or cremated. She had insisted Stephen tell her exactly how Peter had died, but had fainted again when he'd told her he'd been caught up in the submarine's propeller. *He got his wish to be buried at sea*, Kaisa had thought later. The cremation would be a formality, as there would hardly be any ashes to put in the urn. Yet Kaisa wanted a place where she could visit Peter, so there was to be a stone.

As the funeral party made their way into the chapel, Stephen spotted a gaggle of newspaper photographers outside. He asked Kaisa if it would be okay for them to have a few pictures, and she nodded. He organised everyone to pose in front of the double doors, then asked the journalists politely but firmly to leave.

When the music started Kaisa sat in the chapel, staring at Peter's coffin, trying to comprehend what had happened and that he wasn't ever going to be in their little house in Chepstow Place ever again. She clutched the single red rose she was going to place on the gravestone, and Ravi held her other hand the whole of the time.

Beside her, Pirjo and Peter's mother sat and wept quietly. Peter's father stared ahead of him, sitting upright, holding his wife's hand. Peter's siblings and their partners sat in the next row. Kaisa had hugged his family briefly, unable to look at Nancy or Simon's sad faces for long. Rose and her husband Roger sat behind them, and afterwards they, along with Stephen and the rest of the family, came back to Chepstow Place, where Ravi had organised a buffet and drinks.

In the kitchen, Kaisa could hear the voices of people talking in hushed tones in the lounge. She knew she needed to get back to the guests, but her legs were numb, and she was unable to move. Shifting in her seat, she suddenly realised her tummy was touching the edge of the table. She looked down at the growing baby inside her and realised she had to cope, she needed to be sane and well for Peter's child. She got up from the table and, wiping the tears from her eyes, walked into the lounge.

Among all the people drinking wine and chatting and making the room seem tiny, the first person Kaisa spotted was her mother. She wanted to bury her face in Pirjo's embrace and ask the people to leave. But Pirjo took hold of her arm, supported her to an empty sofa, and sat down next to her daughter. With her mother's help, Kaisa managed to get through the day.

28

On the day before she was about to fly back to Helsinki, Pirjo asked Kaisa if they could go out for lunch. Kaisa didn't know if she was ready to face the world yet, but guessed this was some kind of test her mother had devised to see if she could leave her alone. So Kaisa nodded and chose a place nearby, The Earl of Lonsdale, which she knew served decent food. She'd been to The Earl many times with Peter, and with Rose, as well as Ravi, and had to steel herself when she walked inside. Of course, the landlord was about and gave Kaisa a nod. 'I was so sorry to hear about Peter.'

'Thank you,' Kaisa said. She'd forgotten that Peter's horrible accident had been in the papers. In one way that helped her, because she didn't have to tell people, but on the other Kaisa didn't want to share her grief with the world. There had been a couple of reporters ringing the doorbell asking for an interview. Kaisa had told Ravi and then Pirjo to tell them a simple 'No.' She couldn't face anyone, not talk about Peter with anyone.

'I'll have a Coke – and a glass of wine,' she now said to the landlord, and she glanced at her mother. 'And the menu please.' The man nodded and went to get the drinks.

'I'll find us a table, can you bring them over?' Kaisa said to Pirjo, and her mother nodded.

She sat in the far corner of the pub, which was half full of lunchtime drinkers, some of them tourists studying their maps, and a few builders in paint-splattered overalls hugging their pints of beer. Kaisa turned her eyes away from a couple drinking a bottle of wine, who were sitting close to one another and smiling. She looked at her mother, who was speaking in hushed tones with the landlord and sighed with relief. With her little English, Pirjo had managed to talk to the man about Peter so Kaisa didn't have to. Now all Kaisa needed to do was avoid his gaze when he came to bring them the food.

When Pirjo came back with the drinks, she smiled. 'I'm going to be drunk on my plane home.'

She was changing the subject on purpose, Kaisa knew, and gratefully replied, 'No you won't.'

Kaisa would have been glad of the numbing effect of alcohol, but even if she'd allow herself to have a glass, which the midwife had said would be OK, she felt nauseous at just the thought of it.

After they'd chosen their meals and Kaisa had been back to the bar, taking her chance to order the food with a new barmaid she didn't recognise, Pirjo said, 'I wanted to talk to you, Kaisa, before I leave.'

'Oh yes?' Kaisa said.

They'd been doing nothing but talk all fortnight. After the first few days, when Peter's parents had been in the house, and then after the funeral, a day that was mostly a haze in Kaisa's mind, when all Kaisa wanted to do was sleep, Kaisa and Pirjo had been talking about everything.

Kaisa had told her how wonderful Peter had been on the phone, and how he'd said she'd made him the happiest man alive. She had poured her heart out to her mother, telling her about her regrets, speaking again about the awfulness of the first year of marriage and her unfaithfulness with Duncan, and her friendship with Rose, who had promised to come up to London when Pirjo had gone home. Of course, Pirjo knew all of it already, but it helped Kaisa to say it all again, to tell her mother how happy Peter had made her in spite of everything.

Pirjo had listened and had hugged Kaisa, even sleeping with her when Kaisa couldn't settle in the middle of the night.

'I want you to think about what you are going to do now.'

'What do you mean?'

'You need to think about your future. It's not easy to bring a child up on your own.'

'I know,' Kaisa said. She was looking at Pirjo's face trying to find out what she was talking about.

'Come back to Finland!'

'No!' Kaisa said, a little too loudly.

People around them looked up from their drinks. Even the love birds lifted their gaze and stared at Kaisa and Pirjo.

Pirjo put her hand on Kaisa's arm, 'All I'm saying is that you should think of yourself.'

Kaisa was silent for a while then said, quietly, 'I am thinking of myself.'

'And the baby? Do you think you will be able to give the baby a good life in England?'

'Yes!' Again Kaisa raised her voice, but when she saw the landlord put down a glass he was wiping, she lowered her voice and whispered to her mother, 'This is my home now. I was very happy here with Peter.' Kaisa swallowed hard. She couldn't' go on. She removed her hand from the table and from under her mother's grasp and placed both hands on her lap, looking down at them. *Keep calm, keep calm.*

Pirjo leaned back in her red velvet chair and sighed. 'All I wanted to do is make you understand that it'd be easier for you to be at home.'

Kaisa lifted her eyes to her mother's. 'The Navy is looking after me financially, and I have my job. And Ravi and Rose.'

It was Pirjo's time to be quiet. She looked down at her glass, then lifted her eyes up at Kaisa again. 'But are you sure? You're a foreigner here and always will be, won't you?'

Kaisa took a deep breath, and then another, in an attempt to calm down. She felt stronger now and had her eyes squarely on her mother. 'This is my home now. I will have this baby here, and he or she will be English, just like Peter. Our home and place is here.'

Pirjo nodded. 'OK, but just think about what I said.'

'Mum, I know you're thinking of me, but this baby I'm carrying is half English. He or she is part of Peter, and the only thing I have left of him now.' Tears were welling inside Kaisa, but she continued, 'and for now I can't think about moving anywhere.'

In the last few hours Kaisa spent with Pirjo, she tried not to show her frustration with her, and kept quiet. Of course, Pirjo noticed, and when they parted at Heathrow, her mother said, 'Don't think badly of me for what I said. I was only thinking of you. At least think about coming back home, eh?'

Kaisa had nodded and hugged her mother hard. She was fighting tears again, and wondered if she had been right to dismiss moving back to Finland so hastily.

. . .

The day after Kaisa'a mother had returned to Finland, the telephone in the hall rang. It was just past 6 pm and Ravi and Kaisa were sitting in front of the TV in the lounge, watching the evening news.

'You expecting a call?' Ravi said.

Kaisa shook her head. They'd got into a routine during those few first weeks after Peter's passing: if the telephone went, Ravi, or her mother, would reply in case Kaisa wasn't up to talking to yet another Navy Wife who felt she needed to convey her and her husband's condolences.

Kaisa was surprised how little of this English etiquette she could take before she felt close to tears, so Ravi, bless his heart, had taken upon himself to listen to the same platitudes over and over. He was excellent at making excuses for Kaisa not being able to come to the telephone; she was asleep, in the bath (Kaisa never took baths; she preferred the shower), or at the shops. One time, Ravi even told someone that Kaisa had nipped out to buy milk for his tea, an excuse that particular Navy Wife (whom Kaisa couldn't even remember meeting) swallowed easily. Why wouldn't a woman take care of the man in the house – even a 'Paki friend' as Ravi put it when they laughed about the call almost a year later, when Kaisa found she could see the funny side to life again.

Kaisa knew she was being selfish and impolite, but she didn't care. She had pulled the short straw in life, and she didn't need to pander to anyone's sensibilities anymore. She couldn't care less what any Navy Wife – or anyone in the Navy for that matter – thought of her behaviour. If they didn't like it, they could try losing a husband in the senseless way she had. She bet they'd not care about being polite or doing things the right way either in the circumstances.

'It's your sister, I think?' Ravi now said, looking at Kaisa and holding onto the receiver.

'Hello Sirkka, you feeling any better?' Kaisa tried to put on a jolly voice for her sister.

Kaisa had spoken to Sirkka several times after Peter's death. They'd had long, long phone calls in which Kaisa had poured her heart out, and they had both cried and cried. Sirkka had been feeling too sick with her pregnancy to come to the funeral.

'No, still throwing up daily. But I wanted to talk to you about something.'

'Oh yes?'

'I might as well come out with it.'

'What?' Kaisa sighed. Since Peter had gone, she had no patience for anything. 'C'mon what is it?'

'Come home to Finland!'

'You've been speaking with mum.'

'You know she isn't usually right about much, but this time she has a point. You know the best place to give birth is here in Finland. Helsinki has a fantastic new maternity ward, really close to where mum lives. All you'd need to do is to come over a month before you're due, and stay six weeks after the birth. If you want to go back to London, well then you could. Just for the duration of your maternity leave. I'm sure the BBC would let you go earlier under the circumstances.'

Kaisa didn't reply. She wondered if Sirkka might be right. How lovely it would be to be looked after by your own family. To let Sirkka and Pirjo make the decisions for her, and to be in a familiar place when the baby was born. That would be wonderful, wouldn't it?

Sirkka continued, 'Just think, the cousins would get to know you, and you could come over for long visits to Rovaniemi. We could go for a walk with the babies in their prams! How fantastic it would be to have so much time together.'

'OK, I'll think about it.' Kaisa thought there was nothing stopping her from going to see her sister in Lapland whether she was in London or Helsinki, but she let it drop. She didn't want the same argument with Sirkka as she had had with her mother.

'That's wonderful!'

'I said, I'd think about it, not that I'd do it!'

'OK! How are you feeling anyway?'

Kaisa told Sirkka about the end of the hormone injections and how she was actually feeling pretty good. Poor Sirkka had been very sick from almost the beginning. The sisters exchanged a few more pregnancy stories, before Kaisa said she had to go. Ravi had made a mild curry and was gesticulating from the kitchen to say the food was ready.

Over supper, Kaisa told Ravi how tempting it would be to just go back to Finland.

'I can't rely on you forever,' she said and looked down at her plate.

Ravi put his hand over Kaisa's and she was struck how pale her skin looked against Ravi's mocha shade. 'I want to help.' His eyes were gazing directly at Kaisa. 'So no more nonsense about my generosity. You're like a sister to me, Kaisa. I don't know what I'd do without you.'

Kaisa could feel tears welling up inside her, but she held them back and smiled at Ravi instead. 'That's decided then. I want the little one to be born in England, however much less fabulous and world class the facilities!'

'That's my girl.'

. . .

That night, waking after just a few hours sleep, Kaisa thought about her conversation with Ravi and about her sister's words. Would she be better off moving back to Finland after all? She knew she might be able to get a job with the national broadcaster, YLE, or possibly with one of the commercial radio stations that had sprung up all over Finland. They were relaying programmes that Kaisa and the other reporters at the BBC were producing, so she would be known to the management teams in these companies.

The thought of being at home again, with family around her, was very appealing. Especially if she could find work and a place to live. But the thought of leaving the Notting Hill house that she had shared with Peter was unthinkable. There were so many memories here: the white, impractical sofa they'd bought together; the bench in the hall; the wobbly kitchen table that Peter had found in the second-hand shop on Portobello Road; and the pictures on the walls bought during their trips to France with Ravi.

The house itself seemed to breathe Peter. She smiled when she recalled the day they moved in, how they'd vowed to make love in each room, and how they had. They'd even made love in the kitchen, where on one afternoon in the middle of a London heatwave, Peter had entered Kaisa from behind, while she leaned onto the wobbly kitchen table. Kaisa remembered how much they had wanted each other. No, this house held too many wonderful memories. Kaisa couldn't leave this place, or this country. Britain was – had been – Peter's home, and it would be the home of his child too.

The next morning when Kaisa woke after another restless night, there was a letter on the mat. She recognised the writing immediately, and tore open the envelope.

'Dear Kaisa,

I hope you are coping, but I know it must be hard. I have been speaking with your mother ...'

Kaisa put her hand to her mouth. Her father had been speaking with her mother! She walked into the kitchen, flicked the kettle on and continued reading.

'We both agree that you should come back home. Unlike your mother, I don't interfere in the lives of my grown-up daughters, but on this occasion I must give you my opinion. You are expecting a child.

As your father, I know that having a baby when there are two parents isn't easy. To do it on your own is very difficult indeed. And you are planning to have this baby on your own in a foreign country.

You know I very much respected Peter and know he was a good husband and would have made a good father. But, it is not to be. So you need your family around you.

Come home to Finland, this is isänmaasi.

Greetings, Dad.'

Kaisa sat down at the kitchen table and stared at the words. She tried to think when – if ever – she'd had a letter from her father. And he had used that word, *isänmaa*, fatherland, which he must have known would bring a lump to her throat.

'Bad news?' Ravi stood in the doorway, with a concerned look on his face. He was wearing a thick, dark green Prince of Wales checked dressing gown and his smart black leather slippers.

Kaisa translated the letter for Ravi, fighting tears, while Ravi picked up a mug from the wooden tree next to the kettle and made himself tea. He then measured coffee into a cafetière and poured the rest of the hot water over the top.

He turned back to face Kaisa. 'It's OK. If you want to go back to Finland, you should.'

Kaisa sighed and closed her eyes. 'I don't know what to do.'

29

Kaisa had come to fear the nights since Peter's death. During the initial weeks, she'd fallen into bed in a kind of coma from all the crying, usually forced there by her mother or later by Ravi, who would make her a cup of soothing camomile tea and sit by the bed until she fell asleep (or pretended to).

Thinking about the baby usually made her settle, but she'd be awake again a few hours later, in the dead of night, at first blissfully unaware of Peter's death. When reality hit her, she would feel as though someone had punched her in the stomach. She'd feel winded and close to being sick. To calm herself she'd often place her hand on her growing belly and try to think about what Mrs D, her therapist, had told her.

'Try to be grateful and think about what Peter gave you during his life.'

After Kaisa's mother had left, Ravi had got Kaisa in touch with the analyst. 'Just go and see her once,' he'd said. 'For me.'

Kaisa had promised and had immediately liked the grey-haired woman with wise, kind brown eyes. Mrs D, whose second name, she said, was 'unpronounceable', saw her 'clients' as she called the people who came to her home in smart Holland Park.

Kaisa sat opposite Mrs D in a small room while they talked about Kaisa's feelings. For the first sessions, Kaisa spoke less than Mrs D, fearing she'd embarrass herself with an inconsolable crying fit, or even rage, as she'd done when her mother had been staying with her.

Gradually, however, she managed to talk about Peter without tears. She told Mrs D how they had met under the sparkling chandeliers of the British Embassy in Helsinki, about her engagement to the Finnish Matti, about his death, about Kaisa's difficulties in getting used to life as a Navy Wife in Britain, and about the short separation from Peter.

Finally, she told her about her miscarriages and how happy Peter had been during that last phone call home, when he'd found out she was pregnant and receiving treatment that would ensure the baby's survival.

'You must be so glad that he knew about the baby,' Mrs D said to Kaisa on her fourth or fifth visit, and Kaisa, looking up at the wise grey eyes of the older woman, nodded.

'You were lucky.'

'Lucky?' Kaisa replied, her mouth open in amazement.

'Many of the bereaved people I see didn't get the chance to share good news or express their love, like you and Peter did, before their partner is taken away.'

Kaisa looked at her hands resting below her round belly. The baby inside her now kicked properly. When this happened, she'd feel tears prick her eyelids at the thought that she wasn't able to tell Peter about it. She hadn't once considered herself lucky (*lucky!*) for being able to tell Peter she was pregnant again, or for being able to say she loved him. Those words, *You've made me the happiest man alive*, now rang in Kaisa's ears and she saw she was indeed fortunate.

After she'd been seeing Mrs D for a few weeks, Kaisa began to sleep better. At the same time, she started to have vivid dreams about making love to Peter. Waking after such a dream, she'd feel so happy at the prospect of his homecoming, until she remembered that he would never again walk along the front garden and hurriedly take her into his arms, while closing the front door with his foot.

Sometimes Kaisa would dream she was kissing him at a cocktail party onboard a ship, in full view of everybody. He'd grab her behind, just as he had when they'd first met at the British Embassy in Helsinki all those years ago. He had been slightly drunk that evening, having already represented Britain at three other embassies. On the dance floor, in front of the Finnish Foreign Minister and his wife, a former model, Peter had squeezed her bottom. But unlike on that first wonderful evening with her beloved Englishman, when Kaisa had removed his hand and told him off, in the dream, Kaisa ignored the gasps of the other wives and honoured guests.

Once she dreamed that Lady Di came to speak to her at such a party and told her that if she'd been married to Peter she would never let him out of her sight. After that dream Kaisa woke with an intense feeling of jealousy, until she remembered that Peter was no longer alive. She then felt queasy, as if a heavy plate had been placed on her chest and she couldn't breathe. After she'd calmed herself down, she put the light on and pulled a letter out from a pile in her bedside drawer. She lost count of how many notes she'd received from people who had known Peter. Some of the messages were short, some beautifully written with the same kind of old-fashioned fountain pen that Peter had used. But one letter was more special than the others. The sheet of heavy yellow paper had a beautiful crest made out of her initial, with a crown perching on top of the 'D' above the text 'Kensington Palace'. It had arrived a few days after Peter's death, but Kaisa hadn't read any of the notes until weeks later.

'*Dear Kesa,*

I was so distressed to hear that your husband, Lieutenant Commander Peter Williams, who I had the pleasure to meet onboard HMS Redoubt in May this year, perished during an accident. I remember him as a very polite and charming naval officer and can only imagine what sorrow his passing has caused you and your family.

Please accept my warmest condolences.

Yours sincerely,

Diana'

The letter was typed, but the Princess had hand-written the greeting and signed it. She'd misspelled Kaisa's name, but Kaisa knew it was probably a mistake by one of her courtiers, or whatever the people working for her were called. The words alone were lovely, as was the personal touch. She guessed that correspondence from the Princess had caused that particular succession of images in her dream.

Kaisa placed the heavy sheet of paper back in its envelope and put the letter on top of the others in her bedside drawer and climbed back into bed. She tried to rekindle the dream, just to feel Peter's hands on her and his breath close to her skin again.

30

LONDON, SEPTEMBER 1992

Kaisa was lying on her bed, waiting for Rosa to wake up. It was nearly six am, and she knew it would be a matter of minutes before she heard her daughter call out for her. It wasn't quite light yet, but Kaisa hadn't slept well, and around five am had given up and begun reading a new book that Ravi had given her, *A Secret History* by Donna Tart. Ravi had become Kaisa's new supplier of fiction, as well as her best friend, an excellent cook and her private fashion adviser. Kaisa would be starving and in rags if it wasn't for Ravi. She sighed. She'd miss him dreadfully.

She was so grateful for everything he had done for her; especially now she knew about his secret. She worried for him, because after the accident, he had been with her night and day, and he didn't seem to have a steady boyfriend. She'd wanted to ask him if he had casual relationships and to urge him to be careful, but each time she approached the matter, even in a roundabout way, he'd change the subject.

Once, when they'd been sitting at the kitchen table, a few days after Rosa's birth, and the radio was playing 'These are the days of our lives' by Queen, Kaisa had been brave enough to speak honestly with him. Ravi had been holding Kaisa's hands between his, and Kaisa had looked at the few dark hairs growing between the knuckles on the back of his fingers, fighting the memory of Peter's beautiful long fingers, which had hairs growing on them in exactly the same way. Ravi's skin was a shade darker, and his fingernails looked almost feminine in their paleness and cleanliness. Kaisa looked up at Ravi's dark brown eyes and said, 'Ravi, you are being careful, aren't you?'

The death of Freddie Mercury the year before had brought back the memory of Duncan struggling to breathe as he lay in the iron bed in Dorset.

'I couldn't bear to lose another ...'

Ravi had straightened up and looked startled. 'Of course.' He dropped Kaisa's hands and ran one of his own hands through his black, shiny hair. He'd grown it longer, Kaisa now saw, and wondered if it was because he didn't have time to go to the barbers anymore. She knew he didn't want to leave her at home in the afternoons, so each day he hurried back from his job in the City.

'Ravi, I'm just worried about you,' Kaisa had added.

'Oh Kaisa,' he'd said and leaned back on the ancient pine chair, which creaked slightly under his weight. 'I can't talk about it.'

Kaisa had hugged Ravi, and at that moment they'd both heard Rosa stirring. She got up and said, 'Just promise you're careful?'

Ravi had looked down at the table and nodded.

'I promise.'

Kaisa was feeding Rosa her morning porridge in the kitchen when she heard the doorbell go. She looked at her watch; it was only just gone eight so this had to be Peter's parents. She wiped the little girl's mouth, marvelled at her beautiful dark green eyes, which were the exact shape and shade of Peter's, and lifted her up.

'Shall we go and say hello to Granny and Grandpa?'

Rosa giggled and said, 'Ganny, Ganny!'

The girl, who looked almost nothing like Kaisa, having inherited the dark hair and eyes of the Williams family, loved her 'Ganny'. Peter's mother, Evelyn, or 'Evie' as everyone called her, had turned out to be a real rock; after the accident, she and Peter's father had rushed up to London from their home in Wiltshire.

Kaisa had never been very close to Evie, mainly because of the events in Scotland, which had caused so much heartache for her son, not to mention the harm it had done to Peter's career. Kaisa fully understood how she felt; if it had been her, she too would have been sceptical about a daughter-in-law who cheated on her husband after only six months of marriage.

But since the terrible accident, Peter's mum had been an angel, visiting

Kaisa often after her own mother had gone back to Finland, initially shedding tears with her, sharing her grief, which, after all, to her, must have been even worse. Now a mother herself, Kaisa could only imagine how much Evie suffered from losing a child.

Kaisa didn't want to think about what she had to tell them later that day.

When Rosa was born, Evie, together with her own mother, were once again at Kaisa's side, holding her hand as Kaisa cried and screamed her way through the labour. Now Evie popped up to London once of twice a month, babysitting for Kaisa as often as she could, and saving on Rosa's nursery costs.

Sometimes when Kaisa was saying goodbye to Rosa, as Peter's mother held the little girl on her lap, singing nursery rhymes to soften the blow of her mother's departure, she wondered if there was criticism in Evie's voice when she told Rosa, 'Mummy has to go to work, darling, doesn't she?'

She'd often have a look in her pale eyes, a look that said, 'How can you leave this little girl, a gift you were so desperate to have, and all you have left of Peter?' But true to her English manners, she never voiced those criticisms and Kaisa was too tired and too afraid to hear the truth to begin a discussion on the matter. And perhaps she was imagining such criticism.

Kaisa knew she didn't have to go to work, because of the generous pension she was getting from the Navy. Lieutenant Commander Crowther, who still wrote to her and even telephoned to ask how she was, and if there was anything he could do for her, had organised all the paperwork regarding the pension and the death certificate. He had also put Peter's affairs in order, including the mortgage, which was paid off with a life policy. He had communicated all the details to Ravi. A month or so after the funeral, Ravi had sat Kaisa down and told her that she was quite a wealthy woman.

'Peter certainly made sure you would be alright, and the Navy are being very generous.'

Kaisa had nodded. *What was money compared to having Peter alive and with her?* But she had thanked Ravi and thought about what Mrs D kept telling her: *Think of the positives.* Peter had loved her and had made sure she would not have to worry about money if he died before her.

She knew she was being selfish for staying at the BBC, but she needed time away from her home life and the dreadful longing she had for Peter. Sitting at home alone with Rosa, she would, she was sure, obsess about Peter. She wanted to see him just once more; to hear his voice; to feel his lips on her; and his body pressed against hers. She needed an escape from that longing, even if it lasted only as long as her news broadcasts on John

Major's new, flailing government, or the IRA terror attacks in London and elsewhere.

It was her job at the BBC that had saved her from going crazy after Peter's funeral. She knew the only way she'd keep herself sane was to get back to the work she loved, the only place that hadn't changed.

31

I t was a sunny day on the second anniversary of Peter's death. As if to mock her grief, there wasn't a cloud in the sky. Her psychiatrist said she needed to 'let go of her guilt'.

During the sessions she'd taken with the grey-haired analyst, Kaisa had learned more about herself than she thought possible. How she blamed herself for Peter's accident; how she couldn't accept that it was just a random event with disastrous consequences; how she fretted about having no control over it.

Although Kaisa now saw Mrs D only every two months, she had insisted on weekly sessions during the month before the anniversary. Before making Kaisa do the customary relaxation exercises, she'd reminded Kaisa that the only thing she could control was how she spent the rest of her life. Did she want to find the negative, and be sad on the second anniversary of Peter's death, or did she, for her own sake as much as for her daughter's and Peter's family's sake, want to celebrate her late husband's life? Did she want to feel grateful for the love she had shared with Peter and the love she now had for her daughter and her family and friends?

Kaisa had cried and wanted to mourn. She wanted to be sad, she wanted to cry until it was all over, and Peter walked through the door of their little house again, carrying his Pusser's Grip, smiling at her before he bent down and kissed her lips.

She wanted to howl at the unfairness of it all. She wanted to scream and shout at Mrs D, tell her how unfair it was that her memory of Peter's kisses was fading. If only she'd had the chance to take more pictures of him, to record the sound of his voice. All she had was the wedding video made by her uncle, which didn't include Peter's voice. But deep inside, she knew Mrs D was right; she couldn't let Rosa grow up in a home that was sad, and she needed to consider Peter's family too.

Peter's parents drove Kaisa to Kensal Green cemetery in their new Ford Mondeo. Kaisa still had Peter's old Golf GTi, but if it was a sunny day she'd often visit Peter's grave by walking to Westbourne Park Tube station and taking the number 18 bus from there, pushing Rosa in her pram when she was a baby and later in her buggy.

She still hated driving in London, even though she'd done it for years. The traffic around Notting Hill seemed only to get worse and finding a space to park near her home was becoming more and more difficult.

As she fixed Rosa into her car seat, and watched her kick her feet in excitement at being with her grandparents, 'Gampi' and 'Ganny', she resolved that she would heed Mrs D's advice and celebrate Peter's life rather than mourn him today. But she was also worried about how Peter's parents would react to her news. Kaisa decided not to think about that now; she'd tell them later when there was a quiet moment before the guests arrived. She knew she was putting it off, but she needed Ravi's support when she told them what she knew would be a great blow to them.

'Alright?' Evie said from the front seat, turning around to smile at Kaisa and Rosa.

Kaisa nodded quickly, feeling caught out by the older woman's straight gaze. Rosa kicked and waved her hands, pulling her body towards her granny, so that her seatbelt cut into her tummy.

'We'll soon be there, lovey,' Evie cooed and stroked the little girl's stubby fingers.

Kaisa gave her daughter a stick of carrot to suck at. She was teething and would chew at anything Kaisa gave her. 'Ready to go,' she said, and Peter's father started the engine.

Once the four of them were out of the car, and walking underneath the tall arches of the cemetery entrance, Kaisa felt a longing so severe in the pit of her stomach that she had to gasp. Evie was next to her, with one hand resting on Rosa's buggy. She put her other hand behind Kaisa's back, supporting her during their walk towards Peter's grave. Kaisa gave her mother-in-law a grateful smile. She pointed at a flower stall set up to the left of the chapel where they had attended the short ceremony two years ago.

'Let's get some flowers,' Evie said.

Kaisa nodded, unable to speak. Although she came here almost every week, and always made the same purchase of a single red rose to put on Peter's grave, today the ritual felt more poignant, more final. She felt tears well behind her eyelids when she remembered the very first time Peter had given her a red rose at Helsinki airport, just before he boarded a plane to London.

Kaisa had cried all the way home on the bus, desolate that she had to say goodbye to her beloved Englishman. How she wished she'd understood that those were the happy times. How lucky she had been then! To be able to look forward to seeing Peter again, to be able to count the weeks and days until she could feel his lips on hers, his body pressed against hers.

Now the counting was backwards; how long since their last conversation on the telephone, how many days, weeks, months and years since they'd made love, how long since she'd seen his smile, or smelled his familiar scent of coconut aftershave and something else, something musky and manly.

She needed to remember all these things, and yet she was afraid that little by little she was forgetting them. She had the photographs of him smiling next to his yellow, open-top Spitfire, another one in which he is dressed up for a wedding, from the time before she knew him. There were pictures from their own wedding in Finland, and the first hastily arranged registry office ceremony in Portsmouth. There were a few photographs of Peter and Kaisa together on various submarines and ships, at parties and naval dances, holding each other close, smiling into the camera.

Kaisa often examined her own face, as well as that of Peter, and wondered who that smiling woman was, and how Peter felt about her. She regretted each row they'd had, and they had had many. Too many.

She couldn't comprehend how she had been so stupid to sleep with another man, and then foolish enough to leave Peter alone in Scotland, a decision that had parted them for nearly a year. Her head had been full of feminist rhetoric, of pacifism, and opposition to the Navy. The Royal Navy that had been Peter's first love. How remote those beliefs now seemed! But Kaisa knew – as Mrs D had helped her remember – that they'd also had many happy times, as witnessed by the smiling couple in those pictures.

Yet she didn't recognise herself in those photographs; in spite of all the sessions with Mrs D, she had to work hard to find joy in life since Peter's death. If it hadn't been for the pregnancy, and for Rosa, this wonderful, beautiful girl – Peter's daughter – Kaisa didn't know what would have happened to her. She sighed and paid the florist for her rose.

'Here you are, Mrs Williams,' the woman said kindly. She had messy grey hair, which was trying to escape from a stripey scarf tied around her head. She knew Kaisa, and knew what she would order. 'Special day today, is it?' she said, nodding with a smile at Peter's mother and father, who, holding onto the handlebar of Rosa's buggy, were standing a little further away, looking at the buckets of flowers on the other side of the stall.

'Two years today,' Kaisa managed to say.

'I'm so sorry,' the woman said, and then lifting her brown eyes at Kaisa, added, 'It gets better, my dear.'

'Thank you,' Kaisa said and turned away. Kindness, or kind words, were almost the worst, she'd found. Although it was better than the silence many people offered when they heard about what had happened to Peter. It was strange to her how many people were afraid of the word 'death' and preferred talking about 'passing away' or 'loss', as if by simply being careless, Kaisa had let Peter slip away.

Now, two years later, Kaisa had learned to fight the images of the accident running through her head, how Peter must have fought to try and get breath as his body was pulled under the dark waves. After Lieutenant Commander Crowther, or Stephen, had told her the gruesome details, she'd tried to ask Nigel, who, after all, had been there, how Peter had fallen into the water. It was during a phone call months afterwards, but Nigel had only said, 'He slipped up.' His wife, Kaisa's friend Pammy, had told her of Nigel's breakdown after Peter's death. Neither of them had been able to come to the funeral. Nigel had been on strong medication for six months and was now on permanent sick leave from the Navy.

At the graveside, or at the memorial stone as it was correctly called, since what was left of Peter had been cremated and wasn't in the ground, Kaisa remembered how she hadn't been able to take any tranquillisers after the accident, due to the baby. She had been almost jealous of the oblivion Nigel's drugs had given him. Pammy had told her over the telephone that he seemed to do nothing but sleep at the unit he'd been taken to. For weeks he hadn't even recognised Pammy or their two daughters.

'Gampi is going to say a few words,' Evie said, now at her side, bringing Kaisa back to the present day.

She nodded and saw that Rosa was sitting still in her buggy for once, staring at the small patch of grass where Peter's mother had placed the pot of bright red geraniums she'd bought, next to Kaisa's red rose, which she had placed in the vase she'd bought a few weeks after the funeral. The green, plastic vial stood in front of the stone, with the inscription:

Peter, My Beloved,
Our Dearest Son
Brother and Uncle
We Love You Always
Born 10 April 1960
Died 30 September 1990

32

Ravi was already standing by the door when Peter's father double parked in front of the house to drop everyone off. Kaisa removed the sleeping Rosa from the car seat and Peter's mum went to get the buggy out of the back. Evie suffered from back pain, but the older woman straightened herself up and said, 'I'm fine.' Kaisa smiled. Evie wanted to be useful.

'I'm early,' Ravi said, walking up to the car. He still held keys to the house and had obviously let himself in. He kissed Kaisa on the cheek.

Peter's father wasn't used to parking in small spaces, so Ravi got into the driver's seat and smartly manoeuvred the Ford into a space a little way along the road.

'Thank you very much, young man,' Peter's father said when Ravi handed him back the keys.

Kaisa smiled, theirs was an unusual friendship. From what she knew of Peter's parents they were not exactly racist, but at the same time they were not used to seeing anything other than white faces where they lived. The only immigrants were the Free Polish who'd come over during and immediately after the Second World War.

'Brave people, brave people,' Kaisa had heard Peter's dad say about the Poles in their town.

Apart from the race issue, Kaisa also knew her friendship with Ravi could be misconstrued, especially as she knew Peter's parents had no idea about Ravi's sexuality. However, both parents seemed to be grateful to Ravi for all the time he spent looking after Kaisa and Rosa.

It was amazing how a death and a birth brought people together, Kaisa thought, as she watched Peter's father and Ravi walk side by side along the front path to the house. The men's heads were bent over in conversation, and Peter's dad had his hand on Ravi's shoulder. His white head against Ravi's jet-black hair and darker skin made the pair look positively exotic.

'Alright?' Kaisa heard Peter's mum ask behind her. Ravi had managed to wrangle the heavy buggy out of the older woman's hands, before he'd helped to park the car, and she was now standing behind Kaisa on the narrow path. Kaisa realised Peter's mother was cold; she had her arms crossed and was rubbing her arms with her hands.

'Yes, sorry, miles away,' Kaisa said and moved towards the house, carrying Rosa.

Ravi came up to her. He smelled of his usual orange-scented aftershave. When he bent down to give the sleeping Rosa a peck on her forehead, the girl squirmed in Kaisa's arms.

'I'm going to take her up for her nap. We might then get an hour or so to have lunch. Anyone else arrived yet?' she asked Ravi.

'No,' Ravi shook his head. 'I can take her up,' he added, giving Kaisa a look, which said, 'Here's your chance.'

Kaisa shook her head. She went up the stairs and settled the sleeping child into her cot. For a while she sat on her bed; she needed to steel herself. She looked at her watch, there was still time to speak with Peter's parents before her guests arrived.

She put her hand on Rosa's tummy. She'd decided to keep the cot in her bedroom even though there was a smaller bedroom at the back of the house, which she and Peter had thought might become a nursery one day. Ravi had been using it as his bedroom and an unofficial office when he had papers to read for work, and Kaisa wasn't in any hurry to move Rosa away from her bedroom.

Kaisa gazed at the sleeping child. She'd covered Rosa's legs with her favourite pink blanket, which Evie had crocheted for her. Sleepily, the child had grabbed a corner with one hand and was now holding onto it with her chubby fingers. She was so beautiful, with her dark curls mussed around her head on the pillow and her long black eyelashes resting on her pale round cheekbones. Her little mouth was pale pink, with the arch of her lips perfectly drawn. For a moment, the thought that Peter would never see how beautiful she was hit her with such force that her chest felt as if it had collapsed and she struggled to breathe. *Think of the positives, think of the positives*, she repeated in her head, and she concentrated on taking in air through her nose and blowing it out of her mouth as Mrs D had taught her.

'Celebrate his life, instead of mourning his death. And don't worry about upsetting others. This is your life to lead the way you decide is best for you and Rosa,' she'd said as Kaisa had left her office.

When Kaisa's breathing had returned to normal, she gave her daughter a last glance, made sure the baby alarm on the bedside table had its green lights on, and returned downstairs.

All the guests arrived at the same time; Rose and Roger had driven up from Dorset, Peter's best man Jeff and his wife, Milly, from Portsmouth, Nigel and Pammy from Plymouth and even Stephen had made it. Kaisa knew he was now working up in Whitehall, and they'd met a few times at the Army Navy Club in St James's, but he still lived up in Scotland.

Peter's brother Simon had grown very grey during the last year. His wife Miriam gave Kaisa a present for Rosa.

'Thank you, that's very kind of you,' Kaisa said.

'Even though she doesn't understand, I'm sure she'll find this day diffi-cult, so here's something to take her mind off it,' Miriam said, giving Kaisa a short, efficient hug.

Peter's sister Nancy had brought her twins, but said she was sorry her husband couldn't make it. The boy and girl, Oliver and Beth, who had just turned seven, ran in and out through the French doors, in a game no one understood.

Kaisa thought how lucky they were to have a sunny day. She was also not sorry, if she was truthful, that Nancy's loud husband hadn't come. He had the knack of saying the wrong thing, and she knew Peter hadn't much cared for him. The twins were wild, but no one minded. It was good to have children around. They were oblivious to the sadness of the occasion, and happily munched on sandwiches while running around the adults. Kaisa thought how strikingly similar they looked to Peter, and to Rosa, with their mops of dark hair, pale skin and long, lean bodies. Rosa, however, was still chubby, although her long legs and arms hinted at a lankiness to come.

Rose hugged Kaisa hard; and Kaisa held onto her friend for a bit longer than was safe. Too much kindness was still a problem, and could set her off crying at any moment, but she held it together, reminding herself that she needed to be grateful for what she had: the love of Peter's family, her friends and her lovely daughter Rosa.

Rose, after whom Kaisa had partly named her daughter, had also been a great support to Kaisa after Peter's death. She'd been to stay with Kaisa a few times, and had co-ordinated her visit with Ravi, so that it coincided with a work trip Ravi had to take to the States. The two of them had laughed and cried, remembering all the crazy days at the feminist magazine, *Adam's Apple*.

'Without you, I'm not sure Peter and I would have ever got back together,' Kaisa once said during such a conversation.

Rose had looked down at her hands, then lifted her eyes to Kaisa and remarked, 'I'm not sure without my family's interference you would have ever separated.'

Duncan's passing hadn't been mentioned by either Rose or Kaisa, nor Ravi. It was as if Rose didn't want to lump the two men together and Kaisa was grateful for her friend's tactfulness.

The memory of Duncan, of the one stupid drunken night, of the AIDS scare it had led to, and his sad, sad death, made Kaisa want to howl with anger and frustration with herself. Rose had put her arms around Kaisa and rocked her back and forth. 'I'm sorry, darling, I don't mean to upset you.'

'You look well,' Rose now said, eventually letting go of Kaisa.

'So do you!' Suddenly Kaisa noticed that Rose was wearing a loose, sky-blue dress. She looked at her tummy, then at her eyes, which looked bluish, reflecting the bright colour of the dress.

'You're not?'

A wide smile brightened Rose's face, 'It's early days yet.'

'Congratulations!' Kaisa gave her friend another hug.

'I'm over forty, so I know I'm too old, but apparently I'm as healthy as a horse.' Rose turned to her husband, who also had a wide smile on his face. Kaisa shook Roger's hand and gave him a kiss on the cheek. 'I'm so very, very happy for you both.'

Kaisa had spoken with Pammy and Nigel on the phone several times, but this was the first time since Peter's death that the two friends had seen each other.

When they arrived at the door, Kaisa was shocked to see how frail Nigel looked; he'd lost a lot of weight and didn't look at all well. His eyes looked watery and sad, and for a moment Kaisa thought he'd cry when he hugged Kaisa without being able to speak.

Right after the funeral, when Pammy had phoned and apologised for not coming, and told Kaisa about Nigel's breakdown, Kaisa had wanted to apologise to Nigel, and Pammy. She felt responsible for his grief. Peter's death had nothing to do with Nigel, she knew that.

When Kaisa saw Jeff, she had to fight tears once more. Peter's best friend had been such a support to her in the early days of their marriage when they still lived in Portsmouth. Kaisa had often wondered whether, if they'd stayed in Southsea instead of moving up to Scotland, she would have been happier and, with Jeff's friendship, been able to resist Duncan.

Jeff had put on a little weight, and was beginning to resemble his father, one of the witnesses at Peter and Kaisa's hastily arranged registry office wedding all those years ago. When Jeff enveloped Kaisa in his arms, just like the bear hug his father usually gave her, Kaisa felt a little guilty for not inviting Jeff's parents. They'd made the journey up from Portsmouth on the day of Peter's funeral two years ago, and she'd been surprised to see them then. But today, she'd decided on just her and Peter's closest friends and family.

Looking at the now crowded room, she wondered how everyone had fitted in on the day of the funeral. The memory of that day was so hazy. She remembered spending some of it sitting alone in the kitchen, being unsociable and not caring if she was.

'You OK, darling?' Jeff asked, letting go of Kaisa and rubbing her back with his hand.

'Yes, I'm good,' Kaisa replied and turned to Milly, Jeff's wife. She too had got a bit rounder in the middle. She was wearing a loose navy dress, with a single string of pearls around her neck and a pair of flat suede pumps on her feet.

'You didn't bring the girls?' Kaisa asked. Milly had given birth to two children in quick succession after the wedding. Peter had said that she was 'up the duff' already, before they got married. Their first daughter, Catherine, had been born only five months afterwards.

'God no, they're with their grandparents,' Milly said and gave a short laugh.

Kaisa had never really got to know Milly. When Jeff had met her and married very quickly, Peter and Kaisa had been separated, and after they got back together again and settled in London, there hadn't been many opportunities to meet up with Peter's old friend and his new wife. Kaisa now wondered if Milly didn't like her because of what she had done to Peter and this was why there had been no invitations to visit Portsmouth. Mind you, Peter and Kaisa had also not asked them to visit London. Weekends together had seemed so precious that Kaisa rarely wanted to share them with anyone.

A stab of longing suddenly took hold of Kaisa and she forced herself to think of the good times, just as Mrs D had told her. She smiled at Milly, 'How old are they now?'

'Oh,' Milly regarded Kaisa critically. Had she noticed Kaisa's fake smile and interpreted it wrongly?

'Cath is six and Poppy five. Complete nightmare ages – can't wait to ship them off to boarding school,' Milly said turning her face towards Jeff.

Kaisa nodded. She looked to the side and saw Rose, standing on her own by the French doors. She raised her eyebrows at Kaisa, who returned the look with a smile. She turned to Ravi, who'd appeared beside her, 'You've met Peter's friends Jeff and Milly, haven't you?'

'Yes, two years ago,' Ravi said carefully, and shook their hands. He asked what they wanted to drink and Kaisa excused herself and moved towards Rose.

'You OK?' Rose said, leaning against the doorframe of the French windows.

'I'm just about to tell everyone the news.'

Rose nodded. Kaisa had phoned her friend as soon as she'd made her decision and although Rose had been quiet at the end of the phone, she'd admitted that she knew why Kaisa was doing what she was planning. She looked at Rose's kind face and said, 'Would you stay here for a bit of moral support?'

'Of course,' Rose said, and placed her hand on Kaisa's arm. 'I'm here for you. Always.'

With Rose by her side, Kaisa got an empty glass and gave it a tap with a spoon. She wanted everyone present for her announcement, but now that it came to it, she felt nervous.

Suddenly the low chatter that had accompanied the sound of cutlery against the white china plates, stopped and all the faces in the room looked up at Kaisa. She swallowed. It was going to be hard to deliver her news. She glanced at Peter's mother, who had looked pale and serious since she'd spoken to her and Peter's father in the lounge that morning. Evie now seemed to have tears in her eyes. It had been terrible to tell them, and Kaisa had been glad of Ravi's presence. She knew it wasn't easy for him, especially when Peter's mother had blurted out, 'I thought you two were going to get married and that was what this was all about.'

Ravi had looked at his hands, not able to face Kaisa, it seemed, nor the couple opposite.

Kaisa had felt anger towards Peter's parents at that point. She knew Ravi wasn't ashamed of being gay, but at the same time she knew he wouldn't want Peter's parents to know, because it had nothing to do with them. Still, Kaisa felt the unfairness of it all acutely. Why would Peter's parents assume that everyone was the same? But Kaisa had kept her voice steady when she'd said, 'Actually I only made the decision after I'd invited you all to celebrate Peter's life on the second anniversary. I thought it very important we commemorate it every year.'

'Of course,' Evie had replied.

Now she moved her eyes away from Kaisa, and put her hand through the crook of her husband's arm. His eyes were steady on Kaisa, but she couldn't help seeing a hardness in them. Was he also angry with Kaisa for wanting a new life for her and Rosa?

'I wanted to thank you all for coming today. Especially Peter's parents, for whom I know this day is a difficult one. I'd also like to thank, you, Ravi, for being my rock, and Rose,' Kaisa's mouth felt parched and she smiled at her friend, but turning back to the room carried on, 'All of you who are dear friends: Jeff, Milly, Pammy and Nigel. And thank you Stephen for all your help,' Kaisa nodded to the tall man in the corner of the room who she'd convinced to come to the lunch. 'Peter's brother and sister and Miriam. I am very grateful to all of you for your support over the past two years. I hope you know that.'

Kaisa glanced around the room, meeting the eyes of the people she'd thanked. Her gaze came to rest on Ravi. His brown eyes looked even more like liquid than usual. Kaisa knew he was unhappy about her decision. There was a general murmur around the room and the twins, Oliver and Beth clapped their hands. Everyone laughed.

Kaisa cleared her throat. She wasn't finished yet. 'I also wanted to let you know that after having thought about this long and hard ever since ...' Kaisa swallowed again, her mouth feeling too dry to carry on. 'Excuse me for a moment,' she said and reached for a glass of water.

'What I wanted to tell you is that I am moving back to Finland.'

33

A week before she was due to move, amidst all the packing, Kaisa met Rose to say goodbye. She'd taken a cab to make it easier to get to Terroni's with Rosa and her buggy. As she stepped out, she was met by Toni outside the café, and soon the little girl was in Toni's arms and being taken into the café to be fussed over by the whole Terroni family.

'Bella, bella, Rosa!' Mamma said and fed the little girl tiny pieces of pink Italian meringue.

Rose was already sitting at 'their table' in the corner, sipping herbal tea.

'You've gone off coffee, then?' Kaisa asked.

Rose nodded, and Kaisa looked at Rosa sitting on top of the counter, held by Mamma. 'She'd be a little fat girl if I stayed here, with Toni and his family feeding her all the wrong things!'

Toni was convinced Kaisa had given her daughter an Italian name, however much she tried to explain that Rosa was also common in Finland.

Both Rose and Kaisa laughed. Then, after Toni had brought Kaisa a cup of coffee, the two women were quiet.

'You'll come and visit, won't you?'

Rose touched her tummy and said, 'Yes, once this one is out and ready to face travelling.'

Kaisa looked at her friend. She had so much to be grateful for, and she knew she would miss her dreadfully.

'You know I have to do this, right?' she said and Rose, not looking at Kaisa, nodded.

Kaisa took Rose's hands into hers and said, 'Don't be sad. I promise to write often and phone too. And I will come and visit you as soon as the baby is born. Just try to stop me!'

Kaisa told her friend about the large house she was buying in Lauttasaari, a few steps away from the sea.

'There's a beach with a children's play area just along the shore, and I can even get a small boat if I want to. I actually have a private jetty!' she said.

Kaisa hadn't believed how much cheaper the houses in Helsinki were compared to London. The place she'd bought was one of the massive villas she'd admired as a teenager, in the area close to where her old school friend Vappu had lived. Never in her wildest dreams would she have imagined she could ever afford such a place.

Rose smiled. 'It sounds idyllic.'

After a succession of hugs from Toni, Mamma and the rest of the family, Rose and Kaisa, with Rosa now fast asleep in the buggy, walked along the Clerkenwell Road. It was a Tuesday afternoon, around four pm, just before the after-work rush. Seeing the pub, The Yorkshire Grey, where Rose had told Kaisa about Duncan barely two years previously, made Kaisa feel so very old and experienced. She placed her hand in the crook of Rose's arm. 'We'll be OK, won't we?'

Rose stopped in the middle of the road and looked at the sleeping child in the buggy and then at Kaisa. 'Of course you will!'

Kaisa glanced around the empty house. She was holding Rosa's hand, and now pulled the girl up into her arms. She walked slowly up to the French doors and surveyed the perfectly cut lawn. She'd had a specialist company to sort out the garden before she put the house up for sale. She'd never been much of a gardener, and Peter had never had enough time to do anything more than mow the lawn. It had cost her a pretty penny, but the estate agent had said that it was the only 'home improvement', as he'd put it, that she needed to do to get a good price for the little house. The same company had been commissioned to maintain the garden too, and had cut the lawn and weeded the borders, which were now immaculate with evergreen bushes on both sides of the square space.

Kaisa closed and locked the doors, putting the squirming Rosa onto the floor. Rosa had a new doll, given to her as a leaving present by Peter's parents. It had been a painful farewell visit to Wiltshire, although 'Ganny' had told Kaisa she understood she needed to be close to her own family 'since Peter was no longer here'. For Rosa's sake, there had been no tears, and Kaisa was glad of that.

Rosa now stood up and began tottering around the empty living room, making bubbles with her mouth and hugging the doll close to her. Rosa had already been on an airplane several times during her short life, and loved being pampered by the Finnair air hostesses.

'Gone?' she asked, looking at Kaisa with her dark green eyes.

'We are going soon,' she said, and took the little girl's hand. 'Let's just check we haven't forgotten anything.'

Together with Rosa, Kaisa went slowly up the stairs and walked from room to room, all empty now, except the carpets and light fittings with their shades, which she'd agreed to leave behind.

She'd spent so many happy days with her beloved Peter in this house, but Kaisa knew that even if she wasn't here, she would always hold the happy images in her heart. Whatever their love affair and marriage with Peter had been, it had been true.

All the misunderstanding, rows, secrets and infidelities didn't matter. What mattered was that they had deeply and truly loved each other. And that heartfelt love had produced the little, beautiful marvel that Rosa was.

Kaisa carried her daughter down the stairs and as she did so, she heard the horn of a car outside. Ravi was getting out of his brand new BMW.

'Your chariot awaits,' he said and smiled.

ABOUT THE AUTHOR

Helena Halme grew up in Tampere, central Finland, and moved to the UK via Stockholm and Helsinki at the age of 22. She is a former BBC journalist and has also worked as a magazine editor, a bookseller and, until recently, ran a Finnish/British cultural association in London.

Since gaining an MA in Creative Writing at Bath Spa University, Helena has published 13 fiction titles, including six in *The Nordic Heart* Series.

Helena lives in North London with her ex-Navy husband. She loves Nordic Noir and sings along to Abba songs when no one is around. You can read Helena's blog at www.helenahalme.com, where you can also sign up for her *Readers' Group*.

- facebook.com/HelenaHalmeAuthor
- twitter.com/helenahalme
- instagram.com/helenahalme
- bookbub.com/authors/helena-halme
- pinterest.com/helenahalme

Printed in Great Britain
by Amazon

67820633R00440